VIRGIN EARTH

Philippa Gregory has a history degree from the University of
Sussex and a PhD in eighteenth-century literature from the
University of Edinburgh. She is a fellow of Kingston
University. She lives with her family in Sussex.

By the same author

WIDEACRE
MERIDON
THE FAVOURED CHILD
THE WISE WOMAN
MRS HARTLEY AND THE GROWTH CENTRE
FALLEN SKIES
A RESPECTABLE TRADE
PERFECTLY CORRECT
THE LITTLE HOUSE
EARTHLY JOYS
ZELDA'S CUT

PHILIPPA GREGORY

VIRGIN EARTH

HarperCollins*Publishers*

Inside front and back cover illustrations reproduced by courtesy of
The Bodleian Library, University of Oxford (the Red Gooseberry and the White
Cherry from Tradescant's Orchard, MS. Ashmole 1461 ff 13r and 27r); map of
Virginia c.1612: The Royal Geographical Society; engraving by Theodor de Bry of a
'Virginia' Indian village from Thomas Harriot's *A brief and true report*; view of a
fish weir, after Elliott, *Fox Hill: Its People and Places*, 1976.

All reasonable efforts have been made by the author and publishers to trace
the copyright holders of the material contained in this publication. In the event
that any of the untraceable copyright holders comes forward after the publication
of this edition, the author and the publishers will endeavour to rectify the
situation accordingly.

HarperCollins*Publishers*
77–85 Fulham Palace Road,
Hammersmith, London W6 8JB

The HarperCollins website address is:
www.**fire**and**water**.com

This paperback edition 2000

1 3 5 7 9 8 6 4 2

First published in Great Britain by
HarperCollins*Publishers* 1999

Copyright © Philippa Gregory Ltd 1999

The Author asserts the moral right to
be identified as the author of this work

ISBN 0 00 651176 7

Set in Minion

Printed and bound in Great Britain by
Caledonian International Book Manufacturing Ltd, Glasgow

All rights reserved. No part of this publication may be
reproduced, stored in a retrieval system, or transmitted,
in any form or by any means, electronic, mechanical,
photocopying, recording or otherwise, without the prior
permission of the publishers.

This book is sold subject to the condition that it shall not,
by way of trade or otherwise, be lent, re-sold, hired out or
otherwise circulated without the publisher's prior consent
in any form of binding or cover other than that in which it
is published and without a similar condition including this
condition being imposed on the subsequent purchaser.

For Anthony

VIRGIN
EARTH

Winter 1638, At Sea

He woke to the sound of the moving ship, the creaking of the timbers and the aching sigh of the full sails spread, the sudden abrupt rattle of a pulley as a sail was reefed in, the drumming of booted feet on the deck just above his face, the holler of an order, and the continual attack of the sea – the bang of the waves against the prow and the groan of the tiny ship as she climbed up one wave and then wallowed and turned to confront another.

He had slept and woken to this ceaseless din for six long weeks and now he found it familiar and soothing. It meant that the little ship was soldiering on through the terrifying expanse of wind and water, still headed westwards, faithful to the hope that westwards would be the new land. Sometimes J imagined their progress as a seagull might see it looking down, the vast waste of sea and the fragile ship with its lamps burning at dusk, headed trustfully towards where they had last seen the sun.

He had set sail in deep grief, in flight from grief. Even now he dreamed of his wife with bright joyful immediacy, dreamed that she came to him on board the ship and laughingly complained that there was no need for him to set sail, no need for him to run off to Virginia alone, for see! here she was on board herself, and it had all been a game – the plague, her long days of dying, the terrible white-faced grief of their daughter – all a May game, and here she was well and strong, and when would they go home again? Then the noises of the ship were a terrible interruption and J would pull his damp blanket over his face, and try to cling to the dream of Jane and the certainty that she was alive and everything was well.

He could not. He had to wake to the bleak truth that she was dead, and his business half-bankrupt, his father hanging on to their house

1

and their nursery garden and their collection of rarities by the old combination of luck and the love of his friends, while J played the part of the indulged son – fleeing from all of it, calling it a venture, a chance at wealth, but knowing it was an escape.

It was not an enviable escape at first sight. The house at Lambeth was a grand house, set among its own twenty acres of nursery garden, famous for its collection of rarities from all around the world. His father, John Tradescant, had named it the Ark, and had sworn they would be safe there whatever storms rocked the country with king and Church and Parliament all set on different and opposing courses. There were half a dozen bedrooms and the great room for the rarities, a dining room, a drawing room and a kitchen. A little son, Johnnie, to inherit it all and his older sister Frances to insist on her own claims. These riches J had exchanged for a single five-foot, four-inches-long bunk built into the damp wall of the ship. There was no room to sit up, barely room to roll over. He had to lie on his back, feeling the huge movement of the waves lifting and dropping him like driftwood, looking at the planks of the bunk above him. To his right against the skin of the ship, he could feel the slap of the waves and the whisper of their ripples. To his left was the slatted door for which he had paid extra for the little space and privacy it gave him. The other, poorer emigrants slept side by side on the floor of the 'tween deck like animals in a barn. They had been loaded like baggage into the waist of the ship with the crews' quarters at the stern behind them, and the captain's tiny cabin and the cook's galley and cabin – all in one – in the prow before them.

The captain would not allow passengers out on deck except for the briefest and most grudging spells in fine weather. The crew going on watch trampled over the passengers and, when they were returning to their shared hammocks in the stern, dripped water all over them. The emigrants were always in the way, they were regularly cursed, they were less than cargo.

Their bundles and boxes were piled up among their owners in a careless muddle; but as the days wore on into weeks families established their own little seats and bunks out of crates of chickens and bags of clothes. The stench was appalling. There were two buckets provided, one for washing water, one for excrement, and there was a strict rota for emptying the soil bucket over the side. The captain would not allow them to do this more than once a day and when it was J's turn to carry the brimming pail to the side his stomach heaved.

There was scarcely enough water to drink, and it came warm and tasting of the barrel, there was hardly enough food. A lumpy porridge for breakfast, the same for dinner, and a biscuit and a slice of old cheese at night.

It would have been a nightmare but the voyage was sustained by hope. They were a shipful of gamblers, a handful of families who had thrown in their lot with a land they had never seen and whose dangers and promises they could hardly imagine. J thought they were the most foolhardy, impulsive, brave people he had ever met, and he did not know whether to fear them as madmen or admire them as heroes.

They were lucky. Seventy days into the voyage, as the temperature rose and the children cried and cried for fresh water and a breath of air, they sighted Barbados and sailed into port for one blissful week of rest as the captain sold his English goods and took on rum and sugar, food and fresh water. They were allowed to go ashore and barter for provisions, to eat fresh fruit for the first time in more than two months. When the ship was due to sail, the return to the festering hold was more than many of them could bear. A number of emigrants left the ship; but most of them gritted their teeth and endured the next leg of the voyage, J grimly among them. It was another full forty days at sea before a sailor opened a hatch and bellowed down: 'Make yourselves ready! We've sighted land.'

Even then they were not allowed up on deck. J gathered with the others looking imploringly upwards to the open hatch. The sailor laughed unkindly. 'Wait below,' he said. 'There's no room for you all!'

It was evening. J, accustomed to the foul smell of the 'tween decks, smelled a fresh new scent on the air – damp earth which reminded him suddenly, poignantly, of the garden at Lambeth after rain, and the wet fresh smell of leaves.

'Land,' the woman next to him said, her voice hushed with awe. 'Land. The new land. Our new land.'

J guessed from the noises of running feet and the shouted commands that they were dropping sail. The waves stopped heaving the ship up and down and instead they felt the insistent pattering slaps of a tidal river. Then there were shouts of greeting and replies from the sailors, and a jolt as the boat ran gently against the quayside and the strange steadying of her motion as the ropes drew her alongside.

'Thank God,' J muttered.

The woman beside him breathed, 'Amen.'

The single women aboard who expected to find husbands as well as gold in the new land primped their hair and put on their clean caps, saved for this very moment. Those children who were not weak with sickness could not be contained; they leaped about on bags and crates

3

and barrels and were cuffed indiscriminately, whenever they stumbled to a standstill. Husbands and wives exchanged apprehensive or hopeful glances. J wondered at the coldness around his heart; he felt no relief that the voyage was over, no excitement at the thought of a new country, of a new land, of a new horizon. He realised then that he had been half-hoping that the ship would founder and take him and his sadness down below the waves to Jane; and then he shook his head at his sin of selfishness that he should ill-wish a voyage because of his own pain.

The sailor stood at the open hatch at last. 'Come on up!' he called. 'Welcome to paradise.'

There was a moment's hesitation and then a rush up the narrow wooden steps and the first emigrants stepped out on deck, and J followed.

It was evening. The skies were a colour that J had never seen before, the palest of mauves lying in stripes like gauze over the enormous river which reflected the colours back up in pink and blue and purple. The river was still, like a tarnished silver mirror, and as J watched it went suddenly dark and stirred and then went still again as an immense shoal of fish swooped by. It was a stretch of water greater than J had ever seen, except for the sea itself. Only dimly behind the ship could he see the distant southern bank as a dark shadow of trees. All around him was the smooth sheen of river water and as he looked inland, away from the sea, it seemed to him that it went on forever, flowing as wide forever, making no compromise with narrowing banks, impossibly wide, impossibly rich, impossibly beautiful.

J looked towards the shore. The emigrants were disembarking in haste; already a chain had been formed, tossing their goods down the line to land with a careless thump on the dockside. Half of Jamestown had turned out to greet the ship, there were shouted enquiries for news of England, demands of the captain for commissions completed, bills paid, and then coming through them all was the governor, Sir John Harvey, grandly shabby in an old coat spruced up for the occasion with worn gold lace, moving through the colonists with his head turned away, as if he despised them.

J could see the walls of the original fort, still manned, with cannon at the ready; but the houses of the town had sprawled beyond their narrow compass and the fort served only as the end point of what would have been, in England, a little market town. The handsomest, biggest houses were stone-built, in a row, in a style that would not have disgraced London, and behind them and to the side of them was a range of styles from frame buildings half-completed, to little wattle-and-daub shanties.

Mostly they were built of wood, planks of untreated crudely sawn boards overlayed one across the other, roofed with mats of badly thatched straw.

No gardens, J noted at once. But everywhere, in every patch of ground, at every corner, even lining the roadside, were tall ungainly plants with leaves broad and flat like those of tulips, flopping over.

'What plant is that?' J asked a man who was pushing up the gangplank to greet a newcomer.

He hardly glanced over his shoulder. 'Tobacco, of course,' he said. 'You'll learn to recognise it soon enough.'

J nodded. He had seen the plant before but he had not thought they would grow it to the exclusion of everything else, in the very streets of their new city.

He took his bag and made his way down the gangplank to the crowded quayside.

'Is there an inn here?'

'A dozen,' a woman replied. 'But only if you have gold or tobacco to pay.'

'I can pay,' J said steadily. 'I come with a warrant from the king of England.'

She looked away as if she were not much impressed with his patent. 'Then you had best tell the governor,' she said, nodding towards the man's broad back. 'If he'll stoop to speak with you.'

J hefted his bag onto his other shoulder and stepped up towards the man. 'Sir John?' he asked. 'Let me introduce myself. I am John Tradescant the younger, gardener to the king. He has commanded me to make a collection of rare plants, and rarities of all sorts. Here is his letter.' He bowed and produced the patent marked with the royal seal.

Sir John did not take it. He merely nodded his head in reply. 'What's your title?'

'Esquire,' J said, still uncomfortable with the lie which claimed his right to be a gentleman when he was in truth nothing more than the son of a working man, and the grandson of a labourer.

The governor turned and extended his hand. J shook the proffered two fingers. 'Call tomorrow,' the governor said. 'I have to collect my letters and some bills of purchase from the captain here. Call tomorrow and I shall be at leisure to receive you.'

'Then I'll find a bed at an inn,' J said uncertainly.

The governor had already turned his back. 'Do that. Or the people are extraordinarily hospitable.'

J waited in case he would offer anything more; but he moved away and there was nothing for J to do but pick up his other bulkier bag, which had been slung down on the quayside, and trudge up the hill, past the bulging walls of the fort, towards the little town.

He found the first inn by the haunting smell of stale ale. As he paused in the doorway there was a loud baying noise of a big dog and a shrill shout commanding it to be silent. J tapped lightly on the door and stepped in.

It was dark inside, the air was thick with smoke, almost unbreathable for a stranger. J's eyes stung and he felt his breath catch.

'Good day,' a woman said abruptly from the back of the room. J blinked tears from his eyes and saw her better: a woman of about fifty with the leathery skin and hard eyes of a survivor. She wore rough wooden clogs on her feet, a homespun skirt kilted up out of the way, a shirt that had once belonged to a man twice her size and a shawl tied tightly around her shoulders.

'I'm new-come from London,' J said. 'I want a room for the night.'

'You can't have one to yourself, you're not at Whitehall now.'

'No,' J said politely. 'Might I share a room?'

'You'll share a bed and like it!'

'Very well,' J said. 'And something to eat? And drink?'

She nodded. 'Paying in gold? Or tobacco?'

'Where would I get tobacco?' J demanded, his irritation finally breaking through. 'I landed five minutes ago.'

She smiled, as if she were pleased to see him rise to the bait. 'How would I know?' she demanded. 'Maybe you'd had the sense to ask in London how we do things over here. Maybe you'd had the sense to buy some on the quayside, seeing as every planter in the colony was selling there today. Maybe you're a returning planter coming back to your rich fields. How would I know?'

'I'm not a planter, and I was not advised to bring tobacco to Virginia,' J said. 'But I am hungry and thirsty and weary. I should like a wash too. When will my dinner be ready?'

The woman abandoned her teasing of him abruptly. 'You can wash under the pump in the yard,' she said. 'Don't drink the water, it's only a shallow well and it's foul. You'll sleep in the attic along with the rest of us. You'll share a pallet bed with my son, or with whoever next comes through the door. Dinner will be ready as soon as it's cooked, which will be the quicker if I can get on now.'

She turned her back to him and stirred something in a pot hanging over the fireplace. Then she moved to a barrel in the corner and drew him a mug of ale.

'Here,' she said. 'Four mugs for a penny. I'll keep the tally.'

'I'm sure you will,' J said under his breath and went out into the yard to wash.

She need not have warned him not to drink the water. It came out of the pump in a brown brackish spout, stinking horribly. Still, it was better than seawater, and J stripped and washed all over, and then pulled on his breeches and sat himself down on a pile of sawn wood and shaved himself, feeling his skin with his fingertips to guide his razor.

The ground still heaved uneasily under his feet, as if he were on board ship. But he knew that his father had felt the same when they had made landfall at Rhé or in Russia after his long voyage across the North Sea. He had told him that it was the same after any long voyage. For a moment J thought of his father at home, and the two children. For a moment he had the sweetest of illusions that Jane was there too, caring for them, awaiting his return. It seemed so much more likely that she would be there, waiting for him, than that she should be dead and he never see her again. The moment was so strong that he had to remind himself of the orangery and the pallet bed, and her white-faced determination that she should die alone rather than pass the plague to him and to her children. The thought of it made him sick to the stomach with grief, and he dropped his head in his hands as the cool Virginia twilight wrapped him in darkness, and he knew that he had sailed to the new world, to the new land, but brought his three-year-old grief all that long way with him.

Spring 1638, Virginia

J opened his eyes and saw, instead of the whitewashed walls and ceiling of his Lambeth home, a thatched roof, close to his face. Beneath him, wooden boards, not even a straw mattress; a pace away, a young man on a pallet bed, still deep in sleep. He took in, slowly, the watery smell of something cooking, the discomfort of the hard floor, and the irritating itch of a fresh fleabite. He sat up cautiously, his head swimming. The solid wooden floor of the loft heaved under his gaze with the illusion of movement.

'You can stir yourselves or it'll be cold!' came a shout from the woman who kept the lodging house. In one fluid movement the lad, her son, was up and out of bed and down the ladder to the kitchen below. J pulled on his boots, brushed down his breeches, shrugged his waistcoat over his grubby shirt, and followed him.

The woman was spooning a pale yellow mixture from the pot, suspended over a miserly fire, into four wooden bowls. She slapped them onto the table and bowed her head over her calloused hands for a brief grace. Another man who had stayed the night sleeping on the floor beside the fire drew up his stool, took out his own spoon and ate with relish.

'What is it?' J asked cautiously.

'Porridge made with Indian corn,' she replied.

'You'll have to get used to it,' the man said. 'Indian corn is almost all we eat.'

J smiled. 'I wasn't expecting milk and honey.'

'There's many that do,' the woman said shortly. 'And many that die still hoping.'

There was a short silence.

'You here prospecting?' the man asked.

'No,' J said. 'I'm a gardener, a plant collector. I've come to collect

8

plants. Authorised by King Charles himself.' He hesitated for a moment, wondering if he should tell them about the great garden in Lambeth and his father's reputation as the greatest gardener that had ever been, advisor to the Duke of Buckingham, gardener to the king and queen, one of the greatest collectors of rarities in the world. He looked at the woman's enfolded, bitter face and thought that he would not.

The man nodded. 'Will you see the king when you get home? If you get home,' he added.

J nodded and took a spoon of the porridge. It was bland, the corn boiled to the consistency of paste. 'Yes. I work for him in his garden at Oatlands Palace,' he said.

'Well, tell him that we can't do with this governor,' the man said bluntly. 'Tell him that we *won't* do with him, and that's a fact. We've got enough worries to deal with here without having a fat fool set over us from England. We need a general assembly with a voice for every planter. We need a guarantee of our rights.'

'You'd be imprisoned if you spoke like that in England,' J pointed out mildly.

'That's why I'm not in England,' the man said shortly. 'And I don't expect to live as if I were. Which is more than can be said for the governor who expects to live like a lord with servants in a land where men and women have come to be free.'

'I'm not his advisor,' J said. 'I speak to the king – when I ever see him – about plants and his garden.'

The man nodded. 'So who does advise him now?'

J thought for a moment. It all seemed a long way away and of little interest in this new country. 'The queen,' he said. 'And Archbishop Laud.'

The man made a grimace and turned his head to spit but then checked the movement when he saw the woman glare. 'Beg pardon. So he hasn't called a parliament?'

J shook his head. 'He hopes to rule without one.'

'I heard he was halfway to being a Papist.'

'I don't know anything about that.'

'I heard that he has taken so many fines and so much wealth into his own hands that he does not need to call a parliament for them to vote taxes, that he lets his wife worship openly as a Papist, and that daily there are men and women in the country crying out for him to change,' the man said precisely.

John blinked at the accuracy and malice of the description. 'I thought you were royalists in Virginia?'

'Not all of us,' the man said with a hard smile.

'Where are you going to find your plants?' the woman interrupted. 'There's nothing grown up and down the river but tobacco.'

'Surely people farm other crops?'

She shook her head. 'We keep beasts – or at any rate they keep themselves. But with the fish jumping out of the river and the animals in the forest it's not worth the labour of doing more than fishing and hunting. Besides, we can trade for anything we need with the Indians. They can do the labour of farming for us. We can all be squires here.'

'I thought I'd travel round,' J said. 'Hire a horse and ride round the country, see what I can find.'

They both looked at him and rudely laughed in his face.

'Hire a horse!' the woman exclaimed. 'There's not more than half a dozen horses in the whole plantation. You might as well ask for a coach and four.'

J kept his temper. 'I see I have much to learn.'

She rose from the table and went to the fire. 'Dark morning,' she said irritably. She bent to the fire and lit what looked like a little twig of kindling. To J's surprise it burnt with a bright clear flame at the very tip, like a specially made taper. She rested it on a small holder, placed on the stone hearth for that purpose, and came back to the table.

'What's that?'

She glanced back without interest. 'We call it candlewood. I buy it from the Indians every autumn.'

'But what sort of wood is it?'

'Candlewood,' she said impatiently.

'But from what sort of tree?'

She looked at him as if he were foolish to be asking something that no-one else cared about. 'How should I know? I pay the Indians to fetch it for me. D'you think I go out into the woods to gather my own candlewood? D'you think I make my own spoons from spoonwood? D'you think I make my own sugar from the sugar tree or my own soap from the soapberry?'

'Candlewood? Spoonwood?' J had a moment of wild imagining, thinking of a tree growing candles, a tree growing spoons, a bush growing soap. 'Are you trying to make a fool of me?'

'No greater fool than you are already – what else should I call them but what they are?'

'What you want,' the man said pacifically, pushing away his empty bowl and taking out a pipe and filling it with rich golden tobacco leaves, 'is an Indian, a savage. One to use as your own. To take you out into

10

the forest and show you all these things. Take you out in a canoe up and down the river and show you the things you want to know.'

'Don't any of the planters know these things?' J asked. He felt fearful at the thought of being guided by an Indian. There had been too much talk in London of brown men armed with knives of stone who crept into your house and cut your throat while you slept.

The woman hawked and spat into the fireplace. 'They don't hardly know how to plant!' she said. 'Everything they know they learned from the Indians. You can find yourself an Indian to tell you what the soap-berry tree is. Civilised folks here aren't interested in anything but gold and tobacco.'

'How shall I find an Indian to guide me?' J asked. For a moment he felt as helpless as a child, and he thought of his father's travels – to Russia, to the Mediterranean, to Europe. He had never asked his father if he had felt fear, or worse than fear: the babyish whimper of someone lost, friendless in a strange land. 'Where would I find a safe Indian?'

'No such thing as a safe Indian,' the woman said sharply.

'Peace!' J's fellow lodger said quietly. 'If you're serving the king you must have papers, a safe pass, that sort of thing.'

J felt inside his shirt where the precious royal order was wrapped in oilskin. 'Of course.'

'Best see the governor then,' the man suggested. 'If you're from the king and you've got some influence at court, the governor'll have time for you. God knows he has no time for honest working men trying to make a living here.'

'Does he have a court?' J asked.

'Knock on his door,' the woman said impatiently. 'Court indeed! He's lucky to have a girl to open the door for him.'

J stood up from the table. 'Where shall I find his house?'

'Set beyond the Back Road,' the man said. 'I'll stroll over with you now.'

'I have to wash first,' J said nervously. 'And get my hat and coat.'

The woman snorted disparagingly. 'He'll want to paint and powder next,' she said.

The man smiled. 'I'll wait for you outside,' he said and went out, closing the door gently behind him.

There was neither jug nor ewer in the attic, nor a mirror. Everything that had to be brought from England was at a premium in the new

11

colony. The most trivial things which J had taken for granted in England were rare luxuries here. J washed under the pump in the yard, flinching from the icy splash, and unconsciously keeping his lips tight shut, fearful of drinking the foul water.

His fellow lodger was waiting for him outside the house, in the shade of a tree, sipping from a mug of small ale. The sun beat down on the blinding dust all around him. He nodded when he saw J and slowly got to his feet. 'Don't rush,' he advised him. 'A man can die of hurry in this climate.'

He led the way down the track that ran between the houses. The road was no dirtier than a back road in London but somehow it seemed worse, with the heat of the sun beating down on it and the bright light which dazzled J and made him squint. Hens clucked around in the dust and shied away from their strolling feet at every street corner, and every garden, every drainage ditch, was filled with the ungainly sprout and flapping leaves of the tobacco plant.

The governor, when J managed to gain admission to the small stone-built house, did nothing more than repeat the lodging-house woman's advice. 'I shall write you a note,' he said languidly. 'You can travel from plantation to plantation and the planters will make you welcome, if that is what you wish. There's no difficulty there. Most of the people you meet will be glad of the company and a new face.'

'But how shall I find my way around?' J asked. He was afraid that he sounded humble, like a fool.

The governor shrugged. 'You must get yourself an Indian servant,' he said. 'To paddle you in a canoe. To set up camp for you when you can find nowhere to stay. Or you can remain here in Jamestown and tell the children that you want flowers from the woods. They'll bring a few things in, I dare say.'

J shook his head. 'I need to see things where they are growing,' he said. 'And see the parent plants. I need roots and seed heads, I need to gather them myself. I need to see where they thrive.'

The governor nodded, uninterested, and rang a silver bell. They could hear the servant trotting across the short hall and opening the badly hung door.

'Take Mr Tradescant to Mr Joseph,' the governor ordered. He turned to J. 'He's the magistrate here at Jamestown. He often puts Indians in the stocks or in prison. He'll know the names of one or two. He might release one from prison to you, to be your guide.'

'I don't know the ways of the country . . .' J said uneasily. 'I would rather have a law-abiding guide –'

The governor laughed. 'They're all rogues and criminals,' he said simply. 'They're all pagan. If you want to go out into the forest with any one of them you take your life in your own hands. If I had my way we should have driven them over the Blue Mountains into the western sea. Just over the distant mountains there – drive them back to India.'

J blinked, but the governor rose to his feet in his enthusiasm. 'My plan is that we should plant the land from one river to the other – from the James River to the Patowmeck River – and then build a mighty fence and push them behind it, expel them from Eden as if we were archangels with flaming swords. Let them take their sins elsewhere. There'll be no peace for us until we are undisputed masters of all the land we can see.'

He broke off. 'But you must take your choice, Mr Tradescant. The only people who know anything of plants or trees in Virginia are the Indians and they may slit your throat once you are in the woods with them. Stay here, safe inside the city, and go home empty-handed; or take your chance. It is a matter of complete indifference to me. I cannot rescue you if you are in the woods with them, whatever the king asks of me, whatever safe passes you have in your pocket.'

J hesitated. He had a moment to appreciate the irony that he had thought he might die on the voyage and had welcomed the thought of his own death, which he had recognised as the only thing to ease his grief. But the thought of meeting his death violently and in fear in unknown woods at the hands of murderous pagans was a different matter altogether.

'I'll speak to this Mr Joseph,' he said at last. 'See what he advises.'

'As you wish,' the governor said languidly. 'I hope you enjoy your stay in Virginia. Please assure His Majesty that I did everything in my power to assist you, when you get home; if you get home.'

'Thank you,' J said levelly, bowed and left the room.

The maid would not take him even for the short walk to Mr Joseph's house until she had tied a shawl around her shoulders and put a broad-brimmed hat on her head.

'It's cool,' J protested. 'And the sun is not even overhead.'

She shot him a swift defensive look. 'There are bugs that bite and a sun which strikes you down, and the heat that comes off the marshes,' she warned. 'The graveyard is full of men who thought that the Virginia sun was not yet up, or that the water was good enough to drink.'

With that she said nothing more but led the way to the magistrate's house, past the fort where the bored soldiers whistled and called to her, and inland up a rough dirt road until she stood before a house which was grand by Virginia standards but would have been nothing more than a yeoman's cottage in England.

'Mr Joseph's house,' she said shortly, and turned and left him at the rough wood front door.

J knocked, and opened the door when a voice shouted to him to come inside.

The house was divided into two. The largest room, where J was standing, served as the kitchen and dining room. There was no separate parlour. There was a ladder at the back of the room leading to attic bedrooms. A light wooden partition, hardly a wall, divided the master bedroom on the ground floor from the rest of the house. Mr Joseph was sitting at the roughly made table in the living room, writing in a ledger.

'Who are you?'

'John Tradescant, from England,' J said, and proffered the governor's note.

Mr Joseph read it quickly. 'I've got no native guide for you,' he said abruptly. 'I've got no messengers due to arrive either. You will have to wait, sir.'

J hesitated. 'I wonder if a white person might be free to take me out, now and then. Perhaps a servant or a labourer might be spared from their work.' He looked at the man's unhelpful expression. 'Perhaps just for a few hours?'

Mr Joseph shook his head. 'How long have you been here?' he demanded.

'Just arrived.'

'When you have been here a little longer you will realise that there is never a spare hour,' the man said grimly. 'Never a spare moment. Look around you. Every single thing you see here has to be wrested from this land. Remember your ship – did you see houses as cargo? Ploughs? Baker's shops? Market stalls?' He paused for emphasis and then shook his head.

'You did not, and that is because we can ship hardly anything. All that we need has to be made or grown or wrought here. Everything. From the shingles on the roof to the ice in the cellar. And this by people who did not come here to farm; but came hoping to pick up gold plates from the seashore, or emeralds from the rivers, or pearls from out of every oyster. So not only are we farming with wooden ploughshares that we have to carve ourselves, but we are farming with labourers who have never seen a ploughshare before, wooden or metal! Who have to learn every step of the way. Who are taught by men who came out to mine gold but find themselves growing tobacco. So there is no-one, not a man nor woman nor child, who has a moment to do anything but work.'

J said nothing. He thought of his father who had travelled half way round the world and never came back without his pockets filled with treasures. He thought of the debts at home which would be mounting and only his father and two young children to care for the business of nursery plants and rarities.

'Then I shall have to go out alone. On my own. For I must go home with plants and rarities.'

'I can give you an Indian girl,' the man said abruptly. 'Her mother is in prison for slander. She's only in for the month. You can have the child for a month.'

'What good will a child be?' J demanded.

The man smiled. 'This is an *Indian* child,' he corrected. 'One of the Powhatan people. She can pass through the trees as quiet as a deer. She can cross deep rivers by stepping on stones that you cannot even see. She can eat off the land: berries, roots, nuts, the earth itself. She'll know every single plant and every single tree within a hundred miles of here. You can have her for a month, then bring her back.'

He threw back his head and shouted an order. From the yard outside came an answering shout and the back door opened and a child was thrust into the room, her hands still full of the flax which she had been beating.

'Take her!' Mr Joseph said irritably. 'She understands some English, enough to do your bidding anyway, she's not deaf, but she's dumb. She can make noises but not speech. Her mother is a whore for the English soldiers, or a servant, or a cook, or something. She's in prison for a month for complaining of rape. The girl knows enough to understand you. Take her for a month and bring her back here three weeks on Thursday. Her mother comes out of prison then and she'll want her back.'

He waved the girl towards J and she stepped slowly, unwillingly forward.

'And don't rape her,' he warned matter-of-factly. 'I don't want a half-breed baby nine months from now. Just order her to find your plants and bring you back within the month.'

The magistrate waved them both from the room and J found himself on the doorstep in the bright morning sunlight with the girl like a shadow at his elbow. He turned and looked at her.

She was an odd mixture of child and woman; that was the first thing he saw about her. The roundness of her face and the open gaze of the dark eyes was that of a child, an inquisitive, bonny child. But the straightness of her nose and the high cheekbones and the strength of her jaw would make her a beautiful woman in only a few years' time. Her head was not yet level with his shoulder, but the long legs and slim long feet showed that she would grow taller. She was dressed according to Jamestown convention in someone's cast-off shift which reached down to her calves and flapped around her shoulders. Her hair was long and dark, flowing loose on one side of her head; but the other side, around her right ear, was shaved close, giving her a curious, exotic appearance. The skin of her neck and her shoulders, which he could see around the gaping gown, was painted with outlandish blue ridges of tattoos. She was looking at him with apprehension, but not outright fear; looking at him as if she were measuring his strength, and thinking that whatever might happen next she would survive it.

It was that look that told J she was a child. A woman fears pain: the pain inside her body, and the pain of a man's command. But this was still a girl, since she had a girl's confidence that she could survive anything.

J smiled at her, as he would have smiled at his own nine-year-old daughter Frances, left so far away in London. 'Don't be afraid, I won't hurt you,' he said.

Years later he would remember that promise. The first thing he, a white man, had said to an Indian: 'Don't be afraid. I won't hurt you.'

J led the girl away from Mr Joseph's house to the shade of a tree in the centre of what would in England have been the village green, but here was a dusty piece of waste ground between the river and the Back Road. A couple of cows foraged pessimistically around them.

'I need to find plants,' J said slowly, watching her face for any signs of understanding. 'Candlewood. Soapberry. Spoonwood.'

She nodded, but whether she understood him, or was merely trying to please him, he could not tell.

He pointed to the tree. 'I want to see trees.' He pointed to where the thick line of the forest fringed the river, beyond the desert of waste ground that the settlers had made around the little town, tree stumps still showing in the new fields, dust blowing away from the exhausted tobacco rows.

'Will you take me into the woods?'

She looked at him with sudden keen intelligence, and stepped towards him. She put a hand on his chest and then turned from him and mimed walking: a wonderful vivid mime that made J laugh at once. It was the English walk, the rolling swagger of a self-important man walking in ill-fitting shoes. She rolled her hips as English men do when they walk, she picked up her feet as English men do when their blisters are nipping their toes. She nodded at him when she saw that he understood, and then she turned and pointed far out beyond the felled trees to the dark, impenetrable wall of forest. She stood for a moment, and then spread her arms and with a little shudder of movement from the crown of her dark head to her bare feet made him see – see the inexpressible: a tall tree with wide spreading branches. It was an illusion, like a mountebank's trick; but for a moment J, watching her, saw not girl but tree; saw the movement of wind in the branches, saw the sway of the trunk. Then she stepped away from her mime and looked at him inquiringly.

'Yes,' J said. 'Trees. I want to see trees.' He nodded and smiled at her, nodded again. Then he stepped closer and pointed to himself. 'And flowers,' he said. He bent down and mimed delightedly finding something on the ground, picking it and smelling it.

He was rewarded by a bright smile and then a tiny, half-suppressed chuckle of laughter.

He mimed picking berries and eating them, he mimed gathering nuts or digging roots from the ground. The girl nodded; she had understood.

'We go now?' J demanded. He gestured towards the woods, started to march forward to indicate his readiness.

She looked at him from his heavy leather boots to his tall hat. She said not a word but J sensed that his clothes, his boots, his walk, even his very body – so heavy and stiff – seemed to her an impossible burden to take into the woods. But then she sighed, and with a little lift of her shoulders seemed to shrug away the difficulty of how a lumpish overdressed white man could be taken into the forest. She stepped forward and with a gesture of her hand indicated that he should walk behind her, and headed towards the trees at a gentle trot.

Sweat poured off J before they were halfway through the cultivated fields outside the half-opened walls of Jamestown. A crowd of midges and strange, sharply biting moths spun around his head and stung and nipped at every exposed inch of skin. He wiped his face with his hand and it came away dirty with the wings and legs of little bloodsucking insects and left his face sore. They reached the shade of the forest edge;

but it was no better. At every pace a small cloud of insects bloomed around his big feet and fastened themselves to every piece of reddening skin.

J swatted and wiped and smoothed his face and his neck and his hands, making a thousand awkward ungainly movements to each one of her gliding paces. She trotted like an animal, with no wasted energy. Her arms were relaxed at her side, her upper body still, only her feet pattered forward in little steps, steadily one before the other in a thin one-track path. J, watching her run, at first thought it was the pace of a little child; but then found he could hardly keep up with her as she crossed the fields and headed for the trees.

The edge of the forest was like the face of a friend with half the teeth knocked out. The girl looked around at the ragged stumps of trees as if she was grieving for the loss of someone's smile. Then she made that little gesture of her shoulder which said so eloquently that there was no accounting for what a white man might do, and went forward with that slow, very slow trot that was just faster than J's normal walk, and too slow for his running stride. He was continually walking and then breaking into a run to catch her up and then walking again.

As soon as they were beyond the felled trees she stepped off the path, looked around her, listened for one intent moment and then went to a hollow tree at the side of the path. With one fluid movement she flung the shift over her head, folded it carefully, and stowed it in the roots of the tree.

She was all but naked. A little buckskin skirt covered her privates in front but left her long thighs and buttocks exposed. Her breasts were those of a young girl, pointed and as firm as muscle. J exclaimed, not with desire but with fear, and looked around him. For a moment he thought he might have been entrapped by her, and that someone would spring up to witness that he was with her, looking at her shameful nakedness, and some dreadful punishment would follow.

The forest was silent, there was no-one there but the two of them. At once J imagined that she must be inviting him, seducing him; and he could not deny that she was halfway to being desirable. But then he saw that she was not even aware of him, blind to his rapid succession of fears and thoughts. Without fear, without any sense of her own nudity, without the shame she should feel, she bent to the foot of the tree and drew out a small black jug. She dipped in her fingers and drew out a handful of a reddish grease. She smoothed it all over her body as a rich woman will stroke perfume on her skin, and smiled at J when she straightened up and her body glistened with it.

He could see now that the blue and red tattoos which ringed her shoulder blades went down her narrow back in wild spirals. Only her small breasts and belly were bare of them. The grease had added a redder colour to her skin and a darker sheen to the tattoos. She looked stranger and older than she had on the Jamestown green. Her hair looked longer and thicker, her eyes darker and wilder. J watched this transformation from a child in someone's hand-me-down clothes to a young woman in her own gleaming skin with a growing sense of awe. She had changed from a serving maid – the child of a criminal serving maid – into a creature of the wood who looked as if she belonged there, and whose skin, dappled with the light through the shifting canopy of the leaves, was almost invisible against the dappled light of the forest floor.

She held out the pot for him to take some grease.

'No, thank you,' J said awkwardly.

Again she proffered it.

J shook his head.

Patiently she pointed to the cloud of insects around his face and neck, and J noticed for the first time that there were no midges and moths around her. She thrust the pot towards him.

Squeamishly, J dipped his hand into the pot and brought out a little grease on the tips of his fingers. It smelled rancid like old sweat and well-hung meat. J could not help a swift expression of distaste at the powerful stink, he wiped the grease away on a leaf and shook his head again. The girl was not offended. She merely shrugged and then corked the pot with a bundle of leaves, and put it in a woven bag which she drew out from under the tree trunk along with a small quiver made of reeds holding half a dozen arrows, and a small bow.

The quiver she hung at her side, the bow over her shoulder, the soft woven bag across her body to hang on the other hip. Then she nodded to him briskly, to indicate she was ready. She gestured towards the river – did he want to go along the shoreline?

J pointed towards the deeper trees to their left. She nodded and stepped before him, made that little confident gesture that told him to follow behind her, and led the way.

She moved as quietly as an animal through the shadows and the trees. Not even the arrows in her quiver rattled together. The tiny, almost invisible, track was blocked at every pace by a fallen log or a strand of creeper stretching from one tree to another. She trotted over the one and ducked beneath the other without ever breaking her steady stride. J, out of breath, breaking twigs and kicking stones with his heavy shoes, ducking beneath vines, rubbing his face against the trailing disagreeable stickiness of spiders' webs and the stinging moths, stamped behind her like a pursuing cart horse.

She did not look around. 'Well, she hardly needs to look to know that I am following her,' J thought. The noise alone was enough to alert all of Virginia. But she did not even glance to see if all was well with him. She just went at her slow steady trot, as if having been assigned the task of taking him into the deep forest she need no longer consult him until she delivered him to his destination.

They jogged for about half an hour as J's breathing went from a pant to a straining, painful snatching for breath, until at last they came to a clearing where she paused and turned. J, who had been watching every step on the treacherous path, though blinded by his own sweat and dazzled by a cloud of stinging insects, dropped to the ground and whooped for air. Courteously she hunkered down beside him, sitting on her heels, and waiting, composed and silent, for the white man to stop panting and mopping his face, and grabbing at his side where he had a stitch and at his ankle where he had a sprain.

Slowly J fell silent. The noises of the wood which had been obscured by his trampling progress rose up all around him. There were frogs croaking from the river behind them, there were crickets singing. There were birds singing in the thick canopy of leaves above them, pigeons cooing, jays calling, and an interweaving of sounds which J, a town boy, could not recognise.

He heard the rasp of his own breath subside and he turned to look at her. She was quiet and composed.

J gave her a small, almost apologetic, smile, and lifted his hand to the neck of his thick linen shirt and flapped it to indicate his heat. She nodded solemnly and pointed to his thick jacket.

J, feeling every inch a fool, slid his arms out of the sleeves and handed it to her. She folded it as carefully as a housewife in England and put it beside them and scattered a handful of leaves and moss on it. At once it had disappeared. J blinked. He could not even see the outline of it. She had hidden it completely.

She turned and pointed at his breeches and his boots. J shook his head.

Again she pointed at his breeches and mimed pulling them down. J, feeling like an aged virgin clutching to modesty, held the waistband tighter to him. He saw the glimpse of a smile cross her face but then she moulded her expression into impassivity. She gave a little shrug which said as eloquently as any words that he might wear his breeches if he chose to be hot and uncomfortable, and keep his boots if he wanted to alert the whole forest by his heavy tread.

She made a small gesture with her hand that said: 'Here. Trees,' and then she sat back on her heels and looked at him expectantly.

The trees were coming into leaf. J gazed around in wonderment at the height of them, at the richness of the growth, at the vines which looped one to another and twisted around them. Some of them he could recognise as English trees and he found he was nodding towards them, almost as a man might greet the welcome sight of an acquaintance in a strange land. He saw elderberry bushes, oak, hornbeam, cherry trees, walnut trees and dogwood with a sense of relief. But there was also a jumble, an overwhelming richness of foliage and trunk, bark and small flowers, that he could not name, could not identify, that crowded upon him, all beautiful or interesting, large or shapely, calling for his attention and competing with each other. J rubbed his hand across his sweating face. There was a lifetime's work here for a plant collector; and he had promised his father to be home by early summer.

He glanced at the girl. She was not watching him, she was sitting on her heels, waiting patiently, as steady and still as the trees around them. When she felt his gaze upon her she looked up and gave him a small shy smile, a child's smile, as if to say that she was proud of her little cleverness in bringing him to the heart of the wood, happy to wait until she could demonstrate her cleverness at fetching him home. It was a smile that no father could have resisted. J smiled back at her. 'Well done,' he said. 'This is just what I wanted.'

The girl did not lead him home until the evening and then her little bag was packed with seedlings that J had dug from the forest floor. J was carrying his hat like a bowl, filled to the brim with tiny tree seedlings, each showing no more than a pair of leaves, a white stem and a trail of little roots. There were more plants packed into the pockets of his breeches. He had wanted to put some in her quiver but she had shaken her head decisively, and when he proffered the plants again, she had stepped back from him to show him why she refused.

In one swift movement the bow came off her shoulder and into her hand, with the other hand she had an arrow out of the quiver and notched on the bow. She was ready with a sharpened reed arrow head in moments. She nodded; her meaning was clear. She could not waste time fumbling with plants in her quiver.

J tried to hide a smile at this child's seriousness over a child's toy. She was certainly deft; but the bow was a tiny one and the arrows were as light as their flights: made of reed, tipped with sharpened reed.

'May I see?' he asked.

She unstrung the arrow from the bow and handed it to him. At once he realised his mistake. The arrow in his hand was a killing blade. The reed at its head was honed to razor sharpness. He drew it against his thumb and there was no pain, but a fine line of blood bloomed at its touch.

'Damnation!' he swore, and sucked his thumb. It might be made of reed, it might be so light that a young girl could carry it all day; but the arrow head was sharper than a knife.

'How exact is your aim?' J asked her. He pointed to a tree. 'Can you hit that?'

She stepped towards the tree and pointed instead to a leaf which was shifting slightly in the wind before the trunk. She stepped back, notched the arrow into the bow and let fly. The arrow whistled softly in the air and thudded into the tree trunk. J stepped forward to look. There were traces of the leaf around the arrow shaft: she had hit a moving leaf at twenty paces.

J made a little bow to her, and meant the gesture of respect.

She smiled, that little gleam of pride again, and then pulled the arrow from the tree trunk, discarded the broken arrow head and replaced it with another, put the arrow back in her quiver and led the way from the forest clearing at her usual trot.

'Slower,' J commanded.

She glanced at him. He was clumsy with tiredness, his leg muscles singing with pain, and unbalanced by his burden of seedlings. Again he saw that small smile and then she turned and walked before him with a loping pace which was only a little slower. She paused for a moment in the clearing where he had thrown off his jacket and picked it up, dusted off the leaves and handed it to him. Then she led the way back to the hollow tree at the edge of the forest. She hid her bow and arrow in the trunk and drew out her servant's shift.

J, after a long day of jogging behind her dappled flanks, was now accustomed to her nakedness. He found that he liked the gleam of her skin better than the crumpled mess of the shift. He thought she was diminished by the gown, she looked less modest than in her proud tattoos and buckskin. He made a little shrug to show his sense that she was returning to some sort of unnatural constraint and she nodded at his sympathy, her face grave.

'You will stay at my inn tonight,' J said, pointing down to Jamestown where there were already lights showing and chimneys smoking.

She neither nodded nor shook her head, she was frozen still, her eyes never leaving his face.

'And tomorrow we shall go out into the forest again. Mr Joseph said you should come out with me every day for a month, until your mother is freed.'

She nodded her consent to that. Then she stepped forward and pointed at the little plants in his pocket and gestured towards the river. She mimed the strong paddling of a canoe, out towards the sea. Her hand gestured to the right, they should go south, she waved, a long way, waved again, a very long way; then she stepped back from him and with her arms spread and her shoulders rounded she mimed for him a tree: a tree with branches that bowed down, bowed down low over still water, spread her fingers: with branches that trailed into the water.

J was entranced. 'But can we get a canoe?'

The girl nodded. She pointed to herself and held out her hand, pointing to her palm, the universal mime for money. J proffered a silver coin, she shook her head. He drew out his tobacco pouch. She nodded and took a fat handful. Then she pointed his face towards Jamestown, looked into his eyes again as if she were reluctant to trust so stupid a man to find his own way home, and then she nodded at him and turned towards a shrubby bush.

In a second she had disappeared. Disappeared without trace. J saw the little branches of the bush quiver and then she was gone, not even a glimmer of the servant's smock showing in the darkness. For a moment he waited, straining his eyes against the failing light to see if he could spot her, but she had disappeared as surely as a roe deer will vanish by merely standing still.

J, realising that he would never find her against her will, knowing that he had to trust her, turned his face towards Jamestown as she had bid him and trudged home.

❧

When the lodging-house woman knew that J had spent all day with the Indian girl in the woods, and would spend nights away with her, she was scathing.

'I'd have thought a man fresh out of England could have done without,' she said. She dumped in front of him a wooden bowl filled to the brim with a pale porridge.

'Suppawn,' his fellow lodger said out of the side of his mouth. 'Indian cornmeal and milk.'

'More corn?' J asked.

The man nodded grimly and spooned his portion in silence.

'I'd have thought you could have brought a woman from England, if your needs are that urgent,' the woman said. 'God knows, the town needs more women. You can't make a plantation with nothing but soldiers and fools.'

J bent his head and slurped porridge from his spoon.

'Don't you have a wife you could have brought?' the woman demanded.

Grief stabbed J like a knife in the belly. He looked up at her and something in his face silenced her nagging.

'No,' he said abruptly.

There was a short embarrassed silence.

'I'm sorry,' she said, 'if I spoke wrong . . .'

J pushed away the bowl, the familiar feeling of grief choking him from his belly to his throat.

'Here,' the man offered. He produced a leather bottle from the folds of his breeches and poured a slug over J's unwanted porridge. 'Have a drop of Barbados rum, that's the thing to give it flavour.' He poured a measure for himself and stirred it in. He waved to J with his spoon. 'Eat up,' he said with rough kindliness. 'This is not a land where a man can go hungry and eat later. Eat up and drink up too. You never know where your next meal is coming from here.'

J pulled his bowl towards him, stirred in the rum and tasted the porridge. It was much improved.

'The girl is guiding me to plants and trees,' he said to them both. 'As I told you, I am a collector. Neither the governor nor Mr Joseph could think of anyone else who could assist me. But she is a good little girl. She is not much older than my own daughter. I should think she is little more than thirteen. She leads me to the forest and then waits quietly and leads me home.'

'Her mother is a whore,' the lodging-house woman remarked spitefully.

'Well, she is but a little maid yet,' J said firmly. 'And I would not be the man to abuse her.'

The woman shook her head. 'They're not like us. She's no more a maid than my young mastiff bitch is a maid. When she's ready she'll couple like an animal. They're not like us, they're half-beasts.'

'You speak badly of them because of your losses,' J's fellow lodger said fairly. He nodded to J. 'Mistress Whitely here lost her man and her child in the Indian rising of 'twenty-two. She doesn't forget. No-one who was here at the time can ever forget.'

'What happened?' J asked.

The woman lowered herself to the bench opposite him and leaned her chin on her hand. 'They were in and out of Jamestown every night and day,' she said. 'The children stayed in our houses, our men went out hunting with them. Again and again we would have starved if they had not traded with us – food, fish, game. They taught us how to plant: corn and the rest. They taught us how to harvest it and cook it. We would have died over and over again if they had not sold us food. The vicar was going to have an Indian school. We were going to teach them our ways, Christian ways. They were to be subjects of the king. There was not the slightest warning, not the hint of a warning. The chief had been their leader for years and he came and went through Jamestown as free as a white man. We had his own son as a hostage, we feared nothing. Nothing.'

'Why did you have hostages then?' J asked.

'Not hostages,' she corrected herself swiftly. 'Adopted children. God-children. Children in our care. We were educating them in our ways. Turning them from savagery.'

'And what happened?' J asked.

'They waited and planned.' Her voice was lowered, the two men leaned forward to hear her, there was something fearful in the way the three white faces went closer together, and her voice dropped to a haunting whisper. 'They waited and planned and at eight o'clock one morning – Good Friday morning they chose in their blasphemy – all over the country they came out of the bushes, to each little farm, to each little family, to each lone man, they came out and struck us dead. They planned to kill every single one of us without a word of warning reaching the others. And they'd have done it too; but for one little turncoat Indian boy who told his master that he had been ordered to kill him, and the man ran to Jamestown and raised the alarm.'

'What happened?'

'They opened the arsenal at Jamestown and called the settlers in. Everyone who was near enough came in and the town was saved, but up and down the river, in every isolated farmhouse, there was a white man and woman with their skull staved in by a stone axe.'

She turned her bleak face to J. 'My husband's head was cleaved in two, with an axe of stone,' she said. 'My little boy was stabbed through the heart with an arrow head of shell. They came against us without

25

proper weapons, they came against us with reeds and shells and stones. It was like the land itself rose up and struck at us.'

There was a long silence.

She rose from the table and stacked the bowls, callous again. 'That's why I have no time for even the smallest girl of theirs,' she said. 'They are like stones and reeds and trees to me. I hate every stone and reed and tree in this land, and I hate every one of them. I hate them to their death and destruction. This land will never be home for me until everyone of them is gone.'

'How many of us died?' J asked. He said 'us' without thinking. This was a war of the dark forests against the white men; of course he counted himself among the planters.

'Not quite four hundred,' she said bitterly. 'Four hundred men and women who wanted nothing more than to live in peace in a little part of a great great land. And then the hunger came.'

'Hunger?'

'We had to leave the crops in the field, we were too afraid to bring them in,' she explained. 'We all crowded into Jamestown and manned the guns over the wooden walls. It was a bitter winter, and there wasn't enough to eat. And we couldn't trade with them as we usually did. We had always traded with them for their winter stores, they always had plenty and they always sold to us. But now we were at war with the very people who had fed us.'

J waited for more.

'We don't talk about that time,' she said shortly. 'About that winter. We ate what we could, and no blame to those who found what they could.'

J turned to his fellow lodger for an explanation.

'The graveyard,' the man said in an undertone. 'They dug up their dead and ate them.'

The woman's face was stony. 'We ate what we could get,' she said. 'And you'd have done the same. There's no such thing as Christian behaviour when you're starving. We did what we had to do.'

J felt the suppawn dinner rise up in the back of his throat at the thought of what the cook had tasted.

'We survived,' she said flatly.

'I'm sure –' J stammered.

'And when the weather got warmer those who were not dead of their wounds, or of grief, or of starvation, died of the plague,' she went on. 'All of us packed in to this little town, all of us sick with grief and fear. Hundreds died that winter, and it was all the Indians' fault. As soon as we could muster men and supplies we went against them. We passed a law and we swore an oath, that not a man or a woman would be left alive.'

The man nodded. 'We hunted them down like dogs and we pushed them further and further away. It was an order – kill all the men and women and enslave the children. We pretended to be at peace for a while and we watched them plant their crops and commit themselves to their fields, and then, and only then, we went in and destroyed their harvest. They make fish weirs, intricate clever things, we destroyed them wherever we saw them. We drove away the game so that they would starve when they went hunting, we burned them out of their villages so they were homeless, we trampled their crops in the field so they would know hunger as we had known hunger. We took our revenge.'

'We had some good hunting,' the woman said reminiscently. She drew three mugs of ale and set them on the table. 'I remember the soldiers from the fort coming in with the heads of the savages at their belt, and then setting them up along the gate like a gamekeeper stakes up a dead weasel.'

'And are they finished now?' J could hear the nervousness in his own voice.

'Oh yes,' the man said. 'This was sixteen years ago, remember, and there's not been a word from them since. They cannot live without the spread of land for their game and farming, and we have pushed them backwards and backwards towards the mountains. They used to live always on the move you see: winter inland, summer down towards the sea, spring to the fields. Once we built our houses and cleared the forest we drove them out, drove them like a herd of deer into bad foraging.'

'They must hate us as their worst enemies,' J said.

Neither of them answered. The man shrugged and lowered his face into his mug.

'We won, and that's the main thing,' the woman said firmly. 'It's our land now and if they want to live here they have to serve us. There's no more schools and teaching of them. There's no more peace and promises of friendship. If they want to stay in our borders they do as they are bid. They can be our slaves or their blood can water the fields. Nothing else.'

〰

At dawn J was down at the quayside, Jamestown silent behind him and only the gleam of the fires in the bread ovens showing that anyone was awake.

The girl was there before him. She had a small dugout canoe bobbing in the dark water. J surveyed it uneasily. It too much resembled the tree it recently had been. The bark had been stripped off and the sides roughly chiselled so that it was shaped to a point at both ends, the inside had been scorched and then scraped clean; but it still looked nothing more than a small tree: stripped, shaped, and hollowed.

She was seated in the prow, a paddle in the water, waiting for him. When she saw him she looked up and gestured, with a tiny authoritative movement, that he should take his place behind her.

'Won't it sink?' J demanded.

Again she made that small gesture.

J assumed that she could swim, and reminded himself that they were alongside the dock and the ship which had brought him from England was moored at the quayside, within hailing distance. He put his little travelling satchel in the boat and then stepped in himself. At once it rocked and nearly overturned.

J dropped to his knees, and found that the canoe steadied immediately. Before him was a paddle. He drew it out, careful not to move too fast, and put it in the water, on the same side as hers.

She glanced over her shoulder, her child's face serious, and shook her head. J transferred his paddle to the other side and was rewarded by a grave nod. Then she leaned forward and dug the blade of her paddle into the lapping river water, and they moved slowly away from the wooden pier.

At first J could see nothing, but all his other senses were fully alert. He felt the canoe moving smoothly and easily on the water, the current of the river and the ebb of the tide together drawing them out to sea. He sensed the immensity of the water around them, a great desert of water, and their canoe moving among it like a sleek, dark fish. He could smell the land ahead of them: the salt mud, rank tidewash weed and rotting driftwood; and from Jamestown, falling away behind them, the homely smell of woodsmoke and the rancid stink of the household waste which they tipped at the water's edge for the tide to take away.

Slowly the sky lightened and J could see the girl's outline, kneeling in the canoe ahead of him. She bowed forward, digging her paddle into the inky black water. J tried to copy her motion and the canoe suddenly skidded as he got the stroke right. She did not turn her head, she was absorbed in her own task of weaving air and water together.

He could hear the birds stirring in the woods on either side of the river. A thousand single calls and coos and cries were building to a cacophony of sound that drifted over the glassy water towards them.

There must be hundreds of thousands of birds in the wood to make such a sweep of sound, and then the river birds started to wake. J heard a clatter of quacking and a huge flight of ducks took off from the bank on his left and headed towards the brightening sky. Gulls were swirling and calling overhead, and then the whole world suddenly went dark as a flock of pigeons, innumerable birds, fled across the sky, blocking the light for minutes and filling the whole shadowy world with the creaking of their wings and the rush of their passage.

J had a sense of a virgin world: a place where man was a stranger, an interloper, who had not left a mark, a world where vast flocks and herds of animals and birds moved, obeying their natural order, and nothing could prevent them. It was a new world, another Eden, a paradise for a plant collector. For the first time in years, for the first time since Jane's death, J had a powerful sense of hope, of the possibilities before him. If men could make their home in this new land they could make a country like a paradise, rich and easy. Perhaps even he could make a home here. Perhaps he and the children could make a new home here and the old life at Lambeth, London, and the old losses of Lambeth, could be left far behind.

They paddled for an hour to cross the wide river and reach the other bank. Then they turned and followed the south bank eastward, towards the sea. Even though the ebbing tide was taking them downriver they had to paddle to hold the canoe on course, and J's shoulders and arm muscles were tight with strain after the first hour, but the girl still moved fluidly and easily, as if the delicate feathering of the paddle and the deep digging movement to push the boat forward were nothing to her.

As they drew closer to the bank J saw the virgin woods coming down to the water's edge and brightly coloured birds flirting from trees to water and back again. Every now and then there was a clearing in the woods and the bare earth of a ploughed field. Sometimes there were black men and white men planting side by side, and they raised their heads to watch the canoe go by. J waved, but the girl stared straight ahead as if she were a little statue, with no curiosity about her fellow men at all.

The sun came up, a pale yellow sun swimming in cloud. The mist was burned off the river and the stinging moths came out and formed a cloud around J's red, sweaty face. He puffed them off his lips but he could not spare a hand from the paddle to swat them away. He shook his head irritably and the canoe made a little wobble in the water.

At that movement she glanced back and saw him, hot, flushed, irritable, and with one smooth stroke she turned the canoe and plunged towards the shade of an inlet.

The trees closed around them, over their heads, around their backs, they were hidden in a world of green. The girl ran the canoe up on a sandbank and stepped out. She slipped off her servant's smock, folded it carefully and stowed it in the canoe. Then she pointed commandingly at him.

J took off his jacket, then she pointed at his boots.

'I'll keep my boots on,' J said.

She shook her head. Pointed to the vast reach of water, closed her eyes and mimed a man plunging downwards, dragged under by the weight of his boots.

'Oh,' J said. 'All right then.'

He sat on the wet sand and pulled off his boots, stood before her in his stockings, breeches and shirt. She gestured at the rest of his clothes.

J smiled, shook his head. 'I'll keep them on . . .'

She tugged at his shirt with an impatient little hand, and produced from the canoe, with a flourish, a little buckskin skirt, like her own.

'Indian breeches?' J asked.

She nodded.

'I cannot dress like a savage,' J said reasonably.

She pointed to the dugout canoe, to herself, to the distance they had come and the distance they were to go. Her meaning was clear. You are travelling like one of the Powhatan, with one of the Powhatan. Why not be comfortable?

'I'll get bitten,' J protested. He made little pinchers of his thumb and finger and pinched at the skin of his forearm, showed her the tiny irritating swellings on the skin of his face.

The girl nodded and produced the jar of grease she had used in the forest the day before, held her own smooth arm for his inspection, turned her little unmarked face towards him.

J looked around him in embarrassment. But the woods were loud only with birdsong and impervious to his shame. There was no-one within ten miles in any direction.

'Oh, all right,' he said awkwardly.

He stripped off his breeches, grateful for his long shirt tails which hid his nakedness from her. She held out the buckskin skirt. J struggled to put it on, under his shirt. She stepped lightly around to his back, pulled the shirt out of the way and tied the strings of the apron for him. The soft leather nestled against him like another skin. The air was

30

cool on his legs. J felt white and ungainly, a bleached leviathan beside her slight brown body; but he also felt comfortable for the first time since he had arrived in this painfully humid country.

She gestured that he should take off his shirt. J shucked it over his head and then she presented him with the jar of grease. With a sense of nothing left to lose, J put his fingers into the pot and smoothed it all over his face, his neck and his chest. It smelled dreadful and felt as sticky as honey.

She gave a tiny trill of laughter, and he looked down and saw his white skin streaked with red. She held out her bare arm to show him the comparison. Against her treacle-coloured skin the grease showed only as a darker brown, but J was striped white and red.

He paused, but she clicked at him like someone encouraging an animal, took the pot herself and ducked under his arm. He felt her little hands painting the stuff on his back. Despite himself he felt the tiniest flicker of arousal at the touch. But then she came before him again, and he saw that grave child's face and the swinging black plait of hair, and remembered that she was a little maid, not much older than his daughter, and under his protection.

J rubbed the grease into his skin. He thought he must look like a mummer at a feast, painted and dressed like a fool. But at least he felt cool. His embarrassment faded, and then he realised also he was no longer being bitten. The grease was repelling the insects that danced in a cloud on the waters all around them.

The girl nodded at him with evident approval and picked up his discarded clothes, folded them and stowed them in the canoe. Then she steadied the canoe while he climbed in again.

Without his breeches and awkward boots, J found he was more comfortable. There was a hollow carved in the wooden floor and without the bulk of his breeches and boots his knees fitted into the space. The wood, slightly porous, was cool and pleasantly damp on his bare legs, the river air blew gently against his naked chest. He put his face up, enjoying the cool breeze on his neck, feeling the sweat on his face cooling and drying. The girl gave him a small triumphant smile and pushed off, stepping into the canoe before him and kneeling in one smooth movement. The canoe barely bobbed in the water. Then she turned it around and paddled it strongly towards the main river once more.

They paddled until midday. J was troubled neither by insects nor by the growing heat of the sun in his face. When the sun was at its highest, the girl turned the canoe into an inlet of the river and ran it ashore.

At once the cool greenness of the trees engulfed them. J got out of the canoe, and staggered a little on his cramped legs. She smiled and went sure-footed as a deer up the sandy beach to the forest. J reached for his satchel and followed her.

She offered him the forest with a little wave of her hand, as a princess might gesture to a visiting ambassador as if to say: 'my lands'.

J nodded. The girl took his hand and pulled him a little way towards the trees. He was to go and collect whatever specimens he wanted. J paused.

'What will you do?'

She made a gesture to show that she would stay there. She picked up a few dry sticks and piled them together: she would make a fire. She took a little hoeing stick from the purse at her belt, and mimed digging up roots: she would find food. She gestured towards the trees and mimed sleep: she would find some shelter for them.

'We stay here tonight?' J asked, repeating her mime of sleep.

She nodded.

'I will come back here in a little while,' he said. He pointed to himself and to the forest, and showed his walking fingers. She nodded, and then mimed herself calling and then a mime of listening.

'I'm to stay where I can hear you?' J asked, and was rewarded with a nod and a smile.

Feeling like a child sent out to play, J went to the canoe and pulled on his leather boots, took his bag and went along the shoreline. He glanced back.

She was drawing the canoe higher up the beach, away from the reach of the tide. Then she turned and started collecting firewood. She seemed as comfortably at home in this wilderness as a young woman in the kitchen of her own house. J turned away and wandered further along the shoreline, his eyes at the edge of the wood looking for saplings and little plants in their first flush of spring growth that he might get safely home to England.

He obeyed her order that he stay within earshot, and worked his way in a sweep around their little camp until he emerged on the shoreline on the other side, his satchel bulging with seedlings and cuttings wrapped in damp linen.

She was putting the finishing touches on a shelter for the night. She had bent three saplings together and lashed them to make a low bender.

She had roofed them with some wide green leaves and filled in the walls with rushes. The canoe was drawn up before the open mouth of the little hut and tipped on its side as protection, and there was a small fire smoking before the hut and two fishes staked on sharp sticks, waiting to be roasted. J came quietly but she did not jump when she saw him, he imagined that she had heard his every move since he had left her at midday. She nodded gravely as she saw him and then pointed to his satchel.

'Yes. I've done well,' he said. He opened the flap of the bag and showed her. She nodded her approval and then indicated behind him. She had weeded and dug a little patch of ground.

J felt a sense of real delight. 'For my plants?' He pointed to his satchel. She nodded and looked at him, querying if it was what he wanted.

'That is excellent!' J beamed. 'I shall collect more tomorrow and plant them up here, and only move them again when we go back to Jamestown. Thank you!'

The girl nodded with a little smile and he saw that she relished his praise just as his daughter Frances did. 'You're very, very clever,' he said, and was rewarded by a slight blush and another smile.

She turned to the fire and threw on some dry kindling, and the blaze flickered up. She hunkered down on her heels and fanned the flame with a handful of stiff reeds until the twigs were glowing red, then she took one stick with the spitted fish and gave J the other. She showed him how to hold it above the glowing twigs so that it roasted in the heat but did not catch fire, and to turn it when the skin was brown and crispy.

When it was cooked she tipped the one on her stick on to a broad green leaf and proffered it to J, and then took the one he had cooked which was too dark on one side, and still a little raw on the other. She bowed her head over it for a moment, for all the world as if she were saying grace in a Christian home, and extended a hand to the sky, then turned it palm down to the earth. J realised that she *was* saying grace, which he had quite forgotten, and he had a momentary uncomfortable sense of confusion as to which of them was the ignorant pagan and which the civilised human. Then she smiled at him and started eating.

It was a firm white fish with a wonderful spicy taste from the scorched skin. J ate with relish, leaving only the bones, the head, tail and fins. When he had finished she drew from inside the canoe a little basket of dried fruit and gave him a handful of berries, dried blueberries. They were like a handful of pebbles in his mouth at first and then their taste seeped out, making his face pucker with their sourness, which made her laugh.

It was growing cold. The sun was behind them, inland behind the high trees. J put some more wood on the fire, and the girl got to her feet. She took a small glowing twig from the fire, went down to the water's edge, and laid the twig on a shell at her bare feet. From the purse at her waist she took out a small pinch of something and then, without embarrassment, untied the thong of her buckskin skirt and laid it to one side. She picked up the burning twig and the pinch of herbs and, naked, waded into the water. J heard her gasp a little at the coldness of it.

The tide was coming in; the river, a mixture of salt and sweet, lapped at the sand beach. The girl was nothing more than a dark shadow against the dancing, gleaming water. J watched her blow on the glowing end of the twig and then put it to her cupped hand and blow again. She was lighting the herbs. J smelled a sharp, acrid smell like tobacco, carried to him on the onshore wind. Then he saw her scatter the smoking herb on the water.

She washed her face and her body, and then raised her wet head to where the moon was showing low on the horizon and lifted her hands in prayer. Then she turned back to the land and waded out of the water.

J thought of evening prayers at Lambeth, of his dead wife's faith, and of the lodging-house woman who had assured him that these people were animals. He shook his head at the contradictions. He pulled off his boots and went into the shelter she had built them.

Inside she had heaped two beds of leaves. They were soft and aromatic. J's clothes were neatly spread over the top of one heap, his travelling cloak on top of it all. J rolled himself up in its comforting smelly wool and was asleep before she had come inside.

J and the Indian girl stayed for nearly a month in the shelter she had built. Every day they went further afield, paddling in the morning in the canoe, and then she would run it aground and fish, or set snares for birds, while J foraged in the undergrowth for saplings and young spring growth. They would come companionably home in the light of the setting sun to the little camp and J would heel in his collection while she plucked the birds or cleaned the fish and prepared the evening meal.

There was a powerful dreamlike quality to the time. It was a relationship like no other. The grieving man and the silent girl worked together day after day with a bond that grew but needed no words. J was absorbed in one of the greatest pleasures a man can have – discovering a new country, a country completely unknown to him – and she, freed from the conventions and dangers of Jamestown, practised her woodcraft skills and observed the laws of her own people for once without a critical white observer judging and condemning her every move, but only with a man who smiled at her kindly and let her teach him how to live under the trees.

They never exchanged words. J would talk to her, as he would talk to his little seedlings in the seed bed she had made for him, for the pleasure of hearing his own voice, and for the sense of making a connection. Sometimes she would smile and nod or make a little grunt of affirmation or give a trill of laughter, but she never spoke words, not in her language nor his own, until J thought it must be as the magistrate had said and that she was dumb.

He wanted to encourage her to speak. He wanted to teach her English, he could not imagine how she could survive in Jamestown, comprehending only the outflung pointing arm or a clip to the head. He showed her a tree and said 'pine', he showed her a leaf and said 'leaf', but she would only smile and laugh and refuse to repeat what he told her.

'You must learn to speak English,' J said earnestly to her. 'How will you manage if you cannot understand anything that is said to you?'

The girl shook her head and bent over her work. She was twisting supple green twigs into a mesh of some sort. As he watched she made the final knot and held it up to show him. J was so ignorant that he could not even tell what it was that she had made. She was smiling proudly.

She set the little contraption on the forest floor and stepped back a few paces. She dropped to her feet, hunched her back and sidled towards it, her arms stretched before her, her hands shaped like beaks, snapping together. At once she was a lobster, unmistakable.

J laughed. 'Lobster!' he said. 'Say "lobster"!'

She pushed back her hair where it fell over the left side of her face and shook her head in her refusal. She mimed eating, as if to say, 'No. *Eat* lobster.'

J pointed to the trap. 'You have made a lobster pot?'

She nodded and stowed it in the canoe ready for setting at dawn the next day when they went out.

'But you must learn to speak,' J persisted. 'What will you do when I go back to England? If your mother is put in prison again?'

She shook her head, refusing to understand him, and then she took a twig from the fire and walked towards the river and J fell silent, respecting the ritual of casting tobacco on the water, which was the same at dawn and dusk, and which marked her transition from day to night to day again.

He went into the shelter and pretended to sleep so that she might come in and sleep beside him without any fear. It was a ritual he had developed of his own to keep them both safe from his growing fascination with her.

Only on the first night, when he had been so weary from paddling that he could not keep his eyes open, had he slept at once. All the other nights he had lain awake listening to her near-imperceptible breathing, enjoying the sense of her closeness beside him. He did not desire her as he might have desired a woman. It was a feeling more subtle and complicated than that. J felt as he might have done if some precious rare animal had chosen to trust him, had chosen to rest beside him. With all his heart he wanted neither to frighten nor disturb her, with all his heart he wanted to stretch out a hand and stroke that smooth, beautiful flank.

Physically, she was the most beautiful object he had ever seen. Not even his wife Jane had ever been naked before him, they had always made love in a tumble of clothes, generally in darkness. His children had been bound in their swaddling bands as tight as silkworms in a chrysalis from the moment of their birth, and dressed in tiny versions of adult clothing as soon as they were able to walk. J had never seen either of them naked, had never bathed them, had never dressed them. The play of light on bare skin was strange to J, and he found that when the girl was working near him he watched her, for the sheer pleasure of seeing her rounded limbs, the strength in her young body, the lovely line of her neck, the curve of her spine, the nestling mystery of her sex which he glimpsed below the little buckskin apron.

Of course he thought of touching her. The casual instruction from Mr Joseph not to rape her was tantamount to admitting that he might do so. But J would not have hurt her, any more than he would have broken an eggshell in a drawer of the collection at Lambeth. She was a thing of such simple beauty that he wanted only to hold her, to caress her. He supposed that of all the things he might imagine with her, what he wanted to do most was to collect her, and take her back to Lambeth to the warm, sunlit rarities room where she would be the most beautiful object of them all.

J would have lost track of time in the woods, but one morning the girl started to take the thatch from the roof of the little hut and untie the saplings. They sprang back undamaged, only a slight bend in the trunks betraying the fact that they had been walls and roof joists.

'What are you doing?' J asked her.

In silence she pointed back the way they had come. It was time to go home.

'Already?'

She nodded and turned to J's little bed of plants.

It was filled with heads and leaves of small plants. J's satchel was bursting with gathered seed heads. With her hoeing stick she started to lift the plants, tenderly pulling at the thin filaments of roots and laying them in the dampened linen. J took his trowel and worked at the other end of the row. Carefully they packed them into the canoe.

The fire which she had faithfully kept glowing for all the days of their stay she now damped with water, and then scuffed over with sand. The cooking sticks which they had used as spits for fish, game birds, crabmeat and even the final feast of lobster she broke and cast into the river. The reeds which had thatched the walls and the leaves which had thatched the roof she scattered. In only a little while their campsite was destroyed, and a white man would have looked at the clearing and thought himself the first man there.

J found that he was not ready to leave. 'I don't want to go,' he said unwillingly. He looked into her serene uncomprehending face. 'You know ... I don't want to go back to Jamestown, and I don't want to go back to England.'

She looked at him, waiting for his next words. It was as if he were free to decide, and she would do whatever he wished.

J looked out over the river. Now and then the water stirred with the thick shoals of fish. Even in the short weeks that they had been living at the riverside he had seen more and more birds flying into the country from the south. He had a sense of the continent stretching forever to the south, unendingly to the north. Why should he turn his back on it and return to the dirty little town on the edge of the river, surrounded with felled trees, inhabited by people who struggled for everything, for life itself?

The girl did not prompt him. She hunkered down on the sand and looked out over the river, content to wait for his decision.

'Shall I stay?' J asked, secure in the knowledge that she could not understand his rapid speech, that he was raising no hopes. 'Shall we build ourselves another shelter and spend our days going out and bringing in fine specimens of plants? I could send them home to my father, he could pay off our debts with them, and then he could send me enough money so that I could live here always. He could raise my children, and when they are grown they could join me. I need never go back to that house in London, never again sleep alone in that bed, in her bed. Never dream of her. Never go into church past her grave, never hear her name, never have to speak of her.'

She did not even turn her head to look at him, to see if there was meaning in his quiet whispering.

'I could make a new life here, I could become a new man. And this year, next year, you will be a beautiful woman,' J said, his voice very gentle. 'And then . . .'

She turned at that, as if she understood the tone of his voice. Turned and looked directly at him, without shame, as if she were about to ask him what he meant – if he were serious. J broke off and flushed. He managed an awkward smile.

'Well!' he said. 'Just as well this all means nothing to you! Better be off!'

She rose to her feet and gestured to the river. Her half-tilted head asked: 'Which way?' South into the country, which neither of them knew, or upriver to Jamestown?

'Jamestown,' J said shortly, pointing north-west. 'I have been rambling like a fool. Jamestown, of course.'

He seated himself in the canoe and steadied it with his paddle. It was easier now that they had gone out every day and he had grown skilful. She pushed off the prow of the boat and stepped aboard. They paddled as a team and the boat wove easily along the shoreline, and then they felt the stronger push of the river.

An hour out of Jamestown, where the river started getting dirty and the bank was pocked with felled trees, she called a halt and they ran the canoe ashore. Slowly, unwillingly, they washed off the grease in the water. She took a handful of leaves and scrubbed his back so that his white skin shone through the dark grease and the familiar smell, which he had hated so much on the first day, was dispersed. Together they put on the clothes they must wear in the town, and she shrank into the confines of the ragged shift and looked no longer like a deer in dappled sunlight but instead like a sluttish maidservant.

J, shrugging back into his shirt and breeches after the freedom of the buckskin loincloth, felt as if he were taking on the shackles of some sort of prison, becoming a man again with a man's sorrows and no longer a free being, at home in the forest. At once the cloud of insects settled greedily on his sunburned arms and shoulders and face. J swatted at them and swore, and the girl smiled with her lips but with no laughter in her eyes.

'We'll come out again,' J said encouragingly. He pointed to himself and to her and to the trees. 'We'll come out again some day.'

She nodded but her eyes were dark.

They got into the canoe and began to paddle upstream to Jamestown. J was plagued all the way by the biting moths and the sweat in his eyes, the tightness of the shirt across his back and the rub of his boots. By the time they came alongside the little wooden quay he was sweating and irritable. There was a new vessel in port and a crowd on the quayside. No-one wasted more than a quick glance on the little Indian girl and the white man in the dugout canoe.

They ran the canoe aground at the side of the quay and started to unload the plants. From the shadow of the dockside building a woman came and stood before them.

She was an Indian woman but she wore a dress and a shawl tied across her breasts. Her hair was tied back like a white woman's and it exposed her face which was badly scarred, pocked all over with pale ridges of scar tissue as if someone, long ago, had fired a musket at point-blank range into her face.

'Mr Tradescant?' She spoke with a harsh accent.

J spun to hear his name and recoiled from the bitterness in her face. She looked past him at the girl and spoke in a rapid string of words, fluting and meaningless as birdsong.

The child answered, as voluble as she, shaking her head emphatically and then pointing to J and to the plants and to the canoe.

The woman turned to J again. 'She tells me you have not hurt her.'

'Of course not!'

'Not raped her.'

'No!'

The bowstring-tight line of the woman's shoulders suddenly slumped, and she gave a sharp sob, like a cough of vomit. 'When they told me you had taken her into the woods I thought I would not see her again.'

'I am a plant collector,' J said wearily. 'See. There are the plants. She was my guide. She made a camp. She hunted and fished for us. She has been a very, very good girl.' He glanced at her and she gave him a swift encouraging smile. 'She has been very helpful. I am in her debt.'

The Indian woman had not followed all of the words but she saw the glance that passed between them and read correctly the affection and mutual trust.

'You are her mother?' J asked. 'Just . . . er . . . released?'

The woman nodded. 'Mr Joseph told me he had given her to you for the month. I thought I would not see her again. I thought you had taken her to the woods to use her and bury her there.'

'I'm sorry,' J said awkwardly. 'I am a stranger here.'

She looked at him with a bitter line around her mouth. 'You are all strangers here,' she observed.

'She can speak?' J remarked, tentatively, wondering what it might mean.

The woman nodded, not bothering to answer him.

The girl had finished unloading the canoe. She looked at J and gestured to the plants, as if asking what should be done with them. J turned to the woman. 'I have to fetch some barrels and prepare these plants for my voyage home. I may take a passage on this ship. Can she stay and help me?'

'We'll both help,' the woman said shortly. 'I don't leave her alone in this town.' She hitched her skirts a little and went down to the shoreline. J watched the two women. They did not embrace; but they stood just inches away from each other and gazed into each other's faces as if they could read all they needed to know in one exchange of looks. Then the mother nodded briefly and they turned side by side and their shoulders brushed as they bent over the plants together.

J went up to his lodging to fetch the barrels for packing the plants.

They worked until it was dusk, and then they worked again the next day, wrapping the cuttings in earth and damp linen, layering them in the barrel separated by damp linen and leaves, and packing the seeds in dry sand and sealing down the lid. When it was done, J had four half-barrels of plants which he would keep open to the air and damp with fresh water, and one sealed barrel of seeds. He shouted up to the ship and a couple of sailors came down and loaded them for him. At least he would have room to care for them on the voyage home. There were only a couple of people making the return voyage to England. The rest of the space was taken up with the cargo of tobacco.

'We sail in the morning at first light,' the captain warned him. 'You'd best get your things aboard tonight and sleep aboard yourself. I can't wait for passengers, when the tide ebbs we go out with it.'

J nodded. 'I will.' He had no desire to return to the inn and the embittered landlady. He thought if she called the girl a beast in his hearing then he would speak in her defence and then there would be a quarrel and perhaps worse.

He turned to the two women. 'What is her name?' he asked the mother.

'Mary.'

'Mary?'

She nodded. 'She was taken from me when she was a baby and baptised Mary.'

'Is that the name you use for her?'

She hesitated, as if she was not sure she would trust him. But then there was a murmur from the girl at her side.

'She is called Suckahanna.'

'Suckahanna?' J confirmed.

The girl smiled and nodded. 'It means "water".'

J nodded, and then the fact of her speaking his own language suddenly struck him. 'You can speak English?'

She nodded.

He had a moment of profound, unhappy bewilderment. 'Then why did you never . . . ? You never . . . ? I did not know! All this time we have travelled together and you have been dumb!'

'I ordered her never to speak to a white man,' the woman said. 'I thought she would be safer if she did not answer.'

J opened his mouth to argue – it must be right that the girl should be able to speak, to defend herself.

But the mother cut him off with an abrupt gesture of her hand. 'I have just come from a month in prison for saying the wrong thing,' she pointed out. 'Sometimes it is better to say nothing at all.'

J glanced at the ship behind them. Suddenly he did not want to leave. The realisation that the girl had a name, and could understand him, made her intensely interesting. What had she been thinking during their days of silent companionship? What might she not say to him? It was as if she had been a princess under a spell in a romance and suddenly she had found her tongue. When he had confided in her and told her of his feelings, for his home, for his children, for his plants, she had met his confession with an impassive face. But she had understood, she had understood everything he said. And so, in a way, she knew him better than any woman had ever known him before. And she would

41

know that only yesterday morning he was tempted to stay in this new land; to stay with her.

'I have to go. I am promised in England,' he said, thinking that they might contradict him, that he might not have to go, as if the breaking of the spell which had kept her silent might release him too.

The two women said nothing, they simply watched the indecision and reluctance in his face.

'What will become of you two now?' he asked, as if their plans might affect him.

'We will leave Jamestown,' the woman said quietly. 'We will go back into the forest and find our people. I thought we would be safer to stay here, my husband and my father are dead. I thought I could live inside the walls and work for the white men. I thought I could be their servant.' She shook her head. 'But there is no trusting them. We will go back to our own.'

'And Suckahanna?'

The woman looked at him, her eyes bitter. 'There is no life for her,' she said. 'We can find our people but not our old life. The places where we used to grow our crops are planted with tobacco, the rivers are thin of fish and the game is going, scared away by the guns. Everywhere we used to run, there is the mark of a boot on the trails. I don't know where she will live her life. I don't know where she will find a home.'

'Surely there is room for your people as well as the planters,' J said passionately. 'I can't believe there is not space in this land . . . we were out for nearly a month and we saw no-one. It's a mighty land, it stretches for miles and miles. Surely there is room for your people as well as mine?'

'But your people don't want us here. Not since the war. When we plant fields they destroy our crops, when they see a fish weir they break it, when they see a village they fire it. They have sworn we shall be destroyed as a people. When my family were killed they took me into slavery and I thought that Suckahanna and I would be safe as slaves. But they beat me and raped me, and the men will soon want her too.'

'She could come with me,' J suggested wildly. 'I could take her to my home in England. I have a son and a daughter there, I could bring them up all together.'

The woman thought for a moment and then shook her head. 'She is called Suckahanna,' she said firmly. 'She must be by the river.'

J was about to argue but then he remembered seeing Pocahontas, the great Princess Pocahontas, when he was just a boy himself and had been taken to view her as a child might be taken to see the lions in the Tower.

She had not been Princess Pocahontas by then, she had been Rebecca Rolfe, wearing ordinary English clothes and shivering in an English winter. A few weeks later she had died, in exile, longing for her own land.

'I will come again,' he said. 'I will take these things to England and come out again. And next time, when I come, I shall build a house here and you shall be my servant and she shall be safe.'

'How could she be safe with you?' her mother asked swiftly. 'She's not a child, though she's so slight. She's near thirteen now, by the time you come back she'll be a woman. There's no safety for a Powhatan woman in the white man's town.'

J thought for a moment and then took the step, the next step, speaking without thought, speaking from his heart, his unexamined heart. 'I shall marry her,' he promised. 'She will be my wife and I will keep her safe and she shall have her own house and fields here. I shall build her a house beside the river and she need fear for nothing.'

He was speaking to her mother but he was looking at the girl. A deep rosy blush was spreading from the coarse linen neck of the shift up to her forehead where the bear grease still stained her brown skin at the dark hairline. 'Should you like that?' J asked her gently. 'I am old enough to be your father, I know. And I don't understand your ways. But I could keep you safe, and I could make a house for you.'

'I should like that,' the girl said very quietly. 'I should like to be your wife.'

The older woman put out her hand to J and he felt the roughened palm in his own. Then she took her daughter's hand and joined them together in a hard grip. 'When you come back she shall be your wife,' she promised him.

'I will,' the girl said.

'I will,' J swore.

The woman released them and turned away as if there was nothing more to be said. J watched her go, and then turned to Suckahanna. She seemed at once very familiar, the easy companion of weeks of travelling and camping, and exquisitely strange, a girl on the edge of womanhood, a virgin who would be his wife.

Carefully, as if he were transplanting a seedling, he put his hand to her cheek, stroked the line of her jaw. She quivered as he touched her but moved neither forwards nor back. She let him caress her face for a moment, for one moment only; and then she turned on her heel and ran from him.

'Come back soon,' she called, and he could hardly see her in the darkness as she went swiftly after her mother, only her linen shift gleaming in the dusk. 'Come in the good time, the fruitful time, Nepinough, and I shall make you a great feast and we will build our house before winter comes.'

'I will!' J said again. But she was already gone, and the next day at dawn the ship sailed and he did not see her.

Summer 1638, London

J's ship arrived at London docks at dawn in early April and he came blearily out of his cabin into the cold English air, wrapped in his travelling cloak with his hat pulled down on his head. A wagoner was idling on the dockside, fiddling with the feedbag at the head of a dozing horse.

'Are you for hire?' J shouted down.

The man looked up. 'Aye!'

'Come and fetch my goods,' J called. The man started up the gangplank and then recoiled at the waving fronds of saplings and small trees.

'Goods?' he asked. 'This is a forest!'

J grinned. 'There's more than this,' he said.

Together they humped the barrels filled with damp earth down the gangplank and into the wagon, the whippy branches of trees stirring above their heads. Then J brought another barrel of seeds and nuts, and finally his own small bundle of clothes and a chest of rarities.

'I know where we're headed,' the man said, climbing on to the box and waking the horse with a slap of the reins on its back.

'You do?'

'Tradescant's Ark,' the man said certainly. 'It's the only place in the world that you'd go to with half a forest on board.'

'Quite right,' J said, and put his feet up on the board. 'What's the news?' he asked.

The carter spat accurately over the side of the wagon and hit the dirt road. 'Nothing new,' he said. 'A lot worse.'

J waited.

'Everything you can eat or drink is taxed,' the carter said. 'But that was true before you went away, I dare say. Now they've got a new tax, a rotting crime of a tax: ship money levied on everyone, however far they are from the sea. It's the ports that should pay ship money, they're the ones that need the navy to keep them free of pirates. But the king is making all the towns pay, even inland towns. My sister lives in Cheltenham. Why should she pay ship money? What are the seas to her? But she has to.'

J nodded. 'The king won't call a parliament, then?'

'They say he won't even hear the word mentioned.'

J allowed himself a pleasurable 'tut tut' of disapproval.

'If he called a parliament and asked them to set a tax they would tell him what they think of him as king,' the carter said baldly. 'They would tell him what they think about a Privy Council which is advised by a Papist French queen, and a court which is run by Frenchmen and Jesuits.'

'That can't be so,' J said firmly. 'I've only been gone a few months.'

'It's well known the Tradescants are the king's servants,' the man said unpleasantly.

'It is indeed,' J agreed, remembering his father's regular warnings against gossip that could be overheard as treason.

'Then I'll say no more,' the carter remarked. 'And see how you like it when they knock on your door and tell you that now there is a monopoly declared on the dirt in your garden and you have to pay a fine of ten per cent to some courtier if you want to plant in it. Because that's what's happened to every other trade in the kingdom while the king taxes the traders but won't call a parliament which could tax the gentry for their rents.'

The man paused, waiting for a shocked response. J discreetly kept silent.

'You'll have heard that the Scots have sworn they won't read their prayers from the new book?'

'No?'

The man nodded. 'All of 'em. Taken against Archbishop Laud's prayer book. Say they won't read a word of it. Archbishop is put out. King is put out. Some say he'll make 'em, some say he can't make 'em. Why should a king order what you say to God?'

'I don't know,' J said tactfully. 'I've no opinion on the matter.' And he tipped his hat over his eyes and dozed as the wagon jolted down the familiar road to his home.

He did not lift his hat as they went down the South Lambeth road towards the common; but he looked sharply all around him from under the brim. It was all well. His father's house still stood proudly, set back from the road, the little bridge spanning the stream that ran alongside the road. It was a handsome farmhouse in the old timbered style, but on the side of the house was the ambitious new wing, commissioned by his father for the housing of the rarities, their great collection of oddities from the monstrous to the miniature. At the back of the house was the garden which made their name and their livelihood, and the rarities room overlooked the garden through its great windows of Venetian glass. J, taught by a long-standing habit, looked at the ground as the cart drove around the south side of the building so that he did not see his father's vainglorious stone crest, affixed to the new wing in defiance both of the college of heralds and of the simple truth. They were not Tradescant esquires and never had been, but John Tradescant, his father, had drawn up and then commissioned a stonemason to carve his own crest; and nothing J could say could persuade him to take it down.

J directed the carter past the rarities room, where the terrace over-looked the orderly gardens, on to the stable yard so that the plants could be unloaded directly beside the pump for watering. The stable lad, looking out over the half-door, saw the waving tops of small trees in the cart and shouted, 'The master's home!' and came tumbling out into the yard.

They heard him in the kitchen and the maid came running up the hall and flung open the back door as J mounted the steps to the terrace and stepped into his house.

At once he recoiled in surprise. A woman he did not know, dark-haired, sober-faced, with a pleasant confident smile, came down the stairs, hesitated when she saw him looking up at her, and then came steadily on.

'How d'you do,' she said formally, and gave him a small nod of her head, as if she were a man and an equal.

'Who the devil are you?' J asked abruptly.

She looked a little awkward. 'Will you come in here?' she said, and showed him into his own parlour. The maid was on her hands and knees lighting the fire. The woman waited until the flame had caught and then dismissed the girl with a quick gesture of her hand.

'I am Hester Pooks,' she said. 'Your father invited me to stay here.'

'Why?' J demanded.

Hester hesitated. 'I imagine you don't know . . .' She broke off. 'I am very sorry to have to tell you that your father is dead.'

He gasped and swayed. 'My father?'

She nodded, saying nothing.

J dropped into a chair and was silent for a long moment. 'I shouldn't be surprised . . . but it is a dreadful shock . . . I know he was a great age, but he was always . . .'

She took a chair opposite him without invitation, and sat quietly, folding her hands in her lap. When J turned to her she was waiting, judging her time to tell him more.

'He didn't suffer at all,' she said. 'He grew very tired, over the winter, and he went to bed to rest. He died very peacefully, just as if he fell asleep. We had brought many of his flowers into his room. He died surrounded by them.'

J shook his head, still incredulous. 'I wish I had been here,' he said. 'I wish to God I had been here.'

Hester paused. 'God is very merciful,' she said gently. 'At the moment of his death he thought that he saw you. He was waiting and waiting for you to return, and he woke as his bedroom door opened, and he thought that he saw you. He died thinking that you had come safe home. I know that he died happy, thinking that he had seen you.'

'He said my name?' J asked.

She nodded. 'He said: "Oh! You at last!"'

J frowned. The old fear that he was not first in his father's heart returned to him. 'But did he say my name? Was it clear that he meant me?'

Hester paused for a moment and then looked into the gentle, vulnerable face of the man that she meant to marry. She lied easily. 'Oh yes,' she said firmly. 'He said: "Oh! You at last!", and then as he lay back on the pillow he said "J."'

J paused, and took it all in. Hester watched him in silence.

'I can't believe it,' he said. 'I don't know how to go on without him. The Ark, and the gardens, the royal gardens – I have always worked beside him. I have lost my employer and my master as well as my father.'

She nodded. 'He left a letter for you.'

J watched her as she crossed the room and took the sealed letter from a drawer in the table.

'I think it's about me,' she said bluntly.

J paused as he took it from her. 'Who *are* you?' he asked again.

She took a little breath. 'I am Hester Pooks. I'm all but alone in the world. Your father liked me, and my uncle told him I had a good dowry. I met him at court. My uncle is a painter, commissioned by the queen. My family is a good family, all artists and musicians, all with royal or noble patrons.' She paused and smiled. 'But not much money. Your father thought I might suit you. He wanted to make sure that there was someone to bring up his grandchildren, and to keep them here. He didn't want them living in London with your wife's parents. He thought I would marry you.'

48

J's jaw dropped open. 'He has found me a wife? I'm a man of thirty years of age and he found me a wife as if I were a boy? And he chose you?'

Hester looked him squarely in the face. 'I'm no beauty,' she said. 'I imagine your wife was lovely. Frances is such a pretty girl, and they tell me she takes after her mother. But I can run a house, and I can run a business, I love plants and trees and a garden, and I like children, I like *your* children. Whether or not you want to marry me, I should like to be a friend to Frances in particular. It would suit me to marry you and I wouldn't make great demands on you. I don't have great expectations.'

She paused. 'It would be an arrangement to suit ourselves,' she said. 'And it would leave you free to garden at the royal palace of Oatlands or to go abroad again and know that everything was safe here.'

J looked from her to his letter. 'This is outrageous! I have barely been home a moment and already I learn that my father is dead and that some woman, who I've never met before in my life, is half-betrothed to me. And anyway . . .' He broke off. 'I have other plans.'

She nodded soberly. 'It would have been easier if he had lived to explain it himself,' she said. 'But you are not half-betrothed, Mr Tradescant. It is entirely up to you. I shall leave you to read your letter. Is it your wish that I wake the children and bring them down to see you?'

He was distracted. 'Are they both well?'

She nodded. 'Frances especially grieves for her grandfather but they are both in perfect health.'

J shook his head in bewilderment. 'Bring them in to me when they wake,' he said. 'No need to wake them early. I will read this letter from my father. I need time. I do feel . . .' He broke off. 'All my life he has managed and controlled me!' he exclaimed in a sudden explosion of irritation. 'And just when I think I am my own man at his death I find that he had my future life in his hands, too.'

She paused at the doorway with her hand on the brass door ring. 'He did not mean to order you,' she said. 'He was thinking that I might set you free, not be a burden. And he told me very clearly that you had buried your heart with your wife and that you would never love me nor any woman again.'

J felt a pang of deep guilt. 'I shall never love a woman in my wife's place,' he said carefully. 'Jane could never be replaced.'

She nodded, she thought he was warning her. She did not realise that he was speaking to himself, reproaching himself for that runaway sense of freedom, for his sense of joy with the young girl in the wood so far from home and responsibilities and the normal rules of life.

'I don't expect love,' Hester said simply, recalling him to the shadowy room. 'I thought we might be able to help each other. I thought we might be . . . helpmeets.'

J looked at her, looked at her and saw her for the first time as she stood in the doorway, framed by the dark wood. He saw the simple plain face, the smooth white cap, the intelligent dark eyes and the strength of her jaw. 'What on earth put it into his head?' he asked.

'I think I did,' she said with a glimmer of a smile. 'It would suit me very well. Perhaps, when you are over the surprise of it, you will think that it will suit you too.'

He watched her close the door behind her and opened his father's letter.

> *My dear son,*
>
> *I have made a will leaving the Ark entire to you. I hope that it will bring you much joy. I hope that Baby John will succeed you, as you succeed me, and that the name of Tradescant will always mean something to people who love their gardens.*
>
> *If I am dead when you return then I leave you my blessing and my love. I am going to join your mother, and my two masters, Sir Robert and the Duke, and I am ready to go to them. Do not grieve for me, J, I have had a long life and one which many men would envy.*
>
> *The young woman called Hester Pooks has a substantial dowry and is a sensible woman. I have spoken to her about you and I believe she would make a good wife to you and a good mother to the children. She is not another Jane, because there never could be another Jane. But she is a straightforward, kind young woman and I think you need one such as her.*
>
> *Of course it is your decision. But if I had lived long enough to see your return I would have introduced her to you with my earnest recommendation.*
>
> *Farewell my son, my dear son,*
> *John Tradescant.*

J sat very still and watched the kindling twigs in the fire flicker and turn to knotted skeletal lace of dry ash. He thought of his father's determination and his care, which showed itself in the meticulous nursery and seed bed, in pruning and weeding and in the unending twisting and training of his beloved climbing plants, and showed itself here too, in providing a wife for his adult son. He felt his irritated sense of thwarted independence melt before his affection for his father. And at the thought of the gardens being left to him in trust for another John Tradescant coming behind them both he felt the anger inside him dissolve, and he slipped to the floor and rested his head in his father's chair and wept for him.

❧

Frances, coming in a little later, found her father composed and seated in the window where he could look out at the cold horse chestnut avenue and the swirls of fog in the early-morning darkness.

'Father?' she said tentatively.

He turned and held out his arms to her and she ran into his embrace. He brought her close to him and felt the light tiny bones of her body and smelled the warm clean smell of her skin and hair. For a moment he thought vividly and poignantly of Suckahanna, who was no heavier but whose every muscle was like whipcord.

'You've grown,' he said. 'I swear you are nearly up to my chest.'

She smiled up at him. 'I am nine,' she said seriously. 'And Baby John is bigger than when you left. And heavier. I can't lift him now he's five. Hester has to.'

'Hester does, does she? D'you like Hester?'

He thought she looked at him as if she needed help in saying something, as if there were something she could not say. 'Yes.'

'Your grandfather thought she might marry me, he thought she might be a mother to you.'

A look of relief crossed her face. 'We need a mother,' she said. 'I can't lift Baby John now he's so big, and I don't always know what to do when he cries. If he were to be sick, like Mama was sick, I wouldn't know how to care for him and he might die . . .' She broke off and gulped on a sob. 'We need a mother,' she said earnestly. 'A cook isn't the same.'

'I'm sorry,' J said. 'I didn't know.'

'I thought you would bring us one home from Virginia, with other things in the cart,' she said childishly.

J thought for a moment of the girl, only a few years older than this one, thanked his luck that he had not been so misled as to bring her back here and burden himself with her care as well as that of his children. 'There's no-one in that country who could be a mother to you,' he said shortly. 'No-one who could be a wife to me here.'

Frances blinked back her tears and looked up at him. 'But we need one. A mother who knows what to do when Baby John is naughty, and teaches him his letters.'

51

'Yes,' J said. 'I see we do.'

'Hester says breakfast is ready,' she said.

'Is Baby John at breakfast?'

'Yes,' she answered. 'Come.'

J took her hand and led her from the room. Her hand was cool and soft, her fingers were long and her palm had lost its baby fatness. It was the hand of an adult in miniature, not the soft plumpness of a little child.

'You've grown,' he observed.

She peeped up a little smile at him. 'My uncle Alexander Norman says that I will soon be a proper young lady,' she said with satisfaction. 'But I tell him that I shall be the king's gardener.'

'You still want that?' J asked. She nodded and opened the door to the kitchen.

They were all waiting for him at their places around the dark wooden table: the gardener and the two lads, the cook and the maid and the boy who worked in the house and the stables. Hester was at the foot of the table with Baby John beside her, still half-asleep, his drowsy eyes barely showing above the table top. J drank in the sight of him: the beloved boy, the Tradescant heir.

'Oh, Father!' Baby John said, mildly surprised.

J lifted him up, held him close, inhaled the sweet warm smell of sleepy child, hugged him tight and felt his heart turn over with tenderness for his boy, for Jane's boy.

They waited for him to sit before they took their own places on the benches around the table and then Hester bowed her head and said grace in the simple words approved by the church of Archbishop Laud. For a moment it struck a discord with J – who had spent his married life in the fierce independent certainties of his wife and listening to her powerful extempore prayers – but then he bowed his head and heard the rhythm and the simple comfort of the language.

He looked up before Hester said 'Amen'. The household was around the table in neat order, his two children were either side of Hester, their faces washed, their clothes tidy. A solid meal was laid on the table but there was nothing rich or ostentatious or wasteful. And – it was this which decided him – on the windowsill there was a bowl of indigo and white bluebells which someone had taken the trouble to uproot and transplant from the orchard for the pleasure of their bright colour and their sweet, light smell.

No-one but J's father, John Tradescant, had ever brought flowers into the kitchen or the house for pleasure. Flowers were part of the work of the house: reared in the orangery, blooming in the garden, shown in the rarities room, preserved in sugar or painted and sketched. But Hester had a love of flowers that reminded him of his father, and made him think, as he saw her seated between his children, and with flowers on the windowsill, that the great aching gaps in his life where his wife and his father had once been might be resolved if this woman would live here and work alongside him.

J could not take his young children from their home to Virginia, he could not imagine that he might be able to go back there himself. His time in the forest seemed like a dream, like something which had happened to another man, a free man, a new man in the new land. In the months that followed, busy anxious months, in which John the Younger had to become John Tradescant, the only John Tradescant, he hardly thought of Suckahanna and his promise to return. It seemed like a game he had played, a fancy, not a real plan at all. Back in Lambeth, in the old world, the old life closed around him and he thought that his father was probably right – as he generally was – and that he would need Hester to run the business and the house.

He decided that he would ask her to stay. He knew that he would never ask her to love him.

J did not formally propose marriage to Hester until the end of the summer. For the first months he could think of nothing but clearing the debts caused by the crash of the tulip market. The Tradescants, father and son, had invested the family fortune in buying rare tulip bulbs, certain that the market was on the rise. But by the time the tulips had flowered and spawned more bulbs under their perfect soil in their porcelain pots the market had crashed. J and his father were left with nearly a thousand pounds owed to their shareholders, and bound by their sense of honour to repay. By selling the new Virginia plants at a handsome profit and by ensuring that everyone knew of his new maidenhair fern, an exquisite variety which everyone desired on sight, J doubled and re-doubled the business for the nursery garden, and started to drag the family back into profit.

The maidenhair fern was not the only booty that visitors to the garden sought. John offered them new jasmine, the like of which no-one had ever seen before, which would climb and twist itself round a pole as rampant as a honeysuckle, smelling as sweet, but flowering in a bright primrose yellow. A new columbine, an American columbine, and best of all of the surviving saplings: a plane tree, an American plane tree, which John thought might grow as big as an oak in the temperate climate of England. He had no more than half a dozen of each, he would sell nothing. He took orders with cash deposits and promised to deliver seedlings as soon as they were propagated. The American maple which he brought back with such care did not thrive in the Lambeth garden though John hung over it like a new mother; and he lost also the only specimen he had of a tulip tree, and nearly came to blows with his father's friend the famous plantsman, John Parkinson, when he tried to describe the glory of the tree growing in the American wood, which was nothing but a drying stick in the garden in Lambeth.

'I tell you it is as big as an oak with great greasy green leaves and a flower as big as your head!' John swore.

'Aye,' Parkinson retorted. 'The fish that get away are always the biggest.'

Alexander Norman, John's brother-in-law and an executor of John Tradescant's will, took over some of the Tradescant debts on easy terms as a favour to the young family. 'For Frances's dowry,' he said. 'She's such a pretty maid.'

J sold some fields that his father had owned in Kent and cleared most of the rest of the debts. Those still outstanding came to two hundred pounds – the very sum of Hester's dowry. With his account books before him one day, he found he was thinking that Hester's dowry could be his for the asking, and the Tradescant accounts could show a clear profit once more. On that unromantic thought he put down his pen and went to find her.

He had watched her throughout the summer, when she knew she was doubly on trial: tested whether she was good enough for the Tradescant name, and how she matched up to Jane. She never showed a flicker of nervousness. He observed her dealing with the visitors to the rarities. She showed the exhibits with a quiet pride, as if she were glad to be part of a house that contained such marvels, but without boastfulness. She had learned her way around the busy room quicker than anyone could have expected, and she could move from cabinet to wall-hanging, ordering, showing, discussing, with fluid confidence. Her training at court meant that she could be on easy terms with all sorts of people. Her artistic background made her confident around objects of beauty.

She was good with the visitors. She asked them for their money at the door without embarrassment, and then showed them into the room. She did not force herself on them as a guide; she always waited until they explained if they had a special interest. If they wanted to draw or paint an exhibit she was quick to provide a table close to the grand Venetian windows in the best light, and then she had the tact to leave them alone. If they were merely the very many curious visitors who wanted to spend the morning at the museum and afterwards boast to their friends that they had seen everything there was to see in London – the lions at the Tower, the king's own rooms at Whitehall, the exhibits at Tradescant's Ark – she made a point of showing them the extraordinary things, the mermaid, the flightless bird, the whale's mouth, the unicorn's skeleton, which they would describe all the way home – and everyone who heard them talk became a potential customer.

She guided them smoothly to the gardens when they had finished in the rarities room, and took care that she knew the names of the plants. She always started at the avenue of chestnut trees, and there she always said the same thing:

'And these trees, every single one of them, come from cuttings and nuts taken from Mr Tradescant's first ever six trees. He had them first in 1607, thirty-one years ago, and he lived long enough to see them flourish in this beautiful avenue.' The visitors would stand back and look at the slim, strong trees, now green and rich with the summer growth of their spread palmate leaves.

'They are beautiful in leaf with those deep arching branches, but the flowers are as beautiful as a bouquet of apple blossom. I saw them forced to flower in early spring and they scented the room like a light daffodil scent, a delicious scent as sweet as lilies.'

'Who forced the chestnuts for you? My father?' J asked her when some visitors had spent a small fortune on seedlings and departed, their wagon loaded with little pots.

She turned to him, slipping the coins into the pockets of her apron. 'I had the gardener bring them into flower for your father as he lay sick,' she said simply.

'He saw them in bloom?'

She nodded. 'He said he was lying in a flowery mead. It was something we once talked about. He lay among a rich bed of scents and colours, tulips all around him, and over his bed were great boughs of flowering horse chestnut. It was a wonderful sight. He liked it.'

J thought for a moment of the other deaths in the house: his mother's in the room ablaze with daffodils, and the boat laden with Rosamund roses going slowly downriver to the City for Jane's funeral. 'Did he ask you to do it?'

Hester shook her head.

'I am glad you thought of it,' he said. 'I am glad there was someone here to do that for him.' He paused and cleared his throat. 'About his plan that we should marry . . .'

She flushed a little but the face she turned towards him was serene. 'Have you come to a decision?'

He nodded.

'I'm glad. I cannot in all conscience stay here much longer. Your mother-in-law Mrs Hurte is bound to wonder what I am doing here, and the servants will talk.'

'I have thought about it,' he said, sounding as detached as she. 'And I have thought that we might suit very well.'

She stole a quick look at his face. 'You want to marry me?'

'If you desire it,' J said coldly. 'As my father wrote to me in his letter, I have two children and work to do. I must have someone reliable at my home. I have observed you these last months and you are clearly fond of the children and you do the work well. I cannot think of a better wife for me, especially since I have no preference in women.'

She bowed her head. For a moment she had an odd sentimental thought that by accepting Tradescant's loveless proposal she was cutting herself off from all the other possibilities which might have unfurled before her. Surely there would have been men, or even just one man, who might have loved her for herself, and not because she was good with his children and reliable with his business? Surely there might have been just one man who might have proposed and waited for her answer with his heart pounding? Surely there might have been just one man who might have put her hand to his lips so that she felt not a polite kiss but the sudden warm intake of breath which reveals desire?

She gave a small unnoticed shrug. No such man had yet appeared and she was nearing thirty. The agreement with John Tradescant was the best she had ever been offered in a country where success was measured in terms of intimacy with the court. The king's gardener and a favourite of the queen was a good catch, even for a spinster with a dowry of two hundred pounds.

'I have no preference in men,' she said, as coolly as he. 'I will marry you, John.'

He hesitated. 'No-one ever calls me John,' he said. 'I've always been J. It was my father who was John.'

Hester nodded. 'I know that. But your father is dead now, and you are the head of the household and a son no longer. I shall call you John. You are the head of the household, you are John Tradescant.'

'I suppose I am . . .'

'Sometimes it is hard when your father or mother dies,' she said. 'It's not just their death which causes you grief, but the fact that you are no longer someone's little child. It's the final stage of growing up, of becoming a man or a woman. My mother used to call me a pet-name, and I have never heard that name since she died. I never will hear it again. I am a grown woman now and no-one calls me anything but Hester Pooks.'

'You are saying that I must take my manhood.'

'You are the head of the household now. And I will be your wife.'

'We will have the banns called at once then,' he said. 'At St Mary's.'

She shook her head at the thought of him walking to his wedding past the headstone of his only beloved wife. 'I am a resident of St Bride's in the City,' she said. 'I will go home and get the banns called there. Shall we marry at once?'

He looked indifferent. 'It would be more convenient for me,' he said politely. 'But you perhaps have clothes to order? Or things you want to do?'

'A few things. We can be married in October.'

He nodded as if it were the completion date of some routine gardening work. 'In October then.'

October 1638

John wondered if he should feel himself faithless to his promise to Suckahanna, but he did not. He could not remember her well enough, only foolish details like the pride of her smile or the cool clasp of her hand when he had pledged himself to her. He dreamed one night that he was in the woods with her and she was setting a fish trap. When he woke he wondered at the power of the image of her bending over the little stream and setting her trap of woven withy. But then Baby John marched determinedly into the room and the dream was gone.

He wondered occasionally what was happening to her, whether she and her mother were safe in the woods as they had planned to be. But Virginia was so far away, a two-months' voyage, and such a leap of the imagination that he could not keep her in his mind. Surrounded by the business worries and demands of his home J could not retain the picture of Suckahanna. Every day she seemed more exotic, more like a traveller's tale. She was a mermaid, a barnacle goose that swam underwater and then flew from the barnacle shells, a being with its head beneath its shoulders, a flying carpet. One night when he was drunk he tried to tell a fellow gardener that he had collected his Virginia plants with an Indian maid who was covered in blue tattoos and wore nothing but a buckskin pinny; and the man roared with laughter and paid for another round of ales to praise John's bawdy invention.

Every day she receded further from him. Whether he tried to speak of her or kept silent, whether he dreamed of her or let her image go, every day she seemed less likely, every day she floated down the river of his memory in her little canoe, and never looked back at him.

On the first of October Hester went to stay in her City lodgings to prepare for her wedding: buying a few pieces of lace to stitch on her petticoats and her shift, packing her bags, warning her landlady that she would need the little room no longer for she was going to be married to the queen's gardener – Mr John Tradescant.

Her uncle John de Critz gave her away and his family and the de Neve relations made an impressive show in the little church. It was a quiet ceremony. John did not want to make a fuss and the de Critz family were refined, artistic people with no desire to throw rice or ears of wheat, or shout and riot around the bedroom door.

The bridal couple went soberly home to Lambeth. Before she left Hester had given orders that the great bedroom which had once been John and Elizabeth's should be hung with new curtains, swept out and cleaned, and fully aired. She felt that she would rather sleep in the bed where John Tradescant had died than share the bed that had belonged to John and Jane. Frances was moved into her father and mother's old room and Baby John had his nursery room to himself.

John had made no comment about the arrangements except to say that it should all be done as she wished. He did not show any grief at moving from his first wife's bedroom, nor did he object to the cost of replacing the curtains and wall hangings throughout.

'They are ten years old.' Hester justified the expense.

'It doesn't seem so long,' he said simply.

The children were dancing on the garden wall, waiting for them to come down the road from Lambeth.

'Are you married?' Frances demanded. 'Where's your new dress?'

'I just wore this one.'

'Am I to call you Mother?' Frances asked.

Hester glanced at John. He had bent to scoop Baby John from the wall and was carrying him into the house. He took care not to reply.

'You can call me Hester, as you always have done. I am not your mother who is in heaven, but I shall do my best to love you and care for you as well as she would have done.'

Frances nodded carelessly, as if she were not much concerned, and scrambled down from the wall and led the way into the house. Hester nodded, she was not disappointed in Frances's lack of warmth. This was not a child who could easily ask for comfort; but no child needed love more than she did.

The new family went into the parlour and Hester seated herself in the chair on one side of the fire opposite John. Baby John sat on the rug before the fire and Frances hesitated, unsure where she should sit.

Without looking at Hester she sank to her knees before the warmth of the fire and then slowly leaned backwards against the arm of Hester's chair. Hester dropped her hand gently on the nape of her stepdaughter's neck and felt the tight, thin muscles of her neck relax at the touch. Frances let her head lean back against her stepmother's touch, trusted her caress.

'We shall be happy,' Hester promised in an undertone to her brave little stepdaughter. 'All will be well, Frances.'

At bedtime the household gathered for evening prayers and John read from the new book of common prayer, enjoying the rhythm of the language and the sense of security which came from using the same words at the same time of day, every day. The household, which had prayed aloud, speaking freely from their hearts under Jane, now bowed their heads and listened, and when the prayers were over they went about their work of bolting the doors for the night, damping down the fires, and snuffing the candles.

Hester and John went up the stairs together to the big bedroom for the first time. The housemaid was waiting in the room.

'Cook thought you might want helping off with your gown, Miss Hester – Mrs Tradescant, I should say!'

Hester shook her head. 'I can do it.'

'And Cook sent up this tray for the two of you,' the maid persevered. There had evidently been a strong sense in the kitchen that more should have been done to mark the occasion. 'She brewed a wedding ale for you,' the maid said. 'And there's some cake and dainty blackberry pudding.'

'Thank you,' Hester said. 'And thank Cook too.'

John nodded and the maid left the room.

The couple looked at each other, their embarrassment dissolved by the maid's intervention.

'Clearly they think we should be carousing and singing,' John said.

'Perhaps they think *they* should be carousing,' Hester observed astutely. 'I imagine that not all the wedding ale is in these two tankards.'

'Shall you have a drink?' John asked.

'When I'm ready for bed,' she said, keeping her tone as light and inconsequential as his. She moved towards the bed and climbed up into it. She did not draw the bed curtains against him, but managed, in their shadows, to undress from her gown and to get into her night shift without embarrassment. She emerged with her hair still braided to put her fine gown in the press at the foot of the bed.

John was seated in his chair before the fire, drinking his wedding ale. 'It's good,' he recommended. 'And I've had a little cake too.'

She took up the tankard and sat opposite him, curling up her feet under her night shift. She sipped at the ale. It was strong and sweet. At once a heady sense of relaxation spread through her. 'This *is* good,' she said.

John laughed. 'I think it probably serves its purpose,' he said. 'I was more nervous than for my first day at school and now I am feeling like a cock o' the walk.'

Hester flushed at that single accidental bawdiness. 'Oh.'

John buried his face in his tankard, as embarrassed as his new wife. 'Go to bed,' he said shortly. 'I shall join you in a minute.'

She put her thin white feet down on the bare floorboards and went with her quick boyish stride to the bed. John did not turn around as she climbed in. He waited until she had settled and then got up and blew out his candle. He got undressed in the half-darkness and then pulled on his nightgown.

She was lying on the pillow, lit only by a single candle and by the flickering light from the fire. She had unbraided her hair and it spread dark and sweet-smelling on the pillow. A sudden anguish of longing for his lost wife Jane, and the serious passionate desire that they had shared, swept over John. He had promised himself he would not think of her, he had thought it would be fatal to this night if he thought of her, but when he saw Hester in his bed, he did not feel like a bridegroom, but like an unwilling adulterer.

It was a business contract, and it must be fulfilled. John turned his mind to the outrageously half-naked painted women of the old king's court. He had seen them at New Hall when he was little more than a boy and remembered them still with an erotic mixture of disapproval and desire. He held the thought of them in his mind and moved towards Hester.

She had never been touched by a man who was in love with her, or she would have known at once that John was offering her the false coin of his body while his mind was elsewhere. But she too knew that the contract of marriage was not completed until consummation. She lay still and helpful beneath him while he pierced her and then brutally moved in the wound. She did not complain, she did not comment. She lay in silence while the pain went on and then suddenly stopped as he sighed and then moved away from her.

She rose up, biting her lip against the hurt, and wrapped a cloth tightly around her groin. There was only a little blood, she thought; it probably felt worse than it was. She thought that she would have taken the whole thing easier if she had been younger, fresher, warmer. It had been a cold-hearted assault and a cold-hearted acceptance. She shivered in the darkness and got back into bed beside her husband.

John had turned to lie on his side with his back to her as if he would shut out the sight of her and shut out the thought of her. Hester crept back under the covers, careful not to touch him, not to breach the space between them, and set her teeth against the pain, and against the bitterness of disappointment. She did not cry, she lay very still and dry-eyed and waited for the morning when her married life would begin.

'I shall go to Oatlands this week,' John remarked the very next morning at breakfast. Hester, seated beside Baby John, looked up in surprise. 'This week?'

He met her gaze with bland incomprehension. 'Yes.'

'So soon?'

'Why not?'

A dozen reasons why a newly wed husband should not leave his home in the first week of his marriage came to her. She folded her lips tightly on them. 'People may think it looks odd,' was all that she said.

'They can think what they like,' John retorted bluntly. 'We married so that I should be free to do my work and that is what I am doing.'

Hester glanced at Frances, seated at her left, opposite Baby John. Frances's white-capped head was bowed over her bowl, she did not look up at her father, she affected to be deaf.

'There is the planting of the spring bulbs to finish,' he said. 'And pruning, and planning for winter. I have to make sure the silkworm house is sound against the weather. I shall be a month or so away. If you are in any need you can send for me.'

Hester bowed her head. John rose from his place and went to the door. 'I shall be in the orchard,' he said. 'Please pack my clothes for me to go to Oatlands and tell the boy I shall want a horse this afternoon. I shall ride down to the docks and see if anything has come in for the king's collection.'

Hester nodded and she and the two children sat in silence until the door closed behind John.

Frances looked up, her lower lip turned down. 'I thought he would stay home all the time now you are married.'

'Never mind!' Hester said with assumed cheerfulness. 'We'll have lots to do. There's a bonfire to build for Guy Fawkes's day, and then Christmas to prepare for.'

'But I thought he would stay home,' Frances persisted. 'He will come home for Christmas, won't he?'

'Of course,' Hester said easily. 'Of course he will. But he has to go and work for the queen in her lovely gardens. He's a royal gardener! He can't stay home all the time.'

Baby John looked up and wiped his milky moustache on his sleeve.

'Use your napkin,' Hester corrected him.

Baby John grinned. 'I shall go to Oatrands,' he said firmly. 'Pranting and pranning and pruning. I shall go.'

'Certainly,' Hester said, and she emphasised the correct pronunciation: 'Planting and planning and pruning are most important.'

Baby John nodded with dignity. 'Now I shall go and look at my warities.'

'Can I take the money from the visitors?' Frances asked.

Hester glanced at the clock standing in the corner of the room. It was not yet nine. 'They won't come for another hour or so,' she said. 'You can fetch your school work, both of you, for an hour, and then you can work in the rarities room.'

'Oh, Hester!' Frances complained.

Hester shook her head and started to pile up the empty porridge bowls and the spoons. 'Books first,' she said. 'And, Baby John, I want to see all our names written fair in your copybook.'

'And then I will go pranting,' he said.

Hester packed John's clothes for him and added a few jars of bottled summer fruit to the hamper which would follow him by wagon. She was up early on the day of his departure to see him ride away from the Ark.

'You had no need to rise,' John said awkwardly.

'Of course I had need. I am your wife.'

He turned and tightened the girth on his big bay cob to avoid speaking. They were both aware that since the first night they had not made love, and now he was going away for an indefinite period.

'Please take care at court,' Hester said gently. 'These are difficult times for men of principle.'

'I must say what I believe if I am asked,' John said. 'I don't venture it, but I won't deny it.'

She hesitated. 'You need not deny your beliefs but you could say nothing and avoid the topic altogether,' she suggested. 'The queen especially is touchy about her religion. She holds to her Papist faith, and the king inclines more and more to her. And now that he is trying to impose Archbishop Laud's prayer book on Scotland, this is not a time for any Independent thinker; be he Baptist or Presbyterian.'

'You wish to advise me?' he asked with a hint of warning in his voice which reminded her that a wife was always in second place to a man.

'I know the court,' she said steadily. 'I spent my girlhood there. My uncle is an official painter there, still. I have half a dozen cousins and friends who write to me. I do know things, husband. I know that it is no place for a man who thinks for himself.'

'They're hardly likely to care what their gardener thinks,' John scoffed. 'An undergardener at that. I've not even been appointed to my father's post, yet.'

She hesitated. 'They care so much that they threw Archie the jester out with his jacket pulled over his head for merely joking about Archbishop Laud; and Archie was the queen's great favourite. They certainly care what you think. They are taking it upon themselves to care what every single man, woman, and child thinks. That's what the very quarrel is all about. About what every individual thinks in his private heart. That's why every single Scotsman has to sign his own covenant with the king and swear to use the Archbishop's prayer book. They care precisely what every single man thinks.' She paused. 'They may indeed question you, John; and you have to have an answer ready that will satisfy them.'

'I have a right to speak to my God in my own way!' John insisted stubbornly. 'I don't need to recite by rote, I am not a child. I don't need a priest to dictate my prayers. I certainly don't need a bishop puffed up with pride and wealth to tell me what I think. I can speak to God direct when I am planting His seeds in the garden and picking His fruit from His trees. And He speaks to me then. And I honour Him then.

'I use the prayer book well enough – but I don't believe that those are the only words that God hears. And I don't believe that the only men God attends are bishops wrapped up in surplices, and I don't believe that God made Charles king, and that service to the king is one and the same as service to God. And Jane –' He broke off, suddenly aware that he should not speak to his new wife of his constant continuing love for her predecessor.

'Go on,' Hester said.

'Jane's faith never wavered, not even when she was dying in pain,' John said. 'She would never have denied her belief that God spoke simple and clear to her and she could speak to Him. She would have died for that belief, if she had been called to do so. And for her sake, if for nothing else, I will not deny my faith.'

'And what about her children?' Hester asked. 'D'you think she would want you to die for her faith and leave her children orphans?'

John checked. 'It won't come to that.'

'When I was at Oatlands only six months ago, the talk was all about each man's faith and how far each man would go. If the king insists on the Scots following the prayer book he is bound to insist on it in England too. If he goes to war with the Scots to make them do as he bids, and some say he might do that, who can doubt that he will do the same in England?'

John shook his head. 'This is nothing,' he said. 'Nonsense and heartache about nothing.'

'It is not nothing. I am warning you,' Hester said steadily. 'No-one knows how far the king will go when he has to protect the queen and her faith, and to conceal his own backsliding towards popery. No-one knows how far he will go to make everyone conform to the same church. He has taken it into his head that one church will make one nation, and that he can hold one nation in the palm of his hand and govern without a word to anyone. If you insist on your faith at the same time as the king is insisting on his, you cannot say what trouble you might be running towards.'

John thought for a moment and then he nodded. 'You may be right,' he said reluctantly. 'You are a powerfully cautious woman, Hester.'

'You have given me a task and I shall do it,' she said, unsmiling. 'You have given me the task of bringing up your children and being a wife to you. I have no wish to be a widow. I have no wish to bring up orphans.'

'But I will not compromise my faith,' he warned her.

'Just don't flaunt it.'

The horse was ready. John tied his cape tightly at the neck and set his hat on his head. He paused; he did not know how he should say farewell to this new, common-sense wife of his. To his surprise she put out her hand, as a man would do, and shook his hand as if she were his friend.

John felt oddly warmed by the frankness of the gesture. He smiled at her, led the horse over to the mounting block and got up into the saddle.

'I don't know what state the gardens will be in,' he remarked.

'For sure, they will appoint you in your father's place when you are back at court,' Hester said. 'It was only your absence which made them delay. It is out of sight, at once forgotten with them. When you return they will insist on your service again.'

He nodded. 'I hope they have not mistook my orders while I was gone. If you leave a garden for a season it slips back a year.'

Hester stepped forward and patted the horse's neck. 'The children will miss you,' she said. 'May I tell them when you will be home?'

'By November,' he promised.

She stepped back from the horse's head and let him go. He smiled at her as he passed out of the stable yard and round the path which led to the gate. As he rode out he had a sudden sense of joyful freedom – that he could ride away from his home or ride back to it and that everything would be managed without him. This was his father's last gift to him – his father who had also married a woman who could manage well in his absence. John turned in his saddle and waved at Hester who was still standing at the corner of the yard where she could look after him.

John waved his whip and turned the horse towards Lambeth and the ferry. Hester watched him go and then turned back to the house.

❧

The court was due at Oatlands in late October so John was busy as soon as he arrived planting and preparing the courts which were enclosed by the royal apartments. The knot gardens always looked well in winter, the sharp geometric shapes of the low box hedging looked wonderful thinned and whitened by frost. In the fountain court John kept the water flowing at the slowest speed so that there would be a chance for it to make icicles and ice cascades in the colder nights. The herbs still looked well, the angelica and sage went into white lace when the frost touched their feathery fronds behind the severe hedging. Against the walls of the king's court John was training one of his new plants introduced from the Ark: his Virginian winter-flowering jasmine. On warm days its scent drifted up to the open windows above, and its colour made a splash of rich pink light in the grey and white and black garden.

The queen's orangery was like a jungle, packed tight with the tender plants which would not survive an English winter. Some of the more handsome shrubs and small trees were planted in containers with loops for carrying poles and John's men lifted them out to the queen's garden at first light, and brought them in again at dusk so that even in winter she would always have something pretty to see from her windows. John placed a lemon and an orange tree, both trained into handsome balls, on either side of the door to her apartments, like aromatic sentries.

'These are pretty,' she said to him from her window one day as he was supervising the careful placing of some little trees in the garden below.

'I beg your pardon, Your Majesty,' John said, pulling off his hat, recognising the heavily accented voice of Queen Henrietta Maria at once. 'They should have been in their places before you looked out.'

'I woke very early, I could not sleep,' she said. 'My husband is worried and so I am sleepless too.'

John bowed.

'People do not understand how hard it is sometimes for us. They see the palaces and the carriages and they think that our lives are given up to pleasure. But it is all worry.'

John bowed again.

'You understand, don't you?' she asked, leaning out and speaking clearly so that he could hear her in the garden below. 'When you make my gardens so beautiful for me, you know that they are a respite for me and the king when we are exhausted by our anxieties and by our struggle to bring this country to be a great kingdom.'

John hesitated. Obviously it would be impolite to say that his interest in the beauty of the gardens would have been the same whether she was an idle vain Papist – as he believed – or whether she was a woman devoted to her husband and her duty. He remembered Hester's advice and bowed once more.

'I so want to be a good queen,' she said.

'No-one prays for anything else,' John said cautiously.

'Do you think they pray for me?'

'They have to, it's in the prayer book. They are ordered to pray for you twice every Sunday.'

'But in their hearts?'

John dipped his head. 'How could I say, Your Majesty? All I know are plants and trees. I can't see inside men's hearts.'

'I like to think that you can give me a glimpse of what common men are thinking. I am surrounded by people who tell me what they think I would like to hear. But you would not lie to me, would you, Gardener Tradescant?'

John shook his head. 'I would not lie,' he said.

'So tell me, is everyone against the Scots? Does everyone see that the

Scots must do what the king wishes and sign the king's covenant, and use the prayer book that we give them?'

John, on one knee, on cold ground, cursed the day that the queen had taken a fancy to him, and reflected on the wisdom of his wife who had warned him to avoid this conversation at all costs.

'They know that it is the king's wish,' he said tactfully. 'There is not a man or woman or child in the country who does not know that it is the king's wish.'

'Then it should need nothing more!' she exclaimed. 'Is he the king or not?'

'Of course he is.'

'Then his wish should be a command to everyone. If they think any different from him they are traitors.'

John thought intently of Hester and said nothing. 'I pray for peace, God knows,' he said honestly enough.

'And so do I,' said the queen. 'Would you like to pray with me, Gardener Tradescant? I allow my favourite servants to use my chapel. I am going to Mass now.'

John forced himself not to fling away from her and from her dangerous ungodly Papistry. To invite an Englishman to attend Mass was a crime punishable by death. The laws against Roman Catholics were very clear and very brutal, and clearly, visibly, flouted by the king and queen in their own court.

'I am all dirty, Your Majesty.' John showed her his earth-stained hands and kept his voice level though he was filled with rage at her casual flouting of the law, and deeply shocked that she should think he would accept such an invitation to idolatory and hell. 'I could not come to your chapel.'

'Another time, then.' She smiled at him, pleased with his humility, and with her own graciousness. She had no idea that he was within an inch of storming from the garden in a blaze of righteous rage. To John, a Roman Catholic chapel was akin to the doors of hell, and a Papist queen was one step to damnation. She had tried to tempt him to deny his faith. She had tried to tempt him to the worst sin in the world – idolatory, worshipping graven images, denying the word of God. She was a woman steeped in sin and she had tried to drag him down.

She closed the window on the cold air without saying farewell or telling him that he could rise. John stayed kneeling until he was sure that she had gone, and that the audience was over. Then he got to his feet and looked behind him. The two assistant gardeners were kneeling where they had dropped when the window opened.

'You can stand,' John said. 'She's gone.'

They scrambled to their feet, rubbing their knees and complaining of the discomfort. 'Please God she does not look out of the window again,' said the younger one. 'Why will she not leave you alone?'

'She thinks I am a faithful servant,' J said bitterly. 'She thinks I will tell her the mood of the people. What she does not realise is that no-one can tell her the truth since any word of disagreement is treason. She and the king have tied our consciences in knots and whatever we do or think or say we are in the wrong. It makes a man want to cut loose.'

He saw the gardeners looking at him in surprise. 'Oh, waste no more time!' John snapped impatiently. 'We've kneeled enough for one day.'

Winter 1639

The court always spent the long Christmas feast at Whitehall, so John was able to leave the royal gardens at Oatlands dormant under a thick frost, and go home to Lambeth in November and spend Christmas at home. The children had made him little presents of their own for Twelfth Night, and he gave them sweets and fairings bought from Lambeth winter fair. To Hester he gave a couple of yards of grey silk for a gown.

'They had a blue silk too but I did not know what you would like,' he said. He would have known exactly what Jane would have preferred; but he seldom observed what Hester was wearing. He had only a general impression of demure smartness.

'I like this. Thank you.'

After the children had gone to bed, Hester and John stayed by the fireside, drinking small ale and cracking nuts in companionable domestic peace. 'You were right about being cautious at Oatlands,' John said. 'In Lambeth the news was all of a war against Scotland. The northern counties are armed and ready, and the king has called a council of war. They say that the militia will be called up too.'

'Do they really think that the king would go to war over a prayer book? Does he really think he can fight the Scots into praying with Archbishop Laud's words?'

John shook his head in disagreement. 'It's more than the prayer book. The king thinks that he has to make one church for all his kingdom. He thinks one church will bind everyone together, bind us all together under his will. He has taken it into his head that if the Scots refuse their bishops then they will refuse their king.'

'You'll not have to go?' Hester asked, going straight to the point.

John grimaced. 'I may have to pay for a substitute to go soldiering in my place. But perhaps they will not muster the Lambeth trained bands. Perhaps I may be excused since I serve the king already.'

Hester hesitated. 'You would not publicly refuse to serve, as a matter of conscience?'

'It would certainly go against my conscience to fire on a man who has said nothing worse than he wants to worship his God in his own way,' John said. 'Such a man, be he Scots or Welsh or English, is saying nothing more than I believe. He cannot be my enemy. I am more like a Scots Presbyterian than I am like Archbishop Laud, God knows.'

'But if you refuse you might be pressed to serve, and if you refuse the press, they could try for treason.'

'These are difficult times. A man has to hold clear on to his conscience and his God.'

'And try not to be noticed,' Hester said.

John suddenly realised the contrast in their opinions. 'Hester, wife, do you believe in nothing?' he demanded. 'I have never had a word from you of belief or conviction. All you ever speak of is surviving and avoiding awkward questions. You are married into a household where we have been faithful servants of the king and his ministers since the start of the century. My father never heard a word against any of his masters in all his days. I didn't agree with him, that's not my way; but I am a man of conscience. I hold very strongly to the belief that a man must find his own way to God. I have been a man of independent belief since I was old enough to think for myself, praying in the words of my own choosing, a Protestant, a true Protestant. Even when I have wavered in my faith, even when I have had doubts, profound doubts, I am glad to have those doubts and think them through. I have never run to some priest to tell me what I should think, to speak to God for me.'

She met his gaze with her own straight look. 'You're right. I believe in surviving,' she said flatly. 'That's all, really. That's my creed. The safest route for me and mine is to obey the king; and if I do happen to think differently to what he commands – I keep my thoughts to myself. My family works for noble and royal patrons, I was brought up around the court. I am loyal to my king and loyal to my God; but, like any courtier, my first interest is in surviving. And I fear that my creed is going to be as thoroughly tested as any other in the next few months.'

〰

The press gang did not come for John. But he did receive a letter from the Mayor of London. John was to pay a tax demanded personally by the king to finance the war against the Scots. The king was marching north and desperately needed money to equip and arm his soldiers. And more soldiers would be coming, soldiers from Ireland, and mercenaries from Spain.

'The king is bringing in Papists to fight against Protestants?' John demanded, scandalised. 'What next? French soldiers from his wife's country? Or the Spanish army? What was the point of us defeating the Armada, fighting to stay free of Papist powers, if we now invite them in?'

'Hush,' Hester said. She closed the door of the parlour so that the visitors in the rarities room could not hear her husband's shout of outrage.

'I will not pay!'

'Wait and see,' Hester advised.

'I will not,' John said. 'This is a matter of principle to me, Hester. I will not pay money to an army of Papists to march against men who think as I do, whose consciences are as tender as mine.'

To his surprise she did not argue but bit her lip and bowed her head. John looked at the top of her cap and had a sense at last of being master in his own house and impressing on his wife the importance of principle.

'I have spoken,' he said firmly.

'Yes indeed,' she said quietly.

Hester said nothing to disagree with John, but that day, and every day thereafter, she stole from the little collection of coins which the visitors paid until she had enough to pay John's tax without him knowing, if the tax collector came back.

He did not return. The Lord Mayor of London, with the great men of the City behind him, was not inclined any more than John to hand over thousands of pounds' worth of City gold for the king's war against an enemy who was a natural ally. Especially when the king was demanding money without the agreement of a parliament.

1640

In the absence of any voluntary money the king was forced to call a parliament. For the first time in ten years the squires and landlords returned to Westminster with a belief that they might now get back to the proper task of advising the king and running the country.

Hester went to find John in the orchard with the news of the new parliament. The buds on the apple trees were fattening and splitting and showing white and pink petals as crumpled as ribbons crammed into a pocket.

'Perhaps the king will listen to the voice of the people,' John said hopefully.

'He might,' she said. 'But he is listening to the old Earl Strafford and to the queen. Two voices instead of the one. Will he listen to the voice of the people in preference to the voice of his own wife, who is trying to gather an army of English Papists and a Spanish army for him?'

John thought for a moment. 'No,' he said. 'Of course not.'

Hester nodded. 'Takings are down for the gardens,' she warned. 'People are not ordering plants and seeds. This should be our busiest time of the year but it's as quiet as winter. No-one can think about gardens while the king is half at war with the Scots and has called a parliament which is filled with men who disagree with him.'

'We can manage for a short spell,' John said.

'We earn more in the spring than we do for all the rest of the year,' she said. 'I have been looking at the account books. We have to make money in spring. A war starting in springtime is the worst thing that could happen for us. If the uncertainty carries on till June or July we will not make a profit this year.'

'What about the rarities?'

'There are more visitors because there are more people in the city,'

Hester said. 'The country gentry who have come in for the parliament are curious to see Tradescant's Ark. But if the business between the king and Scots grows more serious I think they'll stop coming too. A trade like ours depends on people feeling safe enough to spend money on pleasure: on visiting, on rarities, and on their gardens. A country at war does not plant gardens.'

'I still have my post at Oatlands,' John pointed out. 'And I will succeed my father as chief gardener and draw his wage.'

Hester nodded. 'If the worst comes to the worst we can live on your wages.'

'At the very worst we can close the Ark and live at Oatlands,' John said. 'The house there is only little; but we could manage for a while if we cannot afford to keep the Ark open.'

'I'm not sure that I would want to live in the grounds of a royal palace in times like these,' Hester said cautiously.

'I thought you were such a royalist?'

'I don't want to take sides,' Hester said. 'Not when I don't know exactly what the sides will be. Nor when I don't know which side will win.'

The sides became rapidly clearer after the king's army, unenthusiastic and poorly paid, were defeated by the Scots who went on to occupy Newcastle and Durham and hammer out a peace with the king which would force him to call a new parliament in England. It became clear to everyone in the country, except perhaps to the king and the queen, that the Scots and the Independent English thinkers had the king on the run. Hester started a correspondence with Mrs Hurte, the mother of John's first wife, who kept her eyes and ears open in the City and was as sceptical as Hester, and rightly concerned for the safety of her grandchildren.

> *The new Parliament will impeach Strafford, just as the old one was wild to impeach Buckingham. If J has ever had any dealings with the Earl, or if his father kept any correspondence, it should be hidden or, better yet, burned. They are saying that Strafford is a traitor prepared to wage war against his own country for the benefit of the king and queen. They will accuse him of treason – treason against the people of England, and once one royal servant is accused how many others will be charged?*

Hester went upstairs to the attic and opened John's old chest of papers. The Tradescants had supplied seeds and young saplings to the Earl but there were no incriminating letters left from the years when John Tradescant had been known as a discreet man who regularly visited Europe and could be trusted with a letter or a message.

The Earl was a loud-mouthed unattractive old man, twisted with gout and losing his sight. He had been a relentless force in Ireland, hammering a Protestant will on a Catholic people; but he was old now. The king had recalled him to England only for the unscrupulous clarity of his advice, and been indebted to him for the suggestion that if towns did not send enough money for the king's army their aldermen should be hanged in their robes to clarify the urgency of the situation. The Earl had walked past John in the gardens of Oatlands a dozen times and never wasted more than a glance on him.

The Tradescants were safe from any accusation of complicity with the king. But many royal servants slipped away and went abroad, or retired to their country estates. Others were not so quick or careful. In December, Archbishop Laud was arrested and imprisoned in the Tower to await the pleasure of the Houses of Parliament.

Hester did not pray from any prayer book at evening prayers that night but read from the King James Bible as the only text which did not define the household as for or against the king.

'No prayers?' John asked her quietly as the household went about its last tasks of the day and Hester counted out the bedtime candles.

'I don't know any more what words God would prefer,' she said drily. 'And no-one knows what man requires.'

Spring 1641

The day that Strafford was called to account in the great hall at Westminster there were no visitors to the Ark at all. Everyone who could get a ticket or a pass to see Strafford at bay before his accusers was in the city. Even the streets were deserted.

In the unnatural silence of the house at Lambeth there was suddenly a thunderous knock on the front door. Frances went running to open it, but Hester darted out from the rarities room and caught her in the hall.

'Frances! Don't answer it!'

The girl halted at once.

'Go round to the gardens and find your father. Tell him to go to the stables, saddle a horse, and wait till I send a message.'

Frances caught the note of urgency in her stepmother's voice, nodded, white-faced, and ran. Hester waited until she was out of sight, smoothed down her apron, straightened her cap, and opened the door.

It was a gentleman usher of the royal household. Hester showed him into the parlour. 'My husband is not here at the moment,' she said, deliberately vague. 'I can send a message for him if it is urgent.'

'The king is at Whitehall and wishes to see him.'

Hester nodded. 'I shall have to write to him at Oatlands,' she said. 'He is the king's gardener at Oatlands, you know. May I tell him why the king wants him?'

The gentleman usher raised his eyebrows. 'I should have thought it would be enough to tell him that he is wanted,' he said rudely.

Hester bowed slightly. 'Of course,' she said. 'But if the king requires some plants or seeds then we need to know at once, so that we can prepare them. Or if he wants some rarities delivered . . .'

'Oh,' the man said. 'I see. The king is buying a hunting lodge at

Wimbledon for the queen. They want Mr Tradescant to design a garden.'

No trace of her relief appeared on Hester's face. 'I will send for him at once,' she said. 'He may not even have arrived at Oatlands yet. He left only this morning. I may catch him on the road, and tell him to come back.'

The gentleman usher nodded.

'Can I offer you some refreshment?' Hester asked. 'A glass of wine?'

The gentleman usher shook his head. 'I shall return to Whitehall,' he said. 'These are difficult times.'

'Very difficult,' Hester agreed with feeling. She showed him to the door and then went to the stables to find John. He was leaning against the pump in the stable yard, enjoying the early warm sunshine on his face.

'Frances came flying out as if all the devils in hell were at the door,' he said carelessly. 'Why are you so fearful?'

'I thought it might have been the press gang or the tax collectors, or a message from the court that you would be safer to miss,' she explained. 'I don't know *what* I fear except I am uneasy, I am afraid for us. If the king's own advisor can be on trial for his life then the king can protect no-one. Indeed, it's the loyal servants of the king who are the most endangered. And we have been known as royal servants for two generations. I don't want this family suddenly named as enemies of the people of England because we have taken royal gold. We all have to make our own safety in these days.'

John put his hand on her shoulder. It was his first ever gesture of affection. Hester stood very still, as if she had been approached by a wary wild animal and did not want to scare it away. She felt herself lean, very slightly, towards his caress.

'You're very careful for me,' he said. 'I appreciate it.'

She could have stood like that, in the warm sunny yard with his hand on her shoulder, forever. But John dropped his hand. 'So who was it?'

'It was a message from the court. The king is buying a manor at Wimbledon for the queen and they want you to design a garden.' She paused for a moment. 'The king's advisor and chief minister is at bay before his enemies and on trial for his life, and yet the king has time to send to you to tell you to make a new garden.'

'Well, at least that solves the problem of selling seeds and plants,' he said. 'If I am making a new royal garden we will need all our stocks. We're back in profit, Hester. Am I to go at once?'

'I said you were on the road to Oatlands, before I knew what the message was. So you can go today or tomorrow.'

'So our troubles are over!' John exclaimed happily. 'A new garden to design, and all our seedlings and plants bought by the king.'

'I don't think our troubles will be over that quickly,' Hester said cautiously. 'Take great care, John, when you meet the king and queen.'

When John got to Wimbledon the king and queen were not to be found.

'Their Majesties are walking privately in the garden,' one of the courtiers told him. 'They said you were to go and meet them there. You may approach Their Majesties.'

John, accustomed to the ways of the court, expected to find twenty to thirty people with the king and queen walking privately, but for once they were indeed alone, just the two of them, with her hand in the crook of his arm and her embroidered silk skirts brushing against his legs as they walked together.

John hesitated, thinking that for once they might have chosen to be alone and might be enjoying their privacy. But when they turned at the edge of the grass court and saw him the queen smiled and the king beckoned him forward with one of his little gestures. Although they wished it to be always understood that they were very much in love, they preferred each other's company before an audience. The queen liked to be seen publicly basking in the king's adoration, even more than she enjoyed a private moment.

'Ah, Gardener Tradescant!' the queen said. John bowed low and dropped to one knee. The king flicked his finger to permit John to rise and John got up. At once he saw that they were not having a carefree stroll in the garden. The queen was flushed and her eyelids were red, the king looked pale and strained.

'Your Majesties,' John said warily.

'The king has bought me this pretty house to take our minds off our troubles,' the queen said in her lilting accent. 'We are much troubled, Gardener Tradescant. We want to be diverted.'

John bowed. 'It could be a fine garden,' he said. 'The soil is good.'

'I want it done all new,' the queen said eagerly. 'A pretty style to match the house.' She gestured back at the manor house. It was a handsome place new-built of red brick, with two arching flights of steps down from the terrace and gardens terraced down the slope. 'I want many fruit trees. The king and I will come here in midsummer to escape from the noise and fuss of the court and we will eat fruit off the trees and grapes off the vine and melons off the . . .' She broke off.

'Off the ground,' the king suggested. 'They g . . . grow on the g . . . ground, do they not, Tradescant?'

'Yes, Your Majesty,' John said. 'My father learned the way of making them grow rich and ripe when he was with Sir Henry Wootton at Canterbury, and he taught me the way. I can grow you melons here and all sorts of fruit.'

'And pretty flowers,' the queen added. 'White and blue flowers in the knot garden.'

John bowed his assent, keeping his face hidden. White and blue were the flowers of the Virgin Mary. The queen was asking for a Papist knot garden on the very edge of a London on the brink of revolt.

'We need somewhere to retire in these troubled times,' the king said. 'A little hidden garden, Tradescant. Somewhere that we can b . . . be ourselves.'

The queen stepped to one side to look at a neglected watercourse, lifting her silk dress carefully away from the wet ground.

'I understand,' John said. 'Will you be here only in summer, Your Majesty? It helps me if I know. If you are not to be here in autumn then I do not need to plant for that season.'

'Yes,' the king said. 'A summertime p . . . place.'

John nodded and waited for further orders.

'It pleases me to give her a p . . . pretty little h . . . house of her own,' the king said, watching the queen at the end of the little terrace. 'I have great work to do – I have to d . . . d . . . defend my crown against wild and wicked men who w . . . would pull me down, I have to d . . . defend the church against levellers and s . . . and s . . . and sectaries and Independents who would unstitch the very fabric of the country. It is all for m . . . me to do. Only I can preserve the country from the m . . . madness of a few wicked men. Whatever it costs me, I have t . . . to do it.'

John knew he should say nothing; but there was such a strange mixture of certainty and self-dramatisation in the king's voice that he could not remain silent. 'Are you sure that you have to do it all?' he asked quietly. 'I know some sectaries, and they are quiet men, content to leave the Church alone, provided that they can pray their own way. And surely, no-one in the country wants to harm you or the queen, or the princes.'

Charles looked tragic. 'They d . . . do,' he said simply. 'They drive themselves on and on, c . . . caring nothing for my good, c . . . caring nothing for the country. They want to see me cut down, cut down to the size of a little P . . . Prince, like the D . . . Doge of Venice or some catspaw of Parliament. They want to see the p . . . power my father gave me, which his aunt g . . . gave him, cut down to n . . . nothing. When was this country t . . . truly great? Under King Henry, Queen Elizabeth and my f . . . father King James. But they do not remember this. They don't w . . . want to. I shall have to fight them as traitors. It is a b . . . battle to the death.'

The queen had heard the king's raised voice and came over. 'Husband?' she inquired.

He turned at once, and Tradescant was relieved that she had come to soothe the king.

'I was saying how these m . . . madmen in Parliament will not be finished until they have destroyed my ch . . . church and destroyed my power,' he said.

John waited for the queen to reassure him that nothing so bad was being plotted. He hoped that she would remind him that the king and queen he most admired – his father James, and his great-aunt Elizabeth, had spent all their lives weaving compromises and twisting out agreements. Both of them had been faced with argumentative parliaments and both of them had put all their power and all their charm into turning agreements to their own desire, dividing the opposition, seducing their enemies. Neither of them would ever have been at loggerheads with a force which commanded any power in the country. Both of them would have waited and undermined an enemy.

'We must destroy them,' the queen said flatly. 'Before they destroy us and destroy the country. We must gain and then keep control of the parliament, of the army and of the Church. There can be no agreement until they acknowledge that Church, army, and Parliament is all ours. And we will never compromise on that, will we, my love? You will never concede anything!'

He took her hand and kissed it as if she had given him the most sage and level-headed counsel. 'You see how I am advised?' he asked with a smile to Tradescant. 'You see how w . . . wise and stern she is? This is a worthy successor to Queen Elizabeth, is sh . . . she not? A woman who could defeat the Sp . . . Spanish Armada again.'

'But these are not the Spanish,' John pointed out. He could almost hear Hester ordering him to be silent while he took the risk and spoke. 'These are Englishmen, following their consciences. These are your own people – not a foreign enemy.'

'They are traitors!' the queen snapped. 'And thus they are worse than the Spanish, who might be our enemies but at least are faithful to their king. A man who is a traitor is like a dog who is mad. He should be struck down and killed without a second's thought.'

The king nodded. 'And I am s . . . sorry, Gardener Tradescant, to hear you sympathise with them.' There was a world of warning despite the slight stammer.

'I just hope for peace and that all good men can find a way to peace,' John muttered.

The queen stared at him, affronted by a sudden doubt. 'You are my servant,' she said flatly. 'There can be no question which side you are on.'

John tried to smile. 'I didn't know we were taking sides.'

'Oh yes,' the king said bitterly. 'We are certainly t . . . taking sides. And I have paid you a w . . . wage for years, and you have worked in my h . . . household, or in the household of my dear D . . . Duke since you were a boy – have you not? And your f . . . father worked all his life for my advisors and servants, and my f . . . father's advisors and servants. You have eaten our b . . . bread since you were weaned. Which side are you on?'

John swallowed to ease the tightness in his throat. 'I am for the good of the country, and for peace, and for you to enjoy what is your own, Your Majesty,' he said.

'What has *always* b . . . been mine own,' the king prompted.

'Of course,' John agreed.

The queen suddenly smiled. 'But this is my dear Gardener Tradescant!' she said lightly. 'Of course he is for us. You would be first into battle with your little hoe, wouldn't you?'

John tried to smile and bowed rather than reply.

The queen put her hand on his arm. 'And we never betray those who follow us,' she said sweetly. 'We are bound to you as you are bound to us and we would never betray a faithful servant.' She nodded at the king as if inviting him to learn a lesson. 'When a man is ready to promise himself to us he finds in us a loyal master.'

The king smiled at his wife and the gardener. 'Of course,' he said. 'From the highest servant to the l . . . lowest, I do not forget either loyalty or treachery. And I reward b . . . both.'

Summer 1641

John remembered that promise on the day that the Earl of Strafford was taken to the Tower of London and thrown into the traitors' prison to be executed when the king signed the Act of Attainder – his death warrant.

The king had sworn to Strafford that he would never betray him. He had written him a note and gave him the word of a king that Strafford would never suffer 'in life, honour or fortune' for his service – those were his exact words. The most cautious and wily members of the Privy Council fled the country when they recognised that Parliament was attacking the Privy Council rather than attacking the king. Most of them were quick to realise too that whatever the king might promise, he would not raise one hand to save a trusted servant from dying for his cause. But the Bishop of Ely and Archbishop William Laud were too slow, or too trusting. They too were imprisoned for plotting against the safety of the kingdom, alongside their ally Strafford in the Tower.

For all of the long spring months, Parliament had met on Strafford's case and heard that he had recommended bringing in an army of Irish Papist troops to reduce 'this kingdom'. If the king had interrupted the trial to insist that Strafford was referring to the kingdom of Scotland he might have saved him then from the executioner. But he did not. The king stayed silent in the little ante-room where he sat and listened to the trial. He did not insist. He offered, rather feebly, to never take Strafford's advice again as long as the old man lived if they would but spare his life. The Houses of Parliament said they could not spare his life. The king struggled with his conscience for a short, painful time, and then signed the warrant for Strafford's execution.

'He sent little Prince Charles to ask them for mercy,' Hester said in blank astonishment to John as she came back from Lambeth in May with a wagon full of shopping and a head full of news. 'That poor little boy, only ten years old, and the king sent him down to Westminster to go before the whole Parliament and plead for the Earl's life. And then they refused him! What a thing to do to a child! He's going to think all his life that it was his fault that the Earl went to his death!'

'Whereas it is the king's,' John said simply. 'He could have denied that Strafford had ever advised him. He could have borne witness for him. He could have taken the decision on his own shoulders. But he let Strafford take the blame for him. And now he will let Strafford die for him.'

'He's to be executed on Tuesday,' Hester said. 'The market women are closing their stalls for the day and going up to Tower Hill to see his head taken off. And the apprentices are taking a free day, an extra May Day.'

John shook his head. 'So much for the king's loyalty. These are bad days for his servants. What's the word on Archbishop Laud?'

'Still in the Tower,' Hester said. She rose to her feet and took hold of the side of the wagon to clamber down but John reached out his arms and lifted her down. She hesitated for a moment at the strangeness of his touch. It was nearly an embrace, his hands on her waist, their heads close together. Then he released her and moved to the back of the wagon.

'You've bought enough for a siege!' he exclaimed, and then, as his own words sunk in, he turned to her. 'Why have you bought so much?'

'I don't want to go into market for a week or so,' she said. 'And I won't send the maids either.'

'Why not?'

She made a little helpless gesture. He thought he had never before seen her anything other than certain and definite in her movements. 'It's strange in town,' she began. 'I can't describe it. Uneasy. Like a sky before a storm. People talk on corners and break off when I walk by. Everyone looks at everyone else as if they would read their hearts. No-one knows who is a friend and who is not. The king and Parliament are splitting this country down the middle like a popped pod of peas and all of us peas are spilling out and rolling around and not knowing what to do.'

John looked at his wife, trying to understand, for the first time in their married life, what she might be feeling. Then he suddenly realised what it was. 'You look afraid.'

She turned away to the edge of the wagon as if it were something to be ashamed of. 'Someone threw a stone at me,' she said, her voice very low.

'What?'

'Someone threw a stone as I was leaving the market. It hit me in the back.'

John was dumbfounded. 'You were stoned? In Lambeth?'

She shook her head. 'A glancing blow. It was not thrown to hurt me. I think it was an insult, a warning.'

'But why should anyone at Lambeth market insult you? Or warn you?'

She shrugged. 'You're well-known as the king's gardener, the king's man, and your father before you. And these people don't inquire where your heart lies, what you think in private. They think of us as the king's servants, and the king is not well-regarded in Lambeth and the City.'

John's mind was whirling. 'Did it hurt you? Are you hurt?'

She started to say 'No', but she stumbled over the word and John, without thinking, caught her into his arms and let her cry against his shoulder as the torrent of words spilled out.

She was afraid, very afraid, and she had been afraid every market day since Parliament had been recalled and the king had come home defeated from the war with the Scots. The women would not always serve her, they overcharged her and leaned on the scales when they were weighing out flour. And the apprentice boys ran after her and called out names, and when the stone had struck her back she had thought it would be the first of a hail of stones which would hit her and knock her from the box of the wagon and beat her down in the street.

'Hester! Hester!' John held her as the storm of crying swept over her. 'My dear, my dear, my little wife!'

She broke off from crying at once. 'What did you call me?'

He had not been aware of it himself.

'You called me little wife, and your dear –' she said. She rubbed her eyes, but kept her other hand firmly on his collar. 'You called me dear, you've never called me that before.'

The old closed look came down on his face. 'I was upset for you,' he said, as if it was a sin to call his own wife an endearment. 'For a moment I forgot.'

'You forgot that you had been married before. You treated me like a wife you are . . . fond of,' she said.

He nodded.

'I am glad,' she said softly. 'I should like you to be fond of me.'

He disengaged himself very gently. 'I should not forget I was married before,' he said firmly, and went into the house. Hester stood beside the cart, watching the kitchen door closing behind him, and found she had no more tears left to cry but only loneliness and disappointment and dry eyes.

Summer 1641

Hester did not go to market again all summer. And she had been right to fear the mood of the village of Lambeth. The apprentice boys all ran wild one night and the fever was caught by the market women and by the serious chapel goers, who made a determined mixed mob and marched through the streets shouting, 'No popery! No bishops!' Some of the loudest and most daring shouted, 'No king!' They threw a few burning brands over the high walls of the empty archbishop's palace, and made a half-hearted attempt at the gates, and then they broke the windows down Lambeth High Street at every house that did not show a light at the window for Parliament. They did not march down the road as far as the Ark and John thanked God for the luck of the Tradescants, which had once again placed them on the very edge of great events and danger and yet spared them by a hair's breadth.

After that, John sent the gardener's lad and the stable lad together to market and though they often muddled the order and stopped for an ale at the taverns, at least it meant that any muttering about the king's gardener was not directed at Hester.

John had to go to Oatlands and before he went he ordered wooden shutters to be made for all the windows of the house, especially the great windows of Venetian glass in the rarities room. He hired an extra lad to wake at nights and watch out down the South Lambeth road in case the mob came that way, and he and Hester went out one night in the darkness with shaded lanterns to clear out the old ice house, and put a heavy bolt on the thick wooden doors to make a hiding place for the most valuable of the rarities.

'If they come against us you will have to take the children and leave the house,' he ordered.

She shook her head and he found himself admiring her cool nerve.

'We have a couple of muskets,' she said. 'I won't have my house overrun by a band of idle apprentice lads.'

'You must not take risks,' he warned her.

She gave him a tight, determined smile. 'Everything is a risk in these days,' she said. 'I will see that we come safe through it all.'

'I *have* to leave you,' John said anxiously. 'I am summoned to Oatlands. Their Majesties will visit next week and I have to see the gardens are at their best.'

She nodded. 'I know you have to go. I shall keep everything safe here.'

John was at Oatlands ready for the full court, but the queen came alone. The king and half the court were missing, and the rumour was that he had gone north to negotiate with the Scots himself.

'He is in Edinburgh and all will be mended,' the queen said with her complacent smile when she came upon John dead-heading the roses. She was concealing her boredom as best as she could. She was accompanied only by a few ladies, the old flirtatious, artistic, idle entourage was broken up. The more adventurous and more ambitious men were riding with the king. There was the smell of opportunity and advancement in the court of a king at war, and the young men had been sick of peace and a court devoted to marital love for so long. 'It will all be resolved,' the queen promised. 'Once they meet him again he will charm them into seeing that they were wrong to march against him.'

John nodded. 'I hope so, Your Majesty.'

She came close to him and lowered her voice. 'We will not go to London again until it is all agreed,' she confided. 'Not even to my little manor at Wimbledon. We shall go nowhere near to Westminster. After the death of my Lord Strafford –' She broke off. 'They said they would try *me* after the Earl! Try *me* for treasonous advice!'

John had to resist the temptation to take one of her little white hands. She looked genuinely afraid.

'He should have stood against them,' she whispered. 'My husband should not have let them take Strafford, nor Laud. If he lets them pick us off one after another we will all be lost. And then he will be left all alone and they will have tasted blood. He should have stood against them for William Laud, he should have stood against them for Strafford. How can I be sure he will stand for me?'

'Your Majesty, matters cannot go so far,' John said soothingly. 'As you say yourself, the king will come home and it will all be resolved.'

She brightened at once. 'He can scatter a few baronies around the Houses of Parliament, and places at court,' she said. 'These are all lowly men, commoners up from the provinces. They have neither learning nor breeding. They will forget their folly if the price is high enough.'

John felt the familiar rise of irritation. 'Majesty, I think they are men of principle. They did not behead Lord Strafford on a whim. I think they believe in what they are doing.'

She shook her head. 'Of course not! They are scheming with the Scots, or with the Dutch, or with someone for their own ends. The House of Lords is not with them, the court is not with them. These are little men come up from the country, crowing like little cocks on their own dunghills. We just have to wring their necks like little cocks.'

'I pray that the king can find a way to agree with them,' John said steadily.

She flashed him her charming smile. 'Why, so do I! He shall make all sorts of promises to them, and then they can vote us the taxes we need and the army we need to crush the Scots and they can go back to their dunghills and we can rule without them again.'

Autumn 1641

It might have gone either way for the king, and the queen, but for their fourth kingdom of Ireland. The news that Strafford was dead ran through Ireland like a heath fire. Strafford had held Ireland down with a mixture of legal rigour and terrible abuse of power. He had ruled them like a cynical old soldier and the only law in the land was that of superior military power. Once he was dead the Papist Irish rose up in a defiant storm of rage against their Protestant masters. Strafford had kept them brutally down, but now Strafford was gone. The rumours and counter-rumours had flown around the kingdom of Ireland until every man who called himself a man took up a pitchfork or a hoe and flung himself against the newly arrived Protestant settlers, and the greedy land-grabbing Protestant lords, and spared neither them nor their women nor children.

The news of what had taken place, horrifically embellished by the terrified imagination of a minority in a country they did not own, reached London in October and fuelled the hatred against Papists a thousand times over. Even Hester, normally so level-headed, departed from discretion that night and prayed aloud in family prayers that God might strike down the dreadful savage Irish and preserve His chosen people, settled in that most barbaric land; and the Tradescant children, Frances and Johnnie, round-eyed with horror at what they heard in the kitchen and in the stable, whispered a frightened, 'Amen'.

The Papist rebels were spitting Protestant children on their pikes and roasting them over the fires, eating them before the anguished gaze of their parents. The Papist rebels were firing cottages and castles with the Protestant owners locked inside. Everyone knew a story of fresh and unbelievable horror. No-one questioned any report. It was all true, it was all the worst of the worst nightmares. It was all worse than reports told.

John was reminded, for a brief moment, of the bitter woman who kept the lodging house in Virginia, and how she had called the Indians pagans and beasts, and how she too had stories of skinning and flaying and eating alive. For a moment he stepped back from the terror which had caught up the whole of England, for a moment he wondered if the stories were as true as everyone swore. But only for a moment. The circumstances were too persuasive, the stories were too potent. Everyone said it; it had to be true.

And there was worse. In the streets of Lambeth and in London they did not call it the Irish rebellion, they called it the queen's rebellion, in the absolute certainty that all the nightmare tales from Ireland were gospel truth, and that the rebellion was fomented by Henrietta Maria herself in support of the devilish Papists. What the queen wanted was a free Roman Catholic Ireland and then, as soon as she dared, the queen would ship her fellow Papists from Ireland to England so they could butcher and eat English babes as well.

Spring 1642

Parliament, still in session, drew ever closer to accusing the queen. It was a steady, terrifying approach, which would not waver nor hesitate. They impeached twelve bishops for treason, one after another, until a round dozen had appeared before the bar of the House, with their lives on the line. And then the word was that the queen was next on the list.

'What shall you do?' Hester asked John. They were in the warmth of the rarities room where a large fire kept the collection warm and dry though there was a storm of wintry sleet dashing against the grand windows. Hester was polishing the shells and precious stones to make them gleam on their beds of black velvet, and John was labelling a new collection of carved ivories which had just arrived from India.

'I don't know,' he said. 'I shall have to go to Oatlands to see to the planning for the gardens next season. I will learn more there.'

'Planning gardens for a queen who will be beheaded?' Hester asked quietly.

John met her gaze, his mouth twisted with anxiety. 'I am following your creed, wife. I'm trying to survive these times. I don't know what's best to do other than to behave as if nothing has changed.'

'But John –' Hester started, but was interrupted by a knock at the front door, and they both froze. John saw Hester's colour drain from her cheeks, and the hand that held the duster trembled as if she had an ague. They stood in complete silence and then they heard the maid answer and the reassuring chink of a coin as a visitor paid for entrance to the collection. Hester whisked her cloth out of sight into the pocket of her apron and threw open the handsome double doors to him. He was a well-dressed man, a country man, by the look of his brown suit and his weather-beaten face. He paused in the doorway and looked around at the grand, imposing room and the warm fire.

'Well, this is a treat,' he said in the round tones of the west country.

Hester moved forward. 'You are welcome,' she said pleasantly. 'This is John Tradescant, and I am his wife.'

The man dipped his head. 'I am Benjamin George,' he said. 'From Yeovil.'

'A visitor to London?'

'Here on business. I am a Parliament man representing the borough of Yeovil.'

John stepped forward. 'My wife will show you the rarities,' he said. 'But first can you tell me what news there is?'

The man looked cautious. 'I can't say whether it is good or bad,' he said. 'I am on my way home and Parliament is dissolved, I know that much.'

John and Hester exchanged a quick look. 'Parliament dissolved?'

The man nodded. 'The king himself came marching in to arrest five of our members. You would not have thought that he was allowed to come into Parliament with his own soldiers like that. Whether he was going to arrest our members for treason or cut them down where they stood, I don't know which!'

'My God!' John exclaimed, aghast. 'He drew a sword in the House of Commons?'

'What happened?' Hester demanded.

'He came in very civil though he had his guards all about him, and he asked for a seat and sat in the Speaker's chair. But they were gone – the men he wanted. They slipped out the back half an hour before he came in the front. We were warned, of course. And so he looked about for them, and made a comment, and then went away again.'

John was struggling to hide his irritation with the slowness of the man's speech. 'But what did he come for, if he left it too late to arrest them?'

The man shrugged. 'I think myself it was some grand gesture, but he bodged it.'

Hester looked quickly at John. He made an impatient exclamation. 'Are you saying he marched his guard into the House to arrest five members and failed?'

The man nodded. 'He looked powerfully put out,' he observed.

'I should think he was. What will he do?'

'As to that . . . I couldn't say.'

'But then what will Parliament do?'

The man slowly shook his head. Hester, seeing her husband on the edge of an outburst and the man still thinking his answer through, had to bite her lip to keep silent herself.

'As to that . . . I couldn't say either.'

John took a swift step to the door and then turned back. 'So what is happening in the City? Is everything quiet?'

The country squire shook his head at the mystifying speed of change. 'Well, the Lord Mayor's trained bands are to be called out to keep the peace, the king's men have all gone into hiding, the City is boarded up and ready for a riot or . . . something worse.'

'What could be worse?' Hester asked. 'What could be worse than a riot in the City?'

'War, I think,' he said slowly. 'A war would be worse than a riot.'

'Between who?' John asked tightly. 'A war between who? What are you saying?'

The man looked into his face, struggling with the enormity of what he had to say. 'War between the king and Parliament, I'm afraid.'

There was a brief shocked silence.

'It has come to this?' John asked.

'So I am come to see the greatest sight of London which I promised myself I would see before I left, and then I am going home.' George looked around. 'There is even more than I thought.'

'I will show it all to you,' Hester promised him. 'You must forgive our hunger for news. What will you do when you get home?'

He bowed courteously to her. 'I shall gather the men of my household and train them and arm them so that they can fight to save their country from the enemy.'

'But will you fight for the king or for Parliament?'

He bowed again. 'Madam, I shall fight for my country. I shall fight for Right. The only thing is: I wish I knew who was in the right.'

Hester showed him the main features of the collection and then, as soon as she could, left him to open the drawers and look at the smaller things on his own. She could not find John in the house, nor in the orangery. As she feared, he was in the stable yard, dressed in his travelling cloak, waiting for his mare to be saddled.

'You're never going to court!' she exclaimed.

'I have to,' he said. 'I cannot bear having to wait for scraps of news like this.'

'You are a gardener,' she said. 'Not a courtier, not a Member of Parliament. What is it to you whether the king is quarrelling with Parliament or not?'

'I am on the edge of it all,' John said. 'I know too much to sit quietly at home and nurse up my ignorance. If I knew less of them then I would care less. If I knew more then I could decide better what to do. I am halfway between knowledge and ignorance and I have to settle on one side or the other.'

'Then be ignorant!' she said with sudden passion. 'Get into your garden, John, and set seeds for the gardens at Wimbledon and Oatlands. Do the trade you were born to. Stay home where you are safe.'

He shook his head and took both her hands. 'I won't be long,' he promised her. 'I shall go over the river to Whitehall and find out the news and then come back home. Don't fret so, Hester. I must learn what is happening and then I'll come home. It is better for us if I know which way the wind is blowing. It is safer for us.'

She left her hands in his, enjoying the warmth of his callused palms. 'You say that, but you are like a boy setting out on an adventure,' she said shrewdly. 'You want to be in the heart of things, my husband. Don't deny it.'

John gave her a roguish grin and then kissed her quickly on both cheeks. 'Forgive me,' he said. 'It's true. Let me go with your blessing?'

She was breathless with the sudden casual embrace and felt herself flushing. 'With my blessing,' she repeated. 'Of course you have my blessing. Always.'

He swung himself into the saddle and let the horse walk out of the yard. Hester put her hand to her cheek where his lips had briefly touched, and watched him go.

He had to wait for a place on the horse ferry at Lambeth, and then the traffic on the City side of the river was busier than he had ever seen it. There were hundreds of people milling around in the narrow streets, asking for news and stopping ballad sellers and pedlars of news-sheets to demand what they knew. There were armed groups of men marching down the road, pushing people aside and demanding that they shout, 'Hurrah! for the king!' But then down another road would come another group shouting, 'Hurrah! for Pym! No bishops! No Papist queen!'

John drew his horse back into a sidestreet, fearful of being caught up in a fight, when he saw two of these groups heading towards each other. But the royalists wheeled off quickly to one side, as if they were on an urgent errand that took them away; and the others took care not to see them, and not to give chase. He watched them go and saw that they, like himself, were not ready for a fight yet. They didn't even want a brawl, let alone a war. He thought the country must be filled with men like himself, like the honest Member of Parliament for Yeovil, who knew that they were in the grip of great times, and wanted to take their part in the great times, who wanted to do the right thing; but were very, very far from knowing what the right thing might be.

John's father would have known. He would have been for the king. John's father had had a straightforward faith that his son had never learned. John made a wry face at the thought of the certainties of the man and of his own confused layering of doubts, which left him now still mourning one woman, half in love with another, and married to a third; in the service of a king while his heart was with the opposition; always torn both ways, always on the fringe of everything.

The crowds grew thicker around the palace of Whitehall and there were armed guards looking grim and frightened with their pikes crossed at the doorways. John rode his horse round to an inn and left her in the stable, and then walked back to the palace, jostled all the way. The crowd was the same strange mix of people. There were beggars and paupers and ill-doers in rags and shabby old livery who were there to shout and perhaps collect a few coppers for their hired loyalty. There were working men and women, young apprentices, artisans and market people. There were the serious black-coated preachers of the independent churches and sectaries, and there were the well-to-do merchants and City men who would not fight themselves, but whose hearts were in the fight. There were sailors from the ships in port, shouting for Parliament since they blamed the king and his French wife for the dangers of the Dunkirk pirates, and there were members of the London trained bands, some of them trying to impose order and find their men, and others running wild and shouting that they would die to defend the rights of Parliament. This motley crowd had a motley chant which ranged from the catcalls and boos of those who did not know what they cared for, to the regular call of those who knew their cause: 'No bishops! No queen!', and the new call which had come about since the king had taken a sword into the House of Commons: 'Privilege! Privilege!'

John fought his way to the front of the mob at the gates to the palace of Whitehall and shouted, over the noise, to the guard.

'John Tradescant! The king's gardener.'

The man shifted slightly, and John ducked under the pike and went in.

The old palace of Whitehall was the most disorganised of all the royal palaces, a jumble of buildings and courts and gardens, dotted with statuary and fountains and alive with birdsong. John, hoping to find a face he knew, made his way towards the royal apartments and then was brought short as he rounded a corner and nearly collided with the queen herself.

She was running, her cape flying behind her, her jewel box in her hands. Behind her came the king, carrying his own travelling desk of papers and a dozen maidservants and manservants, each burdened with whatever they had been able to snatch up. Behind them came two royal nursemaids, running with the two royal babies in their arms, the five-year-old Princess Elizabeth trotting to keep up, and the two young princes, James and Charles, lagging in the rear.

John dropped to his knee as she saw him but she rushed towards him and he jumped to his feet as she pushed her jewel box at him.

'Gardener Tradescant!' she cried. 'Take this!' She turned to the king. 'We must wait!' she insisted. 'We must face the rabble! We must face them down!'

The king shook his head and motioned for her to go on. Unwillingly, she went before him. 'I t . . . tell you they have run mad!' he said. 'We must get out of the C . . . City! There's not a loyal heart here. They have all run m . . . mad. We must go to Hampton Court and c . . . c . . . consider what to do! We must summon soldiers and take advice.'

'We are running like fools from our own shadows!' she shrieked at him. 'We must face them and face them down or we will spend the rest of our life on the run.'

'We are l . . . lost!' he shouted. 'L . . . lost! D'you think I want to see you dragged before the b . . . bar and impeached for treason? D'you think I want to see your h . . . h . . . head on a pike? D'you think I want to see the rabble take y . . . you, and the children, t . . . take you now?'

John joined the train of servants running behind them and followed them to the stables. All the way the quarrel between the king and queen grew more inarticulate as her French accent deepened with her temper and his stammer grew worse with his fear. When they reached the stable yard she was beside herself.

'You are a coward!' she spat at him. 'You will lose this city forever if you leave it now. It is easier to run away than to retake. You must show them that you are not afraid.'

'Ha . . . Hi . . . I fear nothing!' He drew himself up. 'N . . . Nothing! But I must have you safe and the children safe before I can m . . . make m . . . my m . . . move. It is your safety, Madam, that I am securing now. For myself I care nothing! N . . . ha . . . N . . . Nothing!'

John pressed forward and put the jewel box on the coach floor. He was reminded of the king's odd mixture of shyness and boastfulness. Even now, with a mob hammering on the doors of the palace, the two of them were playing out their parts in a masque. Even now they did not seem to be completely real. John looked around, the servants were like an audience at a great play. No-one urged a course of action, no-one spoke. The king and queen were the only actors; and their script was a great romance of danger and heroism and lost causes and sudden flights. John felt his heart pounding at the noise of the crowd outside and knew the deep visceral fear of a mob. He had a sudden vision of them breaking down the gates and tumbling into the stable yard. If they found the queen beside her travelling coach with her jewel box beside her, anything could happen. The whole power of the royal family which the old Queen Elizabeth had so powerfully cultivated depended on the creation and maintenance of distance and magic and glamour. Let the people once see the queen swearing at their king like a French lace-seller, and the game would be up.

'I will see you s . . . safe at Hampton Court and then I will return and crush these traitors,' Charles swore.

'You shall crush them now!' she shrieked. 'Now, before they gain their strength. You shall face them and defy them and destroy them or I swear I shall leave this kingdom and never see it again! They know how to respect a princess of the blood in France!'

At once the mood of the scene shifted. The king took her hand and bowed over it, his silky hair falling to shield his face. 'N . . . never say it,' he said. 'You are q . . . queen of this country, queen of all the h . . . hearts. This is a faithful country, they l . . . love you, I love you. Never even th . . . think of leaving me.'

There was renewed shouting at the door. John, forgetting that he should stay silent, could not bear to see them taken like a pair of runaway servants in the stable yard. 'Your Majesty!' he urged. 'You must either prepare for a siege or get the coach out! The crowd will be upon you in a moment!'

The queen looked to him. 'My faithful Gardener Tradescant!' she exclaimed. 'Stay with us.'

'G . . . Get up at the back,' the king ordered. 'Y . . . You shall escort us t . . . to safety.' John gaped at him. The only thing he had thought to do was to bring the two of them to a sense of urgency.

'Your Majesty?' he asked.

The king handed the queen into the coach where the two little princes, Charles and James, white-faced and silent, were waiting, their eyes like saucers with terror. Then the nursemaids and the babies bundled in and the king climbed in himself. John slammed the door on them. He wanted to tell them that he could not possibly go with them but he heard the rising volume of the crowd at the gates and he was afraid that they might argue with him, command his service, question his loyalty, delay again.

John stepped back from the coach, waiting for it to draw away; but it did not move. Nobody would do anything without a specific order and the king and queen were arguing again inside.

'Oh! Damnation! Drive on!' John shouted, taking command in the absence of any authority, and swung himself up beside the footmen clinging on the back. 'Westward, to Hampton Court. And drive steadily. Don't for God's sake run anyone down. But don't stop!'

Even then the footmen hesitated at the stable doors.

'Open the doors!' John shouted at them, his temper at breaking point.

They leaped to obey the first clear order they had heard all day and the great wooden doors swung open.

At once the men and women in the very front of the crowd fell back, as the doors opened up and the coach pulled out. John saw they were taken aback at the sudden movement of the doors, at the progress of the fine horses, and the wealth and richness of the gilding on the royal coach. The king's ornate carriage with the plumes of feathers on each roof corner, and the huge high-stepping Arab horses harnessed with tack of red leather and gold studs, still had the mystique of power, divine power, even with a traitorous Papist queen inside. But those in the front could not get back very far; they were held steady by the weight of the crowd behind them, still pushing forward.

The crowd had pikes but they were using them as banners, not yet as weapons. On each one was tied a white flag scrawled with the word 'Liberty!' and they jogged them up and down at the windows of the coach. John prayed that the queen kept her face turned down and for once in her life kept quiet. The prestige of the king might get them safely through the mob if she did not antagonise them.

John heard a frightened child crying from inside the coach. 'Drive on!' he ordered the coachman above the noise of the crowd. 'Go steady!', and he shouted as loud as he could: 'Make way for the king! For the rightful king!'

'Liberty!' someone yelled, jabbing a pike dangerously close to his face.

'Liberty and the king!' John replied, and heard another voice at once echo the new slogan. The footman beside him flinched as someone spat. 'Stay still, you fool, or they will drag you down,' John muttered.

At any moment the mood of the crowd could change from boisterous protest to murder. John looked over the roof of the carriage to where the streets narrowed for the way out of town.

'Make way for the rightful king!' John shouted.

The crowd grew denser at the crossroads. 'Keep going!' John yelled at the coachman. He had an absolute certainty that if they stopped, even for a moment, the doors would be pulled open and the royal family dragged from the coach and torn apart on the very street. Once the mob learned that they could stop the king in his carriage, then they would know they could do whatever they wished. All that was holding them back was the old superstitious belief in the king's power, the divinity of kingship that King James had preached and that Charles so passionately believed. The crowd kept reaching towards the coach as it crawled slowly past them but their hands would drop back as if they feared a burning from the gold paintwork. If they touched and snatched just once, then they would all know that the king was not a god, a vengeful god. If they found the courage to touch just once, they would snatch at everything.

'Keep back,' John shouted. 'Make way for the king!'

Everything depended on the coach maintaining the painfully slow walking pace, and never checking, and never stopping, all the way westwards where the sun shone on the water in the open sewers, like a pointer to safety.

Someone pulled at his coat, nearly hauling him off balance. John grabbed tighter at the footman's strap and looked down. It was a woman, her face contorted with rage. 'Liberty!' she cried. 'Death to the Papists! Death to the Papist queen!'

'Liberty and the king!' John shouted back. He tried to smile at her and felt his lips stick on his dry teeth. As long as the queen kept her face hidden! 'Liberty and the king.'

The carriage lurched over the cobbles. The crowd was thicker but the road further ahead was clear. Someone threw a handful of mud at the coach door but the crowd was too dense for them to start stoning, and though the pikes still jogged to the cry of 'Liberty!' they were not yet aimed towards the glass of the windows.

As the road went on, out of town, the crowd thinned, as John had hoped it would. Most of these people had homes or market stalls or even businesses in the City, there was nothing to be gained by following the coach out along the West Way. Besides, they were out of breath and tiring of the sport.

'Let's open the doors!' someone exclaimed. 'Open the doors and see this queen, this Papist queen. Let's hear her prayers, that they're so keen that we should learn!'

'Look!' John yelled as loud as he could. 'An Irishman!' He pointed back the way they had come. 'Going into the palace! An Irish priest!'

With a howl the mob turned back and ran, slipping and sliding over the cobbles back towards the palace, chasing their own nightmares.

'Now drive on!' John yelled at the driver. 'Let them go!'

The carriage gave a great lurch as the driver whipped the horses and they leaped forward, bumping on the cobbles. John clung like a barnacle on the back of the great coach, swaying on the leather straps, and ducked his head down as the wind blowing down the street whisked his hat away.

When they reached the outskirts of London the streets were quiet, the people either boarded inside their houses and praying for peace, or roaming in the city. John felt the slackening of tension around his throat and he loosened his grip on the footman's strap and rocked with the sway of the coach all the way to Hampton Court.

The king was not expected at Hampton Court. There was nothing ready for the royal family. The royal beds and furniture, rugs and pictures were all left at Whitehall. The family stepped down before the solidly closed great doors of the palace and there was not even a servant to open up for them.

John had a sense that the whole world was collapsing around him. He hesitated and looked towards his monarch. The king leaned back against the dirty wheel of the coach, as if he were exhausted.

'I did not expect this sort of welcome!' Charles said mournfully. 'The doors of my own palace closed to me!'

The queen looked pleadingly at Tradescant. 'What shall we do?'

John felt an irritable sense of responsibility. 'Wait here,' he said. 'I'll find someone.'

He left the royal coach before the imposing grand front doors and went around to the back. The kitchens were in their usual careless state; the whole household always took a holiday during the king's absence.

'Wake up,' John said, putting his head around the door. 'The king, queen and royal family are outside waiting to be let in.'

It was as if he had set off a fire-ship among the cockle boats at Whitby. There was a stunned silence and then instantaneous uproar.

'For God's sake get the front door open and let him in,' John said, and went back to the courtyard.

The king was leaning back against the coach surveying the high, imposing roofs of the palace as if he had never seen them before. The queen was still seated in the carriage. Neither of them had moved since John had left them, although the children were whimpering inside the coach and one of the nursemaids was praying.

John pinned a smile on his face and stepped forward and bowed. 'I am sorry for the poor welcome,' he said. As he spoke the great doors creaked open and a frightened-looking footman peeped out. 'There's a couple of cooks here, and a household of servants,' John said reassuringly. 'They'll make Your Majesties comfortable enough.'

At the sight of a servant the queen brightened. She rose to her feet and waited for the footman to hand her down from the carriage. The children followed her.

The king turned to John. 'I thank you for the service you have given us this day. We were glad of your escort.'

John bowed. 'I am glad to see Your Majesty safe arrived,' he said. At least he could say that with a clear conscience, he thought. He was indeed glad to get them safe out of London. He could not have stood by and seen the queen and the royal princes pulled out of their carriage by a mob, any more than he could have watched Hester and the children abused.

'Go and see that there are r . . . rooms made ready for us,' the king commanded.

John hesitated. 'I should return home,' he said. 'I will give orders that everything shall be done as you wish, and then go to my home.'

The king made that little gesture with his hand which signified 'No.'

John hesitated.

'S . . . stay until we have some order here,' the king said coolly. 'Tell them to prepare our p . . . privy chambers and a dinner.'

John could do nothing but bow and walk carefully backwards from the king's presence and go to do his bidding.

There was only so much that could be done. There was only one decent bed in the house fit for them; and so the king, queen, and the two royal princes were forced to bed down together in one bed, in the only aired linen in the whole palace. There was a dinner which was ample, but hardly royal; and no golden plate and cups for the service. The trappings of monarchy – the tapestries, carpets, gold plate and jewels, even the richly embroidered bed linen that always travelled with the king in his great progresses around the country – were still at Whitehall. All that was ever left in the empty palaces was second-rate goods, and Hampton Court was no exception. The queen ate off pewter with an air of shocked disdain.

Dinner was served by the kitchen staff and the lowly gentlemen of the household who maintained the palace in the king's absence. They served it as it should be done, on bended knee, but all the ceremony in the world could not conceal that it was plain bread and meat on pewter plates on a plain board table.

'You will escort the queen and I to Windsor tomorrow,' the king said, when he had finished eating. 'And from thence to Dover.'

Tradescant, who was seated at a lower table down the hall, got up from his bench and dropped to his knee on the stale rushes on the floor. 'Yes, Your Majesty.' He kept his head down so that he showed no surprise.

'See that the horses are ready at dawn,' the king ordered.

The royal family rose from their places at the top table and left the great hall by the door at the back of the dais. Their withdrawing room would be cold and smoky with a chimney which did not properly draw.

'Are they running for it?' one of the ushers asked John as he rose from his knees. 'All of them?'

John looked appalled. 'They cannot do so!'

'Did they need to run from London? Like cowards?'

'How can you tell? The mood of the rabble around Whitehall was angry enough. There were moments when I feared for their lives.'

'The rabble!' the man jeered. 'They could have thrown them a purse of gold and turned them around in a moment. But if they run from London, will they run from the country? Is that why they're going to Dover? To take a ship to France? And what will become of us then?'

John shook his head. 'This morning I was taking leave of my wife in my stable yard at Lambeth,' he said. 'I hardly know where I am, let alone what is to become of the king and the queen and their kingdoms.'

'Well I bet you they run for it,' the young man said cheerfully. 'And good riddance,' he added under his breath, and then snapped his fingers at his dog and left the hall.

It was a long, cold journey to Dover; the royal family were muffled up inside the coach but John was standing in the footman's place behind, holding on to the strap. By the time the coach rumbled in to Dover castle John was clinging on with fingers that were blue, his eyes running with tears from the cold wind in his face, every bone in his face aching as if he had an ague. From his place on the back of the coach he had heard, over the rumble of the wheels, the queen steadily complaining, all the way down the long frosty roads.

They slept that night in Dover castle, in better comfort; and then lingered undecided for a week. First they were waiting for news, then deciding to sail to France, missing the tide, changing their minds, waiting for more news. Courtiers slowly reassembled from the rout of London, noblemen were recalled from their country seats. Everyone had different advice, everyone was listened to with kingly courtesy, no-one could agree, no-one could act. Eleven-year-old Princess Mary, setting sail to live with her bridegroom in Holland, joined them during the week that they hesitated, havering between one choice and another, and found that the queen, her mother, was very bitter with her daughter for marrying a Protestant and leaving the family in such distress. Princess Mary made no undutiful replies to her mother, but sulked in eloquent silence.

A couple of heavy bags arrived at dawn from the Tower of London and John assumed, but did not ask, from the dour expression of the guard who never let them out of his sight, that the king was sending the country's treasure overseas with his wife and that once again the most precious stones in England would be hawked around the moneylenders in Europe.

The king and queen finally came to a decision to separate. Princess Mary was bound for Holland in one ship, the queen and the three babies were to set sail for France in another: the *Lion*. The two princes – Charles and James – and the king were to stay in England and find a solution to the demands of Parliament. John and the other attendants waited at a distance on the quayside as the royal couple forced themselves to the brink of parting. The king held both her hands and kissed them tenderly.

'You will not yield one inch to them,' the queen said, her voice demanding and penetrating so that every man on the quayside could hear how the king of England was hag-ridden. 'You will not make one concession. They must be brought to heel. They must know their master. You will not even speak with them without keeping me informed.'

Charles kissed her hands again. 'No,' he promised. 'M . . . My love, my dear love. I will not have a m . . . moment when I do not think of you.'

'Then think that I will never be able to come back until the traitor Pym is executed for treason,' she said fiercely. 'And think of your son and his inheritance which must be passed to him entire. And I shall raise such an army in Europe that if they will not agree they will be destroyed! So make no concessions, Charles, I will not permit it!'

'My dear, d ... dear love,' he said quietly.

He raised his head from her hands and she kissed him full on the mouth as if to pledge him to an oath.

'Don't forget!' she said passionately. 'We have lost too much already by your weakness! Not one concession without my agreement. You must tell them that *they* will have to concede to us: Church, army, and Parliament. I am a queen, not a market trader to huckster over the price. Not one concession.'

'God speed, m ... my love,' he said tenderly.

She smiled at him at last. 'God bless you,' she said. Without thinking of the effect it would have on the king's waiting servants, she made the sign of the cross, the dreadful Papist gesture, over his head; and Charles bowed his head beneath the sign of the Anti-Christ.

Henrietta Maria picked up her full silk skirts and went carefully up the gangplank to the sailing ship. 'And don't forget,' she called, raising her voice from the ship. 'No concessions!'

'No, my love,' the king said sadly. 'I would d ... die rather than disappoint you.'

The ship moved away from the quayside and the king called for his horse. He mounted and rode alone, up the steep cliffs behind the little town, keeping the queen's sail in sight, riding and waving his hat to her until the little ship was vanished into the pale mist lying sluggishly on the waves, and there was nothing for God's anointed monarch to do but ride slowly and sadly back to Dover castle and write to his wife promising that he would always do whatever she thought best.

John subtracted himself carefully from the men who surrounded the king as they returned to break their fast in Dover castle. He ordered a horse from the tavern, and when he was ready to leave went to seek the king.

'With Your Majesty's permission I will go to my home,' he said carefully. He saw at a glance that the king was in one of his moods of high drama. John did not want to be the audience to one of the tragic speeches. 'I promised my wife I would only be away a matter of hours, and that was weeks ago. I must return.'

The king nodded. 'You may travel w ... with me for I am going to London.'

'Back to the City?' John was astounded.

'I shall see. I shall see. Perhaps it is n . . . not too late. Perhaps we can agree. The queen would be pleased, d . . . don't you think, if my next letter to her came from my palace at Whitehall?'

'I am sure everyone would be pleased if you could reclaim your palace by agreement,' John said carefully.

'Or I could go to B . . . Bristol,' the king said. 'Or north?'

John bowed. 'I shall pray for Your Majesty.'

'I hope you will do . . . do more than that. I hope you will be with me.'

There was an awkward silence. 'In these troubled times . . .' John began.

'In these troubled times a man must bid farewell to his wife and then do his duty,' the king said flatly. 'P . . . Painful duty. As I have done.'

John bowed.

'You may go and bid her farewell and then j . . . join me.'

John bowed again, thinking rapidly of how he could escape from this service. 'I am only a gardener,' he said. 'I doubt that I can assist Your Majesty better than by keeping your palaces in beauty. And when the queen returns I would want her to have a pretty garden to greet her.'

The king softened at that, but he had the needy anxiety of a man who hates to be left alone. The loss of the queen made him cling to anyone, and John's presence was a reassuring reminder of the days of gardens and masques and royal progresses and loyal speeches. 'You shall s . . . stay with me,' he said. 'I shall send you back to the garden when I have more men about me. In the meantime you shall write your f . . . farewell to your wife and join me. I am separated from my wife – you would not w . . . wish to be more happy than your king?'

Tradescant could see no escape. 'Of course not, Your Majesty.'

He sent Hester a note before they left Dover.

Dear Hester,

I am commanded by His Majesty to stay with him until he takes up his new quarters, wherever they may be. We are travelling northwards at present and I will return home as soon as I am permitted, and write to you if not. Please keep my children and rarities safe. And preserve your own safety. If you think it best, you may store the rarities in the place you know, and take the children to Oatlands. These are troubled times and I cannot advise you at this distance. I wish I were with you. If I were free from my duty to my king, I would be with you.

He did not dare to say more for fear of someone stealing and opening the letter. But he hoped she would read between the lines and understand his reluctance to travel with the king and the two princes, and his deep anxiety that none of them, least of all the king, seemed to know where they should go or what they should do next.

They rode north, still uncertain. The king was instantly diverted by the pleasure of being on the road. He loved to ride and liked being free of the formality of the court. He spoke of the time that he and the Duke of Buckingham had ridden across Europe – from England to Spain – without a courtier or a servant between them. He spoke of his present journey as if it was the same playful piece of adventure and the two young princes caught his mood. Prince James and Prince Charles for once in their lives were allowed to ride alongside their father, as his companions, and the country people lined the roadsides as they entered market towns and called out their blessings on the handsome bare-headed king and the two charming boys.

The courtiers, returning from their country houses and from White-hall, joined the train, and the whole trip became an adventure: riding through the spring countryside and staying each night in a hunting lodge or a fine Tudor mansion.

A court formed around the king, and many of the loyal gentlemen dug deep into their own fortunes to support him, and tried not to begrudge the cost of the hunting and the dancing and the music which the king had to have wherever he went. Even so, there were many debts that remained unpaid. Many gentlemen stayed at home, although they were summoned more than once; many did not send money. When the king, tired of provincial minstrels, sent for the court musicians they sent back a polite letter saying they would come if they could, but since they had not been paid any wages for months they could not afford to attend His Majesty without payment in advance. The king had to do without his own musicians for the first time in his life. There was no money to pay them, neither in advance nor in arrears.

John said nothing, and did not remind the king that his wages also had not been paid since the end of last summer when he had been appointed gardener at Oatlands in his father's place and also given the care of the Wimbledon garden. He was not following the king for gold, after all. He was not following him for love nor loyalty either. He was neither mercenary nor courtier. He was following him because the king refused to release him, and John was not yet ready to insist on his freedom. The habit of obedience was ingrained in him, he was not yet ready fully to rebel. Loyalty to the king was like honouring his father whose loyalty had never wavered; honouring his father was one of the ten commandments. John was trapped by habit and by faith.

He did not cease to try for his release. He spoke to the king in the stable yard of a pretty hunting lodge that they had commandeered for the week. Charles was out hunting on a borrowed horse and was in light-hearted mood. John checked the tightness of the girth under the saddle flap and looked up at his king.

'Your Majesty, do I have your permission to go to my home now?'

'You can ride with us to Theobalds,' the king said casually. 'It was one of your father's gardens, was it not?'

'His first royal garden,' John said. 'I didn't know the court was moving again. Are we going back to London?'

The king smiled. 'Who can say?' he said mysteriously. 'The game is not even opened yet, John. Who can say what moves there are to b . . . be made?'

'It is not a game to me,' John burst out incautiously. 'Nor to the men and women that are drawn into it.'

The king turned a frosty look down on him. 'Then you will have to be a reluctant player,' he said. 'A s . . . s . . . sulky pawn. For if I am prepared to gamble my future with daring then I expect the lesser men to throw in their all for me.'

John bit his lip.

'Especially those who were b . . . born and b . . . bred into my service,' the king added pointedly.

John bowed.

❧

The stay at Theobalds brought them closer to London, but no closer to an agreement. Almost every day a messenger came and went from the palace at Theobalds to Parliament at Westminster but no progress was made. The king was certain that the country was solidly behind him – in his journey northwards from Dover people had brought invalids to him at every stopping point and the mere touch of his hand had cured them. Every loyal address at every inn and staging post assured him that the country was solidly his. No-one had the courage to point out that anyone who disagreed with the king was likely to stay away from his progress, and no-one reminded the king that at every major town there had also been petitions from common people and gentry begging him to acknowledge the rights of Parliament and to reform his advisors, and live at peace with the Scots and with his Parliament.

From London came the rumours that the Lord Mayor's trained bands were out drilling and practising every Sunday and they would fight to the death to defend the liberty of Parliament and the freedom of the city of London. The city was solidly for Parliament and against the king and was preparing itself for a siege, entrenching both to the west and north. Every workman was bidden to dig great ditches which would run all around the city, and women, girls, and even ladies saw it as their patriotic duty to ride out on Sundays and holidays and help the men dig. There was a great wave of enthusiasm for the Parliamentary cause against the impulsive, arrogant, and possibly Papist king. There were great fears of an army coming from Ireland to put him back inside his capital city and to force Roman Catholicism back on a country which had only been free of the curse for less than a hundred years. Or if the king did not bring in the Irish then he might bring in the French, for it was well-known that his wife was openly recruiting for a French army to subdue the city and its supporters. Chaotic, excited, fearful, London prepared itself for siege against hopeless odds, and decided to choose a martyr's death.

'We go to York,' the king decided. John waited to see if he would be released from royal service.

The king's heavy-lidded gaze swept over the men in the stable yard, saddling up their horses for the ride. 'You will all come too,' he said.

John mounted his horse and edged it through the courtiers to the king's side.

'I should like to go to Wimbledon,' he said cunningly. 'I want to make sure that all is well there. So that it is fit for the queen when she comes home again.'

Charles shook his head and John, glancing sideways, saw that his king was beaming. The king was enjoying the sense of action and adventure, the end of the effeminate routine of masques and plays and poetry of the peacetime court.

'W ... We have no time for g ... gardens now!' he laughed. 'M ... March on, Tradescant.'

John wondered for a moment if there was anything he could say to abstract himself from the small train, and then shrugged his shoulders. The king had a whim that Tradescant should stay with him, but the whim would pass, as did all royal whims. When his attention was diverted elsewhere Tradescant would ask and receive permission to leave.

John pulled his horse up and fell in at the rear of the royal train as they trotted down the great avenue of Theobalds Park, through the sea of golden daffodils between the trees. He thought for a moment of his father, and how his father would have loved the ripple of cold wind through the yellow bobbing heads, and then he realised with a smile that his father had probably had a hand in planting them. As the party trotted out through the great gates John looked back at the avenue of trees and the sea of gold washing around their trunks and thought that his father's legacy to the country might last longer than that of the royal master he had served.

When they reached York in mid-March the king and his immediate friends settled in the castle, while the other courtiers and hangers-on found billets in all the inns and ale houses in the town. John lodged in the stables on a pallet bed in the hay store. After a few days when he had not been summoned he thought that the king had finished with his service and he might go home. He went to find the king in the main body of the castle. He was in his privy chambers, books and maps all around him.

'Your Majesty, I beg your pardon,' John said, putting his head around the door.

'I did not send for you,' the king said frostily.

John came no nearer. 'Spring is here, Your Majesty,' he said. 'I seek your permission to go and supervise the planting of the queen's gardens. She likes the flower gardens at Oatlands to be well-planted, and she wants fruits from her manor at Wimbledon. They need to be planted soon.'

The king softened at once at the mention of his wife.

'I would hate Her Majesty to be disappointed.'

'You shall go,' the king decided. He thought for a moment. 'After we have taken Hull.'

'Hull, Your Majesty?'

He beckoned Tradescant in and gestured him to shut the door against eavesdroppers. 'The queen bids me to make the garrison of Hull my own,' he said. 'So that I may have a strong port for our allies to send supplies. She has bought up half the armies of Europe, and her brother the king of France will aid us.'

John closed his eyes briefly at the thought of French Papist troops marching against the English Protestant Parliament.

'She wants us to take Hull for her – and so we will,' the king said simply. 'After that you can go home.'

John dropped to one knee. 'Your Majesty, may I speak freely?'

The king smiled his tender smile. 'Of course,' he said. 'All my people can speak to me freely, and in safety. I am their father, I am their only true friend.'

'A French army, a Papist army, will not aid your cause,' John said earnestly. 'There are many men and women in the country who do not understand the rights and wrongs of this quarrel between you and Parliament; but they will see a French army as their enemy. People will speak ill of the queen if they think she has summoned the French against her own people, English people. Those that love her and love you now will not accept a French army. You will lose their love and trust.'

Charles looked thoughtful as if he had never had such counsel before. 'You believe this, Gardener Tradescant?'

'I know these people,' John urged. 'They are simple people. They don't always understand arguments, they often cannot read. But they can see the evidence of their own eyes. If they see a French army marching on the English Parliament they will think we have been invaded and that their right course of action is to fight against the French. My own father went with your friend, the Duke of Buckingham, to make war against the French. They have been our enemies for years. Country people will think that the French have invaded us, and they will take up arms against them.'

'I had not seen it that way.' Charles looked undecided. 'But I must have an army and I must have munitions and H . . . Hull has the mightiest store of weapons outside of London . . .'

'Only if you have to fight a war,' John said persuasively. 'You only need arms if you fight. But if you could come to an agreement . . .'

'I l . . . long to come to an agreement,' the king said. 'I have sent them m . . . message after message offering talks and concessions.'

John thought of the queen's tempestuous demands that the Members of Parliament should be hanged before she would return to her city.

'I shall take Hull, and then I shall be able to make concessions,' the king said decisively.

John felt the sense of frustration that all the king's advisors were learning to endure.

'If you came to an agreement you would not have to take Hull,' he pointed out. 'If you could agree with Parliament, then the country would be at peace and there would be no need for a fort, Hull or any other. There would be no need for a position of strength.'

'She wants me to take Hull,' the king said stubbornly. 'And it is mine own. I am claiming nothing but what is mine by right.'

Tradescant bowed. When the king started speaking of his rights it was difficult to make any headway. By right everything in the four kingdoms was his; but in practice the countries were ruled by all sorts of compromises. Once the king assumed the voice he used in his masques and spoke grandly of his rights nothing could be agreed.

'When do we go to Hull?' John asked resignedly.

The king smiled at him, a flash of the old merriment in his eyes. 'I shall send the P . . . Prince James in to Hull on a visit,' he said. 'They cannot refuse a visit from the prince. He shall g . . . go with his cousin, the Elector Palatine. And then I shall f . . . follow him. They cannot separate father and son. And once he is inside he will open the gates to me. And once I am there –' he snapped his fingers '– it is mine! As easily and peacefully as that.'

'But what if . . .'

The king shook his head. 'No. N . . . No carping, Tradescant,' he said. 'The city of Hull is all for me, they will throw open the gates at the sight of Prince James, and then when we are installed we can make what terms we wish with Parliament.'

'But Your Majesty . . .'

'You may go now,' the king said pleasantly. 'Ride with me at n . . . noon tomorrow to Hull.'

They left late, of course, and idled along the road. By the time they finally arrived on a little rise before the town it was getting cold with the sharp coldness of a northern spring afternoon, and growing dark, getting on for dinner time. The king had brought thirty cavalrymen, carrying his standards and pennants, and there were ten young gentlemen riding with him as well as Tradescant and a dozen servants.

As they came towards the city Tradescant saw the great gates swing closed, and his heart sank.

'What's this?' the king demanded.

'A damned insult!' one of the young men cried out. 'Let's ride at the gates and order them open.'

'Your Majesty . . .' Tradescant said, bringing his horse a little closer. The young courtiers scowled at the gardener riding among them. Tradescant pressed on. 'Perhaps we should ride by, as if we never intended coming in at all.'

'What use would that be?' the king demanded.

'That way, no-one could ever say that an English town closed its gates to you. It did not close its gates because we were not trying to enter.'

'Nonsense!' the king said easily. One or two of the young men laughed aloud. 'That's the way to teach them b . . . boldness. Prince James's party will open the gates to us if the governor of Hull does not.'

The king took off his hat and rode down towards the town. The sentries on the wall looked down on him and John saw, with a sense of leaden nausea, that they were casually pointing their crossbows towards him, their monarch, as if he were an ordinary highwayman coming towards the city walls.

'Please God no fool fires by accident,' John said as he followed.

'Open the gates to the king of England!' one of the courtiers shouted up at the sentries.

There was a short undignified scuffle and the governor of Hull, Sir John Hotham himself, appeared on the walls.

'Your Majesty!' he exclaimed. 'I wish we had known of your coming.'

Charles smiled up at him. 'It does not m . . . matter, Sir John,' he said. 'Open the gates and let us in.'

'I cannot, Your Majesty,' Sir John said apologetically. 'You are too many for my little town to house.'

'We don't m . . . mind,' the king said. 'Open the gates, I would see my son.'

'There are too many of you, it is too large and too warlike a party for me to let in at this late hour,' Sir John said.

'We are not warlike!' Charles exclaimed. 'Just a small party of pleasure-seekers.'

'You are armed,' the governor pointed out.

'Only my usual g . . . guards,' the king said. He was still smiling but John could see the whiteness around his mouth and his hand trembling slightly on the reins. His horse shifted uneasily. The royal guards stared, stony-faced, at the sentries on the towers of Hull.

'Please, Your Majesty,' Sir John Hotham pleaded. 'Enter as a friend if you must enter. Bring in just a few of your men if you come peacefully.'

'This is my t . . . town!' the king shouted. 'Do you . . . do you . . . do you deny your king the right to enter his own town?'

Sir John closed his eyes. Even from the road before the gate the king's party could see his grimace. John felt a deep sense of sympathy for the man, torn between loyalties just like himself, just like every man in the kingdom.

'I do not deny Your Majesty the right to enter into your town,' the governor said carefully. 'But I do deny these men the right to enter.' His gesture took in the thirty guards. 'Bring in a dozen to guard Your

Majesty and you shall dine with the prince in the great chamber this night! I shall be proud to welcome you.'

One of the courtiers edged his horse up to the king. 'Where is the prince's party?' he said. 'They should have thrown open the gates to us by now.'

Charles shot him an angry look. 'Where indeed?' He turned back to the governor of Hull. 'Where is m . . . my son? Where is Prince James?'

'He is at his dinner,' the governor said.

'Send for him!'

'Your Majesty, I cannot. I have been told he is not to be disturbed.'

Charles spurred his horse abruptly forward. 'Have d . . . d . . . done with this!' he shouted up at the governor. 'Open the gates! That is an order from your k . . . king!'

The man looked down. His white face had gone paler still. 'I may not open the gates to thirty armed men,' he said steadily. 'I have my orders. As my king you are always welcome. But I do not open the gates of my town to any army.'

One of the king's courtiers rode forward and shouted at the people whose curious faces were peering over the tops of the defensive walls. 'This is the king of England! Throw your governor down! He is a traitor! You must obey the king of England!'

No-one moved, then a surly voice shouted, 'Aye, and he's the king of Scotland and Ireland too and what justice do they have there?'

The king's great horse reared and shied as he pulled it back. 'Then b . . . be damned to you!' the king shouted. 'I shall not forget this, John Hotham! I shall n . . . not forget that you locked me out of my own town!'

He wheeled the horse around and flung it into a gallop down the road, the guards thundering behind him, the courtiers, servants and John with them. He did not pull up till his horse was blown and then they turned and looked back down the road. In the distance they could see the gates finally open, the drawbridge come down, and a small party of horsemen ride out, following in their tracks.

'Prince James,' the king said. 'Ten minutes too l . . . late.'

The king's party waited while the horsemen rode nearer and nearer and then pulled up.

'Where the devil were you, sir?' the king demanded of his nephew, the Elector Palatine, who had led the party.

'I am sorry, Your Majesty,' the young man replied stolidly. 'We were at our dinner and did not know you were outside the gates until Sir John came to us just now and said you had ridden away.'

'You were supposed to open the g . . . gates to me! Not idle with your no . . . noses in the trough!'

'We were not sure you were coming. You were due before dinner. You said you would come in the afternoon. We gave up waiting for you. I thought the governor would have opened the gates to you himself.'

'But he refused! And there was no-one to force him, b . . . b . . . because you were at your dinner, as usual!'

'I'm sorry, Uncle,' the young man replied.

'You will be sorrier yet!' the king said. 'For now I have been refused admittance to one of my t . . . t . . . towns as well as being banned from my City! You have done evil, evil work this day!' He turned on his son. 'And you, J . . . James! Did you not know that your father was outside the gates?'

The prince was only eight years old. 'No, sire,' he said. His little voice was scarcely more than a thread in the cold evening air.

'You have disappointed your f . . . father very much this day,' Charles said gloomily. 'Pray to G . . . God that we have not taught disloyal and wicked men the lesson that they can defy me and travel in their w . . . wicked ways and fear nothing.'

The prince's lower lip trembled slightly. 'I didn't know. I am sorry, sir. I didn't understand.'

'It was a harebrained plan from first to last,' the Elector said dourly. 'Whose was it? Any fool could see that it would not work.'

'It was m . . . my plan,' the king said. 'But it required speed and decisiveness and c . . . courage, and so it failed. How am I to succeed with such servants?' He surveyed them as if they were all equally to blame, then he turned his horse's head towards York and led them back to the city through the darkening twilight.

April 1642

When they got back to York John found a letter waiting for him from Hester. It had taken nearly a month to reach him instead of the usual few days. John, looking at the dirt-stained paper, realised that, along with loyalty and peace, everything else was breaking down too: the passage of letters, the enforcement of laws, the safety of the roads. He went to his pallet bed in the hayloft and sat where a crack in the shingles of the roof let in the cold spring light and he could see to read.

> *Dear Husband,*
>
> *I am sorry that you have gone away with the court and I understand that it was not possible for you to come and say farewell before you rode away. I have hidden the finest of the rarities where we agreed, and sent others into store at the Hurtes' warehouse where they have armed guards.*
>
> *The city is much disturbed. Every day there is drilling and marching and preparations for war. All the apprentice boys in Lambeth have given up their rioting around the streets and are now formed into trained bands and drilled every evening.*
>
> *Great ditches are dug outside London against the coming of a French or Spanish army and all of our gardeners have to go and take their turn with the digging whether they will or no.*
>
> *Food is scarce because the markets are closed as country people will not travel from their homes, and carters are afraid of meeting armies on the roads. I am feeding vagrants at the door with what we can afford but we are all doing very poorly. All the dried and bottled fruit is finished and I cannot get hold of hams to salt down for love nor money.*
>
> *These are strange and difficult times and I wish you could*

be with us. I am keeping up my courage and I am caring for your children as if they were mine own, and your rarities and gardens also are safe.

I trust you will come home as soon as you are released from service.

God be with you,
Your wife,
Hester Tradescant.

John turned Hester's letter over in his hands. He had an odd, foolish thought that if she were not his wife already, he would admire and like this woman more than any other he knew. She cared for the things that mattered most to him as if they were her own. It was a great comfort to him to know that she was in his house, in his father's house, and that his children and his rarities and his garden were under her protection. He felt an unexpected tenderness towards the woman who could write of the difficulty of the times and yet assure him that she was keeping up her courage. He knew he would never love her as he had loved Jane. He thought he would never love another woman again. But he could not help but like and admire a woman who could take control of a household as she had done, and confront the times that they lived in as she did.

John rose to his feet, picked hay off his doublet, and went to his dinner in the great hall of York castle.

The king and his noble friends, splendidly dressed, were already in their place at the top table as John slipped into the hall. They were dining off gold plate but there were only a dozen dishes. The county was finding it hard to feed the appetite of the court, the provincial cooks could not devise the dishes that Charles expected, and the farms and markets were drained by the hunger of the enlarging, idle, greedy court.

'What news?' John asked, seating himself beside a captain of the guard and helping himself from the shared dish placed in the middle of the table.

The man looked at him sourly. 'None,' he said. 'His Majesty writes letters to all who should be here, but the men who are loyal are already here, and the traitors merely gain the time to make themselves ready. We should march on London now! Why give them more time to prepare? We should put them to the sword and cut out this canker from the country.'

John nodded, saying nothing, and bent over his meat and bread. It was venison in a rich, dark sauce, very good. But the bread was coarse and brown with gritty seeds. The rich wheat stores of Yorkshire were slowly emptying.

'While he is waiting I might go to my home,' John said thoughtfully.

'Lambeth?' the captain asked.

John nodded.

'You'd be seen as a traitor,' the man said. 'London is solid against the king, you'd be seen as a turncoat. You'd never plant another bulb for him.'

John grimaced. 'I'm doing next to nothing here.'

The man spat a piece of gristle on the rushes of the floor and one of the dogs squirmed forwards on its belly to lick it up. 'We're all doing next to nothing here,' he said. 'Nothing but waiting. It is war. All that is undecided is when and where.'

July 1642

All that spring and summer the country was waiting, like the captain, to see when and where. Every gentleman who could command men to follow him armed them, drilled them, and trained them, and then wrestled with his conscience night and day as to which side he should join. Brothers from the same great house might take opposite sides and divide the tenants and servants amongst them. The men of one village might come out as passionate royalists, the men of the village next door might side with Parliament. Local loyalties set their own traditions: villagers in the shadow of a great courtier's house that had felt the benefits of royal visits might sharpen their pikes and put a feather in their hat for the king. But villagers along roads from London where the news was easily spread, knew of the king's evasions and lies before the demands of Parliament. Those who prized their freedom of conscience, or those who were prosperous, free-thinking men, said that they would leave their work and their homes and take up the sword and fight against papacy, superstition and a king who was driven to sin by his bad advisors. Those whose habits of loyalty had gone deep with Elizabeth and deeper with James, and were far from the news of London, would turn out for the king.

In early July, as the court at York started to complain of the smell of drains and to fear the plague in the overcrowded town, the king announced that they were to march to Hull once again. This time the plan was better laid. The royalist George Digby was inside the garrison and he had forged a plan with Hotham the governor that the town would open its gates to a besieging force from the king, as long as the force was sufficiently impressive to justify a surrender.

Charles himself, dressed in green as for a picnic, rode out at the head of a handsome army on a warm summer day in early July. Tradescant rode at the tail end of the courtiers, and felt that he was the only man in the chattering, singing, light-hearted band who wished that he was elsewhere, and who doubted what they were about to do.

The city's defenders were bolstered by soldiers sent by the Scots. 'It makes no difference, we have an agreement,' Charles said contentedly.

The foot soldiers laid aside their pikes and got out spades. The royal army started to dig a ring of trenches around the city. 'They will surrender before we are more than a foot deep,' Charles assured his commanders. 'No need to dig the lines t . . . too straight or too well. If they do not surrender t . . . tonight, we will attack at dawn tomorrow. As long as we make a sh . . . show.'

As the soldiers dug their trenches, and as Charles broke his fast with some red wine and bread and cheese, a simple meal, as if he were out on a hunting trip, the great gates of Hull slowly opened.

'Already?' Charles laughed. 'Well, this is gracious!' He shaded his eyes with his hand, and then shook his head and stared harder. The bread fell from his hand, unregarded. Slowly, his laughter died.

A regular well-drilled army marched steadily out from the gates of the town towards them. The front flank kneeled down and the musketmen, steadying their weapons on the shoulders of the front rank, took aim and fired straight at the royalist army.

'Good G . . . God! What are they doing?' Charles cried.

'To horse!' one of the quicker courtiers shouted. 'Get the men saddled up! We've been betrayed!'

'It can't b . . . be . . .'

'Save the king!' Tradescant shouted. The royal guard, recalled to their duties, dropped their dinner in the dust and threw themselves on their horses.

'Mount! Your Highness!'

There was a dreadful scream as another volley of shots pocked the dry ground around them, and some of the musket balls found a target.

'Retreat! Retreat!' someone yelled.

All the orders of command were broken, as the men scattered, running like panicked sheep across the stubbly hayfields, pushing through hedges and trampling down the ripening corn. Still the defenders of Hull came forward, the first rank dropping to their knees and reloading as the second rank fired over their shoulders and then marched on. Then they too dropped down and reloaded as the men behind them fired.

It was an unstoppable progress, John thought. The king's soldiers did not even have fire lit ready for their muskets. They had no cannon ready, they did not even have their pikes. All they had were their trenching spades, and the men who had been digging had been the first to fall, toppling down into their shallow ditches, and screaming and crawling in the dirt.

At last someone found a trumpeter and ordered him to sound the retreat, but the foot soldiers were already up and running, running from the well-disciplined lethal ranks that were pouring, like little toy soldiers, out of the gates of Hull, firing and reloading, firing and reloading, like a monstrous toy which could not be stopped or escaped.

The king's guards surrounded his horse and galloped him away from the battle. Tradescant, his own horse snorting and pulling, looked wildly around him and then followed the king. His last view of the battlefield was a horse, its stomach blown open by a cannon shot from the walls of the city, and a lad, not much more than fourteen, trying to shelter behind the body.

'This is the end,' John found he was saying as his horse wearily found the road to York and followed in the train of the ragged retreat. 'This is the end. This is the end. This is the end.'

August 1642

For the king it was the beginning. The second humiliation outside the walls of Hull had decided him. The queen's continual demands that he confront and defeat his parliament drove him on. He issued a proclamation that every able-bodied man in the country should rally to his army, and on Eastcroft Common outside Nottingham he paraded three cavalry troops and a battalion of infantry while the herald read the proclamation of war. John, standing behind his master in the pouring rain, thought that never in the history of warfare did any campaign look less promising.

The rain dripped in a steady stream from his hat. No-one had thought to bring a spade and they could not get the royal standard to stand properly in the stony ground. John thought of his father and his last service to the Duke of Buckingham when he had followed him to Portsmouth and waited to take ship to the Ile de Rhé, knowing that the battle would be lost and that it was, in any case, a cause not worth fighting for. John thought of his father's face when he had met him, riding home on the Duke's cart, of the half-hidden look of relief in his eyes. And he understood at last what it was to follow a master unwillingly, when that master will lead you to death from pure folly.

John looked at the king, the feather in his hat drooping in the pouring rain, as he listened, nodding approval, to the herald shouting the proclamation into the wind which whipped his words away. John thought that his family had served the kings and their favourites for long enough, and that any debt owed, had surely by now been paid – by his father's heartbreak in the Ile de Rhé, and now, a generation later, by his own fear and despair before the walls of Hull.

In the rain outside Nottingham John found his determination to leave the king, whatever might be the outcome of his desertion. When they turned away from Eastcroft Common and went back to their billets in Nottingham, John turned southwards and rode alone to London without asking permission, without giving notice.

The royal standard blew down that night.

Hester, roused from sleep by the sound of a tap on the back door, ran downstairs, pulling on her nightgown, her heart pounding with fear. She peered out of the kitchen window into the pale greyness of the summer dawn and saw the familiar outline of John's head.

She threw open the door. 'John!'

He opened his arms to her, as if they were husband and wife in their hearts as well as by name, and Hester ran towards him and felt his arms come around her and hold her close.

He smelled of sweat and fatigue and the warm erotic male smell which lingered around his clothes when she brushed them. Hester felt herself long for his touch, and she tightened her grip around his back and held him close. He did not move away from her, he did not unclasp her hands. He held her as if he wanted her as she wanted him, and made no move to put her aside.

They stumbled together over the threshold, not releasing each other until they were at the fireside and the embers of the fire cast a warm glow. Then she leaned back, her arms still tightly around him, so that she could see his face.

She was shocked. The eight months of his absence had put grey into his hair at the temples and bags beneath his eyes. His beard was still a true dark brown, but matted and dirty, his face was smudged with dirt, his forehead carried new lines. He looked desperately weary. He looked like a man on the run.

'Was there a battle?' she asked, trying to understand what this mute look of suffering might mean.

He shook his head, released her, and dropped into the chair by the fireside. 'Not one that is worth mentioning,' he said bitterly. 'When they come to write the history of these days it will not have more than a line. We rode out like fools, thinking that we would win without having to fight. We went out like the chorus in one of his masques – all show and pretence. For all the good we were, we might as well have had swords of wood and helmets of painted paper.'

Hester was silent, shocked by his vehemence, and by the bitterness in his tone. 'Were you hurt?'

He shook his head. 'No – only in my pride.' He paused. 'Yes. Deep in my pride,' he corrected himself.

She did not know how to question him. She turned and threw some kindling on the fire and then some small twigs and broken branches of applewood. Coal was short in London, the Tradescants were living off their land.

He leaned forward to the blaze as if he were chilled to the heart. 'All along it has been like a masque,' he said, as if he was gripping some truth about the king at last. 'As if it were some pretty play with a script which everyone was to follow. The threat of Parliament, the flight from London, his parting with the queen when he rode along the cliffs waving to her ship and wept, the ride north to victory. It has all been a masque – beautifully costumed. But when the time came for the king to defeat his enemies –' He broke off.

'What happened?' Hester kneeled at the fire and kept her eyes on the flames, afraid to interrupt him.

'The chorus didn't arrive,' John said sourly. 'The engines which should show Jove descending or Neptune rising up from the sea failed to work. Instead of the gates of Hull opening and the governor coming out with the golden key on a velvet cushion and some poetry from Ben Jonson, it all went wrong. The gates opened and the soldiers came out and just went fire . . . reload . . . fire . . . reload . . . like dancers – but they weren't doing our dance. They were following another script. And . . . and . . .' He was silent for a moment. 'I don't know what the end of this play will be.'

'The king?' she asked in a little whisper.

'The king is sticking to his masque,' John said savagely. 'Act two was raising the royal standard. But the weather was all wrong. It should have been balmy skies or perhaps a bright comet overhead. Instead it poured with rain on him and we looked like sodden fools. But he will not realise that the scenes are going wrong. He thinks it is a rehearsal, he thinks it will be the greater on the night if it all goes wrong now.'

'And what of you?' she asked softly.

'I am finished with him,' John said. 'I am finished with his service. I went back into his service to please my father and because I longed to work on the great gardens which are in his gift, and besides, when I was a young man there was almost nowhere else to work but for the king or the court. But I will die in his service if I go on. I am a gardener and he would not give me leave to go and garden. He has to have everyone in the masque, everyone has to carry a standard or a spear. He will never cease with this until we are all dead, or all defeated, or all persuaded that he is the Lord's Anointed and can do no wrong.'

Hester quickly looked towards the kitchen door, but it was safely closed and all the household was still asleep.

'I saw my father go out to certain death in the service of the Duke of Buckingham, and I saw him ride home, spared only by the death of his master,' John continued. 'I saw his eyes on that day. He never recovered from the death of the Duke. He was never his own man again. The loss of the Duke lay like a shadow over our family, and my father was torn between relief that he had survived and grief that the Duke was dead.

'I swore then that I would never be like that, I swore I would never pledge myself to follow a man until death, and I meant it. I will never be a servant like that. Not even for the king. Especially not for this king, who cannot reward service and never says that he has had enough. He will not stop until every one of his servants is lying dead before him, and then he will expect a miracle from God himself to raise up more foot soldiers for his insatiable theatre. I will have no more of it. I can bear no more of it.'

'You won't join with Parliament?' Hester asked, aghast. 'Oh, John, you won't fight against the king?'

He shook his head. 'I'm not a turncoat. I won't fight against him. I've eaten his bread and he has called me his friend. I've seen him weep and I've kissed his hand. I won't betray him. But I won't play that part in this damned mockery.'

'Will you stay here, quiet at home with us?' she asked. She had a low sinking feeling in the pit of her belly. She knew that he would not.

'How can I?' he demanded of her. 'People know who I am. They will ask me who I serve. I won't deny him – I'm not a Judas. And he will send for me.' He nodded. 'Sooner or later he will realise that I am not at court and he will send for me again.'

'Then what shall we do?'

'We'll go to Virginia,' John said with decision. 'All of us. We'll take ship as soon as we can get a passage. We'll take what we can carry and leave the rest. Leave the house and the garden and even the rarities. We'll get out of this country and leave it to tear itself to pieces. I won't see it. I won't be here. I can't bear it.'

Hester sat very still and measured the despair in her husband's voice against her love for him, and her love for their home.

'Will you have a glass of ale?' she asked.

He lifted his gaze from the fire, as if he suddenly remembered where he was. 'Yes,' he said. 'And then let's go to bed. I have wanted you in my bed for night after long night, Hester. I have missed you, and thought of you here, missing me. I have wanted you and cursed the miles that were between us. And in the morning I shall see my children and we'll tell them that we are leaving.'

'You have wanted me?' she asked, very low.

He put his hand out and turned her face up to him, one gentle finger under her chin. 'Knowing that you are here has kept me going through one dark night after another,' he said. 'Knowing that you are here and that I have someone to come home to. Knowing that you will open your bed to me, and open your arms to me, and that whatever is going wrong all around me, I have somewhere that I can call my home.'

She could have moved forwards, she could have kneeled before him as he sat in his chair, he would have drawn her to him and on to his lap and he would have kissed her, as he had never yet kissed her, and they could have gone to bed as he wanted to do, and as she had wanted to do from the moment she had first seen him.

But Hester caught hold of her determination, forced herself to wait, and drew back from him, drew back and sat on her seat on the other side of the fireplace.

'Now wait a minute,' she said. 'Not so fast, husband. I cannot leave here.'

For a moment John did not hear her. He was so conscious of the fall of her nightgown, and of her dark hair only half-hidden by her cap, of the play of the firelight on her neck and the glimpse of her shoulder. 'What?'

'I cannot leave here,' she said steadily. 'This is my home.'

'You don't understand,' he said abruptly. 'I have made up my mind. I have to go. I cannot stay here, I will be torn apart by the two of them – king and Parliament. Parliament will have me out entrenching and drilling for their defence, and the king will summon me to court. I cannot be faithless to them both. I cannot watch the king ride into war as if it were a masqued ball. I cannot stay in England and see him die!'

'And I cannot leave.' She spoke steadfastly, as if nothing would ever move her.

'You are my wife,' John reminded her.

She bowed her head.

'You owe me absolute obedience,' he said. 'I am your master before God.'

'As the king is yours,' she said gently. 'Isn't that what this war is all about?'

He hesitated. 'I thought you wanted to be my wife?'

'I do. I agreed to be your wife, and to rear your children, and to care for the rarities and the garden and the Ark. How can I do these things in Virginia?'

'You can care for me and the children.'

Hester shook her head. 'I won't take the children there. You know yourself how dangerous it is there. There are wild Indians, and hunger, dreadful disease. I won't take the children into danger.' She paused for a moment. 'And I won't leave here.'

'This is *my* home,' John reminded her. 'And I am prepared to leave it.'

'It is my home too.'

They locked gazes like enemies. John remembered his first impression of her as a plain-faced managing woman who had been put in his house without his consent. 'Hester, I am going to Virginia,' he said coldly. 'And it is my wish that you come with me and the children.'

Her straight gaze never wavered. 'I am sorry,' she said evenly. 'I cannot do that. I will not take the children into danger and I have no wish to leave my home. If you go then I will keep everything safe for your return, and I will welcome you when you return.'

'My father . . .' he started.

'Your father trusted me with the care of this house and with the care of the children while you were away,' she said. 'I promised him on his deathbed that I would keep it all safe: plants, rarities, and children. I will not leave this house for any wandering battalion to take it over and to chop down his trees for firewood. I won't leave his chestnut avenue for them to spoil. I won't leave it unprotected for any vagrants to steal the fruit or pick the flowers. I won't leave the rarities stored in a warehouse with no idea of when I can return. And I will not take Jane's children to a country far away where I know they cling to survival against all the odds.'

'Jane's children!' he shouted. 'Jane was my wife! They are my children! She is nothing to you! They are nothing to you!'

John saw her flinch as if he had slapped her face. But it did not shake her steadiness. 'You are wrong,' she said simply. 'I have long thought of myself as caring for Jane's children and trying to care for them as she would wish. And sometimes I think that she looks down from heaven and sees them, growing strong and beautiful, and that she is happy for them. But they are my children too, I have loved them without fail for four years and I will not take them from their home because you have decided to leave your master and leave your country and leave your home.'

'I'm not faithless!' he said, stung.

126

Hester gave him a long, level look. 'You and your father are the king's gardeners,' she said. 'You are in his service.'

'He doesn't own my soul!' John shouted. 'I am his servant, not his slave! I can withdraw my service. I can work for myself, I can leave. I have just left.'

She nodded. 'Then a man has a right to choose where he lives and who he calls master?'

'Yes,' John said firmly.

'A woman too?'

'Yes,' he said begrudgingly.

'Then I choose to live here, and you will not take the children without me to care for them.'

'You want to stay here and face who knows what dangers?'

'I shall face the dangers when they come,' she said. 'I am not such a fool as to think that we are safe here. We're too near to the city – if the king brings in a Papist army we will be in the worst place. But if that happens I shall take them to Oatlands, or away into the country. We will have a warning of the dangers. I can prepare for them. And Jane's parents will warn us and protect them, and Alexander Norman knows to the minute where the king's army can be found, he makes the barrels for the gunpowder. My own family have refuges planned. I shall have advisors, I shall have protectors.

'But in Virginia there would be no-one to keep us safe but you; and you don't know the country, and you are not a farmer or a labourer, and I think only a farmer or a labourer can get a living there.'

John got to his feet and spoke bitterly. 'I won't argue with you,' he said spitefully. 'Because I don't care enough to take the trouble. It doesn't matter to me if you will come with me to Virginia as my wife or if you prefer to stay at home like a housekeeper. It is your choice. I shall go to Virginia a single man, if that is your wish.'

She felt a pain inside her which was worse than anything she had suffered from him so far. She heard the threat of infidelity in his words but she would not let him frighten her into abandoning her home. 'I am sorry to stand against you,' she said steadily. 'But I promised your father I would guard his trees and his grandchildren, and I cannot escape that promise.'

John got to his feet and stalked to the door. 'I am tired. I shall sleep. I don't want to be disturbed. I am used to sleeping alone.'

Hester bowed her head, not commenting on the fact that she was no longer invited into bed with him. 'Take your bed,' she said politely. 'I shall make up the bed in the spare bedroom.'

'And as soon as possible I shall take ship,' John said. 'Don't doubt me, Hester. I shall leave for the new world. I am sick of this country. I am sick of this house.' He did not say it but the words 'and I am sick of you' hung in the air, unspoken, between them.

She bowed her head. 'I shall guard the children and the trees for your return.'

'And if I never come back?'

'Then I shall guard them for the next John Tradescant, your son,' she said. 'And I shall guard them for the people of England who will want the trees and the plants when they stop making war. And then they will remember and honour the name of Tradescant, even if you are no longer here.'

October 1642

The luck of the Tradescants was still running John's way. There was a ship due to leave for Virginia in October and he could get a place aboard her. Half a dozen new settlers were sailing too, loading their goods and getting ready for their new life. John was on the dock with them when someone shouted that the king had fought a battle and had triumphed, at a place called Powick Bridge.

John joined the crowd that gathered around the trooper. He was a Parliament man and his tale of terror was growing greater with every telling.

'We were serving under my Earl of Essex,' the man said. 'And ordered badly, no-one can deny it. We were to cut off the king's cousin, Prince Rupert, from the main army. But as we went down the lane towards them there was firing on either side of us, from the hedges. Dirty work, you couldn't see where it was coming from. The officers shouted "Wheel about" – but none of us knew how to wheel about. Easier to say than do in the narrow lanes anyway. Some were shouting that "wheel about" meant retreat, and they tried to force their way back through the others coming forward. Those at the back still didn't know of the danger so they were coming on. It was all confusion, d'you see?

'There was a charge from the king's devils, cavalry, riding like madmen, and we went down and around and were thrown about. It was every man for himself all the way back to our camp and the next day the Earl said we should all be trained properly, and that he would have us trained at once.

'But Prince Rupert trained his men before he took them out. He told them what "wheel about" meant before he marched them into the very jaws of the enemy. Prince Rupert learned his fighting all over Europe. Prince Rupert is going to win this war for his cousin King Charles, he knows all the tricks. Prince Rupert has changed our plans completely, he has beaten us before we began.'

Bertram Hobert, a fellow passenger with John, glanced at him. 'Does this change *your* plans, Mr Tradescant?' he asked.

'No,' John said discreetly. 'My going or staying is nothing to do with the progress of the war. I have interests in Virginia, a plantation there, some land where I have a fancy to build a house. And I made a good sum on the plants I brought back last time. Whether Parliament or the king wins, some day there will be peace and men will want to garden.'

'Are you not for the king? Won't you join him now? Now that he is on the road to victory?'

'I have been in his service all my life,' John said, hiding his resentment. 'The time has come for me to do some travelling and gardening for myself. He does not need a gardener now, he needs soldiers, and – you heard that man – he has them.'

Hobert nodded.

'What about you?' John asked.

'I was leaving whatever happened,' the man said. 'I can make no progress here. I work as hard as any man; but what the taxes don't take, the tithes do. I wanted a country where I can see real wealth for me. I've seen how a man can prosper in Virginia. I'll stay a dozen years and come back a rich man and buy a farm in Essex. What about you? Will you stay for long?'

John thought for a moment. It was a question he and Hester had carefully skirted, in all the weeks while she packed for him and took orders in her careful script from gardeners who had heard he was going collecting again. With his boat creaking at the dockside and the wind blowing offshore, with the tide running and a sense of his freedom rising in him, John felt young and reckless again; a young man fit for a young country, full of promise.

'I shall make a home there,' he said. 'My wife and children will stay in England and I shall be back often. But Virginia is the country for me. I shall build a house there and . . .' He broke off, thinking of Suckahanna's small, sideways smile, her tattooed nakedness which had become more erotic for him since his first innocent sight of her. He thought that by now she would be a woman, a woman fully grown, and ready for love and desire.

'It's a country where a man can grow,' the farmer said, throwing his arms wide. 'There's land for the asking, and earth which has never been ploughed. There's a new life there for me.'

'And for me,' John said.

130

John welcomed the long idle days of the voyage. He became accustomed to the movement of the ship and his stomach stopped swooping with terror at the long, frightening slide into the troughs of the waves. The captain was liberal with the passengers, letting them come up on deck, almost as they wished, as long as they did not distract the crew; and John spent days leaning on the rail of the deck and looking down into the moving green muscles of the ocean. A couple of times they caught sight of a pod of whales, chasing a school of fish that stretched for more than a mile across. Once or twice they saw large white birds whose names John did not know and he asked the captain if one could be shot so that he could have it stuffed for the rarities room. The captain shook his head. He said it was unlucky to shoot a bird at sea, it would summon up a hurricane. John did not press the point, it seemed a long, long way from the rarities room at Lambeth, a long way from Hester, a long way from the children, and a long way from the king and his costumed play-acting wars.

John had thought that he would use the time of the two-month voyage to make some plans, come to some decisions about his future. He had thought he would write down his own timetable: how long he would spend building a new house in Virginia, when he would send for the children, even if Hester still refused to come. But as the ship went westward, and still more westward, as he spent every evening watching the sun sink lower and lower through the clouds and then into the sea, he found he could not think or plan; all he could do was dream.

It was not a journey, it was an escape. John's inheritance of a business which was at the same time a duty had nearly strangled him. He had been bound by loyalty and even in the end a begrudging sympathy in service to a king whom he despised. His father's choice of his wife had forced him into a new marriage, one he would not have chosen for himself. His burdensome work and his duty to his family conspired to close down the ways that were open to him: like untrimmed hedges overshadowing a lane. John had a sudden exhilarating sense of having vaulted a gate and starting to make his own way across fields towards the open country, where there were no paths and no lanes, and no restrictions. Somewhere he could make his own life, build his own house . . . even choose his own wife.

He dreamed of her – Suckahanna – almost every night. It was as if his dreams had been locked down inside him, and only freed once he freed himself from England, from Hester, from home. Once the ropes keeping the ship at the quayside were dropped and trailed through the cold water of the Thames, John felt his desires rocking like the boat as it headed for freedom.

He dreamed of the month they had spent in the forest together and the light shining through the leaves to dapple her bare brown skin. He dreamed of the line of her spine as she squatted before the fire, of the asymmetric tilt of her head where the hair was cut short on one side to keep the bowstring free, and black and flowing on the other. In his dreams he could taste the food she had found and cooked for them, the bitterness of the dried blueberries, the richness of the roasted lobster, the nuts, the seeds, the roots. He remembered the clean cold taste of water, an exotic drink for a man who had drunk small ale or milk for all his life. He woke in the mornings to the sudden pang of disappointment that they were still so many days out of Jamestown, and he woke aroused and embarrassed. He had the little enclosed bed with doors around the bunk all to himself but anyone sleeping outside could have heard him groan in desire in his dreams, and he was afraid that he might have said her name in his sleep.

The cold winter mornings at sea were hard for John. While he had been in Lambeth, trapped between the demands of the king and the duties to his family, he had managed to forget the last words she had called to him – 'Come at Nepinough', the harvest time. He had not gone back to her as he had promised. Perhaps she had waited, perhaps her mother had waited with her, and met every boat from England for all of the summer season, and then? And then? Would they have waited a full year, would they have waited two, four?

John hoped that they would have heard that England was at war with itself. The Virginia colonists were sworn to the royalist cause but there would have been a ready stream of gossip and fears running around the colony. Enough talk, surely, for the Indian woman and her daughter to realise that perhaps John could not get away? But perhaps they had never thought that he would come. John remembered Suckahanna's ability to say nothing for a whole month, even though he spoke to her, and laughed with her and worked beside her and watched her every move with tenderness and desire. She had said nothing to him, even though she had understood every word that he had said. She had said nothing to him because she had been ordered by her mother to stay silent. Perhaps, after Nepinough had come and gone, her mother had ordered her to forget him, or to marry a man of her own people, or – worst thought of all – to go and lie with a white man and earn their safety that way. At that thought, John would pull on his boots and stamp up to the deck and look out over the bowsprit to where the horizon of sea and air lay empty and unhelpful, miles and miles away.

'I've never seen a man in such a hurry to go and see some flowers,' Bertram Hobert remarked as he came beside John one morning near dawn to lean on the rail and look westward with him.

For a moment John thought of confiding in him – his anxious desire for Suckahanna, his undeniable betrayal of Hester – but then he shrugged and nodded.

'Running from? or running to?' Hobert pursued.

John shook his head at the tangle of his life. 'Both, I suppose.'

They ran into a storm just a week before they were due to sight the coast of the Americas and John had some bad days of sickness and fear as the ship rolled and shuddered and felt as if she was foundering in the troughs of the waves. He opened the hatch and looked out to try and ease his sickness but he was met by the sight of a wall of water, a towering mountain of water, rearing over the narrow deck and about to fall. The other passengers, a young family and a couple of men, shouted at him to shut the hatch, and he dropped it down and then heard the crash of the wave on the deck, felt the ship shudder under the impact and stagger under the weight of the water. They were in such terror that they did not speak, except Mrs Austin who prayed constantly, her arms around her children, her eyes tight shut, and Bertram Hobert, who maintained his own whispered litany of swearing. John, huddled in the hold beside them, wedged in with goods, was certain that they were all going to sink to the bottom of the heaving ocean, and that he would deserve such a fate, because he had betrayed not one but two women, and had abandoned them both.

Slowly, painfully slowly, the waves eased a little, and then the terrifying howling of the wind in the mast and the rigging eased, the ship steadied, and once again they could hear the everyday noises of the crew on deck. The hatch opened and dripping and exhausted sailors dropped down into the hold and shouted into the galley for bread and a hot drink before turning into their hammocks to sleep, all wet and sea-stained, with their boots still on. The bread was rationed, the water rationed too. The ship had made the voyage without the usual stop at the West Indies and everything was running short.

John, cautiously going up on deck, found a clear, freezing day with the storm a dark smudge on the horizon to the north, and before them,

and ahead of them, and growing clearer all the time, the stark white
and black of the forests of Virginia in midwinter.

'Home,' John said, as if the storm had blown his doubts away, and
the terror of the storm had earned him the right to claim his own land
and his own future. 'Home, at last.'

As they sailed up the river John looked around eagerly for changes. He
could see at once that settlers had spread out along the river in the four
years he had been away. Every three or four miles there was newly
cleared land and a little house set facing the water, a small wooden
pontoon to serve as a quay for loading of the only crop: tobacco. John
thought that Suckahanna's mother had been right to predict that there
would be no room for the two races to live alongside each other. The
British were spreading themselves so prodigally that their new lands and
houses lined the riverside like a ragged ribbon on both banks.

Bertram Hobert joined John at the rail. 'That's Isle of Wight County.'
He nodded towards it.

'Isle of Wight?' John exclaimed, taking in the thick forest, deep green
with pine and fir tree, black and white with naked boughs filled with
deep snow. Hobert laughed shortly. 'Sounds odd, doesn't it? Isle of
Wight County there, and Surrey County next door to it.'

John looked to the other bank. 'And there's Jamestown at last,' Hobert
said, following his gaze. 'I'll tell my wife to be ready.' He turned and
went below. But John stayed on deck, straining to see the settlement,
to see all the changes. The derelict land around Jamestown had spread
further in the four years, like a wound gone bad, festering in the marshy
ground. The tree stumps were left in the ground to rot and the unused
branches were left where they had fallen. New patches of ground had
been cleared by burning and were black and charred, ready to come
under the plough for tobacco to be planted in spring. Drifts of snow
were heaped around the cleared area as if the loss of the trees had left
an opening for fierce winds and cold weather. Even the snow was dirty.

Jamestown itself looked as if it were thriving. The stone quay had
been extended to handle more and more ships coming to the country
for tobacco, and the warehouses along the quayside were a storey higher
and broader than they had been before, laden with drifts of grimy snow
which rested on the cold roofs.

There was a new paved road running parallel with the river, and
someone had planted a row of trees for shade. Behind the new road

were substantial stone-built houses, still no greater than a yeoman's cottage in England, but better made than their predecessors, and with windows of oiled paper rather than shutters. In some small square panes John could see the bright glint of expensive glass.

The quayside was still filthy with garbage and the deep gutter in the new road showed that no-one had thought it worth while to consider drainage for the new town. The score of houses still tipped their nightsoil on the riverbank or threw it out in the yard where it froze and then leached into the drinking water supply. It was still a town where men, and an increasing number of women, were coming only to seek their fortunes. They did not care what sort of life they led nor what sort of place they were making. Most of them still thought of England as 'home'.

The fort was still there but the gates were stuck open and the guns were rolled back, as if they were only kept in place because no-one could be bothered to move them.

On the quayside people were waiting for news, goods, and to greet the new settlers. They were broad as bears, every one of them, muffled up against the cold air in thick skins, each breath a cloud before every face.

'What news of the king?' a man shouted as he caught the rope and made it fast. 'What news of the war?'

'Victory for the king!' one of the sailors shouted jubilantly back. 'We left just as his cousin Prince Rupert had wiped out Parliament's men. One of the survivors swore there was no doubt about it, the king will have beaten them by now.'

'Thank God for that,' the man replied. And another one cheered. John noted that the report by one trooper of one skirmish had now been elevated into a total defeat and the end of the war, but said nothing. That was how the king's masquing worked. Only one battle was ever enacted. There was no long, bitter exchange of small victories and small defeats, little setbacks and petty humiliations. One glorious cavalry charge by Prince Rupert had concluded the matter and the colonists could go back to growing tobacco and making money with light hearts.

John shrugged and went below to fetch his bags. He was as far from England and the news as everyone else. He had no reason to think that the war would be a longer and more painful business than the sailor and the colonists believed. Perhaps they were right and he was wrong and already the king was back in Whitehall and planning some new triumph: war with the Irish, or war with the Scots, or – since it was King Charles, as changeable as March weather – war with the Spanish or French. John hefted his bag holding his clothes and his money over his shoulder and went up on deck to the head of the gangplank.

She was not there. Not among the crowd on the quayside, nor back in the shadow of the warehouse walls where he had left her. He shook his head, he had not really expected her to be there, on the quayside; but he could not help the pang of childish disappointment. Somewhere, in a corner of his mind, he had seen himself coming down the gangplank and Suckahanna, a little older, a little more beautiful, running towards him and into his arms. It had been a foolish dream by a man who had already buried one wife and deserted another, a man who knew that love and desire do not always have a happy ending. But John still looked for her, and still knew disappointment that she was not there.

He watched his box being unloaded and then took hold of it and dragged it through the slush up to the inn where he was absolutely certain that he would find the landlady as sour-tempered and as inhospitable as four years before.

His first visit was to Mr Joseph.

'Of course I remember you,' the magistrate said. 'You went out into the woods in an Indian canoe and came back with barrelfuls of plants. Were they any good in England?'

'Most of them took,' John said. 'Some of them did very well. One of them, the spiderwort, is one of the most beautiful flowers I have ever grown. We had the purple one before, but this is white like a little three-petalled star.'

'And what news of the king?' Mr Joseph interrupted.

'Good news. Prince Rupert's cavalry had a great victory at a place called Powick Bridge,' John said, repeating the popular belief. 'They say he can't be stopped now.'

Mr Joseph nodded. 'Well, thank God for that,' he said. 'I don't know what would have been our case if Parliament had won. We're a royal colony. Do we become a Parliament colony? No-one thinks of these things. What about you? Would you have been a gardener to Parliament?'

'I'm here because I don't know what I would have been,' John admitted. 'I couldn't see my way clear at all.'

The magistrate nodded. 'Now what can I do for you? D'you want another Indian guide?'

'I want the same one,' John said, keeping his tone deliberately casual.

He wondered if the man could hear the pounding as his heart raced. 'I want that girl again. Do you know where she is?'

'What girl?'

John had to force himself to speak quietly and steadily. 'You sent me out with a girl, d'you remember? Her baptised name is Mary. Her mother was in prison for a month for accusing someone of rape. You had the girl in service here, d'you remember? When I came back her mother met us and took the girl away. She said they might go back to their own people. Have you seen her since then?'

'Oh, the harlot and her daughter,' Mr Joseph said, remembering. 'No. They must have gone into the woods. I've not seen them.'

John had expected anything but this blank refusal. 'But . . . but you must have?'

Mr Joseph shook his head. 'No. D'you want another guide?'

'I want that girl!'

The man shrugged. 'I can't help you, I'm afraid.'

John thought rapidly. 'How could I find her? D'you know of other Indians who come in from the forest who might know her?'

Mr Joseph shook his head again. 'They're settling down at last,' he said with satisfaction. 'The ones who have been taken into service are kept here, in town, or safe on the plantations. The ones who have kept to the forest are pushed back, almost every day, further and further away from the river, away from the coast. We're cleaning the land of them. We're getting them out of the way. If she's out in the forest with them you'll not see her again. She could be over the mountains or the other side of York River by now if she's got any sense.' He paused for a moment. 'What d'you want her for?'

'I promised I would take her into my service,' John said smoothly. 'I said when I came back and built my house she could come to work for me. She's skilled with plants.'

'They're all skilled with plants,' Mr Joseph said. 'Get another one.'

Every new immigrant to Virginia was awarded a headright of land, fifty acres a person. John, arriving for the second time, was awarded a further fifty acres, marked solemnly on a map held in the new building of the burgesses' assembly. His father had been persuaded to purchase two headrights when the Virginia Company was founded, so John had his land put together in one spreading acreage of two hundred acres: as big as an English farm. It was upriver from Jamestown, not the most

137

desirable of sites since the tobacco ships would not go too far upstream. The earliest assignments had all been around Jamestown or downriver. Latecoming planters had to ship their goods in their own boats downriver to Jamestown and catch the ocean-going boats there.

John looked carefully at the burgesses' map. The lines of rivers and mountains were indistinct and vague. The only part of the country that John knew well was the woods where he had lived for the month with Suckahanna, and they were indicated with a rough scribble suggesting inlets and islands and swampy ground. It hardly mattered. There was so much land to be had in the new colony that disputes over boundaries had been left behind in overcrowded England. No-one in this new huge country was going to quibble over a mile to the east or ten miles to the west, scale was a different thing in this vast emptiness.

Bertram Hobert was consulting the map alongside John. 'Next to my land,' he remarked. 'What d'you say we build one house together and then live in it while we work on the other?'

John nodded thoughtfully. 'When could we start?'

'Not till spring. We'd die of hunger and cold out there in the winter. We'll stay snug in town until spring, and go out as soon as we can.'

John looked out of the open slit of the window at the iron-grey sky and the falling snow and thought of Suckahanna, barefoot in the frozen woods where the snow was dozens of feet deep and where the wolves howled at night. 'How could anyone survive out there in winter?'

Hobert shook his head. 'Nobody can,' he said.

Winter 1642–3, Virginia

Bertram Hobert rented lodgings in town for himself, his wife Sarah and his slave, a black man called Francis. After John complained of the treatment he got at the inn, Hobert said he could stay with them until the spring, and then the whole party would go upriver to look at their new land.

John found the town much changed. A new governor, Sir William Berkeley, had arrived from England and had equipped the official residence with beautiful furniture and goods. His wife, who was already a byword in the community for her looks, was giving parties and all those who could remotely pass as a gentleman and his lady were dressing in their best and walking up the drive to the governor's house. The roads were paved now, and the tobacco was no longer grown at the street corners and on any corner of spare land. A man could buy or sell using coin and not pinches of tobacco or bills drawn on a tobacco merchant's. 'It's become a town and not a camp,' John remarked.

Those were the beneficial changes of the four years. There were others that filled him with worry for Suckahanna and her mother. The river was now lined with plantations from its mouth right up to James's Island. Before each of the planters' houses the land had been cleared and the fields stretched down to the little wooden piers and quays. On James's Island itself the fields ran into each other, there was no forest left at all. On the more distant banks the land was black where it had been burned and not yet ploughed. John could not see how Suckahanna and her people could survive in a country which was turning itself into fields and houses. The woods she had roamed every day for mile after mile, hunting turkey or wood pigeon, or looking for roots or nuts, were burned back to a few scorched trees among ploughed fields. Even the river, where she had followed the schools of fish ready to catch them wherever the flow of the water was right, was enclosed by riverfront acres and penetrated by landing piers.

John thought he might be imagining it – or perhaps it was the effect of the freezing-cold weather – but it seemed to him that the flocks of birds were fewer, and he no longer heard the wolves howling outside the walls of Jamestown. The countryside was being tamed, and the wild animals and the people who lived alongside them were being driven inland and away. John thought that if Suckahanna was with her people they might have been driven far away to where the burgesses' map showed nothing more than a space marked 'forest'. He started to fear that he would never find her again.

Bertram busied himself with trade while they were waiting for the weather to change. Since it was his second visit to Jamestown, he had judged his market well. He had brought a store of the little European luxuries that the colonists missed so much. Most afternoons he was welcomed in the better homes to show his supplies of paper and ink, pens and soap, real candles, rather than the green wax of the Virginian candleberries, French brandy rather than the eternal West Indies rum, lace, cotton, linen, silk, anything carved with skill or made with artistry that reminded the colonists of home where skill and artistry had been easily hired.

John went with him on these visits and met a new sort of people, people for whom the old divisions of gentry and labourers no longer applied, for they all laboured. What mattered now was the gradation of skills. A clever carpenter or an able huntsman was more respected in this new country than a man with a French surname, or knowledge of Latin. A woman who could fire a musket and skin a deer was her husband's helpmeet and partner, and more valuable to him than if she could write poetry or paint a landscape. Hester would have thrived in this place where a woman was expected to work as hard as a man, and to take her own share of responsibilities, and every day John found himself wishing that she had come with him, and, contradictorily, longing for news of Suckahanna.

Sarah Hobert reminded John of Hester. She prayed every morning, and said grace at every meal, and in the evenings she taught Francis the slave his letters and the catechism. When John saw her with a chicken over her knees plucking and saving the feathers for a pillow, or scraping cobs of corn by the fireside in the evening, and then carefully setting the empty cobs in the woodbasket for fuel, he remembered Hester: hardworking, conscientious, and with an inner strength and silence.

For a while he thought the cold weather would never lift and free them from the idle life of Jamestown, but Hobert swore he would not go upriver while the snow was still thick on the ground. 'A man could die out there and no-one ever know, and no-one ever care,' he said. 'We stay in town until the ground warms up and until we can row upriver without great bergs of ice crashing down around us. I won't take the risk of moving from the town until spring.'

'And then it would be more dangerous to stay,' his wife said quietly. 'They have terrible fevers here in the hot weather, Mr Hobert. I would rather be well away from here before the summer comes.'

'In good time,' he said with a glance at her under his eyebrows which warned her to hold her peace and not join in with the councils of men.

'In God's time,' she said pleasantly, not the least overawed.

John knew that Hobert was right but still he felt impatient. He asked all the townspeople he met if they remembered the girl or her mother, but people told him that one Indian looked like another, and if the girl had vanished then no doubt she had been stealing or betraying her master and had run off to the woods to her own people.

'And precious comfort she'll get there,' one woman told him as she waited by the town's only deep well for her turn to draw water.

'Why?' John asked urgently. 'What d'you mean?'

'Because every day they get pushed back a little more. Not now in the winter, because our men don't go out into the woods in winter, it gets dark too early and the cold can kill a man quicker than an arrow. But when spring comes we will make up packs of dogs and bands of hunters and go hunting the redskins, we force them back and back and back, so the land is clear for us and safe for us.'

'But she's only a girl,' John exclaimed. 'And her mother a woman all alone.'

'They would breed if left alone,' the woman said with stout indifference. 'I don't mean to shock you, mister, but it's us or them on this land. And we're determined that we shall be the victors. Whether it's wolves or bears or Indians, they have to fall back and give way before us or die. How else can we make this land our own?'

It was a ruthless logic that John could hardly condemn, for he himself held four headrights of riverside land and virgin forest and he heard himself talking with anticipation of the trees he would clear and the house he would build, and he knew that his own land was another two hundred acres where the Powhatan would never hunt again.

April 1643

He had to wait until April, and then he and the Hoberts rowed upriver and saw their adjoining plots. It was good land. The trees reached down to the water's edge and their thick canopy shaded the banks. Their wide grey roots stretched out into the flooded river. John tied the canoe he had borrowed to an overhanging trunk and stepped ashore on his own new land.

'My Eden,' John said quietly to himself.

The trees were alive with the singing of birds, birds courting and chasing, fighting and nesting. He saw birds that looked like familiar English species but which were bigger, or oddly coloured, and he saw others that were wholly new to him in this new and wonderful world, birds like little herons which were white as doves, strange ducks with heads as bright as enamelled boxes. The soil was rich, dark and fertile, an earth which had never known the plough but which had made and remade itself with centuries of tumbling leaves and rotting vegetation. Feeling almost foolish, John went down on his hands and knees, took a handful of the rich soil, crumbled it between his hands and raised it to his nose and his lips. It was good dark earth that would grow anything in rich abundance.

The bank sloped steeply up from the river, there would be no flooding on his fields, and there was a little hillock, perhaps half a mile back from the river frontage, where John would build his house. When the trees were cleared he would have a fine river view, and he would be able to look down the hill to his own landing stage where his own tobacco would be loaded to take downstream.

John thought his house would be set square to the river. A modest house, nothing like the grand size of Lambeth: a pioneer's house of one room downstairs and a ladder leading up to a half-floor for storage set in the eaves. A fireplace in one wall, which would heat the whole of the little building, a roof of reeds or maybe even wooden shingles. A floor of nothing more than beaten earth in the first few years, perhaps later John would put down floorboards. Windows which would be bare and open, empty of glass, but with thick wooden shutters to close in winter and bad weather. It would be a house only a little grander than an English pauper might build to squat on common land and think himself lucky. It would be a normal house in this new world, where nothing could be taken for granted and where men and women rarely had anything more than they could build or make for themselves.

Thoughtfully, John reached towards a sprouting vine and pulled away a cutting, tucking it in his pocket. He would grow it around his door-frame. It might be a little hovel in a great wilderness but it would still have a garden.

The house did not take long to build. There were men in Jamestown who would work at a daily rate, and Bertram and John hired them as a gang to work first on the Hobert house and then on John's smaller version of the same design. The gang specified that they were to have their food and their ale, and that the nails, the most costly part of the house, were to be supplied: counted out each morning, and checked in at nightfall. They told John that when he wanted a new house built elsewhere, he should burn his old house down and then sift through the ashes for the nails. New timber could be had simply by clearing the woods around the foundations, but new nails had to come from England.

'But then you never have houses for sale,' John remarked. 'You never have houses for newcomers.'

'They can build their own,' the man said in the rough frankness of the new world. 'And if they cannot build their own they can go homeless.'

Sarah Hobert cooked for the men while they built her house, roasting meat over a camp fire on long skewers in a way that the colonists had learned from Indian guides. John thought of Suckahanna squatting beside the little fire with trout skewered on green sticks. Sarah made bread in a heavy dark dough from rye flour; the colonists could not grow wheat in this land. When her own house was finished and the builders moved on to John's house, she came too and cooked for them there, never complaining that she would have preferred to start digging her own fields or planting her own vegetable patch.

143

'Thank you,' John said awkwardly as the Hoberts got into their native canoe to travel the little way downriver to their own homestead. 'I could not have built it without you.'

'Nor could we have built ours so quick without you,' Bertram said. 'I will come over in the next month or two to see how you are faring. We will have to be like brothers if we are to survive in this land, John.'

'It's funny,' John said. He took the rope and cast it off, throwing it into Sarah's waiting hands. 'I thought this was an easy country to live in, easy to build a shelter, easy to find food. But now it seems to me that we are on the very edge of surviving, all the time.'

They looked at him blankly, their pale faces turned towards him as the current nudged the canoe away from the bank.

'Of course it is a struggle,' Sarah replied, stating the obvious. 'The Lord God ordains that we should struggle our way through this difficult world to righteousness.'

'But a new world –' John suggested. 'A new world of natural goodness, of natural wealth?'

She shook her head and the canoe bobbed. Bertram took up the paddle. 'Men and women are born to struggle.'

'See you soon,' Bertram called over the widening gulf of water. 'I'll come over some time, when we are settled.'

John raised his hand in farewell and stood watching them. Bertram paddled the canoe awkwardly, with none of Suckahanna's easy grace, and Sarah sat stiffly in the front for all the world like a Thames fishwife in a wherry. The current flowing swiftly downriver took them, so that Bertram need do no more than steer. John watched the flowing water for a long while after they had gone from sight around a bend in the river, then he turned and went slowly up the little track to his new house.

It stood, a plain little box made of green wood, in a square of cleared ground. John had felled no more than the trees he had needed to build it, and their unwanted branches and lesser wood was heaped in wasteful confusion all around. He stopped on his way up the river bank to admire it. It was a square-built house, little more than a shed or a hovel, but he had felled the wood which had built it, and planed the planks of the door, and set the rough frame for the window and packed the reeds for the thatched roof, and he felt proud of it.

Then he looked a little closer. On one side of the door was the cutting he had picked when he first set foot on his new land. It had struck, he could see the fresh green growth of the trumpet vine which would flower in early summer as golden and as prolific as Turkish nasturtiums. But on the other side of the door, which he had not yet touched, someone had dug the earth, cleared it of stones, and planted another creeper, one he did not recognise, which already was putting out a little shoot to touch the new wall so that soon, perhaps as early as this summer, the door would be wreathed in some other new flower, planted by someone else.

His first thought was that Sarah must have put it in, working in an idle moment, while the rest of the building gang had been up on the roof. But then he realised that Sarah would have thought that such a task was a waste of time, and a vanity – neglecting the real work of the day. None of the builders would have troubled themselves with such a piece of frivolity. Bertram Hobert could not tell one plant from another unless it was tobacco from maize. And there had been no-one else near the little house in the woods. John paused for a moment and then turned towards the darkening forest.

'Suckahanna?' he whispered into the green shadows. 'Suckahanna? My love?'

%

She did not come to him, though that night he lay wakeful on the bare floor of his house, and waited for her, certain that she was out in the forest, waiting for him. At dawn he lifted the wooden latch on his new door and stepped out into the forest, already singing its way into morning, and looked around, expecting her to emerge from the trees and come to him. She was not there.

He went down to the river, half-expecting to see her surface from the icy water, with a knife in her hand and a handful of freshwater mussels in her little purse; but the water was grey and ruffled only with the morning breeze.

John thought with a pang of cold fear that maybe she was tormenting him, to repay him for the delay, to make him wait for her as she had waited for him.

'I'm sorry,' he said, speaking to the indifferent trees, to the blithely singing birds in the high branches. 'As soon as I got home I found my father was dead and there was much for me to do. My children needed me, and I had to work –' He hesitated. Even speaking before nothing but thick woodland, he was conscious of the lie of omission when he did not mention Hester. 'I never forgot you,' he said. 'Even when I was at war and fighting for my king I thought of you every day and I dreamed of you every night.' That part at least was mostly true.

145

He waited. From the river behind him came a loud splash. John whirled around. But there was only the spreading ring of water where a salmon had leaped or an otter broken the surface in a dive. She was not there. Not in the river and not in the trees.

John shrugged his coat a little closer around his shoulders and went into his house.

John opened a new sack of cornmeal and put his pot on the embers of the fire. He heated up enough water for a wash, a drink, and to make suppawn porridge for his breakfast.

'I must hunt this evening,' he said to the empty house. 'I can't live on this swill.'

He washed his face but did not trouble to shave. 'I shall grow a beard and a moustache like my father,' he said to the empty room. 'Who is there to see me after all?' He poured half the hot water into a beaker, threw a spoonful of the cornmeal into what was left and stirred it till it thickened. It was warm and he was hungry. He tried to ignore the fact that it tasted of nothing.

He took his bowl, spoon and pot down to the river and washed them, watching the reeds to his left for movement, in case Suckahanna was hiding there, watching him, and laughing at him having to do woman's work. Then he filled the pot with fresh water and went back up to his house.

The room was still silent and empty. John took down his axe from the hook above the fireplace and went out to cut wood from the felled timber before the house. The great felling of trees to clear land for planting would have to wait. Firewood was the most important. The fire must not, on any account, go out. Enough people had warned him of the danger in Jamestown, and that was in a town where you could borrow a couple of glowing embers from the house next door and carry them home on a shovel. Here in the wilderness, a fire was like a spark of life itself. If it went out it might take a couple of hours to get it lit again, even with a good tinderbox and dry wood, and if darkness and cold were coming on, that would seem a very long time. If a pack of wolves had found the courage to come to the door, it would feel like an eternity with neither light nor fire to scare them away, and no means of firing the musket.

John cut and split logs for most of the morning and then piled them on either side of the fireplace to dry. He opened the rough-planed door of his house and looked down to the river. He was aching with fatigue and yet all he had done was get in one, perhaps two, day's supply of firewood. He had nothing for dinner but more suppawn porridge, and nothing at all for supper. He set the pot on the fire to heat the water and felt, for the first time, a dark sense of foreboding that surviving would be a struggle in this country which no longer seemed rich and easy.

'I must think,' John said into the silence of the house. 'Suckahanna and I ate like princes, every day, and she was not chopping trees all morning. I must try to live like her, and not like an Englishman.' He scraped the last of the porridge from his wooden bowl and put it to one side. 'I'll put down a fish trap,' he resolved. 'And at dusk when the birds are coming back to the trees to roost I'll shoot a couple of pigeon.'

He felt the juices rush into his mouth at the thought of roast pigeon. 'I can do that,' he promised himself. 'I can learn to live here, I am a young man still. And later, when Bertram and Sarah come over, Sarah can teach me how to make bread.'

He set his bowl and spoon to one side and went to his pile of belongings, to find a length of twine. 'Now a fish trap,' he said.

John had seen a fish trap in Jamestown, and had watched Suckahanna weave one out of the tendrils of vines and a couple of sticks. She had spent two evenings on it, and on the third evening they had eaten roasted carp. John had bought the withy hoops and the string in Jamestown, all he had to do was knot a net that would keep a fish inside. He took the string and the hoops outside, sat on a tree stump in the afternoon sunshine and started to work. First he made a row of knots around the large entrance hoop. The fish was to swim in, and then through a series of hoops, each one smaller, until it was trapped in a little space at the end of the maze, and could not find its way out. John knotted his first row and then set to work on the second. It was intricate, difficult work but John was a patient man, and determined. He bent over the task, twisting the string, knotting, moving on to the next row. He did not notice the sun was falling behind the trees until the shadow had chilled his back. Then he straightened and sighed.

'By God, this is weary work,' he said. He took string and hoops inside the house and put them down at the fireside. The fire was burning low. He put on another couple of logs and took his musket down. He loaded it, tipping the powder and then the ball down the muzzle, and then sprinkled a pinch of powder at the top of the powder pan, ready for lighting. He bent over the fire to light the long coil of oiled string which served as the fuse. When it was glowing brightly he held it between first and second finger, well away from the powder pan, and went quietly out of his house.

The trees were so near that John could hunker down on his doorstep, his two vines on either side, and watch the open sky above him for the wood pigeons coming home to roost. A great whirling flock of them came in all at once, and John waited for them to settle in the trees. One plump, confident bird landed on an extended branch which dipped under its weight. John waited for the branch to stop swaying and then took careful aim, touching the glowing string to the powder.

He was lucky. The sound of the shot was like a cannon blast going off in that innocent land and the flock of pigeons exploded out of the trees in a flurry of whirling wings. But John's target bird could not fly up, it spiralled downward, one wing broken, bleeding from the breast. John dropped his musket and taper and ran across the cleared ground, crossing it in five giant strides. The bird was scrabbling to get away, one wing trailing. John snatched it up and wrung its neck quickly and mercifully. He felt the little heart pound and then stop. He went back to the doorstep, put the bird inside, near the fireplace with the unfinished fish trap, and reloaded the gun.

The light was going fast and it was getting cold and dark. The pigeons, recovering from their fright, circled the little clearing and landed in the trees again. John took aim and fired and the birds dashed skyward again, but this time nothing fell to earth.

'Just the one,' John said. 'Well, that will do for my supper at least.'

He plucked the bird carefully, saving the feathers in a fold of linen. 'That'll make me a pillow some day,' he said with assumed cheerfulness to the shadowy room. He gutted and beheaded the bird, tossing the entrails into the water in his cooking pot which he set on the fire for soup. Then he split the pigeon into four, and skewered the pieces carefully on a sharp green stick and set it before the fire with the pot beneath it to catch the dripping juices.

It was a long while for a hungry man to wait but John did not allow himself to hurry, nor to be distracted from the task of turning and turning the fowl while its stubbly skin grew golden, and then brown, and then finally crisp and black. 'Pray God it's cooked through,' John said fervently, his stomach rumbling with hunger.

He took the skewer, and with his knife pushed the pieces off the charred wood on to his trencher. The meat was speckled with burned wood. John flicked the splinters away and then took up a little leg joint. It was wonderful: hot, tasty, and strong. John burned his lips against the hot skin but nothing could have stopped him biting into the flesh. He ate every scrap of meat and then dropped the bare bones reverently into his cooking pot. For the first time in his little house he looked around with something like confidence.

'That was good,' he said quietly. He gave a quiet, satisfied belch. 'That was excellent. I shall hunt again tomorrow. And I shall have the soup for my breakfast. A man cannot work on the land with only porridge in his belly.'

He picked a scrap of meat from his teeth. 'By God, that was good.'

He kicked off his boots and drew his satchel and spare jacket towards him, folded them under his head for a pillow, and then pulled his travelling cloak and a rug over him. He opened one eye to see that the fire was banked in, and his fish trap was safe, and then he was asleep in moments.

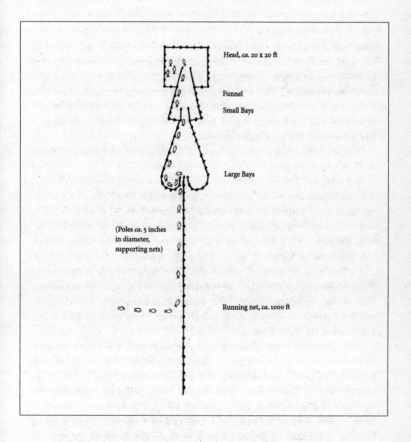

Head, *ca.* 20 x 20 ft

Funnel

Small Bays

Large Bays

(Poles *ca.* 5 inches in diameter, supporting nets)

Running net, *ca.* 1000 ft

May 1643

Next day John set to work on the fish trap for an hour and set it in the cold, swift-flowing water. The meat from last night's supper stayed in his stomach more comfortably than porridge, he felt stronger and more competent all day; but the following morning he felt hungrier, as if his body were expecting meat again. He had the soup from the pigeon bones for breakfast and then had it again, thinned down and less satisfying, for his dinner at midday.

In the afternoon he went to look at his fish trap and found a small trout in the keep-net.

'Praise God!' John said devoutly, inwardly praising himself. He lifted the trap from the river, carefully supporting his trophy, and smacked the squirming little fish on the head. He cleaned it and gutted it. There was not much left of it after he had cut its head and tail off but he set it in the pot with a little water and dried maize flour to make a stock and simmered it for a few moments, and then left it to cool until supper.

These foods became his staple diet. The monotonous blandness of the cornflour – as porridge, as vegetable, as sauce, and the occasional treat of fish or meat. Slowly, John adapted, and only ate well and with relish in poignant dreams of Lambeth feasts: great dinners at Twelfth Night, rich tables at Easter.

Every day he chopped wood, and went out into the forest to see if he could recognise any berries or nuts which Suckahanna had gathered, but the branches were showing nothing more than fresh green leaves and the nuts had all blown down in the winter gales or been eaten by squirrels and mice. The woods were not as friendly to John as they had been to her. Everywhere that she had looked there had been food or tools or medicines or herbs. Everything that John saw was strange.

After weeks and weeks of this he thought that he had had his fill of strangeness. His father had loved the rare and the unusual and John had inherited that love. Their whole lives were based on the joy of difference: different plants, flowers, artefacts. But now John was in a different world, where everything was strange to him and he felt that perhaps he liked strangeness only against the background of the familiar. He liked the exotic flower when it grew in his English garden at Lambeth. It was harder to admire when it was growing against an exotic tree, under a foreign sky.

'I'm heartstruck,' John said in sudden amazement in the middle of the second month, and a great longing for Lambeth and the children and even for Hester rushed over him so powerfully that he staggered, as if from physical sickness, and had to steady himself with a hand on a tree trunk. 'God! I am longing for my home. It has been weeks, no, months since I came to live here and I have spoken to no man and seen no woman since the Hoberts left. I miss my home. And, my God, I am lonely.'

He turned to look back at the little clearing and, plumb in the centre of it, the house as small and as rough as a wooden box made by a thick-handed apprentice. A sense of the minute scale of the house and the enormity of the forest rushed upon John, leaving him breathless and fearful. 'But I'm making my home here,' he said stubbornly.

The wind, the massive wind, stirred the tops of the high, strong trees as if the very woods themselves were laughing at the false pride of a man who thought he could make a home among such wildness. John could labour here all his life and never manage to do more than survive. He could never build a house like the one at Lambeth, never make a garden like Oatlands. Those were achievements which took years of labour in a society rich in labour. Take away those riches, the work of many hands and many brains, and a man was like an animal in a wood – less than an animal, because every animal in the wood had its place in the scheme of things, food that was suited to it, a home which was right for it, whereas John had to fight to get enough food in this land of plenty, and had to struggle to keep his fire burning to keep his house warm.

A sense of despair as real as darkness swept over him. 'I could die out here,' John thought, but he no longer spoke aloud. The very silence of the woods seemed too great to challenge, it silenced his little voice. 'I *will* die out here.' Every thought seemed to open a greater gulf beneath his feet. 'I am making my home here, far from my children, from my wife, from my friends. I am making a place where I am all alone. And sooner or later, by accident or illness or old age, I will die here. I will die alone. In fact, if I fail for just one day, just *one* day, to get up and fetch water, chop wood, hunt or fish I *will* die here. I could starve to death before anyone came.'

John pushed away from the tree but found that his legs could hardly support him. His sense of loneliness and fear had weakened him. He staggered back towards his house and thanked God there was at least a curl of smoke coming from the chimney, and suppawn in the cooking pot. John felt his throat close at the thought of eating cold porridge again. He fell to his hands and knees and retched. 'God, my God,' he said.

A little saliva dribbled from his mouth. He wiped it on his sleeve. The strong brown homespun of the sleeve was stinking. He noticed it when he brought it to his face. 'My clothes smell,' he said in quiet surprise. 'I must smell.'

He touched his hand to his face. His beard had grown and was matted and dirty, the moustache was long around his mouth. 'My breath must smell, I am filthy,' he said softly. 'I am so foul that I cannot even smell myself.' He felt humiliated at the knowledge. John Tradescant, the apple of his mother's eye, his father's only heir, had become a dirty, bedraggled vagrant, clinging to the edge of the known world.

He dragged himself to his feet again. The sky seemed to look down on him, as if he were a tiny, tiny insect making its arduous way across a massive leaf on a tree in a forest in a country that was too great for any man to cross.

John stumbled to his door and pushed it open. Only in the cramped room could he restore his sense of scale. 'I'm a man,' he said to the four rough wood walls. 'Not a tiny beetle. I am a man. This is my house.'

He looked around as if he had never seen it before. The four walls had been made of newly felled green wood, and as the fire heated the room and the weather warmed, the wood had shrunk. John would have to take clay and twigs to patch the gaps. He shuddered at the glimpse of the forest through the cracks of the house walls, as if the wildness outside was seeping in through his house to attack him.

'I can't,' he said miserably. 'I can't build the house and find food and wash and hunt and clear the land as well. I can't do it. I've been here for nearly two months, and all I can do is survive, and I can barely do that.' His throat closed again and he thought he was going to retch but instead he spat out a hoarse sob.

He felt the waistband of his trousers. He had thought that, for some reason, his belt had been stretching but now he realised that he was thinner. 'I'm not surviving,' he finally acknowledged to himself. 'I'm not getting enough to eat.'

At once the tiredness which was now familiar, and the ache in his belly which he had thought was some kind of mild illness, made a new and terrifying sense. He had been hungry for weeks and his hunger was making him less and less competent to survive. He missed his shot more and more often, his stock of logs for the fire was harder to cut every day. He had fallen back on gathering firewood rather than making the effort of swinging an axe. This meant that the wood was drier and burned quicker so that he needed more, and it also meant that the land around the little house was no clearer than it had been when Bertram had come over to help him build his house at the start of their time in the wilderness when they had been confident and laughing.

'Spring is here and I have planted nothing,' John said dully, holding a fold of his waistband in his calloused hand. 'The ground is not clear, and I cannot dig. I have no time to dig. Just getting in food and water and fuel takes all my time, and I am tired . . . I am so tired.'

He stretched out his hand for his cloak. It was not folded tidily away in the corner of the room any more but left in the corner where he kicked it to one side in the mornings. He wrapped himself in its thick warmth. Hester had bought it for him when he said that he was going away, he remembered. Hester, who had not wanted to come. Hester, who had sworn that the new country was not for men and women who were used to the ease and comfort of town life, that it would suit only farmers who had no chance of doing well in their home country, farmers and adventurers and risk-takers who had nothing to lose.

John lay down on the bare earth floor before the glow of the fire and pulled the collar of the cloak up over his face. Although it was morning he felt he wanted to pull the cloak over his head and let himself sleep. He heard a small, pitiful sound, like Frances used to make when she woke from a bad dream in the night, and realised that it was himself, and that he was weeping like a frightened child. The little sound went on, John heard it as if he were far away from his own fear and weakness, and then he fell asleep, still hearing it.

He woke feeling hungry and afraid. The fire was nearly out. At the sight of the grey ash in the grate John leaped to his feet with a gasp of fear and looked out of the open window. Thank God, it was not dark, he had not slept away the whole day. He stumbled outside, the cloak clinging to his feet, making him stumble, and gathered armfuls of wood from his outside store. He tumbled the logs into the grate and prised off the dry pieces of bark. With little twigs he poked the bark into the heart of the red embers and put his head down into the ash and blew, gently, softly, praying that they would catch. It took a long time. John heard himself muttering a prayer. A little flame flickered yellow like a candle, and then went out.

'Please God!' John breathed.

The little flame flickered yellow again and caught. The twist of bark crisped, burned, and was consumed. John laid a couple of twigs across it and was rewarded by them catching alight at once. Immediately he fed the fire with bigger and bigger twigs until it was burning brightly and John was safe from the coming darkness and cold once more.

He realised then that he was hungry. In his cooking pot was porridge from last night, or if he wished to give himself the labour he could clean out the pot and set some water to boil and try to shoot a bird for meat. There was nothing else to eat.

He put the cooking pot a little closer to the flames so that the porridge would not be stone cold, and went to the door.

The evening was drawing in. The sun had gone behind the trees and the sky above the little house was veiled with strips of thinnest cloud, like the shawl the queen used to wear over her hair when she was on her way to Mass. 'Mantilla clouds,' John said, looking up at them. The sky was pale, the colour of dead lavender heads in winter, the colour of heather in summer, violet and pink with all the brightness drained away.

John shivered. His momentary admiration of the sky had suddenly changed. At once it looked again too vast, too indifferent, it was impossible that a man as small as him could survive under the great dome of it. From the mantilla clouds looking down, John's home would be nothing more than a little speck, John peeping out would be smaller than an flea. The country was too big for him, the forest too wide, the river too rich and cold and fast-flowing and deep. John had a sense that all his new life was nothing more than an arduous crawling like a little ant from one place to another and that his survival was of no interest to the sky, any more than the life of an ant was of interest to him.

'God is with me,' John said, summoning Jane's faith.

There was a silence. There was no sign that God was with him. There was no sign that there was any God. John remembered Suckahanna casting smoking tobacco on the river at sunrise and sunset, and thought for a blasphemous moment that perhaps this land had strange gods, different gods, from England; and that if John could somehow creep under the protection of the gods of the new world then he would be safe from the indifferent gaze of the swelling sky.

'I should be praying,' John said quietly. He did not observe Sundays here in the wilderness. He did not even pray before his meals nor before he lay down to sleep at night. 'I don't even know when Sunday is!' John exclaimed.

He could feel panic rising up in him at the thought that he had slept during this day; but he did not know how long he had slept. He did not know how far the town was downriver, how long it would take him to get there, that he did not even know what day it was.

'I cannot go into town dressed like this and stinking like an animal!' John said. But then he stopped. How was he to get clean if not in town? He could hardly wash and dry the clothes he needed unless he was prepared to run as naked as a savage in the forest. And how could he pay for all his laundry to be done in the town like some fine gentleman? All his money should be spent on hiring labourers to clear his land, buying seed corn, buying tobacco seeds, new axes, more spades.

John thought of the wealth of the house at Lambeth. He thought of the servants who did the work for him: the cook who prepared the meals, the maid who waited in the house, the garden and the gardeners, his wife Hester who ordered it all done; and how he had wildly, madly decided that none of it was for him any longer, and that his life belonged somewhere else, with another woman. Now he looked ready to die in that somewhere else. And the other woman was lost to him.

'That is all this place is to me,' he said softly. 'Somewhere else. I am living in somewhere else and I am going to die in somewhere else unless I can get myself home again.'

A sharp, acrid scent reminded him abruptly of his dinner. He turned with a cry of distress. The cooking pot was spewing a dark smoke into the room, it had overheated and the porridge had stuck to the bottom of the pot and was burned.

John lunged to pull it away from the fire and then recoiled as the hot metal handle scorched into his hand. He dropped the pot and cursed, his hand burning with pain. He had a little water left in his cup and he poured it over the burn. The skin puckered up and turned white. John felt the sweat break out on his face at the pain and he cried out again.

He turned from the room and ran out of the door, down to the river. At the little beach before the house he knelt down to the water and plunged his hand in. The cold water felt like a blow from a whip against the damaged skin but slowly the pain eased. 'Ah God, my God,' John heard himself saying. 'What a fool! What a fool I am!'

When the pain had eased a little he took his hand from the water and looked at it fearfully. The handle of the cooking pot had left a white stripe along his palm. The skin was dead-looking, swelling fast. John tried to flex his fingers; at once a sharp pain ran like a blade across his hand.

'So now I have only one good hand,' he said grimly, 'and burned dinner.' He looked again at the sky. 'And night coming on.'

He turned and walked slowly back up to the little house, his head full of thoughts and fears. The fire was still lit, which was one good thing. He pushed the overturned cooking pot with his booted foot. It rolled on the earth floor. It was cool, he had been down by the river for perhaps an hour. He had not known that the time was passing. He set it on its little feet and peered inside. There was nothing that he could eat. The porridge was blackened and charred almost to ashes.

John took the pot and went down to the river once more, picking his way in the twilight which was coming on in a rush like a dark cloak thrown over the forest. He left the pot to soak in the water while he looked at his fish trap. It was empty. John went back to his pot and arduously, with his good left hand, tried to scrape out the charred remains, swill it and rinse it clean.

He filled the pot with water and, carrying it in his left hand, went back up the beach and up the little hill to his house. Where the trees had been felled before the house the forest was already regaining the land. Small vines and little weeds and ground-covering plants were invading the space. If John did not get out and dig soon the forest would crowd back in and his house would be all but forgotten, marked only on a map in the governor's office as a headright, once claimed but then neglected, ready for another fool to take the challenge and try to make a life in the wilderness.

In the house John poured his drinking water into his cup, spilling some on the floor in his one-handed clumsiness, then he put a scoop of powdered cornflour into the water and set it to heat. This time he did not take his eyes from it, but stood over it, stirring as it thickened and came to the boil, and then set it to one side to cool before serving it into his trencher. He had made enough for breakfast tomorrow so he could eat when he woke in the morning. His stomach rumbled. He could not remember the last time he had eaten fruit or something green. He could not remember when he had last eaten meat that was not wood pigeon. He thought, absurdly and suddenly, of English plums and the sharp sweetness of their flesh. In his father's garden there were thirty-three different varieties of plum tree, from the rare white diapered plum of Malta, which the Tradescants alone grew in all of England, to the common dark-skinned plum of every cottage garden.

He shook his head. There was no point thinking about home and the wealth his father had left him. There was no point thinking about the richness of his inheritance, the flowers, the vegetables, the herbs, the fruit. There was no point thinking about any food which he could not catch or grow in this unhelpful land. All there was for dinner tonight, and breakfast the next day, was an unappetising mess of corn porridge. And unless he could find a way to fish and shoot with only one hand, that would be all there was for a day or so, for a week or two, until his hand healed.

With his belly full of porridge John drank water and took off his boots, ready to sleep. His cloak was missing. He looked around for it, cursing his own laziness in not hanging it up every morning. It was nowhere to be seen. John felt a disproportionate alarm. His cloak was missing, the cloak Hester had given him, the cloak he always slept in. He could feel an absurd panic rising up in him and threatening to choke him. He strode to the corner of the room where his goods were piled and turned them over, tumbling them to the ground in his haste. His cloak was not there.

'Think!' he commanded himself. 'Think, you fool!'

He steadied himself and his breathing, which had become hoarse and anxious, settled down. 'I must stay calm,' John said to himself, his voice quavery against the darkness. 'I have left it somewhere. That's all.'

He went through his movements. He had slept in his cloak in the afternoon and then he had run outside when the fire had burned out. He remembered then. His cloak had been tangled around his feet and he had kicked it away in his haste to get some dry wood to relight the fire.

'I left it outside,' he said quietly. 'Now I'll have to get it.'

He went slowly to the door and put his hand on the wooden latch. He paused. Through the cracks between the planks the colder night air breathed against his face like an icy sigh. It was dark beyond the wooden door, dark with a density that John had never seen before in his life, a blackness which was not challenged by firelight nor candlelight nor torchlight for dozens of miles in one direction, and hundreds, thousands, perhaps millions of miles westwards. It was a darkness that was so powerful and so completely void of light that John had a foolish, superstitious fear that if he opened the door, the night would rush into the room and extinguish the fire. It was a darkness which was too great for him to challenge.

'But I want my cloak,' he said stubbornly.

Slowly, fearfully, he opened the door a little way. The clouds were thick between him and the stars, the darkness was absolute. With a little whimper John dropped to his hands and knees like a child and crawled over the threshold of his house, his hands before him feeling his way, hoping to touch his cloak.

Something brushed against his outstretched fingers and he recoiled with a sob of fright but then he realised that it was the soft wool of his cloak. He gathered it up to him as if it was a treasure, one of the king's most beautiful sacred tapestries. He bundled it to his face and smelled his own strong scent, not with distaste but with a sense of relief at smelling something human in this icy empty darkness.

He did not dare to turn his back on the void. With one arm tucking his cloak to his chest, he backed, still on his hands and knees, into his doorway like a frightened animal retreating into its lair, and then he shut the door.

His eyes, strained wide open against the darkness, blinked blindly when he was back in the fitful flickering light of the cottage. He shook out his cloak. It was wet with dew. John hardly cared. He wrapped himself in it and lay down to sleep. Lying on his back, his eyes still wide open in fear, he could see the steam rising off himself. If he had not been so deep in despair he would have laughed at the sight of a hungry man supping on porridge, a cold man wrapped in damp cloth, a pioneer with one hand. But none of it seemed very funny.

'Dear God, keep me safe through the night and show me what I must do in the morning,' John said as he closed his eyes.

He waited in the darkness for sleep to come, listening to the sounds of the forest outside his door. He had a moment of acute terror when he heard a pack of wolves howling in the distance, and thought that they might smell the food and come and ring the cottage with their bright yellow eyes and their lean, serene faces. But then they fell silent and John fell asleep.

When he woke in the morning it was raining. He put his cloak to one side and put the pot by the fire to heat. He stirred the porridge but when he came to eat it he found he had no appetite. He had gone through hunger into indifference. He knew he must eat; but the grey porridge, dirty with the old ash from the inside of the pot, was tasteless in his mouth. He forced himself to swallow five mouthfuls and then put the pot in the fireplace to stay warm. If there were no fish in the trap, and if he could not shoot something, then it would be porridge for dinner as well.

The stocks of wood beside the fire were low. John went outside. The woodpile was low too and damp from the rain. John took nearly all of it and stacked it inside the house to dry. He went to grasp his axe to go and cut some more but the pain from his burned hand made him cry out. He could not use the axe until the burn was healed. He would have to gather wood, break up what he could by stamping on it, and burn the longer branches from one end to another, pushing them into the heart of the fire as they were consumed.

He went out into the rain, his head bowed, wearing only his homespun coat, leaving his cloak behind to dry. He had seen a fallen tree rather like an oak when he had been out with his gun a few days ago. He trudged towards it. When he got there he saw that some of the branches had split from the main trunk. There was wood that he could use. Using only his left hand, he pulled a branch away from the rest of the tree, and tucked the limb under his arm. It was hard work getting it home. The broad sweep of the branch kept getting caught in the undergrowth, wedged against trees, enwrapped in ground vines. Again and again John had to stop and go back and break it free. The forest of John's headright was thick, almost impenetrable, it took John all the morning to travel just one mile with his firewood, and then another hour to break it up into manageable logs before bringing it inside the house to dry.

He was soaked through by the rain and by sweat and aching with tiredness. The burn on his hand was oozing some kind of liquid. John looked at it fearfully. If the wound went bad then he would have to go to Jamestown and put himself in the hands of whatever barber surgeon had set up in the town. John was afraid of losing his hand, afraid of the journey to Jamestown, one-handed in a dugout canoe, but equally afraid of staying on his own in the cottage if he became ill. He could taste the sweat on his upper lip and recognised the scent of his own fear.

He turned to the fire, wanting to think of something else. The fire was burning well and the room was warm. John looked out through the open window and through the gaps in the plank walls. The forest outside seemed to have come a little closer, to have advanced through the sheets of rain to press a little nearer to the solitary house.

'Don't let it destroy me,' John whispered, knowing himself to be absurd. 'Don't let me come all this way and try so hard, to be just grown over as if I were nothing more than the dead body of a dog.'

There was nothing to eat but yesterday's porridge. John did not bother to heat it. Warm or cold, it was equally unpleasant to him. He took a spoon and made himself eat four spoonfuls and then took a draught of water. He knew that he should go out into the forest with his gun and shoot a wood pigeon, a squirrel, anything he could get, for its meat. But the rain was too forbidding and the darkening sky was threatening thunder. John felt a sense of deep, helpless terror at the thought of being out there amid all that powerful green life, with the rain pouring more life and more energy into the avid earth, and him the only thing in the woods which was cringing and growing weaker every day.

'I'll sleep while it rains,' he said, trying to comfort himself. 'I'll take the gun out at twilight, that's always a good time.'

He took off his wet coat and his sodden breeches and spread them out to dry, then he pushed one of the big branches into the heart of the fire, wrapped himself up in his warm cape, and fell asleep.

John felt as if he had slept for perhaps a minute and then he woke with a start of terror to the realisation that it was dark. He could not see the window. The whole cottage was in darkness. Only the embers of the fire glowed, the branch of the tree had quite burned through and fallen away from the hearth.

His first thought was that it was a terrible storm which had darkened the sky, but then he heard the silence of the outside, all he could hear was the patter of rain on leaves, an awful, remorseless, unforgiving patter of steady rain on fresh leaves. John struggled to his feet. He found that he was half-naked, wearing only his shirt, and remembered that only minutes ago he had taken off his sodden trousers and jacket and lain down for a rest. He pulled them on; they were dry, they had been dry for hours.

'It's night,' John suddenly realised. 'I slept all the afternoon and now it is night.'

He looked around the room as if everything might have changed during his long, enchanted sleep. His heap of goods, the tools he had thought he would use to farm his new land, his stores of dried goods, were all there; and higgledy piggledy beside them was the pile of wood that he had brought in only this morning.

He took a couple of logs and put them on the fire. When they burned up the shadows in the room leaped and flickered at him; but the window and the cracks in the walls looked darker and more ominous than ever.

John bit back a sob of misery. It might be the middle of the night or just before dawn but he could not lie down and sleep again. All his senses were alert, he felt surrounded by danger. His certainty was that it was afternoon, early afternoon, and that he should be out fetching firewood, checking the fish trap, hunting, or at the very least starting to clear a patch of ground and digging so that he could plant his seeds. But the darkness, the strange, inexplicable darkness outside the house was impenetrable.

'I shall have to wait until dawn.' John tried to speak calmly but the quaver in his voice frightened him and made him fall silent. He thought instead, arranging the words in his mind so they sounded like calm good sense. 'It will be good to start early in the morning. I shall take my gun and shoot wood pigeon while they are still roosting. I might get a couple and then I could dry the meat. I might get several and then I could smoke them in the chimney and always have meat to eat.'

The darkness outside the window did not lift at all.

John sat down before the fire, stretched his legs before him and looked into the flames. Hours passed. His head nodded and he stretched out before the fire and closed his eyes. He slept. At dawn he woke, warned by the growing chill that the fire was dying down, got up and heaped more wood on the embers. He slept again. It was not until the middle of the morning that he woke. His empty stomach rumbled but he did not feel hungry; he felt weak, light-headed and weary.

'I'll sleep again,' he said. He glanced towards the closed shutters of the window. Around the frame was a line of bright golden light. The storm had blown away and it was a beautiful sunny day.

John looked at it without interest. 'I'm tired,' he said to the silent room. He slept.

🐾

When he woke it was early afternoon. The ache in his belly was hunger, but all he felt was thirst. There was no water left in his beaker. 'I shall have to go down to the river,' he said unhappily to himself. He heaped more wood on the fire and looked at the ash-filled hearth as if it were a greedy enemy. 'I suppose I could let it go out,' he said thoughtfully, rejecting the wisdom of those who had told him never to let the fire go out, that the fire was his light and protection and saviour. 'I could let it go out during the day. Just light it at night.'

He nodded to himself as if approving a statement of good sense, and opened the door. Then he stopped dead.

On the doorstep was a small basket, beautifully woven in coloured strings. Inside it were three warm new-laid duck eggs, a loaf of pale yellow corn bread, a handful of nuts and a leaf wrapped around some dried fruits.

John exclaimed and looked out at once towards the forest where the trees were thick at the edge of his felled patch. Nothing moved. There was no skirt of buckskin flicking out of sight, no gleam of dark oiled hair.

'Suckahanna?' he called. His voice was low, he had spoken in nothing but a low whisper for so many weeks he thought he had forgotten how to shout her name. He tried again. 'Suckahanna?'

There was no answer. A jay shrieked and a wood pigeon clattered in the branches as it flew away, but there was no other sound.

John bent and picked up the basket. Surely this was a gift from her, seeing his door closed, guessing how low this country had brought him? He took the basket inside and set it down by the fireplace, and then, feeling his desire for food rekindled at the sight of the eggs, he went quickly down to the river and filled his cooking pot with water.

He set the eggs on to boil but he could not wait for them to cook before tasting the other food. While they were bubbling in the pot he broke the bread and ate it, and then cracked the nuts on the hearthstone and ate the sweet kernels. The juices rushed into his mouth, the taste of a food which was not cornflour porridge was so strange and desirable that the corners of his jaw suddenly pained him sharply, as if he had bitten into a lemon. It was passionate desire for food, for a new taste. When the eggs were boiled John broke off the tops, careless that he scalded his mouth, and ate the whites and sucked the yellow yolks down in great desirous gulps. The yellow tasted like blood, he could feel the strength of it coursing through him, making him whole-hearted again, courageous, enterprising, making a pioneer out of a man who moments ago had been a lost boy.

'My God, I was hungry!' he said. He took the last piece of bread and ate it, relishing the slightly sweet taste of it and the pale yellow colour. Then he took a handful of the dried fruit and put it in his mouth. At once his mouth was filled with flavour as strong as sherbet, as sharp as redcurrants. It was a fruit he did not know, wrinkled like raisins but as sharp-tasting as sour greengages. John held the sweet mass in his mouth and sucked it and sucked it as the sharpness and sweetness poured out of the dried skins and into his throat.

He sat entranced, his mouth pursed around the flavour, as if nothing in the whole world could be as good as this moment when he was fed at last, after months of hunger.

When he had finished his meal there were only a few of the fruits left over. He had eaten everything else. 'I should have saved some,' John thought regretfully. 'I am as greedy as a savage to pour it down my throat and not save any for my dinner.' Then he realised that he could not have stopped himself from eating. He simply would not have had the willpower, and that without the strength from the meal he could not have gone on.

'And now I shall check my fish trap, and I shall clear a patch of ground and plant some seeds,' he said determinedly. 'Thank God I have the strength to do it.'

First he loaded the fire with the broken branches, remembering the wisdom of the rule that he should always keep the fire in. Then he went out of the cottage and left the door open behind him so that the cool, clean wind could sweep in and blow away the stench of him living like a dog, sleeping like a dog, and never getting clean. He went down to the river and stripped off his shirt and his breeches and left them piled under stones in the water while he waded into the icy river and washed. When he came out, shivering with cold, he pulled out his clothes and rinsed them roughly until the shirt was evenly pale grey instead of dirty and stained. Then he wrung them, still favouring his hurt hand, and shook them out as he jogged back to the house on his bare feet. The fire was blazing. He upended the cooking pot and balanced a couple of sticks so he could spread the wet clothes before the heat. Then he went back outside, bare-arsed, wearing only his jacket for warmth, and started to break up firewood.

When he had made a good pile he stacked it and then went inside for his spade and pick. He paused for a moment looking over his land, his new land. It was no hunger-born illusion that the forest was creeping back. Long trails of vines were moving in like snakes across the cleared patch, speckles of weeds were springing like a green plague across the clean soil. Nothing would stop this earth regenerating. By felling the trees all John had done was let in the low-growing plants which were colonising the clearing.

John marked out with his eye a line which would run parallel with the front of his house and stop before the doorway. It would be a vegetable bed with young tobacco plants interspersed with eating plants. Salad vegetables would be quick to grow, and he had seed potatoes, turnip, carrot, leek and pea seeds as well. Other planters up and down the river, with labourers to work for them, some of them enslaved, some of them free, had taken the risk of planting nothing but tobacco, assuming that they could buy everything else they wanted, all their food, all their building materials, all their clothes, from the profits of one cash crop. Men like that had died in the early years, or begged from the Indians and called it trade, or gone barefoot into town and pleaded for charity. But when the tobacco grew, and the price of tobacco started to rise, the gamble for some of them had paid off. John thought of the little cottage gardens that his mother had told him about, in the village of Meopham, where every house, however small, had a patch of ground behind it which grew food to keep the worst of the winter hunger away. John realised that he was reduced to a level that his parents had congratulated themselves on leaving behind; but then he thought more cheerfully that perhaps this was his starting place, as Meopham had been theirs.

He hefted the pick and swung it into the ground. At once it jarred on a root and he felt the sudden pain as the new skin on the palm of his hand split open and drained a dripping water. He caught his hand up and looked fearfully at it. The skin which had looked so dead and white had peeled off the wound and was pouring, not blood, but a clear liquor. The pain was so sharp that John's head rang with it for long moments. Then he slowly bent, took the axe and the spade, tucked them under his arm, and brought them back to the house. He could not dig one-handed. His garden would have to wait.

Inside the house he took a strip of linen which had once been destined to be a white stock if he were invited to somewhere fine, and wound it around his hand, tying it tight to staunch the flow. It stung painfully as he wrapped it, and he felt the cloth stick into the wound.

'The thing is,' he said quietly to the empty room, 'is that I don't rightly know what to do for the best.'

John thought he should wait till his shirt and breeches were dry and then walk, though it would be a long walk, to the Hobert plantation and see what Sarah Hobert could do for a grievous burn. 'She may have a salve,' John said. 'And I could stay the night with them, and talk. And they'll have bread.'

The high spirits of the morning were draining out of him. He felt his shirt, anxious now to leave. The shirt was dry and sweet-smelling but the breeches, made of thick homespun, were still wet. John was thinking of wearing them wet when a sudden pain gripped him deep in his belly.

It was the food, shovelled down into his shrunken stomach, too rich for a system which had been living at starvation level. 'Ah God!' John exclaimed. The pang of it was like a sword thrust into his heart.

He doubled up and ran, bent double, for the door. He had scarcely cleared the house when he voided himself and felt his strength burst and then trickle from him. He clung to the doorframe with the pain of it and then felt his hands and even his fingertips grow weaker as the pain seized him in the belly and shook him, like a monster's jaws.

'What a fool I am, what a fool . . .' he gasped between spasms. He thought he should have known that his body could not take the richness of such food after weeks of hunger. 'What a fool . . . what a fool.'

The attack subsided and John half-stumbled and half-crawled back indoors. The stink was very bad but he could not get down to the river again to wash. He wrapped himself in his cloak and lay down before his fire. He realised that he would not be well enough to walk to the Hoberts'. He could not paddle his canoe one-handed. He could not dig his garden until his hand healed, and until this dreadful flux passed he would be fit for nothing. He would be hard-pressed to get down to the river and then he would be unable to walk up the hill again. He lay in the warmth of the fire, thanking God that he had thought to make it big this morning, and then closed his eyes. Everytime the pain in his belly woke him with a spasm of hurt he turned his eye towards the door. If Suckahanna did not come again with food, with water, and with herbs to heal his burned hand, John thought he would probably die there, lying before a dying fire, bare-arsed, sick as a dog, and with one worthless and perhaps poisoned hand, and nothing fit to eat.

She did not come. When dusk fell John crawled to the door and pushed it shut, fearful of the night creatures. If the wolves came closer tonight it would be only the closed door that would keep them from him, and they could break that down with one spring. John himself did not have the strength to load his gun. He felt himself sweating into his cloak and then a wet sensation and a terrible stench which meant that he had emptied his bowels again. He could do nothing but lie in his own filth. Some time in the night he was sick on the floor, the vomit spreading in a pool around him, and then the smell of it made him sick again but he brought up only burning bile from his empty belly. He hauled himself up on one elbow and put more wood on the fire. Then he slept.

He woke in the morning, aching all over and shivering as if he had an ague. His hand was throbbing and the fingers were turning black. The house stank like a kennel and his cloak was stuck to his back by a dried pelt of excrement. He crawled to the door and opened it, kicking the cloak off his back as he went. His skin was raw and sore and his sight kept coming and going, the open door a wavering oblong of gold and green light.

There was a black earthenware pot of clean water on the doorstep, and another pot beside it of warm corn porridge. John heard his sore throat give a little sob of gratitude. He drew the pot of water towards him and sipped it cautiously. His stomach rumbled but the dreadful spasms of pain had passed. He pulled himself round to sit on the doorstep and lifted the pot of porridge to his lips. It was not porridge as he made it, in his dirty scorched cooking pot. It was light, faintly scented with herbs, as yellow as blanchemange, flavoured with something like saffron. John took a cautious sip and, despite a growl of hunger from his belly, made himself wait, sip water, pause. Then he took another.

Cautiously, eating so slowly, that his breakfast took most of the morning, John ate the porridge from the pot and drank most of the water. An hour later, he found he could stand without fainting. Warily, he pulled himself up the doorframe and bundled his stinking cloak out of the house. A row of cleared and dug earth extended along the front of the house, from the point where John had thrown one blow of the pickaxe to where it ended, neatly squared, before the door. John looked at it and then rubbed his eyes as if it were a dream, a dream from fever and from his sickness.

No. It was real. She had come in the night and cleared a row of earth for him to plant his seeds. She had come and seen his sickness and realised that he had eaten too fast and put himself at the very door of death through his own greed and stupidity, and she had left him, not a little feast, but a thin meal of gruel and water, so that he would get well again. She was keeping him as if he were a child, choosing his food for him, doing his work for him. John felt ready to weep for gratitude that she was prepared to give him food, fetch his water, do his work. But he knew also a sharp, contrasting discomfort that she should see him so unmanned, that she had seen he could do nothing in this new land, not even survive.

'Suckahanna?' he whispered.

Still there was no reply, just the calling of birds, and the quacking of ducks in the river.

John gathered his foul cloak and hobbled down to the river to soak it in his washing place, and lowered himself into the cold water to try to get clean. Again he laboured up the slight slope to his house, lugging the wet cloth, his feet tender on the stones of his field. His hand was sore, his head thudding, his stomach quiveringly tender. 'I cannot survive here,' John said as he reached his door after a long, arduous struggle up the little hill. 'I must find a way to get downriver to Bertram, I will die here.'

He wondered for a moment if he should wait for her, if he were to lie before the fire whether she might come and live with him, as they had planned. But he was warned by the cautious way she had approached him. He could not count on her to rescue him. He must help himself. 'I shall go downriver to Bertram,' he said. 'If she wants to come to me she will know how to find me there.'

His breeches and his shirt at least were clean and dry. It took him a long time to pull them on. His boots went on with a struggle which left him panting for breath, and he bent over to ease the swimming of his head. He did not take his gun for he could not load it nor keep the fuse lit in the canoe. There was nothing else that he could carry. This new country which he had been certain would make him rich had made him poorer than a pauper. All he could carry were the clothes that he stood up in, all he could manage to do was to stagger like a drunkard down the hill to where the canoe was pulled up, out of reach of the tide.

He thought for a little while that he would never get it down the small beach and into the deep water. He pushed for a while and it moved no more than an inch. Then he had to rest, and then he had to push again. It was a process that took most of his strength and courage. When the canoe finally rocked in the water he could hardly find the energy to climb in. He thought that his weight had grounded it, but when he took the paddle in his one good hand he managed to lift the weight a little and the canoe slid into the middle of the river into the deeper water.

The tide was on the ebb and the current of the river was flowing seaward. The canoe picked up speed. John tried to use the paddle to steer it closer to the bank but with one hand he could not control it. He thrust the paddle into the water and the canoe spun around it; in a second he would be swamped and the canoe would sink. He made one desperate shove, pointed it downriver, and then clung to the side as it bucked and weaved in the fast current, shaking as it tumbled in the white water. John looked at the bank which seemed to be tearing past him. Nothing seemed familiar though he and Bertram had watched carefully, pointing out landmarks, so that he would be able to make this journey, so Bertram would know when he was nearing John's head-right. He thought he recognised a tall single pine with its roots extending deep into the water, and he dug the paddle in again, trying to turn the canoe towards the shore. The current snatched the paddle, John lunged to grab it back, and then the paddle was flicked like kindling from his hand and the canoe was turning and turning in the dizzying flood and John could neither steer it nor control it, nor do anything but duck down on the wet floor of the canoe and give himself up for lost.

John opened his eyes. Above him was a high, rounded roof made of lashed branches, and thatched with broad leaves. He was lying on some sort of bedstead made of branches spread with mats. He turned his head, half-expecting to see the familiar face of Bertram Hobert or Sarah's restrained smile. The place was empty.

It was not a house built by a normal Englishman, that at least was clear. It was a domed-ceilinged square hut, roofed and walled with leaves, floored with woven mats and deerskins spread on the earth. In the centre of the hut was a small fire with a tiny heart of red which kept the hut warm and filled it with light, acrid smoke. On the walls were hung the skins of animals, and a basket half-woven, and other baskets bulging with goods. The only light filtered in through the hole in the roof above the fire, and flickered at the skins which curtained the door. John swung his feet down to the floor and took two cautious steps to go out.

At once a brown-skinned child popped his head inside the room, took one look at John standing, and, without moving, without taking his eyes from the Englishman, opened his mouth and let out a yell. John froze to the spot, heard running footsteps and then a woman stood behind the child, her hand on his shoulder, and another woman behind her, poised with a bow raised and an arrow on the string.

John dropped to sit on the bed, spread his hands, tried to smile.

'Hello,' he said. He nodded, trying to look reassuring, peaceable. 'Hello.'

The two women nodded in reply, saying nothing. Remembering the weeks of silence from Suckahanna, John did not make the assumption that they could not understand him, although their eyes remained blank and black.

'Thank you for bringing me here. The canoe was too strong for me. I was trying to get to my friend's house – Bertram Hobert – but the current swept me away.'

Again they nodded, saying nothing.

'Is Jamestown anywhere near here?' John asked. He wondered if he had been swept far below the town, down to the edge of the sea perhaps. 'Jamestown? Anywhere near? Jamestown?'

The woman with the arrow on the string smiled briefly. 'Nowhere near,' she said. She spoke with a strange Welsh lilt to her voice.

'You speak English!' John exclaimed.

She did not nod or smile, nor did she release the tension on the bowstring.

'I am a peaceful man,' John said. 'I was trying to farm outside my house, on my land beside the river. I went hungry, and I burned my hand. I was going to find my friend to get help. I am a peaceful man. I am looking for an Indian girl, an Indian woman. Suckahanna.'

Neither of the women responded to the name.

'I want to make her my wife,' John said, plunging in. 'If she will have me. I have come back to Virginia –' He broke off. It occurred to him that perhaps in their ignorance they did not know the name of their country. 'I have come back here, from my home, to be with her.'

'Suckahanna is married to my brother,' the woman with the bow on the string said precisely. 'He went with her when she took her gifts of food to you. We did not realise that you would eat it all at once – like a pig with acorns. We did not mean to make you sick.'

John felt embarrassment burn under the skin of his face. 'I was foolish,' he said. 'I was very hungry.' The thought of these people discussing his greed, and perhaps watching him void himself and retch, made him want to close his eyes and be anywhere else, even back in his own little house facing death, rather than here with the woman looking at him in mild curiosity.

'Why did Suckahanna not show herself?' he asked. 'I would be her friend now she has a husband.' He looked at the arrow on the string again. 'I never wronged her,' he said hastily. 'I wanted to marry her when I thought she was a maid.'

The woman's face did not soften. John thought in sudden, rapid terror that perhaps they had saved him for some dreadful execution. There were stories in Jamestown of men having their bellies cut open and their guts dragged out before their eyes. 'I meant her no harm,' John said. 'I meant none of you any harm.'

'Your house is where we hunt,' the other woman observed. 'You have frightened away the game birds and the deer are making other paths in the woods to get away from your burned field and the smell of you.'

'I am sorry,' John said again. He thought of the governor's map and the empty spaces of forest unmarked by any names. 'I thought the forest was empty.'

They looked at him as if his words were simply incomprehensible. 'Empty?'

'Empty of people,' John corrected himself. 'I knew there were animals living there. But I did not think it was your land.'

'The animals do not own the land,' the woman with the arrow pointed at his body said slowly, as if she were trying to understand some alien logic.

'No,' John agreed.

'But you know they are there, they pass through the forest.'

'Yes.'

'We pass through the forest too, we follow them when we hunt them, we clear land for a season to grow our food. How can land be empty?'

John swallowed on a dry throat, his head thudded sharply. 'It is how we white men speak,' he said helplessly.

The woman with the bow nodded, the arrow still pointing at his belly. 'You people said you would come here for just a little while, look for precious metal and then go,' she observed. 'Now you tell us that the land is empty and you build your houses on the game trails and fell the trees of the forests and never let them grow again.'

'I am sorry,' John said. 'We did not know that you were living here. If you would help me to get to Jamestown I could tell the governor . . .'

He trailed off. Suddenly she turned the arrow away from him as if she had lost interest in the whole conversation. 'We will decide what is to be done with you when the men come home,' she said abruptly. 'Stay here till then.'

John spread his hands, trying to indicate his obedience and harmlessness.

'The child will bring you something to eat,' the other woman said. 'Do not shit in here. You must go to the forest for that.'

John felt his face burn scarlet and cursed himself for a fool to be so ashamed for having diarrhoea when he could be facing disembowelling.

'Of course not,' he said, clinging to his dignity.

The woman looked at him. 'We all saw you,' she said. 'But we are clean. We are the People, the Powhatan. You must do your dirt in the forest while you are with us, and cover it up after.'

'I will,' John said. 'I am thirsty.'

'The child will bring you food and drink,' the other woman said. She slid her arrow into a quiver strapped to her side. 'Don't gorge yourself.'

'And Suckahanna? Is she here?' John tried to ask the question with a calm, neutral voice but his head hammered again at the thought of her.

They looked at him indifferently, and then they turned and went out.

The child brought a pot filled with icy cold water. John sipped at it carefully. The pot was coal-black, as smooth as marble in his hands. He could not think how it had been made, it was as elegant as a funerary urn in the king's collection.

He waited. The child, he could not even tell if it were a boy or a girl, wearing an apron of buckskin but otherwise naked, squatted in the doorway of the hut and regarded him with solemn dark eyes. John tried to smile. The child's face was grave. John leaned back against the wall of the hut and waited.

He could see the shadows lengthen in the little square of the doorway, and then he heard the sound of singing from far away. From the child's silent alertness he guessed that it had heard them some minutes ago. John looked at the child and raised his eyebrows as if to ask what might be happening. The child was solemn as a warrior, and like a powerful warrior merely shook its head.

John leaned back again and waited.

The chorus of singing came nearer. John listened more intently. He was sure, he was certain, he could hear Suckahanna's voice. Reason told him that it was not possible, that he had heard her speak only once or twice, that he surely could not hear her voice among many; but still he felt his heart pound and still he leaned forwards, his ears aching with the effort to hear more clearly.

'Suckahanna?' he whispered.

The child, recognising the name, nodded, and then made a simple, graceful gesture to the door, and she was there, framed by the golden evening light, taller than he remembered, her face a little graver, her hair grown on both sides of her head but still braided away from her face on the right-hand side, wearing buckskin leggings and a little buckskin dress, and her arms and cheeks painted with red spirals.

'Suckahanna!' he said.

She stood before him and looked him over, unsmiling, and then she drew a little closer and put out her hand. John, hesitating, not knowing what he should do, put out his hand in reply, and then, as solemn as Parliament men, they shook.

Her fingers, warm and dry, closed on his and John felt an extraordinary sense of desire at that light touch. His eyes went to her face and he saw, only half-believing, the slow smile spread from her eyes to her lips till her whole face was lightened and joyful.

'John,' she said sweetly, her accent lilting on his name. 'Welcome to my people.'

At once he stumbled into explanations. 'I meant to come, I meant to come when I said. I didn't plan to betray you. It was my intention to come to you. But when I got home my father was dead and my children needed a mother –' He broke off as he saw her shake her head and shrug.

'I knew you meant to come,' she said. 'But when you did not come my mother and I had to leave Jamestown and find our people. And then it was time that I should be married, and so now I am married.'

John would have withdrawn his hand but she held him fast. 'This is my son,' she said with a smile to the child in the doorway.

'Your son!'

'The son of my husband. His first wife died and I am now mother to this boy, and I have a girl-child of my own.'

John felt regret wash over him as painful as sickness. 'I never thought –'

'Yes, I am a woman grown,' she said steadily.

John shook his head as if he would deny the passing of the years. 'I should have come. I meant to come.'

'Your hand is hurt? And you have been sick?'

'The sickness was my own fault,' John said. 'I went hungry for too long and then ate the eggs you sent me – was it you?'

She nodded.

'They were so good. But I ate them too fast. And I burned my hand on the cooking pot and then the wound broke open . . .'

She took his hand and bent her head over it to see the wound. John looked at the crown of her dark head and smelled the faint, familiar smell of her warm skin and the bear-grease fat which deterred insects, and felt desire spread through him until he thought he must draw her close, and that whatever it cost him, he must hold her in his arms, just once, before he died.

She looked up and at once recognised the desire in his face. She did not flinch back as an Englishwoman would have done. But she did not come forward either. She stood very still and steadily took him in, reading his desire, his fear, his need.

'I think we can heal the wound on your hand,' she said gently. 'Come.'

The little boy at the doorway stepped aside for the two of them and Suckahanna led John out of the hut into the evening light.

John blinked. He was in the centre of a town square, all around were other long huts, built of wood, and walled with reeds, intricately woven. Each hut had a little spiral of scented smoke above its roof, and a flock of children playing in the doorway. In the centre of the square sat a handful of men, at their ease, talking in low, confident voices, one of them tightening a bow string, another sharpening reeds for arrow tips. They glanced up as Suckahanna led John by, but they made no comment, nor even acknowledged his presence. They took him in, as one animal takes in another. They saw in one devouring glance the way he walked, the prints his boots made on the ground, the scent of him, the matted, ill-kept hair and the pallor of sickness. They assessed his ability to fight, to run, to hide. They sensed his fear of them and his trust in Suckahanna. Then they turned back to their work and their talk as if there was nothing to be said about him or to him – as yet.

Suckahanna led him towards a little street with the houses set on either side. At the end of it was a large fire and half a dozen of the black pots sitting squat among the embers, and skewers of meat resting on a rack. John felt his stomach clench in hunger but Suckahanna took him past the food to a hut opposite the fire.

She stood outside and called a word, perhaps a name, and the curtain in the doorway opened and an old woman looked out.

'Suckahanna!'

'Musses.'

The woman spoke in a rapid flow of language, and Suckahanna replied. Something that she said made the old woman snort with laughter and she shot a quick smiling look at John as if he were the butt of the joke. Then she stretched out her hand to see the burn on John's palm.

Suckahanna gestured that he should show her. 'This is a wise woman, she will cure the wound.'

Hesitantly, John opened his fingers to show the scar. It was getting worse. Where the blister had burst the raw flesh had got dirty and was now smelling and oozing. John looked at it fearfully. If he had such a wound in London he thought that a barber surgeon would have cut the hand off, to prevent the infection spreading up his arm to his heart. He feared the infection only slightly less than he feared these savages and whatever treatment they might prescribe.

The woman said something to Suckahanna and Suckahanna laughed, a spontaneous giggle, like the girl John had known. She turned to John.

'She says you should be purged, but I told her you had already done that for yourself.'

The woman was laughing, Suckahanna was smiling, but John, in fear and in pain, could muster only a grim nod.

'But she says you should still sweat out your illness before we cure the wound.'

'Sweat?'

'In a –' Suckahanna did not know the English word. 'Little house. In a little house.'

The woman nodded.

'We'll go there now,' Suckahanna said. 'Then we can get the herbs for the wound before nightfall.'

The woman and Suckahanna led him to the boundary of the village. There was a smaller round hut on the very edge of the little town, its roof at ground level, and thick smoke billowing out from the hole in the centre of the roof.

'It's very hot,' Suckahanna explained.

John nodded, it looked like hell.

Suckahanna laid a gentle hand on his dirty shirt. 'You must take off your clothes,' she said. 'All of them, and go down into there, naked.'

Instinctively, John's hands gripped the belt of his breeches and then he gave a little yelp of pain at the touch of the cloth on his raw palm.

'There!' Suckahanna said, as if that proved the point. 'Take your clothes off and go down into the little house.'

Reluctantly, John pulled his shirt off. The old woman regarded his pale skin with interest, as if he were a ham ready for smoking. John shot a swift, frightened look at the little house.

'Suckahanna – am I to be killed?' he asked. 'I would rather die with my breeches on.'

She did not laugh at his fears. She shook her head. 'I would not lead you to your death,' she said simply. 'I kept you safe in the woods for a month, didn't I? And then I told you that I loved you. Nothing has changed.'

It was like that easy rush of desire that he had felt when he met her. All at once he trusted her. He untied the laces of his breeches and dropped them to the floor. He heel-toed out of his boots and shucked off his stinking stockings. He stood before the two of them naked and felt his genitals shrivel at the curious, bright gaze of the old woman and Suckahanna's evident lack of interest.

'Go down in there,' she said, gesturing to the steps which led down into the smoke-filled darkness. 'There is a bed. Lie down. You will be hot, you will sweat like a fever. When Musses calls you, you can come out. Not before.'

John took one step towards the hut and hesitated. Suckahanna's familiar hard little hand pushed him in the small of the back. 'Go on,' she said insistently. 'You always are thinking, John. Just do.'

He smiled at the truth of that and went down the steps in a little rush of temporary courage, and pitched headlong into the darkness.

The hut was filled with acrid herbal smoke and the heat was intense. He understood now that the hut was set deep like a cellar so that the very earth was like an oven, holding the heat inside. At the very centre of the hut was a small fireplace heaped with red embers, and a jar of dried leaves beside it. There was room for a little bench of stones which were so hot to the touch that John had to sit gingerly, and let his skin become accustomed to their warmth.

'Put the pot of herbs on the fire!' Suckahanna called from the outside.

Reluctantly, John poured the dried leaves on to the fire. At once the hut was filled with a billow of black smoke which sucked the very air out of his lungs and left him choking and whooping for breath. The smoke felled him, like a helpless tree, so he stretched out along the stones and felt his eyes run with tears against the acrid fumes. His nose hurt with the heat, the very coils inside his ears ached with the intense heat and the airless, powerful scent. He felt himself drifting into an extraordinary dream state. He saw Frances with a trowel and a watering pot in the garden of Lambeth, he saw the Duke of Buckingham throw back his dark head and laugh, he saw Johnnie at the moment of his birth, scarlet, wet and squalling, he saw Jane smiling through the candlelight on their wedding night. He saw his father dying in a bed of flowers, he saw the Rosamund roses he had sent down the river for Jane's memorial service at her father's chapel.

From far, far away he heard a voice call something in a strange language and he opened his eyes. The smoke had cleared a little, the heat seemed less intense. His skin was pink, like a baby's. He was damp all over with sweat and his skin was smooth as a sun-warmed lizard.

'She says you can come out!' he heard in English. But it was not the command but the sound of Suckahanna's voice which brought him from his daze, up the steps and out into the sunlight.

'Ah,' the old woman said with pleasure at his appearance. She nodded at Suckahanna, and then tossed a buckskin cape around John's shoulders to keep the chill of the evening air from him.

John looked around for his clothes. Everything was gone except his boots. Suckahanna was standing among a small group of women, they were all looking at his nakedness with a cheerful curiosity.

Suckahanna stepped forward and held out a bundle of clothing to him. As John took it he saw that it was a clout – a piece of cloth to twist between his buttocks and tie on a strap around his waist – a deerskin kilt and a deerskin shirt. He recoiled. 'Where are my clothes?'

Suckahanna shook her head firmly. 'They smelled,' she said. 'And they had lice and fleas. We are a clean people. You could not wear those clothes in our houses.'

He felt ashamed and unable to argue.

'Put those on,' she said. 'We are all waiting for you.'

He tied the strings of the clout around his waist and felt better with his nakedness hidden from so many bright black eyes. 'Why are they all here?'

'To find the herb for your hand,' she said.

John looked down into his palm. The wound was cleaner from the sweating, but there was still a crease of rotting flesh at its centre.

He pulled on the shirt and straightened the kilt. He thought that he must look absurd with his big white legs under this beautifully embroidered skirt and then his own heavy boots on his feet; but none of the women laughed. They moved off, one trotting behind another, with the old woman at the front and Suckahanna at the rear. She glanced back at John. 'Follow,' was all she said.

He remembered then the unbearable steady pace she would use when they were in the woods together. All the women moved at that remorseless trot which was too fast for him to walk and too slow for him to run. He walked and then ran after them in short, breathless bursts and Suckahanna never turned her head to see if he could keep up, but just kept her own steady pace as if there were neither thorns nor stones under her light moccasins.

The old woman in the front was running and watching the plants on either side of the path. John recognised a master plantswoman when she stopped and pointed a little way into the wood. She had spotted the one she wanted, at a run, in the twilight. John peered at it. It looked like a liverwort, but a form that he had never seen before.

'Wait here,' Suckahanna ordered him and followed the other women as they went towards it. They seated themselves down in a circle around it and they were silent for a moment, as if in prayer. John felt a strange prickling on the back of his neck as if something powerful and mysterious was happening. The women held out their hands over the plant as if they were checking the heat over a cooking pot, and then their hands made weaving gestures, one to another, above and around the plant in a constant pattern. They were humming softly, and then the words of a song emerged, softly chanted.

The darkness under the trees grew more intense; John realised that the sun had set and in the upper branches of the trees there was a continual rustle and chirping and cooing of birds settling down for the night. On the forest floor the women continued to sing and then the old woman leaned forwards and picked a sprig of the herb, and then the others followed suit.

John shifted restlessly from one sore foot to another. The women rose to their feet and came towards him, each chewing on the herb. John waited, in case he too had to eat it, but they walked around him in a circle. Suckahanna stopped first and gestured that he should hold out his hand. John opened his fingers and Suckahanna bent her mouth to his palm and gently spat the chewed herb into the wound. John cried out as the juice accurately hit the very centre of the rotting flesh, but he could not pull his hand away because she was holding it tight. The other women pressed around him and each spat, as hard and as accurately as a London urchin, so that the chewed juice from the herb did not rest on the wound but penetrated deep inside. John yelped a little at each blow as he felt the astringent juice entering the rotting flesh. The old woman came last and John braced himself. He was right to think that her spit would be as hard as a musket ball, right into the very centre of his damaged palm. As he cried out she whipped out a leather binding from the pocket of her apron, spread a leaf on top of the wound and tied it tight.

John was half-dizzy from the pain and Suckahanna ducked under his arm and supported him as they walked back to the village.

It was growing dark. The women turned off to their own huts, to the cooking fire. The men were already seated, awaiting their dinner. Suckahanna raised a hand in greeting to one of the men who solemnly watched her supporting John back to the hut. They went through the doorway entwined like lovers and she helped him lie down on the wooden bed.

'Sleep,' she said gently to him. 'Tomorrow you will be better.'

'I want you,' John said, his mind hazed with pain, with the smoke, with desire. 'I want you to lie with me.'

She laughed, a low amused laugh. 'I am married,' she reminded him. 'And you are ill. Sleep now. I shall be here in the morning.'

Spring 1643, England

On a cold day in spring, Alexander Norman took a boat upriver, disembarked north of Lambeth and strolled through the fields to the Ark. Frances, glancing idly from her bedroom window, saw the tall figure coming towards the house and dived back into her room to comb her hair, straighten her gown, and rip off her apron. She was downstairs in time to open the front door to him, and to send the maid running out into the yard to look for Hester and to tell her that Mr Norman was come for a visit.

He smiled very kindly at her. 'You look lovely,' he said simply. 'Every time I see you, you have grown prettier. How old are you now? Fifteen?'

Frances cast down her eyes in her most modest gesture and wished that she could blush. She thought for a moment that she should lay claim to fifteen years, but then she remembered that a birthday invariably meant a present. 'I'm fifteen in five months' time,' she said. 'October the seventh.' Without lifting her gaze, modestly directed to the toes of her boots, she could see his hand moving towards the flap on his deep coat pocket.

'I brought you these,' he said. 'Some little fairings.'

They were very far from little fairings. They were three large bundles of ribbon of a deep scarlet silk shot through with gold thread. There would be enough to trim a gown and make ties for Frances's light brown hair. Despite the shortages of the war, the fashion was still for gowns with sleeves elaborately slashed and trimmed, and Frances had a genuine need as well as a passion for ribbon.

Without taking his eyes from her absorbed face, Alexander Norman said: 'You do love beautiful things, don't you, Frances?' and was rewarded by a look of complete honesty, empty of all coquetry, when she looked up and said: 'Oh, of course! Because of my grandfather! I have had beautiful things around me all my life.'

'Cousin Norman,' Hester said pleasantly, coming into the hall from the kitchen door. 'What a pleasure to see you, and on such a cold day. Did you come by the river?'

'Yes,' he said. He let her help him off with his greatcoat and gave it to Frances to take to the kitchen to warm it through, and to order some hot ale. 'I would not trust the roads these days.'

She shook her head. 'Lambeth is quiet enough now that the archbishop's palace is empty,' she said. 'All the apprentice lads are exhausted with their drilling and their mustering and digging the fortifications. They have no stomach left for roaming around the streets and making trouble for their betters.'

She led the way into the family sitting room. Johnnie was seated before a small fire, writing out plant labels with painstaking care. 'Uncle Norman!' he exclaimed and leaped up from his place. Alexander Norman greeted him with a brisk hug and then dived once again into his pocket.

'I have given your sister half a mile of silk ribbon, should you like the same to edge your suit?' he asked.

'No, sir, that is, not if you have anything else . . . that is, I should be very grateful for anything you bring me . . .'

Alexander laughed. 'I have a wicked little toy here which one of the armourers made at the Tower. But you must promise me to only behead dead roses.'

From his pocket he drew a small knife which folded cunningly, like a barber's razor, so the sharp blade was hidden and safe. 'Do you permit, Mrs Tradescant?' Alexander asked. 'If he promises he will take care of his fingers?'

Hester smiled. 'I should like to have the courage to say no,' she said. 'You may have it, Johnnie, but Cousin Norman must show you how to handle it and see that you are safe with it before he leaves us today.'

'Can I carve things with it?'

Alexander nodded. 'We'll set to work as soon as I have drunk my ale and told your mother the news from town.'

'Wooden whistles? And toys?'

'We'll start with something easier. Go and ask them in the kitchen for a cake of soap. We'll work our way up to wood.' The boy nodded, put the cork carefully back in his pot of ink and carried the tray of labels out of the way, and then went from the room. Frances came in and set down a cup of ale before her uncle and then took up some sewing and sat in the windowseat. Hester, glancing across the room, thought that her stepdaughter could have been sitting for a portrait entitled 'Beauty and the Domestic Arts' as she bent her brown head over her work. A swift glance from Frances's bright eyes warned her that the girl was perfectly aware of the enchanting picture she made.

'Any news?' Hester asked.

Alexander Norman nodded. 'You've heard the news of Birmingham?'

Hester glanced towards Frances. 'We won't speak of it now. I heard enough.'

Alexander shook his head. 'Dreadful doings. Prince Rupert lost control of his men altogether.'

Hester nodded. 'And I heard that the king holds the whole of the west country.'

Alexander Norman nodded. 'He's lost the navy but he holds many of the ports. And they face France, so he can land a French army if the queen's promises are fulfilled.'

Hester nodded. 'And no-one is marching on London?'

Alexander Norman gave a small shrug. 'Not that I've heard, but this month alone there have been skirmishes all over the country.'

'Nothing close?'

Alexander Norman leaned forwards and put his hand over Hester's tightly gripping fingers. 'Peace, cousin,' he said gently. 'Nothing close. You know I would warn you the moment I heard of any danger to your little Ark. You and your precious cargo will come safe through this storm.'

He glanced over to the windowseat. 'Frances, would you fetch me another glass of ale?' he asked.

She rose at once and went to the door. 'And give me a moment alone with your stepmother,' he said smoothly. 'I want her advice on a private matter.'

Frances glanced at Hester to see if she demurred, and when Hester gave the smallest of nods Frances slightly raised her eyebrows in a tiny expression of sheer impudent speculation and left the room, closing the door behind her.

'She's impertinent,' Hester said as the door shut. 'But it's only lightness of spirit.'

'I know it,' Alexander Norman agreed with her. 'And I would not see her subdued. She's very like her mother. She was a light-hearted girl but her spirits were kept much in check by her strong sense of religion, and her strict upbringing. But Frances was spoiled from the moment she was born by John and by them all. It's too late to try to weigh her down now, I would rather see her soar.'

Hester smiled. 'I feel that too,' she said. 'Though it falls to me to try to keep her in check.'

'You worry about her safety?'

'I do. I worry for all of us, of course, and for the treasures. But mostly for Frances. She is at an age when she should be venturing out a little more, going into society, to make friends; but she is cooped up here with me and with her brother. The plague is everywhere again this year so I cannot let her stay with her grandparents in the City – and besides they are not sociable people, they meet no-one.'

'She could go to court at Oxford . . .'

Hester's face was a picture. 'I'd as soon throw her into the lion's cage at the Tower than send her among that crowd. Everything that was bad about the king's court when they were properly housed and properly served is ten times worse now they are crowded into Oxford and drunk nine nights out of ten with celebrating victories.'

'I've been thinking the same,' Alexander said. 'I wondered if you would consider me . . . I wondered if you would let me offer her – and yourself of course – a safe haven. I wondered if you would leave here, shut the Ark up until the end of the war, and come and live with me at the Tower of London: the safest place in the whole of the kingdom.'

When she said nothing he added, very quietly, 'I mean marriage, Hester.'

She went quite pale for a moment, and moved her chair back from his a little.

'You did not expect this? Though I have been such a frequent visitor?'

Mutely, she shook her head. 'I thought it was just kindness for Mr Tradescant's family,' she said softly. 'As a family friend, as a relation.'

'It was more.'

She shook her head. 'I am a married woman,' she said. 'I do not consider myself deserted or widowed. Until I hear from John that he is not coming home ever again I shall bear myself as his wife.' For a moment she looked at him as if she were pleading with him to disagree with her. 'You may think he has left us forever, but I am sure he will come home. There are his children, there are the rarities, there is the garden. He would never abandon the Tradescant inheritance.'

Alexander did not answer, his face was very grave.

'He would never abandon us,' she said again but with less certainty. 'Would he?'

Before he could answer she rose from the chair and went quickly over to the window with her light, determined step. 'And if you are thinking that he will die over there, and never return, I must tell you that I would still think it my duty to stay here and guard the house and the garden for Johnnie to inherit when he is a man. I promised John's father that I would keep the place and the children safe. Nothing would release me from that promise.'

'You have misunderstood me,' he burst out. 'I am so sorry. I was not proposing marriage to you.'

She turned at that. The light of the window was behind her and he could not clearly see her face. 'What?'

'I was thinking of Frances.'

'You were proposing marriage to Frances?'

The incredulity in her voice made him wince. Dumbly, he nodded.

'But you are fifty-five!'

'I am fifty-three.'

'And she's a child.'

'She is a young woman, and she is ready for marriage, and these are dangerous and difficult times.'

Hester was silenced, then she turned away from him. He saw her shoulder hunch slightly, as if she were protecting herself from insult. 'I beg your pardon. You must think me a complete fool.'

He took three swift steps across the room and turned her around, held her at arms' length so that he could see her face. 'I think of you, as I have long thought of you, as one of the most courageous and lovable women that I have ever met. But I know John will come home to you, and I know that you have loved him ever since you were married. I think of you now as I will always think of you, as a dear, dear friend.'

Hester looked away, wretched with embarrassment. 'I thank you,' she whispered. 'Please let me go.'

'It was my own shyness and stupidity in what I said that led you to misunderstand me,' he said determinedly. 'Please, don't be angry with me, or angry with yourself.'

She twisted from his hold. 'I feel that I have been a fool!' she exclaimed. 'Refusing a proposal which wasn't being made to me. And you are a fool too!' She suddenly regained her spirits. 'Thinking that you could marry a girl who is hardly out of her short clothes.'

He went for the door. 'I'll take a turn in the garden, if I may,' he said. 'And we'll talk again later.'

He went out without another word and Hester, looking from the window, saw him walk along the terrace on the south side of the house and down the steps into the garden.

The garden was at its mid-May perfection. In the walled fruit garden he could not see the sky for the mass of pink and white blossom, as thick as rose-sugared cream on a pudding. In the long walks in the flower gardens the daffodils and tulips were a wash of colour, red and gold and white. The chestnut avenue was coming into its height of beauty, the blossoms opening up into thick candles, white delicately marked with pink. On the walls on the right-hand side of the garden the espaliered figs and peaches and cherries were already weighted with blossom, showering petals on the flower beds beneath them like unseasonal snow.

The parlour door behind Hester opened and Frances came in with Alexander's glass of ale. 'Has he gone?'

'You can perfectly well see that he has,' Hester snapped.

Frances put down the glass without spilling a drop and turned to examine her stepmother's cross face.

'What did he do to upset you?' she asked calmly.

'He said something ridiculous, and I thought something ridiculous and I feel . . . I feel . . .'

'Ridiculous?' Frances suggested, and was rewarded with a glare of irritation.

Hester turned away from her and looked out of the window again. In the thick window pane she could see, simultaneously, Alexander strolling in the garden and the reflection of her own face. She looked grim. She looked like a woman struggling under the weight of many worries, and still fighting them.

'What did he say that was so ridiculous?' Frances asked gently. She came beside her stepmother and slipped her arm around the older woman's waist. Hester saw that smooth prettiness beside her own worn face and felt a deep pang of envy that her own beauty was past, and at the same time a glow of joy that she had brought that unloved, frightened little girl into this rare, beautiful being.

'He said that you were a young woman grown,' Hester said. She felt Frances at her side. The girl was a girl no longer, her breasts were filling out, the curve of her waist would fit a man's hand, she had lost her coltish legginess, she was, as Alexander had seen but her stepmother had not, a young woman.

'Well, I am,' Frances said, as one stating the obvious.

'He said you should be married,' Hester said.

'And so I shall be, I suppose.'

'He thought sooner rather than later,' Hester said. 'Because these are dangerous times. He thinks you should have a husband to take care of you.' She had thought that Frances would pull away and laugh her reckless laugh. But the girl rested her head on her stepmother's shoulder and said thoughtfully: 'You know, I think I would like that.'

Hester pulled back to look at Frances. 'You still seem like a little girl to me.'

'But I am a young woman,' Frances pointed out. 'And when I go into Lambeth the men shout at me, and call things to me. If Father were at home then it would be different, but he is not home, and he is not coming home, is he?'

Hester shook her head. 'I have no news of him.'

'Then if he does not come home, and if the war goes on, and so everything is still so uneasy . . .'

'Yes?' Hester asked.

'If our lives don't get easier then I would like a husband to care for me, and to care for you and Johnnie. I think we need a man in this house. I think we need a man to care for us.'

There was a long silence. Hester looked into the beautiful face of her stepdaughter and thought that perhaps the first of her promises to this girl's grandfather, John Tradescant, was nearly fulfilled. She had brought up his granddaughter to be a beautiful woman and within a year or two there would only be Johnnie and the treasures for her to guard.

Alexander Norman strolled in the grounds for an hour before he came in to dinner. He found Hester laying the table in the parlour with Frances helping her. Johnnie was showing a visitor around the rarities.

'I think I made a sale for you,' he said informally as he came in the door. Hester glanced up at his entrance and was relieved to see his familiar, reassuring smile. 'A young man from Kent, enquiring about fruit trees. I spoke warmly about John's plums and handed him over to your gardener. I left him writing down an order for a score of trees and being paid in gold.'

Frances laughed and clapped her hands. 'Excellent, Uncle Norman! Now all we have to do is to teach you to weed and you shall come and work for us every day.'

'Twenty trees is a very good sale,' Hester agreed. 'Especially in these times, when no-one can put their mind to gardening. You did say that he had to arrange his own transport?'

'I did. I know you can't undertake delivery.'

'If we had anyone we could spare I still wouldn't send them. I can't risk losing my horse and cart.' Hester turned to Frances. 'Fetch Johnnie, and tell Cook that she can serve dinner.'

Frances nodded and went out of the room.

Alexander held out his hand. 'Am I forgiven for my stupidity?'

Hester took his hand. 'And you must forgive me. It's a curiously uncomfortable mistake for a woman to make. If I'd had more experience I would have known how a man usually proposes to a woman.'

He smiled at her and did not release her hand for a moment. 'And the matter of Frances's future?'

Hester shook her head and withdrew her hand. 'She's too young yet,' she said stubbornly. 'Ask again in a year or two. I must warn you I would rather see her with a young husband in a little house of her own, starting her own life.'

He nodded. 'I understand. But young men are not safe choices these days. Whether he's a royalist or for Parliament he's likely to be called to serve his master, and there are no little houses where young people can be sure that they will be left to live at peace in this kingdom any more.'

'When the war ends . . .'

'When the war ends we shall know whether she should look for a husband at Parliament or at court. But what if it trails on for years? I tell you, cousin, there are stores in the Tower promised to the Parliament army, and stores to match that in royalist hands enough to keep this war going for another twenty years. Parliament is not likely to surrender – that would be to sign their own death warrants for treason – and the king is not a man to come to terms with them.'

Hester nodded. For a moment she looked haggard with worry. 'If she is in any danger I shall send her to you,' she promised. 'I know you would take care of her.'

Alexander gave a small formal bow. 'I would lay down my life for her,' he said simply. 'And I love her so much that I would put her interests before mine. If they make peace, or if she falls in love with a man of her own age who could keep her safe, I will not stand in her way, nor even remind you of this conversation.'

🌹

A few days after Alexander Norman's visit Hester, glancing out of the window, saw a stranger slip around the corner of the house and head for the kitchen door. She got up from the hearth, took off her rough hessian apron, and went to see what he wanted.

He was standing on the back doorstep. 'Mrs John Tradescant?' he asked.

The hair on the back of Hester's neck prickled. 'Yes,' she said levelly. 'And who is asking?'

He slipped in around the doorframe, so that he was in the kitchen. 'Shut the door,' he whispered.

Hester did not make a move to obey him. 'There is a stout man in my employ within earshot,' she said. 'And half the neighbourhood would come running down the road if I called. You had better tell me your business, and swiftly.'

'Not my business. The king's.'

Hester felt dismay like a blow in the belly. Slowly, she shut the door. 'Come in,' she said, and led the way into the rarities room.

'Can we be overheard?' he asked, looking around but not seeing the hanging flags, the dangling birds' skeletons, the whale's head, the polished cases crammed with goods.

'Only if I scream,' Hester said with sour humour. 'Now, what is it?'

The man put his hand inside his jacket and showed her a glint of gold. 'Do you recognise this?'

It was one of the king's favourite rings. Hester had seen it on his finger many times. 'Yes.'

'I am here by the orders of a lady – we need not say her name – who has brought to London the king's Commission of Array. You know what that means.'

'Not the least idea,' Hester said unhelpfully.

'It's a summons. A summons to the king's standard. It'll be read aloud at Whitehall when our army is at the city gates. You have to play your part. Your husband is commanded to proclaim the king's authority in Lambeth and order out the loyal men for His Majesty as soon as he is given the word.'

'What lady?' Hester asked flatly.

'I said we need not say her name.'

'If she's asking me to risk my neck she can tell me her name,' Hester persisted.

He put his mouth to her ear and Hester smelled the familiar scent of sandalwood that the young men of court used as pomade. 'Lady d'Aubigny,' he whispered. 'A great lady and the widow of a hero. Her lord fell at Edgehill and she is trusted by the king to call out the royalists of London to fight for him. And she is trusting you.'

Hester felt a deep sense of relief that John was far away. 'I am sorry,' she said swiftly. 'My husband is away in Virginia, gathering rarities, and making his own plantation.'

'When will he return?'

She shrugged. 'I don't know.'

The man's gleeful, conspiratorial mode deserted him in a moment. He swore and took two hasty paces away from her. 'Then what are we to do?' he demanded. 'Mr Tradescant was to secure Lambeth and the riverside. We were counting on him.'

'You were counting on him to secure the king's safety and you did not think to discover if he was at home?' Hester asked, disbelieving. 'He could be sick, he could be dead of the plague, he could have changed sides!'

The man threw her a swift, angry glance. 'War is a gamble,' he said grandly. 'Sometimes the gamble pays off, sometimes it does not. I was gambling that he would be here, in good health, and keeping faith with his master.'

Hester shook her head. 'He does not break his faith. But he can be of no use to you.'

'His son?'

'Johnnie is not yet ten.'

'What about you? Surely you have influence with local people. You could use this house as a rallying point. I could send you an officer to raise the men, or your father . . . d'you have a father?'

Hester shook her head. 'No father, and no influence. I am a newcomer here,' she said. 'I am Mr Tradescant's second wife. We have only been married four years. I have no friends here. And I have no family.'

'Someone has to do it!' he burst out. 'Someone has to secure the riverside and Lambeth!'

Hester shook her head again and led the way to the front door. The royalist conspirator trailed unhappily after her.

'What about someone at the bishop's palace? What about the local vicar?'

'The Archbishop is in the Tower for his service to the king, as you well may recall. And his servants are long gone.' Hester opened the front door. 'And the vicar here is an Independent. He was one of the first to preach against Archbishop Laud's reforms.'

The man would have hesitated but she ushered him out of the house. 'I shall call on you if we need a safe house this side of the river,' he promised. 'D'you have horses, or barns where a small troop of horse could lie hidden?'

'No,' Hester said.

The man hesitated and looked at her with a sharp look. Hester felt a sudden fear, she had taken him for a fool but the bright assessing gaze he turned on her was not the gaze of a fool. 'I trust you *are* for the king, Mrs Tradescant,' he said, and there was menace in his voice.

'When he comes into London he will expect support from his loyal servants. You will have to put this house at his disposal.'

'I know nothing of these matters,' Hester said weakly. 'I am just conducting the business of the house and the garden in my husband's absence . . .'

'There are wives and widows in the same case as you all around the country,' the man said sharply. 'And they have not forgotten where their loyalties lie. Are you for the king? Or not?'

'For the king,' Hester said unenthusiastically.

'Then His Majesty will call on your services,' the man said. 'You may count on it.'

He nodded to her, turned and walked across the little drawbridge over the stream at the side of the Lambeth road. Hester watched him stride away, his coat flung back, his feathers bobbing in his hat, every inch a nobleman, every inch a cavalier, then she closed the door on the sight of him, and on her fear.

She thought for a moment and then went into the parlour to write a note to Alexander Norman.

> It may be that I need your assistance. Please let me know that
> your neighbourhood is free of the plague. I may wish to come
> and stay with you for a few days.

She sealed the note and went through to the kitchen. The gardener, Joseph, was in there, eating his midday dinner of bread and bacon.

'Can you take this to Cousin Norman at Aldgate?' Hester asked abruptly.

The man wiped his mouth with the back of his hand. 'I was going to cut back the leaves of the early tulips this afternoon,' he said.

Hester hesitated. There were few things more precious in the Ark than the tulips. 'Even so,' she said. 'I think this is more important. Put it into his hands only, and wait for a reply.'

Joseph brought a message back as it was getting dark. Hester was sitting on the terrace before the house, enjoying the setting sun and the slow gathering of the darkness. The garden before her was an enchanted place in the quiet twilight. The apple blossom was like a mist around the heads of the trees in the lower orchard, the tulips were drained of their daytime colour and glowed like white cups in the beds. Hester thought of John Tradescant, the old man she had met, who had willed his grandchildren into her care, and thought that this garden was his memorial, as much as the ornate stone tomb in the churchyard.

'He didn't write it, he spoke it to me.' Joseph made her jump, appearing suddenly before her on the path.

Hester put her hand to her heart. 'You frightened me! Coming out of the gloaming like a ghost!'

'He said: "No plague. Rooms ready. Whenever."'

Hester smiled at the man's frowning delivery. 'Was that all?'

'Absolutely all,' he said. 'I made sure I would remember it, and he heard me say it over and over a dozen times before I left.'

'Thank you,' Hester said. 'Johnnie and Frances and I will help you with the tulips tomorrow.'

He nodded and went round the back of the house to the yard pump and the kitchen door. Hester sat alone, watching the last light leave the tops of the trees, the nodding flowers. When it grew cold she rose to her feet and went towards the door. 'John,' she said softly. 'I wish you would come home.'

Summer 1643, Virginia

The days that followed John's arrival in the Indian village fell into a routine as orderly as the smooth running of John's English home. In the morning Suckahanna's boy would waken him with one of the smooth black bowls filled with hot water for washing. Outside his hut, in the cool dawn light, John would see the People coming and going as they went down to the river for the morning prayer.

When they returned John would look for Suckahanna, her face bright as she walked beside her husband, his son at one side, her baby strapped on her back. The boy was Suckahanna's shadow and she seemed to know his whereabouts, without even turning her head to look for him. It was as if, when she adopted him and married his father, she had made a bond with him that stretched over any distance but was as palpable as touch.

Before he was allowed to eat the boy had marksman training. Suckahanna plucked a piece of moss from a tree and threw it in the air for him. Not until his little arrow had pierced the falling moss could the boy eat his breakfast. Some mornings Suckahanna was out under the trees with him for three, four, five attempts before John heard her word of praise and the quick touch of her fingers on his dark head.

'He had no mother for his early years,' she explained to John. 'He has much to learn.'

'Why did his father not teach him?' John asked. He was tempted to complain of Suckahanna's husband, to make him look foolish in her eyes. She just tossed her head and laughed. 'Bringing a child into the world is work for a woman,' she said simply. 'A man cannot do it.'

As the sun rose and warmed the air they would all gather for a breakfast of fruits or nuts or a gruel made from cornflour and berries. This was the hungriest time of the year – the winter stores were almost exhausted and the summer crops were not yet ripe – but even so no-one went hungry in the village. The stores had been put aside all through the rich fruitful time of the year, and then extra had been laid aside as well in the huge granary building filled with great bowls of dried pulses, huge netted sacks of dried maize, vats as big as a man filled with nuts. John wondered why they did not broach the great store, but no-one would tell him.

After breakfast the men would string their bows, oil their bodies, tie back their hair, paint their faces, and go out to hunt together. John watched the laughing camaraderie of the huntsmen with the knowledge that he would always be an outsider. The men did not speak to him, he did not know if they even understood English. The women understood everything he said, but their replies were brief. Inevitably, John was learning the rhythm of Powhatan speech, picking up individual words and names. He watched the men, understanding that they were planning the hunt. Suckahanna's husband was among them, in the very heart of the preparations. He was acknowledged as a fine hunter, a man who could kill a deer alone, without the help of a hunting party. Other braves could drop a deer with a well-placed arrow when it had been driven from one cover to another and directed towards them; but Suckahanna's husband could throw a deerskin over his shoulder, strap the horns to his head and move so skilfully and so deer-like with his tittupping step and his nervous, flickering head-tossing, with his sudden stag-like stillness, that he could go among a herd of deer and pick one off as it grazed beside him. A man had to be blessed by the deer god to manage such a feat. Suckahanna's husband was treated with loving respect and he alone decided the course of every hunt. Even his name showed his nature. He was called Attone – the arrow.

As the men readied themselves to leave the village, the women gathered children and their gardening tools and went to the fields to plant and to weed. While John was weak from his illness and under Suckahanna's special protection he went with her, and watched them planting. Their crop was set in a field which had been roughly cleared by burning. They left the tree stumps, left even the biggest living trees and planted around them. The edge of the field was ragged, where the fire had not taken hold. Its disorder offended John's sense of how a tidy field should be set square on the landscape, its lines drawn clearly, hedged and ditched.

'You could get the men to help you clear the tree stumps,' he suggested to Suckahanna. 'It wouldn't take long to uproot them and pull them out. Then you could plant your crops in straight rows. Those tree stumps you have left in will only grow back within a season, and then you'll have all the work to do all over again.'

'We want the trees to grow back,' she said. 'We don't want this field for more than a season.'

'But if you cleared it properly then you could use it year after year,' John insisted. 'You would not have to move on. You could have the same fields and keep the village in the same place.'

Decidedly, she shook her head. 'The earth gets weary of working for us,' she said. 'We plant a field here and then we set her free. We move on to another place. If you plant corn in the same field three years running, then in the third year you will harvest nothing. The earth gets weary of hungry men. She has to rest like a woman with a baby at the breast, needs to rest, needs some time alone. She cannot be always feeding.'

'White men plant the same fields, and go back to them year after year,' John observed.

'White men did,' she corrected him. 'All around Jamestown now they are finding that the land is tiring of them. The land is weary of the hungry white mouth which eats and eats and eats and cannot be satisfied and will not move on.'

She moved to the next row with her hoeing stick. In each hole she dropped four grains of corn and two bean seeds. Behind her another woman came sowing pumpkin seeds. Later, beneath the crops, they would plant the quicker-growing amaracocks for their lush, thirst-quenching fruit.

John picked up a stick of his own and hunkered down beside her. 'I'll help,' he said.

She could not repress a giggle at the sight of him, and then she shook her head. 'This is women's work, only women do it.'

'I can do it. I'm a gardener in my own country. I can plant.'

Still Suckahanna refused. 'I know that you can. And any Powhatan man can do it, if he has to. But women like to do it. It is what we do.'

'To serve the men?' John asked, thinking of the delicious idleness of the hunting men when they returned to camp and found their dinner waiting for them and their fields cleared and planted, their houses swept clean, the sweat lodge heated and ready for them.

She shot him a quick, scornful look from under her dark eyebrows. 'Because the earth and the women are together,' she half-whispered. 'That is where the power of the People belongs, not in the war councils or in the hunting parties. It is women who have the power to make things grow, to give birth. The rest – is pipesmoke.'

John felt his view, his comfortable view of the world, shift and rock. 'Men have the power,' he said. 'God made them in his image.'

She looked at him as if he might be joking. 'You may believe that your god did that,' she said politely. 'But we are the children of the Hare.'

'The Hare?'

She stopped her work and sat back on her heels. 'I shall tell you as if you were my little child,' she said with a smile. 'Listen. In the very beginning when there was nothing but darkness and the sound of the running water, the great Hare came out of the darkness and made both man and woman.'

John squatted down beside her in the damp earth, watched the smile move from her eyes to her lips, and the way her hair fell over her bare shoulders.

'They were hungry. Men and women are always hungry. So the Hare put them in a bag until he could feed them. He ran through the darkness with the bag held tight in his mouth and everywhere he ran there was land made, and water made, and the great deer to walk the land and drink the water and feed the new-made man and woman. And everywhere he went there were fierce mouths biting at him from out of the darkness, hungry meat-eating mouths that would snap at his heels and at the bag he was carrying. But everywhere he ran, the mouths were destroyed, and fled back into the darkness until it was safe for him to do what he wished.'

John waited.

Suckahanna smiled. 'Then, and only then, he opened the bag and let out the man and the woman. The man ran to hunt the deer. The man has the great richness of the deer. This is what he wanted. But the woman –' she paused and gave him a sly sideways smile '– the woman has everything else.'

A year ago John would have called it a heathen tale full of heresy and nonsense. But now he listened and nodded. 'The women have everything else?'

'Everything but hunting and war.'

'So what am I to do?' he asked her.

Suckahanna looked momentarily surprised, as if he had moved the conversation onwards in one great bound. 'You will get well,' she said slowly. 'And then you will decide.'

'Decide?'

'Where you want to live. What kind of man you want to be.'

John hesitated. 'I thought I would get well and go back to my home – to my fields up the river.'

She shook her head. 'You must know by now that you cannot live there,' she said gently. 'You cannot live there alone. You must know by now that you cannot survive in this land alone. You would have died there, my love.' The endearment slipped out, she flushed and bit her lip as if she would have taken it back.

'I thought – I thought I might get a servant, or a slave. I thought –' He hesitated. 'I have been thinking that you might come with me?'

'As a servant? As a slave?' Her look blazed at him.

'I meant I must have someone to work under me,' John corrected himself. 'And I have been praying that you would come to me ever since I made landfall. I meant a servant, and you as well.'

'I shall never lie under a white man's roof again,' Suckahanna said firmly. 'I have taken my decision, and I am with the People.'

John jumped to his feet and took a stride away from her and then back again. 'Then there is nothing for me here,' he cried out. 'I came to make a new life for myself, to farm virgin earth, to find you. And you tell me I cannot plough or hoe alone. I cannot keep myself or even keep my fire in. I cannot take you away from your people, and I cannot take you to my people. I have been a fool to run from one life to another and still achieve nothing.'

There was a cry from the little platform shelter where the children played. Suckahanna glanced back, listening for her own baby's voice. They heard another woman call in response and get up from her knees and go to see to the crying child. Suckahanna returned her attention to her gardening, picked up her hoeing stick, picked out little weed seedlings from her row. Without turning her head to see if John was listening she spoke very quietly to him.

'Perhaps you could be with me,' she said slowly. 'Leave your people and join mine.'

'I can't live here, seeing you every day,' John said softly. 'I want you, Suckahanna. I can't bear to live near you and yet to sleep every night only a footstep away from you.'

'I know,' she said, so quietly that he had to lean forward to hear. But still her hands worked, her hoeing stick piercing the fresh soil and the seeds dropping quickly and accurately through her fingers. 'I could ask my husband to release me.'

'Release you?' John asked incredulously. 'This is possible?'

'He might,' she said evenly. 'If it was my wish.'

'Your people let their wives come and go as they choose?'

She shot him a small smile. 'I told you that we were a proud people.

195

Wives are not slaves. If they wish to leave they must be free to do so, don't you think?'

'Yes . . . but –'

'We would have the children,' she went on. 'The little boy and my own baby. You would have to promise to love them and care for them like a father.'

'And where would we live? You said you would not live in my house?'

'We would live here,' she said, as if it were the most ordinary thing in the world. 'Among the People. You would become a Powhatan.'

'I would learn your language? Live among you as an equal?'

'You are learning it already,' she observed. 'You laughed at Musses the other day and she was not speaking English.'

'I can understand some, but –'

'You would have to join the People, as a brother.'

'They would accept me?'

'*We* would accept you.'

John was silent, his head spinning. This was a far greater step than his adventure to Virginia, this was a step into the unknown beyond the plantation, into the darkness of unknowable lands.

'I don't know,' he said.

'You would have to decide,' she repeated patiently, as if she had led a child around a circle of explanation and returned to the key point at last. 'You would have to decide, my love.'

John hesitated at the endearment. 'Do you want me to be with you?' he asked.

At once her hands returned to their work, her head bowed and her veil of dark hair tumbled over her face hiding her expression, brushing her naked brown shoulder. 'You would have to decide, without advice from me,' she said to the earth. 'I don't want a man with half a heart.'

***

At midday the women rested. The fields they were working were distant from home, too far to return to the village for the usual meal, prayers and rest. They ate a little cold gruel and fruit which they had brought with them, they said their brief prayers to the sun which stood precisely above each and every one of them, blessing each and every one with light and warmth on the exact centre of her head. Then they rested in the shade of the trees. Suckahanna's baby was at her breast as she lay back, the little boy playing stalking or marksmanship with his tiny bow and arrow, with the others. John rested near Suckahanna, listened to the ripple of talk, picked out words, one word after another, all of them making more sense to him. He watched her openly now, wondering how it would be if they were married. If she could indeed leave her husband and come to him. If he could indeed become a Powhatan. If he could ever be recognised as a man among the People.

When they returned to camp he touched her arm. 'I need to take advice from a man,' he said. 'Can one of the men speak my language? Someone I can trust to tell me how a Powhatan man might see this? Not a friend of your husband?'

At once her dark eyes lit up with laughter. 'Oh! You don't trust me!'

'I do –' John heard himself stammering. 'Of course!'

Suckahanna turned her head and babbled a string of words at her sister-in-law who was a few paces ahead. The woman screamed with laughter and turned back, laughing at John, and pointed an accusing finger at him. John picked out among the rapid flow the few words: man, Powhatan, talk, talk, talk, everything.

'What is she saying?'

'She says you are a true man, a Powhatan already. She says all men need to talk, talk, talk among themselves, to make the decisions which are already known.'

'Known?' John queried.

Suckahanna veiled her eyes with the downward sweep of her eyelashes. 'Everyone thinks that you love me,' she said quietly. 'Everyone thinks that I love you. We are all just waiting . . .'

'Waiting?'

'For you. To decide.'

❀

John went that night before supper to the house of the werowance, the senior man of the village. It stood four-square at the head of the village street, near the dancing ground, at a distance from the smoke of the cooking fires. It was walled with tree bark, and roofed with bark roughly cut in shingles. In the heat of the day the bark walls would be rolled up like curtains, but as the evening grew cold the old men closed out the chill night air. The werowance himself was sitting on a raised platform at the end of the tent; at his side were two of the old men of the tribe. They all carried their sharp hunting knives, John noticed. They all looked grave.

John stood in the doorway, awkward as a boy.

'You can come.' The werowance spoke in heavily accented English; but there was neither welcome nor warmth in his voice.

John entered the darkness of the house and sat, obedient to the small gesture, on a pile of soft deerskin. For a moment he was reminded of King Charles's wordless gestures to his servants, and the thought gave him a little courage in the darkness of the strange house. He had served the greatest king in England, he could surely bear himself like a man before someone who was nothing more than a savage chief clinging to the edge of unknown land.

'You desire Suckahanna?' the werowance said briefly.

John found he was looking at the length and sharpened cane blades of the hunting knives.

'I knew her before she was a married woman,' he said. His voice sounding weak and apologetic, even in his own ears. 'We were promised to each other. I promised I would come back for her.'

The werowance nodded. 'But you did not come back,' he observed.

John gritted his teeth. 'When I got to my home in my country my father had died and my children needed care. I had to stay.'

'She waited,' the werowance pointed out. The old men on either side of him nodded, their sharp faces like stone eagles on a lectern in church. 'She trusted your word.'

'I am sorry,' John said awkwardly.

'You have a new wife and children in your own country?'

John thought of a swift lie, thought he might tell them that the plague had taken both his children as well as Jane. But a fearful superstition halted his tongue. 'Yes, I have children,' he said quietly. 'And a wife.'

'And is your wife now the one who waits?'

John nodded.

The werowance sighed as if John's infidelity was a riddle, too tedious and complex to unravel. There was a silence that stretched for a long time. John's back ached, he had sat awkwardly and now he felt too uneasy to wriggle back on the pile of skins and lean against the wall of the house.

'Where do you want to be?' the werowance asked him. 'With Suckahanna or your wife?'

'With Suckahanna,' John said.

'You will care for her children as if they were your own?'

'Gladly.'

'You know the children are not to be taken to your people? They will stay with the Powhatan?'

John nodded.

'And their mother stays with us too. She will never go to your country with you.'

John nodded again. 'She told me this.' He could feel a squirm of excitement starting to grow inside him. This had all the signs of an interrogation of a bridegroom, it was not the preamble to a refusal.

'She came to us for a home, she could wait for you no longer. She made her choice and now she is our child. We have taken her to our hearts.'

The older men nodded. One said something low in their language. The werowance nodded. 'My brother says that we love her. We would avenge her hurt.'

'I understand,' John said. He was afraid they would hear the beating of his heart, it sounded so loud in his own ears. 'I don't want to take her from you. I know she has made her choice, and that she and her children will be with you.'

'And any children you may have with her,' came a low growl from another man, speaking clearly in English. 'They will not be Englishmen, remember. They too will be the People of the Hare.'

John had not thought of his children being born here, being raised by Suckahanna, being rocked in the papoose, learning deadly accuracy with a reed arrow. He felt his heart leap at the thought of fathering such a son. He swallowed. 'Yes.'

'If you choose her, you choose to be with her, to be with us,' the werowance repeated.

John bowed his head.

There was a silence.

'Do you wish to be our brother?'

John drew a breath. Lambeth seemed a long way away, Hester more dead to him than his first wife, Jane. His own children half-forgotten. The pulse in his blood, the drumming beat in his ears, was for Suckahanna. 'I will,' he said.

Faster than the eye could follow, like a striking snake, the werowance snatched at John's wrist, twisting it so that he fell to his knees before the basilisk gazes of the three old men. The pain shot up John's arm to his shoulder, the grip on his wrist joint was so powerful that he had to stay on his knees.

'Against your own people?' the werowance demanded.

'It won't come to that,' John gasped. He could feel the bones in his arm starting to bend, an ounce more pressure and they would break. 'I know that they have treated your people badly but they have the land they need now, it won't come to a war.'

'They have driven us back like helpless deer,' the man said, his grip unchanging. 'And they will drive us back and back, every time they need an inch more land. Is that not so?'

John did not dare to answer. He felt the sweat standing on his back, the muscles in his arm singing with the pain. 'I can't say.'

'They use the land and leave it, like a hog in a stall, don't they? They foul it and then it is good for nothing. So always they need more land, and more land, and then more?'

Abruptly the werowance let John go and he pitched face down on the rushes of the floor, biting his lips to keep from crying out. He could not contain his panting breath, he whooped like a hurt child.

'So there will come a time when every inlet of the river and every tall standing tree sees an Englishman hammering in a stake.'

John sat back on his heels, fingered his forearm, his shoulder. 'Yes,' he conceded unwillingly.

'So when you say you are our brother, you must realise that we will call on you as our brother. You will die beside us when we run forward. Your hands will be red with the blood of white men. You will have their scalps tied to your belt.'

John thought of the Hoberts in their little house hidden among the trees, and the inn at Jamestown, the serving maid at the governor's house, the rough kindliness of the planters, the hopeful faces of the emigrants when they first docked at the quay. The werowance clapped his hands, a sharp ringing sound.

'I knew you couldn't do it,' he remarked, and rose to his feet and walked from the house.

John scrambled to his feet and took three rapid strides after him. One of the old men stuck out a bony leg and John tripped and pitched down to the skins on the floor.

'Lie still, Englishman,' the old man said, his speech perfect, his diction Oxford-pure. 'Lie still like a fool. Did you think we would give our daughter to a man with half a heart?'

'I love her,' John said. 'I swear it.'

The two old men got slowly to their feet.

'Love is not enough,' said the old man. 'You need custom and kinship as well. Love her all you like. There is no shame in it. But choose your people and stay with them. That is the path of a brave.'

Without another word the old men went out, their bare feet passing within an inch of John's face. He lay on the skins, the very symbol of a man brought low, and let them walk past him.

It grew dark. John lay still. He did not notice the thickening of the light and the spreading shadows on the wall. He heard the distant sound of singing and knew that dinner had been cooked and eaten and that Suckahanna's people were at the dancing circle, singing down the moon, singing the fine weather in, singing the herds of deer towards them, singing the fish into the weirs and the seeds strong and tall out of the ground. John lay face down in the skins and neither wished nor wept. He knew his own emptiness.

A light came to the doorway, a twig of burning candlewood, bright as the best wax in London. Beneath it, half-lit, half-shadowed, was Suckahanna.

'You told them you did not want me?' she asked from the doorway.

'I failed a test,' John said. He sat up and rubbed a hand over his face. He felt immensely weary. 'They said I should have to fight against my own people and I could not agree to do it.'

'Very well.' She turned to go.

'Suckahanna!' he cried and the desperation and passion in his voice would have made any woman pause but a woman of the Powhatan. She did not even hesitate. She did not drag her feet. She went out as lightly stepping as if she were about to join a dance. John leaped up from the floor and ran out after her. She must have heard him coming, she knew the rhythm of his stride from her girlhood, but she did not hesitate nor look around. She walked without breaking her pace down the little street to her own house, parted the deerskin at the door and slipped inside without even glancing back.

John skidded to a standstill and felt an urge to scream and hammer his fist through the wall of the light, beautifully made house. He took a sobbing breath and turned towards the fire at the dancing circle.

They were dancing for joy, it was not a religious ceremony. He could tell that at once since the werowance was seated on a low stool with only an ordinary cape thrown for warmth around his shoulders, and no sacred abalone shells around his neck. He was clapping his hands to the music of the drums and flutes, and smiling.

John went towards the light but knew that he was not suddenly revealed. They would all have seen him in the shadows, sensed him running after Suckahanna and then turning back to them. He skirted the beaten earth of the dancing floor and worked his way around to the werowance's seat. The three old men glared at him with the bland amusement of cynical old age which always enjoys the diversion of youthful pain.

'Ah, the visitor,' said the werowance.

'I want to marry her,' John announced without preamble. 'And my children will be Powhatan, and my heart will be with the Powhatan. And you may command me as a brave.'

The sharp, beaky face gleamed with pleasure. 'You have changed your mind,' the werowance observed.

'I have learned the price,' John said. 'I am not a changeable man. I did not know what Suckahanna would cost me. Now you have told me and I know. And I agree.'

One of the men smiled. 'A merchant, a trader,' he said, and it was not a compliment.

'Your children to be Powhatan?' the other old man confirmed. 'And you to be our brave?'

John nodded.

'Against your own people?'

'I trust it will never come to that.'

'If it ever does?'

John nodded again. 'Yes.'

The werowance rose to his feet. At once the drumming stopped, the dancing halted. He put out his arm and John, uncertainly, went towards him. The thin arm came down lightly on John's broad shoulders but he could feel the strength of the sinews in the hand as the werowance gripped him.

'The Englishman wants to be a brave of the Powhatan and marry Suckahanna,' the werowance announced in Powhatan. 'We are all in agreement. Tomorrow he goes hunting with the braves. He marries her as soon as he has shown he can catch his own deer.' John scowled at the effort of understanding what was being said. Then the beaky face turned towards him and the werowance spoke in English.

'You have a day to prove yourself,' he said. 'One day only. If you cannot mark, hunt and kill your deer in the day from dawn to sunset then you must go back to your people and their gunpowder. If you want a Powhatan woman then you have to be able to feed her with your hands.'

Suckahanna's husband grinned at John from the centre of the dancing circle. 'Tomorrow then,' he said invitingly in Powhatan, not caring whether John understood or not. 'We start at dawn.'

At dawn they were in the river, in the deep, solemn silence of the prayers for the rising of the sun. Around the braves, scattered on the water, were the smoking leaves of the wild tobacco plant, acrid and powerful in the morning air. The braves and the women stood waist-deep in the icy water in the half-darkness, washed themselves, prayed for purity, burned the tobacco and scattered the burning leaves. The embers, like fireflies, swirled away downriver, sparks against the greyness.

John waited on the bank, his head bowed in respect. He did not think he should join them until he was invited, and anyway, his own strict religious background meant that he shrank in fear for his immortal soul. The story of the Hare and the man and the woman in his bag was clearly nonsense. But was it any more nonsense than a story about a woman visited by the Holy Ghost, bearing God's own child before kneeling oxen while angels sang above them?

When the people turned and came out of the water their faces were serene, as if they had seen something which would last them all the day, as if they had been touched by a tongue of fire. John stepped forward from the bushes and said in careful Powhatan, 'I am ready,' to Suckahanna's husband.

The man looked him up and down. John was dressed like a brave in a buckskin shirt and buckskin pinny. He had learned to walk without his boots and on his feet were Powhatan moccasins, though his feet would never be as hard as those of men who had run over stones and through rivers and climbed rocks barefoot since childhood. John was no longer starved thin; he was lean and hardened like a hound.

Suckahanna's husband grinned at John. 'Ready?' he asked in his own language.

'Ready,' John replied, recognising the challenge.

But first every man had to check his weapons, and sons and girls were sent running for spare arrow heads and shafts, and new string for a bow. Then a woman ran after them with her husband's strip of dried meat which she had forgotten to give him. It was a full hour after sunrise before the hunting party trotted out of the village. John suppressed a smug sense of satisfaction at what he regarded as inefficient delays; but kept his face grave as they jogged past the women, setting off for the fields. There were cat-calls and hoots of encouragement at the men's hard pace and at John, keeping up in the rear.

'For a white man, he can run,' a woman said fairly to Suckahanna, and Suckahanna turned her head to look after them as if to demonstrate that she had not been watching and had not noticed.

John did not permit himself a grin of satisfaction. The fat had been leached off him during his hungry time in the woods and his stay in the Indian village had been hard work. He was always running errands from field to village, or helping the women with the heavy work of clearing the land. The food they gave him had built only muscle, and he knew that though he might be thirty-five this year he had never been healthier. He imagined that Attone would think that he would drop from the line of braves panting and gasping within the first ten minutes but he would be proved wrong.

Ten minutes went by and John was gasping for breath and fighting the desire to drop out from the line. It was not that they moved so fast, John could easily have sprinted past them, it was the very steadiness of their pace which was so exhausting. It was not a run and it was not a walk, it was a walk on the balls of their feet, a fast walk which never quite broke into a run. It was hard on the calf muscles, it was hard on the arch of the instep. It was sweating agony on the lungs and the face and the chest and the whole racking frame of the Englishman as he tried first to run and then to walk and found himself forever out of stride.

He would not give up. John thought that he might die on the trail behind the Powhatan braves, but he would not return to the village and say that he had not even sighted the deer he had promised to kill because he had been out of breath and too weary to walk to the woods.

For another ten minutes, and another unbearable ten after that, the file of braves danced along the path, following in each other's footsteps so precisely that anybody tracking them would think he was following only one man. Behind them came John, taking two steps to their one, then one and a half, then a little burst of a run, then back to a walk.

Suddenly they halted. Attone's fingers had spread slightly as he held his hand to his side. No other signal was needed. The fingers opened and closed twice: deer, a herd. Forefinger and little finger were raised: with a stag. Attone looked back down the line of the hunting party and slowly, one by one, all the half-shaven heads turned to look back at John. There was a polite smile on Attone's face which was soon mirrored down the line. Here was the herd, here was a stag. It was John's hunt. How did he propose they should go about killing one, or preferably three, deer?

John looked around. Sometimes a hunting party would set fires in the forest and drive a herd of deer into an ambush. Even more skill was required for an individual hunter to stalk an animal. Attone was famous among the People for his gift of mimicry. He could throw a deerskin over his shoulders and strap a pair of horns to his head and get so close to an animal that he could stand alongside it and all but slide a hand over its shoulders and cut its throat as it grazed. John knew he could not emulate that expertise. It would have to be a drive and then a kill.

They were near to an abandoned white settlement. Some time ago there had been a house by the river here, the deer were grazing on shoots of maize between the grass. There was a jumble of sawn timber where a house had once been and there was a landing stage where the tobacco ship would have moored. It had all gone to ruin years before. The landing stage had sunk on its wooden legs into the treacherous river mud and now made a slippery pier into the river. John looked at the lie of the land and thought, for no reason at all, of his father telling him of the causeway on the Ile de Rhé and how the French had chased the English soldiers over the island and to the wooden road across the mudflats and then picked them off as the tide swirled in.

He nodded, affecting confidence, as if he had a plan, as if he had anything in his head more than a vision of something his father had done, whereas what he needed now, and so desperately, was something he himself could do.

Attone smiled encouragingly, raised his eyebrows in a parody of interest and optimism.

He waited.

They all waited for John. It was his hunt. It was his herd of deer. They were his braves. How were they to dispose themselves?

Feeling foolish but persisting despite his sense of complete incompetence, John pointed one man to the rear of the herd, another to the other side. He made a cupping shape with his hands: they were to surround the deer and drive them forwards. He pointed to the river, to the sunken pier. They were to drive the deer in that direction.

Their faces as blank as impudent schoolboys, the men nodded. Yes indeed, if that was what John wanted. They would surround the deer. No-one warned John to check the direction of the wind, to think how the men would get into place in time, to disperse them in stages so that each would get to his place as the others were also ready. It was John's hunt, he should fail in his own way, without the distraction of their help.

He had beginner's luck. Just as the men started to move into their places the rain started, heavy thick drops which laid the scent and hid the noise of the men moving through the woodland surrounding the clearing. And they were skilled hunters and could not restrain their skill. They could not move noisily or carelessly when they were encircling a herd of deer even if they wanted to, their training was too deeply engrained. They stepped lightly on dry twigs, they moved softly through crackling shrubs, they slid past thorns which would have caught in their buckskin clouts with the sharp noise of paper tearing. They might not care whether or not they helped John in his task; but they could not deny their own skill.

In seconds the hunting team was cupped around the herd, ready for the signal to move forward. John held back, at the base of the cup, he hoped to see the herd driven before him and struggling in the mud, giving him the chance of a clear shot. He made the small gesture with his hand which meant 'drive on'; and he had the pleasure of seeing all of them, even Attone, move co-operatively to his bidding.

One, two, the deer's heads went up, the does looking for their young. The stag snuffed the wind. He could smell nothing, the wind had veered with the rain. The only scent he got was the clear water smell of the river behind the herd. Uneasily he glanced around and then he turned his head and walked a little back the way they had come, to the river.

The braves paused at John's gesture and then, as he beckoned them, moved forward again. The herd knew that something was happening. They could see nothing in the sudden downpour of rain and hear nothing over the pitter-pat of fat raindrops on summer leaves, but they had a sense of uneasiness. They bunched closer together and followed the stag as he went, his heavy head swinging to one side and then the other, looking all about him, and led the way towards the river.

John should have held back, but he could not. He made the gesture to 'go forward' and was saved from disaster only by the braves' own skill. They could not have borne to have moved forward and stampeded the herd and lost them. Not if there had been a dozen Englishmen to humiliate. They could not have done it any more than John could have mown down a bed of budding tulips. Their skill asserted itself even over their desire for mischief. They disobeyed John's hurried commands and fell back, waiting until the anxious heads dropped again to graze and the flickering ears ceased to swivel and flick.

John gestured again: 'go forward'! And now, slowly the braves moved a little closer as if their own looming presence alone could move the deer towards the river. They were right. The empathy between deer and Powhatan was such that the deer did not need to hear, did not need to see. The stag's head was up again and he went determinedly down the path which the farmer had once trod from his maize field to his pier, and the does and fawns followed behind.

John waved, 'on, on', and the deer went faster, and the hunters went faster behind them. Then, as if they could sense the excitement before they could even hear or smell or see, the deer knew they were being pursued; and they threw their heads back and their dark liquid eyes rolled, and they trotted and then they cantered, and then they flung themselves headlong down the little muddy single-file path to the deceptive safety of the pier as it stretched out into the river like an avenue to a haven.

The braves broke into a run following them, each one fitting an arrow to his bow as he ran, a faultless smooth gesture, even while dancing around fallen trees, leaping logs. John fumbled for his arrow, dropped it in his haste, put his hand to his hip for another and found that his quiver had been torn from him as he ran. He was weaponless. He threw aside his bow in a burst of impatience but his feet pounded faster still.

The deer were following a trail, the braves were filtering through thick forest but still they went as fast as the herd, they kept pace with them, they were the power behind the herd, driving it forwards, exactly to the place where John wanted them to go, to the wooden causeway, out into the river.

'Yes!' he cried. The braves broke from the trees in a perfect crescent, the herd a tossing tawny mass of horn and eyes and heads and thundering feet cupped inside the circle of running men. 'Now!' John yelled, a great passion for the deer and for the hunt rising up in him. He felt a great desire to kill a deer, thus owning it and this moment forever: the moment that John led his hunting party and took his deer.

But just as that moment was there, just as the first deer leaped down to the causeway to the illusion of safety, and lost her footing at once on the slippery betraying timbers, and an arrow went zing through the air and pierced her pounding heart, just as the others were ready to follow her, one young buck jinked to the right, to the bank, to the clear run downriver to freedom, and another, seeing the sudden spurt of his pace, followed him, and Tradescant saw in that split second of time that his cup of braves was not holding, that his herd of deer would be lost, spilled like quicksilver out of an alchemist's goblet, and would run away downriver.

'No!' he yelled. 'No! My deer!' And now he was not thinking of Suckahanna, nor of his pride, nor of the respect of Attone and the other braves. Now he was intent, determined that his plan should work, that his beautiful strategy should be beautifully performed and that no fleet, infuriating beast should spoil the perfection of the moment of the hunt. 'No!'

At once he was running in great jolting, ground-eating strides, running as he had never run before, to plug the gap in the line, to outpace the first hunter on the extreme right, to stop the deer escaping from his goblet, his beautiful, deer-filled goblet. Attone, his arrow on a string, heard the yell as the Englishman, his long hair flying behind him, took breakneck strides, great leaps down the hill, watched open-mouthed, even forgetting the imperative of the hunt, as the Englishman yelled, 'No!' and while yelling outpaced one, two and then three hunters, and flung himself towards the breach.

John's sudden eruption caused terror in the herd. Instead of slipping away through the gap they doubled back and met the upstream wing of the hunters. There was nowhere for them to go but out into the river, on the slippery causeway. One after another they leaped and scrabbled for it. Their sharp hooves could gain no purchase on the greasy, half-rotted wood, they fell, they pitched into the river, there was a hail of arrows.

But John did not see any of this. All he saw was the gap in his plan, the breach in the perfection of his hunt, and a deer jinking and swerving to get past him. He ran, he ran towards it, his hands outstretched as if he would catch it by the throat. The deer caught sight of him and went for freedom, made a great leap down the steep bank to the river, splashed into the water, fought its way to the surface and laid its smooth head back so the wet, dark nose was able to pant, and it was able to swim, sharp legs flailing, to the centre of the river.

John, unable to bear the sight of his prey escaping, let out a desperate 'Hulloah!' and flung himself, as if he thought he could fly, down the six-foot riverbank and into the water, on top of the deer, falling head first in a wild dive so there was a resounding crack as deer skull met John's forehead, and while he was still blinded by the blow they plunged down into the depths of the river and rose up together, and even gazed into each other's startled, desperate eyes. John felt his hands close around the deer's throat before a sharp hoof struck him like a bullet in his chest and pushed him down below the water again.

Attone, far from letting fly with his arrow at the disappearing head, far from picking off the deer which were slithering and plunging off the causeway, found that he was screaming with laughter at the sight of the Englishman, the despised, over-anxious, women-guarded Englishman howling like a spirit from the dark world, bounding as if he could outrun a deer, and then diving head first into a shallow river. A man so filled with blood lust, so insane with desire, that he could come nose to nose in deep water with a deer and still close his hands around its throat.

Attone gripped a tree for support and called in English: 'Englishman! Englishman! Are you dead? Or just mad?'

Tradescant, surfacing and realising suddenly that he was in cold, weedy water, that he had neither bow nor arrow nor kill, but instead a sensation very like a broken rib and a hoof-shaped bruise over his heart, and a cracked head for his pains, heard also the irresistible laughter of a Powhatan engulfed by amusement, and started to laugh too. He paddled like a weak dog to the water's edge and then found he was laughing too much to climb up the bank. It was absurdly high and he recalled that he had dived off the top of it and actually landed head first on the deer. The thought made him collapse in laughter again, and the sight of Attone holding out his hand, his brown face creased in helpless laughter, redoubled Tradescant's own amusement.

He gripped Attone's hand but it was too much for both of them and their grip slipped as their helpless giggles weakened them so that all Attone could do was fall back on the soft grass of the riverbank and give himself up to it, while Tradescant lay back in the river and howled like a dog at the thought of his hunt and his madness and his incompetence.

When Suckahanna saw the men coming back to camp she went out slowly to greet them; she was proud, and this was a difficult matter for any woman. Her husband was the finest hunter among the people but she was proposing to leave him for an Englishman who had been seen by everyone as incapable of even shooting a pigeon with one of the white man's infallible guns.

First she saw the kill. Six of the hunters carried in three deer lashed by their feet to pruned branches. It was a kill that any hunting party would have been proud to bring home, enough to feed the village and leave surplus meat for salting down. Suckahanna breathed in sharply and drew herself a little higher. She would not be seen by anyone running up to the braves and asking them who had done the kill. But three deer was a successful hunt; three deer was undeniable evidence that the braves on the hunt had done well.

Then she saw John. At first she thought he must be wounded, grievously wounded, for the man who was supporting him was her own husband, Attone. She started to run towards him, but then she checked herself after two paces. There was something odd about the way they walked together, it was not the stumble of a sick man and the load-bearing stride of his helper. They were clinging together as if they were both dizzy, as if they were both drunk. She watched, then she put her hand up to shade her eyes from the evening sun. She heard their voices, they were not talking to each other in low, anxious tones, like men helping one another home, nor exchanging the odd satisfied word, like men returning sated from the hunt. They were saying one word and then another and then they would do a little wandering detour in a circle, like drunkards, legless with laughter.

Suckahanna stepped sharply back into the doorway of her house and dropped the curtain of skins to hide herself. In the darkness she turned and lifted the side of the skin so she could peep out. The men carrying the deer were staking them out for cleaning and skinning, but Attone and John were not going to set to work. Arms around each other's shoulders, they headed for the sweat lodge with most of the braves, and even as they went Suckahanna could still hear that sudden explosion of giggling.

'Dived in!' she heard, and then a crow of laughter from Tradescant: 'But what you don't know is that I fell on its head!' That was too much for Attone, his knees simply gave way beneath him.

'I saw you. You had no arrows?'

'Why does he need arrows? If he is going to fall on deer to kill them?'

There was another scream and all the braves flung their arms around each other's shoulders and swayed together, their feet pounding to their bellowing laugh.

A woman came to Suckahanna's doorway. Suckahanna pushed back the deerskin and came outside.

'What are the men doing tonight?' the woman asked.

Suckahanna shrugged with a smile which said at once, 'Men!' and said, 'How I love him!' and said, 'How impossible he is!'

'How should I know?' she asked.

The half-sacred silence of the sweat lodge calmed them and the exhaustion of the day took its toll. They sat against the walls illuminated by the glowing coals, eyes shut, soaking up the healing heat, sweating out the aches and pains. Every now and then one of the braves would grimace and giggle and then there would be a little ripple of laughter.

They stayed in the heat for a long time until their sinuses were hot and dry, until the very bones of their faces were filled with heat. John could feel the bruise on his head swelling like a maggot and the hoof print on his chest growing dark and tender. He did not care. He cared for nothing but the deep, sensual pleasure of this heat and rest.

After a long, long while, Attone rose to his feet and stretched himself like a cat, every vertebra in his backbone extending. He put out a peremptory hand to John and spoke in Powhatan. 'Come, my brother.'

John looked up, saw the proffered hand and reached up his own to clasp it. Attone pulled him to his feet and for a moment the men stood side by side, hand-clasped, looking deep into each other's eyes with a measuring, honest look of respect and affection.

Attone led the way out of the sweat lodge. 'I have a name for you, your tribal name,' Attone said. 'You cannot be John Tradescant any more. You are a brave now.'

John took in the full meaning. So he was accepted. 'What shall my name be?' he asked.

'Eagle,' Attone announced.

The grandness of the name caused a murmur of admiration from the other braves at the honour being done to John.

'Eagle?'

'Yes. Because you kill a deer by dropping on it from the sky.'

There was a scream of uncontrollable laughter and the men were clinging to each other for support again, John in the centre, Attone with his arms around him. 'Eagle!' the braves said. 'Mighty hunter!' 'He who falls like an eagle without warning!'

They turned and ran down to the river together to wash. The women pulled the smaller children out of the way of the laughing, shouting men. They plunged into the river together and splashed like boys before huskanaw. Then Attone caught sight of a shadowy tall figure on the riverbank and straightened up and looked serious.

The werowance was watching them. Attone came out of the river and the men of the hunt followed him. They dried themselves and pulled on clean buckskins and then, when they were all ready, the werowance led the way to the dancing circle and the braves stood before him.

'Did the man who wants Suckahanna kill his deer?' the werowance asked in their own language.

There was a moment's complete consternation.

'We brought three deer home,' Attone said smoothly. 'A fine day's kill, and the man who wants Suckahanna was at my shoulder the whole day. He did not hang back, he did not fail, he did not tire. He planned the hunt and his plan was a good one. It drove the deer to the river and we killed three.'

'Which one did he kill?' the werowance asked.

Attone fell silent.

'We could have killed none without his plan,' one of the other men volunteered. 'He saw that we could drive them to the river. He showed us the way.'

The werowance nodded leisurely as if he were prepared to spend all night on this inquisition. 'And which did he kill?' he asked. 'One of the bucks? The doe?'

John, following this interrogation as well as he could, understood that the hunters could not conceal his failure. He felt a great wave of disappointment wash through him: that the hunt and the laughter and his naming should all come to nothing because an old man, old enough to be his father, should stick to the letter of the law. He thought that the way of a brave would be to acknowledge his failure, like a man, and then walk away from the village and never look back. He stepped forwards, he opened his mouth to speak. He took a moment to think of the word which meant defeat in Powhatan and realised that he did not know one. Perhaps there was no word for defeat in Powhatan. He framed a sentence with the words he did know. Something like – 'I have not killed. I cannot marry.'

'Yes?' The werowance invited him to speak.

There was a cry from the women at the edge of the dancing circle.

'Whose deer is this?' someone asked.

A woman came towards them. She had hold of the front legs of a deer and was dragging it towards them. From the loll of the head it was clear that the neck was broken.

'That's my deer!' John exclaimed. He hammered Attone on the shoulder. 'That's my deer!' He ran towards the woman and took the delicate legs from her hands. 'This is my deer! My deer!'

'I found it at the river's edge,' she said. 'It had been washed downriver. But it had not been in the water long.'

'The Eagle killed it!' Attone announced. At once there was a ripple of laughter from the braves. The werowance shot a quick sharp look around them.

'Did you kill this deer?' he asked John.

John could feel a bubble of laughter, of joy, rising up in his tight throat. 'Yes, sire,' he said. 'That is my deer, I killed it. I want Suckahanna.'

'Eagle! Eagle!' The shout went up from the braves.

The werowance looked at Attone. 'Do you release your wife to this man, your wife and your first-born son, and your second-born child?'

Attone looked straight at John and his hard, dark face creased into an irresistible smile. 'He's a good man,' he said. 'He has the determination of a salmon leaping homeward, and the heart of a buffalo. I release Suckahanna to him. He is my brother. He is the Eagle.'

The werowance raised his ornate spear. 'Hear this,' he said so quietly that all the women at the edge of the dancing circle craned forward to listen, Suckahanna among them.

'This is our brother. He has proved himself in the hunt and he is the husband of Suckahanna. Tomorrow we receive him into the People, and his name shall be Eagle.'

There was a roar of approval and applause and people crowded around John. John had to fight his way through smiling faces and slapping hands to get to Suckahanna and fold her in his arms. She clung to him and lifted her face to his. As their lips met he felt a sudden jolt of passion, a feeling he had forgotten for many years, and a deep hunger for more of her; more, as if a kiss alone would not satisfy him, could never satisfy him, as if nothing would ever be enough but to fold her into his heart and keep her beside him for always.

Suckahanna moved her face from his and reluctantly John released her. She rested her head on his shoulder and his senses shifted again to take in the touch of her slight body tucked beneath his arm, the way her long legs matched his side, the scent of her hair, the warmth of her naked skin against his cool damp chest.

The people were cheering them, linking their names together.

'Why do they call you Eagle?' she asked, turning her head up to look into his face.

He caught sight of Attone, waiting for his answer. 'It is private,' he said with assumed coldness. 'Something for us braves.'

Attone grinned.

❧

John could not sleep with Suckahanna that night, though she moved from Attone's house to stay the night with Musses. Attone himself carried her deerskin, her baskets and her pots to Musses's hut and kissed her tenderly on the forehead as he left her there.

'Does he not mind?' John asked, watching this affectionate farewell.

Suckahanna shot him a quick, mischievous smile. 'Only a little,' she said.

'I should mind,' John observed.

'He married me because he was advised to do so,' she explained. 'And then he had to keep me, and my mother, and we brought no dowry, no bride price at all. So he could never afford to take another wife, if he should like another woman. He was stuck with only one: me. And now everything has changed for him. He is a bachelor again, you will have to pay him for me, he will like that, and he can look about him and choose a girl he really wants this time.'

'How much will I have to pay?' John asked.

'Maybe a lot,' she warned him. 'Maybe one of your guns that you left at your house.'

'Are they still there?' John asked incredulously. 'I would have thought that everything had been stolen.'

She nodded serenely. 'Everything has been stolen. But if it is to be Attone's gun I think you will find that it will be returned.'

'I should like my guns returned to me,' John observed.

She laughed. 'I should think you would. When you are adopted tomorrow, when you are one of the People, then no man or woman or child will steal from you ever again, not even if they are starving. But they took your goods when you were a rich white man, and now your goods are gone.'

She looked at his half-convinced expression.

'What would you want with them? What would you do with them here, when everything that a man wants can be got with a bow and arrow, a spear, a hoeing stick, a knife or a fish trap?'

John thought for a moment and realised that his goods were part of the life he had left behind, part of his old life, better lost and forgotten than standing in the corner of his new Indian house reminding him of the man he had been, of the life he might have lived.

'Very well,' he said. 'If he can get them back he can have them.'

𝗪

John was woken just before dawn by Attone's hand on his shoulder. 'Awake, Eagle,' the man whispered. 'Come and wash.'

They were early, only the men were moving like grey shadows down the village street. It was still dark, only a line of pale grey like a smudge of limewash above the dark of the forest trees showed that dawn was coming.

Tradescant waded into the river beside Attone and followed every move that he made. First the careful washing of the face: eyes, mouth, nostrils, and ears. Then the meticulous washing of armpits, and crotch, and then finally a deep immersion in icy water, while rubbing chest, back, thighs, calves, and feet. Attone emerged blowing water and flinging back his long hair.

He waded for the shore, John followed him. There was a little fire built on the pebble beach and a handful of the tiny Indian tobacco

214

leaves piled beside it. Attone took up an abalone shell, took up a leaf, lit it at one of the glowing embers, and, blowing on the spark, walked back into the river with the burning leaf outstretched and the abalone shell cupped beneath it to catch the sacred ash. He faced towards the sun and murmured the prayer. John copied him exactly, and got very close to the prayer as well, invoking the sun to rise, the deer to eat well and be happy, the rain to come, the plants to grow, Okee the cruel god to withhold his anger, and the People to tread lightly on the earth and to keep the love of their mother. Then he scattered the ash and embers on the water and turned his face to the shore. John followed suit.

Waiting there was Suckahanna, her face grave. When John went to his clothes, the hand-me-down buckskin he had been given on his arrival at the village, she shook her head wordlessly and held out for him a new buckskin clout made of soft new leather, and a little buckskin apron exquisitely embroidered.

John smiled at her, remembering the little girl she had been when she had first showed him the Indian clothes and how reluctant he had been to part with his breeches. She crinkled her eyes at him but she did not smile with her lips, nor speak. It was a moment too solemn for speech.

John stepped forwards and let her dress him as she wished, and then let her and Musses paint him with the red bear-grease ointment so that his skin was as dark as theirs in the greying light of the dawn.

From the village they could hear the roll of drums and then a steady, insistent beat.

'It is time,' said Attone. 'Come, Eagle. It is your time.'

John turned, expecting to see Attone laughing at the name, but the brave's gaze was steady and his face was grave. There was not even a smile in his look.

'My time?' John asked uneasily.

Suckahanna turned and led the way back to the village but when they approached the dancing circle she fell back and joined the crowd of women who were waiting at one side. They linked arms around her so she was at the centre of a circle of women with arms interlinked, like a country dancer in the middle of the ring.

John found himself surrounded by braves, his friends of yesterday. But none of them greeted him with a smile. Their faces were unmoving, as hard as if carved from seasoned wood. John looked from one to another. They no longer seemed like friends; they seemed like enemies.

The door to the werowance's hut was drawn back and the old man came out. He was terrifyingly dressed in a costume completely made of bird feathers, sewed so skilfully that John could see no seams and no cloth. He looked like a man transformed into a dark, glossy bird and he stalked on his long legs with the arrogant pace of an ill-tempered heron. Behind him came the two other elders, wearing black capes which gleamed with beads of jet. They chinked as they walked, they were laden with amulets and necklaces of copper and abalone shells.

At a gesture from the werowance's richly carved spear two young men came awkwardly from his house, carrying something low and square between them. For a moment John thought they had brought a mounting block, a post, or a pedestal for the werowance to stand on and address the people, but then he saw that the centre of it was hollowed to take a man's chin, and the wood on either side had been sharply cut with an axe. With a sensation of dull horror John recognised what it was. He had been on Tower Hill often enough, he knew an executioner's block when he saw one.

'No!' he shouted and flinched back, but there were a dozen men around him. They did not even grab him, they pressed close to him and John was held in a solid wall of hard flesh. They interlocked arms, they held themselves tight, forcing themselves one against each other so John was helpless among them. Even if he had dropped dead in a faint of fear he would still have been standing, they had him so tight.

The werowance smiled his cruel, beak-nosed smile at John and his dark feathers quivered as if he were an English raven come all this way to peck out John's eyes. John heard himself shout against the injustice of it. Why save him when he was burned and poisoned and starving to death to bring him here and behead him? But then he remembered the wisdom of Jamestown and knew that there was no reason to these people, nothing but mischief and meaningless cruelty, nothing but torture for sport and bloodshed for pleasure, and he started to think that a blow from an axe would be a mercy rather than a disembowelling, or a scalping, or being torn apart, or staked out on an anthill. The thought of these horrors made him cry out 'Suckahanna!' and he lunged so that he could see her, trapped as he was trapped, her face white and agonised, pleading desperately with the women around her, and forever looking towards him and calling 'John!'

The braves clutched his arms, there was no chance of escape, and marched him towards the block. John kicked out and swore but they held him, the sheer weight of them forcing his head down and down till his chin met the pitiless coolness of the skilfully shaped wood and he felt his body recognise the place of his death.

'God forgive me my sins,' John whispered. 'And keep my children and Hester safe. God forgive me, God forgive me.' He closed his eyes for a moment against the horror and then he opened them again and looked for Suckahanna. The women had released her and she was standing stock still among them, her face as white as an Englishwoman's with terror.

'Suckahanna,' John said softly.

He tried to smile at her, to reassure her that there was, even now, no bad blood between them, no regrets and no reproaches. But he knew that he could only bare his teeth, that all she would see was his skull beneath the rictus of the smile, that soon she would see the white of his skull as they peeled back his forehead to cut the trophy of his scalp.

The pressure on his back and his neck was gradually released as the men sensed his surrender. John rolled his eyes to look for the executioner and his axe, and saw instead a great war club, beautifully made and counterweighted, and the man holding it, waiting for the signal to step forward and pound John's head into fragments.

His courage failed him completely then, he felt warm water gush between his legs. He heard a little wail which was his own voice of terror.

The werowance lifted his ornate ceremonial spear, the black feathers on his arms rustled like pinions, like a black angel he stood between John and the rising sun, and his face was filled with joy.

The spear fell. The war club rolled back on the upswing, and John waited for the blow.

Something hit him hard, and his whole tortured body flinched from the impact, but it was not a war club to the head, it was the full weight of Suckahanna, broken free of the circle of women, diving across the dancing ground to lie along his back, one knee in his piss, her hair falling over his flinching spine, her head above his, her chin on his skull, offering herself on the block.

The executioner was too late to stop his downswing, he could only shift it to one side, and the mighty club thudded, like a cannon ball, into the beaten mud of the dancing ground. John felt the whistle of its passing lift the hair of his beard, opened his eyes and looked towards the werowance.

The old man was serene. He raised his spear and spoke as quietly as ever.

'See this, people of the forest and river, see this, people of the plains, see this, people of the seashore, and the swamp, see this, people of the sky, of the rain, of the sun, all the people who have run from the mouth of the Great Hare and who run over the land that He made. Suckahanna, our daughter, went to the very edge of the dark river for this man. He owes her his life. She has given him life, he has a Powhatan mother.'

The people nodded. 'He has life from a Powhatan woman.'

John felt Suckahanna tremble down the length of her lean body pressed against his. He saw her shaking hands come down on either side of the executioner's block and clench white as she forced herself up to kneel and then stand before her people. He thought he should stand too, beside her, but he doubted his legs would hold him. Then he thought again that if Suckahanna could dive towards him to have her head smashed in his place then he should stand for her. He should probably kneel to her.

He heaved himself to his feet and found that his legs were trembling and his body icy with sweat. Suckahanna turned to him and took his hand.

'I take you as my husband,' she said shakily. 'I take you into our people. You are one of the People now and you always will be.'

There was a silence. John feared that his voice would shame him with a squeak of terror. He cleared his throat a little and looked at the girl who had become a woman and who had now twice become his saviour.

'I thank you for my life,' he said, speaking their language haltingly, mixing in English words when he was at a loss. 'I will never forget this. I gladly take you to my wife and I gladly join the People.'

'I take *you*,' she stressed very slightly.

'I am glad that you take me to your husband, and I am glad that the People admit me,' John corrected himself.

There was a ripple of pleasure throughout the crowd and then every-one looked to the werowance, dark in his dark feathers, hunched like a heron in a pine tree, brooding over the couple. He raised his spear.

'Eagle!' he shouted.

There was a roar from the braves, and then the women and the children took it up. 'Eagle!' 'Eagle!' 'Eagle!'

John felt his knees give way and he grabbed for Suckahanna as she swayed too. The women were at her side, the braves bore him up, Attone among them.

'Eagle!' Attone cheered, and with a swift sideways grin at John: 'Eagle! who kills by diving on his deer and pisses himself at his own wedding.'

They got intoxicated that night. Dazed and riotous and then stupefied and giggly, then dancing and leaping and singing under a big yellow midsummer moon. They smoked the sacred tobacco until their heads rang with it and their very eardrums grew hot and itchy. They smoked until they saw dozens of moons cavorting in the sky and they danced on the dancing ground beneath them, following the lunar steps. They smoked until they were whimpering for cool water for their aching throats, and they ran down to the river and exclaimed at more moons, floating in the water, like stepping stones into the darkness. They smoked until they grew hungry like children and raided the stores for anything sweet and spicy and ate handfuls of dried blueberries and popped corn on the embers of the fire and burned their tongues in their hurry. They smoked in a great orgy to celebrate that the Eagle had passed the test and put his head on the block, and that a woman of the People had laid her head down beside him for love of him, and such a thing had never been seen since the time of Pocahontas, when Princess Pocahontas herself had laid her head down to save John Smith, though she had been little more than a girl and hardly understood the risk she took.

Suckahanna's story was more passionate and the women made her tell it over and over again. How she had met John and feared him, how he had treated her gently and never known that she had understood every word he said, that she had heard him tell her that she was beautiful, that she had heard him say that she was lovable. The women sighed at that and the young braves giggled and dug each other in the ribs. Then Suckahanna told them how she waited and waited for him, in the cruelty of the white man's world at Jamestown; and that when she gave him up she had been glad of a refuge with the People and glad of the kindness of Attone, who had been a husband that any woman might admire and love. And at this part of the story the young women nodded and glanced over to Attone in neutral judicial appreciation as if it had not occurred to any of them that Attone was now a free man. Then Suckahanna told them how she had heard of a new white man who had made a clearing in the wood and built a house and had planted a flower at his doorstep. She told them that at that word, at that single piece of news, she knew at once that John had come back to the land of the Great Hare and she went alone to stand in the shadow of the trees and see him. And that when she saw him, her heart went out to him and she knew then that he was still the only man she had ever loved and ever would love and she went straight to Attone and to the werowance and told them that the man she loved was an Englishman living alone in the forest and asked their permission to go to him.

But they were wise, she said now, and cautious, and they made her wait and watch him. And they realised as they watched him that he did not have the skill to keep himself. He could not feed himself and dig his fields and keep his fire in. It was too much work for a single white man to do. Even the children of the Great Hare live together so that the women can garden and the men can hunt and they can all work together. Then Suckahanna went to the werowance and to her husband Attone, and told them that she would like to be released to go to the Englishman and help him to make his home in the land of the Hare.

But again, they were too wise. They said that the Englishman could not be trusted with the children of Attone. That when Suckahanna returned to him he might take her as a servant and not as a wife. Or he might take her and then abandon her, as white men like to do. They said she should wait and watch.

She waited and she watched and she kept him alive with little gifts and then finally she saw him so near to death and to despair that he got in his canoe and could have drifted forever down to the Great Sea. Then, and only then, was Suckahanna allowed to take his life in her keeping and bring him to the Powhatan.

It was a good story and it lasted through the last hours of the night when the smoke started to disperse from their wild, dazed heads, and the laughter subsided and the men and women and children drifted away from the dancing ground and the great fire they had built for their revels, and found themselves falling asleep with only an hour left of the night.

Suckahanna and John were among the last to leave. At last there was no hurry, there was no urgency in their meeting. They had their house, the werowance had allowed them to use one of the empty store houses, another house would be built soon. Suckahanna had put deerskin on the sleeping platforms and hung her baskets on the walls. The baby was slung up in its papoose, her little boy was lolled, his heavy head in her lap. Suckahanna smiled at John.

'I'm sleepy too,' she said.

John got to his feet and lifted Suckahanna's son into his arms. The warm boy clung to him in sleep, with the easy trust of a child who has only ever known a loving touch. John followed Suckahanna to their new house and laid the boy, as she directed, on his little sleeping platform in the corner. Then he sat on the warm skins and watched his wife unbraid her hair, untie her little skirt and drop it to the floor. She stood before him naked.

John rose to his feet, his fingers fumbling for the tie of his own loincloth, found it and dropped the buckskin to the floor so that he was as naked as she. Her eyes travelled all over him, without shame, dark with desire, and she smiled a little, as a woman smiles when she sees that her man desires her: partly in vanity, partly in joy.

She turned with a proud little toss of her head and then stretched out on the sleeping platform, pulling the soft deerskin to one side so that it framed the bronze, smooth length of her, her dark hair spread, her lips half-parted, her breath coming a little faster and her eyes hazy with desire. John moved towards her and kneeled on the sleeping platform, moving over her with a sense of unreality, as if, after all his years of dreaming, this could only be another dream. He bent his head and kissed her and at the warmth and taste of her lips he knew himself to be awake and alive, and more powerfully alive than he had ever been in his life before. He gathered her warm buttocks into his hands and entered her with a quiet sigh of pleasure. Suckahanna's dark eyes flickered shut.

Summer 1643, England

Hester woke on the morning of 31 May to the sound of gravel rattling against her bedroom window. For a moment she had the absurd thought that it was John, locked out of his own house, summoning her to let him in, to a reconciliation, a return, and to the end of her loneliness and waiting.

She jumped out of bed, ran to the window and looked down. It was a man, wrapped to the eyes in a cape, but she would have recognised the hat, heavy with plumes, anywhere.

'God rot him,' Hester swore under her breath, threw a jacket over her nightdress and ran barefoot down the stairs to let him in at the back door. In the stable yard a dog barked briefly. Hester let the man slip inside and then closed the door behind him.

'What is it?' she asked tersely.

'It's gone awry,' he said. He dropped the cape from his face and she saw he was drawn and anxious. 'I need a horse to get away from here to warn the king.'

'I don't have one,' Hester said instantly.

'Liar,' he shot back.

'I don't have one to spare.'

'This is the king's business. His Majesty shall hear how I am served.'

Hester bit her lip. 'Will you send the horse back to me?' she asked. 'She's my husband's horse and the saddle horse for my children, and she works on the land as well. I need her.'

'The king's need is greater.'

'Keep your voice down,' Hester hissed. 'D'you want to wake the whole house?'

'Then give me the horse!'

She led the way down the hall to the kitchen at the back. He hesitated

222

when he saw the fire banked in for the night. 'I need food,' he said.

'You're going to Oxford, not to America!' Hester said impatiently. 'Eat there!'

'Give me some bread and some cheese, and I'll drink a glass of ale while you are saddling the horse.'

Hester waved him towards the larder. 'Eat what you want,' she said. 'And come out into the yard as soon as you are done.'

She stepped into a pair of clogs which were on the stone doorstep and unlocked the kitchen door. She pulled the jacket around her shoulders and did up the buttons. John's mare was in her loosebox, she whinnied when she saw Hester and the dog barked again.

'Hush!' Hester called to them both as she went into the tack room to fetch John's heavy saddle and bridle. The mare stood obediently while Hester struggled with her tack, and then shifted when a shadow fell over the stable. Hester looked up, instantly afraid that it was Parliament men come to arrest the royalist, and arrest her too as a conspirator. But it was the cavalier, his hands full of bread and cheese, his hat tipped back on his head.

Hester led the horse out into the yard. 'Give me that,' she said suddenly and snatched the hat from his head. He was too surprised to protest. With one swift movement she plucked the feathers from the hat band and tossed them into the midden heap. 'Why not carry the king's colours while you're about it?' she demanded.

He nodded. 'I shall tell His Majesty that the Tradescant house remembers their master. You will be rewarded for this.'

'The only reward I want is for you to send the horse back,' Hester said. 'D'you promise you will send her back to me?'

'I do.'

Hester stood away from the mare's head as she stepped delicately on the cobbles, and out of the yard and around the house to the road. Hester stood very still and quiet, listening. If the man had been sighted she would hear the horses' hooves on the Lambeth road as they chased him. There was silence. Somewhere in the garden a thrush was starting to sing.

Hester realised that she was shivering with cold and with apprehension. She turned and crept across the yard to the kitchen door, slipped off the muddy clogs and went to the fireside. If he was captured and named her as his ally and the Ark as a safe royalist house, then she could face arrest for treason against Parliament, and the punishment for treason was death. The cavalier might ride with feathers in his hat and a light heart even in the middle of defeat; but Hester was only too well aware that the country was at war, and it was becoming a war in which there was no quarter given.

She waited by the fire until the little square kitchen window became light and then she went upstairs and woke Frances and Johnnie.

'What is it, Mother?' Johnnie asked, seeing her grave face.

'We're going on a visit to Uncle Norman,' she said. 'Today.'

They took a boat down the river and the boatman was full of news of a royalist plot which had been uncovered only yesterday. Hester nodded. 'I have no interest in politics,' she said.

'You'll be interested soon enough if these traitors hand the city back to the king,' the boatman said. 'If the king brings in murdering Irishmen and damned Frenchmen to cut the throats of honest Englishmen!'

'Yes,' Hester said politely. 'I suppose I will be then.'

The boatman hawked and spat in the water and rowed steadily on.

Alexander Norman greeted them as if their visit had been planned for months instead of thrown together in Hester's panic. His housekeeper had prepared two rooms in his small town house next to his work yard in the Minories in the shadow of the Tower. Frances and Hester would share a bed and Johnnie was to have a little attic room.

'My cousin has long promised me this visit,' he said to his housekeeper as she showed Hester into the front parlour and took her hat and cape. 'I insisted it should be May before the City is too hot and unhealthy.'

'There's nothing worth having in the shops,' the housekeeper remarked to Hester. 'So if you were thinking of new fashions you might as well have stayed at home. There are more tailors out of business than you could name.'

Hester nodded. 'My husband's first wife's family are haberdashers,' she said. 'I thought they would let me see if they have anything left in stock.'

The housekeeper nodded. 'They'll surely have some silk saved for the little miss here. Isn't she a beauty?'

Hester nodded. Frances was struggling out of the thick cape and the big bonnet which Hester insisted she wore. 'Yes, she is.'

'Looking for a husband for her?'

Hester shook her head. 'Not yet.'

The woman nodded and bustled off. 'I shall serve you with your dinner in a few minutes,' she promised.

Alexander drew a chair near the fire for Hester. 'Was it cold on the river?'

'A little,' she said, sitting down.

'Are you in trouble?' he asked very quietly.

'A royalist officer came and took John's horse. He was looking for John to help them in a plot to claim Lambeth for the king.'

Alexander looked shocked. 'When was this?'

'He left this morning. But he came for the first time two weeks ago.'

He nodded. 'Did he get safe away?'

Hester shook her head. 'I don't know. There was no-one waiting outside the house, at any rate, and no-one seemed to be watching us leave today. But he was headed for Oxford and the king. I don't know if he got there.'

He turned away from her for a moment.

'What is it?' she asked. 'The boatman said there was some kind of plot.'

'It's Lady d'Aubigny,' Alexander said.

Hester gave a little gasp.

'You knew her name?'

'It was a name I heard when he was swearing me to secrecy two weeks ago. I didn't think that everyone would know it so soon.'

'She's a fool. Edmund Waller and she were plotting together to seize London for the king. They were going to seize the Tower and arrest Parliament and the House of Lords was to gather behind them and royalists were to rise up.'

Hester's face was pale. 'And?'

'And nothing. Everyone in the plot spoke about it from the assemblies to the taverns, and they were arrested this morning. Lady d'Aubigny has disappeared, no-one knows where yet; but Waller is arrested, and half a dozen others.' He paused for a moment. 'Who knows you're here?'

'The household. I said we were coming for a visit. I thought it might look worse if we went into hiding.'

He nodded. 'You were right. But I am wondering if you should leave London.'

'All of us?'

'Just you. D'you have family somewhere outside the City? Somewhere you can go until this panic is over?'

She shook her head. 'John said I was to go to Oatlands if I was in danger. He still has his house there. He is still gardener there.'

The housekeeper put her head around the door. 'Dinner is on the table,' she said.

'I'm starving!' Johnnie exclaimed, and he and Frances, who had been sitting in the windowseat looking at the street below, went to the dining room. Alexander took Hester's cold hand.

'Come and have something to eat,' he said. 'Nothing is going to happen in the next ten minutes. And I will send one of my clerks to Westminster to see what is happening.'

Hester ate nothing at dinner, and every time a cart went by in the street outside she found she was listening, waiting for the knock at the door.

'What is the matter, Mother?' Frances asked. 'I can tell that something is wrong.'

Hester looked at Alexander.

'You should tell them,' he said. 'They have a right to know.'

'A royalist spy came in the night and took Father's mare,' Hester said.

Frances and Johnnie looked stunned at the news.

'A royalist spy?' Johnnie demanded.

'What was he wearing?' Frances asked.

'Oh, why didn't you wake me?' Johnnie cried. 'And I could have helped him!'

'He was wearing a cape and . . .' Hester's voice quavered on a reluctant laugh. 'And an absurd hat with feathers.'

'Oh!' Frances breathed. 'What colours?'

'What does that matter!' Johnnie exclaimed. 'Oh, Mother! Why didn't you tell me? I could have guided him! I could have gone with him and been his page!'

'I expect that's why she didn't tell you,' Alexander said gently. 'Your place is at home, guarding your mother and the Ark.'

'I know,' Johnnie said. 'But I could have gone with him for a battle or two and then come home again. I am a Tradescant! It is my duty to serve the king!'

'It is your duty to protect your mother,' Alexander said, suddenly grim. 'So be silent, Johnnie.'

'But why have we come here?' Frances asked, abandoning interest in the colour of the royalist's hat feathers. 'What is happening? Is Parliament after us?'

'Not after you,' Hester said quietly. 'But if they know that he came to the Ark for help then I may be in trouble.'

Frances turned at once to Alexander Norman and put her hands out to him. 'You'll look after us, won't you?' she demanded. 'You won't let them take Mother away?'

He took her hands, and Hester saw that he had to stop himself from drawing her close. 'Of course I will,' he said. 'And if she's in any danger at all I shall find somewhere safe for her, and for you all.'

Frances, still hand-clasped with Alexander, turned to her stepmother and Hester saw them, for the first time, as a couple; saw the tilt of his head towards her, saw her trust in him.

'Should you go into hiding?' Frances asked her.

'I'll go to the Tower now,' Alexander decided, 'and see what news there is. You keep the door locked until I return. They can hardly have found your name and traced you here so soon. We must be a day ahead at least.'

Hester found that her mouth was dry and reached for a glass of small ale. Alexander gave her a quick, encouraging smile. 'Be of stout heart,' he said. 'I will be back within the hour.'

The little family went back into the parlour and Frances and Johnnie took up their posts in the windowseat again, but this time they were not commenting on the passers-by; they were on look-out. Hester sat, in uneasy idleness, by the fireside. The housekeeper coming in with fresh coal made them jump. 'I'd have thought you would want to go out and walk around.'

'Perhaps later,' Hester said.

❧

Inside the hour, true to his word, Alexander Norman came strolling down the street, stopping for a chat with his neighbour who had a small goldsmith's shop, and then opened his front door and stepped inside. At once his air of leisured cheerfulness deserted him.

'It's bad news,' he said, checking that the parlour door was closed behind him. 'Lady d'Aubigny took sanctuary in the French Embassy under the pretext that her husband's family is French. But Parliament has ordered that the French hand her over and they have done so. She'll be tried for treason, she was carrying the king's Commission of Array. She was trying to raise an army in the very City itself.'

'The French ambassador handed over an English lady of the king's party to Parliament?' Hester demanded, incredulously.

'Yes,' Alexander said, looking grave. 'Perhaps His Majesty has fewer friends in Paris than he thinks. Perhaps the French are preparing to deal with Parliament direct.'

Hester found she was standing by her chair, as if ready to run. She forced herself to sit down and to start breathing normally. 'And what else?'

'Edmund Waller, who passes for the brains behind this brainless scheme, was taken up and is singing like a blinded thrush,' Alexander said. 'He is naming everyone he spoke to, in the hopes of escaping Tower Hill and the block.'

'Would he have my name?' Hester asked quietly. She found her lips were numb and she could not speak clearly.

'I can't tell,' Alexander said. 'I didn't want to ask too detailed questions for fear of attracting attention. We can hope that your man got clear away, and that he was too small a link in the chain to connect you to the plot.'

'As long as he was not captured on Father's horse,' Frances pointed out.

'If I said it was me who gave him the horse . . .' Johnnie suggested. 'I could say that it was me and that I was a royalist. They wouldn't execute me, would they? I'm not ten yet. They'd give me a whipping and I don't mind that. I'd get the blame and you'd be all right.'

Hester drew him towards her and kissed his smooth fair head. 'I don't want you involved in this, whatever the risks.' She looked up at Alexander Norman. 'Should I stay? Or go?'

He bit his upper lip with his teeth. 'It's the devil's own decision,' he said. 'I think you should go. We gain nothing from you being here and we risk everything. If your man is captured and he follows the example of his betters he will volunteer information and he is bound to name you. Even if he goes free then the king's men are so indiscreet that your name might still be mentioned. Go to Oatlands and stay in John's house in the garden for a week. I'll send you a message if it's all clear and you can come home again.'

'Oatlands?' Johnnie demanded. 'With Prince Rupert?'

'Yes, he's said to be quartered there,' Alexander Norman said. 'At least you'll be safe from Parliament while he is there.'

'Oatlands!' Johnnie exulted. 'Prince Rupert! I'll have to go with you. To defend you.'

Frances was about to say 'I'll come too', but she hesitated and looked towards Alexander Norman. 'Should I?'

'You'll all go,' he said. 'You're safer there than anywhere if Rupert is still there. Parliament can't arrest you there, you'll be under royalist protection; and when you come home we can say you were only doing John's work on the gardens.'

Frances was about to argue, but then she held her peace.

'You could go now,' Alexander said. He led the way out of the room to the narrow hall.

Hester hung back and looked at her beautiful stepdaughter. 'Did you not want the risk of being with me?' she asked. 'I would understand if you didn't want to come to Oatlands. You can go to your grandparents if you wish, Frances.'

'Oh no!' Frances cried out, and suddenly she was a girl again. 'Mother! Oh no! Whatever risks you were taking I should want to be with you. I'd never leave you alone to face danger! I was just thinking that perhaps Uncle Norman could come with us. I'd feel so much safer if he was with us.'

'The safest way is for him to be here, gathering news, and for us to be tucked out of the way in the country,' Hester said. 'And when it is all quiet again we can go home. I don't like to leave the rarities and the gardens.'

'In case Father comes home this month?' Johnnie asked.

Hester managed a smile. 'In case Father comes home this month,' she agreed.

Oatlands Palace was beautiful in early summer. The garden was showing signs of neglect and most of the rooms of the house were shut up. There was a regiment of soldiers occupying the main hall and the regimental cooks working in the kitchens. The cavalry's horses were stabled in the old royal stables and there was constant drilling and training and parading over John's precious turf at the front of the palace. Prince Rupert was only rarely with his troops. Half the time he was at Oxford with the court, arguing against the negotiations for peace, bolstering up the king's erratic determination to conquer the Parliament and not negotiate with them. The royalist cavalry troops paid no attention to the silkworm house nor to the gardener's house next door to it. The commander saw Hester when he was walking in the gardens and Hester mentioned that since her husband was still nominally gardener to the palace she had thought it her duty to make sure that the gardens were not suffering too badly.

'Very commendable,' he said. 'What needs doing?'

'The grass wants mowing,' Hester said. 'And the knot garden needs weeding and trimming. The roses should have been pruned in winter, it's too late now, and the fruit trees.'

He nodded. 'These are not the times for gardening,' he said flatly. 'You do what you can and I shall see that you are paid for your time.'

'Thank you,' Hester said.

'Who's the pretty maid?' he asked abruptly.

'My stepdaughter.'

'Keep her out of the way of the men,' he said.

'She'll stay by me,' Hester said. 'Can she walk in the gardens?'

'Yes. But not near the house.'

Hester dipped a little curtsey.

He was about to walk away but he hesitated. 'I visited the Ark once,' he said. 'When I was little older than your lad. The old Mr Tradescant showed me around himself. It was the most wonderful place I had ever been. A palace of curiosities. I could hardly believe the things I saw. A mermaid, and the jaw of a whale!'

Hester smiled. 'We still have them,' she said. 'You are very welcome to visit us again when you come to London. You may come as our guest. I should be glad to show you the new things too.'

The commander shook his head. 'It seems extraordinary to me that while I am fighting for the king against his own deluded people that you are still collecting mice skins and glassware and tiny toys.'

'For one thing there is nothing else for me to do,' Hester said tartly. 'My husband left the rarities and the garden and the children in my care. A woman should do her duty, whatever else may be happening.'

He nodded his approval of that.

'And when it is all over, when it is finished, then the men who have been fighting will want to go home to their houses and their gardens,' Hester said more gently. 'And then it will be a great joy to them to find rare and beautiful things have survived the war, and that there are strange and lovely plants to grow, and tulips are as bright and fiery as ever, and the chestnut trees are as rich and as green as ever they were.'

There was a little silence, and then he bowed low and took her hand and kissed it. 'You are keeping a little piece of England safe for us,' he said. 'Pray God we all come safely home to it at the end of all this.'

'Amen,' Hester said, thinking of John so far away, and of the war going on for so long, and of the young men who came to the Ark to order trees only for their heirs to grow. 'Amen.'

Hester found a youth who had so far avoided both the excitement of the war and the recruiting officers to mow the courts around Oatlands under her supervision, and then weed the gravel of the knot garden. Little could be done with the kitchen garden except to leave it to grow what vegetables and fruit could struggle through the weeds. But judging from the blossom which drifted like snow in the corners of the walled garden there would be a fine show of fruit, especially plums and apples which thrived on neglect.

In the silkworm house the shelves were full of dusty little corpses. When the king and queen had left the court and abandoned the old life, the boiler had gone out and all the worms had died. Hester, with her instinctive hatred of waste, cleaned out the trays and swept the floor with a bustling irritation against a queen who could command such things into being, and then forget them completely. Every day Hester and Frances hitched up their skirts, rolled up their sleeves and worked in the gardens, noting the positions of the tulips which should be lifted in autumn, tying in climbing plants to the bowers and arbours, and weeding, weeding, weeding: the white gravel of the stone gardens, the drive, the terrace, the stone-flagged arbours. Johnnie put himself in charge of the watercourses and drained and scrubbed them, coming home at dusk wet through with triumphant tales of streams running clean, and cracks in the watercourses repaired with his own sticky mixture of clay and white chalk.

In the afternoons he was allowed to watch the cavalry drilling, practising turning and wheeling at a shouted order, and once he saw Prince Rupert himself on his huge horse with his poodle held over his saddle-bow and his dark hair in a curled mane over his shoulders. Johnnie came home full of joy at the sight of the handsome prince. Prince Rupert had seen him and smiled at him and Johnnie had asked if he could serve in his regiment as soon as he was old enough and could find another horse.

'You didn't say anything about the cavalier who took Father's horse?' Hester asked quickly.

At once all the boyish wildness drained from his face and he looked cautious. 'Of course not,' he said quickly. 'I'm not a child.'

Hester had to stop herself from drawing him on to her knee and taking him in her arms. 'Of course you're not,' she said. 'But we must all mind our tongues in these dangerous days.'

She smiled to reassure him that she was not afraid; but at night, in all long dark nights, Hester remembered that she was in exile from her home and in danger of her life, and sometimes she feared that while they were safely hidden at Oatlands the other army, who were at least as well-armed and perhaps as well-trained as this one, might march on the little house at Lambeth and destroy it with all the treasures and all the plants as a nest of treason.

She could get neither news nor gossip. The soldiers stationed at Oatlands Palace knew nothing more than they would get their marching orders any day, and Hester was too fearful to go into Weybridge for news. She had to wait for a message from Alexander Norman. In the third week of June he came himself.

Frances saw him first. She and Hester were grubbing in the flower beds of the queen's court, lifting the early tulips and putting the precious bulbs into sacks to take away.

'Look!' Frances exclaimed, and in the next moment she was up and running like a child with her arms outstretched to him.

For a moment he hesitated and then he spread his arms to her and folded her tight. Over her light brown head his eyes met Hester's and he gave her a small apologetic smile. Frances pulled back to see his face but did not unclasp her hands from their grip around his back. 'Are we safe?' she demanded urgently.

'Praise God, yes,' he said.

Hester felt her knees go weak and sank down on a stone seat. For a moment she could not speak. Then she asked: 'The man got safe home to Oxford?'

'And sent your mare back with a hidden note in the saddle which apologised for seizing the animal at swordpoint. If anyone does inquire we can show them the note which will serve as a strong argument in your defence. We have been lucky indeed.'

Hester shut her eyes and breathed deeply for a moment. 'I have been more afraid than I was ready to admit.'

'And I,' Alexander Norman said with a gleam. 'I have been trembling in my boots for the last fortnight.'

'I knew we'd be safe,' Frances said. 'I knew you would keep us safe, Uncle Norman.'

'What other news?' Hester asked.

'Waller, who started the whole plot, is the only one to get off scot-free,' Alexander said, his voice low. 'Every time the king uses such weak reeds as this, he falls in the estimation of every right-thinking person. Waller confessed everything, he named everyone he had spoken to and thanks to his ready tongue two men have been hanged for conspiracy, though they did far less than him, and at his bidding. And there will be more to die.'

Hester shook her head in disapproval.

'Waller himself is fined and imprisoned, but the news of his treachery and of his conspiracy has driven the Parliament men closer together. There's a new oath of loyalty and they're all eager to make close alliance with the House of Lords and with the Scots. The king has done his cause the worst damage he could have done – he has frightened his enemies into friendship with each other, and not advanced himself a single step. And any man of judgement must despise Waller, and his master too.'

Hester rose from the seat. 'So I can go home?'

'Yes. I called in at Lambeth on my way upstream so that I could tell you if things were well there. Joseph tells me that the garden is beautiful and the house has been closed and kept safe. Everything is ready for your return.'

Frances clapped her hands. 'Let's go!' she said. 'I'd rather weed my own garden than the king's any day!'

Alexander took her hands and turned them palms upwards. They were filthy from lifting the bulbs and her fingernails were broken. 'You'll never be a lady with hands like these,' he said. 'You should wear gloves.'

'Oh phoo,' Frances said, pulling her hands away. 'I don't care about being a lady. I'm a working woman like Mother.'

'Well you'll never sew silk with callused hands,' Alexander replied. 'So I shall never bring you ribbons again.'

She knew him too well to fear his threats. 'Then I shall never dance for you or sing to you or speak to you kindly,' she said.

'Enough,' Hester remarked. 'There's enough warfare in the kingdom without it starting at home. We'll finish lifting these tulips and then we'll pack and go home. I am longing to sleep in my own bed again.'

Winter 1643, Virginia

John had not thought it possible that he could become one of the Powhatan but by the autumn he felt as if his London life was left far behind him. There was so much for him to learn that every day was completely absorbing. He was all but fluent in the language – an easy task since once he was adopted into the People not one of them would speak English to him. Within weeks he was speaking nothing but Powhatan, and within months he was thinking in their rich natural imagery. It was not just the language he had to master, but their very way of thinking, of being. He had to learn the pride of a man whose land has been directly given to him, as a favour from the Great Hare. He had to learn the joy of providing food for his family, and for his village to eat. He had to learn the tiny pleasures of family and village life, the easy jokes, the sudden flare-ups of irritation, the appeal of gossip, the danger of making mischief, the delight of Suckahanna's growing boy and baby, and the dark, constant pleasure of the coming of the night.

They never talked when they made love. They never spoke of it. With his first wife, Jane, it had been that some things were not to be mentioned because they were secret, almost shameful; but with Suckahanna the pleasures of the sleeping platform where anything was possible, where any pleasure might be sought and any sensation given, were pleasures of the darkness and silence. In the daytime and during speech they were in abeyance, waiting for the darkness that would come again.

John had thought in the first months of his marriage that he would go insane, waiting for the sun to set and the children to sleep so that he could take Suckahanna into his arms. Then he was glad that the autumn season made the nights longer, and that the cold weather drove the families of the village indoors earlier and earlier. The children would be rolled together in a thick rug on their sleeping platform, the fire at the centre of the house would glow with a warm light and fill the little house with hot smoke, and in the darkness and warmth Suckahanna would enfold him and hold him in her mouth, in her body, until he ached with the urgency of his desire and then finally found the rush and release of his passion, as she closed her eyes and slid into her own joy.

Even on the coldest days the braves went hunting. When the snow was thick on the ground they wore thicker moccasins on their bare feet and buckskin jerkins for warmth. They would laugh at John when they came home if his lips were blue with cold. They threatened to send him stalking stripped naked since his white skin blended so well with the snow.

Attone had John's old gun but there was no powder for it. However, he insisted on carrying it on every hunt, and after he had felled a wild goose or duck with a superbly placed arrow and it came spiralling to earth, he would pull the gun from the deerskin holster he had made to carry it on his back, sight the falling bird and solemnly remark 'Bang.'

'Good shot, sir!' John would say in English, the words awkward and alien on his tongue.

And Attone would turn and beam. 'Good shot,' he would confirm.

Attone was at John's side for all of the autumn hunts, prompting, reminding, explaining. But all of the Powhatan people were quick to teach John the things he needed to know to live among them. That ceremony of adoption and marriage in one had been all they needed. John was one of the People.

He shared their dangers as well as their pleasures. As autumn turned into winter the stores grew low and the people began to go hungry. The food was set aside for the strongest small children and for the braves on the hunting parties. Old people, the weak, and the sickly accepted that when there was scarcity, the food had to go to those most likely to survive. John offered his portion to Musses but she laughed in his face.

'Do you think I am afraid to die?' she asked him as he brought her a bowl of suppawn.

'I thought only that you were hungry,' he said.

'You thought right,' she said sharply. 'I am hungry for meat. So eat your breakfast, Eagle, and go out and drop from the sky on to a deer. The People need food. The hunters must do their work.'

He nodded at the wisdom of what she was saying, but he could not understand how she could refuse a bowl of porridge when his own belly growled with hunger at the sight of it.

'I love the People more than I love a fat belly on myself,' she explained. 'And I was fed from my grandmother's bowl when she went hungry to feed me, and she was fed from hers.'

John dipped his head and ate his porridge and gave thanks for the filling warm sweetness of it.

When he looked up her bright hungry eyes were on him. 'Now go and kill a deer,' she ordered.

It was not always easy to hunt. The days were short and icy cold, and when they had shot a white-coated hare, or a deer, or a skunk, or a foolish foraging squirrel there was less meat on the bones than on summer carcasses. The fish weirs froze and the little treats which supplemented the Powhatan diet, the fruits and nuts and berries, were gone. There were edible roots which the women could dig for, and there was the great temptation of the storehouse.

'Why can we not eat from the store?' John asked Suckahanna.

'We do,' she said. 'But we share it very carefully when there is no food to be had in any other way. It has not come to that yet. It may not come to it this year.'

'But there is enough in the store to keep the village for the whole season!' John exclaimed. 'It will spoil if we don't eat it!'

She gave him a sly sideways smile. 'No it won't,' she said. 'The meat is properly smoked and the fish salted down in pots. The oysters and crayfish are smoked and dried and the seeds and nuts are dry and safe. You are pretending that the food will go bad to give you an excuse to eat.'

John made an impatient noise and turned on his heel.

'Why can we not eat the store food?' he asked Musses.

She shook her head. 'That is the wealth of the People,' she said. 'Our inheritance. We saved it carefully, from good harvests and bad. We keep it through the winter and eat as little as we can. That is the way of this people. They are not Englishmen who eat their seed corn and then find in spring they have nothing to plant.'

'Why can we not eat the store food?' John asked Attone.

'Why not?'

'Yes.'

'Have you asked Suckahanna?'

'Yes, and Musses.'

'And what do the women tell you?'

'One tells me that we may need the food later, though we are halfway through winter already and as hungry as we can be. The other tells me that the People do not eat their seed stores. But these are not seed stores. These are dried oysters.' John felt the juices rush into his mouth at the thought of oysters, and swallowed, hoping that his hunger did not show in his face.

Attone took his shoulder in a hard, friendly grip and put his face close to John's. 'You're right. It's not seed. You're right, it would be good to eat some of it now. Why do you think we have waited and worked and starved ourselves to store a year's supply of food?'

John shook his head. Attone's lips came closer to his ear.

'In the time of the uprising when our king, Opechancanough, went against the white men, do you know what they did to our fish weirs?'

'They tore them down,' John said, as softly as the other man.

'And what they did to our crops in the fields?'

'They trampled them into the mud.'

'They did worse than that. They let the women plant and weed them, so we thought that they would let us get them in. Then, after we had spent a year of our labour in tending the food they came at harvest time and set light to them and to the forest around them.' He dropped back and looked into John's face. 'They burned anything, without thought,' he said. 'I would have understood it if they had stolen the harvest from us. But they did not do that. They just burned it where it stood, ripe and ready for picking. So that winter they went hungry themselves without our food to buy. But we – we starved.'

John nodded.

'I buried my brother that year,' Attone said quietly. 'My older brother, who was like a father to me. He died with a belly full of frozen grass. There was nothing else to eat.'

John nodded in silence.

'So now before any brave would lift his hand against a white man he would want to know that he has a year's supply of food in his house. Don't you think that, my Eagle?'

John gaped. 'This is a supply for war?'

The grip on his shoulder tightened so hard it was like a vice. 'Did you think we would let them push us into the mountains, into the sea?'

Dumbly, John shook his head.

'Of course there will be war,' Attone said matter-of-factly. 'My son has to have a trail to follow. He has to have deer to kill. If the white man will not keep to his treaties, will not share the land, then he will have to be killed.'

John bowed his head. He felt a great sense of impending doom.

'You grieve for your people?' Attone asked.

'Yes,' John replied. 'Both of them.'

The deer were fewer, hunting was hard. The men went out in twos and threes, looking for small game and birds. Attone and John left the usual trails and struck out downriver. Suckahanna watched them go, her baby strapped on her back. She embraced John and then she stood back and raised her hand in a respectful salute to her previous husband. He touched his forehead and his heart to her. 'Suckahanna, guard my son and daughter,' he said.

'Go safely, both of you,' she replied. 'May the trail be smooth under your moccasins and the hunting rich.'

The two men jogged out of the village. John was used to the steady half-running pace of the hunting party now and his calves no longer seized with cramp as his feet ate up the miles. But it was hard running in the snow. Both men were shiny with sweat when they paused to draw breath and to listen to the quietness of the winter woods all around them.

There was a mild thaw. John could hear a steady drip drip of melting water from trees where dark-stained twigs were at last thickening with buds. Attone's head was cocked. 'What can you hear?' he asked John.

John shook his head. 'Nothing.'

Attone raised his eyebrows. He could never become accustomed to the insensitivity of the Englishman.

At once he crouched and his hand went into the gesture with two raised fingers which meant, hare or rabbit. At once John crouched beside him and they both put an arrow on the bow.

It came slowly, quite unaware of their presence. They heard it before they saw it because it was white against the white snow: a winter hare with a coat blanched like ermine. When it dropped on to its haunches the only sign that revealed its presence was the little dimples of dark footprints behind it, and the occasional betraying flick of an ear.

Attone raised his bow and the little thwack of sound as the bow was released was the first thing that alerted the hare. It bounded up and the arrow caught it in the body, behind the foreleg. John and Attone were behind it at once but the animal raced ahead of them, the arrow jinking and diving with it, like a harpoon in a speared fish.

Attone gave a sudden cry as he tripped and fell to the ground. John knew well enough not to check for a moment. He kept running, follow-

238

ing the terrified creature, weaving in and out of trees, jumping over fallen logs, diving around rocks, and finally scrabbling on hands and knees through the winter-thin scrub to keep the wounded animal in sight.

Suddenly there was a crack of a musket shot, loud and startling as cannon fire in the icy silence, and John flung himself backwards in terror. The hare was thrown into the air and fell down on its back. John rose up from the bushes, half-naked in bear-grease-stained skin and buckskin kilt and jerkin, and looked into the wan, half-starved face of his old friend Bertram Hobert.

He recognised Bertram at once despite the marks of hunger and fatigue on the man's face. He was about to cry out in greeting but the English words were sluggish on his tongue; and then he realised that Bertram was pointing his musket at John's belly.

'That's mine,' Bertram snarled, showing his black and rotting teeth. 'Mine. D'you hear? My food.'

John spread his hands in a quick deferential gesture, aware all the time of his razor-sharp reed arrows nestling in the quiver in the small of his back. He could have one on the string and loosed long before Bertram could reload and prime his musket. Was the man mad to threaten with an empty gun?

'Step back.' Bertram waved him aside. 'Step back, or by God I'll shoot you where you stand.'

John went back two, three steps, and watched with silent pity as Bertram hobbled over to the dead hare. There was precious little meat on it and the rich guts and heart had been blasted out by the shot on to the snow. The silvery pelt, which would have been good to trade, had been destroyed too. Half the hare had been wasted by killing it with a gunshot whereas Attone's reed arrow should have gone straight to the heart and left nothing more than a farthing-size hole.

Bertram bent stiffly over the body, picked it up by the limp ears and stuffed it in his game bag. He bared his teeth at John. 'Get away,' he said again. 'I'll kill you for staring at me with your evil dark eyes. This is my land, or at any rate, near enough mine. I won't have you or your thieving people within ten miles of my fields. Get away with you or I'll have the soldiers out from Jamestown to hunt you down. If your village is near here we'll find it. We'll find you and your cubs and burn the lot of you out.'

John stepped back, never taking his eyes from Bertram. The man's face was a twisted ruin hammered from his old sunny, smiling confidence. John had no inclination to step forward now, to greet his old friend and shipmate by name, to make himself known. He did not want to know this man, this weak, cursing, stinking man. He did not want to claim kinship with him. The man threatened him like an enemy. If his gun had been reloaded John thought that it would have been his blood on the snow, and his belly blasted away like the hare's. He bowed his head like a servile, frightened, enslaved Indian and backed away. In two, three paces, he was able to lean into the curve of a tree and know that a white man's eyes would not be able to pick him out from the dapple of white snow and dark tree shadows and speckled bark.

Hobert glared into the shadowy forest which had swallowed up his enemy in seconds. 'I know you're there!' he shouted. 'I could find you if I wanted.'

Attone came up beside John so silently that not even a twig cracked. 'Who's the smelly one?' he asked.

'My neighbour, the farmer, Bertram Hobert,' John said. The name sounded strange and awkward on his lips, he was so accustomed to the ripple of Powhatan speech.

'The winter has rotted his feet,' Attone remarked.

John saw that the brave was right. Bertram was painfully lame and instead of shoes or boots his feet were encased in thick wrappings tied with twine.

'That hurts,' Attone said. 'He should wear bear grease and moccasins.'

'He does not know,' John said sadly. 'He would not know that, and only your people could teach him.'

Attone gave him a quick smile at the unlikeliness of such a meeting and such a lesson. 'He has our hare. Shall we kill him?'

John put his hand on Attone's forearm as he reached for his arrow. 'Spare him. He was my friend.'

Attone raised a dark eyebrow. 'He was going to shoot you.'

'He didn't know me. But he helped me build my house when I came to the plantation. We travelled across the sea together. He has a good wife. He was once my friend. I won't see him shot for a hare.'

'I would shoot him for a mouse,' Attone remarked, but the arrow stayed in his quiver. 'And now we will have to cross the river. There will be no game here for miles where he is stamping on his rotting feet.'

They caught no game though they stayed out for three days, travelling along the narrow trails which the People had used for centuries. Every now and then one of the trails would spread itself to double, even treble, the necessary width and then Attone would scowl and look out for a new house being built, a new headright created where this wide path would lead. Again and again they would see a new building standing proud, and facing the river and around it a desert of felled trees and roughly cleared land. Attone would look for a moment, his face expressionless, and then say to John: 'We have to go on, there will be no game here.'

They struck away from the river on the second day, since the plantations chose the riverside so that the tobacco could be floated down to the quayside at Jamestown. Once they broke away from the riverbanks things were better for them. In the deeper forest they found traces of deer again and then on the third day, as they were bearing round in a wide circle for home, a great shadowy bush caught Tradescant's eye and as he watched, it moved. Then he felt Attone's hand on the small of his back and his breath as he said: 'Elk'.

Something in the quiver of the brave's voice set John's heart racing too. The beast was massive, its antlers as broad as the outspread wings of a condor. Moving almost unconsciously, John fitted his arrow to his bow and felt the thinness of the shaft and the lightness of the sharpened reed arrow head. Surely, this would be like shooting peas at a carthorse, he thought. Nothing could bring this monster down.

Attone was moving away from him. For a moment John thought that they were to make the traditional pincer movement of deer stalking but then he saw that Attone had slung his bow over his shoulder and was climbing the lowest branches of one of the trees. When he was stretched along it with an arrow on the string he nodded to John with one of his darkest smiles.

John glanced back at the grazing elk. It was calm, unaware of their presence. John made a pointing upward gesture: should he climb too? Attone's teeth flashed in a grin, white in the darkness. He shook his head. John should shoot at ground level.

John realised at once why this was apparently amusing. When the elk was struck it would look around for its enemy and it would charge the first thing it saw. That would be John. Attone, in the safety of the branch of the tree, would rain down arrows, but John on the ground below would serve as decoy: as bait. John scowled at Attone, who gave him the blandest of smiles and a shrug – it was the luck of the hunt.

John set his arrow on the string and waited. The elk sniffed the forest floor, searching for food. It turned full face to John and lifted its head for a moment, scenting the air. It was a perfect opportunity. Both arrows flew at the same second. John's arrow, aimed for the heart, pierced the thick skin and layer of fat at the chest, while Attone's plunged deep and unerringly into the beast's eye. It bellowed in pain and plunged forward. A second arrow from Attone's bow pierced its shoulder, severing the muscle of the foreleg so the animal dropped to one knee. John's shaky second shot went wide and then he was running, dodging behind the trees as the beast came on, stumbled on, blood pouring from its head. Attone let fly one more arrow into the head again and then jumped from the tree, his knife in his hand. The flow of blood was weakening the animal, it was unable to charge. It fell to both knees, its head moving from one side to the other, the great sweep of the antlers still a danger. John peeped out from behind a tree and came running back, pulling his hunting knife with the sharp shell blade from its safe pouch. Either side of the wounded animal the two men watched for their chance. Attone, whispering the word of blessing on the dying creature, dived behind the moving antlers and plunged his knife between its high shoulders. The head slumped and John reached down and jabbed a hacking, sawing cut into the thick throat.

The two men jumped clear as the beast rolled on its side and died. Attone nodded. 'Good and quick,' he said breathlessly. 'Go, my brother, we thank you.'

John rubbed the sweat from his face with fingers that were wet with fresh blood. He dropped to sit on the snowy forest floor, his legs weak underneath him. 'What if you had missed?' he asked.

Attone thought for a moment. 'Missed?'

'When the beast was charging at me. What if you had missed your shot?'

Attone took a breath to answer and then John's aggrieved face was too much for him; he could make no sensible reply. He whooped with laughter and dropped back on the cold snow. He laughed and laughed his great belly laugh of joy and John, trying to keep a straight face, trying to stay on his dignity, found it was too much for him and he started to laugh as well.

'Why ask? Why should it matter to you?' Attone demanded, wiping his eyes, and bubbling again. 'You wouldn't care. You'd be dead.'

John howled at the logic of this and the two men lay like lovers, side by side on their backs in the winter forest, and laughed until their empty bellies ached while the blue winter sky above them was darkened with the passing of the geese and the wood was louder with their honking than with laughter.

John was left to guard the carcase while Attone started the long run back to the village. It would be two days before he could bring the braves back to carry the meat into camp. John made himself as comfortable as he could for the wait, built a little bender tent of a pair of saplings and thatched it with thin winter fern, made himself a hearth at one side of it and let the tent fill with smoke for the warmth, and started the work of skinning and butchering the great beast. Attone had left his hunting knife with John, so that when John's knife was blunted cutting the thick hide, fat and meat he would not have to waste time sharpening it. He worked from sunrise in the morning when he rose and said the Powhatan morning prayers at his morning wash in the icy water. At noon he gathered nuts and berries and ate with his dark gaze on the river, watching for shoals of fish. After his dinner he gathered firewood and set to work on the elk again. At night he cut a thin slice of elk meat to barbecue over the fire. John had lost completely the white man's habit of gorging when food was available and starving when times were thin. He ate like one of the People, conscious all the time of the river that brought fish to him, and the winds that blew the birds to him and the woods that hid and offered the animals. It was not the way of a Powhatan to plunge into a trough of food like a hog into acorns. Food was not a free gift, it was part of a giving and taking, a balance; and a hunter must take with awareness.

In the two days and three nights while he waited John realised how much of a Powhatan he had become. The forest was no longer fearful to him. He thought how he had once seemed to be a little beetle crawling across a terrifying and infinite world. He now seemed no bigger, the Powhatan never thought of themselves as owners of the forest. He now felt as if this little beetle called John Tradescant, called Eagle, had found his place and his ordained path in this place, and that he need fear nothing since his place led him from the earth to birth and life and death and then to the earth again.

He knew there were wolves in the forest and soon they would get the scent of the elk, and so he built a rough fence of fallen branches around the carcase, and kept the fire lit. Now that he could eat well from the forest the immense labour of his English life seemed to him absurd. He could hardly remember how he had nearly starved in a wooden house set in a forest teeming with life. But then he remembered the hungry anger in Bertram's twisted face and he knew that a man could live among plenty and never know that he was rich.

On the morning of the third day, as John methodically cut steaks of meat from the big animal's body, he heard a tiny crackle of movement behind him and whirled around with his knife at the ready.

'Eagle, I give you greeting,' said Attone pleasantly.

Suckahanna was with him. John held out his arms to her and she came to him, her body as light as a girl in his grasp, her shoulders bird-like and bony.

'I brought your wife and my children, and some others to help cure the meat and to feast. They were hungry at home,' Attone said. 'Build up the fire, they will come soon.'

John wiped Attone's knife and returned it to him with a word of thanks and then he and Suckahanna piled John's little brushwood fence on to his fire so that it flared up and crackled. As soon as it had burned down into hot embers Suckahanna brought large boulders from the river and heaped them with ashes to make them hot, then she laid dozens of small steaks of meat on the hot stones where they sizzled and spat. By the time the village had arrived – all those able to walk – there was meat cooked and ready for everyone.

Everyone ate a little, no-one ate to excess. Everyone sighed at the end of a couple of mouthfuls and said, 'Good. Good,' as if they had attended a banquet of forty-four courses in Whitehall. Then they all stretched out in the bright winter sunshine and dozed for a little while.

When the shadows lengthened, they set to work. The women made a temporary long house by pegging down saplings and weaving bark and leaves through the twigs. The men set up drying poles for the skin of the beast, and enlarged the fire for cooking and smoking the meat. The children were sent out to gather wood for the fires and for another, wider fence, to encircle the smoking meat and the long house. By sunset, when they all went down to the water to pray and to send the smoking leaves of tobacco downriver, glowing in the darkness, they had a little fortified camp: safe against wolves, defensible in case of attack.

It took another two days for the elk to be butchered thoroughly, smoked and packed ready for carriage back to the village. After the first day a couple of fast-running braves had taken the first consignment back to the village for the elderly and the very young, and those too sick to travel into the forest. The skin was tanned and ready, the meat was smoked. The bones were gathered and tied into a great bundle. Suckahanna poured water over the fires and scuffed the embers with her foot. The women untied the saplings and they sprang back up. It was clear that there had been a house on the site but by spring there would be no mark on the ground; and that was what they wanted. Not only to keep their ways and their paths a secret, but because the forest must be a home to the elk as well as to the Powhatan, and elk will not come near a village nor even a trace of one.

When all the work was done John hesitated with his burden of meat. 'I want to visit Bertram Hobert,' he said to Suckahanna.

'What for?'

'I saw him while we were hunting. He is hungry and he is sick. His feet are falling off him. He was my friend. I should like to take him some meat.'

She looked at him with a long, worried gaze. 'You cannot go looking like this,' she said. 'He will shoot you the moment he sees you.'

'I shall leave a gift of meat on his doorstep,' John said. 'That was done for me once, and it saved my life. I should like to do the same.'

'You ate yourself sick,' she observed. 'Take care you don't kill him by accident.'

John chuckled. 'He has a wife to care for him,' he said. 'Or at least he did have. He is my friend, Suckahanna.'

The look she turned to him was more powerful than tender. 'He cannot be your friend now,' she said. 'You are a Powhatan.'

'He can,' John argued. 'If a Powhatan could not be the friend of a white man then I would have died in the woods and I would never have been called Eagle by one of the finest hunters in the People.'

'That was then,' she said gently. 'The river gets wider every day. The distance between one shore and the other is greater all the time. You cannot cross and recross, my husband.'

He put his hand out to her and barely touched her fingertips. As soon as she felt his touch her eyes flickered closed for just a moment at the pleasure of the warmth of his hand. John knew that he had won.

'Shall I wait for you?' she asked in quite a different tone, as low as a sleepy honey bee in winter.

'Go with the People,' he replied. 'I will catch you up before you reach the village.'

She nodded and picked up her burden of dried meat, and set off. John watched her rangy, long stride until the trees hid her, then he turned and set off at a hunting jog downriver to Hobert's plantation.

John slowed as he recognised the features of Hobert's boundaries, a pine tree where they had slashed a crude 'H', a magnificent oak, bending over the path and shading it with its spreading branches, and then he saw the shingled roof of the Hobert house and a thin spiral of smoke coming from the chimney. John stepped back into the shade of the trees and hunkered down on his heels to watch.

He saw a man bent low under a burden of wood come out of the trees and fling down the cord by the door and straighten up with a sigh. A black man: Francis the Negro slave. He saw the door open and it was Mrs Hobert, speaking sharply and then going indoors. He waited a little longer as it grew cold and the light started to drain from the sky. Bertram must be out late with his gun. John did not move even though the hairs on his arms and his chest stood up, and his skin prickled with goosebumps against the cold. Only when it was nearly dark did he decide that Bertram must already be indoors. He rose to his feet and went silently down the hill to the little house nestling on a piece of flat ground before the river.

He hesitated at the door and then put his eye to the crack to peer into the firelit interior. It was a sparsely furnished room. A table before the fire; two stools and a hewed tree stump served as chairs. A box bed built into the wall was occupied by a man, his shoulder hunched against the room, his head tucked down. A ladder at the back of the room led to a sleeping platform, a string and a piece of sacking serving as a curtain between the two. John thought of the spick and span London house that the Hoberts had left for this venture and felt his heart ache for them, and surprisingly for himself too: another exile in this strange and remote land.

He tapped on the door and called out at the same time: 'A friend, John Tradescant.' His own name was awkward in his mouth.

Despite the reassurance he heard a little scream from Mrs Hobert and heard a stool overturn as Francis leaped to his feet.

'Who?' she demanded.

'John Tradescant, your shipmate and neighbour,' he repeated.

'We thought you were dead!' The door opened cautiously and Mrs Hobert's white face peered out.

John kept back in the shadows. 'I was with the Powhatan,' he said.

'Savages?'

He bit back a retort. 'Yes. So I look strange . . .'

She stepped a little further out, female curiosity driving her onwards. 'Like a savage?'

'Don't be afraid,' John said and came towards the light.

She clapped her hand over her mouth at the sight of him but her eyes widened with terror. 'Is it really you?'

'I swear it,' John said. 'Just dressed as a Powhatan.'

'Your poor, poor man,' she said and took hold of his hand and drew him indoors. 'Good God preserve us all from such a fate. How did you get away from them?'

'I was not captured,' John said. He nodded at Francis, who stood frozen in horror at the sight of him.

'It is me,' John repeated.

Francis nodded, gave a little bow in reply and restored a wood-chopping axe to its place behind the door.

'Sit down, sit down,' Sarah begged him. 'Your hair! and – dear God – they have even stained your skin to their colour!'

'That's bear grease,' John said. 'It keeps off insects in summer and keeps out the cold in winter.'

'God preserve us! How did you get away?' Then her constant terror of the savage men struck her and she shot a frightened look at the thin wooden door. 'Are they after you?'

'No, no,' John reassured her. 'They let me go freely.'

'Are you hungry?' The anxious glance she threw at the cookpot suggested that there was not much to be had, even if he was.

'I have eaten,' John said steadily. 'But I brought you some meat. We killed an elk.'

'Meat?' She choked as the saliva rushed into her throat. 'You have meat?'

John reached for the bundle strapped into the small of his back. 'Here,' he said. 'It's smoked; but you could seethe it in a little water.'

She fell upon it and tossed it into the cookpot as it stood by the hearthside. John, remembering his sickness from food heated and reheated in the same pot, winced a little. But she was already stirring in water from a pitcher, and greedily tasting. 'Bertram, Bertram!'

The shoulder in the bed shrugged still higher, and then the man rolled over on his back and glared into the room.

'We have meat!' she said triumphantly. 'Can you sit up while I spoon you some broth?'

'Meat?' Hobert's voice was a rough croak.

'Neighbour Tradescant has brought us some steaks from an elk,' she said. 'He has been living with the savages but has got away from them now, praise God.'

Hobert heaved himself up to one arm. His face was marked with pain. In the little room John could smell the flesh of his snow-rotted feet and the stench of unwashed blankets.

'John Tradescant?' he asked wonderingly. 'Is that really you?'

John went to the bedside and took the man's hand. 'I have been living with the Powhatan and I dress like them and hunt with them,' he said. 'They treat me as a friend. I saw you in the woods the other day, and I thought you might be in need. I have brought you some meat and I can bring you more. They have medicines as well which would make you well. I would have come sooner if I had known you were in need, Bertram.'

The man's red-rimmed eyes wandered over John's face. 'A savage,' he said, bewildered.

'I am indeed John Tradescant,' John said. 'But I could not live alone in the forest. Thank God I fell among the Powhatan and they have treated me kindly.'

Sarah Hobert came to her husband's bedside with a delicate pot filled with gravy. John recognised at once the work of the People: the perfectly smooth walls of one of their dainty black pots.

'That's Powhatan-made,' he said.

She gave him a swift disapproving glance. 'We used to trade with them, but they became too demanding and dishonest,' she said. 'Now my husband will not have them near his land.' She turned to the wreck of the man in the bed. 'Will you taste, Bertram?'

Eagerly he sat up and reached for the pot, eagerly he sucked at it and gulped until the pot was empty.

'Rest now,' John said, remembering his horrors of illness after he had eaten too richly on a starved belly. 'You can have more later, and I will bring you other food, corn and berries and nuts.'

Sarah reached out and caught his hand. 'Praise God for bringing you back to us,' she said. 'For that which was lost is found.'

John hesitated. 'I must be a visitor only,' he said.

Her face was shining with relief and happiness, deaf to his reluctance. 'Praise God for returning you to your true people,' she said.

It was out of the question for John to leave that night, or even the next day. He slept in the attic on the same side of the makeshift screen as the Negro Francis. In the morning Hobert was in a fever, groaning and counting aloud, counting the sums of money he must save to buy headrights in the new land, counting the percentage of profit he might hope to make, counting the wages he must pay to get his land cleared and tobacco planted.

'Is he mad?' John asked Sarah.

She shook her head. 'It's the fever again,' she said. 'When it comes on him he acts like a madman but then the fever breaks and he is cool-headed again. Francis has to tie him up sometimes.'

'This is impossible,' John said. 'You will have to go back to Jamestown. You cannot stay here with only a sick man and a slave.'

She looked up, her face shining with new hope. 'That's what I had feared,' she said. 'But now you are come, sent by God to help me. You will help me plant the fields, won't you, John? Help me until Bertram is well again? He will be well now that you can bring him food, and when the summer comes he will be well and strong again. He is a man of much strength. This is only the dreadful seasoning of Virginia. They all say that. A man must be seasoned to work under the hot sun. Bertram is burning up now, no sun will ever be too hot for him again.'

'I cannot stay,' John said awkwardly.

'Where else could you go?' she asked. 'Your own headright is over-grown and the savages will have stripped your house of everything you ever owned.'

John felt completely incapable of telling her that he had a new house in the Indian village, and a wife and children waiting for him.

'A cup of ale, for the love of God!' Bertram called loudly from his bed.

Sarah turned and poured him a little pot of water from the pitcher.

'I'll get you some more,' John muttered, and took the pitcher and went outside.

He walked slowly down to the river, filled the pitcher, and strolled back, taking the chance to think. If he left Sarah to fend for herself he was signing her death warrant as clearly as if he were the king in Whitehall condemning some poor soul in the Tower. She and Bertram and Francis would die in the forest and the trees would grow through their earthen floor and the trumpet vine strangle their chimney. There was no chance at all that they would survive in this fruitful, overwhelming land without help. In contrast, Suckahanna and the children would be guarded by Attone, and fed and protected by the village. The land was no danger to Suckahanna, she fed from it as easily as a deer nibbling green shoots in the woods.

John squared his shoulders, picked up the pitcher and went back to the house.

Francis was outside, stacking firewood. 'Go in and guard your master,' John said. 'I must take Mrs Hobert out into the wood and teach her how to gather fruits and roots and berries. You have been starving in the midst of plenty here. Why did you not tell her?'

'Me? How should I know?'

'You must have eaten nuts and berries in your own country,' John said irritably. 'Gathered them in the forests?'

The man raised one eyebrow. 'My own country is not like this one,' he said. 'So we don't have the same fruits. And in any case, I had my meals served to me by my wife or by my slave. I didn't go out clambering in trees for cashew nuts like a monkey.'

'You're a savage!' John exclaimed. 'What d'you mean, slaves, and being served?'

The black man looked from the remnants of his own breeches and shirt to John's embroidered buckskin loincloth and his stained and tattooed skin.

'I see only one savage here,' he remarked.

John swore under his breath and pushed open the door. 'Mrs Hobert!' he said. 'Come out and let me show you how to find nuts and roots for your dinner.'

She brought a basket, Indian-made, John observed, and she was quick to learn how to identify roots which could be cooked and eaten, and roots which could be sliced and eaten raw. John showed her nut-bearing trees and pointed to the wild plum and the wild cherry trees which would blossom and bear fruit later in the year. They came home with a basket full of good things and she sliced the roots to supplement the remainder of the elk in the cookpot for their dinner.

Hobert had lapsed into a deep sleep, the sweat thick and cold on his forehead.

'We won't wake him,' his wife decided. 'The fever may be breaking and he will need his rest.'

'The Powhatan have physic,' John said. 'For fevers and also for frost-bite. I could ask the werowance, or one of the physicians, to come and see Bertram. Or there's a wise woman very gifted with herbs, she made me well. She might come.'

Sarah shook her head in absolute refusal. 'They would poison us and hack us up to eat,' she said. 'You may have been lucky, John Tradescant, that they chose to keep you alive. But they have been our enemies since we came here. At first we traded with them and gave them little trinkets for food and for goods. Then we tried to make them come and work for us, clear the land and dig the fields. But they were lazy and idle and when we whipped them they stole what they could and ran away. After that Bertram has shot at them whenever he has seen them. They are our enemies. I won't have them near me.'

'They have skills that you need to learn,' John persisted. 'This dinner you are eating is Powhatan food. You have to learn how they live in the forest in order to live here yourself.'

She shook her head. 'I shall live as a God-fearing Englishwoman and I shall make this land into a new England. Then they can come to *me* to learn.' She closed her eyes briefly in a prayer. When she opened them she was looking sharply, critically, at John.

'I have unpacked a shirt and pair of breeches belonging to Bertram,' she said. 'You can have them in return for the service you have done us by coming to our door in our time of need. You will not want to walk around half-naked as you are.'

'This is how I live now,' John said.

'Not in a Christian home you don't,' she said sharply. 'I cannot allow it, Mr Tradescant, it is not fit. It is lechery to show yourself like this to me. If my husband were well and in his right mind he would not permit it.'

'I had no thought of lechery, Mrs Hobert –'

She gestured to the clothes spread at the fireside. 'Then dress yourself, Mr Tradescant, please.'

John stayed with the Hoberts for a full week, dressed in English clothes again, but still barefoot. The shirt chafed at his neck, the breeches felt hot and constricting around his legs. But he wore them out of courtesy to Sarah's feelings, and he did not feel he could leave her until Bertram was well again.

The fever broke on the third night, and the next day Bertram was well enough to hobble down to the river, leaning on John's arm.

The little green tobacco shoots were showing through the earth of the nursery beds. Bertram paused and looked at them as dotingly as if they were sleeping children. 'Here is my fortune, Tradescant,' he said. 'Here is my fortune growing. If we can survive the rest of this cold weather without starving, without falling to the savages, then this will be the making of me. I shall see it sold on the quayside at Jamestown. I shall see it packed and sailing for England. I shall hire a servant, a brace of servants, and I will make myself a life here.'

'God willing,' John said.

'Stay with us,' Hobert said. 'Stay with us and you can take a share in this, John. I doubt I can manage without you and Sarah cannot do it all on her own. Francis has no skill with plants, I am afraid to let him touch them. If I am sick when they need planting out who is going to do the work? Stay with me and see my tobacco plants safely into the field.'

'I can't stay,' John said as gently as he could. 'I have made a different life for myself in this country. But I can come back to you and see that you are well. I'll come back gladly and work for you. I'll set out the seedlings for you and show you how the Powhatan plant their food crops so you never need go hungry again.'

'You'll come back to plant out my tobacco? You swear it?'

'I swear,' John said.

'Then we won't need food crops,' Hobert said buoyantly. 'We shall buy all we need with what I can earn from the tobacco. And I'll see you right, John. Next season I shall come to your headright and work for you, as we promised, eh? As we always said we would do.'

On that promise John left the Hoberts and crossed the river just above the falls where he could jump from boulder to boulder in the fast-moving stream. On the far side he stripped off the breeches and the shirt that he had been given and bundled them up into the crook of a tree. It reminded him of Suckahanna's girlhood and her attempt to live in the two worlds. She used to wear a long gown and sometimes a bonnet in Jamestown, but when she was free in the woods she wore her buckskin pinny and nothing more.

The air felt good on his skin again, he felt more of a man in his nakedness than he ever could do in his breeches. He stretched as if he were freed from a constriction greater than a linen shirt, and set off at the Powhatan hunting stride for his home.

Suckahanna greeted him with the careful courtesy of a deeply offended wife. John neither explained nor apologised until they were alone on the sleeping platform, in the darkness of their house, when the soft sighs from both children showed that they were asleep.

'I could not come back when I said I would come,' he said to her smooth naked back. 'Bertram was sick, his wife was hungry and their slave didn't know what to do.'

She said nothing and did not turn to him.

'I stayed to feed a hungry woman and nurse a sick man,' John said. 'When I showed her how to get food and when he was better I came home again, as soon as I could.'

He waited.

'Would you have wanted me to leave them to die?' he asked.

At last she turned back to him. 'Better now and by their own failure than later,' she said simply.

John gasped as the words struck him. 'You speak like a heartless woman,' he protested.

She shrugged as if she did not much care whether he thought her heartless or kind; and then she turned her back on him again and went to sleep.

Spring 1644, Virginia

John did not go back to the Hoberts' homestead for a month. He hunted with Attone and the other braves, he lived as a Powhatan. But there was a coldness between Suckahanna and him which the routine of ordinary life could not conceal.

When he judged it was time for the planting out of Bertram's tobacco he spoke to Attone, rather than Suckahanna.

'My friend who was sick needs me to plant out his tobacco. I should go and help him now.'

'Go then, Eagle,' Attone said unhelpfully.

'Suckahanna will be angry at my going.'

'Stay then.'

'I'm not asking for help –'

'I'm not giving any.'

John paused for a moment and bit back his temper. Attone was smiling. He loved to be annoying.

'I'm telling you that I will be away for a while,' John said patiently. 'I am asking you to watch Suckahanna for me and fetch me if she is in any need. She will not send for me; she is angry with me. She would not send for me even if she needed me.'

'She will be in no need. The game is coming back, the fish are spawning. What would she need you for? You can go to your smelly friends.'

John gritted his teeth. 'If one of the People was in trouble you would go to his help.'

'Hobert is not one of the People. He is not one of mine.'

John hesitated. 'Nor is he mine,' he said, conscious of the pain of divided loyalty. 'But I cannot see him fail or fall sick or die of hunger. He was good to me once, and I have made him a promise.'

'This is a path in a circle,' Attone said cheerfully. 'You are wandering like a man snow-blind, round and round. What is blinding you, Eagle? Why can you not walk straight?'

'Because I am pulled two ways,' John said grimly.

'Then cut one string,' Attone said briskly. 'Before it tangles around your feet and brings you down.' He rose to his feet and loped down the river towards the fish weir without looking back.

The Hoberts' house was amid a sea of green. Bertram had started planting the fields which ran between the house and the river and the absurd flop-leaved plants were three rows thick before the house.

'John, thank God you've come!' Hobert said, kneeling. 'I was afraid you would fail us.'

'Mr Tradescant, you are very welcome!' Sarah said from further down the row.

John, hot in his reclaimed breeches and shirt, waved at them both.

'You should have a hat to shield you from the sun,' Sarah scolded. 'Men have died of sunstroke in this country.'

John put his hand to his face and felt the heat radiating from his flushed skin. 'It's these clothes,' he said. 'How can anyone wear wool in this country in spring?'

'It's the vapours in the air,' Sarah said firmly. 'When we next go to Jamestown I will buy you a hat. We've only just come back from town.'

'There was a letter for you,' Bertram said, remembering. 'I went into Jamestown to buy a hoe and to collect some money sent me from England. I called in at your inn and there was a letter for you there.'

'For me?' John asked.

'It's inside. I put it under the mattress you used last time to keep it safe.'

John put his hand to his head.

'There you are! Sunstroke!' Sarah exclaimed triumphantly.

'No,' John said. 'I just feel . . . It is so odd to have a letter . . .'

He turned and went into the house, jumped up the ladder in one bound. In the loft bedroom was his straw mattress and underneath it was a travel-stained folded and sealed paper. John snatched it up and recognised Hester's writing at once.

A great pain shot through John at the thought of his family in Lambeth and a great fear that one of the children, Frances, or Johnnie, was sick or dead, or that the house had been lost to passing soldiers or the garden destroyed, or Hester herself . . . he pulled himself back from nightmare imaginings, broke the seal and smoothed out the paper.

Lambeth, the New Year, 1644

   Dear Husband,

   Having heard no news from you I pray that your venture is going well and that you have found the land you wanted, cleared it and planted it. It is strange for me not knowing what the view is like from your window, nor what your kitchen is like, nor what the weather may be for you. I try to tell the children about what you are doing now but I do not know whether to tell them you are struggling through deep snow or digging in damp earth. We are reading Captain Smith's True History *in the evenings so that we may understand a little of your life, but I have to keep missing out some of his adventures as the children would be too afraid for you. I pray that you are right and that it is not such a savage place as he describes, and that the planters too have become more kindly and Christian in their doings.*

   Here in Lambeth we are well but troubled, as is everyone in the kingdom, by the continuance of the war. Food is very scarce and there is no coal to be had at all. There has been petty fighting on the roads into London and we never know whether meat for the markets will be driven in or not. Our men are called up to serve in the City trained bands but they have not yet been sent outside the bounds of the City, so when they are stood down they come back to work. We try to keep the Ark and the gardens open as normal and we are trading a little. There are still people who want to live as if the war were not taking place and they still want to know that gardens are growing and that strange and rare beautiful things can still be seen. It is very pitiful to me when a young gentleman comes to order some seeds or plants or trees before he goes off to join either the king or the Parliament army, and I know that he is planting for his heir and does not expect to see the trees grow. It is at those times that I realise what wickedness this war is and will be, and I confess, I blame the king very much for standing so upon his rights and driving his people into rebellion.

   I did not think I would ever be able to say it, but I am glad you are not here, husband. I miss you and so do the children but I do not know how a man could keep his wits and bear the sorrow of this kingdom, especially one like you who had served the king and the queen and seen them reap the consequences of their folly. There are rights, God-given rights, on both sides of the argument and all a woman can wonder is why the two sides cannot come together and resolve to live in peace. But they cannot, they will not, and God help them we all suffer while they hammer out the victory one on the other. Parliament is now in alliance with the Scots and they have sworn to defend each other against the king. But the Scots are a long way away and the king's armies are very close, and everyone seems to think he has the advantage. Also, he has now recruited a Papist Irish army and we are all most afraid of their coming.

What seems more and more certain to me, when this is all over, is that we shall see the king in London again with his liberties barely trimmed, and those who have stood against him will have to pray God that he is more generous in victory than he was in peace time. Prince Rupert is said to be everywhere, and the other commander of the armies is the queen, so you can imagine how the king is advised between those two. Prince Maurice serves also and they have taken Bristol and Devizes this summer. Against the wealth of the king, the Parliament army makes a pitiful showing. The king has commanders who have fought all over Europe and know how it should be done, Prince Rupert has never lost a battle. Against them the Parliament puts ploughboys and apprentice lads into the fields and the gentlemen mow them down like barley. We hear constantly from the Parliament of little battles which are fought at places of no name and mean nothing but are hailed as great victories.

However, the king has not yet approached London – and the City remains firmly against him. Your father-in-law Mr Hurte has provided his own regiment to defend the City, he says – as all the merchants do – that the king cannot rule the City again. But since all the other great towns of the kingdom are falling to the king one by one then clearly, London cannot hold out alone – especially if the queen prevails on her French relations to join her husband. If a French army marches on Westminster the Parliament will have been defeated indeed, and I think it will be harder to be rid of the French Papists than it was to invite them.

Worse than the French Papists will be an Irish army. The

*great fear is that the king is planning all the time to flood the
kingdom with Irishmen, but I cannot believe that such wickedness is in his mind. Not even he, surely, would sow such a
whirlwind. If they could ever be prevailed upon to leave, what
Englishman would ever trust the king's word again?*

*The king holds Oxford of course, and his friends hold garri-
sons all the way up the Great North Road to Scotland. The
queen holds York, and while she is in the field I have no hope
of peace. The king's army must march on London soon, and
those of us who know not what to think (and that is most of
us) can only hope that the city surrenders quickly.*

*The children are well, though running wild with neither
school nor society to tame them. I will not let them go to the
city which is full of the plague again, spread I am sure by the
travelling soldiers who come and go from battle to village. I
have had a one-way door set in our wall so that we can give
food to passing paupers without any one of the servants having
to open our front door. The bridge over the stream I have had
made into a little drawbridge and we pull it up at night. I have
completed the wall around the Ark and garden and sometimes
I feel that I am a Mrs Noah in very truth, peering over the
edge of the Ark as the waters of the end of the world arise and
swirl around me. It is on such nights that I feel very lonely and
very afraid and I wish that I were with you.*

*Johnnie says that he will be a soldier and fight for the king.
He has an etching of Prince Rupert on his black horse pinned
to the head of his bed and makes most bloodthirsty prayers for
his safety every night. He is a handsome, brave boy, as clever
as any child in the kingdom. He is reading and writing in Latin
and English and French, and I have set him to making the
plant labels in English and Latin which he does without error.
He misses you very much but he is proud of having a Virginia
planter for a father, he thinks you are daily wrestling with bears
and fighting Indians and prays for your safety every night.*

*Frances is well too. You would hardly recognise her, she has
grown in these last few months from a girl to a young woman.
She wears her hair pinned up now all the time and her skirts
very long and elegant. I always knew she would be beautiful
but she has surpassed my hopes for her. She has such a dainty
prettiness about her. She is as fair as her mother, Mrs Hurte
tells me, but she has a lightness of spirit which is all her own.*

Sometimes she is too flighty, I am aware of it, and I try to reprove her, but she is such a merry dear that I cannot be too strict. She manages the garden in your absence and I think you will be proud of her when you return. She has a real way with plants and growing things. I often think it is such a shame that she cannot take your place in very truth and be another Tradescant gardener as she always wished to be.

It is her fate which is my greatest worry if the fighting should come near to London. I think that Johnnie and I could survive anything but a direct attack, but Frances is so pretty that she attracts notice wherever she goes. I dress her as plainly as I can and she always wears a cap on her head and a hood to cover her hair when she goes out, but there is something about her which turns men's heads. I have seen her walk down the street and people simply look at her as if she were a flower or a statue, something rare and fine which they would like to take home with them. A wealthy man, whom I will not call a gentleman, visited the garden the other day and offered me ten pounds to give her to him. I had Joseph show him off the premises as quickly as you would wish, but it shows you the anxieties which I suffer over her. One of the kitchen maids − a fool − told Frances that the gentleman had taken a fancy to her and made an offer which was not of marriage, and before he had gone I am sorry to say that she climbed up on the garden wall, turned her back on him, and upended her skirts to show him her bum. I pulled her down and spanked her for indecency, and then thought she was crying most pitiably for shame, but when I had her right way up again I saw she could not speak for laughing. I sent her to her room in disgrace, and only when she was gone did I laugh too. She is a great mixture of minx and child and young lady, and I fancy the fine gentleman would have got more than he had bargained for.

If I think there is a chance of the fighting coming any closer I shall send her up the river to Oatlands, but with the country in this turmoil I do not know where she could be most safe. My choice, of course, is to keep her close by me.

My greatest advisor in these difficult times is your father's friend and your uncle, Alexander Norman, who has the most immediate news of anyone. Since he sends out the ordnance from the Tower of London he always knows where the fiercest fighting has been and how much munition was used in every *battle. He comes out to see us every week and brings us news and satisfies himself that we are well. He treats Frances as a complete young lady and Johnnie as the head of the household, and so they always welcome his arrival as their most favourite guest. Frances is never naughty when he is with us but very sober and careful, an excellent little housewife. When I told him of the man who had offered money for her he was more angry than I have ever seen him before and he would have challenged the man to a duel if I had given his name. I told him that the man had been punished enough but I did not tell him how.*

And as for myself, husband, I will speak of myself though we were not married for love and have never been more than mere friends and for all I fear you do not think of me kindly since we parted on a disagreement. I am doing my duty according to my promise made to you at the altar and to your father on his death bed to be a good wife to you, a mother to your children, and to guard the garden and the rarities. The beauty of the rarities, of the garden and of the children is my greatest joy, even in these difficult times when joy is hard to find. I miss you more bitterly than I had thought possible and I think often of a moment in the yard, a second in the hall, a letter which you once wrote to me which sounded almost loving, and I wonder perhaps if we had met each other in easier times whether we might have been lovers as well as husband and wife. I wish I had felt free to go with you on this venture, I wish you had held me so dear that you would not have gone without me, or felt as I do, tied to the house and the garden and the children. But you do not, and it is not to be, and I do not waste my time in mourning the failure of a dream that perhaps I am a fool to even think of.

So I am well, a little afraid sometimes, anxious all the time, working hard to keep your father's inheritance together for you and for Johnnie, watching Frances, and praying for you, my dear, dear husband, and hoping that wherever you are, however far away you are from me and in such a strange land, you are safe and well and will one day come home to your constant wife, Hester.

John dropped to his knees on his mattress and then hunkered down. He read it all over again. The paper was fragile in parts where it had been wetted by sea water or rain, the ink had run on one or two words but the voice of Hester, her idiosyncratic, brave little voice sounded across the sea to her husband, telling him that she was keeping faith with him.

John was completely still. In the silence of the house he could hear the scratch of a squirrel's claws on the roof above his head. He could hear a log shift in the hearth in the room below. Hester's love and steadiness felt like a thread that could stretch all the way from England to Virginia and could guide him home, or it might wrap around his heart and tug at it. He thought of Frances growing up so mischievous and so beautiful, and of his funny little scholarly son who prayed for him every night and thought he was wrestling with bears, and then he thought of his wife, Hester, a true wife if ever a man had one, fortifying his house with her little drawbridge, managing the business and showing people the rarities even while she watched the progress of the war and planned their escape. She deserved better than a husband whose heart was elsewhere, who exploited her skill and her courage, and then left her.

John dropped his head in his hands. He thought that he must have been mad to leave his wife and his children and his home, madly selfish to leave them in the middle of a war, mad with folly to think that he could make a life for himself in a wilderness and mad with vanity to think that he could love and marry a young woman and make his life all over again, to his own mad pattern.

John stretched out on his mattress and heard a low groan of pain, his own sick heart.

He lay very still for some time. Down below Francis the Negro came in with a load of wood and dumped it by the hearth. 'You in here, Mr Tradescant?'

'Here,' John said. He dragged himself to the ladder and came down, his knees weak, the very grip of his fingers on the rungs seemed powerless.

Francis looked more closely at John and his face slightly softened. 'Was it your letter? Bad news from your home?'

John shook his head and passed his hand over his face. 'No. They're managing without me. It just made me think I should be there.'

The Negro shrugged, as if the weight of exile was unbearably heavy on his own shoulders. 'Sometimes a man cannot be where he should be.'

'Yes, but I chose to come here,' John said.

A slow smile lightened the man's face, as if John's folly was deliciously funny. 'You *chose* this?'

John nodded. 'I have a beautiful home in Lambeth and a wife who was ready to love me, and two healthy children growing every day, and I took it into my head that there was no life for me there, and that the woman I loved was here, and that I could start all over again, that I should start all over again.'

Francis kneeled at the hearth and stacked wood with steady deftness.

'I've been in my father's shadow all my life,' John said, more to himself than to the silent man. 'When I came here for the first time it was virgin earth for me, because it was somewhere he had not been, with plants that he had not seen, a place where he had not made friends and where people would not always know me as his son, a lesser copy of the real thing.

'At home, I worked in his trade, I did what he did. And I always felt I did it less well. And when it came to loyalty to a master, or certainty about my own course –' John broke off with a little laugh. 'He always knew what was the right thing to do. It seemed to me that he was a man of absolute certainty. And I have spent my life blown this way and that with my doubts.'

Francis gave him a brief glance. 'I've seen Englishmen like that,' he observed. 'It always makes me wonder if you are so uncertain, why you are so quick to make rules, to make war, to go into the lives of other people?'

'What about you?' John asked. 'Why did you come?'

The man's face shone in the flickering light from the fire. 'I've been in the wrong place all my life,' he said thoughtfully. 'Being in the wrong place and longing for home is no new thing for me.'

'Where is your home?' John asked.

'The kingdom of Dahomey,' the man replied.

'Is that in Africa?'

The man nodded.

'Were you sold into slavery?'

'I was pushed into slavery, I was dragged into slavery, I was kicking and screaming and biting and fighting from roadside to marketplace to gangplank and down into the hold. I didn't stop fighting and screaming and breaking away until . . .' He suddenly broke off.

'Until when?'

'Until they brought us up on deck for washing and I saw the sea all around me and no land in sight, and I realised I didn't know even where my home was any more, that if I escaped it would do me no good because I didn't know where to go. That I was lost, and that I would stay lost for the rest of my life.'

The two men fell silent. John measured the enormity of that journey across the sea which could suck the courage out of a man, a fighting man.

'Did they bring you to England?'

'Jamaica first, but the captain brought me on to England. He wanted a slave. Lost me in a game of cards to a London merchant, he sold me to Mr Hobert who wanted to bring a horse to Virginia to do his plough-ing for him but was advised that he couldn't ship a horse but a man would do the job as well. So now I am a plough-horse.'

'He doesn't treat you badly,' John said.

The man shook his head. 'For a horse I'm doing well,' he said with quiet irony. 'I get to live in the house and I eat what they eat. And I have a piece of land of my own.'

'You will grow your own food?'

'My own food, my own tobacco, and I will trade on my own account, and when I have earned fifteen shillings Mr Hobert has agreed to sell me my liberty and then I will be his indentured servant, and not his slave, and when I have earned enough to keep myself I shall buy more land and then I shall be a planter, as good as you.'

'You will be freed?'

'Mr Hobert has promised it, the magistrate has witnessed it, and the other black men tell me that it is not uncommon. In a country as big as this a man has to agree with his slaves how long they shall work for him. It's too easy for them to just run from him to a master who will offer better terms. There are always other planters who would give them work, there is always more land for them to plant for themselves.'

'Don't you want to go back to Africa?'

An expression of deep pain passed swiftly across the black face and was gone. 'I have to believe that I will be there at the hour of my death,' he said. 'When they talk of paradise and going to heaven that is where I think I will be. But I don't expect to see it again in this life.'

'Did you leave a family behind?'

'My wife, my child, my mother and two little brothers.'

John was silent at the enormity of this loss. 'You must hate us,' he said. 'All of us white men for taking you away.'

The man looked directly at him. 'I don't hate you,' he said. 'I have no time left for hate.' He paused. 'But I don't know how you can pray to your god and hope that he hears you.'

John turned his head away. 'Oh, I can tell you that,' he said bitterly. 'We do a clever little trick, us Englishmen. We start by assuming that everything in the world is ours, everything that ever was, everything that ever will be.'

He thought of the king's elegant assumption that the world was constructed for his pleasure, that every work of art should belong to him, almost by right. 'In our own country anyone who is not powerful and beautiful is a lesser person, not worth thinking about. When we go overseas we find many men and women who are not like us, so we think they are lesser still. When we find people whose language we can't understand we say they can't speak, when they don't have houses like our houses we say they can't build, when they don't make music like our music or dance like we dance we say they can only howl like dogs, that they are animals, that they are less than animals because less useful to us.'

'So Bertram Hobert takes me as his plough-horse.'

'And I swagger around, thinking that I can come to this country and that the land is empty and I can take a headright, and the woman could have no better future than to love me,' John said bitterly. 'And so I walked away from the land I already owned and the woman to whom I owed a duty. Because I am an Englishman. Because the whole world is to be made for my convenience.'

The door opened and Sarah Hobert stood in the doorway, mud encrusting her boots. 'Pull them off,' she said abruptly to Francis. 'I've come to make dinner.'

Francis kneeled at her feet. John stepped back into the darker corner of the room. Sarah came into the room in her stockinged feet and pulled off her cape, spread it out on the hooks to dry. 'It's raining again,' she said. 'I wish it would stop.'

She put the cooking pot on the edge of the fire and stirred it briskly. It would be suppawn for dinner again. Francis took four bowls from the fireside and put them on the rough trestle table, and pulled up the two stools and the two logs which served as chairs. Bertram came into the room, heeling himself out of his boots, carrying a pitcher of fresh water from the river.

They bowed their heads while Bertram spoke a blessing on their food and then they ate in silence. John looked covertly at Bertram and his wife while they ate their gruel. This land had changed them both. Sarah had been a redoubtable, God-fearing woman in England, the wife of a small farmer, and a trader in her own right. This land had made her hard. Her face was pinched and determined. The fat had been rubbed off Hobert too. In England he had been round-faced and ruddy-cheeked but here he had faced death and terror. His face was engraved with lines of suspicion and hatred. This was a country in which only a man of remarkable courage and persistence could survive. Prosperity was harder and took even longer.

Sarah bowed her head as she finished her dinner and then she rose from the table. There was not a moment to spare for leisure. There was never a moment to spare for leisure.

'Are you ready to work?' she asked John

He felt the letter crackle in his pocket. 'I'm ready,' he said. The suppawn lay heavy in his belly, and although John knew it was old cornflour and stale water, the pain, the deep pain in the centre of his body, was not indigestion but guilt. He should never have left England. He should never have sought and loved another woman. He should have stayed with the woman his father had chosen for him and brought up his children with her. He had run from his life like a schoolboy playing truant and now he realised that a man cannot have two lives. He has to choose. Attone's rough, sarcastic counsel was right – a man pulled two ways by two threads must cut one of them.

Sarah nodded at him and went out of the house, followed by her husband and Francis. She led the way down to the end of the planting, stumping along with a spade in one hand. Bertram carried the pick-axe for the stubborn roots. Francis, behind them both, was pushing Sarah's heavy wooden barrow, loaded with the precious swaying burden of small tobacco plants. John brought up the rear, carrying the two new hoes. He thought for a moment of the carving of his father on the newel post of Hatfield House. That showed a man stepping out to garden for pleasure, with his hat tilted on his head and his hoe in his hand, a rich vase under his arm spilling over with flowers and fruits. All John's life had been filled with plants grown for beauty, filled with the idea of planting and hoeing and weeding to create a solace for the eyes, a source of joy. Now he was working for survival. Some perverse contradictory desire had driven him away from the ease and richness of his father's life into a country where it would take all his skill and strength just to survive. His father's inheritance, the rich joy of his father's work, he had abandoned and left behind him. He paused and watched Hobert, Sarah and Francis as they went down the path towards the river to start planting out their tobacco crop: a small procession of determined people, planting their hopes in virgin earth.

John stayed with the Hoberts for eight nights and when he left, the field before their house was cleared of all big roots, and they had a crop of tobacco set in the ground and thriving. At his insistence they had planted a kitchen garden at the side of the house and it was set with corn, pumpkin, and beans. John would dearly have loved to grow amaracock between the rows, as the Indian women did, so that the Hoberts could have fruit in their garden as well as vegetables. But they had not tasted the fruit since the Powhatan had ceased to trade with them, and they had not thought to keep the seeds.

'I'll see if I can get you some seeds,' John said.

Sarah gleamed at him. 'Steal them,' she said.

John was genuinely shocked. 'I would not have thought you would have permitted thievery.'

'It is not thieving to take from such as they,' she said firmly. 'Do I steal a bone from my dog's bowl? They have no right to the land, it has been claimed by the king. Everything in the land is ours. When they put meat in their mouths they are poaching from us. This land is a new England, and everything in it belongs to English men and women.'

'You'll come back to help me harvest, won't you, John?' Hobert asked.

John hesitated. 'If I can,' he said. 'It is not easy for me to come and go.'

'Stay here then,' Sarah urged him. 'If they are looking askance then you may be in danger. Don't go back to them.'

'It is not them,' John said slowly. 'It's me. It is hard for me to come and go between this world and theirs.'

'Then stay with us,' Sarah said simply. 'You have your bed in the attic, and when our crop is in we will pay you a share. We will come and rebuild your house and clear your field, as we promised. You will be our neighbour again instead of leading this mongrel life.'

John was silent for a moment.

'Don't press him,' Hobert said gently to his wife. 'Come,' he said to John. 'I'll walk up the river with you.'

He took his gun from the hook behind the door, and lit the fuse from the embers in the hearth. 'I'll bring back some meat,' he said, forestalling his wife's protest that there was work to be done in the field. 'I won't be long.'

John bowed to Sarah and nodded his head to Francis, and the two men left.

Hobert walked beside John instead of jogging behind him. John found it strange to have a man at his shoulder, strange to have to curb his stride to a pace as slow as a child's, strange to hear the noise they made as they moved so broad and heavy-shod through the wood. John thought that all the game for miles around would be scared away long before Hobert arrived.

'Is the hunting good now the spring is bringing the deer back into the woods?' John asked.

Hobert shook his head. 'Less than last year,' he said. 'It is the savages. They are taking too much and they are driving the animals deeper and deeper into the woods in the hopes that they can starve us out.'

John shook his head but did not have the energy to contradict him.

'There was news from England at Jamestown,' Hobert said. 'The Scots have come over the border, they're in the war.'

'Against the king?' John asked, astounded.

'Against the king and, more important, on the side of Parliament. There were some saying that the king would have to make terms with Parliament or the Scots. He could never fight against them both.'

'How far south are they?' John asked, thinking of the little house south of the Thames in Lambeth.

'By now? Who knows?' Hobert said carelessly. 'Thank God it is not our war any more, eh, John?'

John nodded absently. 'My wife is still at Lambeth,' he said. 'My son and my daughter.'

'I thought you had all but left them?' Hobert remarked.

'I should not have done so,' John said, his voice very low. 'I should not have left them in the middle of such a war. I was angry with her and I insisted she came with me and when she defied me I thought I was free to go. But a man with a child and a garden planted is never really free to go, is he, Bertram?'

Hobert shrugged. 'I can't advise,' he said. 'It's an odd life you're making, that's for sure.'

'It's two lives,' John said. 'One here, where I live so close to the earth that I can hear its heartbeat, and one there, where I live like an Englishman with duties and obligations but with great riches and great joys.'

'Can a man do both?' Hobert asked.

John thought for a moment. 'Not with honour.'

The moment that Suckahanna saw him come from the shadow of the forest and walk past the sweat lodge, the fields and up the village street she knew that something had happened. He walked like a white man with weight in his heels. He did not stride out as the men of the Powhatan. He walked as if something was pulling his shoulders downwards, pulling his head down to his feet, pulling his feet so that he

267

looked as if he was wading through a mire of difficulties instead of dancing on smooth grass.

She went out slowly to meet him. 'What's wrong?'

He shook his head but he would not meet her eyes. 'Nothing. I have done what I promised to do and now I am come home. I need not go again until harvest time.'

'Are they sick?' she asked, thinking that his slouch might be shielding some illness or pain.

'They are well,' he said.

'And you?'

He straightened up. 'I am weary,' he said. 'I shall go to the sweat lodge and then wash in the river.' He gave her a brief unhappy smile. 'And then everything will be as it was.'

In the warm days when the woods seemed to grow and turn green before his very eyes, John returned to his trade of plant collecting and rarity hunting. Already he had sent home a large parcel of Indian goods: clothing, tools, a case of bands and caps made from bark; now he recruited Suckahanna's son as his porter and every day the two of them left the village for a long stroll in the woods and came back laden with sprouting roots. John worked in companionable silence with the boy, and found that his thoughts often wandered to Lambeth. He felt great affection for Hester and a powerful sense that he should be there with her, to face whatever dangers might come from a country in the grip of an insane war. But at the same time he knew he could not leave Suckahanna and the Powhatan. He knew that his happiness, and his life, lay with the People.

John thought himself a fool: to abandon a wife and then to try to support her, to take a wife and then to think daily of her rival. He wanted so much to be a man like Attone, or even a man like Hobert, who saw life in simple terms, who saw one road and steadily walked it. John did not think of himself as complex and challenged; he lacked all such vanity. He saw himself as indecisive and weak and he blamed himself.

Suckahanna watched him create a nursery bed, heel in the roots, and linger over his cuttings; but she said nothing for many weeks. Then she spoke.

'What are they for?'

'I shall send them to England,' John said. 'They can be grown and sold there to gardeners.'

'By your wife?'

He tried to meet her direct black gaze as frankly and openly as he could. 'My English wife,' he corrected her.

'And what will she think? When a dead man sends her plants?'

'She will think that I am doing my duty by her,' John said. 'I cannot abandon her.'

'She will know that you are alive, and that you have abandoned her,' Suckahanna observed. 'Whereas now she may have given you up for dead.'

'I have to support her in the way that I can.'

She nodded and did not reply. John could not accept the stoical dignity of the Powhatan silence. 'I feel that I owe her anything that I can do,' he said awkwardly. 'She sent me a letter which I got at Hobert's house. She is in difficulties and alone. I left her to bring up my children and to manage my house and garden in England, and there is a war in my country . . .'

Suckahanna looked at him but said nothing.

'I am torn,' John said with a sudden burst of honesty.

'You chose your path,' she reminded him. 'Freely chose it.'

'I know,' he said humbly. 'But I keep thinking . . .'

He broke off and looked at her. She had turned her head away from him, hiding her face with a sweep of black hair. Her shoulders, showing brown and smooth through the veil of black hair, were shaking. He gave an exclamation and stepped forward to comfort her, thinking that she was weeping. But then he saw the gleam of her white teeth against her brown skin, and she flicked around and was running down the village lane, away from him, and was gone. She had been laughing. Not even her immense courtesy could restrain her amusement any longer. The spectacle of her husband struggling interminably forwards-backwards, duty-desire, English-Powhatan, was in the end too helplessly funny for her to take seriously. He heard the wild ripple of her laugh as she ran down the path to the garden where the sweetcorn was already growing high.

'Aye, you can laugh,' John said to himself, feeling himself wholly English, as leaden-footed as if he were wearing boots and breeches and weighed down by a hat. 'And God knows I love you for it. And God knows I wish I could laugh at myself too.'

When the snows were melted from even the highest hills, when there were no sharp frosts in the morning, when the ground was dry beneath the light summer moccasins of the braves, there was a meeting called by the ancient lord, Opechancanough. John the Eagle went with Attone and with one of the senior advisors of the community to represent their village, travelling along the narrow trails, northwards up the river to the great capital town of Powhatan. It nestled in the dry woodlands, at the foot of the mountains on the edge of the river which John had once known as the James River, but which he now called the Powhatan, and the waterfall at the side of Powhatan town was Paqwachowng.

They sighted the town of about forty braves at dusk, and paused outside the city boundaries.

'You're to keep quiet until spoken to,' Attone said briefly to John. 'The elder will do the talking.'

John looked without resentment at the older man who had led the way at a hard pace for the journey of many days. 'I didn't even want to come,' he protested. 'I'm hardly likely to interrupt.'

'Didn't want to come, when you can see new plants and trees and flowers? And take them back to Suckahanna when we sail downriver by canoe?' Attone mocked.

'All right,' John allowed. 'But I'm saying I didn't ask to come. I didn't want a place here.'

The older man's sharp beaky face turned to him. 'But your place is here,' he said.

'I know it, older one,' he said respectfully.

'You will answer questions but not give opinions,' the man ruled.

John nodded obediently and fell into file at the rear.

No-one knew the age of the great warlord Opechancanough. He had inherited his power from his brother the great Powhatan, father of Princess Pocahontas, the Indian heroine whom John had visited when he had been only a little boy and she had been a celebrity visiting London. There was no trace of her beauty in the ravaged face of her uncle. He sat on a great bench at the end of his luxurious long house, his cape of office shining in the gloom with the round discs of abalone shells. He barely glanced at John and his companions as they shuffled up, bowed, deposited their tribute on the growing pile before him, and stepped back.

When everyone had come and bowed to the lord he made a brief gesture with his hand and the priest stepped forward, cast some dust into the fire and watched the scented smoke spiralling upwards. John, weary from many days' walking, watched the smoke too and thought that it made strange and tempting shapes, almost as if one could read the future from it, just as he sometimes lay on his back beside Sucka-hanna's son when they detected shapes and images in the clouds that sailed overhead.

There was a deep mutter from the massed men packed tight into the big house. The priest walked around the fire, people leaning away from the sweep of his cape as he circled, staring into the embers. Finally he stepped back and bowed to Opechancanough.

'Yes,' he said.

Suddenly the old man sharpened into life. He leaned forwards. 'You are sure? We will conquer?'

The priest nodded simply. 'We will.'

'And they will be pushed back into the sea where they came from, and the waves will foam red with their blood and their women and children will hoe our fields and serve us where we have served them?'

The priest nodded. 'I have seen it,' he said.

Opechancanough looked past the priest at the men, waiting in silence, drinking in the assurance that they were unbeatable. 'You have heard,' he said. 'We will win. Now tell me how this victory is to be won.'

John had been dizzy with the scent of the smoke and the sudden warmth and darkness of the hut but suddenly he snapped awake, wide awake, as if someone had slapped his face. He strained his ears and his comprehension to grasp the quick exchange of advice, argument and information: the news of an isolated farmhouse here, a newly built fort with cannon further down the river. He realised with a sinking heart what he had known all along but had continually pushed to the back of his mind: that Opechancanough and the army of the Powhatan were going to fall upon the people of Jamestown, and upon every white settler everywhere in this country which they had called empty and then proceeded to fill. That if the Powhatan won there would not be a white man, woman or child left alive or out of slavery in Virginia. And if the Powhatan lost there would be a dreadful reckoning to pay.

'And what does our brother, the Eagle, say?' Opechancanough suddenly asked. His beaked harsh face turned towards John, where he sat at the back. The men before him melted away as if Opechancanough's gaze was a spear-thrust pointed at his heart.

'Nothing...' John stammered, the Powhatan language sticking on his tongue. 'Nothing ... sir.'

'Will they be ready for us? Do they know we have been waiting and planning?'

Miserably John shook his head.

'Did they think us defeated and driven back, forced out of our forests and away from our game trails?'

'I think so,' John said. 'But I have not been with the white men for a long time.'

'You will advise us,' Opechancanough ruled. 'You will tell us how to avoid the guns and at what time of day we should attack. We will use your knowledge of them to come against them. You agree?'

John opened his mouth but no sound came. He was aware of Attone rising to his feet at his side.

'He is struck dumb by the honour,' Attone said smoothly. Out of sight he trod hard on John's toes.

'Indeed I am,' John said numbly.

'Your hands will be red with English blood,' Opechancanough promised him. His face was serious enough but there was a spark of mischief, that irresistible Powhatan mischief, at the back of his eyes. 'That will make you happy, Eagle.'

Spring 1644, England

Alexander Norman did not speak again of marriage to Frances, but he visited the Ark at Lambeth every week. He took Frances out on the river, he bought her a pony and took her riding in the lanes away from Lambeth and out into the country. Frances came back from these expeditions unusually quiet and thoughtful but she never said more to Hester than that her uncle had been very kind and they had talked about everything under the sun, but nothing that she could remember. Hester felt torn. On one hand she felt she should warn Frances against deepening her relationship with her uncle, which could only bring him pain and disappointment; but on the other hand she did not want to prevent her daughter from enjoying a trusting, loving relationship with a good man old enough to be her father.

It must be Alexander who was principally at risk from heartbreak. Frances enjoyed his company, and learned much from him – from horsemanship to politics. Hester trusted Alexander to spend every day with her without one word of courtship, but she wondered how much pleasure he took when Frances looked up at him and said trustingly: 'You'll know about King Henry, won't you, Uncle Norman? You were a boy when he was on the throne, weren't you?'

He gave Hester a wry smile over his niece's brown head. 'That would be true if I was a hundred years old now. Do you know nothing of history, Frances?'

She made a face. 'Not much. So how old are you, Uncle?'

Hester thought he had to brace himself to answer.

'I am fifty-four,' he said honestly. 'And I have seen three monarchs reign; but never times like these.'

Frances looked at him consideringly, her head on one side. 'Well you don't look very old,' she said bluntly. 'I never think of you as that old.'

273

'I am that old,' he said.

Hester thought that the assertion must be costing him dear.

'I am old enough to be your father.'

Frances's surprised ripple of laughter made him smile. 'I think of you as my friend!' she exclaimed.

'Well, I was your grandfather's friend before you were born. I bounced you on my knee when you were a dribbling little baby.'

She nodded. 'I don't see that that makes any difference at all,' she said, and Hester wondered, but did not ask: 'Difference to what?'

Alexander did not neglect Johnnie or Hester on his visits. He brought Johnnie pamphlets and ballads about his hero Prince Rupert, and he brought Hester welcome news of the progress of the war. He spoke of a new commander, Colonel Cromwell, who had come from nowhere and was said to be little more than a working man, but who had a regiment of soldiers that could withstand a royalist cavalry charge and who had been trained and drilled until they could turn and stand and march forwards on one shouted command.

'I think this Cromwell knows his business as well as Prince Rupert,' Alexander said.

Johnnie shook his head. 'Prince Rupert has fought all around Europe,' he said certainly. 'And he was riding horses, great cavalry chargers, when he was my age. No-one from East Anglia could say the same.'

The news from the king's court at Oxford was of riotous loose living, of scholars and courtiers drunk in the gutters every morning, and of the king celebrating victory after victory, however small the skirmish and insignificant the campaign. It looked as if the kingdom was opening up to him and he would be in London within a year. And then he started his march on his rebellious capital city itself. Alexander Norman sent a message to the Ark at Lambeth.

> *Dear Cousin Hester,*
>
> *I suggest that you hide your most precious treasures in your safe place and pack necessary clothes and goods for yourself. The king is marching on London from the north and the City is preparing for a siege. However, if the king should circle London to besiege it, then I should think it most likely that Lambeth will fall and the Parliamentary forces stand back and hold their ground north of the river. If the fighting is prolonged then you may well be caught between two armies. Therefore, be ready to leave the moment I give you the word and I will take you back to Oatlands.*
>
> *Alexander.*

Hester put the letter at once into the tiny fire of coal dust and kindling and watched it burn sluggishly. She felt very tired, as if the war had gone on forever, and would go on forever, without victory, without peace, with nothing but the wearisome task of surviving. For a moment she sat by the fireside, her head leaning on her hand, watching the note flame, turn to ash, and then fall in soft flakes into the red embers. Then she gave herself a little shake, brushed off her skirt, tied on her hessian working apron and went to the rarities room.

Johnnie was showing a visitor out of the front door.

'What is it, Mother?' he asked as soon as the door was safely closed. 'Not bad news from Virginia?'

She shook her head. 'Not that, thank God. It is a note from your uncle. He says that the king is marching on London and that we must be prepared to leave if the fighting comes close. We must pack up the most precious things for safety at once.'

He nodded, his little face grave. 'I'll call Frances,' he said. 'We'll all help.'

Frances came down from her room, her hair pinned in a new style. 'How do I look?'

'Awful ugly,' Johnnie said with a grin.

Hester was drawing out the big wooden chests which were stored beneath the display cases. 'You pack the glass and porcelain, Frances, you're the most careful. Johnnie, you pack the coins.'

Hester unlocked the cases and then started folding and packing the clothes, vests and coats from all around the world, savages' clothes of feathers and beads, beautifully worked scarves from India and China, and King Henry's own gloves which King Charles himself had given to the Tradescants. She glanced over, Johnnie was carefully laying every coin with its label in the chest.

'You'll have to just pile them in,' she said. 'And when we unpack them we'll have to label them again.'

His little face was shocked. The order of the rarities room had been a sacred charge for the whole family for all of his life. 'But these are Grandfather John's labels!'

'I know,' Hester said grimly. 'And I hope that he would understand that we're doing the best that we can to keep his Ark and all its contents safe. Just tumble all the coins in the chest, Johnnie, and then we can hide it and, even if a dozen regiments come through, when the war is over we can dig it all up and start again.'

He looked reluctant, but did as he was told. Frances, at the other side of the room, was wrapping precious pieces of glass in silks and scarves, and packing them tightly in a wooden box.

Hester looked around the room. It was a collection that had been amassed over years of work, all she could do was to choose the most precious pieces from it and try to save them. 'The little toys,' she said to Frances. 'The mechanical toys. Do them next.'

'What about the mermaid's tail?' Johnnie asked. 'And the whale's jaw?'

'We can't even lift them,' Frances said. 'What will we do? How can we hide them in safety?'

'I don't know,' Hester said. Her hands kept moving, packing, folding, smoothing, but her voice was full of despair and weariness. 'We just pack everything we can, I suppose. And for the rest? I don't know.'

At night Hester and the children and the gardener, Joseph, carried the boxes carefully to the ice house, and stacked them inside. The ice house was lined with brick, it was damp and dark. Frances shivered and pulled her hood over her head, fearing spiders and bats. The boxes filled the small circular room. When they came out they nailed up the door. Hester had an odd, superstitious feeling that it was as if they were mourners before the family vault and that all that was most precious to them had been buried.

'I'll plant a couple of shrubs before it tomorrow,' Joseph promised, 'and grow some ivy over the door. In a month or so you won't know it's there.'

'I hope we have a month or so,' Hester said. 'Cut some branches and lay them over the door to hide it while the ivy is growing. And put a couple of saplings in.'

'Is the king's army coming so soon?' Joseph asked.

'The king himself is coming,' Hester said grimly. 'And please God that whether he wins or loses the battle is over swiftly and the winners bring the country back to peace, because I don't think I can bear another year like this one.'

Within days in the city of London everything was rationed and nothing could be bought. The king's army was coming down the Great North Road and no wagons could get into London to feed the people. The Lord Mayor of London himself set up distribution points where people could buy food and set fair prices so that racketeers could not profit from the city's desperation. Joseph was drafted out every day to dig trenches to protect the city from the cavalry, and there was even an inquiry from the local commander of the trained bands as to how old Johnnie might be, and when he would be old enough to serve.

Johnnie, with his home under siege from the king, was wild to sneak out at night and get to the king's army. 'I could be a scout,' he said. 'I could be a spy. I could tell the king where the ditches are dug, where the cannon are mounted. He needs me, I should go to him.'

'Be quiet,' Hester snapped. The sense of an impending disaster for the house and the children she loved was wearing her patience very thin. 'The king has enough fools running to his standard. You are a child. You will stay home like an obedient child.'

'I am nearly eleven!' he protested. 'And the head of the household.'

Hester gave him a small smile. 'Then stay and defend me,' she said. 'We hold the treasures of the country here. We need to stay at our post.'

He was a little mollified. 'When I am a man I shall train and join Rupert's cavalry,' he promised.

'I hope that when you are a man you will be a gardener in a peaceful country,' she said fervently.

At the end of March there was extraordinary news which came into the city as gossip and was confirmed within the day in broadsheets and pamphlets and ballads. Despite all premonitions and fears, despite all likelihood, the Parliament army, working men officered by those who had never been gentlemen at court, had met the king's army at Alresford outside Winchester, fought a long, hard battle and won a resounding victory. It was all the more impressive because the battle had turned on a cavalry charge by the royalists which, for once, did not end in a rout of terrified Parliament infantry being cut down as they fled. This time the Parliament men stood their ground, and the king's horse, thrown back into the twisting, deep lanes of Hampshire, could not come around again, could not regroup, while the Parliamentary infantry doggedly and determinedly slugged their way uphill to Alresford ridge, and were in Alresford before nightfall.

There were bonfires all over Lambeth that night, and precious candles showed at every window. The next Sunday there was not a man, woman nor child who did not attend a service of thanksgiving. The tide of the war had ebbed for a moment, for a moment only; and no cavaliers would be riding through the narrow streets of Lambeth for a month or two at least. And there would be no Papist Irish murdering soldiers either. The news came filtering through that the Parliamentary forces had captured all the Irish-facing ports of Wales. The king could not bring the Papists into England. Even in Scotland the small royalist forces were being driven back.

'I think the king will have to come to terms with Parliament,' Alexander said to Hester one evening in April. 'He's on the defensive for the first time and the royal army is not one which fights well in retreat. He doesn't have the advisors or the determination to carry on.'

'And what then?' Hester asked. She had a basketful of sweet pea pods from last year in her lap and she was shelling the seeds ready for planting. 'Do I unpack the rarities from their hiding places?'

Alexander considered for a moment. 'Not until peace is declared,' he said. 'We'll wait and see. It maybe that the tide is turning at last.'

'D'you think the king will make peace with Parliament and come meekly home?'

Alexander shrugged. 'What else can he do?' he said. 'He has to come to terms with them. He is still king: they are still Parliament.'

'So all this pain and bloodshed has been for nothing,' Hester said blankly. 'Nothing except to teach the king that he should manage his Parliament as his father and the old queen managed theirs.'

Alexander looked grave. 'It's been an expensive lesson.'

Hester threw a handful of dried empty pods into the fire and watched them spark and flare up. 'Damnable,' she said bitterly.

April 1644, Virginia

John had hoped that he had been summoned to Opechancanough's war council as a simple brave, companion to Attone. But as the days wore on at the town of Powhatan he found he was summoned every morning to speak with Opechancanough. At first the questions were pointed and direct. The fort at Jamestown: was it true that the town had grown so large that all the people could not fit inside the walls? Was it true also that the walls had been allowed to fall into disrepair, that a proper watch was no longer kept, that the cannon were rusty?

John answered as truly as he knew, warning Opechancanough that he had been nothing more than a visitor passing through Jamestown, and not a resident who knew the town inside out. But as the questions went on Opechancanough revealed that he knew the answers as well as John. The wise old commander had many spies watching the fort. He was using John as a check against them, and they against him. He was testing John's own ability to tell the truth, proving his loyalty to his adopted people.

Once he was satisfied that John would honestly tell him all that he knew, then the questions changed. He asked instead what hours the white men rose in the morning, what they drank for their breakfast, if they were all drunkards, half-drowned in fiery spirits by the time darkness fell. Did they have a special magic in their use of gunpowder, cannon, or flintlock, or could the Powhatan people seize these goods and turn them against their makers? Was the god of Englishmen attentive to them in this foreign land, or might He simply forget them if the real people rose up against them?

John struggled with the concepts of magic, warfare, and theology in a foreign language, and in a different way of thinking. Over and over again he found himself saying to the older man, 'I am sorry, I don't know,' and saw the dark brows snap together and the crumpled face darken with anger.

'I really don't know,' John would say, hearing the nervousness in his own voice.

Over and over again Opechancanough would return to the English communications. If a settler discovered the uprising, how quickly could he take the news to Jamestown? Did the English have a method of sending signals in smoke? Or a code of drums?

'Smoke?' John asked disbelievingly. 'No. Nor drums. Soldiers only drum the march forwards or the retreat...'

Opechancanough spat derisively. 'No. To send messages. Long messages.'

John shook his head in bewilderment. 'Of course not. How could you do such a thing?'

Opechancanough's dark smile gleamed. 'Never mind. So if a man was warned and wanted to take the warning to Jamestown, he would have to go himself? By foot or canoe?'

'Yes,' John replied.

There was silence for a moment. 'In the last war we were betrayed,' Opechancanough said thoughtfully. 'It was a couple of our boys who had been treated kindly by their white master and could not bear to hurt him. They warned him. They had grown soft like white boys. They thought they would save him alone; but in warning him they betrayed every one of us. He ran to Jamestown and warned the fort so they were ready for us. And what of the boys who loved their master so much that they betrayed their own people and warned him?'

John waited.

'Shot by the white men,' Opechancanough said. 'That is how the white men reward a faithful servant. We saw it done. And those of us who had fought, and those of us who had not, were all driven further and further away from our villages and watched our fields hoed for tobacco, nothing but tobacco, everywhere the plant for smoke and nothing for life.'

'When will the new war be?' John asked.

Opechancanough shrugged. 'Soon.'

John woke in the night and lay still. Something had disturbed his sleep but he could not trace the noise or the movement or the sense which had woken him. Then he heard it again. From outside the house a twig cracked, and then the skins at the doorway parted and a low voice spoke briefly into the warm darkness: 'It is now.'

Attone at John's side was awake and standing. 'Now!' he said, and his voice was filled with joy.

'What is now?' John asked, as if he did not know, as if he were not near to sinking down on the ground and weeping into the earth for his sense of dread and guilt.

'We are on the warpath,' Attone said gently. 'It is now, my brother.'

Outside the tent the town was in alert silence. Men were stringing their bows and tightening their belts, checking the gleam of the blades of their knives. There was nothing to prepare, for the Powhatan were always ready for travel, for hunting, for war. John fell into line behind Attone and knew that his breath was sluggish and slow beside Attone's light panting, knew his heart was not in this, knew also that there was no way forwards and away from his allegiance to the Powhatan, and no way backwards to the English.

At a signal from Opechancanough, seated on his throne, dark as a shadow in the moonlight, the men moved off, making as little noise as a herd of wolves, silent in their moccasins, their quivers held still at their sides, their bows strung over their shoulders. The moonlight touched each one like a benison, the white gleam falling on a feather plaited into dark hair, on a pale old scar on one high cheekbone, on a smile of excitement, on the gleam of burnished skin. John went silently in Attone's steps, watching the pace of his moccasins, the movement of his haunches beneath the leather skirt, concentrating wholly on the moment of the journey so he could hide from himself the knowledge of the destination.

They were to split into two main parties. One was to travel by canoe downriver to Jamestown, taking advantage of the night to move swiftly and to form a pincer around the town by dawn. The other was to go by land either side of the river, and at every house and cabin, every grand, ambitious building and hopeful shack, they were to go in and kill every man, woman and child in the place, leaving none to escape, and none to take the news downriver.

John was in the land party, Attone with him. He thought that Opechancanough was testing his loyalty to the Powhatan by putting him in the group that would kill so early and so immediately – and not against the fighting men at the fort, but against the vulnerable, sleeping men and women with their children bundled up in the same bed beside them. But then he realised that Opechancanough had placed him where, if he were faithless, he could do no damage. He was at the rear, he could not dash ahead and warn Jamestown. All he could do was botch a few killings upriver and get himself shot.

They came upon a little house near dawn. It was set back from the river on a rise of ground, just as John had built his own house, just as Bertram Hobert had built his. Before it was a little cottage garden, neglected and overgrown, and between it and the river were long fields of tobacco, the plants set in straight rows and growing well. A little quay stretched out into the river for loading the tobacco to sail downriver to Jamestown. No light shone in the window and only a wisp of smoke showed that someone had banked the fire in overnight so that it would be hot to cook the morning breakfast.

It was the smell of woodsmoke clean on the air, unmixed with any other scent, that threw John backwards; he physically recoiled and collided with the man trotting behind him. It was such an English smell. Woodsmoke for the Powhatan was the scent of the interior of their huts, mingled with the smell of cooking, of children, of people sitting around. The smell of smoke from a sooty chimney was the smell of an English homestead.

The man behind shoved John abruptly in the back but did not utter a single sound. John touched Attone's shoulder. 'I cannot do it,' he said.

Attone turned and his glance was as cold as the blade of a knife on bare skin. 'What?'

'I cannot do it. I cannot go in and kill my people.'

'Do you want me to kill *you* now?'

Dumbly John shook his head.

'The others will kill you if I do not.'

John leaned forwards as if he would take Attone in his arms and lie his unhappy face against the man's shoulder. 'They must then. Because I cannot do it.'

'Will you wait here while we do it?'

John nodded.

'And not cry out, nor run off?'

John nodded again.

'My brother will stand guard,' Attone said simply to the others. 'Follow me.'

The men trotted past John without a glance at him. He leaned back against a tree, a useless guard, a faithless friend, a broken warrior, and a shamed husband.

They were quick and clean. There was one surprised cry and no more, and in moments they came back, Attone wiping his shell-bladed knife on a piece of European muslin. 'Go on,' he said briskly to the others.

They nodded and turned to the trail again. One man had something in his hand. Attone reached out and smacked it down. A stone bottle fell to the ground and rolled away. Attone kicked it with his foot so that it spun round and round, spilling out the raw spirit and making the air stink. Then he turned to John.

'Can you find your way back to Suckahanna at the village?'

'Yes.'

'Then go back there. Wait till the men return.'

'She won't have me,' John said certainly.

'No,' Attone said. 'We none of us will want you, Eagle.' He paused as a thought struck him. 'What was your name? Before you were my brother the Eagle?'

'I was John Tradescant,' John said, the name unfamiliar on his tongue.

'Then you will have to be him again,' Attone said flatly. 'Now go to Suckahanna before someone kills you.'

'I am sorry –' John started.

'Go to Suckahanna before I kill you myself,' Attone said abruptly, and disappeared into the darkness.

The village was guarded by Attone's son, who recognised John's footfall and called into the grey dawn: 'Is that you, Eagle?'

'No,' John said. His voice was flat and weary. 'You must call me John.'

'Is my father with you? Are the braves coming home?'

'They are at war,' John said. 'I am alone.'

The boy checked his loving run forwards into John's arms and suddenly looked at him as if a terrible fear was invading him, as if his trust and certainty in John was suddenly unreliable. 'You are not with the men?'

'I could not do it,' John said simply. He had thought that the worst thing would have been to tell Suckahanna; but the bright gaze of her son was hard to meet. The light went slowly out of the boy's face.

'I don't understand,' he said plaintively, willing it to be difficult, too complex for his understanding, tempting John to create another explanation.

'I could not kill an Englishman,' John said heavily. 'I thought I could do it, but when it came to it, I could not. I left my home in England because I could not choose sides and kill Englishmen, and now I am here, in this new land, and I still cannot choose sides and kill.'

The boy's eyes scanned his face. 'I thought you were a brave,' he said reproachfully.

John shook his head. 'No. It seems I cannot be.'

'But you are my father's friend!'

'Not any more.'

'And Suckahanna loves you!'

A movement behind him made him turn. Suckahanna was standing there, watching John. The man and the boy turned and faced her, waiting for her judgement.

'So you have decided at last,' she said calmly. 'You are an Englishman after all.'

Slowly John dropped to his knees, both his knees, in the gesture he had only ever used before to the greatest queen in Europe, and then unwillingly. 'I am,' he said. 'I did not know it until the moment when I could not shed their blood. I am sorry, Suckahanna.'

She looked at him and through him, as if she understood everything about him, and for a moment John thought that he would be forgiven, and that the steady, constant love between them could overcome even this. But then she turned away and snapped her fingers for her boy and walked, light-footed, down the street in the dawn light. She did not look back at him. He knew she would never look at him with love again.

The braves came home jubilant. The first wave of the attack on the isolated houses along the riverside had gone perfectly. The attack on Jamestown had hit the sleeping town and taken it unawares. As many as five hundred colonists had been killed, but as soon as the alarm was given the Indian army had fallen back. Although the fort was taken unawares, the town was now so spread out, and the houses so defended with shutters and stout doors, that no single battle could complete the war. The braves had fallen back to regroup, to heal the wounds and bury the dead, and then they would push forwards again.

Meanwhile in Jamestown the governor was mustering all the able-bodied men and hunting dogs to counter-attack. He had promised the colonists a fight to the death, a solution once and for all.

'We have to move,' Attone said as soon as all the men had returned. 'Deeper into the forest, perhaps across the river and into the wet creeks. Once the village is safely hidden we can come out again and fight.'

The women went to the houses at once to start packing. 'And the crops in the fields?' Suckahanna asked him.

He made a gesture which told her that they were lost. 'Perhaps later. Perhaps we can come back,' he said.

They exchanged a sharp, hard look. He took in the hardness of the lines around her mouth and John, hovering helplessly behind her.

'You are hurt,' she said.

'Just bruised. You?'

She turned away. 'Just bruised.'

❧

They travelled all day. Once, when they paused, they heard a hunting horn and the baying of a dog. It was the governor Sir William Berkeley's hounds on the track, hunting Indians would be the colonists' great sport this season.

They crossed the river at once, the children riding on the shoulders of the men, the women wading through chest-high, rapid-flowing water without a whisper of complaint, and crossed it again, then Attone led them on at a steady run.

John was in the rear, helping the old men and women keep up, carrying burdens for them. Suckahanna had told no-one of what had passed between her and her husband, but she did not need to speak. Everyone could see that the Eagle was not at the side of his friend, not at the side of his wife. Everyone could see that he was a dead man to Attone, to Suckahanna, as surely as if he had gone into Jamestown and fought like a brave and died like a hero. So they let him carry their goods or hold them steady in the river as if he were a rock or a tree, or something of use. But they did not speak to him, nor smile at him, nor even look into his eyes.

All day they travelled as Attone led them closer to the sea, where the mosquitoes rose in clouds from the sodden grass and reeds and the trees bowed down low over dark, silty, salty water. At night they found some ground only a little higher than the tidewash. 'Here,' Attone said. 'Make shelters but no fires.'

An old woman died in the night, and they piled a heap of stones over her face.

'We move on,' Attone said.

All day they travelled at that punishing pace. An old man and an old woman stopped at the side of the trail and said they would go no further. Attone left them with a bow and arrow to do what damage they could to the pursuers, and with a tiny sliver of sharpened bark to open their veins rather than be captured. None of them stopped to say goodbye. The safety of the People was greater than the farewells of individuals. Attone wanted to get the People away.

♆

On the third day they reached a small hill deep inside the swamp and Attone gave the order that they could rest. There was nothing to eat except some dried flour which they mixed cold with the marshy water. Attone sent out scouts, empty-bellied, to go down the trail and see if they were followed. When they returned and said that the trails were safe he sent them out again. Only when the third party had come back on the fifth day did he say that the women could light fires and start to collect food and the men could go hunting.

'What happens now?' John asked one of the old women.

'We live here,' she said.

'In the middle of a foul swamp?'

She gave him a look which told him as clearly as words that she despised his weakness. 'In the middle of a foul swamp,' she said.

Summer 1644, England

Alexander's predictions seemed correct. Through the spring and early summer gossip, wild surmise and news filtered back to London, and finally to Lambeth, of small battles all around the country and then finally, in July, a dreadful battle at Marston Moor. Alexander wrote to Hester:

> *I cannot come out to see you, I am so busy with the demands of the ordnance. There has been a major battle in Yorkshire and it has gone the way of Parliament. I hear that Prince Rupert has met Cromwell himself, and it was Cromwell that triumphed. In haste . . . Alexander.*

Hester waited for news for another few days and then one of her neighbours rapped on the door to say that she was going up to the House of Commons to see the king's standards. 'Forty-eight royal standards laid for all to see on the bar of the House,' she said. 'I'll take Johnnie along with me. The boy should see it.'

Johnnie shook his head. 'Is Prince Rupert's standard taken?' he asked.

'You shall see it,' the woman promised. 'Stained with his own blood.'

Johnnie's brown eyes grew bigger in his pale face. 'I don't want to see it,' he said stubbornly, and then remembered his manners. 'But thank you very much for inviting me, Mrs Goodall.'

She bridled for a moment. 'I hope you're not siding with the enemy?' she said sharply. 'The king has forced us to this battle and now he is defeated and good riddance to him.'

Hester stepped forwards and laid her hand on her stepson's shoulder. 'He's still the king,' she said.

Mrs Goodall looked angrily at her. 'Some say that a king who is his people's woe is no king. The law that says he is king says that he rules for our good, not for our regret. If he does not please us then he is no king at all. There are those who are saying that he should die in one of his bitter battles and we would be a happier land without him.'

'Then his son would be king,' Hester said steadily. 'There would still be a king.'

'Of course you were at court,' the woman remarked pointedly. 'Enriched by the pack of them.'

'I worked there as many did,' Hester said. She sounded defensive and her hand tightened on Johnnie's shoulder as if to draw courage from his narrow little bones. 'But I have taken neither one side nor the other. All I have wanted from the beginning is peace.'

'So do we all,' the woman agreed. 'And there can be no peace with that man or his son on the throne again.'

'You may be right,' Hester said, swiftly stepping back and drawing Johnnie back with her. 'Please God we shall have peace at last and our men can come home.'

October 1644, England

On a cold day in the middle of October, Alexander Norman rode to Lambeth between frosty hedges on icy tracks. Frances was on the look-out for him and ran out into the stable yard with her cape around her shoulders to take his horse and send Alexander into the parlour, to the warmth of the fire.

Hester had mulled wine to greet him. He took a deep draught and set it down. At once Hester knew that he had something important to say. 'Is it peace?' she asked. 'Has the king surrendered?'

'No,' he said. 'He's taken Salisbury, it looks like he's rallying again. But it's not that I came about. It is time for me to speak to you about another matter.'

'Frances,' Hester said, knowing at once what Alexander Norman meant.

'Frances,' he replied.

'I wrote to her father,' Hester said. 'I did not tell him what you had said. But I told him of my worries about keeping her safe. I thought he might make some suggestion.' She paused. 'I have not had a reply. Nothing since that consignment of Indian goods and a barrel of plants.'

'I don't want to wait for his reply,' Alexander said. 'Whether it is for me or against me.'

Hester nodded, taking in the determined tone. 'Why now?' she asked. 'After waiting so long?'

'Because the girl is seventeen next year, because I am fifty-five next year, because peace is as far away as ever. If she waits for peace to come she will lose her young womanhood. She might have to wait another four years, she might wait twenty.'

'Is that what they're saying in the Tower?'

'They're saying that the king will do anything and everything before he surrenders. He's suffered some bitter defeats and he's still summoning help from the Irish, from the Scots, from the French. Nothing will stop him, no defeat can stop him. He has to be king if he is anything. And he has nothing to lose by fighting and fighting forever. And Parliament cannot stop without his surrender. Lord Manchester said it himself in the House of Parliament – they have to go on fighting until the king is completely and utterly defeated, or they are lost. The two sides – King and Parliament – have made the stakes so high that one of them has to be completely defeated, there is no middle course for either any more.'

'I see that,' Hester said.

'He has taken Salisbury this week and he still holds Oxford. As they go into winter quarters nothing is decided. I thought Marston Moor would be the end of the war but nothing will end it until Parliament is routed and the members hanged for treason, or the king dead.'

Out of habit Hester glanced at the closed door. 'Hush.'

Alexander shook his head. 'It's widely said now. People in London think there's no stopping him, no dealing with him, and the mood is getting bitter. But until he's either killed in battle or victorious the war cannot end. I have orders for barrels for gunpowder which will supply the army for the next ten years. It will be a long war, Hester. You cannot doubt it.'

Hester poured him another glass of mulled wine.

'So I am asking for your permission to propose marriage to her,' he said. 'If you refuse me permission I shall wait until she is twenty-one and can please herself.'

Hester sighed. 'You can ask her now,' she said. 'I promised her grandfather that I would care for her and keep her safe, and before God I cannot see how to keep her safe in these times. The garden earns nothing, and the rarities are hidden away and we have nothing to show, and no visitors to show it to. I can barely feed her, we live off fruit and vegetables from the garden. If I could pack her away safely like the precious rarities to bring out when peace comes I would do so. You can ask her, Cousin Norman, and I will abide by her decision.'

She saw his face light up like a young man's in a blaze of joy. 'And do you know how she thinks of me?' he asked. 'You and she are very close. How does she speak of me?'

'With great affection,' Hester said. 'But whether she loves you as a father or a friend I can't say. And I've never asked. I was hoping, perhaps, that I would never have to ask. If she had met a young man, or if John had come home, or if the war ended . . .' She turned away from a dozen regrets. 'I'll go and fetch her.'

Frances was in the stable yard, pumping water into a bucket for Alexander's horse.

'Your uncle wants to see you,' Hester said abruptly. She had to restrain herself from drawing the girl to her, smoothing her hair, holding her once more. 'In the parlour.'

Frances heaved the full bucket into the stable and shut the door. 'Is anything wrong?'

Hester kept her face pleasantly uninformative. 'He wants to ask you something,' she said. 'You must answer however you wish, Frances. Please remember that. Answer however you wish. And think about it. No need for haste.'

The girl looked puzzled and then turned towards the house.

In the parlour Alexander found that his throat was so tight that he could hardly breathe. As the door opened he turned around and saw Frances. She put her cape over the back of one of the chairs. She was plainly dressed in a warm gown of grey and there was a thread of hay in her hair. He took her hands.

'You're cold,' he said.

'I was watering your horse.'

'You should not have done that. I thought Joseph was in the yard.'

'He has too much to do. We have lost all our garden boys. Johnnie and I have to help. I don't mind it.'

His fingers again felt the calluses on her hands. 'I don't want you doing hard work.'

She smiled. 'Mother said you wanted to ask me something?'

Now it came to it Alexander found that he could barely speak. 'I do.'

She said nothing, waited for him. He drew her to the chair before the fire, and when she was seated he remained awkwardly standing before her. Then it was the most natural thing in the world to drop to one knee and take her cold little hand between his two palms and say gently: 'Frances, I have loved you since you were a little girl and I would like you to be my wife.'

All the prepared speech he had rehearsed on the long, cold ride beside the wintry river went from his head. He forgot to caution her against accepting him, he forgot to promise her that he would always be her friend even if he could not be her husband, he forgot all the things he had thought he would say. He just waited for her answer.

She smiled at once, as if he had brought her a ribbon of exceptional magnificence. 'Oh yes,' she said.

He could hardly believe that she assented so easily. At once he wanted to warn her against the wrong decision. 'But I am much older than you, you should take time to think, to talk to your mother, perhaps to write to your father . . .'

She leaned towards him and her arms came around his neck. He felt the warmth of her breath on his cheek and he drew her close and at once knew desire, and a passionate sense of protectiveness.

'I don't need to ask anyone,' she said very quietly. 'I thought you would never ask me. I have been waiting for what seems like forever. I have always known what I would say.'

Winter 1644, Virginia

Winter clamped down on the coastal plain of Virginia as if it had taken sides in the war and was in savage alliance with the colonists. All the food stores of the Powhatan had been looted or fired, there was not enough to eat and even the skills of the women could not feed the tribe from the fish and crabs on the shoreline or the frozen berries left on the trees. The braves went out hunting every day and came back with duck and geese shot on their migrating journey southward. The meat was shared with strict fairness and then mothers gave their portion privately to their children and the old people pretended that they were not hungry.

When they had started the war they had thought that it would be over in one great rush – as battles generally were. There was a persistent belief that the white people would simply go, back to where they came from, especially since they always spoke of that other place as 'home', and talked of it with longing. Why would a man abandon his own fields, his own woods, his own game, and scratch a life on the edge of a strange river? If things went badly for him why would he not take one of the great ships and go, as easily and as unexpectedly as he had come?

Of all the questions Opechancanough had put to John he had never asked him if the colonists would leave if they were defeated – the question never arose in the chief's mind. He knew that land which had been won in a battle could be lost in a battle. He knew that a newly arrived people could be easily dislodged. It never occurred to him until this terrible winter that the white people would renege on their promise to move on, on their promise that they wanted only a small patch of land at Jamestown, and then their promise that they would settle a narrow strip by the river and live in peace with their neighbours.

Opechancanough did not expect men to be honest. He himself had promised peace with a smile on his face and twice gone to war. But he did not expect the depth and consistency of duplicity that the white people brought to the virgin earth. He did not expect their determination, and to his death he never understood their greed.

In the little village there was a strong sense that everything had gone wrong. The first attack had been a victory but since then they had been hunted like frightened hares. Hidden now in the swamps in midwinter they were safe enough but there was a growing fear that the swamps might be all that was left for them, that only the arid land, the brackish water, the desolate and barren places would be left for the People who had been proud to walk safe on their footpaths through fertile woods.

John's share of the food stuck in his throat. He did not go hunting with the braves, he was not invited. He cleared the land around the temporary village with the women and with the old people, keeping his head low and scraping the earth with his hoeing stick, dropping the precious seeds safely into the earth and covering them up. He felt as if he had died on the raid on that little farmhouse and that it was his ghost who worked in the row behind Suckahanna and humbly lay in her little house at night. She did not reject him, she did not invite him. She did not by one gesture or one glance show that she saw him at all. She carried herself with simple dignity as a widow who has lost her man, and John in her shadow found that he was wishing that he had died before seeing that beautiful, loving face look away from him and those dark, veiled eyes go blind.

He thought she might grow kinder to him if he worked without complaint and lay on the floor of her house at night like a dog, like a hunting dog which has been beaten into submission. But she stepped over him when she rose in the morning and went to her prayers in the icy water as if he were a log on the floor. She went past him without disdain, without a glance that might offend him, without a look that might open up a conversation between them, even if it were to be a quarrel. She acted as if he were a dead man, a lost man, a ghost, and as the months went by Tradescant felt that he was lost indeed.

He went to find Attone, who was setting a fish trap by the river and watching the flow of the rising flood water over the markers at the riverbank.

'Can I speak with you?' John asked humbly.

His former friend glanced at him and then away as if the sight of John displeased him. 'What?'

'I need advice.'

There was an unhelpful silence.

'Suckahanna turns from me and says not one word to me.'

Attone nodded.

'Is there anything I can do to make it better between us?'

Attone bent down and raised the trap from the water. The delicate withy-work was bending in the current; he straightened a twig and then carefully bedded it in with pebbles before he answered. He took his time, the whole process took nearly half an hour.

'Nothing.'

'Will she take me back as a husband if I serve her without complaint? Perhaps in Coltayough? In the warm time?'

Attone thought for a moment, his eyes still on his fish trap, and then shook his head. 'I shouldn't think so.'

'At Nepinough?'

Again the dismissive shake of the head.

'Will she ever forgive me for coming home without blood on my hands?'

Attone turned from the river and looked John squarely in the face. The relief of being seen, of gaining a response, was so great that John wanted to fling his arms around his former friend. Just that one look was an affirmation that he was a man still; that he could be seen and acknowledged.

'Never, I should think,' Attone said.

Tradescant drew breath. 'What have I done that is so bad?'

'Don't you know?'

Dumbly, Tradescant shook his head.

'You've shamed her. She stood for you before all the People and said you were a man worthy to be tested. You were tested and you passed and she chose you as her man, before all the People. Now they all look at her and say what a fool that woman is to choose a man who bends like a willow, who is neither white nor brown, who is neither English nor Powhatan, who is neither hunter nor gardener, who is neither Eagle nor John.'

'Will she never forgive me?'

'How can she? Will she ever not feel the shame?'

'If we were to go away –'

Attone laughed a brief bitter laugh. 'Where? D'you think she'd live in Jamestown? D'you think they'd not take her out and hang her or worse? D'you think she'd live with you in that house and send tobacco down the river and pack up your plants for you, and be a wife like the other one, the one you left behind in England? Or d'you think to take her to England and watch her die in exile, as Pocahontas did?'

John shook his head, he felt as bewildered as a scolded child. 'I've been a fool,' he said.

For a moment Attone softened. He dropped his hand on John's shoulder. 'These are foolish times,' he said. 'I think at the end of it all, when the Great Hare runs through the world all alone again, we will all seem fools.'

'Can the People survive?' John asked in a low whisper.

Attone shook his head.

January 1645, England

Johnnie was in the garden at first light, looking for flowers for his sister's wedding bouquet. The frost was as thick on the ground as snow, his boots crunched as he walked across the frozen grass. The sun was bright and hard and the air smelled sharp and exciting: of leaf-mould, of coldness, of the earth waiting for sunshine. Johnnie had a powerful sense of being young and alive and that his life, as the only Tradescant heir, was about to begin.

He wanted to give Frances something beautiful. If she had married in springtime she would have carried a bouquet of flowers from the chestnut tree, their grandfather's pride. If she had married in summer he would have cut the stems and snapped the thorns off a hundred roses. But she had chosen the very heart of the winter and Johnnie feared he could give her nothing from his grandfather's garden but the shiny hardness of evergreen leaves.

Hester, seeing him bare-headed and wearing nothing warm, swung open her bedroom window, hearing the hinge crack against the frost. 'Johnnie! What are you doing?'

He turned and waved. 'I'm picking her a bouquet!'

'There's nothing to be had!'

Johnnie shook his head and went on down the garden. Hester watched him go, the lithe little figure with the determined set to his shoulders: Johnnie Tradescant. Then she turned back into the house to wake Frances for her wedding day.

Frances, bathed, dressed, perfumed and wearing a new gown, came downstairs in a shimmering cloud of palest blue silk. She wore her hair down to her shoulders, curled in ringlets, a tiny scrap of lace for a cap on the back of her head. Her gown, rich pale silk embroidered all over with pale blue patterns, hushed and whispered on the flagstones of the hall. Her wide collar was of the finest Valenciennes lace; the future Mrs Norman could import the very best from France. It matched the deep lace edging of her sleeves, crisp and sweet-smelling with starch. The dress was cut low, the cream of Frances's warm skin contrasting with the coolness of the white lace.

'How do I look?' Frances asked, knowing that she was beautiful.

'Awful ugly,' Johnnie said with a smile, invoking the nursery insult. He whipped out a posy from behind his back. 'I picked you these. But you don't have to carry them if you don't like 'em.'

Frances took the posy from him without any word of gratitude or thanks and looked carefully at it. Hester was reminded that they were children and grandchildren of perhaps the finest gardeners the world had ever known. Neither of them exclaimed over the gift of a plant, they always carefully looked, carefully assessed.

He had cut her fronds of yew, the needles as soft as wool, the green so dark as to be almost black, starred with deep pink berries and smelling hauntingly of winter and Christmas. He had picked her mistletoe from the clumps on the old trees in the orchard and woven the light green wings of leaves around the darker yew so the white berries looked like drops of pearls against the needles. He had found some tiny buds of early snowdrops and woven them into a chain which linked leaves, needles and buds altogether, and he had twisted it around with the lace-like twigs of a rambling rose starred with pink hips.

'Thank you,' Frances said.

'But I have this for your hair,' Johnnie said with simple pride. From the table behind him he produced a spray of primroses, and their sweet, clear smell filled the hall.

'How ever did you get primroses?' Frances asked.

'Potted them up as soon as you said you'd marry him,' Johnnie said proudly. 'I wasn't going to let you catch me out with a winter wedding. We *are* the Tradescants, after all.'

Frances laid down her green bouquet and took the pot of primroses to the mirror in the rarities room. Her high heels sounded hollow on the floorboards; only the big things were left in the room, with a collection of lesser pieces which could be sacrificed to save the others. The room was rich enough to fool a looting soldier into thinking that he had seen all the treasures. Hester kept the key to the ice-house door on a chain round her neck and the ivy was growing thickly over the hinges.

Frances picked the flowers, nipping the soft stems with her fingernails, and tucked them behind her ears and into her ringlets.

'Pretty?' she asked, turning to her brother.

'Well enough,' he said, concealing his pride as he took her hand and tucked it under his arm.

They married at Little St Bartholomew's Church, Old Fish Street, in the City with Hester as one witness and Alexander's friend Thomas Streeter as the other. They dined that night at Alexander's house opposite the Tower of London and raised a glass to the father of the bride.

'I wonder where he is tonight?' Mr Streeter asked thoughtlessly. Alexander glanced quickly at Hester's stricken face.

'I don't mind, as long as he's safe,' she said.

It was hard for Hester to leave Frances. She had cared for her since she had been a fair-headed, sad little girl of nine years old, overwhelmed by the responsibility of looking after her brother, missing her mother every night and every day. She had been too proud to ask for help; she would always have all of the Tradescant stubbornness. She had been too independent to ask for love; but Hester would treasure all her life the memory of the way that Frances had stepped sideways, without glancing up, until she could lean against her stepmother's comforting hip and feel a protective hand rest gently on her shoulder.

'I shall miss you,' Hester whispered as she took her leave in the cramped hall of Alexander's house the next day.

'Oh, Mother –' Frances said, and dived into her embrace. 'But I shall come to the Ark often, and you will come and see us. Won't she, Alexander?'

Alexander Norman, looking years younger as if sheer joy had smoothed the lines from his face, beamed at Hester and said: 'You can come and live with us, if you like. I should think myself a Pasha of Turkey with two such beauties in the house.'

'I have the Ark to see to,' Hester affirmed. 'But I expect you on a visit often. And when there is plague in the city . . .'

'I shall send her to you at once,' Alexander reassured her. 'Never fear. And I shall write you what news there is.'

After that, there was nothing to do but to let her go. Hester held on a moment longer than was necessary, and when Frances stepped back into the encircling arm of her husband Hester felt a pain in her whole body as if something slowly and deeply was peeling away from her. She smiled at once. 'God bless you,' she said, as if the pain was not gripping her inside. 'Be happy.'

She turned from the pretty hall and stepped out into the street. The Tower of London threw a shadow over the street in the morning and the chill struck Hester as she gathered her cape around her. In a second Johnnie was at her side, offering his arm like a cavalier, and Hester managed to step briskly out towards the river and the boat to take them home.

'That was well done,' Johnnie said stoutly, keeping his face turned away from her.

'Very well,' Hester replied, rubbing her gloved hand against her cheeks. 'A plague on this cold wind, it's making my eyes water.'

'Mine too,' Johnnie said.

April 1645, England

Hester felt that the Ark, Tradescant's Ark, was adrift in the spring of 1645. The promise that she had made to John Tradescant – to care for his grandchildren and his rarities – seemed to be slipping away from her; though she had always thought that whatever else slipped away, that promise at least could hold firm.

But Frances was a woman, with a house and a new life of her own, and Johnnie was growing and would be off to war within four, perhaps five, years. Every young man in England knew that he would see fighting before he was old, and Johnnie, even precious Johnnie, could be no exception. The rarities were well-hidden and she could only hope that neither the cold nor the damp would spoil them. The ice house was safely locked and bolted, and Joseph had planted a cherry tree, one of Tradescant's great black cherry trees, before it. The sapling had taken well and was spreading its boughs as if it would deny that there had ever been a door there at all. The springing leaves blurred the outline of the wall, and when the blossom came there would be nothing to see but bobbing flowers.

'We'll have to cut that tree down when we want to get the door open and the treasures out,' Joseph observed to Hester in a quiet voice as she was walking around the garden.

'The way things are going, we'll never be safe to have them out,' she replied, and went on.

The garden was looking as lovely as it did every spring, as if war was not the nation's chief occupation, as if hunger and plague were not a certainty in the coming summer. The daffodils were bobbing in the orchard and in the tulip beds the spears of buds were thickening and blushing with light stripes of colour. If in the autumn there was anyone left alive who cared to buy tulips there would be a fortune in the rich earth of the Tradescant garden.

But nobody was buying, they were not taking money at the door of the rarities room, they were not selling plants. The Ark was slowly sinking under debt. Joseph was working for half-wages and his keep, the lads had left, run away to war, the maids had been dismissed and only Cook stayed on and shared the work of the house with Hester.

The trees were in their first green leaves, Hester could almost smell their freshness in the air. The grass was growing long; as soon as the daffodils had died back then Joseph would scythe it and rake the clippings away. The branches in the orchards were bobbing with their twigs bursting into leaf and the buds thickening with the promise of flowers to come. It should have been a joyous place; but Hester walked among the fertility and over-brimming life of it like a woman chilled to the bone and weary nearly to death.

She walked to the end of the garden and looked out across the pond. It was years since she had brought Johnnie here to feed the ducks, years since they had sat in the little waterlogged boat and he had rowed her backwards and forwards and told her that he would undoubtedly be a great sailor as his grandfather had been – chasing pirates in the Mediterranean, sailing to the very icy doors of Russia. And now she was the wife of another travelling Tradescant and she thought that this would be the year that she would have to find the courage to face the fact that John was never coming home.

Since he had left she had received only one letter, to say that he was leaving Jamestown and going to build his house further up the river and that she should not expect to hear from him again for some time. Then she had received a consignment of Indian rarities and a couple of barrels of plants, badly packed, and badly shipped, which told her that it was not John who had seen them loaded on board. Since then – nothing. And now there was news of an Indian uprising and Jamestown attacked, and all the planters all along the river scalped and skinned and butchered.

She thought she must learn to stop looking for John, learn to stop waiting for him. She thought she would wait till the summer and then, if there was still no news, find a way to tell Johnnie, who was sometimes still her little boy, and sometimes now a young man, that his father was not coming home, and that he was the only Gardener Tradescant left.

'Excuse me,' a voice behind her said politely. 'I am looking for John Tradescant.'

'He's not here,' Hester said wearily and turned around. 'I am his wife. Can I help you?'

The man before her was one of the handsomest she had ever seen in her life. He swept off his hat to her and the plumes brushed the ground as he bowed, one long brown suede boot stretched forwards. He was dressed in grey – a sober enough colour which might indicate he was a Parliament man and one of the dreary Presbyterian sort at that; but his thick, curly head of hair, his rich lace collar, and that laughing confidence in his smile, was that of a cavalier.

Hester's first response was to smile in reply, he was not a man that any woman would find easy to resist. But then she remembered the times they lived in and she glanced towards the house as if she feared a guard of soldiery at his call and a warrant for arrest in his pocket.

'Can I help you?' she asked again.

'I'm looking for tulips,' he said. 'Everyone knows that John Tradescant's is the only garden worth visiting in England, and also these are troubled times to go flower hunting in the Low Countries.'

'We have tulips,' Hester said gravely, not taking advantage of the conversational opening to deplore the badness of the times. 'Was it a special variety you wanted?'

'Yes,' he said. 'What do you have?'

Hester smiled. The verbal fencing was a typical approach to naming a plant which had, in its heyday, cost the value of a house. 'We have everything,' she said with the simple arrogance of a professional at the very top of her profession. 'You had much better tell me simply what you want. We only ever charge a fair price, Mr –?'

He stepped back slightly as if to re-assess her, as if his view of a plain woman plainly dressed had hidden the strength of her character, and her pride. 'I'm John Lambert,' he said. 'And last year I grew half a dozen tulips at my home, and this year I must have more. I simply must. Do you know what I mean, Mrs Tradescant? Or are they nothing more than a crop to you, like wheat to a farmer?'

'They're not my passion,' Hester said. 'But nobody could live in this household and not come to love tulips. They are one of the finest flowers.'

'None finer,' he said quickly.

'Roses?'

He hesitated. 'But the thing about tulips is the shortness of the season, and the way you can buy them in the bulb and hold the bulb in your hand and know that inside it is a thing of such beauty. And you know that if you care for it you will see that thing of beauty, whereas a rose – a rose grows itself.'

Hester laughed. 'If you were a working gardener, Mr Lambert, you would value plants that grow themselves. But let me show you our tulip beds.'

She led the way back through the garden and then paused. The path ran alongside the wall which kept the west wind off the plants. Along the wall, espaliered in regular lines, were apple and pear trees; the south wall was lined with the peaches and apricots. They were Tradescant walls: a double skin of brick with three fireplaces set one on top of each other and a flue running from each fire along the length of the wall to keep the bricks at a steady warmth by night and day. But Hester had not been able to afford the charcoal for the fires for two seasons.

Hester saw Mr Lambert take in the neat planning and the solidity of the building, and the immaculate pruning of the branches, and felt her familiar stir of pride. Then he turned to the garden beds and she heard his sharp intake of breath.

There was bed after bed of tulips. They grew at least twenty of each specimen, and they had more than a hundred different varieties. Each new variety was labelled with a lead spike stuck in the ground at the head of the row and on each spike, in Johnnie's meticulous printing, was the name of each variety. Behind each label, like a row of well-drilled infantry, grew the tulips, with their leaves clasped close to their stalks and their growing heads like multi-coloured soldiers shouldering their pikes.

Hester enjoyed the expression on the cavalier's face. 'We keep the rare ones potted up,' she said. 'These are only garden tulips. I can show you the rarities, we keep them in our orangery.'

'I had no idea,' he said softly. He was walking between the tulip beds, scanning them, bending to read the labels and then going on. 'I had heard you were great gardeners, but I thought you worked on the palace gardens.'

'We do,' Hester said. 'We did,' she corrected herself. 'But we had to have our own garden to stock the palace gardens, and we have always sold our stock.'

He nodded, paced the length of the bed, kneeled down and then got up again. Hester noted the dirt on the knees of his grey suit and that he did not trouble to brush it off. She recognised at once the signs of a besotted tulip enthusiast and a man accustomed to employing others to keep his clothes smart.

'And what rarities do you have?' he asked.

'We have a Lack tulip, a Duck tulip, Agatha tulips, Violetten.' She broke off at the eagerness in his face.

'I've never seen them,' he said. 'D'you have them here?'

'This way,' Hester said pleasantly, and led him towards the house. Johnnie came running out and checked at the sight of the stranger. He gave a neat bow and the man smiled at him.

'My stepson,' Hester said. 'John Tradescant.'

'And will you be a gardener too?' the man asked.

'I am a gardener already,' Johnnie replied. 'I am going to be a cavalry officer.'

Hester scowled a warning at him but the man nodded pleasantly enough. 'I'm in that line of work myself,' he said. 'I'm in the cavalry for the Parliament army.'

'*That* John Lambert!' Hester exclaimed and then flushed and wished she had the sense to be silent. She had read about the talents of the cavalry leader who was said to be the equal of Prince Rupert, but she had not pictured him as a young man, smiling in spring sunshine, and devoted to tulips.

He grinned at her. 'Shall I keep a place among my officers for you, Master Tradescant?'

Johnnie flushed and looked awkward. 'The thing is –'

'He is too young to be thinking of such things,' Hester intervened. 'Now . . . the tulips –'

John Lambert did not move. 'What is the thing?' he asked Johnnie gently.

'The thing is that I am in the king's service,' Johnnie said seriously. 'My family have always been gardeners to the royal palaces, and we have not yet been dismissed. So I suppose I am in the king's service, and I can't, in honour, join you. But I thank you for the invitation, sir.'

Lambert smiled. 'Perhaps by the time you are old enough to ride with me there will be a country united, and only one army and one cavalry and all you will have to choose is your horse and the colour of the feather in your hat,' he suggested diplomatically. 'And both Prince Rupert and I will be proud to serve under the same colours.'

He straightened up and looked over Johnnie's head at Hester's concerned expression. 'Please don't fear, Mrs Tradescant,' he said. 'I am here to buy tulips, not to cause you a moment's uneasiness. Loyalty is a difficult path to tread and these are difficult times. You may well garden in a royal palace once more and I may yet dance off a royal scaffold. Or I might be the new Chief Justice and you Mayor of London. Let's just look at some tulips, shall we?'

The warmth of his smile was irresistible. Hester smiled in reply and directed him to the terrace where the tulips stood in their beautiful ceramic pots. Warmed by the sunshine and sheltered in the orangery at night, these were more developed than those in the bed and they were showing the colours in their petals.

'Now these are our rarities,' she said. 'These are green parrot tulips,

305

very special.' Hester indicated the ragged fringe on the green petals. 'And these are Paragon Liefkens, they have a wonderful broken colour – red and white or red and yellow. The Semper Augustus comes from this family but excels them in shape, it has the true tulip shape and the best broken colour. Here are the Violetten, they come in a different colour in every bulb, very unpredictable and difficult to grow a consistent strain: they can be as pale as a bough of lilac or a true, deep purple-blue like violets. If you were interested in developing your own strain –' She glanced at him and saw the avidity in his face.

'Oh, yes!'

'Then these are the ones I would choose. To get a consistent deep purple would be a wonderful thing to do. Gardeners would thank you forever. And here,' she led the way to the shelter of the terrace and the tulips standing proudly in the precious pots, 'these are our Semper Augustus. We believe them to be the only Sempers in England. My father-in-law bought them and gave one to the queen. When she left the palace my husband brought it back here. As far as I know, no-one else has a Semper.'

Lambert's attention was all that she could have desired. He squatted down so his dark head was on a level with the scarlet and white flower. 'May I touch?'

'Gently,' Hester assented.

He put out a fingertip, the ruby on his hand winked at the scarlet of the petal and he noticed the match of the colour at once. The red of the petal was as shiny as silk shot through with white. One flower, a little more mature than the others, was open and he peered into the cup to see the exotic darkness of the stamens and the sooty black of the pollen.

'Exquisite,' he breathed. 'This is the most beautiful thing I have ever seen.'

Hester smiled. Johnnie glanced up at her and winked. They both knew what would come next.

'How much?' John Lambert asked.

'Johnnie, go and ask Cook for some shortbread and a glass of wine for our guest,' Hester commanded. 'And bring me some notepaper and a pen. You will want to place a large order, Mr Lambert?'

He looked up at her and grinned, the confident smile of a handsome man whose life is going well for him. 'You may command my fortune, Mrs Tradescant.'

Summer 1645, Virginia

John thought that the life at the new village in the creeks would become easier once the crops yielded and the hunting improved, and the fruits were ripe in the forest. When the good weather came there was indeed enough food for everyone; but the easy contentment of the old village life was lost. They dug out a pit and built a new sweat lodge, and dedicated a new dancing circle. They built a grain store and the women made the tall, smooth black jars to hold the dried peas and seeds and maize which would see them through the winter; but the joy that John had thought was inseparable from the Powhatan had gone from them. Expelled from the land where they had chosen to live, and confined to the brackish waters near the shoreline, they were like a people who had lost their confidence and their pride.

They had never thought that they could be defeated by the colonists, or if they thought they could lose, they thought it would be in a great battle, and the braves would lie dead in heaps, and the women would grieve and take their men home and weep over their bodies. Then a price would be paid – the orphans and the widows would disappear into Jamestown and not be seen again and the Powhatan would grieve for them too, as among the lost. Then, after a season, after a cycle of the year, everything would return to normal.

What they had not anticipated was that the war would never stop. What they had not anticipated was that it would not be a battle and a withdrawal of either one side or the other. What they had not anticipated, and John had not thought to warn them against, was the inveteracy of English spite against a native people which takes arms against them.

The colonists were not driven by fear, it was no longer a matter of self defence. The army of half-naked yelling warriors which had come against them had melted away, disappeared back into the woods. The colonists were fuelled instead by a deep sense of outrage and moral righteousness. Ever since the first uprising they had felt that the Indians had escaped punishment, had been pushed back into the woods but not pushed far enough. Even when they had built the wooden palisade to mark the limit of their tolerance of the native people, they had thought that too much land had been left to them. Now, under Sir William Berkeley, there was talk of 'solving' the Indian question. In these terms of speech the families of the Powhatan were now defined as a problem which had to be solved, and not as a people with rights.

Once that shift of thinking took place there could be only one conclusion, and John understood the determination of the colonists who marched out in expedition after expedition to hunt down first one village and then another until it felt as if the trees had ceased to hide the Powhatan, and the leaves ceased to shelter them, as if the colonists could see through the branches and the morning mist, and wherever there was one of the People, a man, a woman or a child, a musket ball would find them.

And then the news came that Opechancanough had been captured. John went to find Attone by the river. He was not fishing, nor sharpening a bow. He was not chipping at the blade of a stone knife, nor tying an intricate knot to flight an arrow. He was standing, uncharacteristically idle, his hands limp at his sides, watching the light on the sluggish water of the river as it lapped at the pebbles at his feet.

'The white men have taken Opechancanough,' John said.

Attone did not turn his head. He had heard John approach from half a mile away and known from the sound of the footsteps that it was John, and that he was looking for someone.

'Yes.'

'I was thinking, should I go into Jamestown and ask them to spare his life?'

Attone turned his bright dark gaze on John. 'Would they spare him if you asked it?'

'I don't know. They might. At least I could speak up for him. I thought I should go to them and explain what the Powhatan believe. At the very least I could make sure that they understand what Opechancanough is saying.'

Attone nodded. 'Yes. Go.'

John stepped forwards and stood beside the man, shoulder to shoulder. 'I have loved you like a brother,' he said suddenly.

Attone flashed him a quick look and at the back of it was a smile. 'Yes.'

'I didn't think it would end here, like this.'

The Powhatan shook his head, his gaze returning to the moving water. 'I didn't think it either, Englishman.'

'You call me Englishman because I am no longer of the People,' John stated, hoping to be contradicted.

Attone simply nodded.

John summoned his resolve. 'Then I will go into Jamestown and plead for his life, and then I will go back to England. I know that there is no place for me with the People any more, and the food I eat robs the hungry men and women.'

'It is time that you went back to your own people. There is nothing for you here.'

'I would stay if Suckahanna asked me –'

Again there was that dark flash and a half-concealed smile. 'You might as well wait for the deer to speak, Englishman. She has turned her head from you, she will not look back.'

'Because of her pride?'

Attone nodded. 'Now *she* is a Powhatan,' he said.

'When I am gone will you tell her that I loved her?' John asked. 'And that I went because I believed she wanted me gone. Tell her it was not uncertainty, and not knowing where I belonged. Will you tell her that my whole heart was with her?'

Attone shook his head, a lazy gesture. 'I will tell her that you loved her as much as a man like you can love.'

'What would a man like you do?' John cried out in frustration. 'If you're saying that my love is less – what would your love be like? What would you do?'

Attone laughed at that. 'Oh! Beat her, I suppose. Love her. Give her a baby to care for. Send her out in the fields to work. Bring her home at night and keep her awake all the night with lovemaking until she is too tired to do anything but sleep. Don't ask me, Eagle, she left me for you. If I knew how to manage her she would never have married you.'

John laughed unwillingly. 'But you will tell her that I love her?'

'Oh go, Englishman,' Attone said, suddenly weary of the whole thing. 'I will tell her the words if I can remember them, but we have no interest in words. And words from Englishmen mean less than nothing. You are a faithless race, and you talk too much. Go and see if your talking can save Opechancanough and then go back to your people. Your time here with us is finished.'

John washed himself clean in the river but the paleness of his skin seemed stained forever by the redness of the bear grease. He asked Musses to cut his hair for him, in a short crop, the same length on both sides, so that he no longer had the side plait of the Powhatan braid. She did it neatly, with two sharpened oyster shells, and gathered up the fallen locks and threw them on the fire.

'Going home?' she asked.

'I have nowhere else to go,' John replied, hoping for sympathy.

'Goodbye,' she said pleasantly and walked away.

John rose up from her fire, took a knife and his bow and arrow and went to find Suckahanna. She was at a corner of the camp, a deerskin strung taut on the curing frame; she was rubbing oil into the skin to keep it supple and sweet.

'I am going to Jamestown to speak for Opechancanough,' John said. She nodded.

'After, I shall take a ship for England.'

She nodded again.

'I may never come back,' he warned.

The tiniest of shrugs greeted that remark and she turned around and tipped some more oil into her palm and worked it into the skin.

'Before I go, I want to tell you that I love you and that I am sorry for not being a true brave,' John said. 'I know I have disappointed you; but I could not spill the blood of my countrymen. If we had found a way to live at peace, white men and Powhatan, then you and I would have been happy together. It is the times which failed us, Suckahanna. I know that I loved you then, and I love you still. Without fail.'

At last she paused in her work, she tossed her head and her black hair slid over her shoulder, and he saw the almost-forgotten sweetness of her smile.

'Go your way, Englishman,' she said. 'You don't snare me with words.'

'And you still love me,' John hazarded.

She gave him that swift, flirtatious, elusive smile. 'Go away.'

It was a long way to Jamestown. John went northwards along the shore-line. He lived off shellfish and berries and early ripening nuts, and occasionally he shot a bird for some meat. He thought it was ironic that now he was preparing to leave the country he had found that he could live off it and that it was the rich and fertile place of his wildest childhood imaginings.

For the first three days he trudged dully, like a London apprentice going to work, watching his feet on the stones of the shore, and looking around him only to check for enemies and to look for game. But on the third day he realised that just over the arid dunes was forest filled with trees and saplings and seeds coming into ripeness, and he left the shoreline, went into the forest and started collecting.

By the time he reached the James River he had made himself a satchel from two duckskins, which were not properly cleaned and were smelling powerfully, and stuffed it with seeds and roots. He approached the first plantation he saw with caution, he did not want to be shot as an Indian by a nervous planter. He saw the man down on his roughly built quay.

'Ahoy!' John called from the shelter of the forest. The English words felt strange on his tongue, for a moment he was afraid he had forgotten his own language.

The man turned to where the sound came from and raked the forest with his gaze. 'Who's there?'

'A friend, an Englishman. But buck-naked.'

The planter lifted his musket. John saw that the fuse was not glowing and the chances were good that it was out. He stepped out of the shelter of the woods.

'You're an Indian dog! Stand still or I shoot you as you stand.'

'I promise,' John said. 'I'm as English as you. I'm John Tradescant, gardener to the king of England, I have a house and a garden in Lambeth and a wife called Hester Pooks and a daughter called Frances and a son called Johnnie.' As he spoke the familiar, beloved names he felt a stirring as if they themselves were calling to him and he should have been listening, he should have heard them earlier.

'Then what are you doing like a savage in the woods?' the man asked, his gun pointed unwaveringly at John's crotch.

John hesitated. Of course, that was the very question.

'Because I didn't know where I should be,' he said slowly. Then he raised his voice and said loudly enough to be heard: 'I was living with the Powhatan, but now I want to go back to England. Can I borrow some clothing and take a boat to Jamestown? I can get money sent to me there, and repay you.'

The man motioned him forwards and John stepped cautiously closer. 'What's the name of the new Parliament commander?' the man asked him quickly.

John spread his hands. 'I don't know. I've been with the Powhatan for the last two years. When I left the king was defeated at Edgehill – I thought it would not be long for him then.'

The man laughed shortly. 'It still is not decided now,' he said. 'What's the name of the king's cousin?'

'Prince Rupert?'

'His son?'

'Prince Charles?'

'Nationality of his wife?'

'She's French, I can tell you the colour of her eyes,' John said. 'I was in court service, I was gardener at Oatlands Palace.'

The man checked. 'You were gardener to the queen of England and here you are as naked as a savage after running wild two years with the Powhatan?'

John stepped forwards and held out his hand. 'Odd, isn't it? I'm John Tradescant, of the Ark, Lambeth.'

They loaned John a pair of breeches and a coarse linen shirt and he crammed his feet into a pair of shoes that should have been the right size but which pinched his feet unbearably. Running barefoot for two years had hardened the skin and spread the bones of his feet, John feared he would never walk comfortably in boots or shoes again.

A tobacco ship called in at the quay to load their crop the next day and John sent a note to Hester at Lambeth and packed his seeds and roots into a watertight barrel addressed to her.

> *Dear Wife,*
>   *I hope this reaches you in good health and fortune. I am on*
> *my way to Jamestown after many months living in the forest.*
> *I have no money. Please send a note of credit for me to draw*
> *twenty pounds for my board and lodging and journey home. I*
> *shall come home as soon as I receive the money.*

John flinched a little at the bareness of the note but he did not feel he could, in all conscience, offer any explanation or any reassurance of love. He feared that perhaps Hester would be hard-pressed to find twenty pounds to pay into a London goldsmith so that the note of credit could be good in Virginia, but he could not bring himself to offer advice as to what she might sell from the collection. He had been too long away. He did not know if she had been able to keep the collection safe. He did not even know for certain that she was still at the Lambeth address. He felt as if he were pitching a rope into darkness and hoping that someone on an unseen quayside might catch it and haul him in. He paused before signing his name. If anyone would haul him in, it would be Hester.

> *I trust you, Hester, and when I come home I shall thank you*
> *for your care of me and mine.*

He signed his name and ran down to the wooden pier and thrust the note at the captain. 'Please see that she receives it,' he said. 'I am trapped here unless she can send me my fare home.' He looked at the ship. 'Unless I could work a passage?'

The captain laughed in his face. 'Work your passage? You're a seaman, are you?'

'No,' John said.

'If you want to go home, mister, you'll have to pay for your voyage, same as anyone.'

'She'll reward you for bringing the note,' John promised him. 'Please see that she receives it.'

The captain tucked it carelessly into his jacket. 'Oh aye,' he said and shouted to the sailors to let go.

The current of the river caught the ship and she pulled away from the quayside. John watched the sails unfurl and heard the shouted orders and the creaks of the rope and timbers as the ship got underway.

'How long before you hear?' the planter asked him.

'It can't be quicker than four months,' John said. 'A voyage there and back, if she has the money, that is.'

The man grinned. 'I could use a hand to work the crop,' he said.

John nodded. Labour was notoriously hard to find in Virginia. He would have to be a hired hand until Hester sent him a note of credit and he could become a gentleman again.

'Very well,' he said. 'But I have to go to Jamestown first. I have a promise to keep.'

John saw the governor for a brief snatched moment as the great man strode from the new assembly room to the governor's mansion. John hobbled after him in his ill-fitting shoes. 'Sir William?'

The young man turned, took in John's humble clothes and strolled on. 'Yes?' he threw over his shoulder.

'I am John Tradescant, gardener to the king.' John followed him. 'I was planting my headright up the river when the Powhatan saved me from starving. I lived with them for years. I have come to Jamestown to ask for clemency for Opechancanough.'

Sir William blinked at the extraordinary story and hesitated. 'Clemency?'

'He's an old man, and he could see no way forward for his people. If they had been allowed to settle fairly after the first uprising he would not have felt so driven. They're ready to make peace now, a lasting peace, if we could only give them the land they need.'

'You are a spokesman for them?' Sir William asked. 'You're on their side?'

Almost imperceptibly a couple of soldiers from the assembly doors edged a little closer.

'No,' John said. 'They have expelled me. I am an Englishman and as soon as I can I shall return to London. But I owe them a debt of gratitude. They took me in and they fed me when I was near to death of starvation. I should like to repay my debt to them and indeed, Sir William, I think they have not been treated fairly by us.'

The young man hesitated for only a moment, then he shook his head. 'This is a new country,' he said. 'We are exploring all the time, south and north and west. The Powhatan, and the other savages, have to know that this is our country now, and if they fight against us, if they break the peace, then death is the only response.'

'The peace was here before we arrived,' John said quickly. 'The country was here before we came. The Powhatan were here before we came. Some might say that it was their country.'

Sir William looked sharply at John. 'Then that man would be a traitor to England and the king of England,' he said. 'You say you were servant to the king himself. He's not a man who accepts half-loyalty, and neither do I.'

John thought for a moment of his long-distant court life and the king who could not distinguish between half-loyalty and play-acting and reality. 'I am faithful to the king,' he said. 'But it is a bad example to kill the king of the Powhatan. He should be like all kings – inviolate.'

'This is not a king,' Sir William said with sudden impatience. 'This is a savage. You insult His Majesty by the comparison. The person of a king is sacred, he stands only below God himself. This dirty old Indian is a savage and we shall hang him.'

He turned abruptly from John and walked away.

'He was a king to us only a few years ago,' John said staunchly. 'Pocahontas was a princess. She was invited to London and treated as a princess of royal blood. I know. I was there and I saw it. The Powhatan then were a free and equal people and their royal family was as sacred as ours.'

The governor shook his head. 'Not any more,' he said simply. 'They're less than animals to us now. And if you choose to go back to them, then tell them this: that there is no place for them in this country. Tell them they will have to go –' he gestured '– south or further west and keep on travelling. It's our land now and we won't share it.'

Autumn 1645, England

Hester received John's letter asking for his fare home in the second week of September. The sailor who brought it was given a penny for his trouble and some thin soup at the kitchen door. Hester took the letter into the rarities room – the tiny fire was burning in there and the light from the tall Venetian windows was good. But she also had a superstitious sense that this was the rarest thing of all – a letter from her husband.

It was crumpled from its resting place inside someone's jacket and grubby as if it had been dropped somewhere and forgotten for a little while. Hester looked at the folded outside of the paper and the tiny splash of wax which sealed it, as if she would read every inch of the paper as well as the message inside. Then she sat at the desk that was set in the window for the convenience of artists who might come to draw the specimens in the collection, and broke the seal.

> *Dear Wife,*
>   *I hope this reaches you in good health and fortune. I am on my way to Jamestown after many months living in the forest.*

Hester paused. She had thought John was living in a planter's house, such as were illustrated in the books about Virginia. A little house made of half-sawn timbers with wood shingles for a roof. What could he mean about living in the forest?

> *I have no money. Please send a note of credit for me to draw twenty pounds for my board and lodging and journey home. I shall come home as soon as I receive the money.*

Hester raised her head from the smudged words. The Virginia venture had ended then, as she had said it would, in bankruptcy and disaster.

There was no profitable crop of tobacco. There was no refuge from the uncertainty of a country at war. John had failed completely, failed so badly that he could not even come home unless she sent him his passage money.

> *I trust you, Hester, and when I come home I shall thank you*
> *for your care of me and mine.*

Hester pressed her finger to her lips and then put it down, as if making a fingerprint in sealing wax on the J at the end of the letter. John was coming home to her. She found she cared not at all that he was coming home penniless, without plantation, or tobacco, or pride. She cared not at all that he was trapped in a foreign land and could not even earn his passage home. All that mattered was that John was coming home, at last.

She sat only for a few minutes in the light of the window and then she set to raising the money to send him at once. Twenty pounds was a substantial sum. Fortunately the letter had come in September, the very time for the sale of tulip bulbs, and the order for John Lambert had been despatched only a week before. Any day now she expected his payment.

Hester threw a shawl over her head and went out to the terrace. Johnnie was working with Joseph, lifting and labelling the tulip bulbs from their beds. When she called him and he looked up she saw his face was still dark with sorrow.

Johnnie's hero Prince Rupert had failed to keep Bristol for the royalists though he had promised his king he would hold it for months. The wildest rumour was circulating: that Rupert had played the king false on purpose. They were saying that he and his brother, the Elector Palatine, now eating his dinner in London at the expense of Parliament having stolidly changed his coat and abandoned his uncle, had conspired all along to have one brother on each side so that they would profit whichever side won. Some people even said that Rupert hoped for the throne of England himself.

Ever since the news had come in of the fall of Bristol Johnnie had come down to breakfast with red eyes, and he had been quiet and moody all the day. When Hester wanted him for work in the garden she had to find him first, and half the time he would be down at the little lake, sitting in the rowing boat, adrift in the middle, slumped in despair over the dripping oars.

'How are the tulips?' she asked.

He nodded, as if he could not take joy even in them. 'They've done well. For every bulb that went in, we are raising three. It's been a good year for tulips, if for nothing else.'

Joseph nodded. 'I've never seen such a crop,' he said. 'Something's going right at least.'

'More than one thing,' Hester said. She tied the ends of the shawl crosswise around her waist and thought it felt like a tight and loving embrace. 'I have a letter here from Virginia.'

The shadow left Johnnie's face and he jumped to his feet from the bed of tulips. 'He's coming home?'

'He's coming home,' she assented. 'At last.'

※

The waiting was the hardest time of all. She had the money from John Lambert for his order of tulips, and then she took some old Roman coins from the rarities room and offered them for sale to a London goldsmith. The price he gave her was little more than theft but Hester realised that portable treasures were flooding on to the market as one grand family after another tried to survive the war years. She went to Alexander Norman to borrow the rest of the money and took the whole amount to the goldsmith who was known to give and receive credit for Virginia. He signed a note of credit for twenty pounds to John Tradescant by name and then Hester had to take it down to the London docks and find a ship sailing to Virginia.

A vessel was waiting to go, almost ready to cast off: the *Makepeace*, going to Virginia by the southern route and stopping at the Sugar Islands.

'I have to see the captain,' Hester said to one of the sailors. She was jostled by a family throwing their bundles on board and pushing their way towards the gangplank. 'Or a trustworthy gentleman.'

'We've got a brace of vicars,' the man said rudely. 'And half a dozen cavaliers. Take your pick.'

'I need a gentleman to assist me,' Hester said stoutly. 'I shall see one of the clerical gentlemen.'

The sailor laughed, turned his head and shouted below. Hester smoothed her cape and wished that she had brought Johnnie with her, or even allowed Alexander Norman to come too. Eventually a white-haired man looked down from the ship's side and said quietly, as if he would not raise his voice over the din of the ship, 'I am the Reverend Walter de Carey. May I help you, madam?'

Hester stepped quickly up the swaying gangplank and held out her hand. 'How do you do, I am Mrs Tradescant, wife of John Tradescant of the Ark, Lambeth.'

He bowed over her hand. 'I am honoured,' he said.

'I am sorry to ask a favour of a stranger but my husband has been –' Hester paused for a moment. 'Plant collecting in Virginia and finds himself without money. I have a note of credit for him but I need to find a trustworthy gentleman to take it to Virginia and give it to him.'

The man smiled wearily. 'I am so little trusted that I have been expelled from my church and the blacksmith stands in my pulpit and tells my congregation what revelation he has gleaned that week from his forge fire,' he said. 'I was twenty years in my vicarage and I baptised every single one of those young men and women who now tell me that I am in league with the Antichrist and a worshipper of the whore of Babylon. *They* would not call me a trustworthy man.'

Mutely, Hester held out the sealed and folded paper. 'If you were twenty years in the vicarage and a good parish priest then you are the man for me,' she said. 'These are hard times of change for us all. Will you help me try to bring my family back together? This is my husband's passage money home.'

He hesitated for only a moment and then he took the paper. 'Forgive me, I am too absorbed in my own sorrows. I will take the paper; but how will I find your husband?'

'He'll find you,' Hester said with certainty. 'He'll be waiting for this. All you have to do is to tell people in Jamestown that you are looking for him and he will find you. Whereabouts are you going in Virginia?'

'I hope to settle there and found a school,' the vicar said. 'The times are against men who believe in the king and God in this country. I trust that the new world will be a refuge for men of steady faith. Half this ship is filled with men like me, who cannot bear the new rule of Parliament and the wild heresies of madmen and self-taught preachers and the like in our own churches.'

'My husband left at the outbreak of the war,' Hester said. 'He could not bear to watch the country being torn apart, and it was tearing him apart too.'

'He will come home to difficult times,' the vicar remarked. 'The fighting may be nearly over, but the bitterness of these years will not be easily restored. And what is to become of the king in the hands of such a crew?'

There was a shout from the bridge and an answering shout from the shore.

'I must go,' Hester said hurriedly. 'I do thank you for accepting the letter for John. He will do all he can to help you when he meets you, I know he will. He will be grateful.'

The vicar bowed. Hester turned for the gangplank and went down it as the lumpers on the dockside shouted to the sailors on the ship and finally cast off from shore.

'God speed,' Hester called to the ship. 'Tell him I am waiting.'

The vicar put his hand to his ear, so Hester waved with a smile on her face and said more quietly, so he would be certain not to hear, 'Tell him I love him.'

Autumn 1645, Virginia

John found that he had learned patience from the Powhatan, as well as the skill of living off the land. When he knew for certain that nothing he could do or say could save Opechancanough from death he went back to the farmer at the edge of the forest and agreed with him that he would work four days a week for his food and bed and a pittance of a wage, and three days of the week he would be free to go collecting in the near-virgin woods around the plantation.

Only a year before he would have been irritable, longing for the ship to come to release him from this service so that he could go home. But John found a sense of peace. He felt this was an interlude between his life with Suckahanna and the Powhatan, and the return – which must be a difficult experience – to Hester and the Ark at Lambeth.

In the days when he worked in the fields he was employed in harvesting the tobacco crop, taking the leaves to the drying sheds, baling them up and then loading them on to the ships which stopped at the little quay as their last port of call before setting off across the Atlantic.

In the days when he was free to roam he took his duckskin satchel, now properly cleaned, and went out into the woods with nothing more than a knife, a trowel, a bow across his shoulder and a couple of arrows in his quiver. It was a secret life he lived once he was out of sight of the planter's house. As soon as he reached the shelter of the trees he stopped and shed his heavy clothes and kicked off his painful shoes. He wrapped them and hid them in a tree, just as Suckahanna the little girl used to do with her servant's gown, and then he went barefoot and naked but for his buckskin through the forest and felt himself to be a free man once again.

Even after his years in the wilderness he had not lost his sense of awe at the strangeness and beauty of this country. He longed to bring it home entire, but he forced himself to choose the best of the shrubs and trees that he found on his long, loping surveys. He found a type of daisy that he thought had never been seen before, a big-flowered daisy with curious petals. He dug up half a dozen roots and packed them into damp soil, hoping they would survive until he had a ship for home. He took cuttings of the vine which Suckahanna had planted at his doorstep all that long time ago. He recognised it now. It was a favourite of hers: a sweet woodbine which some people called honeysuckle, but growing here with long scarlet flowers like fingers. He had a new convolvulus which he would name for himself, 'Tradescantia'. He found a foxglove which was like the English variety but stronger-coloured and bigger in shape. He potted up a Virginian yucca, a Virginian locust tree, a Virginian nettle tree. He found a Virginian mulberry which reminded him of the silkworms and the mulberry trees at Oatlands Palace. He found a wonderful pink spiderwort, the only flower his father had put his own name to, and kept the corms dry and safe, hoping that they would grow in memory of his father. He dug up the dry roots of Virginian roses, certain that they would grow differently alongside their English cousins if he could only get them safe home to Lambeth.

Specimen after specimen he brought back to the little farmhouse and heeled in the growing plants into his nursery beds and laid the seeds in sand or rice to keep them dry. Plant after plant he brought in to add to the Lambeth collection. And as he added a new tree, the Virginian maple, or a new flower, the yellow willow herb, or a new herb, Virginian parsley, he realised that he would bring back to England an explosion of strangeness. If the country had been at peace and ready to attend to its gardens he would have been hailed as a worker of miracles, a greater plantsman and botanist even than his father.

He believed that he thought of nothing but his plants on these long expeditions when he was gone from dawn to dusk and sometimes from dawn till dawn, when he slept in the woods despite the cold winds which warned of the change of season. But somewhere in his heart and in his mind he was saying farewell: to Suckahanna the girl, whose innocence he had prized so highly, to Suckahanna the young woman he had loved, and to Suckahanna the proud, beautiful woman who had taken him into her heart and into her bed and in the end sent him away.

John said goodbye to her, and goodbye to the forest that she had loved and shared with him, and by the time the *Makepeace* sailed by the end of the pier and went upriver to dock at Jamestown, John had said his farewells and was ready to leave.

He had half a dozen barrels of seeds and roots packed in sand. He had two barrels of saplings planted in shallow earth and watered by hand every day. He left them on the end of the pier ready for collection and paddled the canoe upriver to Jamestown to see if this latest ship had brought him a message and the money from Hester.

He hardly expected it. It could be this ship or a later one. But it was part of John's ritual of saying farewell to Suckahanna and making a new troth with Hester that he should be on the quayside to greet every ship, to show his trust that Hester would work as fast as she could to get the money to him. Their plan should not miscarry through his fault.

There was the usual crowd, shouting greetings and offering goods and rooms for hire. There was the usual anarchy of arrival: goods thrown on the quayside, children squealing with excitement, friends greeting each other, deals being struck. John stood up on a capstan and shouted over the heads of the crowd: 'Anyone with a message for John Tradescant?'

No-one replied at first so he shouted again and again like a coster-monger bawling out his wares. Then a white-haired man, looking frail and sick, came down the gangplank with one eye on his sea chest of belongings and lifted his head and said:

'I!'

'Praise God,' John said and jumped down from his vantage point, and knew at the same time the plummet of disappointment that now there was nothing more to stay for, and he must leave Suckahanna's land, just as he had left her.

He pushed through the crowd with a smile of greeting on his face. 'I am John Tradescant.'

'I am the Reverend Walter de Carey. Your wife trusted me with a letter for you.'

'Was she well?'

The older man nodded. 'She looked well. A woman of some courage, I should imagine.'

John thought of Hester's stubborn determination. 'Above rubies,' he said shortly. He opened the letter and saw at once that she had done as he asked. He had only to go to the Virginia Company offices and claim his twenty pounds, Hester had paid the money for him to a London goldsmith and the deed attested to it.

'I thank you,' he said. 'Now, is there any service I can do for you? Do you have somewhere to stay? Can I help you with your bags?'

'If you could help me carry this sea chest,' the man said hesitantly. 'I had thought there would be some porters or servants . . .'

'This is Virginia,' John warned him. 'They're all freeholders here.'

Winter 1645, England

In October Frances and Alexander Norman came upriver to Lambeth to stay for two nights. Hester urged them to stay longer but Alexander said he dared not leave his business for too long, the war must be coming to an end, every day he was sending out new consignments of gunpowder barrels and there were rumours that Basing House had fallen to Cromwell's army at last.

It was not that it was such a strategic point, not like Bristol – the second city of the kingdom – which Prince Rupert had lost only the month before. But it was a place which had captured people's imagination for its stubborn adherence to the king. When Johnnie knew that Rupert was dismissed from the king's service, Basing House became his second choice. It was to Basing House where he planned to run and enlist. Even Hester, with memories of a court which were not all of play-acting and folly but which also had moments of great beauty and glamour, longed to know that whatever else changed in the kingdom Basing House still held for King Charles.

It was owned by the Marquess of Winchester, who had renamed it Loyalty House, and locked the gates when the country around him went Parliamentarian. That defiance seemed to Hester a more glorious way to spend the war than gardening at Lambeth and selling tulips to Parliamentarians. Inigo Jones, who had known Johnnie's grandfather and worked with him for the Duke of Buckingham, was safe behind the strong defences of his own design at Basing House, the artist Wenceslaus Hollar, a friend of the Tradescants, and dozens of others known to Hester had taken refuge there. There were rumours of twenty Jesuit priests in hiding and a giant of seven feet tall. The marchioness herself and her children were in the siege and she had refused free passage out of the besieged house but decided to stay with her lord. She had engraved every window pane of the house with the troth '*Aimez Loyauté*' so that as long as the house stood and the panes were unbroken it would carry a record that one place at least was always unwaveringly for Charles.

'I am as bad as Johnnie, for I long to be there,' Hester confessed to Alexander. They were seated either side of a small fire in the parlour. In the windowseat Frances and Johnnie were playing cards for matchsticks. 'These are the people I knew from girlhood. It feels wrong to be here in comfort while they are facing the guns.'

'They were freer to choose than you,' Alexander said comfortingly. 'You gave your word to John to protect the Ark. And anyway, you have played your part. When the royalist uprising came to your door you lent your horse and did the best you could.'

Hester snorted. 'You know how willing that was!'

'Don't fall in love with the cause just because it is losing,' Alexander warned her. 'He was a reckless and foolish king before he was doomed. John went away rather than serve him, and I've always admired your determination to survive this war and not to join it. Just because it is coming to an end is no reason to want to enlist. It is a foolish man who loves a lost cause only because it is lost.'

Hester nodded. 'Yes,' she said. 'But Basing House is like a fairy story.'

'There will be no romance ending,' Alexander said grimly. 'Cromwell has brought up the heavy guns. There can be no ending but defeat. No walls could stand against them forever.'

Alexander was right, and the news came through the next day, before he and Frances left. Basing House had fallen and a hundred men and women had been killed. Even the engraved window panes were not allowed to survive. Cromwell ordered the house to be destroyed and nothing was left standing.

It was only one battle in the many which now seemed to go inexorably the way of Parliament. Hester's greatest buyer of tulips, John Lambert, was praised in all the reports for being a quick and daring cavalry commander, the Parliament horse were unstoppable. The army under Cromwell had learned their business at last and combined soldierly discipline with an absolute dedication to their cause. They believed they were freeing the country of tyranny and bringing in a new rule of law and justice. They fought as men will fight when their hearts are in the fighting, and there were few underpaid, half-hearted, badly led royal armies that could stand against them.

The king retreated to the hard-drinking, rich-living city of Oxford and the comfort of court life and amused himself as well as he could. His only recognition of his continual defeats was to blame his generals.

Prince Rupert had been dismissed for failing to hold Bristol and nothing he or his friends could say could gain him a fair hearing from the king he had served so faithfully.

It was a bitter winter, colder than any in living memory. Frances wrote to her stepmother that she had been skating on the Thames below the Tower and that if the freeze continued she would take a sledge and travel up the frozen river to visit. Hester, wrapped in John Tradescant's old travelling cape and with a hat made from his Russian furs, went out every morning to brush the snow from the branches of the precious trees to prevent them from breaking under the weight of snow and ice, and sat every night over a fire made of fallen wood and little twigs, dined on potato soup and wondered when spring would come and if it would bring her husband home.

Winter 1646, Barbados

John's ship took the southerly route home and revictualled and took on cargo at Barbados. John, very conscious that he was bringing home a fortune only in seeds and roots which would take an unreliable year before they could be propagated and sold, strolled on the quayside and let it be known that he was prepared to execute errands for the wealthy planters for a small consideration. While the ship was loaded with barrels of sugar and rum John walked inland, past the sugar plantations where gangs of black men and women slaves were bent over the new plants, seeding and weeding the crop while white overseers lounged on their horses with long-tongued hunting whips ready to lash out. John found his way into the woods where the fields stopped and kept his eyes open for new plants.

It was returning from one of these walks, with a couple of seedlings damp in his pocket, that John met a man riding homeward on the road.

'I heard of you,' the man greeted him informally. 'You're Tradescant, the king's gardener, aren't you?'

John uncovered his head and made a little bow. 'Yes, sir. And you?'

'Sir Henry Hants. A planter, these are my fields. I have a little garden of my own, you might like to have a look at some of my things.'

'Indeed I would,' John said eagerly.

'Oh, come for dinner then,' the man said. 'Stay the night.'

He led the way along the lane towards a large white house, as grand as the queen's manor at Wimbledon. John blinked at the opulence of the building, at the best wax candles set at every window so that the house twinkled like a beacon in the soft twilight, and then at the rush of black servants who came running when they heard the sound of the master's horse.

Sir Henry dismounted and let the horse go, secure in the knowledge that two grooms would catch the reins, as he led the way indoors.

There was a terrace at the back of the house and Sir Henry led John through the gleaming hall where the white walls were laden with rich oil paintings, to where the last of the sun was shining on the terrace. A lady gestured languidly from a sofa. 'My wife, Lady Hants,' Sir Henry said briefly. 'Never gets up.'

John bowed and was rewarded by a faint wave.

'Now, let me show you my garden,' Sir Henry said eagerly.

John had been hoping for tropical rarities and was hard put not to show his disappointment. Sir Henry had poured wealth and labour into making a classic English garden in the most unlikely of circumstances. There was a smooth lawn, as good as the king's bowling green at Oatlands. There was a perfect knot garden with low hedges of bay enclosing white stones. John, looking a little more closely, saw that they were not stones but the most exquisite white shining shells.

'Cowries,' Sir Henry said gloomily. 'Cost me a fortune. But actually easier to get than proper English gravel.'

There was a flower garden, planted exclusively with English flowers and shaded with a thatched roof suspended from stakes at each corner. 'Sun's too hot for them otherwise,' Sir Henry complained. 'And the ground's too dry. I keep three boys watering almost constantly all day, and even then I can never grow more than a dozen daffodils every year.'

There was an orchard. John saw that the sun-loving fruits would do well in such a climate. 'I can't grow apples to taste like the ones in Kent.'

They came full circle back to the house. 'You only plant English plants?' John asked carefully.

'Of course,' the man said briskly. 'Why would I want these damn ugly savage flowers?'

'I have a great liking for new plants myself,' John remarked.

'You're a fool,' the man said. 'If you lived here you would find you were longing for the sight of a proper English wood and proper English flowers again. I fight and fight and fight against this soil and against the heat to grow a proper garden.'

John nodded neutrally. 'I see that it takes a very great deal of labour,' he said.

His host nodded and mounted the terrace again. Without a word he put out his hand. At once the black woman presiding behind a great bowl of punch poured a glass, handed it to another woman who put it on a silver tray and bowed and presented it to Sir Henry. John was reminded of the silent, perfect service of the royal court and accepted a glass of his own with a word of thanks.

'Don't thank them,' Sir Henry corrected him swiftly. 'Don't give one word of thanks for service in my house, if you please, sir. It has taken me years to knock some sense of obedience and decorum into them. I don't want them thinking they're doing me a favour by working for me.'

Dinner was a miserable affair of lavish food and the best wines but Lady Hants, half-reclining in her chair at one end of the table, said not one word for the whole of the meal, and her husband drank steadily and deeply of rum and water, becoming more gloomy and irascible with every glass.

One of the slaves among the half a dozen waiting at the table was wearing a strange headdress: a triangular plate bolted over her mouth with straps running from both sides and over her head to keep it in place, a great buckle at the back to keep it pressed tight against her mouth and a padlock to fasten the buckle. John found he could hardly drag his eyes away from the mask-like appearance of the woman, the dark, tragic eyes, and then the sharply geometric shape on the mouth.

'What's the matter with you?' Sir Henry asked irritably. 'Oh! Are you looking at Rebecca? She's been stealing food, haven't you, Becky? Tasting it as she cooks, dirty bitch. So she'll have nothing to eat at all for a couple of days, nothing in her mouth but what I put there.' He gave a shout of laughter and a wink to John at the sexual innuendo. 'Are you sorry now that you tasted my soup, Becky?'

Silently the woman bowed her head.

'Good, good,' Sir Henry said, cheered by the sombre grief of her silence, and waved for another glass of rum and water.

A woman slave escorted John to his bedroom and stood, as still as an obedient dog, at the doorway.

'You can go,' John said, careful not to thank her.

'Sir Henry say you can have me if you want,' she said in carefully spoken English.

John was taken aback. 'Er – I don't –'

'You want a man?'

'No!'

She dropped her dark eyes, a world of despair hidden by the downsweep of her lashes. 'You want a child?'

330

'No!'

She waited. 'What you want to do then?' she asked wearily, dreading some demand more vile than she had faced before.

'I want nothing!' John exclaimed. 'Just to sleep.'

She bowed. 'If he ask you – you tell him I said you can have me.'

'I'll tell him you were very, er, generous,' John corrected himself. 'Obedient.'

'Yes, sir,' she said dully. 'I am obedient.'

In the morning Sir Henry was in a better temper. Over breakfast he asked John about his own garden and about the treasures of the Ark. 'I could send you some things,' he said pleasantly. 'Things I pick up here. If you like savage things.'

'I do,' John said. 'I do indeed. And if there are any plants from England that you desire I could send them out to you. You could grow vines here very well, I would have thought.'

'Could you take a note of credit for me and buy some carpets for me?' Sir Henry asked. 'I want some Turkey carpets for the hall.'

'I should be delighted to do so,' John said. 'And anything else you require.'

'We'll start with this,' Sir Henry said cautiously. 'I'll give you the note of credit and you can buy some carpets and some glass for me, and then I'll send you a few hogsheads of sugar and you can see if you can obtain a better price for me than my normal agent. And then you can send me some more goods. Rarities are no use locked up in a cabinet, you know. They should be traded.'

John nodded. 'I should be glad to do a little trading,' he said. 'My father's rarities have to stay together in the collection we have made. But if you shoot any strange birds I should be glad of their skins and their feathers.'

'I've got some trophies,' Sir Henry said without any great interest. 'I could sell them to you.'

'I have no money until I am at home,' John said awkwardly.

'Note of credit,' Sir Henry said equably. 'We all do it by notes of credit all the time. Just as well there are no damned thieving Jews to redeem the notes before the sugar crop is in, eh?'

By the time John sailed he had a new shrub, a most curious and delightful plant which the islanders called the tree of life because it acted like a living thing, shrinking away when touched. He had a couple of roots of the cabbage tree, and a dozen skins and feathers including a rather fine specimen of the West Indian kingfisher which Sir Henry donated for free. 'Just do me some decent business, when you are in England,' he grumbled. 'An honest agent in London is as rare as a virtuous woman. Which is to say, rare enough to put in your collection.'

'I shall be delighted,' John said politely and watched Sir Henry recede into the distance without any regret as the ship slipped her ropes and drifted away from the shore.

Spring 1646, London

It was a homecoming as ordinary as any man might wish. John hired
a carter at London dock to carry his barrels of seeds and roots, the two
barrels of saplings, the chest of Barbados goods, and sat up on the
wooden seat at the front of the cart as they jolted up the frozen lanes
to Lambeth.

'What's the news of the war?' John asked.

'You'll have heard that Chester surrendered?'

'No?'

'Where've you been?'

'Virginia,' John said. 'Is the king truly defeated?'

'Humbled to dust,' the carter said feelingly. 'And now pray God we
can see some peace and order in this land and that crew of parasites
run back to Rome where they came from.'

John tried to say 'Amen', but found the word did not come out. 'I'll
pray for peace,' he said. 'I've had enough of war for a lifetime.'

'And so have we all. And for some the war lasted longer than their
lifetimes. How many Englishmen d'you think have died to persuade the
king that we want to be governed by Englishmen and pray to God and
not to bishops?'

John shook his head.

'Thousands,' the man said glumly. 'Hundreds of thousands. How
many more died of plague and hardship because of this damned
struggle?'

John shook his head again.

'Thousands more. And how many families d'you think have lost a
son or a brother or a father?'

John shook his head in silence.

'Every single family in the land,' the carter said solemnly. 'This has

333

been a wicked, wicked war, a war without an enemy because we were fighting and killing ourselves.'

Hester was in the stable yard, tossing hay over the door to the horse, when she heard the rumble of the wheels and saw the cart rock as it rounded the corner into the yard. For a moment she saw only the barrels at the back and thought that John had sent some goods ahead, and then she dropped the pitchfork with a clatter on the cobbles as she recognised the man who got down from the carter's seat and turned to face her.

He looked older than she remembered, and weary. The bear-grease stain had faded from his skin but he was still deeply tanned from the hard sun and wind. He had lost a couple of teeth during his time of near-starvation, and he had grown a brown moustache and beard which were flecked with grey. His eyes were sad, an unmistakable sadness which made Hester want to hold him and comfort him without even asking what had grieved him so. He looked as if he had lost something very dear to him and Hester wondered what blade in the new world had cut him so deep.

'John?' she said quietly.

He stepped forwards a little. 'Hester?'

She realised that she was wearing her oldest working clothes, men's thick boots and a brown scarf over her hair which was pinned carelessly on the back of her head. She could not have looked more functional if she had tried. She whisked her scarf off her head and tried not to seem embarrassed. She had always tried to be above vanity, especially with this man who had married his first wife for love and lost her while she was still in her youth and beauty.

Hester brushed the hay from her coat. 'You are welcome home,' she said.

He took two steps towards her and opened his arms to her and she went towards him and felt the intense relief of a man's embrace after more than three years of loneliness.

'Do you forgive me?' he said urgently into her hair. She smelled of hay from the stable and the clean, familiar smell of soap from her skin, and lavender from her linen. 'Can you forgive me for leaving you so unkindly and then disappearing like that?'

'It's you that should forgive me for refusing to go with you,' she said quickly. 'And I regretted it, John.'

He tightened his grip around her. 'I have been unfaithful,' he said quickly, to get the confession over and done with before he was tempted to lie. 'I am sorry.'

She rested her head against his shoulder. 'That's the past,' she said. 'And in another country. You have come home to me, haven't you?'

'Yes,' he said.

She craned her neck to look up into his sad, weary face and realised that he was wearing the same bewildered expression of pain as when they had first met and he had not recovered from the loss of his first wife. 'What happened, John?'

For a moment he was about to answer her, then they were interrupted by the carter. 'I can't unload these on my own,' he said flatly. 'And I can't afford to wait here all day while you two kiss.'

Hester turned with a laugh. 'I'll find Joseph to help you.' She rang the bell which hung at the corner of the yard. 'You go in, John, you must be frozen, and Johnnie will be longing to see you. He'll be in the kitchen eating his breakfast.'

W

John hesitated at the kitchen door, suddenly shy and hardly knowing how to approach his son who had been a boy of nine when he left and was now a youth of twelve. He opened the door slowly and put his head around it.

Johnnie was seated at the scrubbed kitchen table, his bowl of porridge before him, absently spooning it into his mouth, his eyes on his book propped on his mug of small ale. John took in the sight of his son, the fair head with the cropped golden hair, the light hazel eyes, the long nose in the long face and the sweet innocent mouth. You could see his mother in his colouring and the joy in his face, but he was every inch a Tradescant.

He glanced up as the draught from the half-open door blew into the kitchen and put down his book as if he was about to greet his stepmother. Then he saw it was a man looking in at him, and he hesitated.

Very slowly he rose to his feet, very cautiously he looked. John opened the door fully and stepped into the doorway.

'Father?' Johnnie asked uncertainly. 'Is it really you?'

John took two swift steps across the kitchen floor and wrapped his boy in a tight hug and inhaled, half-weeping, half-kissing the top of his silky head. 'It's me. Praise God I am home with you, Johnnie, and you safe and well.'

Hester came in behind him and hung her cape on the hook. 'Did you recognise him?' she demanded.

Father and son answered 'No!' together and then laughed together. John made himself release his son, forced himself to let the boy go.

'He is grown,' Hester said proudly 'And as much help to me in the garden as any man could be. And he is a scholar, he keeps the rarities and garden accounts now, and the planting records.'

'And school?' John demanded.

A shadow crossed Hester's face. 'The school has been closed this last year. The teacher was dismissed, some quarrel about theology. So we do the best we can at home.'

'And where is Frances?' John asked, looking round for her.

Something in Hester's silence made him stop, fear gripping him. 'Where is Frances? Hester, tell me. Please God, tell me that she is not lost.'

'No! No!' She rushed to reassure him. 'She is well, in great beauty and well. It's just . . . you were not here and I did not know you would return. I didn't know what I should do for the best and I was at my wits' end to keep her safe . . .'

'Where is she?' John shouted.

'She's married!' Johnnie interrupted. 'Safe at the Tower with Alexander Norman.'

'She married Alexander Norman?' John demanded.

Hester nodded, her eyes on his face.

'Not my father's executor? Not my uncle? Not that Alexander Norman?'

Hester gave the smallest confirming nod.

'You married my daughter off to a man old enough to be her father? A friend of her grandfather?'

'I did.'

'It was her choice,' Johnnie said stoutly. 'And she is happy.'

'By God, this is most ill-done!' John swore. 'I can't believe it! When did this happen?'

'A year ago,' Hester said quietly.

'Why?' he asked blankly. 'Why did you let it happen? Why did you not write to ask for my permission?'

She turned away from him and tied her house apron around her waist as if she was weary of the whole conversation. 'I could not be sure of keeping her safe,' she said. 'Before Cromwell had the ruling of the army no woman was safe on the streets. I never knew whether the king would retake London or no and then there would have been the cavaliers to face as well. The apprentices rioted every other night, I could not let her step out of the front door.'

'You could have taken her to Oatlands!' he flung at her.

She turned at that. 'Oatlands!' she exclaimed bitterly. 'What do you think the palaces are like now? Oatlands was Prince Rupert's headquarters! D'you think I could keep a pretty girl safe in a barracks? She was as much at risk there as in the stews of the City.'

'You could have put her on a ship to me!'

She blazed up at that. 'And where were you? I had two letters from you in three years, one parcel of Indian goods and one consignment of plants. What was I to imagine? I didn't even know if you were alive or dead. I had to take all the decisions on my own and I did what I thought was the best. Alexander offered her a home and promised me that he would love her and keep her safe. And she wanted to marry him. She accepted him on her own account. And they are happy, anyone can see that.'

'I shall get her home,' John swore. 'I shall have the marriage annulled. She is not to be his wife.'

'She is expecting his baby.' Hester spoke calmly as her heart hammered in her ears. 'She will come home for the confinement, and she visits us often. But she will not leave her husband, even at your bidding, John.'

He flung out of the room at that and she heard him stride across the hall. Johnnie shot one scared look at her and she put her hand on his shoulder. There was a great bellow from the rarities room: 'Mother of God! Where are the rarities? What have you done?'

Hester turned Johnnie on his heel and pushed him gently towards the kitchen door. 'Wrap up warmly and go and sweep the snow off the trees,' she said.

'What will you do?'

'I shall have to explain to him how we live now. It will be hard for him to understand.'

'Then he should never have gone away,' Johnnie said.

They had a bitter row in the half-empty room. John in his horror at the changes could not even hear that the finest of the rarities were safely in hiding. Every confession that Hester had to make, that she had sold one or other of the treasures for food, merely heightened his anger by a further notch.

'You have betrayed me!' he yelled at her. 'You have betrayed my trust, my sacred trust in you. You have sold my treasures, you have sold my daughter!'

'What was I to do?' Hester shouted back, as angry as him. 'You were gone. This summer I was going to tell your son that I feared you must be dead. I had to survive without you. I had to manage somehow. We had one true friend in the whole world and Frances loves and trusts him. She wasn't sold. He took her without a dowry.'

'Sweet God! Am I supposed to be grateful for this charity? He was a friend of her grandfather! A man in his dotage!'

'And where have you been?' Hester turned from the window and suddenly rounded on John. 'For all that you are full of what I have done and failed to do, what do you have to show for three years away? What treasures did you bring back? A barrel of plants and a handful of feathers! The last coins I sold were to buy your passage home when Johnnie and I had not tasted meat for weeks! How dare you accuse me of failing you! It is you that have failed me!'

'You have no idea! You have no idea how I have lived and what I have been trying to do.'

'With some woman? Some Jamestown drab in an inn? Have you been bunked up all these years, spending our money and doing nothing?'

'I've been in the woods, I've been searching to understand what I should do –'

'And the woman?'

'What of her?'

'Her name. Tell me her name.'

'Suckahanna,' he said unwillingly.

Hester screamed in shock and clapped her hand over her mouth. 'You have bedded an Indian? A savage?'

His hand flew out before he knew it, he slapped her face hard. She jerked back and her head banged against the knob of the shutter with a horrible thud. She dropped without another sound, knocked unconscious. For a moment he thought he had killed her and knew a fierce, terrible joy that the woman who had abused Suckahanna should be silenced at once, a feeling instantly succeeded by complete remorse. He dropped to his knees beside her and lifted her up from the floor.

'Hester, wife, forgive me . . .'

Her eyelids fluttered and then opened. 'Take your hands from me,' she spat. 'You are a foul adulterer. I won't have you touch me.'

Hester made up her bed in Frances's old room and moved her clothes out of the master bedroom that night. She cooked a modest dinner for John, she produced a beautifully pressed suit of clothes and set about sewing him a new shirt. She behaved in every way like an obedient and dutiful wife. But he had knocked the love out of her with one impulsive blow, and he did not know how to get it back.

It was as if the heart had gone out of her and out of the house altogether. The garden was neglected, the topiary and the knot garden hedges were growing out and losing their shape. The gravel on the paths was no defence against the constantly springing weeds. The warm nursery beds by the house had not been prepared with sieved earth for the coming of the new season as they should have been. The fruit trees had not been properly pruned in the autumn. Even the chestnuts had not all been planted and grown on ready for sale in the early summer.

'I couldn't do it all,' Hester said stubbornly as she saw John look critically over the garden from the terrace. 'I had no boys, I had no money. We all did what we could but this garden takes a dozen men to keep. Joseph and Johnnie and Frances and I couldn't do it.'

'Of course not, I understand,' John said and he turned away to brood in the half-empty rarities room, and walk with his limping stride around the frozen garden.

Johnnie unpacked the Virginian saplings and left them in their barrels by the house wall. The ground was too hard to dig them in. One of them had died from the salt winds of the voyage but the other four looked strong and likely to put out green leaves when the weather improved.

'What are they?' Johnnie asked.

His father's face lit up. 'Tulip trees, they call them. They grow as round and shapely as a horse chestnut but they have great flowers, white, waxy flowers, as big as your head. I have seen them grow to such a height and breadth –' He broke off. Suckahanna had showed it to him. 'And these are maple trees.'

Johnnie rolled the big barrels of seeds and roots into the orangery and set to work unpacking them and planting them up in pots of sieved earth ready to be set outside and watered when the spring frosts ended. John watched him, disinclined to work himself, horribly quick to criticise when his son dropped a seed or was clumsy with a root.

'Have you never been taught how to do this properly?' he demanded irritably.

His son looked up at him, his resentment veiled. 'I am sorry, sir,' he said formally.

Hester appeared in the doorway and took in the scene in one quick glance. 'Can I have a word with you, husband?' she asked, her voice very even.

John walked towards her and she drew him out of earshot, into the garden.

'Please don't correct Johnnie so harshly,' she said. 'He's not used to it, and indeed he is a good boy and a very hard worker.'

'He is my son,' John pointed out. 'I shall teach him what is right.'

She bowed her head. 'Of course,' she said coldly. 'You must do as you wish.'

John waited in case she should say any more and then he flung himself away from her and stamped into the house, his feet hurting in his boots, knowing himself to be in the wrong, not knowing how to make things right.

'I shall go to London,' he said. 'I shall complete my commissions for Sir Henry. It's clear that we have to make our fortune some other way than by the garden and the rarities since the rarities are gone and the garden half-ruined.'

Hester went back into the orangery. Johnnie raised his eyebrows at her.

'We all have to become acquainted with each other again,' she said as equably as she could. 'Let me help you with that.'

For days John walked around the grounds, trying to accustom himself to the smaller scale of England, trying to accept a horizon which seemed so very close, trying to enjoy his continuing ownership of twenty acres when he had been free to run in a forest which went on forever, trying to be glad of a plain, forthright wife and a bright, fair son and not to think of the dark beauty of Suckahanna and the animal grace of her boy. He arranged the Indian goods in the half-empty rarities room, feeling the arrow head come so easily into his hand, rubbing the buckskin shirt between his finger as if something of the warmth of Suckahanna's skin might still linger.

He made a little money on his commission for Sir Henry and he bought a couple of fine paintings, crated them up and sent them out to him. When the ship came back, in four months' time or so, it would bring him another note of credit and perhaps some more barrels of sugar for John to sell. He drew some satisfaction from being able to make some money, even in these difficult times, but he thought he might never feel a sense of freedom or joy ever again.

Hester did the only thing she knew how to do, and tackled the practical problems of the situation. She asked him to walk with her to Lambeth and took him straight to the best bootmaker still working in the village. He measured John's feet and then looked at the bare soles with horror. 'You have feet like a Highlander, if you'll excuse me saying so.'

'I had to go barefoot. I was in Virginia,' John said shortly.

'No wonder all your boots pinch,' the cobbler said. 'You have no need of boots at all.'

'Yes he does,' Hester remarked. 'He's a gentleman in England and he'll have a pair of boots of best leather, a pair of working boots and a pair of shoes. And they'd better not pinch.'

'I haven't the leather,' the man said. 'They don't drive the cattle to Smithfield, the tanners can't get the hides, I can't get the leather. You've been in Virginia too long if you think you can order shoes like the old days.'

Hester took the cobbler by the elbow and there was a brief exchange of words and the clink of a coin.

'What did you offer him?' John asked as they emerged from the dark shop into the bright March sunlight.

Hester grimaced and prepared for a quarrel. 'You won't like it, John, but I promised to supply the leather from your father's rarities. It was only some leather painted with a scene of the Madonna and Child. Not very well done, and completely heretical. We would invite the troops upon us if we ever showed it. And the man is right, he can't get leather for your shoes otherwise.'

For a moment she thought he was going to flare up at her again.

'So am I to strut around London with Papistical images painted on my boots?' he asked. 'Won't they hang me for a Jesuit in hiding?'

'Not much of a disguise if you're going around with the Virgin Mary on your feet,' Hester pointed out cheerfully. 'No, the painting is almost worn off, and he'll use it on the inside.'

'We are using rare treasures as household goods? What kind of stewardship is this?'

'We are surviving,' Hester said grimly. 'Do you want boots that you can walk in or no?'

He paused. 'Do you swear that nothing else of any merit is missing from the collection?' he demanded. 'That it is safe in hiding as you say?'

'On my honour, and you can see it all for yourself if you cut down the tree and open the door. But John, you had best wait. It's not safe yet. They all say the king is defeated but they have said that before. He has his wife working against us in France, and the Irish to call on, and who knows what the Pope might order if the queen promises to hand over the country to Popery? The king cannot be defeated in battle, for all that they fight and fight. Even when he is down to his last man he is not defeated. He is still the king. They cannot defeat him. He has to decide to surrender.'

John nodded and they fell into stride together for the short walk home. 'I keep thinking. I keep wondering – perhaps I should go to him,' he said.

She stumbled at the thought of him returning to the court and to danger. 'Why? Why on earth would you go?'

'I feel almost that I owe him some service,' he said.

'You left the country to escape serving,' she reminded him.

He grimaced at her bluntness. 'It wasn't that simple,' he said. 'I didn't want to die for a cause I can't believe in. I didn't want to kill a man because like me he had half-heartedly joined, but on the other side. But if the king is ready for peace then I could serve him with a clear conscience. And I don't like to think of him alone at Oxford, without the queen and with the prince fled to Jersey, and no-one with him.'

'There's a whole crowd with him,' Hester said. 'Drinking themselves senseless every night and shaming Oxford with their behaviour. He is in the thick of company. And if he sees you he will only remember you and ask where you have been. If he wanted you he would have sent for you by now.'

'And has there been no word?'

She shook her head. 'Since they wanted us to serve under the Commission of Array there has been nothing,' she said. 'And they risked our lives for a lost cause then. There is nothing you can do for the king unless you can persuade him to come to terms with his people. Can you do that?'

'No.'

As soon as John's new boots were ready he put them on, dressed in his best suit and announced his intention of formally visiting his daughter in her new home. Hester and Johnnie, also dressed in their best, went with him in the boat downriver.

'Will he be angry?' Johnnie asked under the noise of the oars in the water.

'No,' Hester said. 'The moment he sees her she'll have him wrapped around her finger like always.'

Johnnie chuckled. 'Can we shoot the bridge?' he asked.

Hester hesitated. Timorous passengers would make the ferrymen leave them on the west side of Tower Bridge and walk round to rejoin their boat at the other side. The currents around the pillars of the bridge were terrifyingly swift and when the tide was on the ebb and the river was full, boats could overturn and people could drown. It was Johnnie's great passion to shoot the rapids and generally Hester would stay in the boat with him, her hands gripping the side, her knuckles white, and a smile firmly fixed on her face.

'Do what?' John asked and turned around.

'Shoot the bridge,' Johnnie replied. 'Mother lets me.'

John looked in surprise at his wife. 'You can't enjoy it?' he asked.

One glance at her face told him that she was terrified. 'Oh, I don't mind,' she said. 'Johnnie loves it.'

John gave a short bark of laughter. 'Then Johnnie can do it,' he said firmly. 'You and I will land at the Swan Stairs like Christians and Johnnie can meet us on the other side.'

'But I like Mother coming too!' Johnnie protested.

'That's as maybe,' John said firmly. 'But I'm home now, and you're not going to drown my wife to keep you company. You can shoot the bridge on your own, my boy.'

The ferryman set them ashore at the steps. John put his hand under Hester's elbow as they climbed to the top and turned to wave to Johnnie as he sat in the prow of the boat to gain full pleasure from the terrifying ride.

'Look at his face!' Hester exclaimed lovingly.

'You are too indulgent to him,' John said.

She hesitated. John was his father and the head of the household. Restoring the power to him was hard for her, just as regaining his position was for him. 'He's still only a boy,' she remarked. 'Not yet thirteen.'

'If he was in Virginia –' John started and then bit back the rest.

'Yes,' she said softly. 'But he isn't. He's a good boy and he has been courageous and faithful through these difficult years. If he was a planter's son, living in the wilds, then I dare say he would be a quite different boy. But he is not. He is a boy who has had to have his childhood in the middle of a war and he has seen all of the adults around him most terribly afraid. You are right to restore the rules, John, but I won't have him blamed for not being something he has no business to be.'

He turned and faced her but she did not drop her gaze. She stared at him fiercely as if she did not care whether he beat her or sent her home in disgrace. Not for the first time John was reminded that he had married a redoubtable woman and, despite his temper, he remembered also that she was fiercely defending his son, just as she had fiercely defended the garden and the rarities.

'You're right,' he said, with the smile she loved. 'And I will be restored to my place at the head of the household. But I won't be a tyrant.'

She nodded at that, and when they strolled together to the other side of the bridge where the boat was waiting she slid her hand in the crook of his arm and John kept it there.

They paid the boatman and retraced their steps to the Tower. Alexander Norman's timber yard was beside the walls of the Tower on the grounds of a former convent. His house was built alongside, one of the long, thin townhouses pressed against the narrow street. Hester had feared that Frances would be unhappy without a garden, with little more than a dozen pots in the cobbled yard at the back which was overshadowed half the day from the stacks of wood in the timber yard next door. But already the house was draped in climbing roses and honeysuckle was growing up to the very windows, and every window had a bracket fixed outside and a square planting box nailed to the wall with a row of tulips waiting to bloom.

'I'd have no trouble guessing which house was hers,' John said grimly, glancing down the street at the other bare-fronted, bare-faced houses.

'That's nothing,' Johnnie said with pleasure. 'She has a herb garden out the back and an apple tree squashed against the back wall. She says she'll prune it to keep it small enough. She says she'll re-pot it every year and prune the roots too.'

John shook his head. 'She needs a dwarf apple tree,' he said. 'Perhaps if one could graft an apple sapling on to a shrub root it might grow small . . .'

Hester stepped forwards and knocked on the door. At once Frances opened it. 'Father!' she said, and slipped down the step, threw her arms around him and laid her head against his shoulder.

John almost recoiled from her touch. In the three years he had been away she had grown from a girl to a woman of nearly eighteen years, and now, with her slight body pressed against him, he could feel the hard swelling of her baby.

He stepped back to see her and his face softened. 'You're so like your mother,' he exclaimed. 'What a beauty you've become, Frances.'

'She's the very picture of my Jane.' Mrs Hurte emerged from the house and shook John and then Hester by the hand. She enveloped Johnnie in a breathtaking embrace but never stopped talking. 'The very picture of her. Every time I see her I think she has come back to us again.'

'Come inside,' Frances urged. 'You must be frozen. Did you shoot the bridge?'

'Father wouldn't let Mother come.'

Frances shot a brief approving look at her father. 'Quite right. Why should Mother risk drowning because you like it?'

'*She* likes it!' Johnnie protested.

'I swear I never said so,' Hester remarked.

Mrs Hurte surged outwards rather than into the house, took John by the arm and drew him aside. Hester silently admired the tactical skill of her stepdaughter. This was generalship as gifted as Oliver Cromwell's with his New Model Army. Mrs Hurte would change John's mind in favour of the match in two sentences of complaints. Both Hester and Frances strained their ears to hear her do it.

'You're home too late,' Mrs Hurte said reproachfully to John. 'This is a bad business, and you too late to prevent it.'

'I don't see that it is bad,' John remarked.

'A man of fifty-six and a girl of seventeen?' Mrs Hurte demanded. 'What life can they have together?'

'A good one.' John gestured to the pretty house and the tracery of carefully pruned rose branches. 'A boy of her own age could not hope to give her so much.'

'She should have been kept at her home.'

'In these times?' John asked. 'Where safer than beside the Tower?'

'And now expecting a baby?'

'The older the bridegroom, the sooner the better,' John rejoined swiftly. 'Why should you be so against it, Mother? It was a marriage for love. Your own daughter Jane had nothing less.'

She bit her lip at that. 'Jane brought a good dowry and you two were well matched,' she said.

'I will see that Frances is properly dowered when peace is restored and I can sell the Virginia plants and restore the rarities to their proper place,' John said firmly. 'I am trading in a small way with the West

345

Indies and I expect to see a profit on that very soon. And Frances *is* well-matched. Alexander is a good and faithful friend to this family and she loves him. Why should she not marry the man of her choice in these times when men and women are making their own choices every day? When this whole war has been fought for men and women to be free?'

Mrs Hurte smoothed her sombre gown. 'I don't know what Mr Hurte would have said.'

John smiled. 'He would have liked the house, and the business. Cooper for the ordnance in the middle of a war? Don't tell me that he wouldn't have loved that! Alexander is earning twelve pounds a year and that's before he draws his allowances! It's a fine match for the daughter of a man who has little to sell and most of his stock in hiding.'

Hester and Frances exchanged a hidden smile, turned and went into the house.

'That was clever,' Hester said approvingly to her stepdaughter.

Frances gave her a most unladylike wink. 'I know,' she said smugly.

Spring 1646

When the soil warmed in April and the daffodils came out in the orchard and the grass started growing and the boughs of the Tradescant trees were filled with birds singing, courting and nestbuilding, John strode round the brick chip paths in his new Papist boots and learned to love his garden again. He made a special corner for his Virginian plants and watched as the dried roots put up tiny green shoots and the unpromising dry seeds sprouted in their pots and could be transplanted.

'Will they do well here?' Johnnie asked. 'Is it not too cold for them?'

John leaned on his spade and shook his head. 'Virginia is a place of far greater extremes than here,' he said. 'Colder by far in winter, hotter in summer, and damp as a poultice for month after month in summer. I should think they will thrive here.'

'And what will sell the best, d'you think?' Johnnie asked eagerly. 'And what is the finest?'

'This.' John leaned forwards and touched the opening leaves of a tiny plant. 'This little aster.'

'Such a small thing?'

'It's going to be a great joy for gardeners, this one.'

'Why?' Johnnie asked. 'What's it like?'

'It stands tall, almost up to your waist, and white like a daisy against thick, dark leaves, a woody stem, and it grows in profusion. It's a kind of shrubby starwort, like the aster from Holland. In Virginia I have seen a whole forest glade filled with them, like the whiteness of snow. And I once saw a woman plait the flowers into her black hair and I thought then it was the most beautiful little flower I had ever seen, like a brooch, like a jewel. I might name it for us, it's just the sort of little beauty that your grandfather would have liked, and it will grow for anyone. He

347

liked that in a plant. He always said that it was the hardy plants that gave the greatest joy.'

'And trees?' Johnnie prompted.

'If it grows,' John cautioned him. 'This may be our finest tree from Virginia. It's a maple tree, a Virginian maple. You can tap it for sugar, you put a cut in the trunk in springtime, when the sap starts rising, and the sap oozes a juice. You collect it and boil it down and it makes a coarse sugar. It's a great delight, to set a little fire in the woods and boil down the syrup, all the children lick up the spills and run around with sticky faces and . . .' He broke off, he couldn't bear to tell his boy about the other – Suckahanna's boy. 'The leaves turn the deepest, finest scarlet in the autumn,' he concluded.

'And this is a trumpet vine. When I had my house I planted one at the side of my door. It grows as fast as wild honeysuckle, I should think it is up to my chimney pot by now. If it hasn't pulled the whole house down. This I had on the other side of my doorway – the Virginian woodbine tree, like a honeysuckle. But best of all will be the tulip tree.' John touched the saplings, which were planted against the shelter of the wall and were putting out glossy dark leaves at the tips of their branches. 'Please God we can grow it here, it would be a fine thing to see in an English garden.'

'Finer than our horse chestnut?' Johnnie asked, naming the tree that would always be the Tradescant benchmark of beauty.

'It is the only tree I have ever seen to match your grandfather's horse chestnut. Truly, Johnnie, it is a most wonderful tree. If I can grow the tulip tree and sell it to the gardeners of England, as he grew the horse chestnut, then we will have done wonderful work, he and me.'

'And what will there be left for me to do?' Johnnie asked. 'Since he went east to Russia and south to the Mediterranean and you have been west to America. What will there be left for me?'

'Oh,' John said longingly. 'So much still to see, Johnnie. You can't imagine what a great country it is and how far the rivers run inland and how distant the mountains are and how wide the grass meadows stretch. And beyond the mountains they told me there are plains and meadows and forests and more mountains, and inland lakes of sweet water that are as big as the sea, so vast that they have storms which whip up the water into waves that crash on the shore. There will be so much for you to see when you are a man grown and ready to travel.'

'And will you take me, if you go again?' Johnnie asked.

Tradescant hesitated only for a moment, thinking of Attone and

Suckahanna and that other, alien life. Then he looked at the bright face of his son and thought how proud he would be to show him to Attone and to say to him: 'And this is *my* son.' Johnnie was not a child of the Powhatan: a dark-eyed, brown-skinned boy of intense self-discipline and skill. But he was a child of equal beauty: an English boy, blond-headed, round-faced, and with a smile like sunlight.

'Yes,' he said simply. 'If I go again, I will take you too. It will be our adventure next time.'

'We can go when the king has come to his own again,' Johnnie said firmly.

'Mmm.' John was noncommittal.

'You are for the king still?' Johnnie pressed him. 'I know you were away for most of the fighting but you were there when he raised his standard, and you are the king's man, aren't you, Father?'

John looked into the determined face of his son and dropped a hand on his shoulder. 'It's hard for me to say,' he said. 'I am the king's man in the sense that my father was his gardener and I gardened for him too. I don't forget that I have been in his service, or in the service of the court, for most of my life. But I never thought that he was perfect – not like some of the others, not like he would have had us think. I saw him make too many mistakes, I heard too much nonsense for that sort of faith. I thought he was a foolish man, sometimes wickedly foolish. So I don't think him one step below God.'

'But still the king,' Johnnie persisted.

John nodded, resigned. 'Still the king.'

'If he sent for you, would you go?'

'If he sent for me, I would have to go. I would be bound by honour and duty to go if he sent for me by name.'

'Would you take me?'

John hesitated for a moment. 'It's a burden I'd rather not lay on you, my son. If he does not have command of the gardens of the royal palaces then there is no need for you to call him master.'

Johnnie's conviction blazed out of his brown eyes. 'But I long to call him master,' he said. 'If I had been there when he raised his standard I would never have left his side. I'm so afraid it will be all over before I can go into his service, and I'll have missed it all.'

John gave a gruff bark of laughter. 'Aye,' he said. 'I can see you would fear missing it all.'

That night John put his head around the door of Hester's bedroom to see his wife, kneeling at the foot of her bed. He waited in silence till she rose to her feet and noticed him, standing in the doorway.

'I came to ask if I might sleep here.'

She got into bed and held up the covers to him, grave-faced. 'Of course,' she said. 'I am your wife.'

John pulled the nightcap off his head and came into the room.

'I don't want you to have me in your bed as part of your duty,' he said carefully.

'No.'

'I would want there to be warmth and tenderness between us.'

'Yes.'

'I want you to forgive me for going away and leaving you alone and unprotected, and for being with another woman.'

She hesitated. 'Did you leave her of your own free will?'

John could not find a simple answer. 'She saved my life,' he said. 'I was starving in the forest and she took me to the Powhatan and they accepted me for her sake.'

Hester nodded. 'Did you leave her of your own free will? Did you choose to leave her and come home to me?'

'Yes,' John said. 'Yes.' The baldness of the lie dropped like a stone into the pool of candlelight by the bed.

John got into bed beside Hester and took her hand. It was white-skinned after Suckahanna's bronze, calloused by the work she had done for him in his house and in his garden. The backs of her hands were scratched, she had been tying back the climbing roses. John took her hand to his mouth and kissed her fingers one by one.

With a sense of relief he felt desire slowly rising up. At least he would be able to do the physical act, even if his heart were not wholly present. He turned the palm of her hand over and planted a kiss in the middle.

Hester put her hand on his shoulder and stroked the short hair at the nape of his neck.

'Do you love her still?'

He stole a quick glance at Hester's face. She was intent, serious. She did not look enraged as she had every right to be. He risked telling her the truth. 'Not as I love you; but it is true. I do love her.'

'You have never loved me,' she said steadily. 'You married me as an act of convenience and sometimes I think you have felt gratitude or affection towards me. But it was not a marriage for love and I never pretended that it was.'

Her honesty alarmed him. 'Hester . . .'

'I don't want us to pretend,' she said. 'I would rather know the truth than live in a world of pretence.'

'Do you want me to leave you?'

'No!' she said quickly. 'I didn't mean that at all.'

'But you said . . .'

She drew a breath. 'I said that you married me for your convenience, to care for your children and to guard the rarities and the garden. But I married you because I needed a place to live, and a name, and also –' She smiled at him, a friendly, shy smile. 'I was in love with you, John. From the moment that you came home and I walked down the stairs and saw you.'

He put his hand under her chin and turned her face to him. Her cheeks were pink with embarrassment but she met his eyes steadily with her direct, dark gaze.

'And you forgive me?'

She gave a little shrug. 'Since you came home to me – of course.'

'And you love me still?'

'Of course. Why should I change?'

'Because I have wronged you.'

'Are you home to stay?' she asked with her usual practical directness.

'Yes, I am.'

'Then I forgive you.'

He paused for a moment. 'Do you think we could start from the beginning again?' he asked. 'With your love for me and me learning to love you?'

Her colour deepened and he saw the little white bow at the neck of her nightgown trembling as her breath came faster. 'Do you think you could learn to love me?'

John released her hands, put his lips against her throat and then gently untied the fluttering bow. 'I know I could,' he said; knowing at least that he hoped he might.

🌱

At the end of April, Alexander Norman sent a note to the Ark.

> *I write in haste to send you urgent news. The king has ridden off from Oxford and left the court there. No-one knows where he is bound but this must mean the end of the war. He has no more than a dozen gentlemen with him. He must be fleeing to join the queen in France. Thank God at last it is over.*

John took the note through to Hester and laid it down before her where she was working on the household accounts at the drawing desk in the bay of the Venetian windows in the rarities room.

'So it is all over for him at last,' he said.

She glanced quickly up at him. 'You must be glad that it has finished. Just think of getting the country back to normal.'

'Normal!' he exclaimed. 'Who will be king if he is in exile? How will the country be run?'

'By Parliament!' she said impatiently. 'I thought that was what they were fighting for!'

'I can't help but think of him, without the queen, riding out, knowing he has lost everything.'

'Many other people have lost everything,' Hester observed grimly. 'And their sons and brothers and husbands too. Another two years of this and Johnnie would have gone. He's been wild to die in the king's service ever since the war started.'

John nodded and turned to leave the room. 'I just think of him,' he said. 'Riding out on his own. I hope to God he has someone with him who knows the way to Dover.'

🦌

'Newark!' John exclaimed and looked at Alexander Norman in complete disbelief. 'What the devil is he doing in Newark? I thought he was going to France!'

'He rode around,' Alexander said. 'You have to admire the style of it. He came within an hour's ride of London and apparently thought of riding in to test the mood of the people.'

John gasped in horror.

'And then he rode to King's Lynn, and then on northwards to Newark.'

'What the devil is he doing?'

'I think he didn't know what to do,' Alexander said. 'I think he was riding and hoping that something would happen, a stroke of luck, the arrival of a French army or the Irish army or a sudden change of heart in Parliament. I think he was just spinning out the time before he surrendered.'

John shook his head. 'To the Scots?' he said somberly.

Alexander nodded. 'To the Scots army at Newark.'

'Does he think that they will treat him better than his own people?' John demanded. 'Does he think so little of Englishmen that he goes to the Scots who were the first to speak against bishops and the prayer book? Has he forgotten that his own father came south and never went back to Scotland willingly again? His own father said: "no bishops, no king"? And the Scots have never had bishops.'

Frances, sitting by the fireside in the parlour of the Lambeth house sewing a little nightdress, lifted her head at her father's distress. 'If we can only have peace now.'

'But what will they do with him?' John asked. 'They've been his enemies since the start of this. They must hand him over to Parliament at once, and then he is no better off than if he had come direct to London.'

'He must be hoping that he can play them off against the English army and Parliament. If he is there in person, offering them the chance to conquer England, who can say which way they would go? They could fall in behind him and march on England with him as their figurehead. That must be his fondest dream.' Alexander ticked off the options on his fingers. 'Or they can set him up in Edinburgh as their king and not ours. Or they can help him get abroad and pretend they had nothing to do with it, so they don't have his imprisonment on their hands.'

'Or they can hold him as a pawn in their own game,' John exclaimed. 'Who is advising him? Who ever could have advised him to stroll around the kingdom and then go to the Scots in the end? What fools does he have at his side? Why is there no-one there thinking of his safety?'

'I think he is trusting to luck,' Alexander said. 'And still, even now, who knows which way the luck will run?'

When Alexander went back to the City he left Frances at her father's house. The warmer weather had brought the plague into London again and there was talk of it being the worst for many years. The poorer people had gone without fuel and proper food through the hard winter, and when the warm plague winds blew they had no strength to fight the infection. Within months the plague carts were going up and down the narrow streets all night and the white crosses were appearing on door after door. Alexander could do nothing to protect himself but stay in his house and work in his yard, and ban his apprentices from going out as much as possible. But he would not expose Frances to infection.

John found he was absurdly overanxious about his daughter. She looked so like her mother as she grew rounder and her face took on a glow as her pregnancy progressed. He did not want to speak of Jane to his second wife, and he did not want the shadow of her death to hang over the house. He took to spending long hours in the garden, not coming in until the slow early summer dusk, and he found that while he was digging, weeding, and transplanting the Virginian seedlings he was turning over in his mind the different sorts of love a man can have: for his work, for the girl he married for love, for the children she bore him, for the woman he married for convenience, and for the woman he loved hopelessly, helplessly, completely.

He even acknowledged at last his love for the king, the foolish, selfish, intractable master who had so persistently known less and understood less than his servants. John had thought all the loves were threads which pulled him one way and another and would be, as Attone had warned him, a rope to trip him up. But as he walked back to his house past the tulip beds, and saw the shape of their cupped petals against the greater darkness of night, he thought that perhaps the threads could be the warp and woof that wove into the fabric of his life, and made him what he was, a man who had loved very deeply in different ways; and that the different loves were not a betrayal, but a richness.

He was pinching out the buds on the cherry trees in the orchard one day in June when he saw Johnnie come flying out of the kitchen door, and rush to the stable. A moment later he was pulling the saddle horse out of the stall and jumping on her back, bare-back, and trotting out of the yard.

'What is it?' John shouted. He slid down the ladder and ran towards the house. 'Is it Frances?'

He ran into the kitchen and found the cook boiling a pan of water. 'Is it Frances?' he demanded.

'She's taken ill,' the cook said. 'Mrs Tradescant has put her to bed and sent Johnnie for the apothecary. Pray to God that it's not the plague.'

'Amen,' John said and in the same breath: 'Damn you for speaking such fears.' He strode from the kitchen and ran up the stairs in his gardening boots, shedding mud on the polished wood treads. 'Hester? Hester?'

She came out of Frances's room and he saw at once from her face that his daughter was gravely ill. 'What is it?' he demanded. 'Not –' He lowered his voice. 'Not the plague?'

'I don't know,' she said. 'She grew very hot and said she would like to rest, then she just fainted clean away.'

He glanced superstitiously at the closed door. 'Move her into our room,' he said.

'She's in her own room, I don't want to trouble her and move her,' Hester said uncomprehendingly.

He shifted from one foot to another, fearful of even saying the words. 'Please,' he said. 'Her mother took the plague in that room, it was our bedroom. She made me move her from there to the orangery and there she died. Please don't let Frances be in that room.'

Hester stepped towards him and took his dirty hands in her cool fingers. 'John, these are old fears,' she said. 'This is Frances, not Jane. This is a fever, not the plague. She is a strong young woman and I will nurse her as well as I can. I won't move her when she is comfortable in her own bed, and who better to watch over her from heaven than her own mother?'

He hesitated for a moment. 'Does she need anything?'

Hester thought quickly for a task to keep John occupied and to give him a sense of purpose. 'I need herbs,' she said. 'Feverfew and chamomile, and sweet cicely against infection. Can you pick them for me?'

He nodded and went quickly towards the stairs.

'And write a note and send it to Alexander,' Hester said. 'Don't worry him too much, just tell him she has a fever, and she would like to see him, if he can come.'

John paused, obedient as a frightened boy. 'Herbs or letter first?' he asked.

'Letter,' she said. 'Then the herbs, and then why don't you pot her up a couple of tulips? She'd like to see them.'

'I'll bring her up the Semper,' John said, promising the best of them all. 'The Semper Augustus.'

Alexander came up the river at dawn the next day and had the boat set him down on the bank as near to the Ark as he could get. John saw him from the window in the stable yard, taking off his cape and his waistcoat and even his trousers and leaving them in the stable. He shouted for Joseph to work the pump, stripped off his shirt and washed under the stream of icy water before rubbing himself briskly dry with a sheet and pattering to the kitchen door all but naked.

Cook let out a delighted little scream of shock but Alexander Norman paid no attention to her and walked past her to the hall.

'Forgive me,' he said briefly to John. 'But there is a lot of sickness in the City and I wanted to take no risk of bringing it to you here. Are you free of it in Lambeth?'

'Half a dozen dead in the village this week,' John said grimly. 'I thank you for taking care. You can borrow a shirt and breeches of mine.'

'Is she better?' Alexander asked.

John shook his head. 'The fever grew worse overnight and Hester says she is still hot.'

'But it isn't . . . ?' Alexander could not bring himself to name the plague.

'Hester says not.'

The two men looked into each other's anxious faces and for the first time since his return to England John knew the pleasure of finding a man who could understand what he was feeling. His own worry was graven deep into Alexander's face. They both looked as if they had spent the night praying. He reached out his arms and Alexander gripped him tightly.

'Please God it is not . . .'

'Please God,' John replied.

'She is so precious to me . . .'

'I know, I know.'

'I sent her away from the City the moment I thought there was a risk . . .'

'It's in Lambeth anyway. There is nowhere you could be sure that she would be safe.'

'But not her . . .'

'I feel so fearful,' John said very low. 'I think of her mother and her prettiness – and Frances is so like her – and I think that perhaps there is a weakness?'

Alexander shook his head. 'There's no way of tracing where it comes from or who takes it,' he said. 'That's the very devil of it. You just don't know. Is everyone else well? Johnnie? Hester?'

'We're all well,' John said. 'And God knows we would all willingly take it for her.'

Alexander bowed his head for a moment. 'D'you forgive me for marrying her?' he asked irrelevantly.

John gave a short laugh. 'For everything she has ever done or ever can do, if only she will be well again,' he said. 'I knew I loved her but I never knew that the very thought of losing her would be like my own death to me.'

'And the baby?'

'They're both hanging on,' John said. 'Hester says that they are both hanging on.'

There was nothing for the two men to do. A couple of times there was a knock at the door and John went to admit a visitor to the rarities room and one to walk around the garden; but the rest of the time he and Alexander sat in silence in the parlour, either side of the cold fireplace, straining to hear footsteps upstairs, waiting for news. Johnnie took up a position on the top of the stairs outside Frances's room carving at a twig with his pocket knife. All the day, he sat like a little choirboy at a vigil, listening to the gentle murmur of talk and the irregular sigh of Frances's breath.

There was little Hester could do, though she never left Frances's bedside. She sponged her forehead with vinegar and lavender water, she changed the sheets when they grew wet with sweat, she held her hand and spoke to her quietly and reassuringly when Frances tossed in fever-coloured nightmares, and she held her shoulders so that the young woman could sip a drink of cool well water.

But when Frances dropped back on her pillows and lay still, and the flush died away from her cheeks and her skin grew waxy and pale, there was nothing Hester could do but sit at the head of the bed and pray that her stepdaughter would live.

Hester watched all the night at the bedside and at three in the morning her head drooped and she slept. She was wakened only a few minutes later by a movement in the bed and she heard Frances say, 'Oh Hester!' in a tone of such sorrow that she was awake and on her feet as her eyes opened.

'What is it? Have you found a swelling?' she demanded, naming the greatest fear.

'I'm bleeding,' Frances said.

Hester saw at once that the fever had broken but the young woman was white and drained, and her nightdress was stained a deep cherry red.

'My baby,' Frances whispered.

Hester twisted a strip of sheet and held it against the flow. 'Lie quietly,' she said urgently. 'I'll send John for the midwife, you may be all right.'

Frances lay back obediently, but shook her head. 'I can feel it gone,' she said.

Hester, a childless woman, felt herself adrift in a tragedy that she had never experienced. 'Can you?'

'Yes,' Frances said, in a little voice which Hester recognised from the lonely little girl she had first met. 'Yes. My baby's gone.'

357

At seven in the morning Hester went wearily downstairs with a pile of cloths for burning and some sheets to wash, and found Alexander Norman and John alert and silent at the foot of the stairs.

'Forgive me,' she said slowly. 'I forgot the time, I forgot that you would be waiting and worried.'

John took the bundle from her and Alexander took her hand. 'What's happened?' John demanded.

'The fever has broken and she has no swellings,' Hester said. 'But she has lost the baby.' She looked at Alexander. 'I am sorry, Alexander. I would have sent for the midwife but she was sure that it was too late. It was all over in a moment.'

He turned and looked up the stairs. 'Can I go to her?'

Hester nodded. 'I'm sure it's not the plague, but don't wake her, and don't stay long.'

He went up the stairs so quietly that the treads did not squeak. John dropped the laundry on the floor and enfolded his wife in his arms. 'You haven't slept at all,' he said gently. 'Come. I'll give you a glass of wine and then you must go to bed. Alexander can look after her now, or me, or Cook.'

She let him draw her into the parlour, seat her in a chair and press a glass of sweet wine into her hand. She took a sip and some of the colour came back into her cheeks. She had never looked more plain than now, when she was strained and weary. John had never loved her better.

'You cared for her very tenderly,' he said. 'No mother could have done better.'

She smiled at that. 'I could not love her more if I had given birth to her myself,' she said. 'And I have long thought that she has two mothers: Jane in heaven and me on earth.'

He took the chair beside her and he drew her on to his knee. Hester wound her arms around his neck and laid her head on his shoulder and for the first time allowed herself to weep for the baby that was lost.

'There will be other babies,' John said, stroking her hair. 'We will have dozens of grandchildren, from Frances, from Johnnie.'

'But this one is lost,' Hester said. 'And if it had been a boy she was going to call him John.'

Summer 1646

Frances stayed at the Ark for all of the summer, promising Alexander that she would not return to his house in the City until the cold autumn weather had frozen out the plague. But they were not parted for many nights. The fighting was over and there was little demand for barrels for gunpowder. Many evenings Alexander took a boat from the Tower running with the incoming tide up the river to Lambeth, and then strode down the lane to the Ark to see his wife sitting on the front wall, waiting for him as if she were still a little girl.

It was a bad year for sickness, as everyone had predicted, and the town was full of soothsayers and prophesiers and men and women who were prepared to stand up and give witness on street corners that while the king was with the Scots, who had taken him away to Newcastle, the nation could not be at peace. The king must come to London and explain himself, the king must come before the widows and fatherless children and beg their pardons, the king must come before Parliament and agree how to live in peace with them. What the king should not do was to continue debating, sending arguments to Parliament in favour of himself, discussing theology with the covenanting Scots and generally enjoying his life as blithely and as happily as if the country had not battled for years and got nowhere.

'He can't be happy.' John disagreed with Johnnie, who brought back this news from Lambeth market. 'He can't be happy without the queen and without the court.'

'He only has to wait and Montrose will rescue him!' Johnnie declared. 'The Scots are his enemy, he has played a clever game by going to them. They shield him from his enemies, the English Parliament, and all the time he is waiting for Montrose. Montrose will fight his way across the Highlands for the king.'

'Johnnie has a new hero,' Hester told her husband with a smile. She was checking the purchases off the back of the wagon and Cook was taking them into the kitchen. 'He was all for Prince Rupert but now it is Montrose.'

'They say no-one will ever catch him, that he runs around the Highlands like a deer,' Johnnie said. 'The Covenanters will never catch him, he's too quick and too clever. He knows all the passes through the mountains, when they wait for him at one place he melts away over the hills and then attacks them in another.'

'It always sounds so easy when it is told like a ballad,' John said soberly. 'But real battles are not so quick. And real defeats can make a man sick to the heart.'

Johnnie shook his head and would not be persuaded then; but later in the summer he tasted a little of the bitterness of defeat. He spent the day of 25 June at the little lake, rowing his boat around in aimless circles. The king's town of Oxford had surrendered and Prince Rupert – the darling of the court, the hope of the royalists, the most dashing, the most glamorous, the most beautiful general that the war had seen – was sent out of the country into exile and would never be allowed to return.

Hester went down to the lake at dusk to find Johnnie. It was getting cold and the frogs were croaking in the reeds at the side of the pond and the bats dipping like night-time swifts to snatch the insects which still danced over the grey waters. She could just see the little rowboat with the oars shipped and Johnnie curled up in the stern, with his long legs trailing over the side of the boat and the heels of his boots dipping in the water and making circular ripples like rising fish.

'Come in,' she called, her voice gentle across the still water. 'Come in, Johnnie. The war is over and that's a thing to be glad for, not a matter of grief.'

The little huddled figure in the boat did not move.

John came down the path and stood beside Hester.

'He won't come in,' she said.

John took her hand. 'He will.'

She resisted him as he tried to draw her away. 'He has adored Prince Rupert for years. He cried the night that Rupert lost Bristol.'

'He'll get hungry,' John said. 'There is loyalty and love and there is a thirteen-year-old boy's belly. He'll come in.' He raised his voice. 'We have some strawberries for dinner tonight. And Cook has made marchpane pastry to go with them. Have we got some cream too?'

'Oh yes,' Hester said clearly. 'And a rib of beef with Yorkshire pudding and roasted potatoes and the allspick lettuce.'

There was a small movement from the becalmed boat.

John tucked Hester's arm firmly under his elbow and drew her away from the bank of the pond.

'I don't like to leave him,' she whispered.

John chuckled. 'If he's not in by the time dinner is on the table you can send me to swim out to him,' he said. 'It's a pledge.'

🌹

John could make light of Johnnie's despondency at the news of Prince Rupert's exile, but the thought of the king in the hands of the Scots at Newcastle haunted him too. In July there was news of an English mission to try to persuade the king to come to agreement with Parliament, and all the time the king was being worked on to sign a treaty with the Scots.

'If he cannot agree with either the English or the Scots, what will become of him?' John asked Hester. 'He has to give up either his right to the army and come home to England, or give up his religion and join the Scots. But he can't just wait and do nothing.'

Hester said nothing. She thought the king was perfectly capable of waiting and doing nothing while the queen campaigned for him in France, Montrose risked his life and his men in the Highlands and Ormonde tried to fight his way through a maze of the king's own self-betraying plotting in Ireland. 'If the Irish were to come over and join with Montrose and fight for the king –' she suggested.

John flashed her a quick, irritated look. 'Papists and Scotsmen?' he asked. 'Fighting for a Protestant king? An Irish army? The alliance would last half a day and the country would never forgive him.'

'If he *is* a Protestant king,' Hester said carefully.

John dropped his head into his hands. 'No-one knows what he believes any more, nor what he stands for. How could it have come to this?'

'And what do *you* believe?' Hester asked him. 'You were always against the court, and against Papacy?'

John shrugged wearily. 'I didn't go to Virginia just because I had no stomach for killing Englishmen,' he said. 'I went because I was torn. I served the king, and my father served the king or his servants all his life. I can't just turn away and pretend that I don't care for his safety. I *do* care. But he's in the wrong and has been in the wrong since –' He broke off. 'Since he marched his soldiers into the House of Commons,' he said. 'No, before. Since he allowed the government of this country to be run by that madman, Buckingham. Since he took a Papist wife and thus ran the risk of Papist children. From the moment that he set his heart on having a kingdom run as a tyranny and would not listen to his advisors.'

Hester waited.

'I want the kingdom free of his tyranny, I have always wanted that. But I don't need the kingdom free of him. Or his son. Does that make any sense at all?'

Hester nodded and then turned to a more pressing topic for her. 'Shall we unpack the rarities?'

John gave a short laugh. 'D'you think we are at peace? With the king held by the Scots at Newcastle and refusing to agree with his own Parliament?'

'I don't think we're at peace,' she said equably. 'But if we could show the rarities and summon people to the garden to see the Virginian plants we might make some money this summer. And we are in debt, John. This war has been hard on everyone and we are taking no more than a few shillings each month.'

He rose from the chair. 'Let's go and have a look at that tree,' he said.

They stood before the great black cherry tree. It had not liked the situation before the ice-house door and there had been few blossoms in spring and now only a few buttons of green berries which might, in time, ripen and swell.

'I can't bear to chop it down,' John said. 'It has grown to a good size even if it is not bearing much of a crop.'

'Can you move it?' Hester asked. Her gaze went beyond the tree, to the doorway of the ice house where the ivy and the honeysuckle were planted. No-one could have spotted its outline unless they were looking for it. She liked the thought of the garden plants helping to hide the rarities. There was some unity in the Ark if they all worked together to save the precious things.

'My father had a way of moving even big trees,' John said thoughtfully. 'But it takes time. We'll have to be patient. It will be a couple of months at the earliest.'

'Let's do it,' Hester said. 'I am ashamed of the rarities room as it is, I want the treasures back inside.' She did not tell John that while the king was held by the Scots she had no fears for the safety of the treasures or of the family. Hester had great faith in Scottish efficiency, and in the dour Covenanters' immunity to Stuart charm. If the Scots were holding the king, even if they took him far away to Edinburgh, then Hester felt safe.

Hester remembered the moving of the cherry tree as an event which coincided with the death of the hopes of the runaway king. Both processes happened in slow stages. John dug a trench around his father's cherry tree and watered it every morning and night. The news from Newcastle was that the king would agree to nothing: neither the proposals from England, nor those from his hosts the Scots.

With the help of Joseph and Johnnie pulling the trunk slowly first one way and then the other, John dug underneath the tree and gently shovelled earth away from all but the greatest roots. A Scottish cleric who had wrestled with the king's conscience for two months went home to Edinburgh and died, they said, of a broken heart, blaming himself that the most stubborn man in England could not be brought to see where his own interests lay.

John watered the tree richly with his father's mixture of stinging-nettle soup, dung, and water, three times a day. They heard that the queen herself wrote to the king and begged him to make an agreement with the Scots, so that he might be king of Scotland at least.

John pruned the tree, carefully cutting away the branches which would sap the tree's strength. The Scots Covenanters, debating with their royal prisoner, privately declared among themselves that he was mad, he must have been mad to come to them without an army, without power, without allies, and then imagine that they would fight a war for him, on his terms, against their co-religionists for nothing more than his thanks.

Johnnie and Joseph, with John and Alexander on the other side, gently thrust poles from one side of the crater around the tree to the other until it was supported, and then John went down into the mud-filled ditch and freed the last of the roots. The longest, strongest root he pulled gently from the mud and then cursed when it broke and he fell back into the slurry with a bump.

'That's killed it,' Joseph said gloomily, and John climbed out of the ditch soaked through and irritable. Then the four men gently lifted the tree out of the ground and carried it down to the bottom of the orchard where a new hole was dug and waiting. They put it in, lovingly spread out the roots, backfilled the earth, and gently pressed it down. John stood back and admired his work.

'It's crooked,' Frances said behind him.

John turned wrathfully on her.

'Just joking,' she said.

With the doorway clear, Hester tied a duster over her head to keep off the cobwebs and spiders and set to pulling aside the ivy and the honeysuckle. The key still worked in the lock, the door opened with a creak on the dirty hinges. John peered inside. The little round chamber was lined with straw and piled high with chests and boxes of his father's treasures. He caught Hester's dirty hand and kissed it. 'Thank you for keeping them safe,' he said.

Autumn 1646

Hester, Johnnie and Joseph were lifting tulip bulbs in the garden of the Ark. They worked with their fingers in the cold soil. Even the common bulbs were too valuable to risk spearing with a fork or slicing with a spade. On the ground beside Hester were the precious porcelain bowls of the most valuable tulips, their expensive bulbs already lifted and separated, the sieved earth tipped back into the beds.

Joseph and Johnnie filled the labelled sacks with the Flame tulip bulbs. Almost every one had spawned a second, some of them had two or three bulblets nestling beside the first. All three gardeners were smiling in pleasure. Whether the price for tulips ever recovered or stayed as low as it had been thrust by the collapse of the market, still there was something rich and exciting about the wealth which made itself in silence and secrecy under the soil.

There was a step on the wooden floor of the terrace and Hester looked up to see John Lambert. He was looking very fine, dressed as well as always, with a deep violet feather in his hat, and a waterfall of white lace at his throat and cuffs. Hester got to her feet and felt a pang of annoyance at her dirty hands and dishevelled hair. She whipped off her hessian apron and walked towards him.

'Forgive me coming unannounced,' he said, his dark smile taking in her rising blush. 'I am so honoured to see you working among your plants.'

'I'm all dirty,' Hester said, stepping back from his proffered hand.

'And I smell of horse,' he said cheerfully. 'I am on my way from my home in Yorkshire. I couldn't resist calling in to see if my tulips were ready.'

'They are.' Hester gestured to the three bulging sacks at the corner of the terrace. 'I was going to send them to your London home.'

'I thought you might. That's why I have come. I am on my way to Oxford and I wanted the special tulips there. I shall plant them in pots and have them in my rooms.'

Hester nodded. 'I am sorry you will not meet my husband,' she said. 'He is in London today. He has gone into trade in a small way with a West India planter and he is sending some goods out.'

'I am sorry not to meet him,' John Lambert said pleasantly. 'But I hardly dare to delay. I am to be governor of Oxford while my health mends.'

Hester risked a quick glance at him. 'I had heard you were ill – I was sorry.'

He gave her his warm, intimate smile. 'I am well enough, and the work I set myself to do is all but done. Pray God we will have peace again, Mrs Tradescant, and in the meantime I can sit down in Oxford and make sure that the colleges get back into some kind of order, and their treasures are safe.'

'These are hard times to be a guardian of beautiful things.'

'Better times coming soon,' he whispered. 'May I take my tulips now?'

'Of course. Shall you want them all at Oxford?'

'Send the Flame tulips to my London house, my wife can plant them for me there. But the rare tulips and the Violetten I must have beside me.'

'If you breed a true violet one then do let us know,' Hester said, gesturing to Joseph to take the sack of labelled rare tulips out to the wagon waiting in the street beyond the garden gate. 'We would buy one back from you.'

'I shall present it to you,' John Lambert said grandly. 'A mark of respect to another guardian of treasure.' He glanced down the garden and saw Johnnie. 'And how's the cavalry officer these days?'

'Very disheartened,' Hester said. 'Would you let him make his bow to you?'

John Lambert cupped his hands around his mouth and shouted: 'Ho! Tradescant!'

Johnnie looked up at the shout and came up from the tulip beds at a run, skidded to a halt, and dipped in a bow.

'Major!' he said.

'Good day.'

Johnnie beamed at him.

'You must have been disappointed in recent months, I am sorry for it,' John Lambert said gently.

'I can't see what went wrong,' Johnnie said passionately.

John Lambert thought for a moment. 'It was mostly how we used the infantry,' he said. 'Cromwell has them trained in such a way that they change formation very fast, and they can hold their ground even against a charge. And once the king dismissed Rupert then the morale among his commanders was very low. That's one of the keys, especially in a war inside a country. Everyone's got to trust each other. That's what Cromwell got right, when he got the Members of Parliament out of the army. We made the army a family which prays together and thinks together and fights together.'

Johnnie nodded, listening avidly. 'It wasn't Prince Rupert's fault that he lost Bristol!' he exclaimed.

'Indeed it was not,' John Lambert agreed. 'It was mostly the weather. It rained and their gunpowder was soaked. They were going to mine the city walls, rather than let us take a fortified town. They had the mines dug and the gunpowder in place – but then it was wet and didn't fire. No commander could have done anything about that. But there was another thing –'

'What, sir?'

'It's about belief,' Lambert said slowly. 'There are very few like you, Johnnie, who have such certainty about the king. But there are very many, most of my army in fact, who truly believe that if they can win the war that we can make a better country here, better for everyone. They think they are doing God's work and man's work. They think that they will make a world of greater justice and fairness – *we* think that.'

'Are you a Leveller, sir?' Johnnie asked. Hester would have interrupted but Lambert was unruffled.

'I think we all are in a way,' he said. 'Some of us would go further than others, but all the honest men I know think that we should be governed by our consent, and not by the king's whim. We think we should have a parliament elected by everyone in the country and that it should sit all the time and return to the country for election every three years. We don't think that the king and only the king should decide when and where it sits, and whether or not he will listen to it.'

'I'm still a royalist,' Johnnie said stubbornly.

Lambert laughed. 'Perhaps we can find a way to persuade you royalists that it is for the good of us all – king to beggar – that we live in some order and harmony. And now I must go.'

'Good luck,' Hester called, her hand on Johnnie's shoulder. 'Come again.'

'I'll come next spring and bring my Violetten!' he called, and with a swirl of his cape he was gone.

Spring 1647

Johnnie sat in his rowing boat on the little lake at the bottom of the garden, a news-sheet spread before him, his coat turned up around his ears against the sharp frost. He was reading one of the many royalist papers that spread a mixture of good cheer and open lies in an effort to keep the king's cause alive, even while he squabbled with his Scots hosts at Newcastle. This edition assured the reader that the king in his wisdom was forging an agreement which would convert the Scots from their stubborn determination never to accept the English prayer book or the English system of bishops. As soon as the Scots had agreed they would then sweep down through England, return the king to his throne and all would be well again.

Johnnie looked up and saw his father coming through the orchard. John waved and walked to the bank where a little pier stretched into the water.

'You must be freezing,' John remarked.

'A bit,' Johnnie said. 'This can't be right. The Scots aren't likely to surrender all they believe in when they have all but won the war. They aren't likely to start fighting for the king *against* Parliament when they've been allies with Parliament for the last few years.'

'No,' John said briefly. 'You bought the paper. What did you think it would tell you: the truth?'

'I just want to know!' Johnnie sat up abruptly and the boat rocked. 'He has no chance, has he?'

John shook his head. 'What your paper doesn't tell you is that they've refused to take him to Edinburgh unless he too signs their covenant, against Laud's prayer book and against the bishops. Of course he can't sign. He's just turned the kingdom upside down to try and make us do it his way. But the Scots are going back to Scotland, and they don't know what to do with him. Nobody knows why he went to them in the first place. There was never any chance of an agreement. They'll send him to Parliament.'

Johnnie went pale. 'Betray him to his enemies?'

'He's with his enemies already but he wouldn't see it,' John said bluntly. 'The Scots and Parliament have been allies since the war started. Of course they would work on him to try and make a peace. Of course if he won't bend they have to hand him over.'

'What will he do?' Johnnie asked, anguished.

John shook his head. 'He must surrender and accept the terms Parliament imposes. Parliament and the army have defeated him. He has to give up.'

❦

John was wrong. The king did not give up. He attempted to escape, an ill-planned, unlikely attempt which was as successful as it deserved to be. The guard around him was doubled, he was warned that he should know that he was a prisoner of the English Parliament, and taken to Holdenby House in Northamptonshire.

Hester found John at the bottom of the orchard, scowling at the cherry tree. 'I think I killed it,' he said. 'And I watched my father moving trees twice the size of this when I was a boy and never learned the knack of it.'

'It looks no worse than the others,' Hester said, looking round the orchard where the whippy bare boughs of the trees flailed against a white sky.

'I've killed it,' John said. 'For all the care I took. I don't have my father's talent. I worked at his side all my life and still I'm not half the gardener he was. He knew where he belonged, he knew who he served, and he knew his trade and I –' He broke off and put his hand on the bough of the tree as if for support.

'What's the news?' Hester asked, guessing at once the source of John's discomfort.

John gave her a quick look from under his lowered brows. 'Just some lads at the back door, begging for bread on their way home,' he said. 'Discharged from the army and heading homeward.'

Hester waited. John put his hand out and held the trunk of the dead cherry tree. 'They said that the army would rule Parliament and they would have their revenge on the king,' he said. 'They said they would make him pay because a new day is coming when all men will have land and all men will have a vote to choose their rulers and all men will be equal with one another.'

'These are young men's thoughts,' Hester said quickly. 'You were a young man wild for change yourself once, John.'

He nodded. 'But these were not young men, they were men of my age. And they said that many think as they do. They are Levellers and they say the best men of the army are with them. They want to finish what Parliament started. They want to exile the king and turn the country into a new land of freedom and equality.'

Hester looked around the security of the walled orchard. 'Parliament would not give away land?' she asked.

John shook his head. 'I don't think they'll wait for Parliament,' he said. 'These are men of action and determination. They've been fighting to make a better country for working men. They have little patience for the gentlemen in Parliament. They want to see the land given to working men. They want the royal estates, the church estates, the commons, and the wastes.'

'And every man would have his own little piece of land and grow things?'

'So they say.' John smiled grimly. 'It's what I always wanted. It's how I always thought things should be. And now it looks as if the army might destroy Parliament and do it.'

'Turn on their masters?'

'Why not? Didn't Parliament turn on the king?'

'Would they take from landowners like us? Tax us?'

John shrugged. 'How would I know what they might do? They might think that these walls should be pulled down as any other.'

Hester nodded and turned back towards the house. He could tell by her slow stride that she was thinking. Halfway to the house she turned and came back to him.

'I think we should be growing vegetables,' she said. 'That's what they'll be wanting now.'

The whole family helped in the restoration of the rarities to the room with the high Venetian windows and the smooth, polished floor. They wanted to return it to its previous state, they wanted it restored, without loss of beauty, without loss of richness, without loss of the glamour that hung around it: the scent of the skins, the delight of the multiplicity of things, the joy of the ordered jumble; the big things hanging from the ceiling, the tiny things in their cabinets, the exotic next to the mundane, the historic next to the inventions.

There were some terrible gaps in the collection. The coins had fared the worst and the items made of precious metals. Hester had made inroads into anything which had held its value during the war years and she could not conceal from John that there were trays of Roman and mediaeval coins which would never be stocked again.

Some things had suffered from damp. A triptych altar screen had been leaned against the ice-house wall and its bright colours had been leached away by the moisture of the brick. Many rare skins had rotted and decayed, and some of the woollen clothes were pitted with moth-holes. Vellum pages of illuminated manuscripts had been eaten by ants and the foul dirt of rats and mice was all over the cases which held the flowers dried in sugar.

'I am sorry, I am sorry,' Hester cried as one parcel after another was brought out into the light. 'If I had only known that we would be safe I would never have hidden the things away.'

'You didn't know,' John said generously. 'And if the soldiers had suddenly swept through we could have lost everything in one night.'

Frances, her hair tied in a kerchief, and Johnnie in his gardening clothes gently beat the dust and the moths from the clothes, rugs and skins outside and then carried them in for Hester and John to rearrange and hang.

Bit by bit, piece by piece, drawer by drawer, object after object, the rarities room was reassembled, and when they stepped back and looked around after a full fortnight of work they saw an impressive collection of wealth and novelty. Only someone who had grown up in the room, as the Tradescant children had done, rocked in the light of those great windows, would have known that anything was missing. The visitors, who would surely come again now that peace was here, could not fail to be amazed.

Summer 1647

John was digging in the new vegetable bed and setting in lettuce seeds to see which would grow the fastest when Hester came out of the house, shading her eyes against the bright sunshine, and then hurried down the path towards him.

'The king's been taken,' she said baldly.

He looked up with as much anxiety as if she had said one of the children was ill. 'Taken?'

'Some whippersnapper Cornet marched up to Holdenby House and arrested His Majesty,' Hester said, nearly spitting with rage.

'How did you hear this?' John asked, wiping his muddy hands on his leather gardening apron.

'The ferry boatman. Frances has come for a visit, I went down to the river to meet her. London is buzzing with the news.'

'Who has him?'

'A man of no importance,' Hester said. 'A nobody. One of the new men of the New Model Army, rode to Holdenby House and captured the king as if he was a piece of baggage in the baggage train. It is these people who will bring us down. People who have no respect. Men who have spent four years learning that nothing matters, not pictures in church, not music, not gardens, not kings.'

'And where has he taken His Majesty?' John asked.

'To Maidenhead,' she said. 'And they say Oliver Cromwell himself is going out to meet him.'

'Cromwell?'

She nodded. 'D'you think that means peace?'

John shook his head. 'I suppose it means that the game has changed again,' he said, baffled. 'When the king was held by the Scots he was in the power of Parliament. But now the army has him, I don't know what will become of him, or us for that matter.'

'We may be in danger,' Hester said. 'The ferry boatman said that the soldiers of the New Model Army may march on Parliament. They're determined to have their pay. And they recognise no loyalty to anyone but their commanders and their levelling ideas. They are saying that Parliament and the City may hold out against the army. But if the army comes to the City from the south then they will march right through here. We may have to pack up the rarities again. They are marching for their pay, they are hungry and desperate men. And they have sworn that all the land and all the property shall be held in common.'

John shook his head. 'It's like living in the middle of a thunderstorm,' he complained. 'It has all changed again. If the army fights against the Parliament which brought it into being, then what becomes of the country?'

In July the news was that the king was to be taken, under guard, to Oatlands.

Hester looked at her husband across the kitchen table. Cook, Joseph, the new gardening boy, Frances and Johnnie all turned to the head of the table and waited for John to speak.

'Now, I have to go,' he said simply. 'He cannot be at Oatlands and not see me working in the garden. That was my work, that was my place.'

Hester hesitated for only a moment. 'I'll pack your bag,' she said, and went out of the room.

Johnnie turned to his father, his face suddenly flushed. 'May I come too?' he asked. 'And see him?'

When his father hesitated he went on in a rapid torrent of speech. 'I've never seen him, and my father and my grandfather were in his service. And I've never even seen him. Frances saw him and the queen. Can I come? Please?'

John gave a short laugh. 'I cannot be sure that I will see him,' he said. 'And if he sees me, he may not speak to me. I just feel the royal court under his window should be tidy, I don't know what state it's in.'

'I can tidy it,' Johnnie said desperately. 'I can weed. I worked there while you were away. I can do it. I am a Tradescant, I am gardener to the king. I should be there.'

Hester came back into the kitchen and John turned to her with relief. 'It depends on what your mother says.'

373

'Can I go with Father to Oatlands?' Johnnie scrambled over his stool to get to his stepmother. 'And work for him? He'd have such a lot of work to do, I could help.'

'I don't know if it's safe,' Hester said hesitantly.

'It's probably safe,' John said shortly. 'Safer than it's ever been with him under guard and forced to make peace at last.'

She nodded. 'He can go if you wish it,' she said to John.

Johnnie turned his bright hazel eyes on his father.

'Oh, very well,' John said. 'But not a word do you speak unless spoken to – and then you just answer "Yes, Your Majesty", or "No, Your Majesty". Not a word about me being in Virginia. Not a word about the cavalier who came here. Not a word about John Lambert buying our tulips. Not a word about anything.'

Johnnie was dancing on the spot with excitement. 'Yes! Yes!' he shouted. 'Yes! Of course. And I shall be absolutely silent. Absolutely. I shall be absolutely discreet.'

John met his wife's eyes across the boy's bobbing head. 'I don't know about you; but I feel very confident,' he said wryly.

They went by the river, rowed in a wherry, Johnnie seated beside his father and looking all around him. When they were past the village of Staines, John said quietly, 'There it is,' and pointed to the little rose-pink palace, sitting on the terraces with the unkempt lawns running down to the river. 'D'you know, I never thought I'd see it again,' John said softly. 'I never thought I'd be here, working in these gardens again.'

Johnnie glanced quickly at his father's darkened expression. 'But you're glad of it?' he asked. 'Glad you came home and that the king is back in his palace, and soon everything will be as it was?'

John dropped his hand on his son's thin shoulder. 'I don't think everything will be quite as it was,' he said. 'There's a lot of men dead and a lot of tears shed, and the king is in his palace but not on his throne. We'll have to mind our tongues here, and beware even of our thoughts.'

The boatman shipped the oars and the wherry nudged against the landing stage. John stepped quickly ashore and caught the mooring rope, dug in his pocket for a coin and dropped it down into the boat as Johnnie tossed up their bags and then handed up, one at a time, a dozen pots with nodding blooms.

John shouldered his bag. 'We'll come back for the pots,' he said, and led the way up the slope to the palace.

Prince Rupert had allowed his cavalrymen's horses to graze on the lawns and they were pocked with hoofprints and lumpy with droppings but at least the animals had kept the grass down. As John approached the palace he saw that the creepers and the wall climbers which he had trained so carefully to take blossoms and scent up to the windows were doing well – overspread, sometimes pulling away from their ties, but thriving on neglect.

The beds at the feet of the rose-brick walls were overrun with weeds but some flowers were still struggling through. Pansies and gillyflowers, irises and peonies had thrust their heads above the encroaching green. 'Soon hoe that out,' John remarked, nodding to his son.

The yew tree *allée* was overgrown but looked thick and bushy, throwing a welcome green shade against the brightness of the afternoon sunshine. The orangery which John's father had rebuilt was dilapidated – the white paint was peeling and some of the ornamental woodwork had been wrenched off for the troopers' campfires – but the silkworm house and the neighbouring gardener's house were as Hester had left them, swept clean and bare and empty.

John left his son collecting firewood for the empty grate and unrolling their travelling cloaks for beds as he prowled around the deserted palace.

The strangest thing was the quiet. Instead of a bustling royal court filled with folly and flirtation, shouted orders, voices calling and musicians playing, there was nothing but the occasional rattle of a shutter banging in the breeze and the insistent coo of the wood pigeons nesting in the trees. The stable yard, which had housed more than a hundred horses, was empty, straws blowing in the yard, the stalls heaped with dung, stale water in the troughs.

The great front door was shut and bolted. John tried the massive brass handle and then stepped back. The king was due in a few days, surely there should be servants inside setting the palace to rights. Not a face showed at the windows, there was not a movement in the courts.

John went around to the kitchen quarters and to the bake-house. The fires were out, the place was silent. A heap of ash and a few scattered utensils showed that the cavalrymen had dined before they left, but all the food had been eaten by rats or mice and their droppings were heaped even on the kitchen tables.

John shook his head in wonder at the desolation of the place, at its transformation from the pinnacle of the social life of the kingdom, with the queen singing about the platonic ideal and the king going hunting on his high-bred Arab horses, to this shell. He turned and trudged back across the bowling green to the silkworm house.

Johnnie had brought up the pots from the riverside.

'Good lad,' John said with pleasure, glad of the chance to set about his work and restore normality at least to the flowerbeds. 'Let's take these up to the royal court. At least that can be looking right in a couple of days.'

They worked hard, side by side, and John enjoyed his son's company. The boy had inherited the Tradescant gift with plants, he handled them as if he loved the touch of the silky white roots, the caress of damp earth. When he hefted a pot in his hand he could tell from the weight whether it needed watering. When he tipped a plant out into his palm he never knocked the blooms. When he set it into a hole and pressed down the earth there was something about his touch which was both precisely judged, and quite unknowing.

'You may be the greatest gardener of us all,' John said at the end of the second day as they walked homewards with their tools over their shoulders. 'I don't believe I had your way with plants when I was your age.'

Johnnie gleamed. 'I love the plants. Not so much the rarities,' he said.

'Not the rarities?' John asked, amazed.

His son shook his head. 'What I'd rather do, more than anything else, would be to collect new plants, to go with you to the Americas, the West Indies, travel, find things, bring them home and grow them. The rarities – well, they just sit there, don't they? Once they're in place there is nothing more to do with them except keep them dusted. But plants grow and blossom and fruit and seed and then there's next year to plant them again. I like how they change.'

John nodded. 'I see.'

He was about to remark that the rarities played their part in the Tradescant family fortune when he heard hoofbeats on the drive. 'What's that?' he asked.

'Could it be the king?'

'Could be.'

John turned and ran towards the silkworm house, cast down his tools, grabbed his coat and turned to run back to the palace. Johnnie danced on the spot. 'Can I come? Can I come?'

'Yes. But remember what I said about keeping silent.'

Johnnie fell into line behind his father, mirrored his father's long stride, composed his face to a scowl of what he hoped was dignified discretion, and spoiled the effect only slightly by a great bounce at every fourth step as his excitement proved too much for him.

They ran round to the stable yard and there, in the dirty stall, was the king's Arab, and a dozen other horses of his escort.

'The king here?' John asked a trooper.

'Just arrived,' the man said, easing the girth of his horse. 'We had to stop at every village for him to touch people.'

'Touch people?'

'They turned out in dozens,' the man said abruptly. 'With all sorts of illnesses and sores and God knows what. And again and again he stopped and touched them, so that they would be cured. And they all went off, back to their hovels, back to their porridge of nothing and water, thinking that he had done them a great favour and that we were some kind of beast to imprison him.'

John nodded.

'Who are you?' the man asked. 'If you want a favour of him, he'll do it. He's the most charming, generous, agreeable man to ever take a country into disaster and death and four years of war.'

'I'm the gardener,' John replied.

'Then you'll see him,' the man said. 'He went out to sit in the garden with his companions, while someone cooks his dinner, and sweeps his chamber, and makes everything ready for him so that he can dine in comfort and sleep in comfort. While I and my men do without.'

John turned on his heel and went round to the royal court.

The king was seated on a bench, his back against the warm brick wall, looking around him at the newly weeded, newly planted garden. Standing behind him were a couple of gentlemen that John did not know, another stranger strolled on the newly raked paths. When the king heard John's footsteps he glanced up.

'Ah . . .' For a moment he could not remember the name. 'Gardener Tradescant.'

John dropped to his knee and heard Johnnie behind him do the same.

'Your w . . . w . . . work?' the king asked with his slight stammer, gesturing to the dug-over beds.

John bowed. 'When I heard you were coming to Oatlands I came to do what I could, Your Majesty. With my son: John Tradescant.'

The king nodded, his dark eyes half-lidded. 'I thank you,' he said languidly. 'When I am returned to my proper place I shall see that you are returned to yours.'

John bowed again and waited. When there was silence he glanced up. The king made a small gesture of dismissal with his hand. John rose to his feet, bowed, and walked backwards, Johnnie skipping nervously out of the way as his father suddenly reversed, and then quickly copying him. John bowed again at the gateway to the garden and then stepped backwards till he was out of sight.

He turned and met Johnnie's astounded face. 'And that's it?' Johnnie demanded. 'After we came here without being asked, and worked without pay for all this time to make it lovely for him?'

John gave a little snort of amusement and started to walk back to the silkworm house. 'What did you expect? A knighthood?'

'I thought –' Johnnie started and then broke off. 'I suppose I thought he might have some task for us, or he might be glad of us, he might see that we were loyal and thank us –'

John snorted again and opened the little white wooden door. 'This is not a king who has plans or gives thanks,' he said. 'That's one of the reasons he's where he is.'

'But doesn't he realise that you needn't have come at all?'

John paused for a moment and looked down at the stricken face of his boy. 'Oh Johnnie,' he said softly. 'This is not the king of the broadsheet ballads and the church sermons. This is a foolish man who ran into the war because he would not take advice, and when he took advice at all, always chose the wrong people to guide him.

'I came today as much for my father as for the king. I came because my father would have wanted to know that when the king came to his palace, the gardens were weeded. It would have been a matter of duty for him. It was a matter of pride for me. If I had freely chosen my way I would have been for the rights of working men and against the king. But I could not choose freely. I was in his service, and there have been some days – most days – when even seeing him as a fool I pity him from the bottom of my heart. Because he is a fool who cannot help himself. He does not know how to be wise. And his folly has cost him everything he owned.'

'I thought he was a great man, like a hero,' Johnnie remarked.

'Just an ordinary man in an extraordinary place,' John said. 'And too much of a fool to know that. He was taught from birth that he was half-divine. And now he believes it. Poor foolish king.'

John and Johnnie stayed the month working at Oatlands. The cook that Parliament had sent with the king needed fresh vegetables and fruits from the kitchen garden and by picking and choosing from the overgrown beds the two Tradescants were able to send fresh food up to the house each day. The king was surrounded by a small court and his imprisonment seemed more like a guard of honour. He hunted, he shot at archery, he ordered John to roll the bowling green smooth so that they could play at bowls.

John was considering paying for some boys to help with the weeding and planting in winter greens, when the news came that the king was to be moved to Hampton Court. Within a few hours the horses were saddled and the retinue was ready to move on.

The king was in the garden, waiting to be told that his escort was ready. John found he could not keep away from the excitement of great events, and took his pruning hook to the climbers on the far wall of the royal court.

The king, strolling around with two of his courtiers, came upon John and paused to watch him work as the two men stood aside.

'I shall see you repaid for this,' he said simply. He smiled a sly little smile. 'Sooner perhaps than you think.'

John jumped from his ladder and dropped to one knee. 'Your Majesty.'

'They may have defeated my army, but now they tear themselves apart,' the king said. 'All I must do is wait, p . . . patiently wait, until they beg me to come to the throne and set all to rights.'

John risked an upward glance. 'Really, Your Majesty?'

The king's smile transformed him. 'Y . . . Yes. Indeed. The army will destroy P . . . Parliament, and then t . . . tear themselves apart. Already the army tells P . . . Parliament what it should do. When they have no enemy they have no c . . . common cause. All they could do was to destroy, it needs a k . . . king to rebuild. I know th . . . them. There is L . . . Lambert. He heads the f . . . faction against Parliament. He will lead the army against P . . . Parliament and then I will have w . . . won.'

John paused before he could find the words to reply. 'So Your Majesty will greet them kindly when they come? And make an agreement with them?'

The king laughed shortly. 'I shall w . . . win the argument, though I lost the b . . . battle,' he said.

A trooper came to the garden gate. 'We are ready to leave, Your Majesty,' he called.

King Charles, who had never before this year ever done another man's bidding, turned and went from Tradescant's garden.

☙

John and his son went down to the gatehouse to see them leave. John was half-expecting a summons to Hampton Court, but the king went by with only a flicker of recognition that his gardener was on his knees at the roadside.

'And that's it?' Johnnie demanded again.

'That's it,' John replied shortly. 'Royal service. We'll set things in order tomorrow and we'll go home the next day. Our work here is done.'

❧

They discovered why the king had been moved when they got home. The City was in uproar with the apprentices rioting in favour of the king's return and the army had thought it safer to have him at Hampton Court with a larger garrison around him. Alexander Norman had sent Frances to the Ark for safety and forbidden her to return to the City until the riots were over – whether they were ended by the return of the king to his throne, the seizing of control by Parliament, or the arrival of Cromwell's army. There were now three players in the game for England. The king, playing one side against the other and hoping; Parliament, increasingly directionless and fearful of its future; and the army, which seemed to be the only force with a vision of the future and the discipline and determination to make it happen.

The soldiers under Cromwell had forged their faith in themselves, in their cause, and in their God during the long, hard years of fighting; they were not men who would now welcome a compromise. They wanted their pay; but they also wanted the country new-made. They had worked out their beliefs and philosophy in between battles, on forced marches, on dark nights when the rain doused their camp fires. They had given up four years of peaceful life at home to fight for the causes of religious and political freedom. They wanted to see a new world in return for their sacrifice. They were under the command of Thomas Fairfax and John Lambert, two great generals who understood them and shared their beliefs, and marched them on the faithless, fearful city of London to ensure that Parliament did not bow to pressure and make a peace with a king who should be deep in despair and not radiant with hope.

Frances took her husband's note to her father, who was hoeing the new vegetable bed. He looked at it briefly, and handed it back to her.

'You'll stay here,' he said.

'If I may.'

He tipped his hat over his eyes and grinned at his daughter. 'I imagine we can endure your company. Will you keep an eye on Johnnie for me? I don't want him marching up to Parliament with a pruning hook over his shoulder, thinking he is bringing the king home to his own.'

'Mother is more afraid that it'll be you running off to enlist.'

John shook his head. 'I'll not take up arms ever again,' he said. 'It's not a trade I do well. And the king is not a captivating master.'

Alexander wrote almost daily, reporting the fluctuations in the mood of the city. But it was all resolved in August when the army, under the command of General John Lambert, marched into London and declared that they could and would make peace with the king. With the House of Lords they drew up proposals to which any king could agree. Cromwell himself took the proposals to King Charles at Hampton Court.

'He will agree to them and be restored,' Alexander Norman said over a comfortable bottle of wine on the terrace. Frances sat on a stool at her husband's feet and he rested his hand on her golden-brown head. Hester sat opposite John, who was in his father's chair – facing out over the garden, watching the fruit in the orchard gilded with the last rays of sunshine. Johnnie sat at the top of the terrace steps. At Alexander's words he gave a radiant smile.

'The king will be returned to his palaces,' he said wonderingly.

'Please God,' said John. 'Please God that the king sees where his interests lie. He told me that he would set the army against Parliament and conquer them both.'

'Not with John Lambert in command,' Hester remarked. 'That man is not a fool.'

'Can it all be as it was?' Frances asked. 'The queen come home, and the court restored?'

'There'll be some missing faces,' Alexander pointed out. 'Archbishop Laud for one, Earl Strafford.'

'So what was it all for?' Hester asked. 'All these years of hardship?'

John shook his head. 'In the end, perhaps it was to bring the king and Parliament to realise that they have to deal together, they cannot be enemies.'

'A high price to pay,' Frances said, thinking of the years when she and Hester had struggled on their own at the Ark, 'to get some sense into that thick royal head.'

Autumn 1647

'He's gone,' Alexander said flatly the moment he entered the kitchen
door and surprised the Tradescants at breakfast. His horse stood sweating in the stable yard outside. 'I came at once to tell you. I rode over.
I couldn't bear to wait. I couldn't believe it myself.'

'The king?' John leaped to his feet and strode to the door, checked
and turned back.

Alexander nodded. 'Escaped from Hampton Court.'

'Hurrah!' Johnnie shouted.

'My God, no,' John said. 'Not to the French? Not when they were
so near agreement? The French haven't rescued him? Kidnapped
him?'

Alexander shook his head and dropped into John's vacated seat.
Frances put a mug of small ale beside him and he caught her hand and
kissed the inside of her wrist in thanks. 'I heard the news this morning
and came straight here with it. I couldn't bear even to write it. What
days we live in! When will we ever see an end to these alarms!'

'When will we ever see peace?' Hester murmured, one eye on her
husband who was standing at the window gazing out into the yard as
if ready to run himself.

'Who's got him?' John demanded. 'Not the Irish?'

'He just slipped away on his own, by the looks of it. There's not
word of him being broken out by soldiers. Just away with his gentlemen.'

'Sir John Berkeley,' John guessed.

Alexander shrugged. 'Maybe.'

'And where has he gone? France? To be with the queen and Prince
Charles?'

'If he has any sense,' Alexander said. 'But why break away now? When

383

things were going so well? When they were so close to agreeing to what he wanted? When he had an agreement with the army that he could sign? All he had to do was wait. The City is for him, Parliament is for him, the army has nothing but fair demands, Cromwell has destroyed the opposition. He has nearly won.'

'Because he always thinks he can do better,' John exclaimed despairingly. 'He always thinks he can do a little more by a grand gesture, a great chance. My father saw him ride out to Spain with the Duke of Buckingham when he was a young prince, and wild and reckless. He never learned the line between taking a risk and ripe folly. No-one ever taught him to take care. He likes the masque – the style and the action. He's never seen that it is all pretend. That real life isn't like that.'

Hester sank back in her chair and glanced down the table at her stepson. Johnnie was looking mutinous. She put out a hand to warn him to hold his silence, but the boy burst out:

'It's the greatest of things! Don't you see? He'll be safe in France by now, and they can beg his pardon from there! The queen will have an army ready for him to command, Prince Rupert will take the cavalry again. They said that he was defeated but he was not!'

John turned a dark look on his son. 'You're right about only one thing,' he said sombrely. 'He's never defeated.'

'That's the wonderful thing about him!'

John shook his head. 'It's the worst.'

Alexander stayed for breakfast and then agreed to stay on for the rest of the week. John was restless all day and at mid-afternoon he went to find Hester.

She was in the rarities room, bringing the planting records up to date in the big garden book.

'I can't stay here, not knowing what's going on,' John said briskly. 'I'll go into Whitehall, see if I can hear some news.'

She put down her pen and smiled at him. 'I knew you'd have to go,' she said. 'Make sure you come home, don't be caught up in whatever is going on there.'

He paused in the doorway. 'Thank you,' he said.

'Oh! For what?'

'For letting me go without badgering me with a dozen questions, without warning me a dozen times.'

She smiled but it did not reach her eyes. 'Since you would go whether I give you leave or no, I might as well give you leave,' she said.

'That's true enough!' John said lightly and went from the room.

Whitehall was in a frenzy of gossip and speculation. John went into a tavern where he might find an acquaintance, bought a mug of ale and looked around for a face he knew. At a nearby table were a group of Africa merchants.

'Mr Hobhouse! Any news? I have come up from Lambeth especially and all I can get is what I know already.'

'You know that he's gone to the Isle of Wight?'

John recoiled. 'What?'

'Carisbrooke Castle. He's set himself up in Carisbrooke Castle.'

'But why? Why would he?'

The merchant shrugged. 'It's not a bad plan. No-one can trust the navy, and if they declare for him how is Cromwell's army going to lay hold of him? He could be snug enough at Carisbrooke, create his court, build his army, and when he is ready sail straight into Portsmouth. He must have had some secret arrangement with the governor Robert Hammond, though everyone thought that Hammond was a Parliament man through and through. The king must have had a deep plan. He'll be waiting for the queen's army from France and then we'll be at war again, if anyone has the stomach for it.'

John briefly closed his eyes. 'This is a nightmare.'

The merchant shook his head. 'I cannot tell you how much money I am losing every day this goes on,' he said. 'I can't induce men to serve, my ships are harassed by pirates in the very mouth of the Thames, and I never know when a ship comes in what price I can command on the quayside or what taxes I shall have to pay. These are times for a madman. And we have a mad king to rule over us.'

'Not another war,' John said.

'He must have laid his plans very deep,' the merchant said. 'He was promising to agree with Cromwell and Ireton only the day before, he gave his word as a king. He was about to sign. What a man! What a false man! Y'know, in business we'd never deal with him. How would I manage if I gave my word and then skipped away?'

'Deep-laid plans?' John asked, seizing on the one unlikely feature.

'So they say.'

385

One of the other merchants glanced up. 'D'you know better, Mr Tradescant? You were at Oatlands with him, weren't you?'

John sensed the sudden intensity of interest. 'I was planting the garden. He hardly spoke to me. I saw him walk by, nothing more.'

'Well God save him and keep him from his enemies,' one of the men said stoutly and John noticed that while only a few months before the man would have been booed into silence or even thrown out of the tavern there were now a few men who muttered 'Amen' into the bottom of their mugs, and no-one who denied the wish.

'So what happens now?' John asked.

'We wait on his whim,' one of the merchants said sourly. 'As we have been doing for this past year and a half. He was defeated fair and square but he still dances around the country and we still have to wait till he tells us what he will agree to. It makes no sense to me.'

'He won't lie down till he's dead,' one of the men said frankly. 'Would to God that he might fall sick and die and then we could deal with his son, any of the sons. Anyone rather than this man.'

'I'll not ill-wish him,' another man said stoutly.

'Then why will he not come to the City and make an agreement?' someone demanded. 'God knows all we want is to have things at peace.'

John looked from one angry, worried face to another and drained his ale. 'I must go back to my garden,' he said. He had a sense of relief at the thought of the rarities room restored and the garden in its autumn order. 'Whether the king has his own again or no, I have my work to do.'

'You won't go and garden for him at Carisbrooke?' one of the men asked mischievously.

John did not rise to the bait. 'I bid you good day,' he said gently, took his hat in his hand and went out.

They learned the rest of the news in dribs and drabs over the week. The king had no deep-laid plans, just as John had suspected. King Charles had taken an impulsive leap into freedom at the very moment when he was about to sign the agreement with Cromwell which would have brought peace between king and Parliament and stability to the kingdom riven by civil war.

Cromwell had faced down his own army, the men who had fought for him in the long and bitter war. The men had told their commander and told Parliament that they expected more from the peace than a king restored to his own, they wanted changes. They wanted justice for the common people, and a living wage. They wanted Parliaments which would represent all the working men of the country and not just the gentry. Cromwell had taken the hard line against them, defending the king against his own men. He had shot the leaders for mutiny, he had made the men drop down their pamphlets into the mud, and then he had returned to Hampton Court with the blood of his own soldiers on his hands, to meet with Charles and conclude the other side of the bargain which would bring the king home. Cromwell had defeated the men who would have shouted against a restoration of the king, and then returned to the king for his signature on the document, as they had agreed it.

But Charles had gone. He had given his word, his word of honour as a king, and then slipped away in the night. He rode with two gentlemen to the New Forest where he had hunted so often with Buckingham in the old days, and taken a boat across to the Isle of Wight, putting his faith in the belief that the governor, Robert Hammond, would take his part on the slight evidence that Hammond had once said he disliked the Levellers in the army, because he was a nephew of one of the king's chaplains, and cousin, many times removed, to the Marquess of Winchester.

'He trusted a man because he knows his uncle?' John asked Hester in despair as they sat by the fireside before going to bed.

She shook her head. 'Oh, John. What else could he do but dodge and dive and scrape about?'

'He could come to an agreement!' John exclaimed. 'And have his throne again!'

She picked up the sewing from her lap. 'He is the king,' she said. 'He would not feel that he has to agree. He has always thought that others should agree with him.'

❧

Hester was right. When the king arrived at Carisbrooke Castle and found that Governor Hammond imprisoned him, rather than hailing him as a hero, he gave his parole and immediately set to scheming. He sent secret messages to the Scots and told them that he was ready now to agree to the very things he had sworn he would never accept when he had been their prisoner. The Scots, tempted by the thought of a king who would accept their parliament and their church, secretly betrayed their allies, the English Parliament, and made a secret solemn engagement to restore Charles to his throne. In return he swore that for a trial period of three years he would abolish the position of bishops and run the English church on the Scottish model. He promised that all the senior posts in the land (and their fat fees) would be given to Scotsmen.

But Charles was no better at keeping his secrets than keeping his word. News of the agreement soon leaked out, especially when a proposal from the English Parliament was insultingly rejected by the king who was visibly, excessively, puffed up with confidence. Soon everyone knew that the king was dealing a false hand again.

'He would make an alliance with the Scots Covenanters?' Johnnie asked his father in bewilderment. 'But he refused to agree with them for all those months at Newark.'

'He has changed his mind,' John said quietly. 'He wants to make a new agreement. He wants to beat Parliament and Cromwell's army at any price. He hated the covenanting Scots and could not agree with them, but they are now the only allies he can get. He is agreeing to things he denied completely only a few months ago. He refused them when he was their prisoner but now he has been seized by the English army he is looking kindly on the Scots again.'

Johnnie scowled. 'So what *does* he believe in?' he demanded in exasperation. 'I thought that he would never give up the English church and the bishops. You told me he thought that was sacred. You told me he would never give up his rights as a king.'

'I think now he is looking to survive,' John said grimly. 'And if he can get back on the throne then who can force him to keep to agreements he made when he was in prison?'

'He would play false?'

John softened at the sight of his son's distress. 'A king must be on his throne,' he said gently. 'You can understand that he might think it was worth anything to get back to his place.'

'And will he do it?' Johnnie asked. 'Will he come back to London? Will I see him on his throne?'

John shook his head. 'They'll never let him off the Isle of Wight again,' he said. 'I wouldn't, if I were General Cromwell.'

Spring 1648

John was in his garden, planting out his tender rarities which had wintered in the orangery. The great tufted American daisy was putting out fresh shoots from its rosette of leaves, and the Virginian woodbine was throwing out scarlet snaky shoots with little unfurling green leaves from its dry, dead-looking trunk. John thought for a moment of Suckahanna with the scarlet honeysuckle flowers in her dark hair, and the night-time scent of honeysuckle on their sleeping platform when he kissed her neck and crushed the flowers beneath his cheek. He patted the earth gently around the roots, saw that the climber could extend and find footholds on the strings hammered in to the rough wall and then turned his back on them to admire his tulip beds.

'There is nothing, *nothing* to compare with them,' he remarked to Hester as she came down the path towards him. Then he broke off abruptly at the sight of her face. 'What's wrong?'

He glanced towards the lane as if he feared a troop of horse there. Even with the king imprisoned at Carisbrooke Castle no man could be certain that the nation would stay at peace. There were too many nations that might wish to meddle, there were too many armies that the queen or Prince Charles might prevail upon to muster.

'I don't know,' Hester said, producing a letter from her apron pocket. 'A letter. For you. From the Parliamentary commissioners.'

John scowled and held out his hand. He broke the seal, spread the paper, read it, and then read it again. He chuckled incredulously.

'What is it?' Hester demanded, trying to read upside down.

'I am to go to Oatlands and make good,' John said. 'Who would have thought it? They want me to mend the walks in the vineyard garden and mow the bowling green, and make good.' He paused and looked up at her. 'How times change and yet change not at all,' he observed.

'I am gardener to Oatlands Palace still it seems, though there is no king and no court to see my work.'

'You'll go —' she suggested, looking at him warily.

He folded the letter, very businesslike. 'Of course. Why not?'

'I thought you might have some feeling that you wouldn't garden for them, where you had gardened for the king, and for her.'

John shook his head. Unconsciously he put out a hand and tucked a stray shoot of the Virginian woodbine beneath a guiding piece of twine nailed into the wall. 'I've been torn all my life, Hester. I'm growing quite resigned to divided loyalties.'

'Johnnie'll take it hard,' she said. 'He's held to being one of the king's gardeners through all this time.'

'We're gardeners to the best gardens in the kingdom,' John said firmly. 'And Oatlands has always been one of the best. I'd stay faithful to my garden before I stayed faithful to any master, you know that. Especially a master as faithless and as changeable as the king. The garden comes first, Hester. If someone will pay me to plant it and tend to it I'll go at once and I'll take Johnnie to help me. He has to learn. King or no king, we have to work for our living. And our living is the gardens. Our great duty is to the gardens.'

'But why would Parliament care for the gardens?' Hester mused. 'With so much else to do? And they were the queen's own gardens. Unless they're putting them in order for her return? And there's been some secret agreement?'

John shook his head. 'Could be. Or maybe they're just men of sense. If the king never returns and Parliament owns Oatlands and all the other royal palaces, then they will sell it at a better profit if it is set in a handsome garden and not in a wilderness. But if the king comes back to his own again and finds it overgrown, then he will only make them pay to set it right.'

'Will you be gone long?' she asked.

'A month at least,' he replied. 'I have duties now, Hester. I am gardener to the Parliamentary commissioners! I am a Parliament man!'

She laughed with him. 'But Johnnie may not find it so easy to change masters,' she warned.

'Johnnie will have to learn,' he ruled. 'It is one thing to be a boy and love stories of Prince Rupert. It is another thing to be a man and to know that if you serve a master who changes as often as the weather then you had better not cleave too tight to him. The king is spinning like a weathercock. The rest of us must look to our own lives.'

April 1648, Oatlands Palace

A troop of Parliamentary horse was still quartered at Oatlands and John's first action, after he had opened up his old house next to the silkworm house, was to find the commander and demand that the horses be banned from grazing in any of the courts or on the bowling lawns.

The commander was happy to agree and promised John the use of as many troopers as he needed to help him in the weeding and the setting of the garden to rights.

'I visited your garden ten years ago,' he said. 'It was a wonderful sight. D'you still have that service tree? I remember it so well.'

'Yes,' John said. 'It still grows. And we have many more rare trees that I have brought back from Virginia. I have a tulip tree with great green leaves that flowers with a blossom like a tulip as big as your head. I have a maple tree which has leaves of scarlet. I have a creeper called a passion flower since some say it shows the marks of Jesus. I have a beautiful new convolvulus, I can sell you the seeds for that, and a Virginian foxglove.'

'As soon as I am discharged and in my own home again I shall come and see what you have for sale,' the officer promised.

'Where is your home?' John asked.

'Sussex, in the west of the county,' the man replied. 'I have a light, sandy soil, very fertile and easy to work. A little dry in summer perhaps, and I'm on the edge of the South Downs so I get a cold wind in winter; my Lenten lilies only come at Easter. But my summer flowers last for longer than my neighbours'.'

'You will grow almost anything then,' John said encouragingly. 'Some of my new Virginia plants can tolerate very cold weather and very hot summers since that is the weather of their home. They would do well with you. I have a creeper with leaves that turn as red as a cardinal's

391

cloak in autumn. It would look well against any wall, red as a rose.'

'I should like to see it,' the man said. 'And what will you do here?'

'Just set the place in order again,' John said. 'I was not ordered to do any planting.'

'Is His Majesty to be brought here?' Johnnie asked, driven to interrupting.

The officer heard the hero-worship in the boy's voice and looked hard at him. 'I think we should all pray that he never comes near any of his palaces again,' he said sternly. 'His greed has taken me and all my men away from our homes and our families and our gardens for six long years. He can rot in Carisbrooke Castle forever, for all I care.'

John leaned on his son's shoulder and the boy obediently said nothing, only the scarlet flush up to his ears showed his distress.

'But you were in his service,' the man said irritably. 'I suppose you're all royalists.'

'We're gardeners,' John said steadily. 'And now I am gardening for Parliament. Still gardening. My enemies are inclement weather and pests. I need no other.'

Unwillingly the commander laughed. 'I know no worse, actually,' he said.

Summer 1648

There was a knock on the big front door of the Ark in mid-May and Hester, putting aside her working apron, went to open it with her usual sense of apprehension. But when she saw the visitor on the doorstep her expression turned to pleasure. 'Major Lambert!' she exclaimed. 'Come to see our tulips?'

'Yes indeed. I couldn't resist.' He stepped into the hall and bent over her hand.

'Is it still Major?' she asked, looking at the rich feather in his hat and the shining leather of his boots.

'Ah no!' he said with a flourish. 'I am a general now, Mrs Tradescant. And before I have done I shall sit in Parliament and bestow a baronetcy on you for your services to gardeners. Or a dukedom. Whatever you would wish.'

Hester giggled. 'Come and see the tulips then,' she urged. 'They are lovely this year. My husband came back last spring and he has many new species which you will want to see, some beautiful plants from Virginia. You will never resist our tulip tree.'

'I beg your pardon?'

Hester laughed. 'I promise. A most beautiful tree which bears white flowers shaped exactly like a tulip. I've not seen them yet because we have only two saplings but we have taken cuttings and my husband swears they will thrive.'

John Lambert followed her through the house and paused on the terrace to look out over the garden. It was the first time he had seen it properly weeded and pruned and looking its best.

'This is a little piece of paradise,' he said, his eyes going over the nodding blossoms of the fruit trees and the flowerbeds and nursery beds before the house. 'It was well-named when you called it the Ark. It has been like a flood of terror outside these walls and yet here it always seems to be like peace.'

Hester stood very still and absorbed the compliment like a blessing. 'I have spent my whole life trying to make it so,' she said. 'I am glad you can see it.'

He glanced at her as if they understood each other very well. 'If we can make the country as peaceful and fertile as this garden, Mrs Tradescant, then it will all have been worth while. If I can make every cottage garden a safe place like this, and every hardworking man in the country with a legal right to his cottage and his garden, then I will have done my duty as well as you have done yours.'

She looked curiously at him. 'Aren't those Leveller sentiments?' she asked. 'I thought the Leveller cause was stamped out?'

He smiled but he did not disagree. 'Not out of the hearts and minds. I think that any man who has seen how the poor suffer in this country, and has seen the way that poor men fought for their rights, would want to see the great wastes and parks opened up so that homeless people could build themselves houses, and hungry people could grow food. I'm a landholder myself, Mrs Tradescant. I don't want my garden walls pulled down. But I don't want huge parks enclosed to feed and shelter deer while men and women outside go hungry.'

Hester nodded and led the way down the garden path towards the blaze of colour that was the tulip beds. She glanced back with a half-smile at John Lambert's transfixed expression.

'They're good, aren't they?'

'They are superb,' he breathed. 'I must, I *must* have some of those.'

'I'll fetch a pen and paper for your order,' Hester said with satisfaction. 'And you must come again next month and see the roses. They are going to be wonderful this year. I like our roses even better than our tulips.'

He shook his head, and something in that gesture alerted her that he was not as carefree as he had suggested. 'I'm afraid I will be busy elsewhere in June,' he said.

🔱

Hester understood what John Lambert had meant when the day after his visit the news came of royalist bands mustered in every town and village in every county. Men who had put away their pikes thinking the battle was over were running and riding up and down the country lanes again, calling men to fight for the king, who needed only one battle to be won against a demoralised and divided Parliament and army to come to his own. The navy suddenly declared for the king and sailed into harbours all along the south coast, and declared every port as royalist. All over the country the retired royalist officers were out again, calling men to arms. Each county, each town, each village had its own royalist headquarters and royalist troop. The nation was at war once more, spontaneously, naturally, and the prize was to release the king and restore him to his throne in a great heave of nostalgia for the days of peace before the war.

Men who had stood by and watched Cromwell's army take the victory in the first king's war were now seized with such an impatience for peace that they turned out for Charles, certain that only by restoring him to the throne could the kingdom find peace. Men who had been indifferent soldiers under Cromwell turned their coats and hoped for pay and a victory under the command of the royalists. And those who had fought for the king over the long four years of the king's war and suffered and feared in the two years since, prayed that this one last chance might restore them to their former fortunes.

They were not summoned by a message. They responded almost individually, spontaneously, in an uprising which was as much an irritated demand for a return to more peaceful days, as a struggle of principle about the existence of bishops.

It was incredible to Hester that the king could be the centre of a second catastrophe, even while he was in his prison. Without even being at liberty his mere presence could be the focus of unrest, and the country which had been at peace for nearly two years was suddenly at war again. It was a full-scale war fought in a hundred different pitched battles all over the kingdom, and then news came to Lambeth that Lord Norwich was besieging the City of London itself and was likely to take it for the king. If London fell then Parliament itself would be taken, and then the war must be over and the king would be the victor.

Hester caught Johnnie sneaking a saddle on to the horse in the stable yard, a pack at his side. Her steady temper suddenly broke. 'And where the devil d'you think you're going?'

He turned to her. 'You can't stop me. I'm going to fight for the king.'

'You're a child.'

'I'm nearly fifteen, old enough to fight.'

It was that spark that fired the charge. Hester sprung on him and seized him by his shirt collar and marched him, like a schoolboy, down the garden path, past the glorious rose beds where waves of perfume billowed in their wake, to the orchard where John was up a ladder disbudding apple trees.

'The king needs fools!' Hester exclaimed. 'A fools' army for a fool of a king.'

'I will go!' Johnnie proclaimed, struggling out from her grip. 'I will not be under your command. I'm a man, I shall play a man's part.'

Hester thrust him at his father. 'He's fourteen,' she announced baldly. 'Says he's a man. I can't rule him any more. You will have to decide. Is he to go to serve the king or not?'

John stepped slowly off the lower rungs of the ladder and looked at his son. 'What's this?'

Johnnie did not look away but faced his father like a young stag facing the leader of the herd. 'I want to do my duty,' he said. 'I want to serve the king.'

'The king is not served by riots and uproar and Englishmen killing each other in the streets of Maidstone and Canterbury,' John said slowly.

'If that is what it takes –'

John shook his head. 'Making peace in a kingdom is done by ceaseless work, ceaseless working towards agreement,' he said. 'Haven't you lived your childhood through a war and seen that at the end there is nothing agreed, nothing is any further forward?'

'I want to do my duty!'

John put his hand on the bough of the apple tree as if he would draw strength from it. 'Your duty is to your God and to your father and mother,' he said.

'You don't even believe in God,' Johnnie shot back. 'You don't believe in anything. You have not done your duty by me as a father – you left us for years. You're the king's man but you don't fight for him, you're in the pay of Parliament and you joke about being a Parliament gardener. You're a Virginia planter but you stay at home in Lambeth. I won't be told my duty by you!'

Hester started forwards to protect her stepson against the blow that must come, and then forced herself to pause, and hold back. John did not strike Johnnie but froze, his hand tightened on the bough of the apple tree until the knuckles went pale.

'I am sorry you think so low of me,' John said quietly. 'And what you say is true. I lost my faith in God when your mother died and I could not even hold her for fear of spreading the infection to you. I have tried to show my respect to others' faith. But the heart went out of me. I did leave you and Frances and your stepmother at a time when I should have stayed and protected you – but I thought the king would draw me into fighting and never let me go. And I was right to fear that – he has drawn the whole four kingdoms of men into fighting and he has never let them go. I have my headright in Virginia but I could not keep it without killing people that I have every reason to love and respect. It was a war between countrymen there too.'

Johnnie was about to speak, Hester knowing him so well, knew that he was fighting not to break down in tears and pitch into his father's arms. He held himself very still, rigid as a soldier under fire.

'But I do have a right to speak,' John said. 'Because I know things that you don't. Because I have thought of things in all this time. I have struggled with one loyalty against another, with one love against another. You might think that I am weak – but this is how my life has come to me. It is not a simple life of simple loyalties. I am not like my father. He found master after master that he could love and follow with a loyal heart. He loved Sir Robert Cecil, and then the Duke of Buckingham, and then the king. He never questioned that they were the master and he the man. But it's not been like that for me. And it won't be like that for you. The world has changed, Johnnie. It's not enough to cite duty any more and go marching off to the rattle of a recruiting drum. You have to think for yourself, you have to pick your own path.'

There was a long silence in the orchard. Somewhere in the high leaves of one of the trees a blackbird started to sing.

'I beg your pardon for speaking as I did,' Johnnie said stiffly. 'And I ask your permission as your dutiful son. I want to go and serve the king. That's my path. I have considered it for myself. I want to fight for my king.'

John shot a look at Hester as if to ask if she could see a way out. One look was enough. Hester's face was tragic, both hands gripped under the shield of her apron.

'God bless you and keep you then,' John said slowly. 'And come back home the minute you have a doubt, Johnnie. You are the only Tradescant heir, and very dear to us.'

Slowly Johnnie dropped to one knee on the grass for his father's blessing. Over his bent fair head John looked at Hester and saw that he had said the right thing – they had to let their son go to war.

❦

Dearest Mother and Father,
    I write this to you on the road to Colchester. I am riding with Lord Norwich and half a dozen gentlemen and a fine

troop of more than a thousand strong. We were rebuffed at London – I got there as they were leaving, unluckily for me – but at least I am in a troop of horse gathering recruits as we go.

The mare is keeping up well and I am sure to feed her every night. We have to forage for our own feed which is hard to do in some of these farms that were poor enough before we arrived and are left worse. Some of the gentlemen use the farmers and labourers very hard, and this does not increase our welcome further down the road.

The ships will supply us when we are in Colchester and an army is coming to our aid from out of East Anglia. There is no doubt that we will win.

My love to Frances and her husband. You can ask Alexander to delay his supply of barrels of gunpowder as a favour to me. I hope you are all well. Your loving and dutiful son – John.

'He signs himself John, not Johnnie,' Hester observed.

'He sounds well,' John answered.

They stood, cheek to cheek in the hall, both of them reading the short letter, and then reading it again.

'She's a good horse, she'll keep him safe,' John said.

'He doesn't sound very happy with the troop.'

John relinquished the letter into her hands and turned towards the garden. 'How could he be? A boy who has seen so little of the world, suddenly ridden off to war?'

'Should you fetch him home?' Hester asked.

John paused, hearing the longing in her voice. 'I cannot,' he said.

She would have argued but he raised his hand to check her. 'Don't reproach me, Hester, it means as much to me as it does to you to see my son enmeshed in this war. I have prayed just as hard as you that we would be at peace before he reached his manhood. I thought it was over. I was sure it was over. But I can't fetch him home like a naughty schoolboy. He has to walk his own path.'

He looked at her and saw the blank agony on her face.

'He is my son!' she said passionately. 'Joking about gunpowder.'

John paused, bleak with worry, nodded, and went out to his garden.

July 1648

Frances was at the Ark for the plague months of the summer and Hester found that her stepdaughter's company was the only one she could bear, as they waited for news of Johnnie. The war was favouring the king and she could hope that Johnnie would march into London as part of a triumphant royal army. In July the Scots confirmed in the most dramatic way that they had changed sides and were now for the king, when they crossed the border with an army of nine thousand men to fling against the battle-weary, underpaid, disillusioned forces of Parliament.

It was an appallingly wet summer. The roses in the garden filled with rain and rotted in their blooms. The strawberries and raspberries were washed into sodden pulp on their stems. Hester spent the days watching the rain pour down the great panes of Venetian glass in the rarities room, looking out at the flooded garden, at her husband splashing around ankle-deep in mud, digging ditches to drain the sodden land into the stream outside the house which was already bubbling over the little bridge and still rising.

Uncharacteristically, Hester did not throw a piece of sacking over her cap and go out to help him. She sat at the desk without books before her, without sewing in her hands. She did not even talk to the few visitors who came to see the rarities, though with the river in flood and the country at war again, they might as well have shut the Ark for all the money they took. Hester sat in silence, watching the rain, Frances in silence at her side.

The news came that the English royalist troops had come under attack on the road to Colchester and had had to rush into the town for shelter. There was a brief and terrible battle as the royalists were driven back into the town, before they got the town gates shut and the Parliamentary soldiers locked out. Hundreds of men were killed in close fighting which was bloodier and more bitter than any known in England before. The names of the hundreds of individual soldiers killed in that spiteful skirmish were lost. Hester sat watching the rain, not knowing if her stepson was alive, or face down in the mud outside the gates of Colchester.

It was not a siege, it was a massacre-in-waiting. General Fairfax with John Lambert was commanding the Parliament army and he had ringed the city with a rampart and ditch with ten forts studding the perimeter. No-one would be able to get out alive. The whole city was not just besieged, it was completely entrapped.

'John Lambert is there?' Hester asked when Frances brought a newssheet and read the report of the siege.

'Yes,' Frances said, and looked at her mother.

'What times these are: that John Lambert should be in one army and my boy in another,' Hester said very softly.

There was another royalist army raised at Kingston upon Thames, commanded by Lord Holland, supported by the Duke of Buckingham, the son of the Tradescants' old master. John had scowled at the mention of his name and stamped out to lay sandbags at the front door of the Ark. The road to Lambeth was completely under water and the little stream before the house had burst its banks and was spreading over the road and into the Tradescants' orchard. John was fearful that the River Thames itself would flood and bring salt water to contaminate his land on the north side of the road but there was nothing he could do to prevent it.

The new royalist army mustered only a few men. Little more than five hundred turned out in the wet and marched first to London and then to Reigate Castle, and then turned in a retreat which quickly became a rout through the villages north of London to defeat at Surbiton. The Earl of Holland was captured by the Parliamentary army and sent to London. Parliament decreed that he would be beheaded for treason to his country. The Duke of Buckingham slipped away to safety in Holland.

'He would,' Tradescant said sourly.

Suddenly, royal fever seemed to have passed as abruptly as it had raged. There was no further uprising in England. It would all depend on the Scots: whether they could get to Colchester in time to relieve the town, whether they would march all the way south and into the very city of London itself.

The royalists besieged in Colchester, their rations running low and any hope for relief now gone, asked for safe passage for women and children, opened the sally port door and sent them out to the Parliamentary army. To their horror the women were stripped and beaten, and sent back to the fort. England had never seen such savagery in fighting. The rules of warfare had been suspended. Men who would have been chivalrous to a defeated enemy six years ago were now in a killing frenzy of rage that war should have broken out again. There were rumours that when the besieged came out of Colchester, as soon they must, they would be cut down where they stood. There would be no quarter, there would be no prisoners. There would not even be trials for treason. When the men lay down their arms the Parliament cavalry would ride over them.

Hester said nothing when John told her this news, she did not weep, she did not whisper Johnnie's name. She looked out of the window and said only: 'When is it ever going to stop raining?'

John went out into the garden and left her watching the drops run down the panes.

They were glad of the rain in Colchester. It was their only drinking water. For meat they had to eat their horses, then dogs, cats, rats, anything they could catch. There was no flour for bread, there were no fruit or vegetables left in the town. Men started to sicken, everyone went hungry.

Hester put a piece of sacking around her shoulders and splashed out into the garden to look at the rain-soaked lettuce, onions, peppers, beans, peas and herbs in their carefully tended beds. 'He's never gone hungry,' she said softly to herself. 'Brought up beside our garden he might have lacked meat once in a while, but he's always had fruit and vegetables. He's never wanted for anything before.'

Hester was hoping that the Scots would march south quickly and relieve Colchester as their first objective. They swept over the border looking like a conquering force and reached Preston Moor, just a mile north of Preston, without anyone standing against them. But there they were met by the Parliament army commanded by Cromwell himself with John Lambert at his side, commanding the cavalry. When Hester heard that it was John Lambert against the only men who could rescue her son, she put her head in her hands at the kitchen table and stayed very still for a long while, as if she were asleep.

When the news reached Colchester of the Scots' defeat there was no hope left for them. The garrison surrendered to a harsh and unforgiving victor. The war was over, the king defeated once more; and the Tradescants had nothing to do but to wait and see if Johnnie would come home, or if he would be among the many hundreds who would never come home again.

Hester left her place at the Venetian window and put a chair and a table at the front door, which overlooked the road from Lambeth. She put her sewing basket on the table and appeared, to any casual passer-by, as if she were sitting at her work and enjoying the September sunshine after the wet summer days. Only John and Frances knew that the shirt she held in her lap was no further forward by the end of September than it had been on the black day that Colchester surrendered.

Autumn 1648

A carter brought him home, a man who had visited the Ark in his boyhood and remembered it as a palace of treasures, and had a fondness for the Tradescant name. Johnnie, pale, jolted by the rough roads, terribly thin, and with a dark, ill-healing scar from his hipbone to his rib, lay in the back on a heap of sacks.

Hester heard the rumble of the wheels and glanced up from her idle hands holding the unsewn shirt and then dropped her work, overturned her chair and flew out of the front door and into the road.

'Johnnie!' she exclaimed as she peered over the tailboard.

He managed a little smile. 'Mother.'

'Drive around to the back,' Hester ordered the driver, her months of passive silence quite forgotten. She jumped up on to the step of the cart, her eyes fixed on her stepson, and held on as they jolted over the little bridge, went past the terrace of the house and into the stable yard. John, picking apples, looked towards the house and saw the cart turning into the yard with his wife clinging like an urchin to the tailgate. He leaped down from the ladder and walked towards the house. He did not run. He feared too much what might greet him.

The carter and Hester had Johnnie on his feet, walking slowly towards the kitchen door, an arm around each of them. Cook flung open the door and Hester guided them through to the parlour and seated Johnnie in his father's chair at the fireside.

He had gone very white, his lips pale in his pale face. Hester snapped over her shoulder, 'Fetch the brandy,' and Cook ran to obey her. John came in, treading mud on to the polished wooden parlour floor.

'Son?'

Johnnie looked up at his father and something in that glance, something vulnerable and unjustly hurt, reminded John so powerfully of

Jane, his lost wife, that his pity for his son and his old grief for her hit him like a renewed blow. He dropped to his knees and took his son's hands.

'You're safe now,' he said. 'Safe home. Are you hurt much?'

'I got a pike in my side,' Johnnie whispered. 'It hurt a lot and bled a lot. But it's healing now.'

Hester held the glass of brandy to his lips and Johnnie sipped.

'We'll have you in bed in a moment,' she promised him. 'And a proper dinner for you.' She smoothed his long fair hair from his forehead. 'My boy,' she said tenderly. 'My poor boy.'

Cook returned. 'His bed is ready for him, sheets warmed.'

The carter and Hester stepped forwards to help him but John put them back. 'I can manage,' he said huskily, and took his son in his arms.

The boy weighed little more than he did when he was only ten years old. Tradescant scowled at the lightness of the body and went towards the stairs. Hester ran ahead and opened the bedroom door, turned down the sheets.

'I'm lousy,' Johnnie protested. 'And covered with fleas.'

'Doesn't matter,' Hester said, slipping off his boots and stripping down his breeches.

He gave a little whimper of pain as she pulled up his shirt and she saw that the dirty linen had stuck to the raw wound.

'We'll soon have you well again,' she said.

Both her husband and her son heard the old determination in Hester's voice. 'We'll soon have you well again.'

❦

King Charles blithely celebrated his forty-eighth birthday at Newport and entertained the Parliamentary negotiators who had been sent from London to make a new peace with a king who had broken every agreement they had made before. This time he was more accommodating than ever; but would not, swore that he could not, allow the sale of the bishops' lands and palaces. The bishops could not be abolished, their position must be maintained. The most he would agree was to rule without them for three years, the promise he had already given to the Scots. But Parliament was firmer than the Scots. It would settle for nothing less than the complete abolition of all the bishops and the freeing of their wealth and lands.

Alexander Norman and Frances, visiting the Ark in November, found

Johnnie sitting at the fireside wrapped in a fine warm gown with his father and mother beside him, discussing the fate of the king.

'Any news?' John asked his son-in-law.

'The Levellers are rising in strength in the army,' Alexander replied. 'And they demand that there be no king ever again and that Parliament be elected every three years by every man with a stake in the country.'

'What does that mean for the king?' John asked.

Alexander shook his head. 'If they gain control of Parliament then it must mean that he is sent abroad. There can be no place for him.'

'Perhaps he will agree,' Hester suggested, one eye on her son. 'Perhaps the king and Parliament can agree at Newport.'

'He must agree,' Alexander replied. 'He must see that he has to agree. He has fought two wars against his own people, and lost them both. He tried the greatest gamble he could play – he brought the Scots in against his own countrymen. And he has lost. He must now agree.'

Johnnie flushed and moved uneasily in his chair. 'How can he? How can he agree to become nothing? He's the king in the sight of God. Does he call God a liar?'

Frances crossed to him and took his hand. 'Now you stop,' she said with the firmness of an older sister. 'You've done your fighting for him. You've done quite enough, and it did no good for anybody. The king must take his own decision, it's nothing to do with you now, or any of us.'

'She's right,' Hester said. 'And none of us can do anything for or against the king. He has travelled his own road. He will have to decide what he should do now.'

The king decided to take the high road of principle – or perhaps he decided he would gamble once again – or perhaps he decided he would make a gesture, a proud theatrical gesture, and see what came of it. He rejected Parliament's proposals boldly, recklessly, outright. And then he waited to see what would happen next.

What happened next rather surprised him. The men of Cromwell's army, Lambert's men, Fairfax's men, furious at the delays and missed opportunities, clear in their own minds that what should happen next was an unbreakable peace and a reform of the laws of the land in favour of hard-working common people, invaded the House of Commons, excluded those Members of Parliament known to be sympathetic to the king, and insisted that the king should be brought to trial for treason against his subjects.

Hester brought the news to John as he was watering the tender plants in the orangery. The frost on the window pane was melting and the glass was dewy and opaque. The citrus trees, their boughs carrying the last glowing fruit of oranges and lemon, scented the room, the charcoal in the hearth shifted and crackled as it glowed. Hester paused on the threshold, reluctant to break the sense of peace. Then she set her lips and marched into the room.

'They have taken the king from the Isle of Wight and are bringing him to London. They have called him for trial,' she said flatly. 'They have accused him of treason.'

John froze where he stood, the watering bottle dribbling cold water on his boot. 'Treason?' he repeated. 'How can a king be charged with treason?'

'They say he tried to steal away the people's liberty and to set up a tyranny,' Hester said. 'And to make war on his people is supposed to be treason.'

The water made a little puddle around John's feet but he did not notice it, and neither did Hester, her gaze fixed on his stunned face.

'Where is he?' John asked numbly.

'On the road to London, that's what they're saying in Lambeth. I suppose they'll put him in the Tower, or perhaps under arrest in one of the palaces.'

'And then?'

'They say that he is to be tried for treason. Before a court. A proper trial.'

'But the punishment for treason . . .'

'Is death,' Hester finished.

Just before Christmas there was a knock at the door. Johnnie, still nervous, started at the loud sound and Hester, hurrying to open it, whispered a blasphemy at whoever had disturbed her boy.

As she opened the door she composed her face into stern serenity at the sight of the armed man.

'Message for John Tradescant, as was gardener to the king,' the man said.

'Not here,' Hester said with her habitual caution.

'I'll leave the message with you then,' the man said cheerfully. 'The king wants to see him. At Windsor.'

'He is summoned to Windsor by the king?' Hester asked, disbelievingly.

'As he likes,' the man said disrespectfully. 'The king orders him there, he can go or no as he likes as far as I'm concerned. I take my orders from Colonel Harrison, who guards the king. And his orders were to tell Mr Tradescant that the king is asking for him. And now I've done that. And now I'm off.'

He gave her a friendly nod and crossed the little bridge to the road before Hester could say another word. She watched him march up the road to the ferry at Lambeth before she closed the door and went to find John in the garden.

He was pruning the roses with a sharp knife, his hands a mass of scratches from his work.

'Why won't you wear gloves?' Hester remarked irritably.

He grinned. 'I always mean to, then I start work and I think I can do it without scratching myself, and then I can't be troubled to stop and go and find them, and then I draw blood and think there's no point in fetching them now.'

'You'll never guess who came to the door.'

'All right. I never will.'

'A messenger from the king,' she said, watching for his reaction.

He stiffened, like an old hunter when it hears the hunting horn. 'The king sent for me?'

She nodded. 'To attend him at Windsor. The man was clear that you need not go unless you wish. The king has no power to order you to obey. But he brought the message.'

John stepped carefully through the rose bushes, disentangling his coat when it was caught by a thorn, his mind already at Windsor.

'What can he want of me?'

She shrugged. 'Not some harebrained scheme of escape?'

He shook his head. 'Surely not. But there's nothing to interest him in the garden at this time of year.'

'Will you go?'

Already he was walking towards the house, his pruning knife slipped in his belt, his roses almost forgotten. 'Of course I have to go,' he said.

They had no horse, there was not enough money to replace the mare who had carried Johnnie to Colchester and been slaughtered for meat during the siege. John walked to the ferry at Lambeth and took a boat upriver to Windsor.

The castle looked much the same: a guard of soldiers at the door, the usual bustle and work which surrounded the royal court. But it was all strangely diminished: quieter, with less excitement, as if even the kitchen maids no longer believed that they were cooking the meat of God's own anointed representative on earth, but instead working in a kitchen for a mere mortal.

John paused before the crossed pikes of the men on guard.

'John Tradescant,' he said. 'The king sent for me.'

The pikes were lifted. 'He's at his dinner,' one of the soldiers said.

John went through the gateway, through the inner court, and into the great hall.

There was an eerie sense of a life lived again. There was the royal canopy billowing a little in the draughts from the open windows. There was the king seated in state below it, the great chair before the great table, and the table crowded with dishes. There were the common people, crammed into the gallery, watching the king eat as they always did. There was the yeoman usher to declare the table ready for laying, the yeoman of ewry to spread the cloth, the yeoman of pantry to lay out the long knives, spoons, salt, and trenchers, the yeoman of cellar standing behind the chair with the decanter of wine. It was all as it had been, and yet it was completely different.

There was no constant ripple of laughter and wit, there was no vying for the eye of the king. There was no plump, ringletted queen at his side, and none of the glorious portraits and tapestries which had always been hung in his sight.

And Charles himself was changed. His face was scarred with disappointment, deep bags beneath his dark eyes, lines on his forehead, his hair thinner and streaked with grey, his moustache and beard still perfectly combed, but paler with white hairs where it had been glossy brown.

He looked down the hall and saw John; but his habitual diffidence did not allow him to greet a friendly face. He merely nodded and with a tiny gesture indicated that John should wait.

John, who had dropped to his knee as he came into the hall, rose up and took a seat at a table.

'What you kneeling for?' a man asked critically.

John hesitated. 'Habit, I suppose. Do you not kneel in his presence?'

408

'Why should I? He's no more than a man, as I am.'

'Times are changing,' John observed.

'You eating?' another man said.

John looked around. These were not the elegant courtiers who used to dine in the hall. These were the soldiers of Cromwell's army, unimpressed by the ritual. Hungry, honest, straightforward men at their dinner.

John drew a trencher towards him and took a spoonful of meat from the common bowl.

When the king had finished dining one yeoman came forward and offered him a bowl to wash his fingertips while another offered the fine linen cloth to dry his hands. Neither of them kneeled, John noticed, and wondered if the king would refuse their service.

He did not even complain. The king took the service as it would have been offered to a mere lord of the manor. He did not even remark that they were not on their knees. John saw the mystery of kingship shrink before his eyes.

John rose at his place, waiting for an order. The king crooked his finger and John approached the high table, paused and bowed.

King Charles rose from his seat, stepped down from the dais and snapped his fingers for a pageboy, who sprang to follow him.

'I d . . . dined on melons two nights ago,' he remarked to John as if no time at all had passed since John and the queen and the king had planned the planting of Oatlands together. 'And I th . . . th . . . thought that we always said we should have a m . . . melon bed at Wimbledon. I saved you the seeds for p . . . planting.'

John bowed, his mind whirling. 'Your Majesty?'

The pageboy stepped forwards and handed John a little wooden box filled with seeds.

'W . . . Will they grow at Wimbledon?' the king asked as he walked past John to his inner chamber.

'I should think so, Your Majesty,' John said. He waited for more.

'Good,' said the king. 'Her M . . . Majesty will like that, when she s . . . sees it. When she comes h . . . h . . . home again.'

'And then he was gone,' John said to an astounded Hester and Johnnie, sitting at the fireside after a long, cold boat trip back to Lambeth.

'He summoned you all that way to give you melon seeds?' Hester demanded.

'I thought it might be some secret,' John confessed. 'I searched the box, and I waited all day in case he should send a secret message for me, once he knew I was in the castle. I weeded the flowerbed beneath the window of his privy apartments so that he would know I was there. But ... nothing. It was truly just for the melon seeds.'

'He is to stand trial for treason, and he is thinking about planting melons?' Hester wondered.

John nodded. 'That is the king indeed,' he said.

'Where will you plant them?' Johnnie asked.

John looked at the taut face of his son, at the shadows under his eyes and the continual frown of pain.

'Would you like to help me?' he offered gently. 'We could make a proper melon bed at Wimbledon. My father taught me the way, and he was taught by Lord Wootton at Canterbury. We were there when I was a boy. Would you like me to teach you how to do it, Johnnie? When the spring comes and you're strong again?'

'Yes,' Johnnie said. 'I'd like to plant them for the king.' He paused for a moment. 'Will he see them grow, d'you think?'

January 1649

John packed a bag. Hester, watching him from the doorway, knew that she was powerless to stop him.

'I have to be there,' he said. 'I can't sit at home while he is on trial for his life. I have to see him. I can't stand not to know what is going on.'

'Alexander could send you a message every day, tell you what has taken place,' Hester suggested.

'I have to be there,' John repeated. 'This was my father's master, and my own. I was there at the start of this. I have to see the end.'

'Who knows when the trial will be?' she asked. 'They should have started this month and yet the date is put back and put back. Perhaps they don't mean to try him at all, but just to frighten him into agreeing.'

'I have to be there,' John insisted. 'If there is to be no trial, then I have to see that there is no trial. I'll wait until it happens – if it happens.'

She nodded, resigned. 'Send word to us then,' she said. 'Johnnie is sick with anxiety.'

John swung his cloak over his shoulder and picked up his bag. 'He's young, he'll mend.'

'He still thinks they should have held out longer at Colchester, or fought their way out,' she said. 'When I think what this war has done to Johnnie, I wish the king was charged with treason. He has broken hearts up and down this country. He has turned against his people.'

'Johnnie will recover,' John said. 'You don't break your heart at fifteen.'

'No,' she said. 'But when he should have been at school or playing in the fields the country was at war and I had to keep him home. When you should have been home to teach and guide him you were away because you knew the king would keep you in his service, wherever that service might lead. Then, when he should have been apprenticed to you and making beautiful gardens or travelling and collecting plants, he was under siege in Colchester for a battle which could neither be won nor lost. Johnnie has never had a chance to be free of the king and the king's wars.'

'Maybe we'll all be free of him at the end of this,' John said grimly.

John could not find a room in an inn near Westminster for love nor money. He could not find a bed. He could not find a share of a bed. They were renting out stables and hayracks as sleeping accommodation for the hundreds and thousands of people who were flocking to see the king on trial.

If there had been half the sympathy that the king so confidently expected, there would have been a riot, or at the least intimidation of the commissioners. But there was no sense of outrage among the men and women who were packing into the City like herrings in a barrel. There was a sense of being spectators at the most remarkable event, of being safely in ringside seats to watch a cataclysm. They were birds above an earthquake, they were fish in a flood. The worst thing that could happen to a kingdom was happening now; and they were able to watch it.

Once the crowd got a taste of history, there was no chance that they would resist it. They had come to see the most extraordinary event in an extraordinary decade, and they wanted to go home having seen it. A reversal in favour of the king that resulted in his agreement with Parliament and resting safe in his bed would have left the crowd, even the royalists among them, with a sense of having been cheated. They had come to see the king on trial. Most of them would even acknowledge that they had come to see the king beheaded. Anything less would have been a disappointment.

John walked downriver to the Tower and knocked on Frances's door, admiring the Christmas rose she had planted at one side.

'One of mine?' he asked her as she opened the door.

She hugged him as she answered. 'Of course. Did you not know you had been robbed?'

'I've not been much in the garden,' he said. It was a statement of his deep distress which she read at once.

'The king?'

'I've come to see his trial.'

'You had much better not go,' she said frankly, drawing him into the little hall and then into the parlour where a small fire of coal was burning.

'I have to,' John said shortly.

'Will you stay here tonight?'

He nodded. 'If I may. There are no beds to be had in the City and I don't want to go home.'

'Alexander is going, but I didn't want to see it. I remember when the king came to the Ark that day, and I saw him, and the queen. They were both so young then, and so rich. They were wrapped in silk and ermine.'

John smiled, thinking of the little girl who had sat on the wall until her fingertips were blue with cold. 'You wanted him to appoint you as the next Tradescant gardener.'

She leaned forwards and stirred the coals so they flamed up. 'It's unbelievable that everything should be so changed. I don't expect to be a gardener; but it is impossible to think that there may be no king.'

'You could be a gardener now,' John offered. 'In these strange days anything is possible, I suppose. There are women preaching, aren't there? And there were women fighting. There were hundreds of women who had their husbands' and their fathers' business in their charge while the men were off to war, and many still working because the men won't be coming home again.'

Frances nodded, her face grave. 'I thank God that Alexander's work was here, and that Johnnie was too young for all but the very end.'

'Amen to that,' John said softly.

'Is Johnnie taking it hard?'

'He's bound to,' John said. 'I wouldn't let him come to see the end of it. But I had to see it for myself.'

'Well then,' she said more cheerfully. 'I shall send to the bake-house for a special dinner for you. And you will need to rise early tomorrow if you are to find a place inside the courtroom.'

Saturday 20 January 1649

Alexander and John went together to Westminster. The trial was to be held in Westminster Hall, open to the public, who were to be herded into pens in the body of the hall to prevent either an attack on the judges or a rescue of the king. Only the wealthy spectators were seated in the galleries running around the sides of the hall. John and Alexander chose to crowd on to the floor.

'Like being in the pit at the theatre,' Alexander complained as they were jostled and pushed.

The galleries started to fill at midday, and then there was a furious scrum in the hall when latecomers tried to push to the front. Tradescant and Alexander battled to keep their places and the pushing was about to generate into an out-and-out fight when the doors opened and the judges entered.

The sword and the mace were brought in first, then the Lord President Bradshaw took his place, a commissioner for advice on the law on either side of him. His big black hat was crammed over his ears. Alexander Norman nudged John.

'He had it lined with iron plates,' he whispered. 'That hat. He is afraid that some royalist will shoot him where he sits.'

John snorted with laughter and glanced across to where Cromwell entered, bare-headed, his face grim. 'You have to admire the man,' he said. 'If anyone was going to be shot it would be him.'

The charge was read, Bradshaw nodded for the prisoner to be brought before the court. John felt the heat and the press of the crowd.

'Are you well?' Alexander asked. 'You've gone white.'

John nodded, his eyes never leaving the south door.

The soldiers came in and pushed back the crowd to make a passageway to the red velvet chair placed before the judges. Then the king came in.

414

He was dressed all in the richest black – black waistcoat, breeches, and cloak, on his shoulder was the dazzling silver star of the Order of the Garter. He did not look at the crowd, he barely glanced at his judges. He walked through the crowd, his head high, dramatically regal, his jewelled heels tapping on the floorboards, his cane held in his hand. He took his seat in the red velvet chair with his back to the audience and his hat firmly on his head, as if he were about to watch a play at Oatlands Palace.

John breathed out and realised that his soft susuration was part of a sigh, almost a moan, from the crowd, as the king took his place, before the men who could condemn him to death.

Bradshaw squashed his armoured hat firmly down on his head, took up the paper and read the charge naming the king as the accused. John Cook, the barrister leading the prosecution, rose to his feet to read the accusations.

'Hold a little,' the king said quietly.

'My Lord, on behalf of the Commons of England and all the people thereof I do accuse Charles Stuart here present of high treason and high misdemeanours –'

The king lifted his cane and tapped John Cook on his arm.

John, hidden in the crowd, said softly: 'Oh no.'

Cook ignored the king completely and continued to read the charge, raising his voice as if to overcome the distraction of the tapping cane and his own sense of bewilderment that an accused man should behave in such a way.

The king reached forward and struck the wing of Cook's gown a vigorous thwack with his cane. There was a gasp from the crowd. Cook abruptly stopped reading. The silver head of the cane fell off and noisily rolled along the uncarpeted boards before coming to rest a few feet from the king's chair. Charles looked around for a servant to pick it up for him. Not a man moved. It took him a long moment to realise that no-one was going to do it; then he shrugged, as if he was indifferent to the slight, and bent and picked it up himself.

John felt his shoulders hunching as if he were ashamed.

Bradshaw, the president of the court, took command of the situation. 'Sir, the court commands the charge be read; if you have anything to say afterwards you may be heard.'

John knew that the king would take any restriction on his speech as an insult. Once, it would have been treason. Surprisingly, the king was silent and Cook started to read the charges from the roll.

After all the rumours and accusations it was odd to hear the charges put so simply. John found he was straining to listen to every word, one hand over his eyes, trying to concentrate. The king was accused of trying to overthrow the rights and liberties of the people by making himself a tyrant. They accused him of making war against his own people and listed the battles where he had been personally in command. Then they accused him of plotting against the kingdom with foreign powers. There was nothing of interest, it was all a matter of fact. The king had undoubtedly done all these things.

The king turned in his chair, as if the long reading of his crimes was not of much interest to him, and looked up at the galleries at the many faces he knew, and out at the body of the court. John raised his head; the king's gaze flicked over him with its usual indifference. John had to fight a desire to call out – and knew also that he had no words to call out.

Cook's accusation went on to what seemed, to most, the worst crime of all – the renewing of the war after the king's defeat. There was a soft groan at that point, many men and women had thought the battles were finished and a peace in the making last year. None of them would forgive Charles for his final throw of the dice which had cost so many more lives and had taught the fighting men a new savagery.

'My God,' whispered Alexander. 'They want to kill him. They are impeaching him for treason.'

John nodded. As soon as he had seen the king dressed as a martyr in black with that dazzling burst of diamonds on his shoulder he had known that this was the greatest masque Charles had ever played. This was no light-hearted interlude, it was full tragedy, and both the king and the court would play it to the full.

'For these reasons,' Cook concluded, 'on behalf of the people of England, I impeach the said Charles Stuart as a tyrant, traitor and murderer, and a public and implacable enemy to the Commonwealth of England.'

There was a dead silence in the court as the people absorbed the accusation and understood that Cromwell and his court were demanding the ultimate punishment: the beheading of the king. The silence was broken by a peal of completely convincing laughter. The king was shaking in his chair, laughing as if at some delightful, ridiculous jest. He threw back his head and shook his curls. The laughter went on, horribly on, prolonged beyond any real amusement, the hard noise of a man defying his own fear.

'Sir,' Bradshaw said steadily. 'You have now heard your charge and the court expects your answer.'

The whole body of people in the court leaned forwards. The fans of ladies in the galleries were frozen still. Everyone listened to hear what the king would say.

'I would know by what power I am called hither?' he asked. 'I would know by what authority – I mean *lawful*?'

The rest of his answer was drowned by an upsurge of voices. 'He's going to challenge them every step of the way,' Alexander shouted over the noise to John.

'God no! If he would just agree, if he would just ask for mercy . . .'

The king was still speaking but he could not be heard above the shouting.

Bradshaw hammered for order and replied to the king. John saw the king shake his head and speak again.

Bradshaw made a gesture: the king should be taken from the court. As he rose to leave the soldiers in the court suddenly shouted 'Justice! Justice!' and John saw the king start back for a moment, and knew that he feared a brawl and death in a struggle more than anything else.

'He wants the scaffold,' John said, suddenly seeing it all. 'So that he can hand the crown entire to Prince Charles. So he can die as a man who was martyred for his beliefs. He's not staking for his own life now, but the condition of kingship itself.'

Charles paused before the table of judges. 'You have shown no lawful authority to satisfy any reasonable man,' he said sternly to Bradshaw.

'We are satisfied.'

'I don't fear *that*,' the king said derisively.

He turned and gave a little half-smile to the people in the courtroom, as a player will do when he has had the best of a scene.

'God save the king!' someone shouted, and then others took it up: 'God save the king!'

The king smiled as he heard the shout and went quietly with his armed escort through the door to the warren of corridors of Westminster. The crowd started to file out into the cold January day. John and Alexander paused outside, a few flakes of snow drifted from the roofs and from the grey sky.

'I'll go home,' John decided. 'There will be nothing until Monday now.'

'I shall come again on Monday,' Alexander agreed. 'If I had not seen it I wouldn't have believed it.'

John shook his head. 'I still don't,' he said.

Hester and Johnnie fell on John the moment he was through the front door. 'What's the news?'

'Nothing yet,' he said. 'They opened the hearing but the king will not recognise the court and they did nothing more than read the charge to him.'

'Will not recognise the court?' Hester asked. 'What can he be hoping to do?'

John tossed his cloak on to the chest at the foot of the stairs. 'God knows. I am frozen through, this is bitter weather to be doing such bitter business.'

'I'll get some hot ale,' Hester said. 'Come to the kitchen with me, I must have the news.'

John followed his wife, Johnnie dogging his footsteps.

'How did he look?' Johnnie asked quietly, as John sat himself on the bench before the scrubbed table and Hester produced mulled ale and hot soup, and a trencher of bread and cheese.

'He looked well,' John said consideringly. 'He had dressed for the part. He was in black but the George was ablaze on his shoulder. He carried his cane – and he tapped at the prosecutor with it –'

'He struck him?' Hester asked.

'Not a hard blow; but it was an awkward moment,' John confessed.

Johnnie's eyes were huge in his pale face. 'Did no-one shout for him?'

'A woman cried from the gallery, and there were a few that shouted "God Save the king", but the soldiers drowned them out with shouting for justice,' John said.

'I wish I could go,' Johnnie said fervently. 'I would shout for him.'

'That's why you won't go,' John said firmly. 'And I keep my head down and my thoughts to myself. They were seeking witnesses to the raising of the royal standard.'

'Did anyone recognise you?' Hester demanded.

John shook his head. 'I am as quiet as a well-fed mouse,' he said. 'I have no wish to be summoned as a witness to either cause. I have no wish but to see the end of this.'

'He's the king!' Johnnie burst out passionately.

'Aye,' John replied. 'And if he would consent to be a little less then he still might get clear of this. He could withdraw and offer them his son in his place. Or he could offer to rule by their assent, not his own. But he will be the king. He would rather be a dead king than a live sensible man.'

'Who were the commissioners?' Hester asked. 'Anyone we know?'

'A few familiar faces,' John said. 'But only half of them named and called have had the courage to sit in judgement on their king. There are a lot of men with pressing business elsewhere.'

'John Lambert?' she asked, deliberately casual.

'With the army in the north,' he replied. 'But his name is down as a commissioner. Why d'you ask?'

'I should hate to think him in it,' she said.

'He wouldn't do it,' Johnnie asserted. 'He'd know that it is wrong.'

John shook his head. 'It's the only way for everyone now,' he said. 'King and commoners. He's left us no way out at all.'

Monday 22 January 1649

On Monday John and Alexander met on the steps of Westminster Hall and went in with the surging crowd as the doors were opened. The press of men and women swept John to the far side of the hall where he could see the king's profile against the red velvet chair. Charles looked drawn and tired, he was finding it hard to sleep while constantly watched, and he knew now that the chances of a miraculous escape were every day diminishing.

The Lord President Bradshaw nodded to the prosecutor John Cook to begin but he had turned away, talking to one of the lawyers. The king, with all his old imperiousness, poked Cook sharply in the back with his cane, and the man spun around in shock, his hand going instinctively to where his sword would be. A gasp went round the courtroom.

'Why does he do it?' Alexander demanded.

John shook his head. 'I doubt any man has ever turned his back to him before,' he said quietly. 'He cannot learn to be treated as a mere mortal. He was brought up as the son of God's anointed. He just can't understand the depth of his fall.'

John Cook ostentatiously pulled his jacket into shape, and completely ignored the blow. He approached the judges' table, and asked them to agree that if the king would not plead then his silence would be taken as a confession of guilt.

The king replied. John noticed that in this crisis of his life he had lost his stammer. His diffidence in speaking directly to people had gone at last. He was clear and powerful as he told the court, in a voice raised loud enough to ensure that he could be heard in the courtroom and by the men scribbling down every word, that he was defending his own rights, but also the rights of the people of England. 'If a power without law can make laws, then who can be sure of his life or anything that he calls his own?'

There was a soft mutter from the courtroom, and a few heads nodded in the galleries where the men of property were especially sensitive to the threat that a parliament free of king and tradition might make laws that did not suit the men of land and fortune. There were Levellers enough to frighten the men of property back on to the side of monarchy. Those that called for the king's execution today might call for park walls to be pulled down tomorrow, for a law which treated commoners and peers equally, and for a parliament which represented the working man.

The Lord President Bradshaw, his metalled hat still clamped on his head, ordered the king to be silent, but Charles argued with him. Bradshaw ordered the clerk to call the prisoner to answer the charge but the king would not be silent.

'Remove the prisoner!' Bradshaw shouted.

'I do require –'

'It is not for prisoners to require –'

'Sir. I am not an ordinary prisoner.'

The guards surrounded him. 'God no!' muttered John. 'Don't let them jostle him.'

For a moment he was back in the Whitehall palace courtyard with the king in the coach and the queen with her box of jewels. He had thought then that if one hand had touched the coach the whole mystery of majesty would be destroyed. He thought now that if one soldier took the butt end of his pike and irritably thumped Charles Stuart, then the king would go down, and all his principles fall with him.

'Sir,' the king raised his voice, 'I never took arms against the people, but for the laws –'

'Justice!' the soldiers shouted. Charles rose from his chair, looked as if he wanted to say more.

'Just *go*,' John pleaded, his hands clapped over his mouth to prevent the words from being heard. 'Go before some fool loses patience. Or before Cook pokes you back.'

The king turned and left the hall. Alexander looked at John.

'A muddled business,' he said.

'A miserable one,' John replied.

421

Tuesday 23 January 1649

The hall doors did not open until midday. John and Alexander were chilled and bored by the time they pushed their way in. At once John's eyes were taken by a great shield, white with the red cross of St George, hung above the commissioners' table which was draped in a richly coloured Turkey rug.

'What does it mean?' he asked Alexander. 'Will they sentence him without another word?'

'If they decide that his silence means guilt then he cannot speak,' Alexander said. 'Once sentence is pronounced he'll just be taken out. That's how all the courts work. There's nothing more to say.'

John nodded in silence, his face dark.

There was a sympathetic murmur as the guards brought the king into court. John could see traces of strain in his face especially around his dark, solemn eyes. But he looked at the commissioners as if he despised them and he dropped into his chair as if it were his convenience to be seated before them.

John Bradshaw, the man with the hardest task in England, pulled the brim of his hat down to his eyebrows and looked at the king as if he were not far off begging him to see reason. He spoke quietly, reminding the king that the court was asking him, once more, to answer the charges.

The king looked up from turning a ring on his finger. 'When I was here yesterday I was interrupted,' he said sulkily.

'You can make the best defence you can,' Bradshaw promised him. 'But only after you have given a positive answer to the charges.'

It was opening a door for the king; at once he soared into grandeur. 'For the charges I care not a rush . . .' he started.

'Just plead not guilty,' John whispered to himself. 'Just deny tyranny and treason.'

He could have shouted his advice out loud, nothing would have stopped the king. Bradshaw himself tried to interrupt.

'By your favour you ought not to interrupt me. How I came here I know not; there's no law to make your king your prisoner.'

'But –' Bradshaw started.

The king's outflung hand meant that Bradshaw should be silenced. The Lord President of the court tried again against the king's torrent of speech. He gave up and nodded to the clerk of the court to read the charge.

John looked over to where Cromwell was sitting, his chin in his hands, watching the king dominating his own trial, his face grim.

The clerk read the long, wordy charge again. John heard his voice tremble at the embarrassment of being forced to read over and over again to a man who ignored him.

'You are before a court of justice,' Bradshaw asserted.

'I see I am before a power,' the king said provocatively. He rose to his feet and made that little gesture with his hand again which was a cue for a servant to bow and go. John recognised it at once but did not think that any other man in the court would realise that they had been dismissed. The king did not care to stay for any longer.

'Answer the charges,' John whispered soundlessly as the guards closed around him and the king walked from the court.

Wednesday 24 January 1649

John spent Wednesday idling at the little house in the Minories with Frances. The court was not sitting.

'What are they doing then?' Frances asked. She was kneading dough at the kitchen table, John seated on a stool at a safe distance from the spreading circle of flour. Frances had learned her domestic skills from Hester, so she would always be a competent cook; but her style was more enthusiastic than accurate and Alexander occasionally had to send out for their dinner after a catastrophe in the bread oven or a burned-out pot.

'They're hearing witnesses,' John said. 'It's to put the gloss of legality on it. Everyone knows he raised the standard at Nottingham. We hardly need witness accounts on oath.'

'They won't call you?' she asked.

He shook his head. 'They're seeking the smallest of trifles. They're calling the man who painted the standard pole. And for the battles they're using the evidence of men who fought all the way through. I was there only at the very beginning, remember. I was there at Hull which everyone has forgotten now. I never saw proper fighting.'

'Are you sorry now?' she asked, with her stepmother's directness. 'Do you wish you had stayed by him?'

John shook his head. 'I hate to see it come to this, but it was a bad road wherever it led,' he said honestly. 'We would be in a far worse case today if he had succeeded, Frances. I do know that.'

'Because of the Papists?' she asked.

John hesitated. 'Yes, I do think so. If he is not a Papist himself then the queen certainly is and half the court with her. The children – almost bound to be. So Prince Charles may be, and then his son after him, and then the door open again to the Pope and the priests and the

424

monasteries and the convents and the whole burden of a faith that is ordered on you by your masters.'

'But you don't even pray,' she reminded him.

John grinned. 'Yes. And I like to *not* pray in my own way. I don't want to not pray in a Papist way.' He broke off at her chuckle. 'I have travelled too far and seen too much to believe in anything very readily. You know that. I have lived with people who prayed very faithfully to the Great Hare and I prayed alongside them and sometimes thought my prayers were answered. I can't see only one way any more. I always see a dozen ways.' He sighed. 'It makes me uncomfortable with myself, it makes me a poor husband and father, and God knows it makes me a poor Christian and bad servant.'

Frances paused in her work and looked at him with love. 'I don't think you're a bad father,' she said. 'It's as you say – you have seen too much to have one simple view and one simple belief. Nobody could have lived as you did, so far from your own people, and not come home feeling a little uneasy.'

'My father travelled further and saw stranger sights but he loved his masters till the day of his death,' John said. 'I never saw him have a single doubt.'

She shook her head. 'Those were different times,' she said. 'He went far as a traveller. But you lived with the people in Virginia. You ate their bread. Of course you see two ways to live. You have lived two ways. And in this country everything changed the moment that the king took up arms against his people. Before then there were no choices to be made. Now you, and many others, see a dozen ways because there *are* a dozen ways. Your father had only one way: and that was to follow his master. Now you could follow the king, or follow Cromwell, or follow Parliament, or follow the army, or become a Leveller and call for a new earth for us all, or a Clubman and fight only to defend your own village, or turn your back on them all and emigrate, or shut the door of your garden and have nothing more to do with any of them.'

'And what would you do?' John asked, secretly rather impressed by his daughter's political acumen.

'I don't have to choose,' she said smugly with a sly little sideways smile. 'That's why I married Alexander.'

'And which side does he serve?'

She laughed outright. 'He serves the master who pays the bills,' she said. 'As do most people. You know that.'

Thursday 25 January 1649

The High Court was sitting in the Painted Chamber in the Palace of Westminster. John knew the room from his days in royal service and guided Alexander through the maze of lobbies and waiting rooms and retiring rooms until they could slip in by a side door. The day was given over to reading out the signed depositions of witnesses who had spoken before the commissioners the previous day. There was little of interest – the halting accounts of the king on horseback riding through the wounded without caring for their condition. Accusations that royalist officers had permitted the looting of dead men's weapons, and rifling the pockets of wounded men.

'That's very bad,' Alexander said softly to John. 'That's one thing Cromwell's very strict on. He won't have looting. That'll count against the king.'

'Hardly matters,' John said dourly. 'Not when you think that he's accused of tyranny and treason.'

One witness, Henry Gooch, gave evidence to show that the king was trying to raise a foreign army to invade England even while he was negotiating with Parliament for an agreed return to the throne.

'Could be a lie,' John said.

Alexander shrugged. 'We know he was raising an army in Ireland and begging the Scots to invade. We know that the queen was trying to move a French army to turn out for him before the people of Paris rose up against their own king and drove him out of the city. This is just evidence on top of evidence.'

'What happens next?' John asked one of the soldiers of the guard as the clerk went on reading the evidence.

'They have to find guilt and pronounce sentence,' the man said solemnly.

426

'But he hasn't pleaded!' John exclaimed.

The man looked away. 'If he chooses not to plead then it counts as guilty,' he said. 'There'll be nothing for you to see or hear until they are ready to pass sentence.'

'Does he know this?' John asked Alexander. 'D'you think he knows that if he goes on and on refusing to plead they'll just execute him anyway? As if he had admitted his guilt?'

'It's his law,' Alexander replied impatiently. 'Men have been executed under his name. He must know what he is doing.'

John felt himself shiver like a man with cold water down his spine.

'I'll wait,' he said to Alexander. 'May I stay with you a few days longer?'

Friday 26 January 1649

John and Frances walked together down to the Tower and then along the path beside the river.

'I might go and stay with Mother for a few days,' she said, looking out over the bright water.

'Why?' asked John. 'Am I crowding you out?'

'I don't want to be here when they do it,' she said.

For a moment he did not understand her. 'Do what?'

'Behead him. They'll do it here, won't they? In the Tower? And put his head on Tower Bridge? I don't want to see it. I know he's been in the wrong, but I remember the day he came to the Ark and he was so handsome, and she was so pretty and dressed so richly. I don't want to hear the drums roll and then stop for him.'

'I have to,' John said. 'I feel I have to see the end of this.'

Frances nodded. 'I think I'll go and stay with Mother for a while when they start to build the scaffold.'

Saturday 27 January 1649

Westminster Hall was more crowded than ever, John and Alexander were pressed against the railings and continually pushed against the broad back of a sentinel soldier. A little after midday the commissioners came into the hall; sixty-eight of them were present, Cromwell among them. When John Bradshaw came in wearing his hat John saw that he was robed in red, red as a cardinal, red as blood.

There was complete silence when King Charles came in, dressed in his rich black. He walked with purpose, and his face was bright. He no longer looked like an exhausted man pushed to his limit, he looked determined and filled with confidence. John, reading his master's stance and face, whispered to Alexander: 'He has a plan or something. He's found a way out.'

Charles did not drop nonchalantly into his chair as he had done before. He seated himself and leaned forwards earnestly and spoke at once, before Bradshaw could begin. 'I shall desire a word to be heard a little,' he started.

Bradshaw at once refused. The proceedings were fixed, the king could not simply speak as he wished. Instead Bradshaw himself started to repeat the charge when there was a stir from the galleries where two masked women were sitting.

'Oliver Cromwell is a traitor!' one of the women shouted clearly.

'Take aim!' shouted the commander of the guard and at once the soldiers in the courtroom turned their muskets on the gallery. There was a scream and a rush away from the armed men, Alexander stumbled and grabbed at the railing. The women were hustled away and the guards went back to their positions. Alexander straightened his coat and brushed down his breeches. 'This is unbearable,' he said to John. 'I thought we were going to die in a riot.'

John nodded. 'Look at Cromwell,' he said.

Cromwell was on his feet, his eyes raking the crowd, taking in the leaded windows through which an attack on the courtroom might be led. There was nothing. It had been nothing more than one woman crying out for her king.

Slowly, Cromwell resumed his seat, he glanced over to the king. Charles raised his eyebrows, slightly smiled. Cromwell's face was grim.

Bradshaw, struggling to regain the attention of the court, ruled that the king's refusal to speak was considered to be a confession of guilt, it would count as a guilty plea. But since the charge was so serious they would hear him speak in his defence as long as he did not challenge the authority of the court.

'They're bending over backwards to give him a fair chance,' Alexander whispered to John. 'There's no precedent for letting him speak in his defence when he won't say whether or not he is guilty.'

The king leaned forwards in his chair, his confidence increasing all the time. 'For the peace of the kingdom and for the freedom of the people I shall say nothing about the jurisdiction of the court,' he said clearly. Again, there was no trace of his stammer. 'If I cared more for my life than for the peace of the kingdom and the liberty of the subject I should have made a particular debate and I might have delayed an ugly sentence. I have something to say which I desire may be heard before sentence is given. I desire to be heard in the Painted Chamber before the Lords and the Commons before any sentence is passed.'

'What?' John demanded.

'What can he be thinking of?' Alexander whispered. 'A proposal of peace at last? Some kind of treaty?'

John nodded, his eyes on the king. 'Look at him, he thinks he has the answer.'

Bradshaw was refusing, insisting on the court's determination not to be delayed again when one commissioner – John Downes – started up. 'Have we hearts of stone? Are we men?' he demanded.

Two judges either side of him tried to pull him down. 'If I die for it I must speak against this!' he shouted.

Cromwell, seated before him, turned, his face black with fury. 'Are you mad? Can you not sit still?'

'Sir, no! I cannot be quiet!' He raised his voice to reach everyone in the hall. 'I am not satisfied!'

John Bradshaw surveyed the sixty-eight commissioners, saw half a dozen irresolute faces, a dozen men wishing they were elsewhere, a score of men who would have to be persuaded all over again, and announced that the court would withdraw to consider.

The king went out first, his step light, his head high, a slight triumphant smile on his face. The commissioners filed out after him, muttering to each other, clearly thrown off their course by this late offer. A draught of clean, cold air swept into the courtroom as the double doors were thrown open at the back and some of the crowd left.

John and Alexander kept their places. 'I'm not leaving,' John said. 'I swear he will escape the hangman. They'll return with an agreement. He's done it again.'

'I wouldn't take a bet against it,' Alexander said. 'He could easily do it. The commissioners are all of them uncertain, Cromwell looking ready to murder. The king has them on the run.'

'What d'you think they are doing now?' John asked.

'Cromwell wouldn't purge them, would he?' Alexander speculated. 'Rid himself of Downes and any that agree with him? He's done it with Parliament, why not with the court?'

John was about to reply when the doors at the back of the hall were slammed shut, the usual signal that the court was about to reconvene, and then the king re-entered, smiling slightly, like a man who is playing a role which is too absurdly easy for him to take seriously, and seated himself in his red armchair. Then the commissioners came in again. Downes was not with them.

'He's not there,' Alexander said quickly. 'That's bad.'

John Bradshaw's face was as grim as Cromwell's. He announced that the court would not accept any more delays. There would be no calling of the Commons and the Lords. The court would proceed to sentence.

'But a little delay of a day or two further may bring peace to the kingdom,' Charles interrupted.

'No,' Bradshaw said. 'We will not delay.'

'If you will hear me,' the king said sweetly. 'I shall give some satisfaction to you all here, and to my people after that.'

'No,' Bradshaw said. 'We will proceed to sentence.'

The king looked stunned, he had not thought they would resist the temptation of an agreement. He sat back in his chair for a moment and John could tell, from his absorbed expression and the gentle beating of his fingers on the arm of his chair, that he was thinking of another plan, another approach.

It was John Bradshaw's great moment. He had a speech in his hand and he started to recite. He read slowly enough for all the writers from the journals to copy down what he was saying. He cited the traditional duty of Parliament and the duty of the king, and the claim that kings could be held accountable for their crimes. The crowd grew restless during the long legal citations but Bradshaw came to the point – that the king, by taking arms against his people, had destroyed the agreement between a king and his people. He was there to protect his people, never to attack.

'I would desire only one word before you give sentence,' the king interrupted.

'But sir, you have not owned us as a court, we need not have heard even one word from you.'

The king subsided into his chair as Bradshaw gestured to the clerk of the court.

'Charles Stuart as a tyrant, traitor, murderer and a public enemy shall be put to death by the severing of his head from his body.'

In silence the sixty-seven commissioners rose to their feet.

'Will you hear me a word, sir?' the king asked politely, as if nothing had taken place.

'You are *not* to be heard after sentence,' Bradshaw said and motioned to the guards to take him away.

The king leaned forwards more urgently. He had not realised that they would not hear him after sentence had been passed. He knew so little of the laws of his own land that he had not realised a man sentenced is not allowed to speak. 'I may speak after the sentence –' Charles argued, his voice a little higher in anxiety. 'By your favour, sir, I may speak after the sentence.'

The guards came closer. John found he was shrinking back, a hand to his mouth like a frightened child.

Charles persisted. 'By your favour, hold! The sentence, sir, I do –'

The guards closed in, forcing him to his feet. Charles shouted over their heads to the stunned crowd: 'I am not suffered for to speak: expect what justice other people will have!'

They hustled him from the hall, there were confused shouts, some for, some against him. The commissioners filed out, John saw them go as if they were floating away, Bradshaw's red gown and absurd hat a dreamlike imagining. 'I never thought they would do it,' John said. 'I never thought they would.'

Sunday 28 January 1649

John would not attend church with Frances and her husband. He sat at the kitchen table, a glass of small ale before him, while the church bells rang and then fell silent, and then rang again.

Frances, entering in a rush to prepare the Sunday dinner, checked at the sight of her father, so uncharacteristically idle.

'Are you sick?'

He shook his head.

Alexander followed his wife into the kitchen. 'They say he is praying with Bishop Juxon. He is allowed to see his children.'

'No clemency?' John asked.

'They are building the scaffold at Whitehall,' Alexander said shortly.

'Not here?' Frances asked quickly.

Alexander took her hand and kissed it. 'No, my dear. Nowhere near us. They are closing off the street before the Banqueting House. They are fortifying it against a rescue attempt.'

'Who would rescue him?' John asked forlornly. 'He has betrayed every one of his friends at one time or another.'

Tuesday 30 January 1649

It was such a bitter, cold morning that John thought the ice on roof and gutter had crept into his own veins and was freezing his belly and bones as he waited in the street. The king was to be executed before noon but though the streets were lined three-deep with soldiers, and the two executioners waited in the lee of the black-draped scaffold, the note-takers and sketch artists gathered at the foot, there was no sign of the king.

The street, crammed with people packed in behind the cordon of soldiers, had a strange echo to it, as the sound of talk, prayers, and the shouts of ballad sellers bawling out the titles of their new songs bounced off the walls of the windowless buildings and boomed in the cold air.

John, looking behind him at the tight-packed crowd and then forwards to the stage, thought it seemed like an exercise in perspective, like Inigo Jones's deceiving painted scenery for a masque, the penultimate scene of a masque which would be followed by the ascension, with Jehovah coming down from a great cloud and the handmaidens of Peace and Justice dancing together.

The two executioners climbed the steps to the platform and there was a gasp at their appearance. They were in costume, in false wigs and false beards and dark brown doublets and breeches.

'What are they wearing? Masquing clothes?' Alexander asked of the man on his left.

'Disguised to hide their identity,' the man said shortly. 'It'll be Brandon the hangman hidden under that beard, unless it's Cromwell himself doing the job.'

John briefly closed his eyes and opened them again. The scene had not changed; it was still unbearable. The chief executioner positioned the block, laid down his axe and stepped back, his arms folded, waiting.

It was a long wait, the crowd grew restless.

'A reprieve?' Alexander suggested. 'The plan he had for peace finally heard and accepted?'

'No,' someone said in the crowd nearby. 'He has been stabbed to death by Cromwell himself.'

'I heard there was an escape,' someone else said. 'He must have escaped. If he was dead they would show the body.'

The rumour and the speculation continued all the morning in a swirl of muttering all around John who stood cold and silent in the middle of it all.

'I must find something to eat,' Alexander said. 'I am famished.'

'I don't want anything,' John said.

'You must be starving, man; and cold,' Alexander exclaimed. 'Let me bring you a loaf of bread when I buy some dinner for myself.'

John shook his head. 'I feel nothing,' he said simply. 'Nothing at all.'

Alexander shook his head and wriggled through the crowd to where an enterprising baker was selling hot bread rolls from a tray. It took him more than an hour to regain his place at John's side but still nothing had happened.

'I brought you some bread,' he said cheerfully. 'And I filled my flask with rum.'

John took the bread in his hand but he did not eat it. His eyes were fixed on the scaffold.

'They are saying that the Scots have visited Colonel Fairfax, who was against this from the start, and that they are all going to Cromwell to beg for a reprieve. The king can be free to live abroad, even Scotland.'

John shook his head.

'I know,' Alexander said. 'If they gave him so much as a farthing's chance he would raise an army and come back again. If he can conspire from prison when he is bound by his word of honour, what would he do loose amid the courts of Europe? He would always come back again. They can't trust him with his life.'

'They've called Parliament,' a man said beside them. 'That's the reason for the delay. They are passing a law in a hurry which says that no-one else can be proclaimed king. No value in beheading a king if another springs up to take his place, is there? And we have one of his sons in England and another two of them in France, and his nephew hanging round like a dog at the door of an abattoir. We've princes enough for pass-the-crown to go on forever. We have to break them of the habit now. So they're making a law to say that no king can be proclaimed in England ever again.'

That sentence shocked John out of his absorption. 'No king can be proclaimed in England ever again,' he repeated.

'Yes,' the man said. 'It has a ring to it, doesn't it? It makes you feel that it's all been worth the struggle. We are free of them forever. There will never be another man to set himself high above all others. There will never be another family who think themselves better than the rest of us by virtue of the bed they were born in. Any masters we have in the future will have to earn their place. They will have to be men that we choose to serve because they are wiser or better or even richer than us. But not because they are born to it. This is Charles the Last. After him there will be freedom.'

'Charles the Last,' John repeated. 'Charles the Last.'

The clocks had struck twelve and then one and then two before there was a stirring among the soldiers which was quickly caught by the crowd, and then a shout: 'He's coming.'

John did not move. He was still and silent as he had been all day. The crowd around him jostled fiercely but John gripped his hands on the railing before him and held tight. Alexander saw that his knuckles were white; but so were his hands, his face, his whole body was bleached by cold and distress.

A window in the Banqueting Hall was open and the king stepped out on to the platform. He was simply dressed in black again: a black cape, a tall black hat, black breeches and a white shirt. The Order of the Garter was a blaze of colour in dramatic contrast. He looked out at the crowd, John felt that sombre, dark gaze pass over him and wanted to raise a hand, to catch at recognition for a moment. He kept his hands and his head down.

The king took some notes from his pocket and spoke quietly to the men on the platform. John, straining his ears, could hear only tantalising snatches of speech; only the last few words rang clear: 'I am a martyr to the people.'

John heard a hiss of breath at the unending, irresistible grandeur and folly of the man, and realised it was cold air through his own teeth. The king swore that he died in the faith of his father, as a Christian, and then spoke quietly to the executioner.

'Oh God, don't let him botch it,' John whispered, thinking not of the executioner who had done this a hundred times, but of the king who must do this beautifully, just once.

The king turned to Bishop Juxon and the bishop helped him to tuck his long hair under his cap to keep his neck free for the blade. Charles handed his George and the ribbon of the Garter to the bishop, and pulled the ring from his finger.

'No, not that, no, no,' John muttered. The details were unbearable. John had nerved himself for an execution; not for a man undressing as if in domestic confidence, tucking his hair out of the way of his pale, fragile neck. 'Oh please God, no.'

Charles took off his doublet but wrapped his cloak around his shoulders again, as if it mattered that he should not catch cold. He seemed to be complaining about the executioner's block. The executioner, a terrifying figure in his masquing disguise, seemed to be apologising. John, remembering the king's ability to delay and prevaricate, found that he was shaking the fence post before him in painful impatience.

The king stepped back and looked up at the sky, his hands raised. John heard the scribble of a pencil behind him as a sketch-maker captured the image of the king, the martyr of the people, his eyes on heaven, his arms outspread like a statue of Christ. Then the king dropped his cloak, knelt down before the block and stretched out his neck.

The executioner had to wait for the signal; the king had to spread out his arms to consent. For a while he knelt there, unmoving. The executioner leaned forwards and moved a wisp of hair. He waited.

'Please, do it,' John whispered to his old master. 'Please, please, just do it.'

There was a wait of what seemed like hours, then with the gesture of a man diving into a deep river the king flung his arms out wide and the axe swept a lovely unstoppable arc downwards, thudded into his neck bone, and his head dropped neatly off.

A deep groan came from the crowd – the sound a man makes at his death, the sound a man makes at the height of his pleasure. The sound of something ending, which can never happen again.

At once there were slow, determined hoofbeats behind them and people screaming and pushing in panic to get away.

'Come on!' Alexander cried, tugging at John's sleeve. 'The cavalry is coming through, out of the way, man, we'll be ridden down.'

John could not hear him. He was still staring at the stage, still waiting for the final act when the king, gorgeously dressed in white, would step down from the stage and dance with the queen.

'Come on!' Alexander said. He grabbed John's arm and dragged him to one side. The crowd eddied, rushing to the sides of the street, many running forwards to the scaffold to snatch a piece of the pall, to scrabble for a bit of earth from under the stage, even to dip their handkerchiefs in the gush of scarlet hot blood. John, pulled by Alexander, and pushed by the people behind him trying to get away from the remorseless cavalry advance down the street, lost his feet and fell. He was kicked in the head at once, someone trod on his hand. Alexander hauled him upwards.

'Come on, man!' he said. 'This is no place to linger.'

John's head cleared, he struggled to his feet, ran with Alexander to the side of the road, pressed against the wall as the cavalry forced their way down to the scaffold, and then slipped away as they went past. At the top of the road he checked, and looked back. It was over. Already it was over. Bishop Juxon had disappeared, the king's body had been lifted through the window of the Banqueting House, the street was half-cleared of people, the soldiers had made a cordon around the stage. It was a derelict theatre at the end of the show, it had that stale leftover silence when the speeches have been finished and the performance is all over. It was done.

It was done but it was not over. John, returning home, found his house besieged with neighbours who wanted to hear every word, every detail, of what he had seen and what had been said. Only Johnnie was missing.

'Where is he?' John asked Hester.

'In the garden, in his boat on the lake,' she said shortly. 'We heard the church bells toll in Lambeth and he knew what it was for.'

John nodded, excused himself from the village gossips and went down the cold garden. His son was nowhere to be seen. John walked down the avenue and turned right at the bottom for the lake where the children had often gone to feed ducks when they were little. The irises and reeds planted in the wet ground at the margin were in their stark frosted beauty. In the middle of the lake the boat was drifting, Johnnie, wrapped in his cape, sitting in the stern, the oars resting on the seat either side of him.

'Hey there,' John said gently from the landing stage.

Johnnie glanced up and saw his father. 'Did you see it done?' he asked flatly.

'Aye.'

'Was it done quickly?'

'It was done properly,' John said. 'He made a speech, he put his head on the block, he gave the sign and it was done in a single blow.'

438

'So it's over,' Johnnie said. 'I'll never serve him.'

'It's over,' John said. 'Come ashore, Johnnie, there will be other masters and other gardens. In a few weeks people will have something else to talk about. You won't have to hear about it. Come in, Johnnie.'

Spring 1649

John was wrong. The king's execution was not a nine-day wonder, it swiftly became the theme of every conversation, of every ballad, of every prayer. Within days they were bringing to John the rushed printed accounts of the trial and eyewitness descriptions of the execution, and asking him if they were the truth. Only the most hard-hearted of roundheads escaped the mood of haunting melancholy, as if the death of a royal was a personal loss – whatever the character of the man, whatever the reason for his death. The country was gripped with a sickness of grief, a deep sadness which quite obscured the justice of the case and the reasons for his death. No-one really cared why the king had to die. In the end, they were stunned that he had died at all.

John thought that perhaps others had believed like him: that a king in his health simply could not die. That something would intervene, that God himself must prevent such an act. That even now, time might run backwards and the king be found alive. That John might wake up one morning to find the king in his palace and the queen demanding some absurd planting scheme. It was almost impossible to accept that no-one would ever see him again. The chapbooks, the balladeers, the portraitists all fostered the illusion of the king's surviving presence. There were more pictures of King Charles and stories about him than there had ever been during his life. He was better beloved than he had ever been when he had been idle and foolish and misjudging. Every error he had made had been washed away by the simple fact of his death, and the name he had given to himself: the Martyr King.

Then came the reports of miracles worked by his relics. People were cured of fits or sickness or rashes like the pox by the touch of a handkerchief which had been dipped in his blood. The pocket knives made from his melted-down statue would heal wounds if laid against them, would protect a baby from violent death if used to cut the cord. A sick lion in the Tower zoo had been comforted by the scent of his blood on a rag. Every day there was a new story about the saint, the people's saint. Every day his presence in the country grew stronger.

No-one was wholly unmoved; but Johnnie, still weak from his injury and defeat at Colchester, was struck very hard. He spent day after day in the boat on the little lake, lying wrapped in his cloak, his long legs folded over the stern and the heels of his boots dipping in the water while the boat drifted around nudging one bank and then another, and Johnnie stared up at the cold sky, saying nothing.

Hester went down to fetch him for his midday dinner and found him rowing slowly to the little landing stage to come in.

'Oh Johnnie,' she said. 'You have your whole life before you, there's no need to take it so hard. You did what you could, you kept faith with him, you ran away to serve him and you were as brave as any of his cavaliers.'

He looked at her with his dark Tradescant eyes and she saw the passionate loyalty of his grandfather without the security of his grand-father's settled world. 'I don't know how we can live without a king,' he said simply. 'It's not just him. It's the place he held. I can't believe that we won't see him again. His palaces are still there, his gardens. I can't believe that he is not there too.'

'You should get back to work,' Hester said, grasping at straws. 'Your father needs help.'

'We are gardeners to the king,' Johnnie said simply. 'What do we do now?'

'There's the trading business for Sir Henry in Barbados.'

He shook his head. 'I'll never be a trader. I'm a gardener through and through. I'd never be anything else.'

'The rarities.'

'I'll come and help if you wish it, Mother,' he said obediently. 'But they're not the same, are they? Since we packed and unpacked them again. It's not grandfather's room any more, it's not the room we showed the king. We have most of the things and it should be the same. But it feels different, doesn't it? As if by packing them and hiding them away, and then unpacking them, and then hiding them again, somehow spoiled it. And people don't come as they used to. It's as if everything is changed and no-one knows yet how.'

Hester put her hand on his arm. 'I just mean you should stop brooding and return to work. There is a time to mourn and you do yourself no favours if you exceed it.'

He nodded. 'I will,' he promised. 'If you wish it.' He hesitated as if he could not find the words for his feeling. 'I never thought that I could feel so low.'

The three of them were at dinner when there was a knock at the door. Hester turned her head and they listened to the cook stamping irritably along the hall to open it. There was the noise of a mild disagreement. 'It'll be a sailor with something to sell,' Hester said.

'I'll go,' Johnnie said, pushing back his chair. 'You finish your dinner.'

'Call me before you agree a price,' John warned him.

Johnnie scowled at his father's lack of trust; and went out of the door.

They heard him shout an oath, and then they heard the noise of his running footsteps down the hall, and the door to the terrace slam as he set off down the garden.

'Good God, what now?' John sprang to his feet and went to the front door. Hester paused by the window to see Johnnie, head down, running blindly towards the lake. She hesitated, and followed her husband.

A bewildered man was at the front door. 'I offered him this for sale,' he said, showing a dirty piece of black cloth. 'I thought it was the sort of thing you would like for your collection. But he jumped back as if it were poison and fled from me. What ails the lad?'

'He's sick,' Hester said shortly. 'What is it?'

The man suddenly gleamed with enthusiasm. 'A piece of pall from the scaffolding of the Martyr King, Mrs Tradescant. And if you like it you can have it and a pen-knife cast from the metal of his statue. *And* I may be able to find you a scrape of earth soaked with his sacred blood. All very reasonable considering the rarity of it and the price you will be able to charge for those coming to see it.'

Hester instinctively recoiled in distaste. She looked to John. His eyebrows were knotted in thought.

'We don't take such things,' he said slowly. 'We buy rarities, not relics.'

'You have Henry VIII's hunting gloves,' the man pointed out. 'And Queen Anne's nightgown. Why not this? Especially as you could make your fortune with it.'

John took a swift turn away from the doorstep and down the hall. The man was right, anything to do with the king would be a goldmine for the Ark, and they were barely making enough money to pay the cook's and Joseph's wages.

He turned back to the front door. 'I thank you, but no. We will not exhibit the king's remains.'

Hester found that her shoulders had been hunched while she waited for her husband's decision. 'But please do bring us any other rare things you have,' she said pleasantly, and went to shut the door.

The man thrust his foot out and stopped the closing door. 'I was certain you would give me a good price for this,' he said. 'There are other collectors who would pay handsomely. I was doing you the favour of coming to you first.'

'I thank you for that,' John said shortly. 'But we won't take anything that remains of the king.' He hesitated. 'He visited here himself,' he said, as if it would make the decision clear. 'It would not seem right to show pieces of him.'

The man shrugged, took his foot from the door and left. Hester closed the door and turned back to look at John.

'That was well done,' she said.

'D'you think we'd ever have got Johnnie to work in the room with the king's own blood in a jar?' John asked irritably and went out to the garden, leaving his dinner untouched on the table.

❦

Johnnie's gloom did not lift as Hester had hoped that it might even when the warmer weather came. In March, when John was planting seeds of nasturtium, sweet pea, and his Virginian amaracock in pots of sieved earth in the orangery, Parliament declared that there would never more be a king or a queen set over the English people. Kingship was abolished forever in England. Johnnie came into the warm room with a small box in his hand, looking grave.

'What have you there?' John asked warily.

'The king's seeds,' Johnnie said softly. 'That he gave you to plant at Wimbledon.'

'Ah, the melon seeds. D'you know, I'd forgotten all about them.'

A swift, burning glance from Johnnie showed that he had not forgotten, and that he thought the less of his father for his absence of mind. 'It's one of the last orders he must have given,' Johnnie said softly, in awe. 'And he sent for you by name, just to ask you to plant them for him. It's like he wanted you to have a task, a quest, to remember him by.'

443

'Just melons.'

'He sent for you, he saved the seeds from his own dinner plate, and asked you to do it. He took the seeds from his own dinner, and he gave them to you.'

John hesitated, dismayed at the tone of worship in Johnnie's voice. The scepticism which everyone in the country had shared when Charles the Cheat was lying and backsliding from his agreements had quite vanished at the man's death when he became Charles the Martyr. John granted grudgingly that Charles had done better than anyone could have imagined in making the throne once more a sacred place; for here was Johnnie, who by rights should be disillusioned after a hopeless siege and a bad injury, with his eyes blazing at the thought of the dead king.

John put his hand on his son's shoulder and felt the strong sinew and bone. He did not see how he could explain to Johnnie that the whim of a man accustomed all his life to command should not be read as significant. Charles the Last had a fancy to pretend that he might live to eat the melons which would be planted at Wimbledon in the spring, and it was no trouble to him that a servant should go all the way from Windsor to Lambeth and back again to fetch John, and that John should go all the way from Lambeth to Windsor and then home again to enact that fancy.

It would never have occurred to him that it might be inconvenient for a man no longer in his service and no longer paid a royal wage to be summoned once more to unpaid work. It would not have occurred to him that his behaviour was arrogant or wilful. It would not have occurred to him that by naming John as his gardener and entrusting him with the commission he would identify him as a royal servant at a time when royal servants were regarded with suspicion. He had put John to inconvenience, he might have put him in grave danger – he would simply never have thought of it. It was a whim and he was always a man who was happy that others should service his whims.

'Would you like to plant them?' John asked, seeking a way out of this dilemma.

Johnnie's face showed the rush of his emotion. 'Would you let me?'

'Of course. You can plant them up, if you like, and when they are ready we'll transplant them to the melon beds.'

'I want to make melon beds at Wimbledon,' Johnnie said. 'That's where he wanted them to be.'

John hesitated. 'I don't know what's happening at Wimbledon,' he said. 'If Parliament wants me to continue working there, then of course we can make a melon bed. But I've heard nothing. They may sell the house.'

'We have to do it,' Johnnie said simply. 'We cannot disobey his command, it was his last order to us.'

John turned back to his nasturtiums and surrendered. 'Oh, very well,' he said. 'When they're ready for planting out we'll take them to Wimbledon.'

Slowly, life began to get back to normal. There was a gradual increase of takings at the door from visitors to the rarities room and orders in the book from the new men who now found themselves in possession of the sequestered estates of royalists who were dead or fled or living quietly in poverty. The new men, officers from Cromwell's army and the astute politicians who had stood against the king at the right time, walked into some fine houses and gardens running to seed which might be restored to beauty.

One by one the visitors started to come back to the Ark, to walk around the gardens and admire the blossoms on the trees and the bobbing heads of the daffodils. Dr Thomas Wharton, a man after John's heart, came to look at the rarities and brought with him a proposal that John should set aside a part of his garden for the College of Physicians. They would pay him a fee to grow herbs and medicinal plants for them.

'I appreciate it,' John said frankly. 'These have been lean years for us. A country at war has no interest in gardening nor in rarities.'

'The country is to be run now by men whose curiosity will not be stifled,' the doctor replied. 'Mr Cromwell himself is a man who likes ingenious mechanisms. He has drained his farmland and uses Dutch windpumps to keep the water out, and he believes that English land could be made to yield as fruitfully as the Low Countries', even the waste grounds.'

'It's a question of not exhausting the soil,' John said eagerly. 'And changing the crops around so that blights don't take hold. We've always known that in gardens and vegetable plots, every convent and monastery garden moved crops from one bed to another each year; but it's true for farmland too. It's how to restore the goodness to the soil that is the difficulty. In Virginia too, the People never use the same field for more than three seasons.'

'The planters?'

'No, the Powhatan. They move their fields each season. I thought it was a mistake till I saw how their crops yielded.'

'This is most interesting,' Dr Wharton said. 'Perhaps you would come to my house and tell me more. I meet with friends once a month to discuss inventions, and rarities, and ideas.'

'I should be honoured,' John said.

'And what d'you use to make your own land fertile?' Dr Wharton asked.

John laughed. 'A soup of my father's devising,' he said. 'Nettles and comfrey and dung stirred up in an evil pot. And if I am disposed to make water I piss in it as well.'

The doctor chuckled. 'So it couldn't be used for a hundred acres?'

'But there are crops which would put the goodness back into the soil,' John replied. 'Comfrey or clover. You'd have to start with a little patch and harvest the seed, plant a greater and greater field every year.'

The doctor tapped him on the arm. 'There's your future,' he said. 'If the new parliament cares little for ornamental gardens, they care a great deal for the richness of the lands. If we are to keep the Levellers from turning us out of our own doors then we have to feed the people from the acres we have under the plough. The country has to be fed, the country has to find peace and prosperity. If you could write a pamphlet about how it could be done then Parliament would reward you.' He hesitated. 'And it would mean that you were seen to be working for the good of Parliament and the army and the people,' he said. 'No bad thing, now that your old master is gone.'

John raised an eyebrow. 'Any news of the prince?'

'Charles Stuart,' Wharton corrected him gently. 'In France, I hear. But with Cromwell in Ireland he might try a landing. He could try a landing at any time and he would always muster an army of a couple of hundred fools. There will always be fools ready to run to a royal standard.'

He paused to see if John disagreed that Charles would only be served by an army of fools. John took meticulous care to say nothing.

'He's called Charles Stuart now,' Dr Wharton reminded him.

John grinned. 'Aye,' he said. 'I'll remember.'

❧

In April John Lambert strolled into the garden with a smile for Joseph, the gardener, and a low bow for Hester.

'General Lambert!' she exclaimed. 'I thought you were at Pontefract.'

'I was,' he said. 'But my business there is done. I am to spend the next few months in London, staying at my father-in-law's house with my family, so I have come to spend the fruits of victory. He only has a little garden so I must not be tempted by one of your great trees. Has Mr Tradescant anything new?'

'Come and see,' Hester said, and led the way out through the glass doors to the terrace and down the garden. 'The tulips are at their very best. We could let you have some in bud in pots. You will be missing your own at Carlton Hall.'

'I might catch them at the end of their bloom. We have a later season in Yorkshire.'

They walked together to the front of the house and Hester paused to enjoy his delight at the sight of the tulips in bloom in the big double beds before the house.

'Every year I catch my breath,' he said. 'It's like a sea of colour.'

Hester smoothed her apron over her hips. 'I know,' she said contentedly.

'And what novelties d'you have?' John Lambert asked eagerly. 'Anything new?'

'A satin tulip, from Amsterdam,' Hester said, temptingly lifting up a pot. 'Look at the shine on it.'

He took the pot in his arms, careless of his velvet jacket and the rich lace at his throat. 'What a beauty!' he said. 'The petals are like a mirror!'

'And here comes my husband,' Hester remarked, curbing her irritation that John was pushing a barrow up from the seed beds in his shirtsleeves with his hat set askew on his head.

Lambert carefully replaced the pot on its stand.

'Mr Tradescant.'

John set down the barrow, came up the steps to the terrace, and bowed to their guest. 'I won't shake hands. I'm dirty.'

'I'm admiring your tulips.'

John nodded. 'Any luck with your own? Hester told me you were going to try with the Violetten?'

'I have been too much away from home to select the blooms for breeding them to a true colour. But my wife tells me they made a pretty show in shades of mauve and purple.'

Further down the orchard Hester saw Johnnie glance up the avenue and then, when he saw that it was Lambert, pick up his watering pot and with assumed nonchalance stroll up the path under the dark sticky buds of the horse chestnut trees.

'Good day to you,' General Lambert said.

Johnnie skidded to a halt and gave a little bow.

'General Lambert is looking for something for his father-in-law's garden in Kensington,' Hester said to her husband. 'I am tempting him with the new tulip.'

'Isn't it fine?' John said. 'It's got a sheen on it like the coat of a bay horse. Does your father-in-law have fruit trees? And you could risk transplanting roses if we do it at once.'

'I'd like some roses,' Lambert said. 'He has some Rosamund roses already. D'you have any in pure white?'

'I have a *Rosa alba*,' John said. 'And an offshoot which I have grown from it with very thick petals.'

'Scented?'

'A very light scent, very sweet. And I have a Virginian rose, there's only two of them in the whole country.'

'And we have a white dog rose,' Johnnie volunteered. 'Since you're a Yorkshireman, sir.'

Lambert laughed. 'That's a pretty thought, I thank you.' He glanced at Johnnie and then looked again. 'Hey now, young man, have you been sick? You're not as bright as when I last saw you.'

There was an awkward silence. 'He was in the war,' Hester said honestly.

Lambert took in the slope of Johnnie's shoulders and the droop of his fair head. 'Where was that, lad?'

'At Colchester.'

The general nodded. 'A bad business,' he said shortly. 'You must be sorry for how it all ended; but thank God we should have peace now, at last.'

Johnnie shot a swift look at him. 'You weren't there for his trial,' he remarked.

Lambert shook his head. 'I was doing my duty elsewhere.'

'Would you have tried him?'

Hester moved forward to hush Johnnie but Lambert stopped her with a little gesture of his hand. 'Let the lad speak,' he said. 'He has a right to know. We are making the country he is going to inherit, he should be able to ask why we made our choices.'

'Would you have found him guilty and had him executed, sir?'

Lambert thought for a moment and then glanced at John. 'May I talk with the boy?'

John nodded and Lambert slid an arm around Johnnie's shoulders and the two of them fell into a stroll, down the little avenue under the

448

resolute strong twigs of horse chestnut and then onwards into the orchard under the bobbing, budding boughs of apple, cherry, apricot and plum.

'I wouldn't have signed his death warrant on the evidence of the trial,' Lambert said softly to Johnnie. 'I thought the trial was mismanaged. But I would have worked with all my power to make him recognise that the king must accept some limits. The difficulty with him was that he was a man who would not recognise any limits.'

'He was the king,' Johnnie said stubbornly.

'No-one's denying it,' the older man replied. 'But look around you, Johnnie. The people of this country have starved while their lords and their kings have grown fat on their labour. There is no justice for them against any man greater than themselves. The profits of running the state, the taxes, all the trade, were in the gift of the king and scattered to the men who amused him, or who delighted the queen. A man could have his ears cropped for speaking out, his hand struck off for writing. Women could be strangled for witchcraft on the evidence of a village gossip. There are very great wrongs which can only be put right by a very real change. There has to be a parliament which is elected by the people. It has to sit by law, and not at the whim of the king. It has to protect the rights of the people and not those of the landlord. It has to protect the rights of the poorest, of the powerless. I had nothing against the king himself – except that he was untrustworthy both in power and out of it – but I have everything in the world against a king who rules alone.'

'Are you a Leveller?'

Lambert smiled. 'Certainly these are Leveller beliefs, yes. And I'm proud to call Levellers my comrades. They are some of the staunchest and truest men under my command. Yet I am a man of property too; and I want to keep my property. I don't go as far as some of them who want everything to be held in common. But to seek justice and the chance to choose your own government – yes, that makes me a Leveller, I suppose.'

'There has to be a leader,' Johnnie said stubbornly. 'Appointed by God.'

Lambert shook his head. 'There has to be a commander, just like in the army. But we don't believe that God appoints a man to tell us what to do. If that were so, we might as well still obey the Pope and have done with it. We know what to do, we know what is right, we know that the hard-working men of this country need to be sure that their lands are safe, and that their landlord will not sell them to another, like

449

a herd of cow, or suddenly take it into his head that their village is in his way and drive them out like coneys from a warren.'

Johnnie hesitated.

'When you marched to Colchester were you quartered on poor farms with nothing to spare?' Lambert asked.

'Yes.'

'Then you've seen how badly some men live in the middle of plenty. The rents they have to pay are greater than the yield of their crops. We cannot have people forever struggling to make that gap meet. There has to be a balance. People must be paid a fair wage for their work.' He paused. 'When you were quartered on a poor farmstead did you take your feed for your horses and a chicken for your dinner and leave them no recompense?'

Johnnie flushed scarlet and shamefacedly nodded.

'Aye, that's the royal way,' Lambert said bitterly. 'That's the kingly way to behave.'

Johnnie flushed. 'I didn't want to,' he said. 'But I had no wages.'

Lambert gripped his arm. 'That's how it happens,' he said. 'If all the wealth is concentrated on the king, on the court, then there must be poverty everywhere else. The king raised an army but had no funds so he didn't pay you, so you had to take forage without paying, so at the end of the line there is some poor widow with one hen and the king's man comes by and takes all the eggs.'

Hester watched her stepson and Lambert walk to the end of the orchard and then turn towards the lake.

'I hope he can say something that will reconcile Johnnie,' she said. 'I've been afraid that he will never be happy again.'

'He might,' John agreed. 'He's had the command of many men. He'll have come across lads like Johnnie before.'

'It's kind of him to take the trouble,' she said.

John gave a wry smile. 'I imagine he'll take away a pot of my best tulips as his payment, won't he?'

Hester gave a little laugh. 'Not the Semper Augustus, at any rate,' she promised.

Summer 1649

With the coming of the summer the numbers of visitors increased at the Ark and the social life of London was restored. There was an explosion of debate as to how the new society should be built, what should be allowed and what should be forbidden. Pamphlets, sermons, diatribes, and journals poured off the little presses which had sprung up everywhere during the war years, new plays were written, new poems commissioned. There was a sense of excitement, of being at the very heart of change, a new world which no-one had ever experienced before. Kings had been killed before in England and elsewhere – but only on the battlefield, or in secret, and their thrones snatched by other claimants. Never before had the whole system of kingship been questioned and found so badly wanting that the people chose to destroy it and put no-one in its place.

Oliver Cromwell was to be known as Chairman of the Council of State, and there would never be another king of England. Even then the new state did not go far enough for many. There was no opening of the electorate: poor men still had no voice in the planning of the nation. There was no abolition of tithes, which many had fought for. There was no reform of the law, nor the ownership of land. The Houses of Parliament were still one House of Lords and a House of Commons packed with landed gentlemen, still serving their own needs before any other; so that the justice that John Lambert had hoped for so passionately was still far away.

But there was a sense of excitement and optimism as palpable as the warmer weather of May and June. There was a sense of changes coming, of hope, of a chance to make England into a country which could be prosperous for the many instead of the few. Families who had been estranged for years, siding with the opposing armies, were able to make friends again. Churches which had been emptied because of doctrinal arguments were now re-established with a new, freer, informal style of preaching. Men wanted to be done with ceremony, with artifice. Men wanted to speak freely to their God, and to speak freely to each other.

An informal association of philosophers, botanists, mathematicians, physicians and astronomers met regularly to debate, Dr Thomas Wharton among them, and John Tradescant too. John Lambert was in London from March and rarely missed a meeting, drawn by their discussion of science and botany. Many of them took to visiting the Ark that summer, to stroll around the garden, to sit by the little lake, to admire anything new and interesting in the rarities room and stay for dinner.

Hester, rather on her mettle as a housewife, took pride both in being able to provide dinner for a dozen men and beds for half of them at a moment's notice, and that it was the Tradescant house and garden which was the centre of attraction.

The conversation would go far into the night, and as the levels fell in the bottles of port the speculation about everything from the functions of parts of the body, to the existence of angels, the movement of the planets in their spheres and the rise and fall of sugar sap in John's maple tree became wilder and more imaginative. Elias Ashmole, a learned lawyer, one evening swore that he could predict to an hour's accuracy the time of a man's death if only midwives would have the sense to record the exact time of birth to let an astronomy chart be rigorously drawn.

'But would you want to know?' John asked, slurring slightly.

'I want to know everything,' Elias replied. 'That is what I mean by being a man of science. I, for instance, am born beneath the planet Mercury, and you can see that I am a completely mercurial man. I'm quick and versatile.'

'And looks like a silver slug, just like the metal!' someone interposed under his breath.

'But a man should separate the personal from the inquiring in his life,' a physician remarked rather confusedly. 'I want to know how blood flows through the veins. But I'm not going to open up my own arm to have a look at it. I am not my own experiment.'

'Not at all!' another man interrupted passionately. 'Unless you are prepared to penetrate, even into your own heart, then you are not inquiring at all. It is mere diversion.'

'Oh yes! If you want to die of the plague in an experiment to see that it is infectious!'

'Truly, one cannot study patients from a distance,' Dr Wharton observed. 'When the plague was in London I . . .'

'And what else have we done in the body politic but make a change and see what flows from it? Cut out the heart and see if the brain can still think?'

'That was not an experiment! It was a decision to which we were driven. I don't see Cromwell as a great physician of the body politic! He was clinging on while the horse bolted!'

'But I don't mean that,' John said, holding to his first thought with difficulty. 'I mean, would you always want to know the future? How would you bear it?'

'Of course you can know it,' Elias replied. 'I have drawn my own chart and I can tell you, for instance, that I shall be a man of considerable fame. I cast my own predictions and they told me clearly: "I shall labour for a fortune with a wife and get it."'

'A rich widow?' someone asked from further down the table.

'Lady Mary Manwaring,' someone muttered. 'Old enough to be his mother. He's been advising her. Guess what he advised?'

'I shall be remembered,' Ashmole insisted. 'I shall have my place in the temple of history.'

'For what?' one of the mathematicians demanded and burped slightly. 'Pardon me. What will earn you your place in the temple of history? Simpling in John's herb garden? Picking his flowers for potions? I don't expect to see you gleaming all over gold with the philosopher's stone in your laboratory. Seems to me that of all of us it will be John's name which will be remembered.'

John laughed. 'I just collect,' he said modestly. 'I don't set myself up as a scientist. Of course, I'm bound to wonder how things grow the way they do. I can't believe that it was all made by God in one week. I can see that man can make new plants, with proper skills. I can see that we can make the earth more yielding, that we can make plants grow better. I have some onions for instance . . .'

'Mr Ashmole has an undeniable reputation in astronomy and astrology –' one of the physicians started.

'I'm just saying that Mr Tradescant's onions, or even his tulips, are likely to yield more lasting joy to the people of this country than all of Mr Ashmole's researches into the history of the masonic order!'

John shook his head. 'It'll be the trees if anything,' he said definitely. 'The greatest joy a man can have in England is the sight of one of our horse chestnut trees in full bloom. And we have my father to thank for that.'

'Hush,' Ashmole said. 'I never speak of the masonic order.'

'Mr Ashmole's work at Brasenose –'

'Is undeniable. And he is my guest.' John recalled his duties as host. 'Pass the bottle, Stephen.'

❦

Johnnie was present at the dinners, but generally kept silent. John, looking down the table, would see his son's intent, dark gaze move from one man to another, taking in the argument, weighing it, and then smiling in agreement or shaking his head. He was as open as a child though he was now nearly sixteen; but he had the politeness and the discretion not to burst out with his own opinions.

He would observe and listen throughout an evening of speculation, but whenever the talk turned to politics he would rise up and leave the room. Most of John's guests were men who thought, like John Milton, that the dead king had been an obstacle to the future of the country, that removing him was like cutting off a worm-eaten bud from a healthy stem. But Elias Ashmole, and some of the Oxford men of learning, continued to favour the king's cause, though they spoke of it with caution. Ashmole's own great work was researching the history of the Order of the Garter, which seemed to most of them at the table as a doomed piece of academia, given that there was now no king in England, and no Order of the Garter at all.

Ashmole would explain that whether the king was present or not, there was still a notion of kingship which could not be so easily dismissed. At moments like that, Johnnie's face would flush and he would lean forwards to listen. But when the other men cried down the notion and said that the king was dead and kingship was finished forever, then Johnnie would silently slip away.

He still could not hear the king named without flinching. It was as if some picture of the king had taken possession of his heart, and the truth about the dead man, his fallibility, his unreliability, and at the end the arrogance of his downright dishonesty, was not enough to shift it.

'This determined loyalty!' John exclaimed to Hester as they sat on the terrace one evening and watched the sun set away to their right in strips of yellow- and peach-coloured clouds. 'It's such a curse to him, he cannot leave the past behind him and move on.'

She was sewing a collar for Frances and she looked up from her work and smiled. 'He's so like your father.'

'Yes.' John was struck. 'Of course. I hadn't thought of it. My father loved Robert Cecil in the old way – a man and his lord – and then the Duke of Buckingham too. When everyone in the country was shouting for the Duke's head my father would still have done his bidding. He was ready to sail with him to France just as the Duke was struck down. Then he was grieving while everyone else in the country was blessing the assassin.'

'Frances has it too,' Hester said. 'That ability to love without doubts. For her it's Alexander, she's not interested in following a master. But that talent to love a man and his cause is a gift, I really admire it. The more so, I suppose, because it's not one that I share. I'm ashamed to say that I am a complete turncoat. I spent much of my early life at court and most of my family and friends were of the king's party; but all I care for now is peace so that we can sell plants and show the rarities.'

'It's a gift that comes with a price to pay,' John observed. 'Johnnie can't accept that the king is dead and that it is all over. I had hoped that General Lambert would have turned him into a Parliamentary man if not a Leveller. I would rather have had him in love with liberty than with a dead king.'

'He'll grow out of it,' Hester said comfortably. 'They were hard years for him. For all of his boyhood he was sure that Prince Rupert would win the war for the king. He thought that King Charles would triumph up to the very last moment. I think even after Colchester he still thought the king might win. But he knows it is all over now.'

In June Johnnie took the king's melon seedlings in their final largest pots on the cart to the river and loaded them on to a little wherry to take them upriver to Wimbledon. He went alone, he did not even tell his father that he was going, anticipating correctly that John had hoped that the seedlings had been forgotten and might be raised among the others in the melon beds at the Ark.

Johnnie took with him some planks of wood to build the frame, his dinner of bread and cheese in his pocket, a saw and a hammer, and a handful of nails in his belt.

'Building a house and planting a garden?' the ferryman asked with a grin.

Johnnie did not smile in reply. 'I am on an errand,' he said solemnly. 'An errand for my master.'

At the manor house he found the garden running to seed and the kitchen garden overgrown. But there was a warm south-facing wall and Johnnie spent the morning setting in his timber framework and banking up earth for the melon bed. Finally he planted the precious seedlings with a good space between each one, and then painstakingly ferried water from the kitchen-yard pump in the empty clay pots with his finger stopping the hole at the bottom.

Johnnie was his father's son; it was hard for him to leave the rest of the garden alone, and only weed the melon bed. He could see the hallmarks of a typical Tradescant garden becoming gradually obliterated. The south face of the house had a large paved terrace before it and an impressive sweep of paired steps coming down in a semicircle. Johnnie saw the stone pots on the terrace and guessed correctly that his father would have filled them with citrus trees pruned into glossy green balls. At the foot of the steps would have been flowerbeds, he could still see the floppy dead leaves of the tulips which had pushed up through the weeds and presented their bright cups to the blind windows above them. There were fountains and watercourses which were once planted with irises and kingcups and were now choked with water weed. There was an ornamental lake which was now evilly bright green but it still had the white and rose plates of water lilies on the scummy surface. There was an old-fashioned knot garden but the pattern of the bay hedges was blurred with weeds and the white stones were dirty. Johnnie looked around at the desolation of the summer garden which had been carefully planted to be the queen's special refuge and knew that the royal cause was lost indeed.

There was nothing he could do for the garden, he decided. But later in the summer, when the melons were in flower, he would visit again and take a soft rabbit's tail from one to another to pollinate them. Then, when they were setting fruit, he would bring his father's expensive glass melon domes to set over each one to make them ripen. He had not thought what he would then do with the fruit. The king had clearly ordered it, so only the king or his son should eat it. Perhaps it would be Johnnie's duty to take the fruit to France, find the king's son, and give him this eccentric piece of his inheritance.

Johnnie shrugged, the fruit was a question for the future. His task was to keep faith with the last order of the king. King Charles had ordered a Tradescant to make him a melon bed in his manor house at Wimbledon; and it was done.

When Johnnie got home he found that his father was irritated with the wasted day's work, and reluctant to promise the loan of the glass melon domes later in the year; but his stepmother defended him.

'Let him be,' she counselled John, as she plaited her hair ready for bed that night. 'He is doing nothing more than putting flowers on the grave. Let him do this one thing for the king and perhaps he will feel that he has done everything that should be done. Then he will feel that his defence of the king is over, and he can be happy and enjoy the peace.'

Summer 1650

Hester might have predicted Johnnie's feelings as accurately as one of Elias Ashmole's astrological projections except for one thing which she had not taken into account: the endless determination of the Stuarts to regain the crown they had lost.

In July Charles Stuart arrived in Edinburgh and forged a new alliance with the Scots, who were always drawn by the temptation of one of their own Stuart kings, and the rich plums that a grateful English monarch might bring them. He promised them anything they asked, and they promised him an army to conquer England, and crowned him king.

Joseph brought the news from Lambeth and came into the dining room to tell it. The family were at breakfast, Frances and Alexander Norman were either side of the table, Philip Harding, a mathematician, and Paul Quigley, an artist, were dining too. A stunned silence at the news was broken by Johnnie dropping his spoon, and the scrape of his chair as he rose to his feet.

'Not again,' John exclaimed. 'When will this stop? Does he not see that he is defeated and his cause defeated and that he owes it to this country, if he owes us any loyalty or love, to let us get on with our lives without another war?'

'I'm going,' Johnnie said determinedly. 'He's certain to march on England and I must be there.'

'Hush,' Hester said, sharply, uncertain of the safety of such an announcement.

The two guests tactfully rose to their feet. 'I'll take a stroll around the garden,' Philip Harding said.

'I'll come with you,' said Dr Quigley.

The door closed behind them. 'That was unwise,' Alexander Norman said gently to Johnnie. 'Whatever your opinions are, you should not let it ever be said that your father is harbouring royalist sentiments and allowing them to be spoken at his table.'

Johnnie flushed. 'I beg your pardon,' he said to his father and to Hester. 'I won't do it again. It was the shock of the news.'

'Joseph had no business blurting it out like that,' Frances said crossly. 'And you can't go, Johnnie. It's too far. And it's bound to fail.'

'Why should it?' he demanded passionately. 'Why should it fail? The Scots army was stronger than the English last time it was out. And Parliament would never have defeated the king in the first place if it hadn't cobbled together an alliance with the Scots. They could march on London and bring the king with them.'

'Not with General Lambert in the way,' Alexander observed.

Johnnie checked. 'Is he going? The Scots have never beaten Lambert.'

'He's bound to. I would think Cromwell will command with Lambert as his second.'

'It makes no difference to me!' Johnnie declared. 'This is the return of the prince. I must be there.'

There was a silence, Frances turned to her father, who had not yet spoken. The silence extended. Johnnie looked towards his father at the end of the table.

'He is the king,' Johnnie said desperately. 'Crowned king.'

'He's not crowned in England,' Hester said sharply. 'He's not our king.'

'He's the third king of England that this family has been called on to serve,' Johnnie pressed. 'And I am the third generation in royal service. This is my service now, this is my king. I must serve him as you served his father and my grandfather served his grandfather.'

There was a long silence. Everyone waited for John to speak.

'You know my heart, sir,' Johnnie said with careful courtesy to his father. 'I hope you will give me leave to go.'

John looked down the table and saw his son blazing with bright intensity. He was restored. He was the Johnnie who had ridden out to the siege of Colchester, nothing like the ghost which they had sent back. John carefully avoided Hester's minatory gaze and spoke softly to his impassioned son.

'I have to weigh your safety against your desire to serve the king. It's not my cause, Johnnie, but you are a grown man and I see that it is yours. But you are the only heir, the only Tradescant to carry the name . . .'

Johnnie cleared his throat. 'I know that,' he said. 'But this is a great cause. It is worth a sacrifice.'

Hester moved quickly as if she would cry out against the thought of Johnnie being sacrificed to a cause, however great. Still John did not let himself look at her.

'If the Scots get as far south as York,' he said carefully, 'then you may join them. You don't want to fight for the king in Scotland, Johnnie, that's their own business. I wouldn't see you fight on their soil. But if they get to York I will buy you a horse and equipment and you can enlist, and I shall be proud to see you go.'

There was a swift intake of breath and a swirl of grey silk at the end of the table as Hester leaped to her feet.

'And your stepmother agrees with me,' John ruled, forestalling the quick exclamation.

'I can see that she does, sir,' Johnnie said gravely, a quiver of laughter in his voice.

'She does indeed,' John repeated.

Hester subsided into her seat again, her hands holding the edge of the table as if physical force was the only way she could restrain her speech.

'And you will promise me not to run off without my permission and blessing,' John stipulated. 'You've been to war now, Johnnie, you know how hard it is. You know it's a hundred times harder for a man without some money in his pocket and the right equipment: a good sword, a warm cloak, a strong horse. If you wait until the Scots have reached York you can join them as an officer. Do I have your word?'

Johnnie hesitated for only a moment. 'You have,' he said. 'But I will start preparing today, so that I am ready the moment I can go.'

'How can you?' Frances interrupted passionately. 'How can you even think of it, Johnnie? After the last time?'

He fired up at the challenge in her voice. 'You wouldn't understand,' he said. 'You're a girl.'

'I understand that you nearly broke Mother's heart last time and that we have none of us been happy since you came back from Colchester,' she said hotly. 'I understand that you have been sick to death ever since that defeat. Why go? Why go all that way to feel despair again? What if you are hurt so far from home? We'd never even know! What if your luck runs out and you get killed in one of these stupid battles at a village where we never even know the name?'

Alexander Norman, looking from his angry young wife to her younger brother, still not yet seventeen years old, hoped for a moment that the two might quarrel like the children they once were and the whole issue be lost in the confusion of words and temper. Johnnie leaped to his feet, ready to blaze back at Frances, but then he reined in his temper and looked at his father.

'I thank you for your permission, sir,' he said formally, and left the room.

Hester waited in silence until they heard his footsteps cross the hall and go out of the back door. Then she spoke bitterly to her husband. 'How could you? How could you agree that he should go?'

John looked at his son-in-law over a mug of small ale. 'Ask Alexander,' he advised. 'He knows how I could.'

Hester, her cheeks blazing, turned to Alexander. 'What?' she spat out.

'They'll never get to York,' Alexander predicted. 'Cromwell can't risk having a foreign army on English soil. He can't even risk having a Scottish army on the march against him. Not after having bloodied his sword in Ireland to keep the people down. He has to bring peace to the kingdom or lose everything. Lose one kingdom and he has lost all four. He'll fight them in Scotland and he'll defeat them in Scotland. He'll never let them come south.'

'But the king will bring out the clans,' Hester whispered. 'Men who would march all night to die for him and for their clan chief. Wild men who won't count the price, who will fight like savages.'

'The clans won't leave Scotland, they never do,' John predicted. 'They'll come no further south than a raiding party.'

'And they'll be poorly equipped,' Alexander agreed. 'They'll come out with daggers and pitchforks and meet Cromwell and Lambert and the Model Army with its cavalry and cannon and muskets and pikes. I'll have to go back to London today, there will be new orders for barrels. But you can be sure that my orders will be to send the ordnance by sea to Scotland to meet the army there – that's where Cromwell will choose his battlefield.'

Hester turned to the window and looked out over the garden. The flowerbeds before the house were filled with pinks, gillyflowers, and the new star-faced spiderwort in pink. The roses on the walls were shedding petals as they bloomed. Johnnie was striding down the avenue, his head up, his shoulders back, his listlessness and sadness quite gone.

'How can we bear it?' she asked softly. 'How could you give him permission and your blessing to go into danger again?'

John was beside her, he slid his arm around her waist and half-reluctantly she let him hold her. 'I am doing the very thing that I think will keep him safe,' he said. 'That is my only intention.'

461

All July and all August Johnnie was in a fever for news, desperate to be ready to go the moment his father said he might leave. He persuaded John to buy him a horse, a reliable old war charger called Caesar with big, strong haunches and broad shoulders that looked as if it would carry Johnnie's light weight for hundreds of miles.

He tied a sack stuffed with hay into the low branch of a tree and practised charging it and stabbing at it with his lance. The first few practices he followed his horse back to the stable after a couple of hard tumbles; but then he learned the knack of thrusting and withdrawing the lance in one smooth motion so the horse and he could go on together.

He bought a travelling cape and a bag that he could strap on the back of the saddle and he kept them packed with everything he might need so that he was ready to leave at a moment's notice. He was alive and vital with excitement and determination, and the whole house rang with the noise of him singing, whistling, running up and down the wooden stairs in his riding boots, shedding mud and creating confusion out of sheer energy.

John had made him promise that he would not tell anyone of the agreement they had made, and Johnnie, who remembered well enough the danger of living as suspected royalists when the king's army was on the march, was careful to make no direct reference as to which side he would be joining as soon as his father said he might go. He was as excited as a child, but he was no fool. Never again did he let slip to visitors or guests that he was only waiting for news from Yorkshire to saddle up his war horse and ride north to join the new, uncrowned king.

The family depended on Alexander Norman to tell them how the war was going. Living in the centre of the city and near the Tower he always had the first of the rumours anyway; but filling Cromwell's orders for supplies of munitions he always knew the latest position of the Model Army, though it might be impossible to tell how they were faring.

'But that's not the point,' Johnnie reminded his father anxiously, finding him in the rarities room, with a tray of recently purchased foreign coins.

'We're running out of space,' John said. 'We have to buy new items, and people like to see different things when they visit. But we cannot show everything we have now properly. We should think about building another room, perhaps.'

'The point was not whether the Scots are winning or losing, it was how far they are advanced,' Johnnie persisted. 'That was our agreement, wasn't it? Because Mother is saying that if they have advanced to York but been defeated then I shouldn't go. But we didn't say that, did we?'

John looked at his son's eager face. 'The letter of our agreement was certainly that you might go if they reached York,' he said. 'But surely, Johnnie, you wouldn't want to join a defeated army. You wouldn't want to volunteer for a lost cause?'

The young man did not hesitate for a moment. 'Of course I would,' he said simply. 'This is not about calculating which side might win and joining that. This is not about trying to end up on the winning side like half the men now in Parliament. This is about serving the king, whether he is winning or losing. His father did not recant when he saw the scaffold. Neither will I.'

John pushed the tray of coins roughly into his son's hands. 'Find a little corner for these, and write out new labels for them,' he said. 'They need to be dusted and polished too. And don't talk to me about scaffolds.'

'But if they get to York, even if they are in retreat –'

'Yes, yes,' John said. 'I remember what we agreed.'

Autumn 1650

For all of Alexander Norman's confidence in the New Model Army, it was a desperate gamble that John was taking with his son's safety. Sometimes he thought of Charles Stuart and himself, at opposite ends of the country, both taking their desperate gambles – one for the crown of England, one for the life of his son. It did not trouble John that he was gambling on Charles Stuart's failure. John's loyalty to the kings, never a strong flame, had flickered fitfully all through the first king's war, and been blown out altogether when the war had been renewed not once, but twice, after defeat. His vigil at the courtroom and scaffold had been a farewell to a man he had served, not the act of a loyal royalist. John's sympathies had always been independent, now, a citizen of a republic, he could call himself a republican.

More than anything else he wanted peace, a society in which he could garden, in which he could watch his children grow to adulthood, make marriages and have children of their own. He would have been hard-pressed to forgive any man for breaking the peace of the new state. And Charles Stuart did not sound like an exceptional man. Cromwell himself complained that the prince was so debauched that he would undo the whole country. All the news of the prince's court over the water had been of popery, folly, and vice.

But it was a close thing. The Scots army first met the English just south of Edinburgh for the battle on Scottish soil that Alexander had predicted. The Scots were in fine form, and filled with confidence at the presence of the young king. The English army were tired from the long march north, and were losing men all the way as individual soldiers changed their minds and turned south for home. The Commander-in-Chief, Cromwell, was in one of his dark moods when he doubted his men's abilities and, worse than that, doubted his own. The voice of God which guided him so clearly had suddenly gone silent and Cromwell was spiralling down into one of his disabling fits of despair. It was only John Lambert's unshakable optimism that kept the army marching north.

Then they nearly lost Lambert at the battle of Musselburgh, just south of Edinburgh, when his horse was shot dead under him and Lambert, falling, was lanced in the thigh. The Scots infantry spotted him, and a band of them were dragging him away from the battlefield when his own regiment, Yorkshiremen most of them, let out a yell of horror which made even the Highlanders check, and charged through the crowd to get to him.

The Scots pressed on southwards for London; the English army chased after them until the Scots chose the ground and turned to face the pursuers outside Dunbar. The English were hopelessly outnumbered; injury, illness, and desertion had taken a dramatic toll. Cromwell was uncertain whether to go forwards against the Scots or fall back. Only Lambert gritted his teeth and said they must fight then and there.

While Cromwell dropped the flap of his tent so that he might weep and pray in privacy, John Lambert mustered the army and told them simply and clearly that the Scots outnumbered them by two to one and thus they must fight with double bravery, double persistence, and double faith. There were about twenty-two thousand Scotsmen drawn up for battle, and only eleven thousand of them. With the smile that Hester Tradescant secretly loved, Lambert pulled off his plumed hat and beamed at his troops. 'I don't think this is a difficulty,' he shouted. 'Come on, Ironsides!'

❦

Early in September, Alexander sent a one line note to John.

Scots defeated at Dunbar.

'Thank God,' Hester said piously when John held out the letter for her to read in the stable yard. She put her hand in her pocket and gave Alexander's boy a coin.

'I already paid him,' John remarked.

Hester smiled. 'I could give ten shillings for this news,' she said. 'Shall you tell Johnnie, or will I?'

She hesitated. 'Where is he?'

'On the other side of the road, picking nuts from the horse chestnut trees.'

'You go,' she said. 'It was your agreement with him that has kept him safe.'

'Praise God,' John said. 'I have had some sleepless nights.'

He strolled around the house, savouring the warmth of the sun reflected from the walls, glancing up in passing at the flamboyant crest which his father had illegally composed and claimed. It didn't matter now, John thought with satisfaction. There were so many newly created titles and such confusion about how titles had come into being, that they could claim to be baronets and no-one would query it. Indeed, Johnnie might one day very well be Sir John Tradescant as his grandfather had always wanted. Who knew what this new world would bring? As long as the family could keep its place, could keep the business, could keep the plants; as long as the horse chestnut trees flowered each year and scattered down the precious nuts like a prodigal rain of wealth, as long as there was always a Tradescant heir to pick them up and set them deep in moist pots.

John walked across the little bridge that spanned the stream at the side of the road and then crossed to the acreage on the other side. He had planted a thick holly hedge as a windbreak and to shield the plant beds from curious passers-by and he thought this year he might trim it to make it thicken out and to square off the top like a handsome green wall. He paused for a moment and looked upwards. It would take more than a week of work to cut back the top boughs of the hedge and it would be a painful, awkward job. He smiled at the thought that at least Johnnie would be at home to help him, and then he opened the door set between brick lintels in the hedge and went into the garden.

It was part physic garden, part vegetable plot, a new sort of garden for a new age which prized science and medicine more highly than luxury and prettiness.

But from ingrained habit, John had made his herb and vegetable beds in a pattern like a knot garden, and they were strictly aligned to a central point where he had dug a deep hole, lined it with clay and filled it with water to use as a dipping pond for watering the garden. The beds nearest the pond were all planted with the rarer and more tender herbs that the College of Physicians had asked him to grow. He had planted the edges with lavender to keep insect pests away, and because lavender was a good paying crop, the flower heads could always be sold to the perfume-makers and the apothecaries. Further away from the central pond radiated other geometrically shaped beds growing greens and brassicas, onions, peas, turnips, purple-flowered and white-flowered potatoes – the food crops of the country gardens which John was breeding and cross-breeding, trying to rid them of their tendency to blight, trying to find the largest and the most nutritious.

If ever they were visited by one of the more dour radicals or sectaries who complained of the riot of wealth and colour in the rarities room or in the garden around the house, John would bring him over here and show how, in these beds, he was using his skills in the service of the people and of God.

Johnnie was at the far end of the garden where they had planted row upon row of saplings, ready for sale, and where they had a chestnut tree at each corner. White sheets were laid under the trees and Johnnie came every day at dawn and dusk to get the very best of the nuts before the squirrels ate them.

'Hey!' John called from the door to the garden. 'Message from Alexander.'

Johnnie looked up and came through the garden at a run, his face ablaze with joy and hope. 'The king's reached York? I can go to him?'

John shook his head and mutely held out the note.

Johnnie took it, opened it, read it. John saw the energy and joy drain out of his son as if a leech of grief had suddenly fastened on his heart.

'Defeated,' he said, as if the word was meaningless. 'Defeated at Dunbar. Where is Dunbar?'

'Scotland,' John said gruffly. 'South of Edinburgh, I think.'

'The king?'

'As you see, he doesn't say. But it's over,' John said gently. 'That was his last throw of the dice. He'll go back to France, I suppose.'

His son looked up at him, his young face bewildered. 'Over? D'you think he'll never try again?'

'He can't keep trying,' John exclaimed. 'He can't keep coming back and coming back and upsetting the country. He has to know that it was over for his father and it is over for him. Their time has gone. The English don't want a king any more.'

'You made me stay and wait,' Johnnie said with sudden sharp bitterness. 'And I stayed and waited, like hundreds, perhaps thousands, of other men. And while I stayed and waited he didn't have enough men. So he was defeated, while I stayed at home, waiting for your leave to go.'

John put his hand on Johnnie's shoulder but the younger man shrugged it off and took a few steps away. 'I betrayed him!' he cried out, his voice breaking. 'I stayed at home obeying my father when I should have ridden out to obey my king.'

John hesitated, choosing his words with care. 'I don't think it was a close-run thing. I don't think hundreds of men would have made a difference. Since Cromwell and Lambert have had command of the army they have rarely lost a battle. I don't think your being there would have made a difference, Johnnie.'

Johnnie looked back at his father and his dark, beautiful young face was filled with reproach. 'It would have made a difference to me,' he said with simple dignity.

He came into dinner in silence. In silence he went to bed. At breakfast the next morning his eyes were sombre and there were dark shadows underneath them. The light had gone out of Johnnie once again.

Hester put her hand on his shoulder as she rose from the table to fetch some more small ale.

'Why don't you go to Wimbledon today?' she asked him gently. 'Your next crop of melons must be nearly ready to pick.'

'What should I do with the fruit?' he asked miserably.

Hester glanced towards John for help and saw the smallest shrug. 'Why don't you pack them up,' she suggested. 'And send them to Charles Stuart in Edinburgh. Don't put your name inside,' she stipulated cautiously. 'But you could at least send them to him. Then you would know that you had served him as you should serve him. You're not a soldier, Johnnie, you're a gardener. You could send him the fruit you have grown for him. That's how you serve him. That's how your father served his father, and your grandfather served King James himself.'

Johnnie hesitated for only a moment then he looked to his father. 'May I go?' he asked hopefully.

'Yes,' John said in relief. 'Of course you can go. It's a very good thing to do.'

468

Spring 1651

In the cold, dark days of February John was glad to go to London and stay with Frances, or with Philip Harding, or Paul Quigley, and join the men in their discussions. Sometimes one of the physicians would conduct an experiment and summon the gentlemen to watch so that they might comment on his findings. John attended an evening in which one of the alchemists attempted to fire a new glaze for porcelain.

'John should be the judge,' one of the gentlemen said. 'You have some porcelain in your collection, haven't you, John?'

'I have some china dishes,' John said. 'They range in size from as big as a trencher to so small that a mouse could dine off it.'

'Very fine?' the man asked. 'You can see light through them, can't you?'

'Yes,' John said. 'But strong. I've never seen the like in this country. I think we don't have china clay which is fine enough.'

'It's the glaze,' said another man.

'The heat of the furnace,' suggested another.

'Wait,' said the alchemist. 'Wait until the furnace is cooled enough and you shall see it.'

'A drink while we wait?' someone suggested and the maidservant brought a bottle of Canary wine and glasses, and they drew up high stools to sit companionably around the alchemist's working bench.

'Have you heard that Oatlands Palace is to be taken down?' one of the men asked John. 'You planted the gardens there, didn't you?'

John checked in the act of drinking. 'Taken down?' he repeated.

Another man nodded. 'They can't sell it. It's too big for a private residence, and it needs too much work done. It's to be destroyed.'

'But – the gardens?' John stammered.

'You should petition Parliament,' one of the mathematicians

recommended. 'Ask them if you may uproot your plants before they start to knock the whole thing down. You have some rarities there, don't you?'

'Indeed I have,' John said, astounded. 'There are some very precious things in the royal courts.' He shook his head. 'Every day there is something new but I would never have thought that they would raze Oatlands.'

John raised the matter of Oatlands' gardens with a Parliament man who visited the Ark to see the rarities and in a few days he received a commission to supervise the selling of the specimen plants from the garden before the demolition of the house. He might take a tithe of the profit and any plants he chose as payment for his trouble, and he was ordered to sell the rest.

'I'll stay there for a week or so, until the work is done,' he told Hester.

'I shall miss our little house there,' she said. 'I liked knowing we had a place out of the city, a refuge.'

'Such a waste,' John said. 'All that work in the gardens, all that beauty in the house. And the new orangery and the silkworm house! All for nothing.'

'Shall you take Johnnie with you?' Hester asked. 'It might do him good to have a change of scene.'

'Yes,' John said. 'I'll take the cart too. I'll bring back some of the chestnut trees if any have survived this winter. And there were some handsome climbers as well which I might be able to cut back from the walls and transplant.'

They harnessed Caesar, Johnnie's war horse, to the cart and John thought that the handsome animal pulling a gardener's cart to a palace which was to be demolished could have served as an illustration for a chapbook entitled: 'How the mighty are fallen'. A war horse harnessed to pull a cart did not seem to him to be a symbol of peace and prosperity when his son sat beside him on the driving seat with his eyes deep-set and dark. Even the horse drooped its head at the unfamiliar weight dragging at its shoulders. It seemed as if both boy and horse should be released from drudgery, should be set free to ride off in some romance of their own devising. The times were too small and too mean for both of them.

They were beautiful creatures, they should have been freed to go their own ways.

John thought that hard work might restore some of Johnnie's spirits, and set him to cutting back and lifting the roses out of the rose garden. There was no time to be troubled with any but the most precious plants in the garden, and the trees in the orchards. The great richness of the nine acres and the terraced courts could not be uprooted and saved in the short February days.

John worked from memory, powerful, evocative memories of planting for the king and queen, remembering what plant was in his hand when she stopped by him on the path, what precious bulbs were stored in the nets hung up high in the roofs of the sheds.

In the evenings they planned the work for the next day and Johnnie would ask over and over again whether the queen had chosen this plant, or that; whether the king had eaten fruit from this very tree. Despite himself, John found that he was remembering with affection the beauty of the garden and the rich frivolity of the court. Despite his own scepticism he drew a picture of a golden time, gardening in summer for a king and a queen who spent money like rain and who walked lovingly arm-in-arm along well-tended paths from one exquisite court and terrace to another.

John and his son spent a week lifting the rarest and most precious plants and potting them up and loading them into the cart. Every other day they drove the cart down to the river and transferred the pots on to a ferry to send to the Ark at Lambeth.

'Hester won't be best pleased,' John remarked as yet another boatload of plants set off downstream. 'She and Joseph will be doing nothing but unloading and watering pots this week.'

'We have to do it,' Johnnie said passionately. 'We're his gardeners. We have to save as much of his garden as we can.'

Something in the desperate note in his voice warned John. He put his hand on his son's arm. 'We're doing this for the plants, not for the king,' he said. 'Some of these are of the best quality, some of these are rare and precious. I couldn't let them go to waste. This work is for the plants and for the Ark.'

Johnnie looked at his father. 'These are the king's plants,' he said with suppressed emotion. 'We're gardening for him now as we always have done. Once it was our duty to put the plants in and safeguard them. Now it's our duty to save them for him. When he comes to his own again he can sit underneath his own father's cherry tree, he can pick roses for his mother from her favourite tree. They've crowned him king in Scotland, haven't they? They've declared him to be their king though they once called his father a prisoner and handed him over to his death. But Charles is an anointed king once more, in a kingdom which acknowledges him?'

'At such a price,' John muttered. 'He agreed to every demand the Scots put to him, and betrayed men who had fought for him in the Highlands for years. Your old hero, Montrose, was captured and executed, and the king dining with the Kirk, his old enemies, looked out of the window and saw Montrose's hand nailed to the door. He said nothing. He went on with his dinner.'

'He does what he has to do,' Johnnie said staunchly.

Once they had rescued the pick of the specimens, and rummaged in the cold soil of the courts for forgotten bulbs, they declared a general sale of plants in Weybridge. The town crier called out the news and it spread from one manor garden to another, from one cottage to another, until everyone in Surrey wanted a flower from the king's garden.

On Saturday John set up a stall on the very front door of the palace and let people come with their own spades to choose, and then dig up their choice. He and Johnnie inspected the booty and set an instant knock-down price on the trees which marched past them, on the little pots of pansies and herbs, on the trailing creepers, torn from the walls, on the endless scarlet-budding roses.

It was a melancholy business to see the garden walking away down the drive, as if even the plants had gone into exile, and John was sorry that he had exposed his son to the sight. He had thought that the work would have given them a project to complete together, that Johnnie would see that the garden was finished, that the palace was destroyed, that the king and kingship were gone forever. But instead there was a powerful sense of loss invoked by the sale. More than one man or woman stopped at John's table, gestured to their purchase and asked reverently: 'He did love these, didn't he? Can you remember if he ever picked a flower from it? Did he touch it?'

John realised that only half of the people were buying plants cheaply; the other half were buying relics, honouring the memory of a dead king, planting a little bit of his martyrdom in their own gardens.

All the cold grey day Johnnie priced, took money, answered questions with endless easy patience. But John, watching him, saw how his head drooped as the light faded from the sky.

'You're tired,' he said gruffly at five o'clock as the winter twilight closed around them. 'And chilled too. I know I am. Let's go down to the ale house and get ourselves a good dinner. I'd like to leave the money in the goldsmith's keeping anyway. I don't want to keep it here.'

Johnnie's face was pale. 'Yes.'

'Are you sick?' John asked.

Johnnie shook his head. 'Weary,' he said. 'I wasn't born to be a huckster. I hate it. How they do go on, don't they? And the smaller the plant the more ado they make about the price.'

John laughed eagerly. 'Yes. It's been a long business. But tomorrow we'll go.'

'And then they'll pull it down and it will be as if it was never here,' Johnnie said dreamily.

John tied the string of the purse and slipped it into his deep pocket. 'Come on,' he said cheerfully. 'Before we are completely benighted.'

He marched briskly down the avenue with Johnnie keeping step beside him. They were warm by the time they saw the yellow light of the ale house and smelled the mixture of woodsmoke and frying bacon.

'You go on,' John said. 'I'll take this purse and put it in the goldsmith's vault.'

Johnnie nodded and went ahead of his father. John stood back and watched his son walk away. 'Johnnie!' he suddenly called.

The young man hesitated and turned, his face a pale blur in the twilight.

'It's being rid of the old to prepare for the new,' John said. 'A baptism. Not a funeral, you know.'

It was a melancholy business the next morning, for all of John's forced brightness. They loaded the cart with leftover tools and the pots which they had filled with the rescued plants during their stay, and then they went round the garden and orchard and orangery in one final tour to see what had been overlooked.

The rose garden was a desert of pitted holes, like the face of a beloved woman pocked with scars. The very shape of the garden had gone, the trees which had given it a structure had been uprooted, the trellised arbours which had been pulled down as people cut off the climbing roses were left as smashed wood in the mud. The lavender borders were ragged, some plants missing, some trodden down. A few snowdrops which had struggled up at the base of the wall in the queen's court had been crushed by someone in their haste to cut down a creeper. A pot had been dropped and smashed and the shards left where they lay, cluttering up the path. The whole palace, once so rosy in pink brick and so immaculately gardened, with smooth lawns and sculpted arbours, was now a tangle of overgrown hedging and churned mud. Even the bowling green which had been John's great pride was pocked with weeds and the richer green of winter moss shone in moist patches among the paler green of weak winter grass.

It had started to rain, an icy, penetrating drizzle, and the clouds sat heavily on the roof of the palace. The glass had been stolen long ago from the windows, or smashed by the successive troops quartered in the palace, and the smell of damp plaster and decay seeped into the courts from the derelict building.

'Let's go,' John said. 'Everything is finished here.'

Johnnie nodded in silence and followed his father to the cart. He climbed on to the box and took the reins of the horse which should have been his war horse, to drive away from the palace which should have been the king's. The avenue was long gone, felled for timber. They drove between pale stumps where grand trees had once shaded the road.

'That was a miserable task,' John said heartily, hoping that Johnnie would agree and that they might share the sadness and then put it behind them.

'It was burying him and his hopes all over again,' Johnnie said sombrely; and then said nothing more.

Summer 1651

Johnnie did not forget the melon bed at Wimbledon. Of the consignment he had sent north to Charles Stuart he had kept one fruit back and from it he had another batch of seeds which he insisted on planting in the Lambeth seed bed, and, when they were grown, insisted on taking to Wimbledon.

'You could grow them here now,' Hester remarked to him reasonably when she saw him loading the earthenware pots into a carrying basket. 'There's no point in taking them all that way.'

'Of course I must plant them at Wimbledon,' he said passionately. 'It was his request.'

'The garden must be overgrown.'

'It's running to seed,' he said, 'and the glass has been stolen from the windows of the house. But you can see it was a lovely place, you can tell it was one of our gardens. Every now and then I come across some special flower struggling through the weeds. Father's Virginian foxgloves, and grandfather's chestnuts in a little avenue in one of the courts.'

'We can't do anything about it,' she said. 'We have to leave the old places behind us. Your father gardened for years at Hatfield and after he left he never went back and it was the same at New Hall. Oatlands will be nothing more than a name in a year or two, in a few years no-one will even remember where it was.'

'I know that,' he said. 'I just plant the melons. I don't deny that everything is changed for the moment.'

'You don't change,' she observed.

For a moment his melancholy lifted. He shot her a small, roguish smile as if he hardly dared to trust her with the hope that he kept hidden. 'Well, everything might change back again one day, mightn't it? And then I will be glad that I kept faith.'

Johnnie had good cause to suggest that everything could change once again. The defeat at Dunbar was not the last battle fought in Scotland, the Scots army did not flee in a rout but in a retreat; and the shaky alliance between the Kirk and the dissolute prince did not completely collapse. Instead, the prince's stature grew and the Scots warmed to him. All through the year, reports of a continuing campaign filtered back to London telling of Cromwell, ill-supported and in a mostly hostile country, trying to gain a decisive victory. Then in midsummer the Scots army, with Charles at their head, did the unthinkable. They broke out of Scotland and crossed the border.

'Can we hide it from him?' Hester demanded urgently of John when he told her the news in the kitchen.

He shook his head. 'He's bound to hear of it sooner or later and I'd not have him think me guilty of double dealing.'

'You swore they'd not come south,' she accused. 'You said Cromwell would defeat them on Scottish soil.'

John's face was taut with worry. 'It was a gamble,' he said. 'And it served us well. They have to go beyond York, remember. That was the agreement.'

'Is Lambert still there?' she asked, as if that were a talisman against the king's advance.

'Oh, for God's sake!' John snapped and turned away from her and marched out into the garden, looking for his son.

He found him dead-heading the roses and tossing the petals into a deep carrying basket for sale in the London markets to the perfumiers or the confectioners. Frances, staying at the Ark to avoid the plague months in town, was working at the opposite end of the bed. John heard their casual chatter and paused for a moment to hold the moment in his mind: his two children doing their work, the family's work, in such easy harmony, in the sunshine, on their own land, in a country so near to peace.

He squared his shoulders and stepped forwards. 'Johnnie –'

The young man looked up. 'Father?'

'There's news. I heard it in London. Charles Stuart is leading a troop over the border. Lambert is chasing after him, but it looks as if he has broken out of Scotland and is determined to invade.'

'Is he south of York?' Johnnie demanded. For a moment John thought that the young man was resonating, like a harp string tuned too tight. 'Is he south of York? Can I go to him?'

'He's headed south,' John said cautiously. 'As soon as we hear from Alexander we'll know for sure.'

Alexander came himself in August.

'I knew you would want to know as soon as I did,' he said. The family were so anxious for news that they greeted him in the hall, as soon as he came through the door, Johnnie at the forefront. 'They were marching on London but they have turned to the west. They're probably hoping to raise recruits from Wales before they face Lambert.'

'And where is Lambert?'

'On a forced march behind them,' Alexander replied. 'There is no other general in the world who could move his men at the speed he does. He'll catch the Scots army, without a doubt. And he'll be the one that chooses the ground.'

'Is he south of York?' Johnnie demanded.

Alexander looked past him to Hester's anguished face. 'I am sorry, Hester,' was all he said.

Johnnie sprang up the stairs, running for his campaign bundle, shouting for Joseph to tell the stable lad to get his horse ready. John turned to his wife and she buried her face against his shoulder.

'Stop him,' she whispered. 'Stop him.'

John shook his head. 'No power on earth can stop him,' he said. He looked at Alexander. 'Can they win?'

Alexander had drawn Frances to his side. 'These are the fortunes of war,' he said. 'You know as well as I do that anything can happen, it can always go either way. But Cromwell and Lambert defeated this army before, and on their own ground. The northern militia will turn out now that the Scots have invaded England, and the northern men hate the Scots worse than anything else. There'll be strong feelings against the king now that he has an army moving through England – no-one has forgotten the last war. It's one thing to mourn the death of a dead king; it's quite another to turn the country upside down again for the claims of a live one. I think they'll lose. But I can't be sure. No-one can be sure.'

'Who cares?' Hester said, her face still hidden, her voice agonised. 'Who cares if they lose or win? Johnnie could be killed, couldn't he? Whether they win or lose?'

John tightened his grip around her. 'We'll have to pray,' he said, and it was a sign of his own desperation. 'That's all we can do now.'

They gathered in the stable yard to see him off. He kissed his sister, he kissed his stepmother and she clung to him for a moment as if she would beg him to stay. She inhaled the scent of him, the newly washed linen which had been stored with lavender bags, the warm straw smell of his hair, the warmth of his skin, the tender stubble of his cheek, the soft apprentice moustache on his upper lip. She held him and thought of the child he had been when she had taken him into her care, and she thought of the terrible gulf in her life that would be carved out if he were lost.

'Let him go,' John said quietly from behind her.

Johnnie briskly embraced Alexander and then he turned to his father. He dropped his head and was about to kneel for his blessing. 'Don't kneel,' John said quickly, as if a patch of damp on his son's knee mattered one way or another when the boy was going out to fight a doomed battle. He wrapped him in his arms and held him furiously tight.

'God bless you and keep you,' he whispered passionately. 'And come home as soon as you feel you can. Don't linger, Johnnie. Once the battle is done there's no shame in riding away.'

The youth was ablaze with joy, he could not hear words of caution. He turned to his horse and he sprang up, swung his leg over and gathered in the reins. The old knowledgeable war horse, Caesar, knew the signs, he pawed the ground, arched his neck and sidled a little, eager to be off.

Hester felt her knees giving way, she put her hand into John's arm and leaned against him.

'I'm away!' Johnnie sung out. 'I'll write! Goodbye!'

Hester folded her upper lip in a tight, admonitory grip between her teeth and raised her hand to wave.

'Good luck!' Frances called. 'God bless you, Johnnie!'

They crowded to the stable-yard entrance to watch him ride out, and then followed him, under the wall with the stone-carved crest, over the little bridge, and then eastwards along the road to the Lambeth horse ferry and the northern roads.

'God bless you,' John called.

The horse's polished haunches moved powerfully. As he reached the firm going of the road, Johnnie let the animal extend into a trot and then into a broad-paced canter. He went too fast for Hester, the big horse's pace took him too swiftly away.

'Johnnie!' she called.

But he did not hear her, and in a moment he was gone.

Autumn 1651

Then there was nothing to do but to wait. The City was alive with rumours and counter-claims of battles and routs and attacks, victory to the Prince or victory to the Model Army. John kept as much of the news from Hester as he could, and asked her to do a dozen tasks in the rarities room, in the garden, to keep her hands busy and to keep her away from the constant litany of bad news in the kitchen between the cook and Joseph. But nothing could stop her longing for her son.

Frances and Hester lit a candle in the window the evening that Johnnie went away, and Hester would not have the shutter closed on it, to hide it from the road, nor ever let it burn out. Every morning she renewed it herself, a great wax candle, more suited for a church than for a home, every night she checked that it was burning safely and its light was showing out towards the Lambeth road where Johnnie had ridden away.

John remarked only that there was a danger of fire if the candle should fall over in a gust of wind, and after that she placed the holder in a dish of water. But nothing would persuade her not to show a light, as if the one candle could guide her boy homewards along the dark, unsafe roads.

In the first week in September Alexander Norman came upriver and marched briskly from the landing stage to the Ark. He found John alone in the physic garden.

'News,' he said shortly.

John scrambled up from the herb bed and waited.

'There was a battle on the third, the anniversary of the Dunbar defeat. Cromwell is a great one for anniversaries.'

'And?'

'Defeat. The Scots were routed and Charles Stuart has gone.'

'Dead?' John asked. 'Dead at last?'

'Disappeared. There's a price on his head and the whole country looking for him. He must be taken any day. The Scots are fled back to Scotland and the English volunteers heading for their homes. Cromwell writes that he is bringing the army home and disbanding the militia. He must think he is completely safe. We must think so.'

'A defeat,' John said.

'It means nothing for a single soldier,' Alexander said swiftly. 'He could be riding home now.'

John nodded. 'I'd better tell Hester before some fool blurts it out to her.'

'Where is Frances?'

'They'll be together,' John predicted. 'This summer has been a long vigil for them both.'

John gathered up his tools and the two men crossed the road. Instinctively they looked east towards Lambeth, as if they might see the big horse and the joyous young man riding back to them.

'I keep looking,' John said gruffly. 'We all of us keep looking for him.'

※

They had no word, they could get no news. Cromwell came home but Lambert stayed in Scotland, ruling from Edinburgh, bringing the Scots gradually into line with a republican England. He sent an order for some tulips to grow in pots in his rooms and Hester, knowing herself to be taking a risk with their whole livelihood and lives, wrote him a note, slipped it in with the bulbs and handed them to his messenger.

> *Forgive me asking for your assistance, but one very dear to me may have been captured at Worcester. Can you tell me how I might discover what has happened to him, or where he is now?*

'Shall I order more candles?' the cook asked, preparing the list for market. 'Or –'

'Or what?' Hester snapped.

The suggestion that there was little point setting out the candle every night for Johnnie was too grave to be named.

'Nothing,' the cook replied.

John Lambert replied by the next courier travelling to London in a note which showed that he understood exactly who might be very dear to Hester and who might have been at Worcester.

> *Dear Mrs Tradescant,*
>
> *I am sorry to hear of your anxiety. The Scots cavalry were not intensely engaged in the battle and retreated in good order to Scotland. There they dispersed. He might well have gone with them till the order came to scatter and thus there is good reason to hope that he may return within the next few months. There were very few captured and he is not among them. I specifically asked for him by name. We are not holding him prisoner. There were very few killed.*
>
> *I thank you for your tulips. You seem to have put in half a dozen more bulbs than I paid for. I wish I could render you greater service in return, but I will be alert for any familiar name and I will write again if I have any news.*

Hester took the letter into the rarities room where the fire was kept burning against the wintry weather and plunged it deep into the heart of the red-hot logs. She very much wanted to keep the note for the little comfort she could draw from it; but she knew that she should not.

Winter 1651

In a dark afternoon of December as Hester was closing the shutters in the rarities room and the parlour she heard a horse walking steadily up the road. She went to the window and looked out, as she always did whenever she heard a single horseman riding by the house. She looked without expectation of seeing her son, but she looked, just as she burned the candle: because he should always be looked for, because a vigil should always be kept for him.

When she saw the size and solidity of the horse, she blinked and rubbed her eyes because for a moment she thought it must be Caesar. But she had thought that she had seen Caesar so many times before that she did not start forwards and cry out.

He came steadily closer and she realised it was indeed Caesar, and that on his back, slumped in the saddle, was Johnnie, his warm cape wrapped around him, bare-headed, finding his way home along the darkened road as much by memory as by sight.

She did not scream or cry or run; Hester had never been a woman for screaming or crying or running. She went quietly to the front door and opened it, opened the garden gate, and stepped quietly across the little bridge over the stream, into the road. Caesar pricked up his ears at the whisper of her skirt, grey against the grey twilight, and quickened his pace. Johnnie, who had been half-asleep in the saddle, glanced up and saw the figure of a woman, waiting in the lane, as if she had waited for him at the gatepost ever since he had left.

'Mother?' His voice was a little hoarse.

'My son.'

He reined in the horse and tumbled down from the saddle. He dropped the reins and stepped towards her outstretched arms. She took his weight in the embrace as his legs buckled as he hit the ground.

'My son, my son,' she said.

He smelled different. He had gone away smelling like a well-washed boy, he came home smelling like a hard-worked man. There was a tang of woodsmoke in his hair, which was tangled and matted. His woollen cloak was heavy with grime, his boots muddy. He was thinner but hard-muscled, she could feel the strength in his shoulders and back as he held her tightly.

'Mother,' he said again.

'Praise God for you,' she whispered. 'I thank God that he heard me pray and sent you home.'

She did not think she could bear to release him but after a moment more she stepped back and led him into the house. Caesar, knowing full well that he was home, walked riderless around the house into the stable yard and as Hester and Johnnie came in the front door there was an explosion of noise from the stables as the lad and John recognised the horse and came running into the house.

'He's home!' John yelled as if he could hardly believe it.

He ran through the kitchen and into the hall and then checked at the sight of his son's weary face and dirty clothes. Then he spread his arms to him and enfolded Johnnie in a powerful hug. 'Home,' he said.

Autumn 1652

The boy was home, the country was at peace. Oliver Cromwell was ruling Parliament with such power and dominance that he might as well have been king himself. Scotland was no longer an independent kingdom but was annexed by England and General George Monck was driving roads through Highland pride and through Highland courage which might never be healed. Charles Stuart was far away in France, or the Low Countries, or wherever he might scrape a living for doing nothing but being his charming self.

The peace brought gardeners back to the orchards and flowerbeds, and men of inquiring minds into the rarities collection. Takings at the door grew every day, and the order book for Tradescant flowers, shrubs, trees and vegetables grew full. John's reputation for strange, beautiful and exotic plants was established and he was gaining increasing respect for his experiments with new vegetables and fruit. He grew potatoes and Indian corn and peaches, nectarines, cherries, grapes for eating and for wine and for drying as raisins; and the scientists and philosophers who dined at the Ark would ask to try the new vegetables and fruits for their dinner.

In the autumn John Lambert came home from Scotland and visited the garden at the Ark and admired John's new collection of cyclamen which he had in a new bed under the chestnut trees. Lambert kneeled down in the dirt of the avenue to look at them, their delicate little petals folded back like a nun's coif. He greeted Johnnie without remarking on the scar beneath his eye, and kissed Hester's hand without mentioning the package of tulips or the hidden note.

'I'm glad to see your boy is home,' was all he said to her.

'Thank you,' she replied. 'And I was glad to see you are now Lord Lambert.'

'Aren't I grand?' he asked her with a smile, and then turned to walk around the flowerbeds with John.

'You gardened for the queen at Wimbledon House, did you not?' he asked when they were seated on the terrace, looking out over the chrysanthemums planted thickly in the beds before the house to give the garden some early autumn colour.

'I did,' John said. 'We planned it and I even planted the beds by the house, a knot garden, and a watercourse; but they had very little time there. She wanted it as a retreat, I was going to make a flowery mead down by the river, I should think it's a hay meadow now.'

'What d'you think of the soil and the situation? There are some good plants still growing.'

'It would have been a most pretty garden,' John said. 'I still have the plans for planting. Johnnie goes up there every summer.'

'I have bought it for my own use. I want a country house not too far from London. I should like to see what you had planned for it.'

'You have it? Well that's –' John broke off.

'A surprise,' John Lambert finished diplomatically for him. 'I think so too. I certainly didn't ever think to find myself in a queen's house, but I think it will suit me very well. I was especially interested to know if any of your plantings have survived. I'd be sorry to spoil a bed of rarities through my own ignorance.'

'Johnnie told me that some things are still there. I know the trees have done well, and Johnnie told me that the horse chestnuts are growing and the fruit trees in the orchards.'

'Horse chestnuts?' John Lambert asked with a gleam.

'Yes.'

'Mature?'

John thought for a moment. 'They'd be, oh, fifteen years old now.' He laughed. 'They'll be flowering and coming into their full beauty. I think you'll find you have a bargain in the garden. And I had planted plum and medlar and quince apples and pears; also the Tradescant great black cherry, and espaliered peaches.'

Hester came out on to the terrace with a bottle of wine and two glasses, Johnnie washed and tidy behind her. 'Will you stay for dinner, Lord Lambert?' she asked. 'Elias Ashmole and his wife are staying with us at the moment, and we expect some other guests too.'

'Thank you, I would like to,' he said.

'His lordship has bought Wimbledon House,' John told her. 'Johnnie, would you go and see if you can find the garden plans for me? They were in the documents in the rarities room.' He looked directly at his son and spoke with emphasis. 'We must be glad that one of our gardens has been bought by a man who will love it,' he said firmly.

It was as if the boy had not heard him.

'That's the queen's house,' Johnnie said bluntly.

Lambert heard the repressed passion behind the words and replied very calmly. 'It was confiscated, as are all the royal houses and palaces. And now I have bought it. I paid good money for it, Johnnie. It was a proper transaction, not booty. I didn't steal it.'

'It wasn't the king's house, it was the queen's,' Johnnie insisted. 'She's never been tried for treason, her estates have never been sequestrated. How can anyone have her house? It has nothing to do with the royal palaces. It's her own house.'

Hester glanced at John.

'Her fortunes go with her husband,' Lambert answered. 'That's the law, Johnnie. And all royalists have lost their houses.'

'Fetch the plans for me.' John tried to stem the rise of his son's temper.

'Fetch the damned things yourself!' Johnnie burst out. 'I'll have no part in robbing the queen of her own. I won't pretend that it's not thievery to live in a queen's palace and steal her fruits! It's nothing better than looting! It's a dead king's goods!'

He flung out of the house and ran down the shallow steps into the garden, they saw him tear down the avenue and through the gate towards the lake. There was an appalled silence.

'I apologise,' John said. 'He will be disciplined, your lordship. He will apologise to you himself. He doesn't realise the gravity of what he is saying.' John shot a swift look at Hester, asking for help. At the very least Johnnie was guilty of appalling rudeness; at the worst, treason.

'I'm so sorry,' Hester said in a whisper. 'He's still very young, you understand. And distressed. I would not have had him speak so to anyone, you least of all. He does realise that the war is over. He is not an active royalist. We are all of us loyal to Parliament here.'

Lambert leaned back against his chair and took up his glass of wine. 'Oh, there's no need to apologise,' he said gently. 'There are many who feel as he does up and down the country, it's bound to take some time for feelings to die down. And there have been enough trials for treason. The lad has strong feelings and it's hard to lose two battles by – what is he? – twenty? Did he get that scar at Worcester?'

'Yes. A scratch from a pike,' Hester said. 'Thank God it missed his eye. It was all but healed up by the time he came home. And he's only eighteen. I am sorry, your lordship. He spent his youth in the shadow of the war.'

'He's at an age when you see things in black and white,' Lambert said easily. 'Things are not so simple in real life. If Charles Stuart would make half the promises to us that he made to the Scots then he could have come home to his throne. But we can't trust him. Those of us who dealt with his father remember that the Stuarts find it easier to promise than to deliver. And the son is even worse than the father for reneging on his debts and word. He's not much of a model for Johnnie to set his heart on.'

'I know,' Hester said sadly. 'But I can't seem to persuade him.'

Johnnie did not reappear for dinner and Hester laid the table, served the gentlemen, and dined on her own in the kitchen before she went out to look for him.

She knew where to go. He was lying in the little rowing boat, his long legs over the back of the boat, gazing up at the sky where a few silver stars were showing against the pale blue.

Hester sat at the foot of the tree where she used to bring him to feed the ducks when he had been such a happy little boy. She observed the gently moving boat for a few moments before she spoke.

'That was ill-done, Johnnie. You will have to apologise to Lord Lambert. He is a good man and he has been kind to me.'

The boat rocked a little as he leaned forwards, saw her, and then reclined again. 'I know I was in the wrong. I will beg his pardon for speaking out.'

'It's foolish to fly out like that. You said enough to be tried for treason tonight.'

'No more than thousands of others.'

'Even so.'

The rocking of the little craft steadied and slowed.

'I know,' Johnnie said. 'I am sorry. I will say I am sorry to father and to his lordship. And I won't do it again.'

She waited for a moment. In the garden somewhere an owl cried hauntingly.

'Are you not cold?'

'No.'

'Hungry?'

'No.'

'Will you come in now?'

'In a little while.'

Hester paused for a moment. 'You know, Johnnie, I doubt that even Charles Stuart grieves more than you do. From what I hear of him he is a light-hearted man who goes from plotting to dancing; and would rather be dancing. He gambles away the money that people risk their lives to raise for him. His friends have given their livelihoods and even their lives for him and yet he dresses in the best clothes and goes to balls, and chases women shamelessly. He's a drunkard and a gambler and a lecher. He's a young man, as you are a young man. But he takes his cause very light-heartedly. Why should you grieve for him? Why grieve more than he does himself?'

'It's not that.' Johnnie's voice came over the still water, she could barely see the boat now in the twilight. 'All that you say about him is true. I was with him at Worcester long enough to see that he is light, as you say. Light-hearted and light-weight. But I don't grieve for the loss of him as a man, I grieve for the loss of everything that kingship means. The loss of the court, the loss of a nation under one ruler, the loss of the beauty of the Church and music and colour, the loss of certainty of every man having a master. The loss of the gardens, the loss of the palaces. The loss of *our* gardens.'

'We still have the Ark,' she said.

'One little garden, more like a farm than a garden,' he said dismissively. 'We're getting a grand reputation for growing onions. This is nothing to a family which had Oatlands, or Hatfield, or Theobalds. Even Wimbledon. All we have now is a tiny patch of ground and no-one plants great gardens any more.'

'They will do again,' she said. 'The country is at peace once more, they will plant gardens again.'

'They'll plant turnips,' Johnnie predicted. 'And marrows. Like father is growing for them. I saw Oatlands Palace and I saw them uproot it, rose by rose. And now the building is pulled down and they made a canal bed with the stone. They didn't even try to make another building of beauty. There's nothing for me to do with my life, there's nothing to do in this country any more. I am a gardener, a gardener who needs great palaces. A physic garden and a vegetable patch is not enough for me.'

'You'll find something,' Hester urged him. 'You'll find your own way, even if it is not our garden, nor a garden fit for a king. You're young, you will find your way.'

'I'll never be a king's gardener in England,' he said slowly. 'That was

489

my inheritance and now I can't have it. There is nothing left for me.'

The boat was drifting away a little to the other side of the lake. Hester paused, taking in the tranquillity of the scene: the sky slowly turning from blue to indigo, the colour of Tradescant spiderwort. The stars were like silver pin-heads against navy cloth. The evening air was cool against her cheek, sweet with the scent of windfall apples, and late-flowering wallflowers.

'We spent hours and hours here together when you were a little boy,' she said tenderly. 'You used to beg to come down here to feed the ducks. D'you remember?'

'Yes,' he said, his voice little more than a whisper. 'I remember feeding the ducks.'

She waited, and when he did not say any more, she rose to her feet. 'Shall I stay with you?' she asked him tenderly. 'Would you like some company?'

'No,' he said and his voice seemed to come from a long way over the still water. 'I'll spend a little time on my own, Mother. I'll come home when I can be merry again.'

Johnnie was not at breakfast.

'Where is he?' John demanded. 'I would have expected him to apologise to Lord Lambert last night.'

'He may have gone into Lambeth and had a late night,' Hester replied diplomatically and she spoke over her shoulder to Cook. 'Would you call Johnnie, Cook?'

Mary Ashmole, a paying guest for the season, helped herself to a slice of ham. 'Young men,' she remarked indulgently.

They could hear Cook labouring up the stairs and then the creak of the floorboards over their heads as she opened Johnnie's door, and then her coming down the stairs again. Her face when she came into the dining room was bright with mischief. 'He's not there!' she announced, smiling. 'And his bed's not been slept in.'

Hester's first thought was not of the ale houses of Lambeth, but that he had run away to join Charles Stuart's court, ridden to the docks and taken a ship to Europe to be with the prince. 'Is his horse in the stable?' she asked urgently.

John took one look at her white face and went quickly from the room. Mary Ashmole rose, hesitated.

'Please don't disturb yourself, Mrs Ashmole,' Hester said, recovering.

'Do finish your breakfast. I expect my son stayed with friends and forgot to send a message.'

She followed John to the stable yard. Caesar's head was nodding over the stable door. John was questioning the stable lad.

'He didn't take his horse out last night,' he said to Hester. 'No-one has seen him since yesterday.'

'Send the boy down to Lambeth and see if he went there,' Hester said.

'This could be much ado for nothing,' John warned her. 'If he is drunk under an ale-house table he won't thank us for sending a search party out.'

She hesitated.

'If he's not back by midday I'll go down to Lambeth myself,' John decided.

At midday John took Caesar and rode down to the village but soon came home again. Johnnie had not been in the ale house, and was not staying with any of his friends in the village.

'Perhaps he was walking to Lambeth and had some accident on the road,' Hester suggested.

'He's not a baby,' John said. 'He knows how to fight. And run. Besides, you know Johnnie: he'd always ride rather than walk. If he was going any distance he'd take his horse.'

'If there was a gang of thieves?' Hester suggested. 'Or a press gang?'

'The press gang wouldn't take him, he's obviously a gentleman,' John said.

'Then where can he be?' Hester demanded.

'You saw him after dinner,' John said. 'Did he say anything?'

'He was in his boat,' she said. 'He always goes there when he wants to be alone and to think. He knew he was wrong to speak out to Lord Lambert, he promised he would apologise to you and to his lordship. I asked him if he wanted me to stay with him and he said he would come home later.'

She paused. 'He said he would come home,' she said. Her voice sounded less and less certain. 'He said he would come home when he was merry again.'

John suddenly scowled as if he had been struck by a pang of pain. He crossed the yard and took her hand. 'Go and sit with Mary Ashmole,' he ordered.

'Why?'

'I'm just going to have a look round, that's all.'

'You're going to the lake,' she said flatly.

'Yes, I am. I'm going to check that the boat is tied up and the oars stowed and then we will know that he rowed ashore and met with some mischance, or changed his mind about coming home.'

'I'll come too,' she said.

John recognised the impossibility of ordering Hester indoors, started to walk towards the avenue, Hester at his side.

Even in autumn the orchard was too lush for the lake to be seen from the main avenue. Hester and John had to turn away from the chestnut trees to the path that ran westwards before they could see the unruffled pewter surface of the water.

It was very quiet. The birds were singing. At the sound of their footsteps a heron rose up from the water's edge and flapped away with its ungainly legs trailing and its long neck working like a pump handle with each arduous wingbeat. The surface was like a mirror, reflecting the blue sky, untroubled by any movement except the speckling of flies and the occasional plop of a rising fish. The boat floated in the middle of the lake, the oars shipped, its painter trailing in the water tying it to the reflected boat bobbing below.

For a moment Hester thought that Johnnie had fallen asleep in the bottom of the boat, had curled his long legs up inside the little rowing boat and that when they called out his name he would sit up, rub his eyes, and laugh at his folly. But the boat was empty.

John paused for a moment and walked out along the little landing stage and looked down into the water. He could see green weed and the gleam of a brown trout but nothing else. He turned and walked steadily back to the house.

'What are you thinking? What are you doing?' Hester tore her gaze away from the still boat and the peaceful water and went after him. 'Where are you going, John?'

'I'm going to get a boat hook and pull the boat in,' he said, without slackening his trudge. 'Then I'm going to get a pole and feel for the bottom of the lake. Then I may have to get a net, and then I may have to drain the lake.'

'But why?' she exclaimed. 'Why? What are you saying?'

He did not slow, nor turn his head. 'Hester, you know why.'

'I don't,' she insisted.

'Wait for me at the house,' he said. 'Go and sit with Mary Ashmole. I will come and tell you as soon as I know.'

'Know what?' she insisted. 'Tell me what?'

They had reached the terrace. Mary Ashmole was waiting for them. John looked up at her and she recoiled from the grimness of his face. 'Take Hester indoors,' he said firmly. 'I will come to her as soon as we know where Johnnie is.'

'You are never going to look for him in the lake,' Hester said. She laughed, an odd, mirthless noise. 'You cannot think he fell out of his boat!'

He did not answer her but walked with that same bent-headed trudge round to the stable yard. Hester and Mary heard him shout for the lad and they waited in absolute silence as the two of them walked back down the avenue. John was carrying a long pole, his pruning hook. The lad was carrying a net which they usually used for securing pots in the cart, and a coil of rope.

Mary Ashmole reached out and took Hester's icy hand. 'Be brave, my dear,' she said inadequately.

❧

John marched to the lake as if he were about to undertake a disagreeable but essential garden chore, like hedging or ditching. The garden lad stole one swift glance at his stern profile and said nothing.

John walked to the edge of the landing stage and stretched out with the pruning hook. The blade just reached the painter as it trailed in the water and on the second try he could draw it in towards him.

'Wait here,' he said to the lad, and stepped into the boat. He rowed out towards the middle of the lake and then shipped the oars and peered downwards. Gently, with meticulous care, he reversed the pruning hook and lowered it into the water, probing with the handle. When he found nothing he rowed one stroke to the side and repeated the whole process in a widening circle.

The lad, who had been gripped by the horror of this task, found that he was getting bored and started to fidget, but nothing could break John's intense concentration. He was not thinking of what he might find. He was not even thinking of what he was doing. He just completed each circle and then went a little wider as if it were some kind of spiritual exercise, like a Papist telling her beads, as if it had to be done to ward off some evil. As if it were meaningless in itself, but should be done as a prevention.

Again and again he rowed another stroke and then probed gently into the dark water. In the back of his mind was a thought of how

Johnnie was probably already home after a night's roistering in the City, or a message would soon come from his sister's house saying that he had decided to make a sudden visit, or he would reappear with an old comrade from the defeated Worcester army. There were so many other explanations more likely than this one that John worked the water of the lake without allowing himself to think what he was doing, divorced from worry, almost enjoying the paddle with the oars and the movement of the wet-handled pole in the water.

When he felt something under the gentle probe of the pole he had a moment of mild regret that now he had to interrupt himself, that now he had a different task to do. Gently, with infinite care, he probed again and felt the object roll and move.

'Bundle of rags,' he whispered to himself, trying to guess at the dimension and weight. 'Hidden household goods,' he assured himself.

He turned to look for the stable lad. 'Throw me the rope,' he said, his voice steady and unshaken.

The lad, who had slumped on the landing stage, got to his feet and inexpertly tried to throw the rope to John. The first attempt fell in the water and splashed John, and the second attempt slapped him with a wet coil.

'Dolt,' John said and enjoyed the normality of the incompetence of the lad. 'Fool.'

He fastened the rope to the ring at the front of the boat. 'When I give the word, you gently pull me in,' he ordered.

The lad nodded, and took a grip on the line.

John pulled the pole out of the water and brought up the pruning hook. He took his leather gauntlet from the big pocket of his coat and pulled it over the sharp blade. Then he plunged the pole back into the water with the shielded hook first. It snagged against the object, lost its grip, and then caught.

'Now,' John called to the lad. 'But steady.'

The lad was so afraid of doing wrong that he started to pull too lightly. For a moment nothing happened at all, then the little boat started to glide back to the landing stage and John felt the weight of the drowned object on the end of his pole. Gently, smoothly, the boat bobbed towards the landing stage, John gripping the pole and waiting to see the object revealed in the shallow water.

He saw first a coat, rendered uniformly black by waterlogging, then Johnnie's white shirt and then his pale, pale face, his open dark eyes, and the swirl and eddy of his fair hair.

'Stop,' John said hoarsely.

At once the lad halted.

The boat rocked, the current of movement which had washed Johnnie up to the surface slipped away and his face sunk out of sight again. For a moment John thought that he could order the world to stop, right there; just as he could command the gardener's lad and then nothing that must follow would need to take place. He could say 'stop' and there would be no drowned child, no heartbreak, no end to the Tradescant line, no silence where Johnnie should have been singing, no terrible gulf where the young man should have been.

John waited for a long moment, trying to understand the reality and then the awful yawning enormity of his loss. The first step in his grief was the realisation that he could not measure it. His loss was too great for him to imagine.

The lad holding the rope stood like a statue, a dragonfly whirred noisily over the surface of the water and settled for a moment.

'Go on then,' John whispered as if this were not his work but he was obeying someone else. 'All right. Go on.'

The lad put his weight on the rope and once again the boat glided towards the landing stage, towing its dreadful freight behind it. At the landing stage when it stopped with a bump, John said gently, 'Tie it fast,' and waited until the lad had done as he was told.

'Take the pole,' John said, proffering it, and when the lad had gripped one end of it, John stepped from the boat into the waist-deep water, felt his way along to the other end and gathered the body of his only son into his arms.

'Step aside and wait,' he said softly to the stable lad. The boy dragged his horrified stare from the waterlogged body and then obediently fled to the shelter of the apple tree where the wasps were feeding drunkenly on fallen fruit.

John waded for the shore, the weight of Johnnie making him stagger as they got clear of the water. He fell to his knees and cradled the white face in his arms and looked down into the sightless eyes and the pale lips.

'My Johnnie,' he whispered. 'My boy.'

They sat together for a long time before John remembered that Hester would be waiting in painful anxiety and that there was much work for him to do.

He laid out the body and draped his jacket over his son's face.

'Watch by him,' he said simply to the stable lad. 'I'll come back with the cart.'

Slowly he walked along the grassy ride and then turned up the main avenue to the house. He could see Hester pacing on the terrace but when she saw him and took in the slump of his shoulders and his wet clothing, and his missing jacket, she froze very still.

John walked towards her, his face numb, his voice lost, then he cleared his throat and said quietly, conversationally, 'I found him. He's drowned. I'm fetching the cart now.'

She nodded, as calm as he, and Mary Ashmole, watching the two of them, thought them completely insensible, thought that they could not have loved their son at all to be so indifferent to his death.

'I thought so,' Hester said gently. 'I knew as soon as I saw the boat, just as you did. I'll ready the parlour for him.' She paused. 'No. He should lie in the rarities room. He was the most precious thing this house ever had.'

John nodded and went with that strange, slow plod round to the stables where, for a fancy, he did not harness the workhorse, but he took Caesar out of his stable and put him between the shafts of the cart to bring his master home.

🦎

They buried him beside his grandfather and his mother at St Mary's, Lambeth. The new vicar was kind enough not to ask how a fit young man came to drown while boating on his own lake. It was assumed that Johnnie had been drunk, or had hit his head as he fell from the boat. Only John knew that the boat had not been overturned but had been floating peacefully with the oars shipped. Only John knew that his son's pockets had been filled with broken pieces of flower pots. Only Hester knew that Johnnie had believed that there was no place for the king's gardeners in England any more. But they neither of them told the other these insights. They both thought that the other had pain enough.

Spring 1653

They could not easily recover. No family can ever fully recover from the loss of a child, and this was a child who had survived infancy during plague years, a childhood during the king's wars, two dangerous battles, and then died when the country was at peace. For a little while they were like lost people, they greeted each other at mealtimes and they went to church together, past the beautifully carved tombstone for John's father and the little crosses which marked Johnnie's and his mother's graves, and they spoke hardly at all.

The meetings of the philosophers and scientists which had made the Ark the centre of intellectual life were broken up and moved elsewhere. John found he could not concentrate on any argument for more than a few moments, and anyway everything seemed meaningless.

Even the uproar which greeted the end of the long Parliament and Cromwell's sudden decision to make a parliament of saints, nominated good men of recognised opinions and sanctity who would bring about the changes which the country so badly needed, failed to raise John from his passive dreaming.

Lord Lambert came to order new tulips in the spring and told John that a new day was dawning for England where there would be the right of every man to vote for his parliament, the legal system would be reformed to make it more just, the poor would be supported and no more landlords would be allowed to enclose the commons and drive squatters and poor people on to the streets. He broke off in the middle of his explanation and said: 'Forgive me, Mr Tradescant. Are you ill?'

'I have lost my son,' John said quietly. 'And nothing matters to me any more. Not even the new Parliament.'

Lord Lambert was stunned for a moment. 'Johnnie? I did not know! What happened?'

'He drowned in our little lake,' John said, speaking the words for what seemed like the thousandth time. 'It was the night you came to dinner.'

Lambert checked. 'When he was so distressed that I had bought Wimbledon?'

John nodded. 'It was that night.'

John Lambert looked stricken. 'Not because of what he said! He didn't drown because of that?'

John shook his head. 'Because he knew his cause was lost. If it had not been that night it would have been another. He couldn't see a way to live in the world that Cromwell and you and I have made. He wanted to be a king's gardener, he could not hear that kings are no good. Johnnie couldn't see it. And I failed to teach him.' John paused for a moment at the pointlessness of regrets. 'I have always been a man of few certainties. So when my son was convinced of a mistake I couldn't correct him. He put his faith in the most foolish prince, the son of a most foolish king. And I couldn't tell him that when you are in the service of a king one of the first things you learn is to not take him too seriously, not to love him too dearly. Johnnie was too close to the king's service, and yet not close enough to see it for what it was.'

He glanced at Lambert. The general was listening intently. He managed a little smile. 'These are private griefs,' he said. 'I don't mean to burden you with them, my lord. Do look around the garden, and anything you desire you can order. Joseph will take the order, my wife is not in the house today.'

'Will you tell her how sorry I am?' Lambert asked, going towards the door to the garden. 'Tell her I am deeply, deeply sorry for your loss. He was a fine young man. He deserved a better cause.'

'He was, wasn't he?' John said, his expression lightening for a moment.

Lambert nodded and went quietly out to the garden to look around at the avenue of horse chestnuts and the beds of exquisite tulips and wondered if they would ever give John any joy ever again, now there was no Tradescant to follow him in the garden.

Winter 1654

The new parliament was short-lived. Its programme of social justice was too radical for the temper of many of the men of influence whose chief hopes of reform had been for a fat slice of the king's wealth and power, and had never gone as far as the soldiers of the army who had fought for an end to greed and tyranny and who truly thought that a new world could be born out of their battles.

When Cromwell saw that he had tried a parliament of selected good men who would have imposed justice on a country too sluggish to become saintly, and then tried a parliament chosen by the voters which could not rise above self-interest, something of the joy went out of him. He took the title of Lord Protector and took the burden of power in a mood of frustration and disappointment and never again thought that he might see the new Jerusalem in London.

'I don't know what the fighting was for if we merely exchanged a king for a Lord Protector,' John said wearily to Hester as they sat at dinner.

'No,' she said quietly.

They sat in the silence which was a constant presence at their table now; it was as if without Johnnie to plan for, there was no business to discuss. The takings at the door were good, the order books were filled. But Hester had withdrawn from much of the business and had lost interest in the garden. She never complained, but she felt as if she had been struggling too hard for too long and that, as it turned out, it had all been for nothing.

'I have been thinking about Virginia,' John said tentatively. 'Bertram Hobert, my old friend from over there, came to see me today.'

Hester raised her head. 'Hobert who nearly died there?'

John nodded. 'He finally brought off a good crop of tobacco and

499

came home to sell it. By making the voyage with his wife he gets another two headrights for free and he wants to make his plantation bigger. He's hired some labourers to take with him and he gets their headrights too. He's full of confidence. He is going back again with the Austin family and they have spare places on their ship.'

John paused. 'I wondered if you would like to come with me, to Virginia. You could see our land, you might be interested in that, and by travelling together we would claim another two headrights. We could sell them, or find someone to farm them for us, or you might like to build a house and settle there. Jamestown is bound to be much improved since my first visit and now –' He broke off.

He had been about to say, 'Now there is nothing to keep us here' – but he did not need to say it. Hester, of all people, knew that there was nothing left in Lambeth but the rarities and the plants.

'What about that woman, the woman you left there?' she asked flatly.

He bowed his head. 'I will never see her again,' he said. It did not have the ring of a promise of a reformed man, his voice had the finality of a man who knows when something is over. 'She will be with her people, and I will be with mine. The time of the Powhatan dealing kindly with the planters is long gone.'

Hester thought for a moment. 'Who would keep this place safe while we are gone?'

'Elias Ashmole would be glad enough to live here for a while,' John pointed out. 'He has promised to help make a catalogue of the rarities collection and he has a great interest in the garden.'

Hester made a little face. 'What if something happens?' she asked.

'He could manage. He's a worldly man, he's managed bigger estates than this little place.'

'Why would he be so helpful?' she asked baldly. 'Why serve us in such a way?'

'He likes the rarities, he likes the garden,' John said. 'He can do his studies here in alchemy and astronomy. He can use my herbs for his medicines.'

'I like his wife Mary better than I like him,' Hester said irrelevantly. 'And she has been very badly treated by him. She told me that he abused her and now they are separated he won't give her any money for her keep. And it was all her money in the first place. He had nothing when he came to advise her, and now her fortune is his.'

John shook his head. 'He's a lawyer by training,' he said. 'I'm not surprised he gives nothing away. He'd make a bad enemy but he's a good friend to us. He would guard this place for us while we were gone.'

She thought for a moment. 'No,' she said reluctantly. 'He would manage well enough if nothing happened. But if there was a fire or another war or an uprising he would never care for the things as we would. Mr Ashmole would think of his own safety before the collection.'

'We could box it all up and store it,' John objected.

'Not again,' she said. 'I couldn't bear it. And even if we did, what about the garden?'

'I do really want to go,' John said. 'I am so weary of this house without our boy, and I miss him in the garden. I hate the lake, I can't go down to that end of the orchard at all, and I can't find the energy to weed and plant and prune and pot on. In every part of the garden I come across tasks which I would give to him to do, or where he was especially skilled. Half of the plants are his plants, nursed up by him while I was away. It's as if I meet him everywhere.'

Hester nodded. 'That's why I'll stay,' she said quietly. 'Because I too feel that I meet him everywhere, and here I can guard the things he loved and watch the things he planted grow tall and beautiful, and it's as if he is still here.'

John raised an eyebrow. 'Shall I go alone? Would you want that?'

She met the little challenge. 'Will you come back again?'

'Yes. There's no life for me there. But I could bring back some new rarities, there is so much more to discover.'

'I will wait for you,' she promised. 'And keep the rarities and the garden safe for you.'

He bowed his head and kissed her hand as it rested on the table. 'You will not blame me for leaving you to your grief?'

She touched his head with her other hand like a blessing. 'I would want it,' she said simply. 'I should like to spend a little time alone. Perhaps I will become accustomed to being without him, if I have a little time alone.'

'Very well then,' he said gently. 'And I promise I will come home.'

Spring 1654

John was at sea, running from grief, once more, and knew that he had chosen the right course. The movement of the ship rocked his sleep at night and the noise of the wind in the sails and the creaking of the timbers were the sounds of mourning to him. He thought of Johnnie constantly and, away from the land and from Hester, he felt free to think of Jane, his first wife, and knew that if there were a heaven and a communion of saints, then she was with her son now. As the seven-week voyage went on, he felt that he could let Johnnie go, as he had once before let Jane go, and love him only in his heart as a memory, and not with that wrenching desire to bring him back.

He was asleep when the ship sighted the Virginia coast and was awakened by the noise and excitement of their arrival in Jamestown. Bertram Hobert hammered on the little wooden shutters around John's bunk and shouted, 'Up, man! We've arrived!' and John tumbled out to find the ship in its usual chaos as sailors slackened off the sails and the look-out man shouted directions, and the passengers still battened-down below the hatches tried to repack their goods which had been scattered during the long voyage.

'Better this time than last,' Bertram said optimistically. 'At least we know the dangers now, eh, John?'

John looked into the face of his old friend. The dreadful hollowed face of hunger had gone, replaced by a rosy round prosperity, but most of Bertram's teeth were missing and the remainder were black.

'We were greenhorns,' John said. 'We knew nothing.'

'Now we do,' Bertram said. 'I will be a man of substance in this land yet, John. I will be a burgess and leave a five-hundred acre plantation.'

'I wonder what changes have taken place since we were last here?'

'Nothing but good,' Mrs Hobert said over her shoulder, throwing linen into a bag. 'I hear that the savages are quite driven back and there is a road made through the woods from Jamestown down to the sea and westwards along the riverbank inland.'

A sailor lifted the hatch above them and shouted that they could come up on deck. John hefted his chest through the hatchway, and took his bundle of clothing.

'You're travelling light,' Bertram remarked.

'It is going home that I hope to be laden,' John said.

They scrambled out on deck and then paused in amazement. For a moment John thought that something had gone ludicrously wrong and they had come to the wrong place. But then he saw that the old wooden fort had gone, the mixture of garrison and town had changed. Before him now was a new town, an elegant town, beautiful and solid and built to last.

A line of stone-built houses with small ornamental gardens before them lined the front road alongside the river and looked down to the quay. Great trees had been left in place to shade the road, and around each tree they had built graceful circular seats so that passers-by could rest in the shade. Each house had a bright new wooden fence before it, one or two even had low stone walls to mark the division between the garden and the street.

There was a pavement slightly raised with wooden beams to keep the ladies' shoes dry and a gutter for storm water and sewage which drained away into the river.

The houses were built two, even three, storeys high, so close that they were all but adjoining and they were built like good London houses, not flung together with wood and mud; but well-planned, proper houses with a central doorway and a window on either side with well-hung shutters and glass in the windows.

The people walking up and down the road and strolling down to the quay were changed as well. The sharp division into the one or two wealthy men and the rest, hungry, work-hardened paupers, was over. There was a more gentle gradation of wealth and status that you could see from the shirts and waistcoats of the labourers through the smart dark homespun of the artisans and smaller planters through to the silks and satins worn by the gentry.

And now there were slaves. John blinked at the numbers of black men and women, fetching, carrying, running at an obedient dog-trot behind a cart, catching the ropes on the dockside and running the gangplank out to the ship, unloading carts and throwing down the bales of cotton, and women with trays on their heads weaving through the crowd at the dockside with fresh produce to sell. Many of them were branded with the mark of their owner on their forehead or cheek. Many of them had the old scars of a whipping on their backs. But some of them, like the women traders, were clearly free to sell their own goods, they walked at their own speed with an arrogant roll of their hips under bright patterned dresses.

A sailor opened the ship's railing, made sure the gangplank was secure and then stepped back. John walked down the plank to the new land.

He had not thought that he would find her again, and he knew she would not look for him; but he did not expect that the country would be emptied of Suckahanna's people. The last Indian war had indeed been the last. Opechancanough's execution was the death of the People as well as the death of their last greatest war leader. Some drifted away, inland, and found other nations that would accept them, and then they too had to move, always westwards, always away from coast and the encroaching white men, the noise of falling timber and the scarcity of game. Some went into service, a service more like slavery for they were paid no wages and allowed no freedoms and worked until they died for no thanks. Some were imprisoned for the crime of rising up to defend their own villages and they served their sentences until illness and despair finished the work that the war had begun.

John stopped every one of the few Powhatan women or children that he saw in Jamestown and asked for Suckahanna, and for Attone, by name, but they all shook their heads at the strange white man and pretended that they could not understand his speech, though he asked them both in English and Powhatan. Ignorance and deafness were their last defence, and they mimed ignorance and deafness and hoped to somehow survive, clinging to the very edge of life in a land which had once been unquestionably their own.

John and the other men on the ship went to the governor's office where the maps of the territory were kept and claimed his headright and then sold it on to William Lea, with his original claim alongside it.

'You don't want it yourself?' Lea asked.

John shook his head. 'I'm no planter,' he said. 'I tried it before and I have not the skills or the endurance. I'm a gardener. You've paid my passage and more and I'm glad for that, but I will spend my time here out in the woods gathering the most interesting plants I can find – my cargo for the return journey.'

A gentleman in the office with them turned at the mention of plants and looked at John keenly. 'Ah!' he said. 'Now I know who you are. I am sure that you must be Mr John Tradescant. I had not known you were coming to visit us again.'

John felt a little curl of pride at his name being known before him. 'How do you do, Mr –?'

'Forgive me,' the planter said. 'I am Sir Josiah Ashley. I saw your garden when I was last in London and I ordered some plants for my garden here.'

'You are gardening?' John asked incredulously. 'In Virginia?'

The man laughed. 'Of course, everything will be very much changed since you were last here. I have a house and before it, running down to the river, I have a garden. Nothing compared to the great gardens you will have worked in, I know. But it is a pretty little couple of acres and it gives me much pleasure.'

'And do you only plant English plants?' John asked, wary of another hopeless attempt at an English garden in foreign soil like the barren attempt in Barbados.

'I grow flowers and plants from the woods too,' Sir Josiah replied. 'I have a great love for English plants, of course, they remind us of our old home. But there are some exquisite flowers and shrubs that I have found and brought into my garden and they thrive.'

'I should so like to see them. And if you had any stock I should offer you a very fair price.'

Sir Josiah bowed. 'You must come and stay with us.'

'I could not impose,' John started shyly.

'This is Virginia,' the man reminded him. 'Guests are not an imposition, they are our only source of entertainment. You will be a great pleasure for us. I am sure you have much news of London.'

'Then I would be delighted.'

'I drive back to my house tomorrow,' Sir Josiah said. 'Shall I collect you from your inn?'

'Drive?' John queried.

'Oh yes, we have a road which runs alongside the river. The tobacco still goes by boat, of course, but I generally drive into town in my cart.'

John blinked. 'I see that everything is indeed changed.' He paused for a moment. 'May I ask one thing: when I was last here I spent some time with the Powhatan people, before the war. They helped me in the woods when I was plant collecting.'

'Oh yes?' Sir Josiah was pulling on his gloves and clapping his hat on his head. John saw that the Virginian belief that the very air was a danger was still prevalent.

'I was wondering where they would be now?'

'Dead, most likely,' Sir Josiah said without regret. 'A bad business. They could have lived with us in such harmony. But they chose not to. A bad business indeed.'

'All of them?'

'There is the village, of course.'

'The village?'

'There is a Powhatan village some ten miles inland. You could go and visit if you liked. I doubt that any that you recognised would be allowed out unless you took them into your service and said you would be responsible for their behaviour.'

'I could do that?'

Sir Josiah hesitated. 'Forgive me. You may not bring savages into my house.'

'You don't have slaves?'

Sir Josiah laughed. 'Of course I do. How else could I grow tobacco? But I won't have the native peoples of this land anywhere near my borders. Africans are my slaves, the others are no use to me at all.'

'But I could go to the village and see if there was anyone I recognised?'

'Of course.' Sir Josiah gestured at the clerk. 'George, give Mr Tradescant here a pass to go to the savages' village. I will countersign it. Shall you go today?'

'Yes,' John said quietly. 'Today. At once.'

He told the woman at the inn that he would be home for dinner and would leave the next day. 'And where are you going now?' she asked with the freedom of speech that the new colony allowed.

'I am going to find someone,' John said. 'At the Powhatan village.'

'An old servant?' she sniffed. 'If you want a servant you can buy a black girl for little more than seven pounds and she will serve you far better than any Indian. The blacks live longer too, and they're more cheerful company. I'd have a black if I were you.'

'I want to find a particular person,' John said, choosing his words with care. 'Not a slave. Can you point out the road?'

'Oh indeed,' she said. 'There is only one road really. There is the road which runs east from here, inland, and there is the road which

506

runs west to the coast. The Indian village is north of here. Take the road upriver and ask whoever you see on the road. Anyone can direct you.'

'Thank you,' said John, and set off.

He had thought he might collect some specimens as he walked upriver but there was almost no forest left at the riverside. The road went past one large house set among field after field of tobacco, and then past another. Some of the houses were still the familiar wooden buildings in the style that John remembered; but they were all growing and sprawling out, with new rooms added on one side, and stables built nearby. The more prosperous were grand with huge pillars and beautiful terraces, like little palaces in miniature, and behind them were little huts made of wood and roofed with reeds, the slave huts, poorer-built than the stables; horses were so much more valuable than slaves.

There were common plants by the wayside but the constant ploughing and reploughing of the land for tobacco had uprooted anything of any size. John thought it incredible that the woods where Suckahanna had run when she was a little girl should now be as tame and as enclosed as the riverside at Surrey.

He passed a gang of slaves working on the road, filling in the potholes with chippings of stone, and they pointed him on: on and then turn right after the next grand house, for the savages' village. The overseer rode up as John left them, tipped his hat to John, confirmed the directions and then went past him to the men. John heard a yelp of pain at a casual blow, and trudged onwards without turning his head.

He turned right as they had advised and found that the track led him through a marsh of foul water. This was land that no-one had wanted, far from the road and from the river, and needing to be drained and cleansed, a project which might take years and never be done. There were rotting trees sunk deep into the marsh and, in their shelter, water-loving plants just coming into bud. John hesitated to step off the single-track causeway and risk a wetting but promised himself that he would stop and collect them on his way back.

He turned another corner and saw a little wooden house, built like his own Virginian shack had been. On either side of it a tall wooden fence ran as if to enclose a huge field. The little hut was a gate house, the only way in to the enclosed acres. On the porch lounging in the sun were two men in remnants of what had once been good jackets, chewing tobacco and spitting into a brass bowl placed conveniently between them. They watched him as he walked up and John felt self-conscious and needlessly guilty as they stared at him, walking along the deserted road towards the village that no-one ever visited.

'Good day,' John said.

One man got to his feet and nodded a greeting.

'I have come to seek a servant of mine,' John said, succumbing to the prejudice of the place. 'I have been a long time in England. I wondered if she was here.'

'Might be,' the man said unhelpfully. 'We've got a hundred and sixty-two of 'em here.'

'And where will I find the others?' John asked, looking around, thinking there must be another village nearby.

'That's all there is,' the man said. 'D'you have a pass?'

John handed over Sir Josiah's letter. 'I mean, where are the other Powhatan? The rest of them?'

The man could hardly read; he only looked at the paper and at the seal on the bottom. 'That's all there is left,' he said simply.

John hesitated at the enormity of what the man was saying. 'There is surely another village elsewhere in the colony with more people?' he asked. 'There were thousands of them when I was last here, thousands.'

The man shook his head. 'This a-one hundred and sixty-two is all that is left of the Powhatan,' he said. 'Unless they start having babies again. But they don't show any disposition at the moment.'

The other man sniggered. 'Most unwillin'.'

'Can I go in?' John asked.

'I'll take you,' the soldier said.

He lit the fuse on his musket and held the gun across his chest, the fuse between his two fingers, the end of it aglow. Then he led the way into the enclosed village.

John walked through the gate, and then stopped and blinked. It was like the village he had known, but in miniature; the long houses were too few and built too small. There was a dancing circle but it was compressed against one of the blank encircling wooden walls. There was the central street leading up to the house of the werowance but it could be walked in forty strides. There was no sweat lodge that he could see. All around the houses, planted with the meticulous care of the Powhatan women, were the food crops, cramped up against the houses. John recognised at once the growing stalks of the Indian corn and the amaracock planted between them, and the little shelter built to overlook the field where the children would wait for their mothers to finish their work.

'Can I talk to them alone?' John asked the soldier.

'They don't speak English,' he said. 'You'd better just look for your girl. I can line them up for you. They understand "Muster".'

'No, no,' John said. 'I can speak Powhatan. Let me speak with them.'

The soldier hesitated. 'Shout if you need help then,' he said and went back to his seat.

The women working in the field did not raise their eyes at this exchange, they did not take more than a glance at John. But John knew that they would have seen every detail of him, and that if Suckahanna or Attone or any of his people were alive in this cage then they would know within minutes that he had come.

He walked up to the little confined field and spoke in Powhatan.

'Sister,' he said. 'I was the husband of Suckahanna and the friend of Attone. They called me the Eagle when they took me into the People.'

She did not break off her work, her hands still moved in the earth, setting the little plants, dropping in seeds. She did not look up at him, she might as well have been deaf.

'I have come to find Suckahanna, or Attone, or any of my people,' John said. 'Or news of them.'

She nodded at that; but did not pause in the steady, sweeping movement of her hands.

'Did you know them?' John asked. 'Suckahanna, Attone, any of them? She had a little boy –'

The woman turned her head and called a single word, the name Popanow, the child of winter, and a young girl came forwards.

'I knew Suckahanna,' she said simply. 'You must be the Eagle. I would not have known you, they spoke of a hunter and you are too fat and old.'

John concealed the hurt to his vanity and looked at the girl. 'I don't remember you.'

'I was born in the village of the bad water,' she said. 'You were long gone.'

'Suckahanna?'

She paused. 'Why d'you want to know, white man?'

John hesitated. 'I am a white man, I know,' he said humbly. 'But once I was a Powhatan. Suckahanna was my wife and Attone was my friend. Tell me, Popanow, what became of my wife and my friend and my people? I was not with them because they sent me away. I have come back to learn what became of them. Tell me, Popanow.'

509

She nodded. 'It was like this. The soldiers were hunting us down, every month they came a little closer. It was like a hunting trip for them, they came out in spring. Winter we were left alone to starve and freeze but spring and summer they came out and destroyed our fields when they could find them, and broke down the fish weirs, and tracked us with their dogs.'

John flinched at the matter-of-fact solidity of her description. 'Attone wanted to lead us upriver and north, away from the white men. We thought that another People might take us in, or if they would not then we could fight the white men and die in the fighting rather than be picked off one at a time. Others thought that the white men would grow weary of the sport of hunting us and start to hunt for food. They would leave us alone after a while. I think Suckahanna was with Attone. She said we should go.

'We started to move out in the winter. We had not enough stores of food, and it was not safe to light fires. A slave saw us.' She was suddenly alight with anger, animated with resentment. 'A black slave who thought more of his master than anything else – the white man's dog, the white man's fool – he ran and told his master, who brought out some other planters and they hunted us through the snow and we were easy to track in the deep snow, and slow-moving with old people and babies to carry.'

John nodded. 'I remember. I was with them when they went to the marshland.'

'We left the people who could not keep up with us. We thought perhaps they would be taken up by the hunting party behind us and sent back to Jamestown for servants. But they did not take them for servants, they killed them where they lay in the snow. The white men cut their throats and scalped their heads where they lay. It was . . .' she sought the word to describe it and found none, '. . . ugly.

'Attone said we should make a stand and fight the hunting party and then we would be safe to go on. They sent the older women and the babies ahead and the rest of us made a trap, a pit in the road, and we hid in the trees, and waited.' She paused. 'It was desperate, digging and trying to hide the pit with branches and fresh snow scattered on top, and knowing they were so close behind.'

'You were there?'

'I was there. I had my bow and my quiver of arrows. I was ready to kill.'

'And?'

'They had horses and guns and dogs,' she said. 'They were hunting dogs, they would keep coming even with an arrow in their eye. They got me at the shoulder and pulled me down. I thought they would eat me alive. I could hear the crunch of their jaws on my bone and smell their breath on me.' She swept back her hair and John saw the ragged scars where a deep bite had been gouged out of her neck and shoulder. 'It's odd to feel an animal licking your blood,' she said.

'My God,' John whispered.

'Half a dozen of us were still alive at the end, and they made us walk back to Jamestown.'

'Suckahanna?'

'Dead.'

The word was like a blow in the pit of his belly, it fell no lighter for being expected. He had known that Suckahanna would never have been taken alive. He had known from the very start that what he was seeking in this strange diminished village was the news of her death.

'Attone?'

'Dead.'

'Suckahanna's son?'

'He got away,' she said. 'He could be anywhere. Maybe dead in the forest.'

'The baby? The little girl?'

'Died of hunger or fever or something. Before we tried to leave the village of bad water.'

There was a silence. John looked at the girl who had seen so much, who was indeed a child of winter.

'I shall go.' He paused. 'Is there anything I can do for you or for the People?'

'Would they set us free if you asked them?'

'No,' John said. 'They would not listen to me.'

'Do you think that they will hold us here forever?' she asked. 'Do you think that they mean us to have enough land to plant, but nothing that we can enjoy, nowhere we can run free? Do they think that now we will do nothing more forever than just cling to life at the edge of the white man's land?'

'No,' John said. 'I am sure not. There is a new government in England and it is pledged to care for the poor and for the men and women who are driven off their land by enclosures. It gives rights to tenants and people who live on the land. Surely they will give you the same rights here.'

She looked at him and for a moment he saw Suckahanna in her eyes with that delicious sense of the ridiculous which had been so often and

so lovingly directed at John. 'Oh, do you?' she said and then turned
and went back to her work.

John walked home dryshod in his English boots across the wooden
causeway, not touching the earth, forgetting the marsh flower, not seeing
anything but the winter battle in the snow and Suckahanna going down,
fighting to the last minute, and Attone falling beside her.

He could see nothing else for the long walk back to Jamestown, not
the new and beautiful houses nor the pretty sailing ships which the
planters now used instead of canoes on the river, not the settled prosperity of the fields drawn like a net of squares thrown over the landscape,
ignoring the contours of hill and slope and stream and imposing their
own order on the wildness. He did not see the outskirts of Jamestown
with the little shanty town of poor wooden houses, nor the town centre
with the governor's beautiful house and the new assembly room for the
burgesses where they were doing their best, by their lights, to build a
new country in this place.

That night when he went to bed he thought he would dream of the
battle and the defeat of the Powhatan and the dreadful death of Suckahanna in the cold snow with dogs snapping at her throat.

But he did not. He dreamed instead of the Great Hare leaping over
the winter snows, with its coat pure white, winter-white, and only its
long ears tipped with chocolate fur, gathering his love Suckahanna, and
his friend Attone, into its gentle mouth and taking them back into the
darkness away from the world which was no longer safe for the People.

Sir Josiah's house was one of the grander stone-built houses and his
garden was richer than John could have imagined. His wife greeted
them and ordered rum and lemons and hot water despite the heat, and
then Sir Josiah took John, punch glass in hand, down the steps to the
garden.

It was a garden poised between two worlds. In many ways it was an
English cottage garden: on the far sides were plants for cutting, for
drying and for medicinal use in a scramble and a muddle of richness.
John strolled over and saw, in their springtime growth, the familiar
herbs and flowers of England, thriving in this virgin earth.

Immediately before the house Sir Josiah had laid out a serpentine knot, an attempt at the formality of the English great gardens. It was edged in bay and planted with daffodils, and between the daffodils were growing some white daisies. John admired the colours and felt the familiar lift to his heart at the sight of spring bulbs but then he looked a little more closely.

'Did you bring these daisies from England?'

'No,' Sir Josiah said. 'I found them growing here. There's a place down by the river, a patch of grassland, I found whole clumps of them and dug them up, and planted them here and they have thrived and multiplied.'

John, oblivious of the snort of laughter from Lady Ashley on the terrace, dropped to his knees and took a closer look. 'I think this is a new kind of daisy,' he said. 'A Virginian daisy.'

'I thought it was just a daisy I might have for very little effort,' Sir Josiah said carelessly.

'And it's very pretty,' John said. 'I'll take a couple home with me when I go. I should like to see it growing in London, I have a good collection of daisies. Could you show me where it grows in the wild?'

'Of course,' Sir Josiah said cheerfully. 'We can go out this afternoon. And you must have a good roam through my woods. And when you have done with me I'll give you a letter of introduction and you can go upriver and stay with my neighbours and see what they have that takes your eye.'

Lady Ashley came floating across the grass towards them. 'Is this your first time in Virginia?' she asked with the slight drawl that the planters all shared.

'No,' John said. 'I was here more than ten years ago for a long stay.'

'And were you plant collecting then?'

'Yes,' John said cautiously. 'But it was not like this.'

Sir Josiah wanted to lend him a horse but John preferred to walk in the woods. 'I miss too much if I am too high and going too fast,' he said.

'I'm sure there are snakes,' Lady Ashley pointed out.

'I have good thick boots,' John said. 'And I was much in the woods when I was last here.'

Sir Josiah had left a good stand of timber to the north of his estate and John started to walk there and then found himself following a stream which drew him deeper and deeper inland. He walked as he always did, as his father had always done – with only the occasional glance towards the horizon and the path ahead and with his eyes mostly on his boots and the little plants under his feet. He had been walking all morning when he suddenly exclaimed and dropped to his knees. It was a sorrel, but what had attracted him was the tiny indentations of the leaves. It was an American version of the familiar plant. John swung his satchel down, took out the trowel and carefully lifted the plant from the moist, dark earth, wrapped it in a broad leaf and tucked it into the pocket of his satchel.

He straightened up and walked on, his eyes glancing up at the trees, and then down to the path. After a little while, amid the buzz of the Virginian spring, the birdsong, the loud cry of the occasional flight of ducks and migrating geese, there was a new sound: a soft tuneless whistling. John was happy.

1655

John stayed in Virginia for two years, travelling from one beautiful house to another, and staying for months at a time enjoying the famous Virginian hospitality. When he went deeper into the country and there were no large stone houses with slave cabins at the back he stayed instead with more humble planters who were building in wood but hoping for greater things. John found that he preferred the humbler sort of man, no-one could help admiring the determination that they showed to cross such a wide sea to find a new land, and to struggle – and John knew what a struggle it was – to wrest a living in a new country.

Sometimes he slept on an earth floor before a fire, in the warm humid days of summer he slept under a tree in the forest. He was never tempted to shed his English clothes and make himself a clout and a buckskin apron. He would have felt a mockery of the People if he dressed in their way and lived in their way, when they were still kept like ferrets in a box. But he could not unlearn the skills they had taught him, and he would not have wanted to forget them. Even wearing his heavy boots he moved through the woods quieter than any Englishman. His eye for plants and trees was his trained Tradescant eye, but he looked the more sharply because these were woods that he had known and loved as his home.

'Don't you fear the woods?' one of the planter's wives asked him curiously as she saw him ready to set out, walking to the next plantation.

John shook his head. 'There's nothing to fear,' he said.

'There's wolves, I sometimes hear them at night.'

John smiled, thinking of his old terror in his little house when he heard the wolves howling and thought that they would come in through the gaps in the walls when his fire went out. 'I lived here once, a long time ago,' he said. 'I learned to love the country then. It feels as familiar to me as my own garden at Lambeth.'

The woman nodded. 'Well, if you keep to the wide track you won't get lost,' she assured him. 'The next plantation starts just three miles up the road. There's only a little stand of trees between their tobacco fields and ours.'

John doffed his hat to her and left. She was right, here and all over the country there were only little stands of trees left between the riverside plantations. For rare plants he had to go deep into the countryside, high into the hills, following rivers and living off the land. He hired a canoe for a few months and took it down the coast to the marshy area that Suckahanna had showed him when she was a little girl. He even went to the place of the bad water where the People had made their stand, and tried to survive before they were hunted down. He found a little plant there, an exquisite valerian, and packed it carefully in damp earth wrapped in leaves to take back to Jamestown with him. He thought if he could persuade it to thrive in Lambeth then it would remind him of the People, even when all other traces of them were gone.

He returned to Jamestown several times during his visit, to pack barrels of plants and send them back to the Ark and on the second visit he found a letter from Hester.

September 1655
   Dear Husband,
   Your new maple has arrived safely and been planted into the garden near to your first Virginia maple so that men may make the comparison and see that it is a little different. I shall write and tell you if it too changes the colour of its leaves in autumn to scarlet.
   Some of the daisy plants were spoiled by salt water by the negligence of the sailors but Frances has potted up the others and says they will live. She says that your Virginia convolvulus must be called Tradescantia. It flowered this summer and is most beautiful with huge flowers very prettily marked. They only live a day but are succeeded by many others. You did not say whether it will over-winter, so we have taken it into the orangery and we also collected seeds and took cuttings. Lord Lambert has begged some seeds for his rare garden and we sold them to him at one shilling for half a dozen.
   Frances is well and stayed with me for the summer, and there have been many other guests too, come to see the rarities

and stay to enjoy the garden. Elias Ashmole has been a constant visitor and many other of your friends send their regards.

You may not have heard but the Lord Protector has established the rule of major generals – one to each county to supervise the work of the magistrates and the churchwardens and the parish overseers. The innovation is not much welcomed in Lambeth, but I will say no more in a letter.

I am caring for your rarities and your garden as ever and I am well.

Your loving wife,
Hester

March 1656

In March, when the worst of the winter storms had died down, John loaded his Virginia treasures on to a ship bound for London. A couple of planters had come down to the quayside to see him off and press him with commissions to complete for them in London. John accepted packages and errands but never took his eyes from his barrels of plants and boxes of rarities.

He was importing a dozen saplings in tubs which would have to stand on deck and be shielded from the spray by a little shelter woven of reeds. Three of them were new Virginian walnut trees, never seen in England before; the others were new poplar trees and whips of Virginian cypress. Safely packed in tubs of damp sand were the roots of some new asters and some new geraniums, and a new vine. Sealed with candlewax in a waterproof chest were seeds that John had gathered the previous autumn: of the aconitum, which the Americans called wolfsbane, Virginian parsley, the exquisitely pretty Virginian columbine, the leopardsbane of America – a flower like a daisy but with a flaming orange petal and a black heart, as bright as any marigold.

John looked at his treasures with the joy of a wealthy merchant bringing home gold. He stuffed letters and packages in the deep pockets of his coat and stepped back from the ship's railing as they ran the gangplank ashore.

'Goodbye!' he called.

'When will we see you again?' Sir Josiah shouted.

'In another few years,' John called back over the widening gulf of water. 'When my stocks are low again. When I want new marvels.'

'Be sure you come!' Sir Josiah called. 'This is a land of marvels.'

John laughed and nodded and waved goodbye, and then stood on deck to watch the town recede swiftly as the current and the wind took the little ship down the river and towards the sea.

'I would never have thought it,' he said to himself. 'From the time when I first came here. I would never have thought that they could have survived and built such a town, almost a city, from the forest.'

The new manicured banks of the river slipped quickly by. John looked upriver, to where the shimmer of light on the water gave the illusion that nothing had changed. 'Goodbye,' he said softly, to the landscape and to the woman he had loved.

April 1656

John came back to his garden, to the Ark and to his wife as the tulips were starting to fatten and show their colour. The wagon rumbled across the familiar bridge and into the stable yard and Hester, looking out of the window of the rarities room at the noise, saw John sitting beside the carter and came running down the terrace and into her husband's arms.

'I should have known you wouldn't miss another spring,' she said. 'But I didn't really expect you till midsummer.'

'I was ready to come home,' John said. 'And lucky to get a fast ship.'

They drew back a little and inspected each other, as old friends will do after a long absence. Hester's hair under her neat cap was nearly as white as the linen, and her face was thinner and more severe. There were lines of grief on her face which would be there forever. John, aged forty-eight, was leaner and fitter than when he had gone away, the days on horseback and on foot had tanned him brown and skimmed off the fat of easy living.

'You look well, but your hair has gone white,' he said.

She gave a little smile. 'It was starting to go as you left,' she said. 'At Johnnie's death.'

John nodded. 'I stopped at his tomb on the way home. I felt I wanted to tell him I was back. I always promised that he would come with me on the next trip. Someone had planted little daffodils.'

'Frances,' she said. 'And when the convolvulus grows she wants to plant some beside your father's tomb so that it climbs around it. She said she wanted them both to see it.'

They left the carter and the garden boy to unload the cart and went towards the house, their arms interlinked. They walked around to the

520

terrace and John leaned on the railing and looked down over the garden.

The flowerbeds at the front of the house were blushing with the colour of the early tulips, beyond them the orchard was carpeted with yellow daffodils, and the white and orange of the narcissi. Above them, the cherry and apricot trees were showing little pink buds, and the thick, powerful twigs of the horse chestnuts were slowly splitting, the fat, sticky buds bursting pale and green out of their shells.

'It's good to be home,' John said with pleasure. 'What's the news?'

'I wrote to you that Cromwell dissolved Parliament and set the army to rule over us directly.'

He nodded. 'And how is that?'

Hester shrugged. 'I don't know about the rest of the country but it works well for Lambeth. They do the work the Justices of the Peace used to do, but more fairly and more evenly. They've closed down a lot of the ale houses and that's nothing but good. They're stricter with paupers and beggars and vagrants so the streets are cleaner. But the taxes!' She shook her head. 'Higher than ever before and now they remember to collect them. They're a hard-working bunch of men; and that will be their undoing. People don't mind the Sunday sports and the maypoles going, they don't even mind the bawdy houses closed down. But the taxes!'

'Are we in profit?' John asked, looking at the rich prosperity of the garden.

'In plants,' she said, following his gaze. 'And to be honest, we're doing well enough. Sending the Members of Parliament back to their homes has done nothing but good for us. The squires and the country gentlemen have little to do but to tend their gardens. Cromwell's major generals are running the country, there is nothing for the gentry to attend to in London, and no work for them to do in the counties. All the work of the squires and the JPs is being done by army men. All they have left is their gardens.'

John chuckled. 'It's an ill wind.'

'Not so ill,' she reminded him. 'Cromwell has brought peace to the country.'

He nodded. 'Have you seen Lord Lambert? What does he say?'

'He was here just a few weeks ago to see our show of daffodils. He has a fancy for a garden in orange, gold and yellow and he wanted some bright yellow lenten lilies. He's not a happy man. He was working on a new constitution for the country, with the backing of the army. He wanted Cromwell to become Lord Protector with an elected parliament. Then Cromwell brought in the major generals and dissolved Parliament.

I think he thought that it smacked of tyranny; but he never said. He stays loyal to Cromwell –'

'He's always loyal,' John interrupted.

'But there's a strain,' she said. 'He doesn't like to see the army put over the people. He wants an elected parliament, not the rule of soldiers.'

John slid his arm around his wife's waist. 'And you?' he asked gently, his lips against her clean cap. 'Are you well?'

She nodded, saying nothing. He did not press the question. They both knew that the answer was now and would always be that she was grieving for Johnnie. They would both always be grieving for Johnnie.

'Your friends have visited in your absence,' she said with forced brightness. 'Mr Ashmole and the others. Mr Ashmole has been very busy working on a catalogue of the collection as you asked him to. I think it's nearly done. It is in Latin. He showed me some pages, it looks very fine. I think you will be pleased with it. He says we can sell the catalogue at the door to guide people around the rarities room and around the garden. And that people can take it away with them to study. Gardeners can see what we are growing and write to us with orders. He says we could charge as much as two shillings.'

'And is Frances well?'

Hester nodded. 'Alexander was ill this winter, a cough which wouldn't ease. She was worried about him for a while but he is mending with the warmer weather.'

John curbed his resentment at his young daughter nursing a husband suffering from the ailments of an old man. 'No signs of another baby?'

'None yet,' Hester said gently.

John nodded, glanced once more at the sunlit beauty of his garden and then turned to his house.

Summer 1657

In early summer John took the wagon and cart over to Wimbledon House with a delivery of bulbs and saplings for John Lambert. He found Lord Lambert in his rare garden – a walled area facing south and west reserved for exotic plants – with an easel before him, paints on a table beside him and an exquisite white tulip in a porcelain blue bowl. In the centre of the garden was a newly planted acacia tree which took John's eye at once.

'Is that one of mine?' John asked.

'No,' Lambert said. 'I had it from Paris last autumn, from the Robins' garden.'

'Very fine,' John said, a hint of envy in his voice. Lambert heard it at once.

'You shall have a cutting,' he promised. 'I know you have so little. I know your garden is so poor.'

John grinned ruefully. 'A true gardener can always squeeze in one more plant. Now, I have brought you some orange plants as you asked. This one they call leopardsbane in Virginia, it flowers in autumn: a wonderful rich, bright orange with a heart as dark as chocolate. And the lily bulbs you ordered. And some whips of orange trees.'

'I have a fancy for a garden in yellow and orange,' Lambert explained, 'with orange trees in tubs at the centre of the beds. And a blaze of colour all around. What d'you think? Are there enough orange flowers?'

'Marigolds?' John suggested. 'Ranunculus? Sunflowers? Turkish nasturtiums? I have some tulips which would pass as orange, and some new narcissi with orange hearts. My father made a golden garden years ago at Hatfield. He used kingcups and buttercups by the watercourses, and yellow flag iris. And my Virginian trumpet vine is a bright true orange.'

'I'll have them all,' Lambert declared. 'And what lily bulbs d'you have for me? I want to plant some great pots with lily bulbs deep in the base, and tulips in the middle, and snowdrops on the top so they succeed each other from spring through to midsummer.'

John shook his head. 'You'll have to repot every three or four years,' he said. 'They won't thrive in such a small space. They'll sap the strength of the earth. But the first two years you could leave them and you would get one flower succeeding another, as long as you keep them damp with comfrey water.'

'Anything else new?' Lambert asked as they walked from the rare garden to the stable yard where John had halted the cart.

'I brought you some day lilies and some white lilies, and there are a couple you could use in your orange garden: a red lily and a flame lily. They could pass for orange and you could breed from them, selecting the most orange colours.'

Lambert nodded to his man to unload the cart.

'I hear you are much at home these days,' John said tactfully, skirting the gossip that Lambert's differences with Cromwell now amounted to an open breach. The rule of the major generals had been replaced by a new parliament which again had failed to agree. Lambert had once more been spokesman for the radical old soldiers of the army who still resisted every attempt to restore the gentry and the lords to their previous power. There was a great suspicion that Cromwell, in an effort to secure peace in the country, was going the way of the Stuart kings, James and then Charles, towards a parliament which served only lords and gentry, an imposed Church which served the needs of the one sole ruler: himself, who might even be called king.

John Lambert had brought a petition from the army to Parliament voicing the old demands of free elections, justice for all, and a fairer chance for working men, as if the Levellers still held the balance of power and could make such demands. He expected a fair hearing from Cromwell who had once been an army man, as Lambert was still.

But Cromwell was an army man no more. He had moved from the clear, godly certainties of the ranks to the complex machinations of the men of power. When Lambert brought the petition asking for the political changes that the army had fought and died for, Cromwell acted swiftly. He reorganised the army, paid some back wages, promoted some men, dismissed others, and broke whole companies. Lambert had to watch the radical leaders of the army posted to service overseas, Jamaica, or Ireland, or simply discharged from their posts.

Then the blow fell on him. Cromwell dismissed Lambert from his own regiment, from the men that had fought behind him every step of the king's wars and had never been separated from their commander before. Lambert had taken the order without argument from Cromwell, because he would not disobey his commander. But he would not take the oath of fealty to him. And he did not admire Cromwell when the republican leader appeared in the robes of state carrying a sceptre.

Lambert scowled for a moment at John, hardly seeing him. 'I am much at home,' he agreed. 'As it turns out, I have little choice. There's no place for me at Westminster, it seems. And no place for me with my regiment. It's been given to Lord Fauconberg.'

'Your regiment?' John asked.

Lambert nodded scowling.

'Who *is* Lord Fauconberg? I never heard of him.'

'A noble lord. A royalist who has become Cromwell's man. I think my regiment is his dowry,' Lambert said wryly. 'He's to marry Oliver's daughter Mary. Quite a little dynasty that Cromwell is making, isn't it? And with a man who was a royalist, and would be a royalist again, especially if his father-in-law was to be king.'

'I never thought that he could govern without you,' John volunteered. 'I never thought he would turn against the army.'

'He's become nervous,' Lambert explained. 'He doesn't want a parliament full of new ideas, he doesn't want an army that might argue with him. So he dissolved Parliament and took my regiment away from me.'

'Could you not have objected?' John asked. 'Surely you command more influence than him, especially in the army.'

Lambert gave a rueful smile. 'And do what?' he asked. 'Lead them out to fight him? Another war fought over the same ground with the same men? Another half-dozen years of heartbreak? I'm not a man for faction, or division. My task has been to pull the country together, I wouldn't tear it apart for my own ambitions. I promised that I wouldn't raise a storm against him if he left my regiment alone, in one piece. I traded: my work and reputation for the integrity of my men. Cromwell agreed. They're under another man's command but no good men have been thrown out in the street for thinking for themselves. It was a fair deal, and I have to stick to my side of the contract.'

'I couldn't believe they were talking of Cromwell for king,' John said. 'I thought that we were building a new country here, and now it seems that we were just exchanging one king for another. The family of Stuart for the family of Cromwell.'

'The person doesn't matter,' Lambert said staunchly. 'Nor the name. What matters is the balance. The will of the people in Parliament, the reform of the law so that everyone can get justice, and the limitation of the king – or Lord Protector – or Council of State. It doesn't matter what the third power is called, but everything has to work in balance. The one with the other. A three-legged stool.'

'But what will you do if the Lord Protector doesn't want to be in balance?' John asked. 'What if he wants the balance tipped all his way? What if the milkmaid on your three-legged stool is thrown down and all the milk spilled?'

Lambert looked at the orange trees in their carrying tubs without really seeing them. 'I don't know,' he said. 'We shall have to pray that he has not forgotten so much of what we all once wanted.' His mood suddenly changed and he grinned at John. 'But I'm damned if I call him Your Majesty though,' he said cheerfully. 'I swear to you, Tradescant, I just couldn't do it. It would choke me.'

Frances and Alexander stayed at the Ark for the spring. Alexander's cough was no better and Frances wanted him away from the smell and noise of the city streets.

John woke one night to hear him coughing in their room and heard Frances go quietly down the stairs. He slipped from his own bed, threw his cape around his shoulders over his nightshirt and went downstairs to the kitchen.

Frances was stirring a saucepan over the embers of the fire.

'I'm making a drink of mead and honey for Alexander,' she said. 'His cough is so troublesome.'

'I'll put a drop of rum in it,' John said, and went to fetch the bottle from the cupboard in the dining room. When he came back he saw that Frances had sunk into one of the kitchen chairs with the saucepan left on the hob. He took it off and poured a hearty slug of rum on the mix, and then poured it into a cup.

'Taste it,' he said.

She would have refused but he insisted.

'Very sweet,' she said.

'Take another gulp,' he said. 'It'll put some spirit in you.'

She did as she was ordered and he saw the colour come into her cheeks.

'I am sorry,' he said.

She met his eyes frankly. 'He's sixty-seven,' she said bluntly. 'We've had twelve good years. We never counted on this many.'

John put his hand over hers.

'And you never wanted me to marry him at all,' she said with a flash of residual resentment.

John smiled wryly. 'Only to spare you this night,' he said. 'And the other nights ahead, while you nurse him.'

She shook her head. 'I don't mind,' she said. 'I'm caring for him now, but he has cared for me for as long as I can remember. I quite like being the one in charge for a change. I like repaying the debt of love. He's always petted me, you know. Petted me so tenderly. I rather like nursing him now.'

John poured a little thimbleful of mead and rum for her. 'You sit by the fire for a while and drink this,' he ordered. 'I'll take this up to him.'

Frances nodded and let him go. John took one of the kitchen candles, lit it at the embers of the fire and went quietly up the stairs to Alexander's bedroom.

Alexander was propped up against the pillow, his breathing hoarse. When he saw John come in he managed a smile of greeting.

'Is Frances all right? I didn't want her running after me.'

'She's having a drop of mead and rum at the fireside,' John said. 'I thought I'd sit with you for a while, if you wish.'

Alexander nodded. 'I brought you this,' John said. 'If it doesn't help you sleep then you have a head stronger than my narwhal tusk.'

Alexander gave a choking little laugh and took a sip of the hot drink. 'By God, John, that's good. What's in it?'

'Herbs of my own brewing,' John said innocently. 'Actually, my Jamaican rum.'

'She'll have a good settlement,' Alexander said suddenly. 'When I go. She's well provided for.'

'Oh yes?'

'The cooperage will go to my manager, but he's agreed a price to pay her, and signed a deed. It's all agreed. She can keep the house if she likes but I thought she'd rather live somewhere else than at the Minories.'

'I'll look after her,' John said. 'It'll be as she wants.'

'She should marry again,' Alexander said. 'A younger man. These are better days now, at last. She can take her pick. She'll be a wealthy young widow.'

John looked cautiously at him, but Alexander spoke without bitterness.

'I'll take care of her,' John repeated. 'She won't make a mistake with her choice.' He paused for a moment. 'She didn't make a mistake last time. Though I disagreed at the time. She made no mistake when she chose you.'

Alexander gave a little laugh which turned into a cough. John held his cup till the paroxysm passed and then gave him another sip of the drink. 'Kind of you,' he said. 'I knew it wasn't your choice. But it seemed like the best life she could have at the time.'

'I know it,' John admitted. 'I know it now.'

The two men sat in companionable silence for a moment.

'All square then?' Alexander asked.

John proffered his hand and gripped Alexander's own. 'All square,' he said fairly.

Summer 1657

Elias Ashmole and the physicians, mathematicians, astronomers, chemists, geographers, herbalists and engineers returned to the Ark to argue, discuss and exchange ideas, on the first Sunday of every summer month. By common accord they avoided the subject of politics. It looked to most men as if Cromwell meant to make himself king. Most of the opposition to him had been dispersed, paid or bullied into silence. General George Monck, another turncoat royalist, held down Scotland for the Lord Protector with a heavy hand and the dour efficiency of the professional soldier. Cromwell's own son Henry held down Ireland. The Cromwells were becoming a mighty dynasty, and the old idealism was lost in the difficulties of ruling a country where any freedom for the many was feared by the powerful few.

The great fear was not political opposition but religious madness. The men and women who would give their form of worship no name because they wanted it to be everywhere, to be the nature of life itself, were growing in numbers. Their opponents called them Quakers because they shook and trembled in religious ecstasy. Their enemies called them blasphemers, especially after one of their number, James Nayler, entered the city of Bristol like Jesus on a donkey with women throwing down palms before him. The House of Commons had him arraigned for blasphemy and savagely punished; but the mutilating of one individual could not stop a movement which threw up adherents everywhere like poppies in a wheatfield. Very soon John's visitors banned the discussion of religion too, as overly distracting from the work in hand.

A couple of times Lord Lambert came from his house at Wimbledon to see any new additions to the garden or the rarities room and sometimes stayed for dinner to talk with the other guests. Sometimes men brought curiosities, or things that they had designed or built. Often at these talks

Ashmole would lead the discussion, his classical education and his acute mind prompting him to take the part of host in John's house.

'I don't like how Mr Ashmole puts himself forward,' Hester remarked to John as she carried another couple of bottles of wine into the dining room.

'No more than any other man,' he answered.

'He does,' she insisted. 'Ever since he catalogued the collection you would think that it was his own. I wish you would remind him that he was nothing more than your assistant. Frances knows her way round the collection better than he does. Even I do. And Frances and I kept it safe through three wars, while he was at Oxford living off the richness of the court.'

'But neither Frances nor I know Latin like Mr Ashmole,' John reminded her gently. 'And he worked very hard for nothing more than my thanks. I couldn't have completed the task without him, you know, Hester. And he's a coming man, mark my words. He'll do great things.'

Hester gave John a brief, sceptical look and said nothing more but turned to go back to the kitchen.

'Is Alexander coming downstairs tonight?' John asked her. It was Alexander's habit now to join the men in the evening after they had dined so that he could listen to their talk. He wore his gown with a rich robe wrapped round his shoulders against the cool evening air. He was often too breathless to speak but he liked to listen to the men discussing, he liked to follow the arguments especially when they talked of astronomy and the new discoveries of the stars.

Hester shook her head. 'He's too weary,' he says. 'Frances will sit with him upstairs.'

The Normans stayed at the Ark through the summer, but still Alexander grew no better. They all maintained the gentle fiction that he would improve when the colder weather came, as before they had pretended that he would be better when he felt the summer sun.

When he said he wanted to go home in August Frances did not argue with him, though the summer months were the most dangerous for the plague in the City. She simply sent the garden boy to the river to hail a boat to take them down to the Tower and told the stable lad to harness the cart.

'He's very ill,' Hester cautioned her. 'He's too ill to make the journey. You should stay here.'

'I know,' Frances said simply. 'But he wants to be home.'

'Settle him in and as soon as he is feeling better you come back here,' Hester said. 'There's plague in the City, I'd rather you were here.'

Frances shook her head. 'You can see as well as I can that he will not feel better, even when he is home. I will stay with him until the end.'

'Oh, Frances.'

'I knew that this was likely to happen when I married him,' Frances said. Her eyes were filled with tears but her voice never faltered. 'And he knew it too. We were neither of us such fools as to think that I would not lose him. We were prepared for this from our wedding day. He warned me of it. I have no regrets.'

'I'll come with you,' Hester decided. 'You'll need someone to run the house while you nurse him.'

'Thank you,' Frances said. 'I'll want you with me.'

Alexander died in his bed, as he had wanted, with Hester at the foot of the bed and Frances holding his hand. He whispered something and she could not hear what he said. She leaned a little closer to hear the words.

'What is it, my love? Say it again?'

'You were the sweetest –' he paused for a breath and Frances leaned a little closer. 'The sweetest flower in all of John's garden.' He smiled at her for a moment, then he closed his eyes and went to sleep.

Frances buried her husband in the church where they had been married and walked back to her house with her father and stepmother on either side of her.

Hester had ordered in a dinner from the nearby bake-house and Alexander's apprentices, his family from Herefordshire, and his friends from the City drank to his memory, ate their dinner and then left.

The house was oddly silent without the tapping of hammers from the yard and continual rasp of the saws.

'Have you thought what you would like to do?' John asked his daughter gently. 'Have you thought where you would like to live? Alexander left you well-provided, and you can sell this house. The sale of the business is already agreed.'

'I had thought,' she said. 'If you would allow it – I should like to come home.'

'To the Ark?'

'Yes.'

John found that he was beaming with delight. 'That would give me much joy,' he said simply.

Autumn 1658

In early September John was wakened at dawn by the noise of the rising wind.

'I'm glad I'm not at sea today,' he said to Hester.

He went to the window and saw the trees in the orchard and the avenue flailing their boughs at the sky where the clouds raced overhead.

'Come back to bed,' Hester said sleepily.

There was a clatter from the stable yard.

'I'm awake now,' John said. 'I'll get up and see that everything's safe. We're in for a storm.'

He spent the day with the lad and Joseph pinning back the creepers and staking the plants which were already rocking in the earth, pulling at their roots. Frances took a sharp knife and went around the garden mercilessly pruning the climbing roses so that the long boughs would not tear the stalks from the soil. She came in for dinner at midday with her arms scratched above her gloves and her hair tumbled about her shoulders.

'Frances Norman,' said Hester, disapprovingly.

'It's wild out there,' Frances said. 'My cap blew off.'

'I can see that,' Hester said.

'We're going to lose half the apples,' John said irritably. 'What a foul wind.'

'And the plums,' Frances said. 'I'll pick as many as I can get this afternoon.'

'I'll come out and help,' said Hester. 'I don't expect any visitors this afternoon, no-one would take a boat on the river unless they had to.'

John had thought that the wind might drop as night fell; but it grew stronger and wilder, and it started to rain. Hester went round the house fastening shutters but still they could hear the thud of the wind against the leaded panes of glass, and in the rarities room they could see the great panes creaking as they moved in their frames.

'I hope to God they don't crack,' John said. 'We'll close the shutters behind them, then at least if they smash the rarities will still have some protection. If I had thought I could have boarded up the house this morning.'

They had an ill-cooked supper. A great gust of wind had come down the chimney and blown soot all around the kitchen. While they ate they heard the clatter of a slate falling from the roof into the stable yard.

Frances declared that she was going early to bed and putting her head under her pillow, and Hester followed her example; but John prowled around the creaking house for half the night, feeling that his Ark was rocking in high seas and that the master should be awake.

In the morning there was less damage than they had feared. The Virginian creeper was stripped of its rosy leaves and would make no show to attract buyers, and there were fallen fruit and broken boughs all down the orchard. The chestnuts had been ripped from the trees too early and they might not ripen, and they had lost most of the apple and plum crop. But the house was still standing and the windows were unbroken, and only a few slates had gone missing from the roof.

'I shall go into Lambeth and order the builder to come,' John said. 'He'll be a busy man this day, I should think.'

He rode Caesar down the lane to Lambeth and thought that the crowd in the market was agog with news of the storm damage until he drew closer and heard what they were saying.

'What was that?' he asked, dropping from the saddle. 'What did you say, sir?'

'Don't you know?' A man turned to him, delighted to be first with the news. 'Haven't you heard? He's dead!'

'Who?'

'The Lord Protector. Oliver Cromwell. Dead in his bed while the storm rattled the roof above him.'

'It's as if God himself was angry,' a man piously asserted. 'It was a sign.'

'A very odd sign then, and rather late in the day,' John said crossly. 'If God didn't like Oliver Cromwell he had plenty of time to demonstrate that before.'

An unfriendly face turned towards him. 'Are you one of his old soldiers?' someone asked unpleasantly. 'Or a servant of the major generals? Or one of the damned tax collectors?'

'I'm a man who thinks for himself,' John said stoutly. 'I serve no master and I owe nothing to any man. And I am absolutely certain that God didn't blow the slates of my roof last night to show me that Oliver Cromwell was dying. If He is all-wise, then He might have found a way to tell me that didn't let the rain in.'

Spring 1659

The storm which blew Oliver Cromwell up to his reward in heaven, or down to the devils in hell, did not helpfully indicate his successor. There were many who said that he nominated his son Richard on his deathbed, but John, recalling what his father had said about the succession of kings, remembered that courtiers were never very reliable about deathbed confessions and that the power of supreme government in England might go to whatever man had the courage to seize it.

The man most fit to succeed was John Lambert, beloved of the army, still the greatest power in the land, and a proven friend of peace, tolerance and reform. But Richard was said to be the heir and a new parliament was summoned to rule with the new Protector.

They were curiously churlish about the job. Richard was not even recognised as Lord Protector until they were forced to acknowledge him so that he could send the fleet to the Baltic to protect English shipping against the Dutch in February. And then in April, the army, impatient with being ignored while they petitioned for back pay and furious at the increasingly arrogant behaviour of the royalists, locked the MPs out of the Commons, Richard among them.

He might be a Cromwell, but he was not an old soldier, and the army suspected that the new breed of politicians and leaders had lost the godliness and republican fire of those who had been forced to fight for their beliefs.

John had promised Hester that he would take her to see Lambert's orange garden at Wimbledon in the spring. They took a boat to the manor house landing stage and walked through Lambert's new plantation to the formal gardens before the house. John hesitated when he saw Lord Lambert on the terrace, his wife beside him. Before them were a couple of soldiers with the standard of his old regiment which had been given to Cromwell's son-in-law.

'What's going on?' Hester asked her husband quietly.

John shook his head.

'Perhaps we should just wave and go back to the plantation,' Hester suggested tactfully. 'It's maybe a private matter.'

'He's beckoning us,' John said. 'Come on.'

The Tradescants went to the foot of the steps. John Lambert smiled down at Hester with a beam that reminded her poignantly of Johnnie when he had just got his own way in an argument.

'You come at a good moment,' he said to them both. 'See. Here's the standard of my regiment. Restored to me.'

'Restored?' Hester asked, coming up the steps and dropping a little curtsey to Lady Lambert.

'Fauconberg and the rest are dismissed from their posts, and so my lads have come to restore the standard to me. We're together again.'

'I'm glad for you,' John said. 'Congratulations, Lord Lambert.'

'Major General,' Lambert said with a gleam. 'And I'd rather be a major general at the head of the best regiment in the army than a lord at my fireside any day.'

Summer 1659

Parliament was dissolved and a new parliament came in, led by a new Council of State, in May. Amongst the new council was John Lambert and he gave his vote to the retirement, with pay, of Richard Cromwell, back pay to the army, the cleansing of schools and universities of ungodly ministers, and the toleration for all religions except for Catholics and those who would bring the bishops back to England. The rule of the Cromwell family was over, England was a true republic again.

'He's asked me to take care of his tulips this autumn,' John remarked to Hester as they worked companionably side by side in the Ark's rose garden. 'He thinks he will be in Whitehall all this year. It'll be odd to work at Wimbledon again.'

'You'll never be his gardener,' Hester said, astonished.

'No, he has his own gardeners. But I said I would lift the tulip bulbs in the autumn. He wants me to choose the colours for the orange garden, and he trusts me with his dark Violetten tulips.'

Hester smiled. 'Not going into service again then, John?'

'Never again,' he said. 'Not even for him. I swore I would never serve another master and then the order came from the king for my father and me, and we couldn't disobey. Anyone else I would have refused.'

'What if Lambert were to become king?' she asked. 'He's the best-loved man in the country. There are many saying that he could be trusted to rule with a parliament. And the army follow no-one but him.'

'I'd like to see a gardener on the throne,' John mused. 'Think of what the palace gardens could be.'

Hester snorted with laughter. 'And that's the main consideration?'

John grinned reluctantly. 'The most important, certainly.'

They heard Frances call from the house and they looked towards the terrace. She was standing with a gentleman at her side. She beckoned to John.

'Who's that?' Hester asked uneasily. 'I don't recognise him.'

'Perhaps someone with something for sale,' John said, stepping carefully round the rose bushes, and picking up his basket filled with the sweetly scented pastel petals. He walked to the terrace and gave the basket to Frances.

'This gentleman says he has private business to discuss with you,' she said briefly.

John absorbed, as a father can do, that his daughter was deeply offended and determined not to show it.

'The gentleman declined to give his name to me,' Frances said in the same clipped tones. 'I'll take these to the stable yard, shall I?'

John smiled pacifically at her. 'If you wouldn't mind,' he said.

'The gentleman asked me to fetch him a glass of wine,' Frances continued stonily. 'Can I fetch anything for you, Father?'

'No indeed,' John said. 'But please ask Cook to serve the gentleman. You are far too busy, Frances.'

He earned a brief smile for that and then she was gone, her back very straight, her head very high. John turned his attention to the mystery guest who had managed, in so short a time, to mortally offend his daughter.

'I beg your pardon,' the man said. 'She was so simply dressed I thought she was your housemaid.' He glanced at John's own muddy homespun breeches, linen shirt, leather waistcoat and scratched dirty hands.

'We are gardeners,' John said gently. 'It's a dirty job. It rather calls for simple dress.'

'Of course –' the man said hastily. 'I did not mean to upset Miss Tradescant.'

John nodded, not bothering to correct him.

'There are far too many women, young and old, trying to meddle in the affairs of men,' the man said in an effort to please. 'You do well to keep her at home and working in her place. The country would be a better place for us all if women were restrained from thinking and bearing witness, and praying, and preaching and all the rest of it. The country will be a better place when the women are back in the kitchens again and everyone back in their proper place. I like to see a young lady dressed as plain as a kitchen maid. It shows she has proper humility.'

'Your business with me, sir?' John prompted. 'I have a rose garden to see to, and petals which have to go fresh to the perfumiers.'

The man glanced around the empty terrace as if he thought they might be overheard.

'Can we talk here?'

'You can talk anything that is fit and legal,' John said shortly.

'My name is Mordaunt. I come from the king.'

John nodded, saying nothing.

'Viscount John Mordaunt,' the gentleman emphasised, as if John were likely to be swayed by a title.

John nodded again.

'There is to be a rising. The country cannot be ruled by a council of nobodies and a parliament of nothings. We have been waiting our time, and now the king has named the day.'

'I don't want to know,' John said abruptly.

'We are counting on you to secure Lambeth for the king,' Mordaunt said earnestly. 'I know where your sympathies lie. You mustn't think that this is a little conspiracy which will get us nowhere but the Tower. This is to be a great uprising on the first day of August. And your part will be to secure Lambeth and this side of the river. You are to secure the horse ferry, and then extend downriver.'

'I don't want to know,' John repeated. 'My sympathies are with peace and order. I won't recognise Charles Stuart until he is crowned king of England. I lost a son –' He broke off.

'Then you will want to be avenged!' Mordaunt said, as if that clinched the matter. 'Your son fought for the king, did he?'

'Twice,' John said. 'And twice wounded. Never paid, never thanked, and never victorious. I don't want to know about the uprising. Don't force secrets on me. I don't want to be in the conspiracy, big or small. Don't tell me, and then I cannot betray you.'

Mordaunt checked suddenly as Hester came up the steps to the little wooden terrace. 'Ssshh! Hush!' he hissed.

Hester glanced interrogatively at John.

'This gentleman is leaving,' John said. 'I'll show him out.'

Mordaunt hesitated. 'When he of whom we were speaking comes back to London you will regret that you did not assist me,' he warned.

John nodded. 'Perhaps,' he said, and showed the man through the double doors of the terrace and into the hall. Frances emerged from the kitchen and stood beside Hester as John eased their unwelcome guest towards the front door.

'When he of whom we were speaking is in his rightful place again then there will be a grave reckoning,' Mordaunt threatened. 'When he is where he should be then he will want to know where you were on the day of which I have spoken.'

'If you mean Charles Stuart,' Frances's voice rang out clearly in the hall, 'then calling him "he of whom you were speaking" is hardly a brilliant disguise. And if *that* is your idea of deep concealment then I don't anticipate great success, on the day of which you have spoken, or any other day, actually.'

Mordaunt exchanged one angry look with her, crammed his hat on his head and flung open the front door. 'When he of whom we were speaking is where he belongs again, then women, especially interfering spinsters, will be kept where they belong,' he said crossly to Frances and stormed out of the door.

Frances lifted up her skirts and ran after him to stand on the front step. 'And we all know where Charles Stuart likes his women!' she shouted down the street to his rapidly retreating back. 'Up against a wall!'

'Should I warn Major General Lambert?' John asked Hester as they prepared for bed that night.

'That Charles Stuart is preparing an uprising?' she asked. She twisted her hair into a loose knot and tied her cap on her head. 'He must know already. There's been nothing but promises of another royal invasion ever since Cromwell died.'

'I don't like to be a spy,' John said uneasily. 'But I don't like being drawn in.'

Hester chuckled. 'I doubt they'll come again for help to you after what Frances said.'

John shook his head, smiling. 'What a fishwife!' he said. 'What ever would Alexander have thought?'

'He knew her,' Hester said. 'It would have come as no surprise to him. She was never a docile girl.'

'She's a complete trooper,' John said. 'I think you must have brought her up very badly, my wife.'

Hester gleamed at him and got into bed. 'I did,' she said. 'But she's a woman who knows her own mind. Give me credit for that at least.'

In the morning John wrote a note to John Lambert and sent it to him at Whitehall.

Your lordship,
    I have heard that there is to be an uprising for Charles Stuart
on 1 August. I know no more than this, and I wish with all my
heart that I did not know this.
    John Tradescant.

He received a reply brought by one of Lambert's troopers, a man with
a head like a cannon ball and a wide toothless grin.

Mr Tradescant,
    If this is the first you have heard of the uprising then you
are too much out of the way in Lambeth. They came to try to
recruit me for it in June.
    In any case, thank you for your loyalty to our great republic.
    Lambert.

Lambert might joke about the royalist indiscretion but there was enough
support for their cause for there to be uprisings all over the country.
Every village, every town, was divided again between men who would
fight for their liberties and men who would fight for their king. Some of
them wanted a more lasting solution than a succession of argumentative
parliaments. Some of them wanted a return to the old days of inefficient
tax collection, and sports in the churchyard on Sunday. Some of them
wanted the rich rewards that an incoming monarch must bring. Some
of them hoped to get their old places back. Some were Roman Catholics,
gambling on the widespread belief that the Stuarts were always Papists.
One or two may even have believed that the libertine in the Hague was
the best hope for the country. None of the fights came to more than a
few broken windows and a couple of brawls except in the case of Sir
George Booth at Chester.

The parliament, in grave fright at the news of an armed uprising,
ordered five regiments to march to Cheshire led by Major General
Lambert. Lambert left his botanical paintings, his rare garden, his orange
garden, and his ornamental pheasants, kissed his wife goodbye and rode
at the head of his restored regiment westwards.

He met Sir George Booth's army at Winnington Bridge. Booth had
one thousand men under the royal standard and Lambert had his full
complement of four thousand. The outcome could not be in doubt.
There was a brief, efficient battle which was notable for its economy
and discipline. Only thirty men died and the rebellion was over. Lambert
held his troops in tight order and there was no cruelty or looting or

taking quarter. The royalist army were relieved of their weapons with careful courtesy and sent back to their homes.

Sir George Booth fled the battlefield disguised as a woman but was arrested when an inn keeper noticed that his 'lady' guest had called for a barber and a razor.

'Inspired,' Lambert said briefly, and ordered that Sir George Booth be taken to London for his trial for treason.

Lambert's popularity rose and he was declared the saviour of the nation in every ale shop and tavern down the Great North Road. More particular were the thanks of the Quakers who came under his protection while he scotched the last of the royalist rebellions. By the end of August he was recognised as the greatest man in the kingdom and a grateful parliament voted him a gift of one thousand pounds.

Autumn 1659

In September, on his way back to London down the North Road, Lambert sent John Tradescant a note which read:

> *You may not have heard that John Mordaunt has left England to join the court of Charles Stuart at the Hague. He has had so many disappointments that I dare say one was no more memorable than another. Whatever happens in the future, Mordaunt's enmity will not be anything to fear.*

Before Lambert returned to London his army sent another petition to the House of Commons. Their list of requests was coming to be known as the 'Grand Old Cause', the cause of the Ironsides, the cause of the Levellers, the cause of the republicans. They demanded godly reforms, a proper command structure for the army, Parliament to be run by elected members advised by a senate, and court martial law in the army.

The House of Commons, always an unfaithful friend when the victory had been won, decided that the army was demanding reforms rather than requesting, and was probably marching on Parliament to seize power. In a frenzy of panic they ordered that the doors should be shut and Major General Lambert, so recently their hero, should be regarded as an enemy of Parliament and arrested for treason.

In early October John Tradescant received a magnificent order for spring bulbs from John Lambert who gave Wimbledon House as his address.

'So he's exiled again,' John observed to Hester. 'They don't have the courage to send him to the Tower but they don't dare let him near Parliament. They must be mad not to make him Lord Protector.'

'They're terrified,' she said. 'They think of nothing but saving their own skins. A parliament run by Lambert would reform them out of existence. He has no patience with time-servers. Did he write all this to you?'

'No, it's just an order for bulbs.'

'Then how d'you know he's in exile?'

John grinned. 'He always orders too many when he has been thrown out of power. He couldn't plant all these if he had three autumns under house arrest.'

John could have sent the lad with the three sacks of bulbs but his curiosity was too great. He himself drove the cart into the stable yard at Wimbledon and was directed to the pheasant garden where his Lordship was feeding his birds.

Lambert, holding a basket of grain, was surrounded by his ornamental pheasants, their plumage brilliant in the autumn sunshine. He turned quickly when he heard a footstep on the gravel behind him, but when he recognised John he smiled his sweet smile. 'Ah, Mr Tradescant, have you brought my bulbs yourself?'

'Yes, my lord,' John said. 'I am sorry to learn that you are confined here.'

'Oh,' Lambert said equably. 'Fortunes rise and fall in politics as well as in battles. In any case you find me bidding farewell to my birds now because I expect to be summonsed today.'

'To battle or to politics?' John asked.

Lambert grinned. 'They're much the same.' He cocked his head. 'Listen. D'you hear anything?'

John listened, then heard the steady beat of a company of horse in trot, and the jingle of armour. 'Soldiers,' he said.

'Then I think this is my summons,' Lambert remarked and John could hear the exultant joy in his voice at the prospect of action. 'Ask them at the stables to saddle my charger for me, would you, Mr Tradescant? I don't think I'm going to be able to plant bulbs today.'

'Can I come too?' John asked.

Lambert laughed. 'If you wish it. D'you have any idea where we are going?'

'No,' John confessed.

'Then you're as wise as I.'

John pulled Caesar from the shafts of the cart, borrowed a saddle from Lambert's groom and waited beside the company of Lambert's horse for the few moments until the general came out of the house.

'What's going on?' John asked one of the troopers.

'They've called out the other regiments against us,' the man said shortly. 'It's between our major general and the Members of Parliament. They've reneged on every promise they've ever given us and when we protest they call it treason. Now they've gone to ground in the Houses of Parliament with two regiments thrown around it and the Parliamentary Horse Guards leading the defence and saying that we must disband. Telling us to throw down our arms as traitors. Us who beat the king for them, then beat the Scots for them, and then beat Charles Stuart for them, and only last month beat George Booth for them. Us, disband! And hand over the general too! So they can throw him into the Tower beside Booth who fought against us!'

'*And* left the battlefield in a petticoat,' someone added to a rumble of laughter.

'And what can you do?' John asked. 'They're the Parliament, and if they've got the Horse Guards out . . .'

'It's what *he* can do,' the trooper replied, nodding towards Lambert, who swung into the saddle and trotted down the road at the head of his troop.

'What can he do?' John asked.

The trooper grinned. 'Anything he likes, is my guess.'

The troop fell in behind the general, bits jingling, hooves clattering on the dry road, and John, with a delicious sense that he should not be tagging on as a spectator, followed behind with Caesar pulling at the reins, his neck arched and tail held high at the prospect of action.

When they reached Scotland Yard at the side of the Palace of Whitehall he saw that the trooper was right, and his sense that he would have been safer to go straight home was right too. It was going to be an ugly scene, a pitched battle between the Parliamentary Horse Guards and Lambert's regiments at the very gateway to the Houses of Parliament. John reined back Caesar, who pulled against the bit as if he too knew that fighting was likely and was ready for the charge.

'Halt!' commanded Lambert and his personal standard dipped to show the signal. The troop of horse halted with a clatter of hooves on the cobbles.

The regiment before the Houses of Parliament tightened their grip on their pikes, blew on the fuses of their muskets and waited for the order to fire. A horse in Lambert's regiment moved restlessly against a too-tight rein, and the chink of the bit was very loud in the silence. There was a long pause as one English regiment eyed another and waited for the command to attack.

John could hear his breathing light and rapid as he sat in the saddle. Any moment he thought he would see the muskets lifted and hear the dreadful crack of their firing. There were probably cannons nearby too, and the Parliamentary Horse Guards had the advantage of being in defence, and near to the stout walls of Whitehall, while Lambert's men were drawn up in the road.

There was a long, long pause as the two troops faced each other, then John Lambert slid from his saddle and dropped to the ground, his spurs ringing as they tapped the cobblestones. He tossed his bridle to his standard bearer and walked forwards as if he were strolling in his orange garden. He left the sheltering ranks of his men, and out across the cobbled gulf which separated the two regiments, as if the men on the other side were not poised to take aim, as if they were not waiting for the order to shoot him down. He smiled at them as if they were his own regiment, his own trusted men. He smiled at them easily and pleasantly, as if he were glad to see them, as if he were greeting them as old friends.

'My God, what is he going to do?' John whispered to himself.

Lambert halted immediately before their commander and looked up at the officer high above him on the big horse, his hand ready-tightened on his sword ready to draw and sweep down in the killing blow. It was a big horse. The man was sixteen hands above Lambert, the general had to look upwards, his eyes screwed up against the evening sunlight.

'Dismount!' Lambert said easily, almost conversationally. There was a moment's pause. Soldiers in both troops held their breath to see what the outcome would be. The officer looked down at the unarmed man before him, Lambert smiled up at him. Then the officer dropped his reins and jumped down from the saddle.

At once there was a roar of approval from Lambert's men and the Parliament guards broke ranks and trotted towards Lambert's regiment to be greeted with smiles and handshakes and laughter. Lambert shook hands with the officer, exchanged a few brief words and then strolled back to his horse, swung into the saddle and then turned to face the men.

'Fall in,' he said pleasantly as if for a routine parade. He nodded to his standard bearer. 'Take my compliments to the Members of the House of Commons and advise them that I have the keys to the House and they must leave. They are no longer welcome. The country will be ruled by a Committee of Safety. We are going to have justice and freedom in this country. And it starts now.'

Lambert had not allowed for General George Monck, out of touch in Scotland, and jealous as a sick dog of his charismatic rival. As soon as he heard of the triumph at Whitehall he sent word to London that as commander of the Parliamentary army in Scotland he did not accept the Committee of Safety and that he was declaring war, and marching south to restore the banned MPs.

'War?' Hester demanded. 'But why?'

'He says he's going to restore Parliament,' John said, reading the latest news-sheet.

'Then why did he not do it before?' Hester asked. 'Why did he not declare war on Cromwell?'

'Because this is a man who thinks he can be Cromwell,' John said astutely. 'He thinks he can put himself at the head of the army and in a little while command Parliament as well.'

'Shall we box up the rarities?' Hester asked John wearily.

John thought for a moment. 'Not yet,' he said. 'But we may have to. General Monck's troops learned their discipline burning out royalists in Scotland.'

'He's for Parliament. He fought against Charles Stuart,' she said. 'Why can he not allow Lambert and the Committee of Safety to bring in their reforms? Why cannot people in this country be given a chance to have the government and the justice they deserve?'

'He believes in nothing, he's a professional soldier,' John said bitterly. 'He fought for King Charles before he saw that Cromwell would win and so changed sides. Then he saw what Cromwell did. He saw one man come to power, nearly to kingship at the head of the army. He won't trust John Lambert not to do the same. And he'll be thinking there's a chance for him.'

'John Lambert is the only man you could trust with that power,' Hester said. 'He's never broken his word, not once, not in all these difficult times.'

'And he paid us for the daffodils that I took to him that day,' John said. 'I hope to God he is able to plant them.'

Lambert never did plant the daffodils that John brought him. In planting time in November, he obeyed his orders from the Committee of Safety to protect England against General Monck and marched north to meet him at the head of eight thousand men.

He would not attack at once. General Monck had been a comrade in arms, and they were both parliamentarians. Lambert believed, trustingly enough, that it must be a misunderstanding. He wrote to Monck to try to explain, to try to convince him of the plans of the Committee of Safety, to persuade him that at last England had a chance to make a free and just society.

Monck pretended to consider, wrote and argued by letter with Lambert, while the Committee in London scraped around trying to find money to pay the soldiers under Lambert's command. They sent nothing. Lambert was caught between the deceit of General Monck and the incompetence of the Committee. He would not attack General Monck when they were still in debate, and by the time he realised that the general was spinning out the argument as a tactic, his army had melted away, and the general had won without a shot being fired.

When he should have been planting his orange-hearted narcissi in his orange garden at Wimbledon House he was watching his army disappear down the Great North Road, knowing that he had been tricked by Monck and betrayed by London.

'What will happen to him?' Hester asked John.

John scowled. 'Monck has had him accused of treason,' he said miserably. 'Treason against the old parliament, who were so lazy and incompetent that no-one cared when Lambert locked them out. Now they'll call themselves martyrs, no doubt. And they'll call him a traitor. Once he's in the Tower it's not a very long walk to the scaffold.'

Spring 1660

In February Lambert turned the remnants of his army south and marched them home in tattered boots. There was no money to buy them provisions or proper clothes. Monck was far ahead of him and marched into Whitehall to be greeted by a stony silence.

George Monck was not a man to be cast down by unpopularity. He put his troops throughout the streets of London, and they were accustomed to doing their duty among a resentful population. London was an easier billet than Edinburgh, and within days there was no-one shouting for a free parliament and John Lambert left on the streets. With a large free feast to celebrate the expulsion of Lambert's Committee of Safety it was possible to generate an enthusiasm for Monck's new council of state, run by himself.

By the time John Lambert brought his exhausted army home it was all over. He was ordered to go to his house at Wimbledon and not approach Parliament.

He wrote to John Tradescant from Wimbledon. The note arrived as the family and guests were eating dinner.

> *Please send me, in pots, your finest specimen tulips of this season to the value of £300.*

'What does he say?' Hester asked John, hovering over his shoulder to read the note.

'He *says* that he wants my best tulips,' John said. 'What that means is something different.'

'It means that he will have to confine himself to gardening and painting,' Elias Ashmole said cheerfully. He helped himself to another slice of baked ham. 'It means that the balance of power has swung to George Monck and he will decide who rules the country from now on.

And if I read the predictions of the planets aright then he will want a king, or at the very least another Lord Protector.'

Hester looked at Ashmole with dislike. 'Then God help us,' she said sharply. 'For since of all the women in England he chose a foul-mouthed washerwoman to take as his wife, what on earth will he choose for a king?'

Elias Ashmole was not in the least downcast. 'I should think it a very good chance that he would choose the rightful heir,' he said. 'And then we shall see some changes.'

'Then we shall see the same thing again,' Hester said bitterly. 'Only this time the battles will have to be fought without anyone's heart in them.'

'Peace, my wife,' John said quietly from the end of the table. 'Mr Ashmole is our guest.'

'A most frequent guest,' Frances observed sweetly, her head bowed demurely over her plate.

In spring, when John Lambert should have been enjoying the daffodils bobbing and the yellow aconite carpeting the beds of his orange garden, he could see only a small square of blue sky from his window in the Tower and George Monck was the undisputed new man of power in London. Lambert was on trial for nothing, sentenced for nothing. They had imposed on him a fine of such a huge amount that not even a man of his fortune and with friends such as his could meet it. It was essential to George Monck that his great rival be safely out of the way while he discovered, for the last and greatest leap of his life, which would be the winning side this time.

Monck had fought as a mercenary for anyone who was prepared to hire an unprincipled sword. He had fought for King Charles before being recruited by Cromwell to fight for Parliament in Ireland. Thereafter he had fought for Parliament. Unlike John Lambert, who had spent his life in pursuit of a written constitution to protect the rights of Englishmen, Monck had spent his life merely trying to be on the winning side.

In April he decided that the winning side was, after all, the Stuarts and, with a packed house of Parliament men who agreed with him, he sent terms to Charles Stuart at Breda.

'It is over then,' John said to Hester, who was seated on the terrace and looking out over the garden where the trees were showing fresh and green and the air was smelling sweet. 'It's over. They are bringing

Charles Stuart back, and all of our struggle for all of these years counts for nothing. When they write the histories our lifetime will be nothing more than an intermission between the Stuarts, they won't even remember that for a while we thought there might have been another way.'

'As long as we have peace,' Hester suggested. 'Perhaps the only way to find peace in this country is with a king on the throne?'

'We must be better men than that!' John exclaimed. 'We must want more than a comedy of ceremony and handsome faces. What have we been doing for all these years but asking questions about how men should live in England? The answer cannot be "as easily as possible".'

'The people want the diversion of a new coronation,' Hester said. 'Ask them in Lambeth market. They want a king. They want the amusements and the entertainments, they want the corrupt tax collectors that you can bribe to look the other way.'

'But what a king!' John remarked disdainfully. 'Half a dozen bastards scattered around Europe already, his tastes formed in Papist courts, and no knowledge of English people at all except what he learned when he was a fugitive. His father ruined us by his devotion to his principles, his son will ruin us by having none.'

'Then he will rule more easily than his father,' Hester pointed out. 'A man with no principles will not be going to war. A man without principles doesn't argue.'

'No,' John said. 'I think the heroic days are over.'

There was a little silence as they both thought of the son who could not wait to see this day, and that if he had lived to see it then even he might have thought that it lacked a little glory.

'And what will happen to John Lambert?' Hester asked. 'Will they free him from the Tower before Charles Stuart arrives?'

'They will execute him for certain,' John said. 'I should think General Monck can hardly wait to sign the order. Lambert is too much of a hero to the army and the people. And when the new king comes home they will be looking for scapegoats to offer him.'

'It cannot be the end for him?' Hester asked incredulously. 'He has never done anything but fight for the freedom of Englishmen and -women.'

'I think it must be,' John said. 'It's a bitter, bitter ending to all our hopes. A king such as Charles restored, and a man like Lambert on the scaffold.'

☙

But that very night, John Lambert climbed from his window in the Tower, slid down his knotted sheets, dropped into a waiting barge on the Thames, and disappeared into the April darkness.

❦

'I have to go to him,' John said to Hester. He was saddling up Caesar in the stable. Hester stood in the doorway, blocking his path. 'I have to go. This is the battle that tests everything I have finally come to believe, and I have to be there.'

'How do you know it is not a story, some ridiculous rumour?' she demanded. 'How d'you know he has raised a standard, is summoning an army to fight for freedom? It could be nothing more than someone's dream.'

'Because only John Lambert would choose Edgehill to raise his standard. And besides, if I go there, and nothing is happening, I can always ride home again.'

'And what about me? What about me if something *is* happening, if a battle is happening and you are in the midst of it and you are killed? Am I to be left here to keep the rarities and the gardens safe forever, with no son and no husband?'

He turned from the horse and came to the door of the stable and took her cold hands in his. 'Hester, my wife, my love,' he said. 'We have lived our lives in some of the wildest and strangest times that this country will ever see. Don't deny me the chance to fight just once, on the side I believe in. That, in a way, I have always believed in. I have spent my life wavering from one view to another, from one country to another. Let me be wholehearted for this, just once. I know that Lambert is right. I know that what he wants for this country, a balance of power and justice for the poor, is what this country needs. Let me go and fight under his standard.'

'Why is it always fighting?' she cried passionately. 'I can't bear it, John. If you should be lost . . .'

He shook his head. 'I want to go back,' he said simply. 'I want to go back to Edgehill where the king was first defeated in the first war. I was never there. I ran from it, just as I ran from the war of the Powhatan in Virginia.'

She would have interrupted him, sworn that it was not a war, sworn that he was not a man who ran from conflict, but he stopped her.

'It was not that I was afraid, I'm not saying that I ran like a coward.

553

But there was nothing that I saw clearly enough to die for. I knew the king was in the wrong; but I pitied him. I knew the queen was a fool; but she was a charming fool. I didn't want to see her driven into exile. I think of her now sometimes, and I can't believe that she has been brought so low. Many women are feather-brained and yet they don't pay for their folly as she has had to pay. The cause didn't seem wholly right to me. It didn't seem wholly clear to me. Right up to the scaffold when they took him out and beheaded him, it didn't seem quite right to me.'

Hester would have pulled her hands away from him but he held her fast. 'You're talking like a royalist,' she said hotly.

He smiled ruefully. 'I know it. That's what I'm saying. I have always been able to see both sides at once. But this time – for the first time in my life – the first time, Hester! – I have a cause I can truly believe in. I don't think that Charles Stuart should come back. I do think that the people of this country should govern themselves without a king or bishops or lords. I do believe – my God, at last I believe – that we are a people who have earned our freedom and deserve to be free. And I want to go and fight for that freedom. Lambert has raised his standard, for freedom, for the good old cause. I want to be there. I want to fight for it. If I have to die for it I will.'

For a moment it looked as if she would cry out against him, then she stepped to one side and opened the stable door. Caesar the war horse stepped out, raising his big hoofs delicately over the threshold, and walked at once to the mounting block and stood still, his neck arched, as if he too wanted to go into battle for the rights of freeborn Englishmen.

John smiled to see the horse and then looked at Hester. 'Are you angry with me?'

'No,' she said unwillingly. 'I'm proud of you, even though this goes against my own interests. I'm glad to see you at last knowing what you believe and going to fight for it. I shall pray that you win. I have always thought that nothing mattered but that we survived these days and it is a change for me to think, like you, that there is something worth fighting for.'

'You think it's worth fighting for?' he asked. 'To keep the king out, to keep Parliament free? To get justice for everyone in this country?'

Unwillingly she nodded. 'Yes,' she said. 'And if any man can do it then Lambert is that man. I know it.'

John took her hand again, kissed it and then caught her to him and held her hard against him. 'I shall come back!' he said passionately.

'Trust me, Hester. I shall come back to you. And God willing we will make this country a place where poor men can be free.'

❀

He came back within a fortnight. All three men who had been so powerful in Hester's life came back to their separate destinations: John Lambert to the Tower on a charge of high treason, Charles Stuart to Dover and the road to London lined with people crowding to touch his sacred hand, and John, head drooping, home to the Ark.

Caesar clip-clopped towards his stable, his ears back, his head low. John dropped off his back in the stable yard and fell to his knees as his legs buckled under him. The garden lad ran to raise him and shouted for Cook. She took one look out of the kitchen door and called for Frances and Hester who were tidying the rarities room.

Hester ran out to the terrace and then round the corner to the stable yard to find John seated on the mounting block, rubbing his stiff muscles. He tried to get to his feet when he saw her, but she went to him and put her arms around him.

'Are you injured?'

'Heartsick.'

'Hurt in your body?'

'No.'

'Your legs?'

'I'm just stiff. I'm too old, Hester, to ride all day and all night.'

'Was there a battle?'

'There was a skirmish. We were hopelessly outnumbered. On the day when it mattered, when it mattered more than anything in the world, there were not enough men ready to stand up and fight for their liberty.'

She wrapped her arms around him and held his weary head close to her heart. She found she was rocking him as she used to rock Johnnie when he woke from a nightmare.

'There was hardly anyone there,' John said flatly. 'Lambert was captured almost straight away. They didn't even bother with us. It was him they wanted. He would have got away but his horse was tired, we were all tired. And discouraged. Because when it really mattered there were not enough men ready to stand up and fight for their liberty.'

He pulled back and stared up into her face as if she could answer him. 'Why is it?' he demanded. 'Why is it that people can see so clearly when it is a question of their safety or their wealth, or their comfort? But when it is a question of their freedom they leave it for someone else to defend. They don't see how they come to their freedom. They don't realise that if the bargees at Wapping are unjustly taxed and the miners in the Forest of Dean are excluded from their rights, if the commoners are driven from the commons and the rich and the mighty encroach, then we are *all* at risk – even if it is not our own gardens which are taken. Even if it is not yet our rights which are threatened. Why don't people see it? When governments persecute the sick, the poor, the women, then everyone has to stand up and defend them. Why don't people see that?'

Hester looked into his angry face for a moment and then pulled him back to her and held him against her heart. 'I don't know,' she said softly. 'You would think people would know by now that when there is an evil you should stop it at once.'

Summer 1660

Charles Stuart, who was to be known as Charles the Second, came home to a country mad with joy. People wanted to get back to a system that everyone knew, many of them hoped to gain from a change of government: a chance to settle old scores and regain old ground. Quakers, sectaries, Roman Catholics and a number of old women who could be named as witches by spiteful neighbours felt the brunt of popular confidence which expected the new king to restore the old persecutions as well as freedoms. Commoners all round the country helped themselves to firewood, poached from the royal forests and the derelict parks, and there was a great rush of burglary from the empty palaces before the new royal servants came to stock-take.

The new king set up a new Privy Council and the great English cake of rewards and places was sliced up between royalists and their friends; but Charles took some care to see that experienced men and those from wealthy or noble families were recruited to office whatever they had done in the wars against his father. Those who had been party to the trial and execution of his father only lost their places of power and were fined, if they fled England.

'I think he'll release John Lambert,' Frances said, bent over a newspaper spread out on the kitchen table. 'It says here that the House of Lords seeks his death but the House of Commons wants him reprieved.'

'Will he be free?' Hester asked, looking up from shelling peas.

Frances shook her head. 'It doesn't say. But if I was Charles Stuart I don't think I'd want Lord Lambert at the head of a regiment again.'

A month after the king was restored to the throne Elias Ashmole asked and got the place of a Windsor Herald. He came to visit the Ark wearing his new regalia, to suggest that John should publish a new edition of the catalogue.

'It should be dedicated to His Majesty,' Elias urged John as they sat on the terrace in the sunshine and looked over the garden which was in full summer bloom. 'Think, if he were to come to visit! His father did, didn't he?'

'Yes,' John said. 'With the queen.'

'I hear she's coming from France in the autumn,' Ashmole said enthusiastically. 'We should have a new edition published by then. I'll pay for it, if you wish. I have some money put by.'

'I can pay!' John said, nettled. 'I'll compose a dedication.'

'I have one already,' Elias said and produced from the deep pocket of his coat a folded manuscript. 'Here.'

John spread the paper on the table.

> *To the sacred majesty of Charles the II*
> *John Tradescant, His Majesties most obedient and most loyal*
> *subject in all humility offereth these collections.*

Frances, looking over John's shoulder, let out a little gurgle of laughter. 'I don't know if you're his *most* obedient subject,' she remarked. 'He surely has some servants that didn't spend the wars as far away as they could get.'

John turned his laugh into a cough. 'Frances, go about your business,' he said sternly and turned to Elias. 'I apologise.'

'A flighty woman,' Ashmole said disapprovingly. 'But if there is any question about your loyalty then you cannot affirm it too loudly, you know, John.'

John nodded.

'Fortunately you have the record of your son's service,' Elias remarked. 'You could always say he died at Worcester. Or died here of his wounds.'

Hester, coming to the terrace with a tray and three glasses of madeira wine, checked at that and exchanged a shocked look with her husband.

'We wouldn't do that,' John said briefly. He got to his feet and took the tray from Hester's hands. 'Look at this that Mr Ashmole has prepared for the printer for me. A new dedication for the front of the catalogue. Dedicated to His Majesty.'

She leaned over the table and read it carefully. To his surprise when she straightened up there were tears in her eyes.

'Hester?'

She turned a little away from the table so Elias Ashmole could not see her face. John followed her.

'What is it?' he asked quietly.

'I was just thinking how proud Johnnie would have been,' she said simply. 'To see our name on the same page as the king's. To have the collection dedicated to the king.'

John nodded. 'Yes, he would have been,' he said. 'His cause won the war in the end.' He turned to Elias Ashmole. 'I thank you for your help, Elias. Let's get it printed at once.'

Elias nodded. 'I'll deliver it to the printers on my way home,' he said cheerfully. 'It's no trouble. I'm glad you approve.'

Hester took her glass of wine and sat with the men. 'Do we have guests for dinner tonight?' she asked. 'Is Dr Wharton and the rest coming for dinner?'

'Yes, and there's news about that too!' Elias said gleefully. 'We are to have royal patronage. The king is very interested in our thoughts and discoveries. We are to be called the Royal Society! Imagine that! We are to be fellows of the Royal Society! What d'you think?'

'That is an honour,' John said. 'Though we'd never have gathered together if it hadn't been for the republic. Under the bishops half what we discussed would have been called heresy.'

Elias flapped his hand dismissively. 'Old days,' he said. 'Old history. What matters now is that we have a king who loves to talk and speculate and who is prepared to advance men of science and learning.'

'Then why does he touch for the king's evil?' Frances asked innocently, bringing a plate of biscuits which she put at John's elbow. 'Is that not the superstition of ignorant people? Would he welcome an inquiry into such nonsense?'

Elias was briefly put out. 'He does his duty, he does everything that is right and courteous and pleasing,' he said with emphasis. 'Nothing more than good manners. Good manners, Mrs Norman, are the very backbone of civilised society.'

'If you are a Royal Society I had best order a royal dinner,' Hester said tactfully. 'Come and help me, Frances.'

Frances shot a grin at her father and followed her stepmother into the house.

It was a good summer for the Ark. The sense of safety and prosperity meant that more and more visitors came to the doors. The spirit of inquiry which the Royal Society represented spread throughout London, and men and women came to see the marvels of the Tradescant collection and then walk in the rich gardens and the orchards.

The horse chestnut avenue which ran from the terrace before the rarities room to the end of the orchard was now thirty-one years old, with broad trunks and wide, swaying branches. No-one who saw the trees in flower could resist purchasing a sapling.

'There will be a chestnut tree in every park in the land,' John predicted. 'My father always swore that they were the most beautiful trees he had ever grown.'

But the chestnuts had their rivals in the garden. John's own tulip tree from Virginia flowered for the first time in the hot summer of 1660, and botanists and painters made special trips up the river to see the huge cupped flowers against the dark, glossy foliage. John had some new roses, Warner's rose and a beautiful new specimen from France that they called the velvet rose for the deep, soft colour of the petals. The fruit trees in the garden had shed their blossoms and were heavy-laden with growing fruits. The early cherries were picked at dawn by Frances to save them from the songbirds, and sold at the garden gate by the lad. One part of the fruit garden was set aside for vines now; John had row upon row of well-pruned bushes, grown low on wires, just as his father had seen them grown in France, with fourteen varieties of grape, including the fox grape from Virginia and the Virginian wild vine.

In the melon beds John grew half a dozen varieties of melon. He always kept one fruit to the side, he called it the royal melon, descendant of the seeds which Johnnie had planted at Wimbledon House. When it fruited in midsummer John sent a great sweet-smelling globe to the king, who was hunting at Richmond, with compliments of John Tradescant. He wondered if this was the second melon that Charles Stuart had received, and if he would ever understand the devotion which had been poured into growing the first fruit.

Autumn 1660

Castle Cornet, Guernsey.
  Dear Mr Tradescant,
Please would you send me, as soon as you lift them, six Iris Daley tulip, six Tricolor Crownes tulip, and two or three tulip which you think I might like that are new to your collection.

If the new tenants of the house at Wimbledon have no objection, I should like you to collect from my garden any specimens which you would like to have as your own. I think the acacia tree was promised to you – all that long time ago. I particularly would like to see my own Violetten tulip again, I had one in particular which I thought might be so dark a purple as to be almost black.

If you can be admitted to the garden I would be very pleased to have some of my lily bulbs returned to me, especially those from my orange garden. I have high hopes of breeding a new variety of lily here and I will send you some bulbs in the spring. I shall call it the Lambert lily and my claim to fame shall not be for the battle for freedom but for one sweet-smelling, exquisitely shaped blossom.

Lady Lambert has joined me here with our children and the castle has become less like a prison and more like a home. All I am in need of, is tulips!

With best wishes to Mrs Tradescant and Mrs Norman –
John Lambert.

John passed the letter to Hester without comment and she read it in silence.

'We'll get him his Violetten back,' she said determinedly. 'If I have to go over the Wimbledon garden wall at midnight.'

Winter 1660

Elias Ashmole came to visit the Ark in midwinter, wearing a new fur-lined cape and very conscious of his new status. He came by carriage with some friends and brought a case of Canary wine to share with John. Hester lit the candles in the rarities room, and ordered dinner for them all, served it and ate her own dinner in the quieter company of Cook in the kitchen.

John put his head around the kitchen door. 'We're taking a stroll down to Lambeth,' he said. 'For a glass of ale.'

Hester nodded. 'I shall be in bed by the time you return,' she said. 'If Mr Ashmole wishes to stay the bed is made up in his usual room, and there are truckle beds for his friends.'

John came into the kitchen and gave her a kiss on the forehead. 'I shall be late home,' he announced with satisfaction. 'And no doubt drunk.'

'No doubt,' Hester said with a smile. 'Goodnight, husband.'

They came home earlier than she expected. She was putting out the candles in the rarities room and raking out the fire when she heard the front door open and John stumble into the hall with Ashmole and his companions.

'Ah, Hester,' John said happily. 'I am glad you are still awake. Elias and I have been doing some business and I need you to witness it for me.'

'Can it not wait until the morning?' Hester asked.

'Oh, sign it now and then we can put it away and have a glass of port,' John said. He spread the paper before her on the painter's table in the window of the rarities room. 'Sign here.'

Hester hesitated. 'What is it?'

'It's a piece of business and we need a witness,' Elias said smoothly. 'But if you are uneasy, Mrs Tradescant, we can leave it until the morning. If you want to read every paragraph and every sentence, we can leave it. We can find someone else to serve us if you are unwilling.'

'No, no,' Hester said politely. 'Of course I can sign it now.' She took the pen and signed the paper. 'And now I shall go to bed,' she said. 'I give you goodnight, gentlemen.'

John nodded, he was opening a case of coins. 'Here you are,' he said to Ashmole. 'In good faith.'

Hester saw the antique milled shilling piece passed to Elias.

'Are you giving away one of our coins?' she queried in surprise.

Ashmole bowed and pocketed the coin. 'I'm very grateful,' he said. He seemed far more sober than John. 'I shall preserve it very carefully as a precious token and a pledge.'

Hester hesitated, as if she would ask him what pledge John had made to him; but one of the men opened the door for her and bowed low. Hester curtsied and went out and up the stairs to bed.

❧

She was wakened by the bang of her bedroom door as John stumbled into the room and then by the shake of the bed as he dropped heavily on to it. She opened her eyes and saw that he had fallen asleep at once, on his back, still wearing his clothes. Hester thought for a moment that she could get up and undress him and get him comfortable in bed. But then she smiled and turned over. John's drinking bouts were rare but she saw no reason why he should not wake up in the morning in some slight discomfort.

🌱

When he woke in the darkness he thought for a moment he had been dreaming his worst dream: of failure and his own inability to inherit his father's work and continue his father's name. He slipped out of the narrow bed without waking Hester, who turned and stretched her hand out over his pillow.

He slipped on his shoes and went downstairs. The parlour which had seemed so bright and jolly only hours ago was now dark and unwelcoming, it smelled of stale ale and tobacco smoke, and the fire was burned down to dark embers. He blew on the coals, was rewarded by a red glow, and then threw on a handful of kindling. The dry wood caught and the shadows leaped high in the room.

On the table was the document and at the foot of the document was his own clear signature, and next to it Elias Ashmole's educated elliptical hand. He touched the wax of his seal. It was hard and cold, there was no escape. The signature was there, the seal was there, the document was there. It stated very clearly that at John Tradescant's death Elias Ashmole was to inherit all the rarities in the collection and all the plants in the garden. John had signed away his patrimony, he had signed away his name, he had signed away his inheritance and all his own work and his father's work would count for nothing.

'I didn't mean this,' John whispered quietly.

With the deed of gift in his hand he went out into the hall. Hester in her white nightgown was like a ghost coming down the stairs.

'Are you ill?' she asked.

Dumbly, he shook his head. 'I have done a most terrible, terrible thing.'

At once her eyes went to the contract in his hand which she had signed as he had bid her. 'The business you were doing with Mr Ashmole?'

'He told me it was a deed of gift, to give the rarities to the University of Oxford at our deaths. He told me that they would put our name to the collection and that everyone would always know that we had the first collection open to any visitor in all the world, that we had the finest things, the rarest, the most beautiful. He told me that I was signing the goods to him as a trustee. He would ensure that the university received the rarities entire, that they would call it the Tradescantean.'

There was the creak of a door opening upstairs.

'Come outside,' Hester whispered as if only in the garden could they be safe. She opened the door to the terrace and slipped out into the icy night, careless of her bare feet on the chill floorboards. 'Does it not say that? The document? Is he not pledged to do that?'

'I just signed it,' John said numbly. 'I just agreed with him that it would be a fine thing to have the collection in the care of the university. So I just signed it. And I made you sign it too.'

'And what *does* it say?'

'I didn't read it carefully enough. And he is a lawyer. He has made sure that it is unclear. It says that the collection is to go to him entire; but there is nothing about the university. He is not a trustee, he will inherit everything for himself. He will have it when we die. He can keep it as he likes. Or he can give it to his heirs. My God, Hester, he can break it up and sell it piece by piece.'

She said nothing, she was aghast. Her face was as white as her nightcap, as her gown.

'And I signed too,' she said, her words a tiny thread of sound.

John took his gardening cape hung on a hook near the door wrapped it around her shoulders, then turned and looked out over the garden, leaning on the rail of the terrace. He thought of the many hours his father had spent, leaning on the rail and looking out at his trees, at his beloved chestnut avenue.

The night was kind to the garden, the trees were as beautiful as black lace against the sky which was slowly growing blue. Somewhere amid the rare plum trees a robin was starting to sing, its haunting ghostly song enhancing the silence. Further down the orchard a duck, disturbed in its sleep beside the lake, quacked once briefly and then was still.

John leaned his head in his hands and blotted out the garden. 'He will have it all when I am gone, Hester. He was witty and helpful, and I thought I was doing a clever thing. And now my head is fit to split and I know that you are married to a fool. There will be no Tradescant collection to carry my father's name to future generations, they will call it the Ashmolean and we will all be forgotten.'

He thought for a moment that she would cry out against him and beat him, but she had turned away and was reading the document by the light of the setting moon. In the pallor of the moonlight she looked sick with the shock. 'I have broken my promise to your father,' she said in a low voice. 'I told him I would guard your children and guard the rarities. I lost Johnnie and now I have lost the rarities too.'

John shook his head. 'You lost nothing,' he said passionately. 'Johnnie died thinking that kings were glorious heroes, not time-serving lechers. He died because he could not bear to live in the new world that the time-servers were making. And it was me that did this; not you. I did it all from my own folly. Because I thought Ashmole was cleverer than me. That's why I was glad to be his friend. That's why I wanted his help with the catalogue of the treasures. And now I wish to God I had inherited my father's caution as well as his treasures. Because I could not keep the one without the other.'

'It might fail,' she said. 'This – paper. We could say you were drunk when you signed . . .'

'I would have to prove more than being drunk. I would have to prove that I was mad for it to fail,' he said. 'And being a fool is not the same as being mad.'

'We could cut off the seal, and the signature, and deny it . . .'

He shook his head again, not answering for a moment. 'We can try but he has the law on his side, and he knows the lawyers. I think there is no escape from my folly. I have failed you and I have failed my father.' He thought for a moment. 'I had no heir,' he continued with deep sorrow. 'No-one to come here after me. And now there will be nothing here, anyway.

'I thought my father's name, my name, my son's name would live forever,' he said wonderingly, looking out over the dark garden, thinking of the riches hidden safe in the frozen soil, waiting for the sun. 'I thought everyone who ever planted a garden would know of us three, would be glad of what we had done. I thought every garden in England would grow a little brighter because of the plants we had brought home. I thought that as long as people loved their gardens and loved trees and shrubs and flowers there would be people who would remember us. But I have thrown it all away. My life's work, my father's life's work: it will all mean nothing. Elias Ashmole will have it all and we will be forgotten.'

Hester stepped forward so she could lean her head on his shoulder, the warmth of her body was familiar and comforting. He put his arm around her and held her close. A little breeze went through the orchard and Tradescant's trees; fifty-seven new plum trees, forty-nine new apple trees, forty-nine new pear trees, twenty-four new cherry trees moved their branches in a gentle dance. Before them the great branches of the chestnut avenue bobbed, their upwinging boughs carrying the hidden sweet spikes of their buds, their proud, broad trunks strong and still. In the orangery, safe in the warmth, were the rare and tender plants, the exotic, precious plants which the Tradescants, father and son, had brought from all over the world for the gardeners of England to love.

'We will be forgotten,' John whispered.

Hester leaned back and picked a sweet-scented winter-flowering jasmine bud, one of the first ever grown in England. The unfurling petals were cream in the yellow moonlight. The tears were hot on her cheeks, but her voice was confident.

'Oh no, they will remember you,' she said. 'I think the gardeners of England will remember you with gratitude one hundred, two hundred, even three hundred years from now, and every park in England will have one of our horse chestnut trees, and every garden one of our flowers.'